# Joseph Sheridan Le Fanu

## Collection of Short Stories

Cape Turnaround™ Collective
A division of Cape Turnaround Productions
Los Angeles, CA

Each of these stories were first published wholly, or as part of a series between the years of 1838 and 1894, by JS Le Fanu.

# About The Author:

Joseph Sheridan Le Fanu ( 28 August 1814 – 7 February 1873) was an Irish writer of Gothic tales, mystery novels, and horror fiction. He was a leading ghost story writer of the nineteenth century and was central to the development of the genre in the Victorian era. M. R. James described Le Fanu as "absolutely in the first rank as a writer of ghost stories". Three of his best-known works are Uncle Silas, Carmilla, and The House by the Churchyard. Sheridan Le Fanu was born at 45 Lower Dominick Street, Dublin, into a literary family of Huguenot, Irish and English descent. He had an elder sister, Catherine Frances, and a younger brother, William

Richard. His parents were Thomas Philip Le Fanu and Emma Lucretia Dobbin. Both his grandmother Alicia Sheridan Le Fanu and his great-uncle Richard Brinsley Sheridan were playwrights (his niece Rhoda Broughton would become a successful novelist), and his mother was also a writer, producing a biography of Charles Orpen.

Within a year of his birth his family moved to the Royal Hibernian Military School in the Phoenix Park, where his father, a Church of Ireland

clergyman, was appointed to the chaplaincy of the establishment. The Phoenix Park and the adjacent village and parish church of Chapelizod would appear in Le Fanu's later stories.

Le Fanu worked in many genres but remains best known for his horror fiction. He was a meticulous craftsman and frequently reworked plots and ideas from his earlier writing in subsequent pieces. Many of his novels, for example, are expansions and refinements of earlier short stories. He specialised in tone and effect rather than "shock horror", and liked to leave important details unexplained and mysterious. He avoided overt supernatural effects: in most of his major works, the supernatural is strongly implied but a "natural" explanation is also possible.

The demonic monkey in "Green Tea" could be a delusion of the story's protagonist, who is the only person to see it; in "The Familiar", Captain Barton's death seems to be supernatural, but is not actually witnessed, and the ghostly owl may be a real bird. This technique influenced later horror artists, both in print and on film (see, for example, the film producer Val Lewton's principle of "indirect horror").Though other writers have since chosen less subtle techniques, Le Fanu's finest tales, such as the vampire novella Carmilla and the short story "Schalken the Painter", remain some of the most powerful in the genre. He had enormous influence on one of the 20th century's most important ghost story writers, M. R. James, and although his work fell out of favour in the early part of the 20th century, towards the end of the century interest in his work increased and remains comparatively strong.

# Table of Contents

# THE DRUNKARD'S DREAM (1838)

_Being a Fourth Extract from the Legacy of the Late F. Purcell, P. P. of Drumcoolagh_

"All this _he_ told with some confusion and
Dismay, the usual consequence of dreams
Of the unpleasant kind, with none at hand
To expound their vain and visionary gleams.
I've known some odd ones which seemed really planned
Prophetically, as that which one deems
'A strange coincidence,' to use a phrase
By which such things are settled now-a-days."

BYRON.

Dreams--What age, or what country of the world has not felt and acknowledged the mystery of their origin and end? I have thought not a little upon the subject, seeing it is one which has been often forced upon my attention, and sometimes strangely enough; and yet I have never arrived at any thing which at all appeared a satisfactory conclusion. It does appear that a mental phenomenon so extraordinary cannot be wholly without its use. We know, indeed, that in the olden times it has been made the organ of communication between the Deity and his creatures; and when, as I have seen, a dream produces upon a mind, to all appearance hopelessly reprobate and depraved, an effect so powerful and so lasting as to break down the inveterate habits, and to reform the life of an abandoned sinner. We see in the result, in the reformation of morals, which appeared incorrigible in the reclamation of a human soul which seemed to be irretrievably lost, something more than could be produced by a mere chimaera of the slumbering fancy, something more than could arise from the capricious images of a terrified imagination; but once prevented, we behold in all these things, in the tremendous and mysterious results, the operation of the hand of God. And while Reason rejects as absurd the superstition which will read a prophecy in every dream, she may, without violence to herself, recognize, even in the wildest and most incongruous of the wanderings of a slumbering intellect, the evidences and the fragments of a language which may be spoken, which _has_ been spoken to terrify, to warn, and to command. We have reason to believe too, by the promptness of action, which in the age of the prophets, followed all intimations of this kind, and by the strength of conviction and strange permanence of the effects resulting from certain dreams in latter times, which effects ourselves may have witnessed, that when this medium of communication has been employed by the Deity, the evidences of his presence have been unequivocal. My thoughts were directed to this subject, in a manner to leave a lasting impression upon my mind, by the events which I shall now relate, the statement of which, however extraordinary, is nevertheless _accurately correct_.

About the year 17-- having been appointed to the living of C----h, I rented a small house in the town, which bears the same name: one morning, in the month of November, I was awakened before my usual time, by my servant, who bustled into my bedroom for the purpose of announcing a sick call. As the Catholic Church holds her last rites to be totally indispensable to the safety of the departing sinner, no conscientious clergyman can afford a moment's unnecessary delay, and in little more than five minutes I stood ready cloaked and booted for the road in the small front parlour, in which the messenger, who was to act as my guide, awaited my coming. I found a poor little girl crying piteously near the door, and after some slight difficulty I ascertained that her father was either dead, or just dying.

"And what may be your father's name, my poor child?" said I. She held down her head, as if ashamed. I repeated the question, and the wretched little creature burst into floods of tears, still more bitter than she had shed before. At length, almost provoked by conduct which appeared to me so unreasonable, I began to lose patience, spite of the pity which I could not help feeling towards her, and I said rather harshly, "If you will not tell me the name of the person to whom you would lead me, your silence can arise from no good motive, and I might be justified in refusing to go with you at all."

"Oh! don't say that, don't say that," cried she. "Oh! sir, it was that I was afeard of when I would not tell you--I was afeard when you heard his name you would not come with me; but it is no use hidin' it now--it's Pat Connell, the carpenter, your honour."

She looked in my face with the most earnest anxiety, as if her very existence depended upon what she should read there; but I relieved her at once. The name, indeed, was most unpleasantly familiar to me; but, however fruitless my visits and advice might have been at another time, the present was too fearful an occasion to suffer my doubts of their utility as my reluctance to re-attempting what appeared a hopeless task to weigh even against the lightest chance, that a consciousness of his imminent danger might produce in him a more docile and tractable disposition. Accordingly I told the child to lead the way, and followed her in silence. She hurried rapidly through the long narrow street which forms the great thoroughfare of the town. The darkness of the hour, rendered still deeper by the close approach of the old fashioned houses, which lowered in tall obscurity on either side of the way; the damp dreary chill which renders the advance of morning peculiarly cheerless, combined with the object of my walk, to visit the death-bed of a presumptuous sinner, to endeavour, almost against my own conviction, to infuse a hope into the heart of a dying reprobate--a drunkard, but too probably perishing under the consequences of some mad fit of intoxication; all these circumstances united served to enhance the gloom and solemnity of my feelings, as I silently followed my little guide, who with quick steps traversed the uneven pavement of the main street. After a walk of about five minutes she turned off into a narrow lane, of that obscure and comfortless class which are to be found in almost all small old fashioned towns, chill without ventilation, reeking with all manner of offensive effluviae, dingy, smoky, sickly and pent-up buildings, frequently not only in a wretched but in a dangerous condition.

"Your father has changed his abode since I last visited him, and, I am afraid, much for the worse," said I.

"Indeed he has, sir, but we must not complain," replied she; "we have to thank God that we have lodging and food, though it's poor enough, it is, your honour."

Poor child! thought I, how many an older head might learn wisdom from thee--how many a luxurious philosopher, who is skilled to preach but not to suffer, might not thy patient words put to the blush! The manner and language of this child were alike above her years and station; and, indeed, in all cases in which the cares and sorrows of life have anticipated their usual date, and have fallen, as they sometimes do, with melancholy prematurity to the lot of childhood, I have observed the result to have proved uniformly the same. A young mind, to which joy and indulgence have been strangers, and to which suffering and self-denial have been familiarised from the first, acquires a solidity and an elevation which no other discipline could have bestowed, and which, in the present case, communicated a striking but mournful peculiarity to the manners, even to the voice of the child. We paused before a narrow, crazy door, which she opened by means of a latch, and we forthwith began to ascend the steep and broken stairs, which led upwards to the sick man's room. As we mounted flight after flight towards the garret floor, I heard more and more distinctly the hurried talking of many voices. I could also distinguish the low sobbing of a female. On arriving upon the uppermost lobby, these sounds became fully audible.

"This way, your honor," said my little conductress, at the same time pushing open a door of patched and half rotten plank, she admitted me into the squalid chamber of death and misery. But one candle, held in the fingers of a scared and haggard-looking child, was burning in the room, and that so dim that all was twilight or darkness except within its immediate influence. The general obscurity, however, served to throw into prominent and startling relief the death-bed and its occupant. The light was nearly approximated to, and fell with horrible clearness upon, the blue and swollen features of the drunkard. I did not think it possible that a human countenance could look so terrific. The lips were black and drawn apart--the teeth were firmly set--the eyes a little unclosed, and nothing but the whites appearing--every feature was fixed and livid, and the whole face wore a ghastly and rigid expression of despairing terror such as I never saw equalled; his hands were crossed upon his breast, and firmly clenched, while, as if to add to the corpse-like effect of the whole, some white cloths, dipped in water, were wound about the forehead and temples. As soon as I could remove my eyes from this horrible spectacle, I observed my friend Dr. D----, one of the most humane of a humane profession, standing by the bedside. He had been attempting, but unsuccessfully, to bleed the patient, and had now applied his finger to the pulse.

"Is there any hope?" I inquired in a whisper.

A shake of the head was the reply. There was a pause while he continued to hold the wrist; but he waited in vain for the throb of life, it was not there, and when he let go the hand it fell stiffly back into its former position upon the other.

"The man is dead," said the physician, as he turned from the bed where the terrible figure lay.

Dead! thought I, scarcely venturing to look upon the tremendous and revolting spectacle--dead! without an hour for repentance, even a moment for reflection--dead! without the rites which even the best should have. Is there a hope for him? The glaring eyeball, the grinning mouth, the distorted brow--that unutterable look in which a painter would have sought to embody the fixed despair of the nethermost hell--these were my answer.

The poor wife sat at a little distance, crying as if her heart would break--the younger children clustered round the bed, looking, with wondering curiosity, upon the form of death, never seen before. When the first tumult of uncontrollable sorrow had passed away, availing myself of the solemnity and impressiveness of the scene, I desired the heart-stricken family to accompany me in prayer, and all knelt down, while I solemnly and fervently repeated some of those prayers which appeared most applicable to the occasion. I employed myself thus in a manner which, I trusted, was not unprofitable, at least to the living, for about ten minutes, and having accomplished my task, I was the first to arise. I looked upon the poor, sobbing, helpless creatures who knelt so humbly around me, and my heart bled for them. With a natural transition, I turned my eyes from them to the bed in which the body lay, and, great God! what was the revulsion, the horror which I experienced on seeing the corpse-like, terrific thing seated half upright before me--the white cloths, which had been wound about the head, had now partly slipped from their position, and were hanging in grotesque festoons about the face and shoulders, while the distorted eyes leered from amid them--

"A sight to dream of, not to tell."

I stood actually rivetted to the spot. The figure nodded its head and lifted its arm, I thought with a menacing gesture. A thousand confused and horrible thoughts at once rushed upon my mind. I had often read that the body of a presumptuous sinner, who, during life, had been the willing creature of every satanic impulse, after the human tenant had deserted it, had been known to become the horrible sport of demoniac possession. I was roused from the stupefaction of terror in which I stood, by the piercing scream of the mother, who now, for the first time, perceived the change which had taken place. She rushed towards the bed, but, stunned by the shock and overcome by the conflict of violent emotions, before she reached it, she fell prostrate upon the floor. I am perfectly convinced that had I not been startled from the torpidity of horror in which I was bound, by some powerful and arousing stimulant, I should have gazed upon this unearthly apparition until I had fairly lost my senses. As it was, however, the spell was broken, superstition gave way to reason: the man whom all believed to have been actually dead, was living! Dr. D---- was instantly standing by the bedside, and, upon examination, he found that a sudden and copious flow of blood had taken place from the wound which the lancet had left, and this, no doubt, had effected his sudden and almost preternatural restoration to an existence from which all thought he had been for ever removed. The man was still speechless, but he seemed to understand the physician when he forbid his repeating the painful and fruitless attempts which he made to articulate, and he at once resigned himself quietly into his hands.

I left the patient with leeches upon his temples, and bleeding freely--apparently with little of the drowsiness which accompanies apoplexy; indeed, Dr. D---- told me that he had never before witnessed a seizure which seemed to combine the symptoms of so many kinds, and yet which belonged to none of the recognized classes; it certainly was not apoplexy, catalepsy, _nor delirium tremens_, and yet it seemed, in some degree, to partake of the properties of all--it was strange, but stranger things are coming.

During two or three days Dr. D---- would not allow his patient to converse in a manner which could excite or exhaust him, with any one; he suffered him merely, as briefly as possible, to express his immediate wants, and it was not until the fourth day after my early visit, the particulars of which I have just detailed, that it was thought expedient that I should see him, and then only because it appeared that his extreme importunity and impatience were likely to retard his recovery more than the mere exhaustion attendant upon a short conversation could possibly do; perhaps, too, my friend entertained some hope that if by holy confession his patient's bosom were eased of the perilous stuff, which no doubt, oppressed it, his recovery would be more assured and rapid. It was, then, as I have said, upon the fourth day after my first professional call, that I found myself once more in the dreary chamber of want and sickness. The man was in bed, and appeared low and restless. On my entering the room he raised himself in the bed, and muttered twice or thrice--"Thank God! thank God." I signed to those of his family who stood by, to leave the room, and took a chair beside the bed. So soon as we were alone, he said, rather doggedly--"There's no use now in telling me of the sinfulness of bad ways--I know it all--I know where they lead to--I seen everything about it with my own eyesight, as plain as I see you." He rolled himself in the bed, as if to hide his face in the clothes, and then suddenly raising himself, he exclaimed with startling vehemence--"Look, sir, there is no use in mincing the matter; I'm blasted with the fires of hell; I have been in hell; what do you think of that?--in hell--I'm lost for ever--I have not a chance--I am damned already--damned--damned--." The end of this sentence he actually shouted; his vehemence was perfectly terrific; he threw himself back, and laughed, and sobbed hysterically. I poured some water into a tea-cup, and gave it to him. After he had swallowed it, I told him if he had anything to communicate, to do so as briefly as he could, and in a manner as little agitating to himself as possible; threatening at the same time, though I had no intention of doing so, to leave him at once, in case he again gave way to such passionate excitement. "It's only foolishness," he continued, "for me to try to thank you for coming to such a villain as myself at all; it's no use for me to wish good to you, or to bless you; for such as me has no blessings to give." I told him that I had but done my duty, and urged him to proceed to the matter which weighed upon his mind; he then spoke nearly as follows:--"I came in drunk on Friday night last, and got to my bed here, I don't remember how; sometime in the night, it seemed to me, I wakened, and feeling unasy in myself, I got up out of the bed. I wanted the fresh air, but I would not make a noise to open the window, for fear I'd waken the crathurs. It was very dark, and throublesome to find the door; but at last I did get it, and I groped my way out, and went down as asy as I could. I felt quite sober, and I counted the steps one after another, as I was going down, that I might not stumble at the bottom. When I came to the first landing-place, God be about us always! the floor of it sunk under me, and I went down, down, down, till the senses almost left me. I do not know how long I was falling, but it seemed to me a great while. When I came rightly to myself at last, I was sitting at a great table, near the top of it; and I could not see the end of it, if it had any, it was so far off; and there was men beyond reckoning, sitting down, all along by it, at each side, as far as I could see at all. I did not know at first was it in the open air; but there was a close smothering feel in it, that was not natural, and there was a kind of light that my eyesight never saw before, red and unsteady, and I did not see for a long time where it was coming from, until I looked straight up, and then I seen that it came from great balls of blood-coloured fire, that were rolling high over head with a sort of rushing, trembling sound, and I perceived that they shone on the ribs of a great roof of rock that was arched overhead instead of the sky. When I seen this, scarce knowing what I did, I got up, and I said, 'I have no right to be here; I must go,' and the man that was sitting at my left hand, only smiled, and said, 'sit down again, you can _never_ leave this place,' and his voice was weaker than any child's voice I ever heerd, and when he was done speaking he smiled again. Then I spoke out very loud and bold, and I said--'in the name of God, let me out of this bad place.' And there was a great man, that I did not see before, sitting at the end of the table that I was near, and he was taller than twelve men, and his face was very proud and terrible to look at, and he stood up and stretched out his hand before him, and when he stood up, all that was there, great and small, bowed down with a sighing sound, and a dread came on my heart, and he looked at me, and I could not speak. I felt I was his own, to do what he liked with, for I knew at once who he was, and he said, 'if you promise to return, you may depart for a season'; and the voice he spoke with was terrible and mournful, and the echoes of it went rolling and swelling down the endless cave, and mixing with the trembling of the fire overhead; so that, when he sate down, there was a sound after him, all through the place like the roaring of a furnace, and I said, with all the strength I had, 'I promise to come back; in God's name let me go,' and with that I lost the sight and the hearing of all that was there, and when my senses came to me again, I was sitting in the bed with the blood all over me, and you and the rest praying around the room." Here he paused and wiped away the chill drops of horror which hung upon his forehead.

I remained silent for some moments. The vision which he had just described struck my imagination not a little, for this was long before Vathek and the "Hall of Iblis" had delighted the world; and the description which he gave had, as I received it, all the attractions of novelty beside the impressiveness which always belongs to the narration of an _eye-witness_, whether in the body or in the spirit, of the scenes which he describes. There was something, too, in the stern horror with which the man related these things, and in the incongruity of his description, with the vulgarly received notions of the great place of punishment, and of its presiding spirit, which struck my mind with awe, almost with fear. At length he said, with an expression of horrible, imploring earnestness, which I shall never forget--"Well, sir, is there any hope; is there any chance at all? or, is my soul pledged and promised away for ever? is it gone out of my power? must I go back to the place?"

In answering him I had no easy task to perform; for however clear might be my internal conviction of the groundlessness of his fears, and however strong my scepticism respecting the reality of what he had described, I nevertheless felt that his impression to the contrary, and his humility and terror resulting from it, might be made available as no mean engines in the work of his conversion from profligacy, and of his restoration to decent habits, and to religious feeling. I therefore told him that he was to regard his dream rather in the light of a warning than in that of a prophecy; that our salvation depended not upon the word or deed of a moment, but upon the habits of a life; that, in fine, if he at once discarded his idle companions and evil habits, and firmly adhered to a sober, industrious, and religious course of life, the powers of darkness might claim his soul in vain, for that there were higher and firmer pledges than human tongue could utter, which promised salvation to him who should repent and lead a new life.

I left him much comforted, and with a promise to return upon the next day. I did so, and found him much more cheerful, and without any remains of the dogged sullenness which I suppose had arisen from his despair. His promises of amendment were given in that tone of deliberate earnestness, which belongs to deep and solemn determination; and it was with no small delight that I observed, after repeated visits, that his good resolutions, so far from failing, did but gather strength by time; and when I saw that man shake off the idle and debauched companions, whose society had for years formed alike his amusement and his ruin, and revive his long discarded habits of industry and sobriety, I said within myself, there is something more in all this than the operation of an idle dream. One day, sometime after his perfect restoration to health, I was surprised on ascending the stairs, for the purpose of visiting this man, to find him busily employed in nailing down some planks upon the landing place, through which, at the commencement of his mysterious vision, it seemed to him that he had sunk. I perceived at once that he was strengthening the floor with a view to securing himself against such a catastrophe, and could scarcely forbear a smile as I bid "God bless his work."

He perceived my thoughts, I suppose, for he immediately said,

"I can never pass over that floor without trembling. I'd leave this house if I could, but I can't find another lodging in the town so cheap, and I'll not take a better till I've paid off all my debts, please God; but I could not be asy in my mind till I made it as safe as I could. You'll hardly believe me, your honor, that while I'm working, maybe a mile away, my heart is in a flutter the whole way back, with the bare thoughts of the two little steps I have to walk upon this bit of a floor. So it's no wonder, sir, I'd thry to make it sound and firm with any idle timber I have."

I applauded his resolution to pay off his debts, and the steadiness with which he pursued his plans of conscientious economy, and passed on. Many months elapsed, and still there appeared no alteration in his resolutions of amendment. He was a good workman, and with his better habits he recovered his former extensive and profitable employment. Every thing seemed to promise comfort and respectability. I have little more to add, and that shall be told quickly. I had one evening met Pat Connell, as he returned from his work, and as usual, after a mutual, and on his side respectful salutation, I spoke a few words of encouragement and approval. I left him industrious, active, healthy--when next I saw him, not three days after, he was a corpse. The circumstances which marked the event of his death were somewhat strange--I might say fearful. The unfortunate man had accidentally met an early friend, just returned, after a long absence, and in a moment of excitement, forgetting everything in the warmth of his joy, he yielded to his urgent invitation to accompany him into a public house, which lay close by the spot where the encounter had taken place. Connell, however, previously to entering the room, had announced his determination to take nothing more than the strictest temperance would warrant. But oh! who can describe the inveterate tenacity with which a drunkard's habits cling to him through life. He may repent--he may reform--he may look with actual abhorrence upon his past profligacy; but amid all this reformation and compunction, who can tell the moment in which the base and ruinous propensity may not recur, triumphing over resolution, remorse, shame, everything, and prostrating its victim once more in all that is destructive and revolting in that fatal vice.

The wretched man left the place in a state of utter intoxication. He was brought home nearly insensible, and placed in his bed, where he lay in the deep calm lethargy of drunkenness. The younger part of the family retired to rest much after their usual hour; but the poor wife remained up sitting by the fire, too much grieved and shocked at the recurrence of what she had so little expected, to settle to rest; fatigue, however, at length overcame her, and she sunk gradually into an uneasy slumber. She could not tell how long she had remained in this state, when she awakened, and immediately on opening her eyes, she perceived by the faint red light of the smouldering turf embers, two persons, one of whom she recognized as her husband noiselessly gliding out of the room.

"Pat, darling, where are you going?" said she. There was no answer--the door closed after them; but in a moment she was startled and terrified by a loud and heavy crash, as if some ponderous body had been hurled down the stair. Much alarmed, she started up, and going to the head of the staircase, she called repeatedly upon her husband, but in vain. She returned to the room, and with the assistance of her daughter, whom I had occasion to mention before, she succeeded in finding and lighting a candle, with which she hurried again to the head of the staircase. At the bottom lay what seemed to be a bundle of clothes, heaped together, motionless, lifeless--it was her husband. In going down the stairs, for what purpose can never now be known, he had fallen helplessly and violently to the bottom, and coming head foremost, the spine at the neck had been dislocated by the shock, and instant death must have ensued. The body lay upon that landing-place to which his dream had referred. It is scarcely worth endeavouring to clear up a single point in a narrative where all is mystery; yet I could not help suspecting that the second figure which had been seen in the room by Connell's wife on the night of his death, might have been no other than his own shadow. I suggested this solution of the difficulty; but she told me that the unknown person had been considerably in advance of the other, and on reaching the door, had turned back as if to communicate something to his companion--it was then a mystery. Was the dream verified?--whither had the disembodied spirit sped?--who can say? We know not. But I left the house of death that day in a state of horror which I could not describe. It seemed to me that I was scarce awake. I heard and saw everything as if under the spell of a nightmare. The coincidence was terrible.

# THE GHOST AND THE BONE-SETTER (1838)

In looking over the papers of my late valued and respected friend, Francis Purcell, who for nearly fifty years discharged the arduous duties of a parish priest in the south of Ireland, I met with the following document. It is one of many such, for he was a curious and industrious collector of old local traditions--a commodity in which the quarter where he resided mightily abounded. The collection and arrangement of such legends was, as long as I can remember him, his _hobby_; but I had never learned that his love of the marvellous and whimsical had carried him so far as to prompt him to commit the results of his enquiries to writing, until, in the character of _residuary legatee_, his will put me in possession of all his manuscript papers. To such as may think the composing of such productions as these inconsistent with the character and habits of a country priest, it is necessary to observe, that there did exist a race of priests--those of the old school, a race now nearly extinct--whose habits were from many causes more refined, and whose tastes more literary than are those of the alumni of Maynooth.

It is perhaps necessary to add that the superstition illustrated by the following story, namely, that the corpse last buried is obliged, during his juniority of interment, to supply his brother tenants of the churchyard in which he lies, with fresh water to allay the burning thirst of purgatory, is prevalent throughout the south of Ireland. The writer can vouch for a case in which a respectable and wealthy farmer, on the borders of Tipperary, in tenderness to the corns of his departed helpmate, enclosed in her coffin two pair of brogues, a light and a heavy, the one for dry, the other for sloppy weather; seeking thus to mitigate the fatigues of her inevitable perambulations in procuring water, and administering it to the thirsty souls of purgatory. Fierce and desperate conflicts have ensued in the case of two funeral parties approaching the same churchyard together, each endeavouring to secure to his own dead priority of sepulture, and a consequent immunity from the tax levied upon the pedestrian powers of the last comer. An instance not long since occurred, in which one of two such parties, through fear of losing to their deceased friend this inestimable advantage, made their way to the churchyard by a _short cut_, and in violation of one of their strongest prejudices, actually threw the coffin over the wall, lest time should be lost in making their entrance through the gate. Innumerable instances of the same kind might be quoted, all tending to show how strongly, among the peasantry of the south, this superstition is entertained. However, I shall not detain the reader further, by any prefatory remarks, but shall proceed to lay before him the following:--

_Extract from the Ms. Papers of the Late Rev. Francis Purcell, of Drumcoolagh_

"I tell the following particulars, as nearly as I can recollect them, in the words of the narrator. It may be necessary to observe that he was what is termed a _well-spoken_ man, having for a considerable time instructed the ingenious youth of his native parish in such of the liberal arts and sciences as he found it convenient to profess--a circumstance which may account for the occurrence of several big words, in the course of this narrative, more distinguished for euphonious effect, than for correctness of application. I proceed then, without further preface, to lay before you the wonderful adventures of Terry Neil.

"Why, thin, 'tis a quare story, an' as thrue as you're sittin' there; and I'd make bould to say there isn't a boy in the seven parishes could tell it better nor crickther than myself, for 'twas my father himself it happened to, an' many's the time I heerd it out iv his own mouth; an' I can say, an' I'm proud av that same, my father's word was as incredible as any squire's oath in the counthry; and so signs an' if a poor man got into any unlucky throuble, he was the boy id go into the court an' prove; but that dosen't signify--he was as honest and as sober a man, barrin' he was a little bit too partial to the glass, as you'd find in a day's walk; an' there wasn't the likes of him in the counthry round for nate labourin' an' _baan_ diggin'; and he was mighty handy entirely for carpenther's work, and mendin' ould spudethrees, an' the likes i' that. An' so he tuck up with bone-setting, as was most nathural, for none of them could come up to him in mendin' the leg iv a stool or a table; an' sure, there never was a bone-setter got so much custom--man an' child, young an' ould--there never was such breakin' and mendin' of bones known in the memory of man. Well, Terry Neil, for that was my father's name, began to feel his heart growin' light and his purse heavy; an' he took a bit iv a farm in Squire Phalim's ground, just undher the ould castle, an' a pleasant little spot it was; an' day an' mornin , poor crathurs not able to put a foot to the ground, with broken arms and broken legs, id be comin' ramblin' in from all quarters to have their bones spliced up. Well, yer honour, all this was as well as well could be; but it was customary when Sir Phelim id go any where out iv the country, for some iv the tinants to sit up to watch in the ould castle, just for a kind of a compliment to the ould family--an' a mighty unpleasant compliment it was for the tinants, for there wasn't a man of them but knew there was some thing quare about the ould castle. The neighbours had it, that the squire's ould grandfather, as good a gintleman, God be with him, as I heer'd as ever stood in shoe leather, used to keep walkin' about in the middle iv the night, ever sinst he bursted a blood vessel pullin' out a cork out iv a bottle, as you or I might be doin', and will too, plase God; but that dosen't signify. So, as I was sayin', the ould squire used to come down out of the frame, where his picthur was hung up, and to brake the bottles and glasses, God be marciful to us all, an' dhrink all he could come at--an' small blame to him for that same; and then if any of the family id be comin' in, he id be up again in his place, looking as quite an' innocent as if he didn't know any thing about it--the mischievous ould chap.

"Well, your honour, as I was sayin', one time the family up at the castle was stayin' in Dublin for a week or two; and so as usual, some of the tenants had to sit up in the castle, and the third night it kem to my father's turn. 'Oh, tare an ouns,' says he unto himself, 'an' must I sit up all night, and that ould vagabond of a sperit, glory be to God,' says he, 'serenading through the house, an' doin' all sorts iv mischief.' However, there was no gettin' aff, and so he put a bould face on it, an' he went up at nightfall with a bottle of pottieen, and another of holy wather.

"It was rainin' smart enough, an' the evenin' was darksome and gloomy, when my father got in, and the holy wather he sprinkled on himself, it wasn't long till he had to swallee a cup iv the pottieen, to keep the cowld out iv his heart. It was the ould steward, Lawrence Connor, that opened the door--and he an' my father wor always very great. So when he seen who it was, an' my father tould him how it was his turn to watch in the castle, he offered to sit up along with him; and you may be sure my father wasn't sorry for that same. So says Larry,

"'We'll have a bit iv fire in the parlour,' says he.

"'An' why not in the hall?' says my father, for he knew that the squire's picthur was hung in the parlour.

"'No fire can be lit in the hall,' says Lawrence, 'for there's an ould jackdaw's nest in the chimney.'

"'Oh thin,' says my father, 'let us stop in the kitchen, for it's very umproper for the likes iv me to be sittin' in the parlour,' says he.

"'Oh, Terry, that can't be,' says Lawrence; 'if we keep up the ould custom at all, we may as well keep it up properly,' says he.

"'Divil sweep the ould custom,' says my father--to himself, do ye mind, for he didn't like to let Lawrence see that he was more afeard himself.

"'Oh, very well,' says he. 'I'm agreeable, Lawrence,' says he; and so down they both went to the kitchen, until the fire id be lit in the parlour--an' that same wasn't long doin'.

"Well, your honour, they soon wint up again, an' sat down mighty comfortable by the parlour fire, and they beginn'd to talk, an' to smoke, an' to dhrink a small taste iv the pottieen; and, moreover, they had a good rousing fire of bogwood and turf, to warm their shins over.

"Well, sir, as I was sayin' they kep convarsin' and smokin' together most agreeable, until Lawrence beginn'd to get sleepy, as was but nathural for him, for he was an ould sarvint man, and was used to a great dale iv sleep.

"'Sure it's impossible,' says my father, 'it's gettin' sleepy you are?'

"'Oh, divil a taste,' says Larry. 'I'm only shuttin' my eyes,' says he, 'to keep out the parfume of the tibacky smoke, that's makin' them wather,' says he. 'So don't you mind other people's business,' says he stiff enough (for he had a mighty high stomach av his own, rest his sowl), 'and go on,' says he, 'with your story, for I'm listenin',' says he, shuttin' down his eyes.

"Well, when my father seen spakin' was no use, he went on with his story.--By the same token, it was the story of Jim Soolivan and his ould goat he was tellin'--an' a pleasant story it is--an' there was so much divarsion in it, that it was enough to waken a dormouse, let alone to pervint a Christian goin' asleep. But, faix, the way my father tould it,

I believe there never was the likes heerd sinst nor before for he bawled out every word av it, as if the life was fairly leavin' him thrying to keep ould Larry awake; but, faix, it was no use, for the hoorsness came an him, an' before he kem to the end of his story, Larry O'Connor beginned to snore like a bagpipes.

"'Oh, blur an' agres,' says my father, 'isn't this a hard case,' says he, 'that ould villain, lettin' on to be my friend, and to go asleep this way, an' us both in the very room with a sperit,' says he. 'The crass o' Christ about us,' says he; and with that he was goin' to shake Lawrence to waken him, but he just remimbered if he roused him, that he'd surely go off to his bed, an lave him completely alone, an' that id be by far worse.

"'Oh thin,' says my father, 'I'll not disturb the poor boy. It id be neither friendly nor good-nathured,' says he, 'to tormint him while he is asleep,' says he; 'only I wish I was the same way myself,' says he.

"An' with that he beginned to walk up an' down, an' sayin' his prayers, until he worked himself into a sweat, savin' your presence. But it was all no good; so he dhrunk about a pint of sperits, to compose his mind.

"'Oh,' says he, 'I wish to the Lord I was as asy in my mind as Larry there. Maybe,' says he, 'if I thried I could go asleep'; an' with that he pulled a big arm-chair close beside Lawrence, an' settled himself in it as well as he could.

"But there was one quare thing I forgot to tell you. He couldn't help, in spite av himself, lookin' now an' thin at the picthur, an' he immediately observed that the eyes av it was follyin' him about, an' starin' at him, an' winkin' at him, wherever he wint. 'Oh,' says he, when he seen that, 'it's a poor chance I have,' says he; 'an' bad luck was with me the day I kem into this unforthunate place,' says he; 'but any way there's no use in bein' freckened now,' says he; 'for if I am to die, I may as well parspire undaunted,' says he.

"Well, your honour, he thried to keep himself quite an' asy, an' he thought two or three times he might have wint asleep, but for the way the storm was groanin' and creekin' through the great heavy branches outside, an' whistlin' through the ould chimnies iv the castle. Well, afther one great roarin' blast iv the wind, you'd think the walls iv the castle was just goin' to fall, quite an' clane, with the shakin' iv it. All av a

suddint the storm stopt, as silent an' as quite as if it was a July evenin'. Well, your honour, it wasn't stopped blowin' for three minnites, before he thought he hard a sort iv a noise over the chimney-piece; an' with that my father just opened his eyes the smallest taste in life, an' sure enough he seen the ould squire gettin' out iv the picthur, for all the world as if he was throwin' aff his ridin' coat, until he stept out clane an' complate, out av the chimly-piece, an' thrun himself down an the floor. Well, the slieveen ould chap--an' my father thought it was the dirtiest turn iv all--before he beginned to do anything out iv the way, he stopped, for a while, to listen wor they both asleep; an' as soon as he thought all was quite, he put out his hand, and tuck hould iv the whiskey bottle, an' dhrank at laste a pint iv it. Well, your honour, when he tuck his turn out iv it, he settled it back mighty cute intirely, in the very same spot it was in before. An' he beginn'd to walk up an' down the room, lookin' as sober an' as solid as if he never done the likes at all. An' whinever he went apast my father, he thought he felt a great scent of brimstone, an' it was that that freckened him entirely; for he knew it was brimstone that was burned in hell, savin' your presence. At any rate, he often heer'd it from Father Murphy, an' he had a right to know what belonged to it--he's dead since, God rest him. Well, your honour, my father was asy enough until the sperit kem past him; so close, God be marciful to us all, that the smell iv the sulphur tuck the breath clane out iv him; an' with that he tuck such a fit iv coughin', that it al-a-most shuck him out iv the chair he was sittin' in.
"'Ho, ho!' says the squire, stoppin' short about two steps aff, and turnin' round facin' my father, 'is it you that's in it?--an' how's all with you, Terry Neil?'

"'At your honour's sarvice,' says my father (as well as the fright id let him, for he was more dead than alive), 'an' it's proud I am to see your honour to-night,' says he.

"'Terence,' says the squire, 'you're a respectable man (an' it was thrue for him), an industhrious, sober man, an' an example of inebriety to the whole parish,' says he.

"'Thank your honour,' says my father, gettin' courage, 'you were always a civil spoken gintleman, God rest your honour.'

"'Rest my honour,' says the sperit (fairly gettin' red in the face with the madness), 'Rest my honour?' says he. 'Why, you ignorant spalpeen,' says he, 'you mane, niggarly ignoramush,' says he, 'where did you lave your manners?' says he. 'If I _am_ dead, it's no fault iv mine,' says he; 'an' it's not to be thrun in my teeth at every hand's turn, by the likes iv you,' says he, stampin' his foot an the flure, that you'd think the boords id smash undher him.

"'Oh,' says my father, 'I'm only a foolish, ignorant, poor man,' says he.

"'You're nothing else,' says the squire; 'but any way,' says he, 'it's not to be listenin' to your gosther, nor convarsin' with the likes iv you, that I came _up_--down I mane,' says he--(an' as little as the mistake was, my father tuck notice iv it). 'Listen to me now, Terence Neil,' says he, 'I was always a good masther to Pathrick Neil, your grandfather,' says he.

"'Tis thrue for your honour,' says my father.

"'And, moreover, I think I was always a sober, riglar gintleman,' says the squire.

"'That's your name, sure enough,' says my father (though it was a big lie for him, but he could not help it). "'Well,' says the sperit, 'although I was as sober as most men--at laste as most gintlemen'--says he; 'an' though I was at different pariods a most extempory Christian, and most charitable and inhuman to the poor,' says he; 'for all that I'm not as asy where I am now,' says he, 'as I had a right to expect,' says he.

"'An' more's the pity,' says my father; 'maybe your honour id wish to have a word with Father Murphy?'

"'Hould your tongue, you misherable bliggard,' says the squire; 'it's not iv my sowl I'm thinkin'--an' I wondher you'd have the impitence to talk to a gintleman consarnin' his sowl;--and when I want _that_ fixed,' says he, slappin' his thigh, 'I'll go to them that knows what belongs to the likes,' says he. 'It's not my sowl,' says he, sittin' down opposite my father; 'it's not my sowl that's annoyin' me most--I'm unasy on my right leg,' says he, 'that I bruck at Glenvarloch cover the day I killed black Barney.'

"(My father found out afther, it was a favourite horse that fell undher him, afther leapin' the big fince that runs along by the glen.)

"'I hope,' says my father, 'your honour's not unasy about the killin' iv him?

"'Hould your tongue, ye fool,' said the squire, 'an' I'll tell you why I'm anasy an my leg,' says he. 'In the place, where I spend most iv my time,' says he, 'except the little leisure I have for lookin' about me here,' says he, 'I have to walk a great dale more than I was ever used to,' says he, 'and by far more than is good for me either,' says he; 'for I must tell you,' says he, 'the people where I am is ancommonly fond iv could wather, for there is nothin' betther to be had; an', moreover, the weather is hotter than is altogether plisint,' says he; 'and I'm appinted,' says he, 'to assist in carryin' the wather, an' gets a mighty poor share iv it myself,' says he, 'an' a mighty throublesome, warin' job it is, I can tell you,' says he; 'for they're all iv them surprisingly dhry, an' dhrinks it as fast as my legs can carry it,' says he; 'but what kills me intirely,' says he, 'is the wakeness in my leg,' says he, 'an' I want you to give it a pull or two to bring it to shape,' says he, 'and that's the long an' the short iv it,' says he.
"'Oh, plase your honour,' says my father (for he didn't like to handle the sperit at all), 'I wouldn't have the impitence to do the likes to your honour,' says he; 'it's only to poor crathurs like myself I'd do it to,' says he.

"'None iv your blarney,' says the squire, 'here's my leg,' says he, cockin' it up to him, 'pull it for the bare life,' says he; 'an' if you don't, by the immortial powers I'll not lave a bone in your carcish I'll not powdher,' says he.

"'When my father heerd that, he seen there was no use in purtendin', so he tuck hould iv the leg, an' he kept pullin' an' pullin', till the sweat, God bless us, beginned to pour down his face.

"'Pull, you divil', says the squire.

"'At your sarvice, your honour,' says my father.

"'Pull harder,' says the squire.

"My father pulled like the divil.

"'I'll take a little sup,' says the squire, rachin' over his hand to the bottle, 'to keep up my courage,' says he, lettin' an to be very wake in himself intirely. But, as cute as he was, he was out here, for he tuck the wrong one. 'Here's to your good health, Terence,' says he, 'an' now pull like the very divil,' 'an' with that he lifted the bottle of holy wather, but it was hardly to his mouth, whin he let a screech out, you'd think the room id fairly split with it, an' made one chuck that sent the leg clane aff his body in my father's hands; down wint the squire over the table, an' bang wint my father half way across the room on his back, upon the flure. Whin he kem to himself the cheerful mornin' sun was shinin' through the windy shutthers, an' he was lying flat an his back, with the leg iv one of the great ould chairs pulled clane out iv the socket an' tight in his hand, pintin' up to the ceilin', an' ould Larry fast asleep, an' snorin' as loud as ever. My father wint that mornin' to Father Murphy, an' from that to the day of his death, he never neglected confission nor mass, an' what he tould was betther believed that he spake av it but seldom. An', as for the squire, that is the sperit, whether it was that he did not like his liquor, or by rason iv the loss iv his leg, he was never known to walk again."

# THE MYSTERIOUS LODGER
## (1850)

### PART I

About the year 1822 I resided in a comfortable and roomy old house, the exact locality of which I need not particularise, further than to say that it was not very far from Old Brompton, in the immediate neighbourhood, or rather continuity (as even my Connemara readers perfectly well know), of the renowned city of London.

Though this house was roomy and comfortable, as I have said, it was not, by any means, a handsome one. It was composed of dark red brick, with small windows, and thick white sashes; a porch, too--none of your flimsy trellis-work, but a solid projection of the same vermillion masonry--surmounted by a leaded balcony, with heavy, half-rotten balustrades, darkened the hall-door with a perennial gloom. The mansion itself stood in a walled enclosure, which had, perhaps, from the date of the erection itself, been devoted to shrubs and flowers. Some of the former had grown there almost to the dignity of trees; and two dark little yews stood at each side of the porch, like swart and inauspicious dwarfs, guarding the entrance of an enchanted castle. Not that my domicile in any respect deserved the comparison: it had no reputation as a haunted house; if it ever had any ghosts, nobody remembered them. Its history was not known to me: it may have witnessed plots, cabals, and forgeries, bloody suicides and cruel murders. It was certainly old enough to have become acquainted with iniquity; a small stone slab, under the balustrade, and over the arch of the porch I mentioned, had the date 1672, and a half-effaced coat of arms, which I might have deciphered any day, had I taken the trouble to get a ladder, but always put it off. All I can say for the house is, that it was well stricken in years, with a certain air of sombre comfort about it; contained a vast number of rooms and closets; and, what was of far greater importance, was got by me a dead bargain.

Its individuality attracted me. I grew fond of it for itself, and for its associations, until other associations of a hateful kind first disturbed, and then destroyed, their charm. I forgave its dull red brick, and pinched white windows, for the sake of the beloved and cheerful faces within: its ugliness was softened by its age; and its sombre evergreens, and moss-grown stone flower-pots, were relieved by the brilliant hues of a thousand gay and graceful flowers that peeped among them, or nodded over the grass.

Within that old house lay my life's treasure! I had a darling little girl of nine, and another little darling--a boy--just four years of age; and dearer, unspeakably, than either--a wife--the prettiest, gayest, best little wife in all London. When I tell you that our income was scarcely £380 a-year, you will perceive that our establishment cannot have been a magnificent one; yet, I do assure you, we were more comfortable than a great many lords, and happier, I dare say, than the whole peerage put together.

This happiness was not, however, what it ought to have been. The reader will understand at once, and save me a world of moralising circumlocution, when he learns, bluntly and nakedly, that, among all my comforts and blessings, I was an infidel.

I had not been without religious training; on the contrary, more than average pains had been bestowed upon my religious instruction from my earliest childhood. My father, a good, plain, country clergyman, had worked hard to make me as good as himself; and had succeeded, at least, in training me in godly habits. He died, however, when I was but twelve years of age; and fate had long before deprived me of the gentle care of a mother. A boarding-school, followed by a college life, where nobody having any very direct interest in realising in my behalf the ancient blessing, that in fulness of time I should "die a good old man," I was left very much to my own devices, which, in truth, were none of the best.

Among these were the study of Voltaire, Tom Paine, Hume, Shelley, and the whole school of infidels, poetical as well as prose. This pursuit, and the all but blasphemous vehemence with which I gave myself up to it, was, perhaps, partly reactionary. A somewhat injudicious austerity and precision had indissolubly associated in my childish days the ideas of restraint and gloom with religion. I bore it a grudge; and so, when I became thus early my own master, I set about paying off, after my own fashion, the old score I owed it. I was besides, like every other young infidel whom it has been my fate to meet, a conceited coxcomb. A smattering of literature, without any real knowledge, and a great assortment of all the cut-and-dry flippancies of the school I had embraced, constituted my intellectual stock in trade. I was, like most of my school of philosophy, very proud of being an unbeliever; and fancied myself, in the complacency of my wretched ignorance, at an immeasurable elevation above the church-going, Bible-reading herd, whom I treated with a good-humoured superciliousness which I thought vastly indulgent.

My wife was an excellent little creature and truly pious. She had married me in the full confidence that my levity was merely put on, and would at once give way before the influence she hoped to exert upon my mind. Poor little thing! she deceived herself. I allowed her, indeed, to do entirely as she pleased; but for myself, I carried my infidelity to the length of an absolute superstition. I made an ostentation of it. I would rather have been in a "hell" than in a church on Sunday; and though I did not prevent my wife's instilling her own principles into the minds of our children, I, in turn, took especial care to deliver mine upon all occasions in their hearing, by which means I trusted to sow the seeds of that unprejudiced scepticism in which I prided myself, at least as early as my good little partner dropped those of her own gentle "superstition" into their infant minds. Had I had my own absurd and impious will in this matter, my children should have had absolutely no religious education whatsoever, and been left wholly unshackled to choose for themselves among all existing systems, infidelity included, precisely as chance, fancy, or interest might hereafter determine.

It is not to be supposed that such a state of things did not afford her great uneasiness. Nevertheless, we were so very fond of one another, and in our humble way enjoyed so many blessings, that we were as entirely happy as any pair can be without the holy influence of religious sympathy.
But the even flow of prosperity which had for so long gladdened my little household was not destined to last for ever. It was ordained that I should experience the bitter truth of more than one of the wise man's proverbs, and first, especially, of that which declares that "he that hateth suretyship is sure." I found myself involved (as how many have been before) by a "d--d good-natured friend," for more than two hundred pounds. This agreeable intelligence was conveyed to me in an attorney's letter, which, to obviate unpleasant measures, considerately advised my paying the entire amount within just one week of the date of his pleasant epistle. Had I been called upon within that time to produce the Pitt

diamond, or to make title to the Buckingham estates, the demand would have been just as easily complied with.

I have no wish to bore my reader further with this little worry--a very serious one to me, however--and it will be enough to mention, that the kindness of a friend extricated me from the clutches of the law by a timely advance, which, however, I was bound to replace within two years. To enable me to fulfill this engagement, my wife and I, after repeated consultations, resolved upon the course which resulted in the odd and unpleasant consequences which form the subject of this narrative.

We resolved to advertise for a lodger, with or without board, &c.; and by resolutely submitting, for a single year, to the economy we had prescribed for ourselves, as well as to the annoyance of a stranger's intrusion, we calculated that at the end of that term we should have liquidated our debt.

Accordingly, without losing time, we composed an advertisement in the most tempting phraseology we could devise, consistently with that economic laconism which the cost per line in the columns of the _Times_ newspaper imposes upon the rhetoric of the advertising public.

Somehow we were unlucky; for although we repeated our public notification three times in the course of a fortnight, we had but two applications. The one was from a clergyman in ill health--a man of great ability and zealous piety, whom we both knew by reputation, and who has since been called to his rest. My good little wife was very anxious that we should close with his offer, which was very considerably under what we had fixed upon; and I have no doubt that she was influenced by the hope that his talents and zeal might exert a happy influence upon my stubborn and unbelieving heart. For my part, his religious character displeased me. I did not wish my children's heads to be filled with mythic dogmas--for so I judged the doctrines of our holy faith--and instinctively wished him away. I therefore declined his offer; and I have often since thought not quite so graciously as I ought to have done. The other offer--if so it can be called--was so very inadequate that we could not entertain it.

I was now beginning to grow seriously uneasy--our little project, so far from bringing in the gains on which we had calculated, had put me considerably out of pocket; for, independently of the cost of the advertisement I have mentioned, there were sundry little expenses involved in preparing for the meet reception of our expected inmate, which, under ordinary circumstances, we should not have dreamed of. Matters were in this posture, when an occurrence took place which immediately revived my flagging hopes.

As we had no superfluity of servants, our children were early obliged to acquire habits of independence; and my little girl, then just nine years of age, was frequently consigned with no other care than that of her own good sense, to the companionship of a little band of playmates, pretty similarly circumstanced, with whom it was her wont to play. Having one fine summer afternoon gone out as usual with these little companions, she did not return quite so soon as we had expected her; when she did so, she was out of breath, and excited.

"Oh, papa," she said, "I have seen such a nice old, kind gentleman, and he told me to tell you that he has a particular friend who wants a lodging in a quiet place, and that he thinks your house would suit him exactly, and ever so much more; and, look here, he gave me this."

She opened her hand, and shewed me a sovereign.

"Well, this does look promisingly," I said, my wife and I having first exchanged a smiling glance.

"And what kind of gentleman was he, dear?" inquired she. "Was he well dressed--whom was he like?"
"He was not like any one that I know," she answered; "but he had very nice new clothes on, and he was one of the fattest men I ever saw; and I am sure he is sick, for he looks very pale, and he had a crutch beside him."

"Dear me, how strange!" exclaimed my wife; though, in truth there was nothing very wonderful in the matter. "Go on, child," I said; "let us hear it all out."

"Well, papa, he had such an immense yellow waistcoat!--I never did see such a waistcoat," she resumed; "and he was sitting or leaning, I can't say which, against the bank of the green lane; I suppose to rest himself, for he seems very weak, poor gentleman!"

"And how did you happen to speak to him?" asked my wife.

"When we were passing by, none of us saw him at all but I suppose he heard them talking to me, and saying my name; for he said, 'Fanny--little Fanny--so, that's your name--come here child, I have a question to ask you.'"

"And so you went to him?" I said.

"Yes," she continued, "he beckoned to me, and I did go over to him, but not very near, for I was greatly afraid of him at first."

"Afraid! dear, and why afraid?" asked I.

"I was afraid, because he looked very old, very frightful, and as if he would hurt me."

"What was there so old and frightful about him?" I asked.

She paused and reflected a little, and then said--

"His face was very large and pale, and it was looking upwards: it seemed very angry, I thought, but maybe it was angry from pain; and sometimes one side of it used to twitch and tremble for a minute, and then to grow quite still again; and all the time he was speaking to me, he never looked at me once, but always kept his face and eyes turned upwards; but his voice was very soft, and he called me little Fanny, and gave me this pound to buy toys with; so I was not so frightened in a little time, and then he sent a long message to you, papa, and told me if I forgot it he would beat me; but I knew he was only joking, so that did not frighten me either."

"And what was the message, my girl?" I asked, patting her pretty head with my hand.

"Now, let me remember it all," she said, reflectively; "for he told it to me twice. He asked me if there was a good bedroom at the top of the house, standing by itself--and you know there is, so I told him so; it was exactly the kind of room that he described. And then he said that his friend would pay two hundred pounds a-year for that bedroom, his board and attendance; and he told me to ask you, and have your answer when he should next meet me."

"Two hundred pounds!" ejaculated my poor little wife; "why that is nearly twice as much as we expected."

"But did he say that his friend was sick, or very old; or that he had any servant to be supported also?" I asked.

"Oh! no; he told me that he was quite able to take care of himself, and that he had, I think he called it, an asthma, but nothing else the matter; and that he would give no trouble at all, and that any friend who came to see him, he would see, not in the house, but only in the garden."

"In the garden!" I echoed, laughing in spite of myself.

"Yes, indeed he said so; and he told me to say that he would pay one hundred pounds when he came here, and the next hundred in six months, and so on," continued she.

"Oh, ho! half-yearly in advance--better and better," said I.

"And he bid me say, too, if you should ask about his character, that he is just as good as the master of the house himself," she added; "and when he said that, he laughed a little."

"Why, if he gives us a hundred pounds in advance," I answered, turning to my wife, "we are safe enough; for he will not find half that value in plate and jewels in the entire household, if he is disposed to rob us. So I see no reason against closing with the offer, should it be seriously meant--do you, dear?"

"Quite the contrary, love," said she. "I think it most desirable--indeed, most _providential_."

"Providential! my dear little bigot!" I repeated, with a smile. "Well, be it so. I call it _lucky_ merely; but, perhaps, you are happier in your faith, than I in my philosophy. Yes, you are _grateful_ for the chance that I only rejoice at. You receive it as a proof of a divine and tender love--I as an accident. Delusions are often more elevating than truth."

And so saying, I kissed away the saddened cloud that for a moment overcast her face.

"Papa, he bid me be sure to have an answer for him when we meet again," resumed the child. "What shall I say to him when he asks me?"

"Say that we agree to his proposal, my dear--or stay," I said, addressing my wife, "may it not be prudent to reduce what the child says to writing, and accept the offer so? This will prevent misunderstanding, as she may possibly have made some mistake."

My wife agreed, and I wrote a brief note, stating that I was willing to receive an inmate upon the terms recounted by little Fanny, and which I distinctly specified, so that no mistake could possibly arise owing to the vagueness of what lawyers term a parole agreement. This important memorandum I placed in the hands of my little girl, who was to deliver it whenever the old gentleman in the yellow waistcoat should chance to meet her. And all these arrangements completed, I awaited the issue of the affair with as much patience as I could affect. Meanwhile, my wife and I talked it over incessantly; and she, good little soul, almost wore herself to death in settling and unsettling the furniture and decorations of our expected inmate's apartments. Days passed away—days of hopes deferred, tedious and anxious. We were beginning to despond again, when one morning our little girl ran into the breakfast-parlour, more excited even than she had been before, and fresh from a new interview with the gentleman in the yellow waistcoat. She had encountered him suddenly, pretty nearly where she had met him before, and the result was, that he had read the little note I have mentioned, and desired the child to inform me that his friend, _Mr. Smith_, would take possession of the apartments I proposed setting, on the terms agreed between us, that very evening.

"This evening!" exclaimed my wife and I simultaneously--_I_ full of the idea of making a first instalment on the day following; _she_, of the hundred-and-one preparations which still remained to be completed.

"And so Smith is his name! Well, that does not tell us much," said I; "but where did you meet your friend on this occasion, and how long is it since?"

"Near the corner of the wall-flower lane (so we indicated one which abounded in these fragrant plants); he was leaning with his back against the old tree you cut my name on, and his crutch was under his arm."

"But how long ago?" I urged.

"Only this moment; I ran home as fast as I could," she replied.

"Why, you little blockhead, you should have told me that at first," I cried, snatching up my hat, and darting away in pursuit of the yellow waistcoat, whose accuaintance I not unnaturally coveted, inasmuch as a man who, for the first time, admits a stranger into his house, on the footing of permanent residence, desires generally to know a little more about him than that his name is Smith.

The place indicated was only, as we say, a step away; and as yellow waistcoat was fat, and used a crutch, I calculated on easily overtaking him. I was, however, disappointed; crutch, waistcoat, and all had disappeared. I climbed to the top of the wall, and from this commanding point of view made a sweeping observation--but in vain. I returned home, cursing my ill-luck, the child's dulness, and the fat old fellow's activity.

I need hardly say that Mr. Smith, in all his aspects, moral, social, physical, and monetary, formed a fruitful and interesting topic of speculation during dinner. How many phantom Smiths, short and long, stout and lean, ill-tempered and well-tempered--rich, respectable, or highly dangerous merchants, spies, forgers, nabobs, swindlers, danced before us, in the endless mazes of fanciful conjecture, during that anxious _tête-à-tête_, which was probably to be interrupted by the arrival of the gentleman himself.

My wife and I puzzled over the problem as people would over the possible _dénouement_ of a French novel; and at last, by mutual consent, we came to the conclusion that Smith could, and would turn out to be no other than the good-natured valetudinarian in the yellow waistcoat himself, a humorist, as was evident enough, and a millionaire, as we unhesitatingly pronounced, who had no immediate relatives, and as I hoped, and my wife "was certain," taken a decided fancy to our little Fanny; I patted the child's head with something akin to pride, as I thought of the magnificent, though remote possibilities, in store for her.

Meanwhile, hour after hour stole away. It was a beautiful autumn evening, and the amber lustre of the declining sun fell softly upon the yews and flowers, and gave an air, half melancholy, half cheerful, to the dark-red brick piers surmounted with their cracked and grass-grown stone urns, and furnished with the light foliage of untended creeping plants. Down the short broad walk leading to this sombre entrance, my eye constantly wandered; but no impatient rattle on the latch, no battering at the gate, indicated the presence of a visited, and the lazy bell hung dumbly among the honey-suckles.

"When will he come? Yellow waistcoat promised _this evening_! It has been evening a good hour and a half, and yet he is not here. When will he come? It will soon be dark--the evening will have passed--will he come at all?"

Such were the uneasy speculations which began to trouble us. Redder and duskier grew the light of the setting sun, till it saddened into the mists of night. Twilight came, and then darkness, and still no arrival, no summons at the gate. I would not admit even to my wife the excess of my own impatience. I could, however, stand it no longer; so I took my hat and walked to the gate, where I stood by the side of the public road, watching every vehicle and person that approached, in a fever of expectation. Even these, however, began to fail me, and the road grew comparatively quiet and deserted. Having kept guard like a sentinel for more than half an hour, I returned in no very good humour, with the punctuality of an expected inmate--ordered the servant to draw the curtains and secure the hall-door; and so my wife and I sate down to our disconsolate cup of tea. It must have been about ten o'clock, and we were both sitting silently--she working, I looking moodily into a paper--and neither of us any longer entertaining a hope that anything but disappointment would come of the matter, when a sudden tapping, very loud and sustained, upon the window pane, startled us both in an instant from our reveries.

I am not sure whether I mentioned before that the sitting-room we occupied was upon the ground-floor, and the sward came close under the window. I drew the curtains, and opened the shutters with a revived hope; and looking out, saw a very tall thin figure, a good deal wrapped up, standing about a yard before me, and motioning with head and hand impatiently towards the hall-door. Though the night was clear, there was no moon, and therefore I could see no more than the black outline, like that of an _ombre chinoise_ figure, signing to me with mop and moe. In a moment I was at the hall-door, candle in hand; the stranger stept in--his long fingers clutched in the handle of a valise, and a bag which trailed upon the ground behind him.

The light fell full upon him. He wore a long, ill-made, black surtout, buttoned across, and which wrinkled and bagged about his lank figure; his hat was none of the best, and rather broad in the brim; a sort of white woollen muffler enveloped the lower part of his face; a pair of prominent green goggles, fenced round with leather, completely concealed his eyes; and nothing of the genuine man, but a little bit of yellow forehead, and a small transverse segment of equally yellow cheek and nose, encountered the curious gaze of your humble servant.

"You are--I suppose"--I began; for I really was a little doubtful about my man.

"Mr. Smith--the same; be good enough to show me to my bedchamber," interrupted the stranger, brusquely, and in a tone which, spite of the muffler that enveloped his mouth, was sharp and grating enough.

"Ha!--Mr. Smith--so I supposed. I hope you may find everything as comfortable as we desire to make it--"

I was about making a speech, but was cut short by a slight bow, and a decisive gesture of the hand in the direction of the staircase. It was plain that the stranger hated ceremony.

Together, accordingly, we mounted the staircase; he still pulling his luggage after him, and striding lightly up without articulating a word; and on reaching his bedroom, he immediately removed his hat, showing a sinister, black scratch-wig underneath, and then began unrolling the mighty woolen wrapping of his mouth and chin.

"Come," thought I, "we _shall_ see something of your face after all."

This something, however, proved to be very little; for under his muffler was a loose cravat, which stood up in front of his chin and upon his mouth, he wore a respirator--an instrument which I had never seen before, and of the use of which I was wholly ignorant.

There was something so excessively odd in the effect of this piece of unknown mechanism upon his mouth, surmounted by the huge goggles which encased his eyes, that I believe I should have laughed outright, were it not for a certain unpleasant and peculiar impressiveness in the _tout ensemble_ of the narrow-chested, long-limbed, and cadaverous figure in black. As it was, we stood looking at one another in silence for several seconds.

"Thank you, sir," at last he said, abruptly. "I shan't want anything whatever to-night; if you can only spare me this candle."

I assented; and, becoming more communicative, he added--

"I am, though an invalid, an independent sort of fellow enough. I am a bit of a philosopher; I am my own servant, and, I hope, my own master, too. I rely upon myself in matters of the body and of the mind. I place valets and priests in the same category--fellows who live by our laziness, intellectual or corporeal. I am a Voltaire, without his luxuries--a Robinson Crusoe, without his Bible--an anchorite, without a superstition--in short, my indulgence is asceticism, and my faith infidelity. Therefore, I shan't disturb your servants much with my bell, nor yourselves with my psalmody. You have got a rational lodger, who knows how to attend upon himself."

During this singular address he was drawing off his ill-fitting black gloves, and when he had done so, a bank-note, which had been slipped underneath for safety, remained in his hand.

"Punctuality, sir, is one of my poor pleasures," he said; "will you allow me to enjoy it now? To-morrow you may acknowledge this; I should not rest were you to decline it."

He extended his bony and discoloured fingers, and placed the note in my hand. Oh, Fortune and Plutus! It was a £100 bank-note.

"Pray, not one word, my dear sir," he continued, unbending still further; "it is simply done pursuant to agreement. We shall know one another better, I hope, in a little time; you will find me always equally punctual. At present pray give yourself no further trouble; I require nothing more. Good night."

I returned the valediction, closed his door, and groped my way down the stairs. It was not until I had nearly reached the hall, that I recollected that I had omitted to ask our new inmate at what hour he would desire to be called in the morning, and so I groped my way back again. As I reached the lobby on which his chamber opened, I perceived a long line of light issuing from the partially-opened door, within which stood Mr. Smith, the same odd figure I had just left; while along the boards was creeping towards him across the lobby, a great, big-headed, buff-coloured cat. I had never seen this ugly animal before; and it had reached the threshold of his door, arching its back, and rubbing itself on the post, before either appeared conscious of my approach, when, with an angry growl, it sprang into the stranger's room.

"What do you want?" he demanded, sharply, standing in the doorway.

I explained my errand.

"I shall call myself," was his sole reply; and he shut the door with a crash that indicated no very pleasurable emotions.

I cared very little about my lodger's temper. The stealthy rustle of his bank-note in my waistcoat pocket was music enough to sweeten the harshest tones of his voice, and to keep alive a cheerful good humour in my heart; and although there was, indisputably, something queer about him, I was, on the whole, very well pleased with my bargain.

The next day our new inmate did not ring his bell until noon. As soon as he had had some breakfast, of which he very sparingly partook, he told the servant that, for the future, he desired that a certain quantity of milk and bread might be left outside his door; and this being done, he would dispense with regular meals. He desired, too, that, on my return, I should be acquainted that he wished to see me in his own room at about nine o'clock; and, meanwhile, he directed that he should be left undisturbed. I found my little wife full of astonishment at Mr. Smith's strange frugality and seclusion, and very curious to learn the object of the interview he had desired with me. At nine o'clock I repaired to his room.

I found him in precisely the costume in which I had left him--the same green goggles--the same muffling of the mouth, except that being now no more than a broadly-folded black silk handkerchief, very loose, and covering even the lower part of the nose, it was obviously intended for the sole purpose of concealment. It was plain I was not to see more of his features than he had chosen to disclose at our first interview. The effect was as if the lower part of his face had some hideous wound or sore. He closed the door with his own hand on my entrance, nodded slightly, and took his seat. I expected him to begin, but he was so long silent that I was at last constrained to address him.

I said, for want of something more to the purpose, that I hoped he had not been tormented by the strange cat the night before.

"What cat?" he asked, abruptly; "what the plague do you mean?"

"Why, I certainly did see a cat go into your room last night," I resumed.

"Hey, and what if you did--though I fancy you dreamed it--I'm not afraid of a cat; are you?" he interrupted, tartly.

At this moment there came a low growling mew from the closet which opened from the room in which we sat.

"Talk of the devil," said I, pointing towards the closet. My companion, without any exact change of expression, looked, I thought, somehow still more sinister and lowering; and I felt for a moment a sort of superstitious misgiving, which made the rest of the sentence die away on my lips.

Perhaps Mr. Smith perceived this, for he said, in a tone calculated to reassure me--

"Well, sir, I think I am bound to tell you that I like my apartments very well; they suit me, and I shall probably be your tenant for much longer than at first you anticipated."

I expressed my gratification.

He then began to talk, something in the strain in which he had spoken of his own peculiarities of habit and thinking upon the previous evening. He disposed of all classes and denominations of superstition with an easy sarcastic slang, which for me was so captivating, that I soon lost all reserve, and found myself listening and suggesting by turns--acquiescent and pleased--sometimes hazarding dissent; but whenever I did, foiled and floored by a few pointed satirical sentences, whose sophistry, for such I must now believe it, confounded me with a rapidity which, were it not for the admiration with which he had insensibly inspired me, would have piqued and irritated my vanity not a little.

While this was going on, from time to time the mewing and growling of a cat within the closet became more and more audible. At last these sounds became so loud, accompanied by scratching at the door, that I paused in the midst of a sentence, and observed--

"There certainly is a cat shut up in the closet?"

"Is there?" he ejaculated, in a surprised tone; "nay, I do not hear it."

He rose abruptly and approached the door; his back was towards me, but I observed he raised the goggles which usually covered his eyes, and looked steadfastly at the closet door. The angry sounds all died away into a low, protracted growl, which again subsided into silence. He continued in the same attitude for some moments, and then returned.

"I do not hear it," he said, as he resumed his place, and taking a book from his capacious pocket, asked me if I had seen it before? I never had, and this surprised me, for I had flattered myself that I knew, at least by name, every work published in England during the last fifty years in favour of that philosophy in which we both delighted. The book, moreover, was an odd one, as both its title and table of contents demonstrated.

While we were discoursing upon these subjects, I became more and more distinctly conscious of a new class of sounds proceeding from the same closet. I plainly heard a measured and heavy tread, accompanied by the tapping of some hard and heavy substance like the end of a staff, pass up and down the floor--first, as it seemed, stealthily, and then more and more unconcealedly. I began to feel very uncomfortable and suspicious. As the noise proceeded, and became more and more unequivocal, Mr. Smith abruptly rose, opened the closet door, just enough to admit his own lath-like person, and steal within the threshold for some seconds. What he did I could not see--I felt conscious he had an associate concealed there; and though my eyes remained fixed on the book, I could not avoid listening for some audible words, or signal of caution. I heard, however, nothing of the kind. Mr. Smith turned back--walked a step or two towards me, and said--

"I fancied I heard a sound from that closet, but there is nothing--nothing--nothing whatever; bring the candle, let us both look."

I obeyed with some little trepidation, for I fully anticipated that I should detect the intruder, of whose presence my own ears had given me, for nearly half an hour, the most unequivocal proofs. We entered the closet together; it contained but a few chairs and a small spider table. At the far end of the room there was a sort of grey woollen cloth upon the floor, and a bundle of something underneath it. I looked jealously at it, and half thought I could trace the outline of a human figure; but, if so, it was perfectly motionless.

"Some of my poor wardrobe," he muttered, as he pointed his lean finger in the direction. "It did not sound like a cat, did it--hey--did it?" he muttered; and without attending to my answer, he went about the apartment, clapping his hands, and crying, "Hish--hish--hish!"

The game, however, whatever it was, did not start. As I entered I had seen, however, a large crutch reposing against the wall in the corner opposite to the door. This was the only article in the room, except that I have mentioned, with which I was not familiar. With the exception of our two selves, there was not a living creature to be seen there; no shadow but ours upon the bare walls; no feet but our own upon the comfortless floor.

I had never before felt so strange and unpleasant a sensation.

"There is nothing unusual in the room but that crutch," I said.

"What crutch, you dolt? I see no crutch," he ejaculated, in a tone of sudden but suppressed fury.

"Why, _that_ crutch," I answered (for somehow I neither felt nor resented his rudeness), turning and pointing to the spot where I had seen it. It was gone!--it was neither there nor anywhere else. It must have been an illusion--rather an odd one, to be sure. And yet I could at this moment, with a safe conscience, _swear_ that I never saw an object more distinctly than I had seen it but a second before.

My companion was muttering fast to himself as we withdrew; his presence rather scared than reassured me; and I felt something almost amounting to horror, as, holding the candle above his cadaverous and sable figure, he stood at his threshold, while I descended the stairs, and said, in a sort of whisper--

"Why, but that I am, like yourself, a philosopher, I should say that your house is--is--a--ha! ha! ha!--HAUNTED!"

"You look very pale, my love," said my wife, as I entered the drawing-room, where she had been long awaiting my return. "Nothing unpleasant has happened?"

"Nothing, nothing, I assure you. Pale!--_do_ I look pale?" I answered. "We are excellent friends, I assure you. So far from having had the smallest disagreement, there is every prospect of our agreeing but too well, as you will say; for I find that he holds all my opinions upon speculative subjects. We have had a great deal of conversation this evening, I assure you; and I never met, I think, so scholarlike and able a man."

"I am sorry for it, dearest," she said, sadly. "The greater his talents, if such be his opinions the more dangerous a companion is he."

We turned, however, to more cheerful topics, and it was late before we retired to rest. I believe it was pride--perhaps only vanity--but, at all events, some obstructive and stubborn instinct of my nature, which I could not overcome--that prevented my telling my wife the odd occurrences which had disturbed my visit to our guest. I was unable or ashamed to confess that so slight a matter had disturbed me; and, above all, that any accident could possibly have clouded, even for a moment, the frosty clearness of my pure and lofty scepticism with the shadows of superstition.

Almost every day seemed to develop some new eccentricity of our strange guest. His dietary consisted, without any variety or relief, of the monotonous bread and milk with which he started; his bed had not been made for nearly a week; nobody had been admitted into his room since my visit, just described; and he never ventured down stairs, or out of doors, until after nightfall, when he used sometimes to glide swiftly round our little enclosed shrubbery, and at others stand quite motionless, composed, as if in an attitude of deep attention. After employing about an hour in this way, he would return, and steal up stairs to his room, when he would shut himself up, and not be seen again until the next night--or, it might be, the night after that--when, perhaps, he would repeat his odd excursion.

Strange as his habits were, their eccentricity was all upon the side least troublesome to us. He required literally no attendance; and as to his occasional night ramble, even _it_ caused not the slightest disturbance of our routine hour for securing the house and locking up the hall-door for the night, inasmuch as he had invariably retired before that hour arrived.

All this stimulated curiosity, and, in no small degree, that of my wife, who, notwithstanding her vigilance and her anxiety to see our strange inmate, had been hitherto foiled by a series of cross accidents. We were sitting together somewhere about ten o'clock at night, when there came a tap at the room-door. We had just been discussing the unaccountable Smith; and I felt a sheepish consciousness that he might be himself at the door, and have possibly even overheard our speculation--some of them anything but complimentary, respecting himself.

"Come in," cried, I, with an effort; and the tall form of our lodger glided into the room. My wife was positively frightened, and stood looking at him, as he advanced, with a stare of manifest apprehension, and even recoiled mechanically, and caught my hand.

Sensitiveness, however, was not his fault: he made a kind of stiff nod as I mumbled an introduction; and seating himself unasked, began at once to chat in that odd, off-hand, and sneering style, in which he excelled, and which had, as he wielded it, a sort of fascination of which I can pretend to convey no idea.

My wife's alarm subsided, and although she still manifestly felt some sort of misgiving about our visitor, she yet listened to his conversation, and, spite of herself, soon began to enjoy it. He stayed for nearly half an hour. But although he glanced at a great variety of topics, he did not approach the subject of religion. As soon as he was gone, my wife delivered judgment upon him in form. She admitted he was agreeable; but then he was such an unnatural, awful-looking object: there was, besides, something indescribably frightful, she thought, in his manner--the very tone of his voice was strange and hateful; and, on the whole, she felt unutterably relieved at his departure.

A few days after, on my return, I found my poor little wife agitated and dispirited. Mr. Smith had paid her a visit, and brought with him a book, which he stated he had been reading, and which contained some references to the Bible which he begged of her to explain in that profounder and less obvious sense in which they had been cited. This she had endeavoured to do; and affecting to be much gratified by her satisfactory exposition, he had requested her to reconcile some discrepancies which he said had often troubled him when reading the Scriptures. Some of them were quite new to my good little wife; they startled and even horrified her. He pursued this theme, still pretending only to seek for information to quiet his own doubts, while in reality he was sowing in her mind the seeds of the first perturbations that had ever troubled the sources of her peace. He had been with her, she thought, no more than a quarter of an hour; but he had contrived to leave her abundant topics on which to ruminate for days. I found her shocked and horrified at the doubts which this potent Magus had summoned from the pit--doubts which she knew not how to combat, and from the torment of which she could not escape.

"He has made me very miserable with his deceitful questions. I never thought of them before; and, merciful Heaven! I cannot answer them! What am I to do? My serenity is gone; I shall never be happy again."

In truth, she was so very miserable, and, as it seemed to me, so disproportionately excited, that, inconsistent in me as the task would have been, I would gladly have explained away her difficulties, and restored to her mind its wonted confidence and serenity, had I possessed sufficient knowledge for the purpose. I really pitied her, and heartily wished Mr. Smith, for the nonce, at the devil.

I observed after this that my wife's spirits appeared permanently affected. There was a constantly-recurring anxiety, and I thought something was lying still more heavily at her heart than the uncertainties inspired by our lodger.

One evening, as we two were sitting together, after a long silence, she suddenly laid her hand upon my arm, and said--

"Oh, Richard, my darling! would to God you could pray for me!"

There was something so agitated, and even terrified, in her manner, that I was absolutely startled. I urged her to disclose whatever preyed upon her mind.

"You can't sympathise with me--you can't help me--you can scarcely compassionate me in my misery! Oh, dearest Richard! Some evil influence has been gaining upon my heart, dulling and destroying my convictions, killing all my holy affections, and--and absolutely transforming me. I look inward upon myself with amazement, with terror--with--oh, God!—with actual despair!"

Saying this, she threw herself on her knees, and wept an agonised flood of tears, with her head reposing in my lap.

Poor little thing, my heart bled for her! But what could I do or say?

All I could suggest was what I really thought, that she was

unwell--hysterical--and needed to take better care of her precious self; that her change of feeling was fancied, not real; and that a few days would restore her to her old health and former spirits and serenity.

"And sometimes," she resumed, after I had ended a consolatory discussion, which it was but too manifest had fallen unprofitably upon her ear, "such dreadful, impious thoughts come into my mind, whether I choose it or not; they come, and stay, and return, strive as I may; and I can't pray against them. They are forced upon me with the strength of an independent will; and oh!--horrible--frightful--they blaspheme the character of God himself. They upbraid the Almighty upon his throne, and I can't pray against them; there is something in me now that resists prayer."

There was such a real and fearful anguish in the agitation of my gentle companion, that it shook my very soul within me, even while I was affecting to make light of her confessions. I had never before witnessed a struggle at all like this, and I was awe-struck at the spectacle.

At length she became comparatively calm. I did gradually succeed, though very imperfectly, in reassuring her. She strove hard against her depression, and recovered a little of her wonted cheerfulness.

After a while, however, the cloud returned. She grew sad and earnest, though no longer excited; and entreated, or rather implored, of me to grant her one special favour, and this was, to avoid the society of our lodger.

"I never," she said, "could understand till now the instinctive dread with which poor Margaret, in _Faust_, shrinks from the hateful presence of Mephistopheles. I now feel it in myself. The dislike and suspicion I first felt for that man--Smith, or whatever else he may call himself--has grown into literal detestation and terror. I hate him--I am afraid of him--I never knew what anguish of mind was until he entered our doors; and would to God--would to God he were gone."

I reasoned with her--kissed her--laughed at her; but could not dissipate, in the least degree, the intense and preternatural horror with which she had grown to regard the poor philosophic invalid, who was probably, at that moment, poring over some metaphysical book in his solitary bedchamber.

The circumstance I am about to mention will give you some notion of the extreme to which these excited feelings had worked upon her nerves. I was that night suddenly awakened by a piercing scream--I started upright in the bed, and saw my wife standing at the bedside, white as ashes with terror. It was some seconds, so startled was I, before I could find words to ask her the cause of her affright. She caught my wrist in her icy grasp, and climbed, trembling violently, into bed. Notwithstanding my repeated entreaties, she continued for a long time stupified and dumb. At length, however, she told me, that having lain awake for a long time, she felt, on a sudden, that she could pray, and lighting the candle, she had stolen from beside me, and kneeled down for the purpose. She had, however, scarcely assumed the attitude of prayer, when somebody, she said, clutched her arm violently near the wrist, and she heard, at the same instant, some blasphemous menace, the import of which escaped her the moment it was spoken, muttered close in her ear. This terrifying interruption was the cause of the scream which had awakened me; and the condition in which she continued during the remainder of the night confirmed me more than ever in the conviction, that she was suffering under some morbid action of the nervous system.

After this event, which _I_ had no hesitation in attributing to fancy, she became literally afraid to pray, and her misery and despondency increased proportionately.

It was shortly after this that an unusual pressure of business called me into town one evening after office hours. I had left my dear little wife tolerably well, and little Fanny was to be her companion until I returned. She and her little companion occupied the same room in which we sat on the memorable evening which witnessed the arrival of our eccentric guest. Though usually a lively child, it most provokingly happened upon this night that Fanny was heavy and drowsy to excess. Her mamma would have sent her to bed, but that she now literally feared to be left alone; although, however, she could not so far overcome her horror of solitude as to do this, she yet would not persist in combating the poor child's sleepiness.

Accordingly, little Fanny was soon locked in a sound sleep, while her mamma quietly pursued her work beside her. They had been perhaps some ten minutes thus circumstanced, when my wife heard the window softly raised from without--a bony hand parted the curtains, and Mr. Smith leaned into the room.

She was so utterly overpowered at sight of this apparition, that even had it, as she expected, climbed into the room, she told me she could not have uttered a sound, or stirred from the spot where she sate transfixed and petrified.

"Ha, ha!" he said gently, "I hope you'll excuse this, I must admit, very odd intrusion; but I knew I should find you here, and could not resist the opportunity of raising the window just for a moment, to look in upon a little family picture, and say a word to yourself. I understand that you are troubled, because for some cause you cannot say your prayers--because what you call your 'faith' is, so to speak, dead and gone, and also because what _you_ consider bad thoughts are constantly recurring to your mind. Now, all that is very silly. If it is really impossible for you to believe and to pray, what are you to infer from that? It is perfectly plain your Christian system can't be a true one--faith and _prayer_ it everywhere represents as the conditions of grace, acceptance, and salvation; and yet your Creator will not _permit_ you either to believe or pray. The Christian system is, forsooth, a _free_ gift, and yet he who formed _you_ and _it_, makes it absolutely impossible for you to accept it. _Is_ it, I ask you, from your own experience--is it a free gift? And if your own experience, in which you can't be mistaken, gives its pretensions the lie, why, in the name of common sense, will you persist in believing it? I say it is downright blasphemy to think it has emanated from the Good Spirit--assuming that there is one. It tells you that you must be tormented hereafter in a way only to be made intelligible by the image of eternal fires--pretty strong, we must all allow--unless you comply with certain conditions, which it pretends are so easy that it is a positive pleasure to embrace and perform them; and yet, for the life of you, you can't--physically _can't_--do either. Is this truth and mercy?--or is it swindling and cruelty? Is it the part of the Redeemer, or that of the tyrant, deceiver, and tormentor?"

Up to that moment, my wife had sate breathless and motionless, listening, in the catalepsy of nightmare, to a sort of echo of the vile and impious reasoning which had haunted her for so long. At the last words of the sentence his voice became harsh and thrilling; and his whole manner bespoke a sort of crouching and terrific hatred, the like of which she could not have conceived.

Whatever may have been the cause, she was on a sudden disenchanted. She started to her feet; and, freezing with horror though she was, in a shrill cry of agony commanded him, in the name of God, to depart from her. His whole frame seemed to darken; he drew back silently; the curtains dropped into their places, the window was let down again as stealthily as it had just been raised; and my wife found herself alone in the chamber with our little child, who had been startled from her sleep by her mother's cry of anguish, and with the fearful words, "tempter," "destroyer," "devil," still ringing in her ears, was weeping bitterly, and holding her terrified mother's hand.

There is nothing, I believe, more infectious than that species of nervousness which shows itself in superstitious fears. I began--although I could not bring myself to admit anything the least like it--to partake insensibly, but strongly of the peculiar feelings with which my wife, and indeed my whole household, already regarded the lodger up stairs. The fact was, beside, that the state of my poor wife's mind began to make me seriously uneasy; and, although I was fully sensible of the pecuniary and other advantages attendant upon his stay, they were yet far from outweighing the constant gloom and frequent misery in which the protracted sojourn was involving my once cheerful house. I resolved, therefore, at whatever monetary sacrifice, to put an end to these commotions; and, after several debates with my wife, in which the subject was, as usual, turned in all its possible and impossible bearings, we agreed that, deducting a fair proportion for his five weeks' sojourn, I should return the remainder of his £100, and request immediate possession of his apartments. Like a man suddenly relieved of an insufferable load, and breathing freely once more, I instantly prepared to carry into effect the result of our deliberations.

In pursuance of this resolution, I waited upon Mr. Smith. This time my call was made in the morning, somewhere about nine o'clock. He received me at his door, standing as usual in the stealthy opening which barely admitted his lank person. There he stood, fully equipped with goggles and respirator, and swathed, rather than dressed, in his puckered black garments.

As he did not seem disposed to invite me into his apartment, although I had announced my visit as one of business, I was obliged to open my errand where I stood; and after a great deal of fumbling and muttering, I contrived to place before him distinctly the resolution to which I had come.

"But I can't think of taking back any portion of the sum I have paid you," said he, with a cool, dry emphasis.

"Your reluctance to do so, Mr. Smith, is most handsome, and I assure you, appreciated," I replied. "It is very generous; but, at the same time, it is quite impossible for me to accept what I have no right to take, and I must beg of you not to mention that part of the subject again."

"And why should _I_ take it?" demanded Mr. Smith.

"Because you have paid this hundred pounds for six months, and you are leaving me with nearly five months of the term still unexpired," I replied. "I expect to receive fair play myself, and always give it."

"But who on earth said that I was going away so soon?" pursued Mr. Smith, in the same dry, sarcastic key. "_I_ have not said so--because I really don't intend it; I mean to stay here to the last day of the six months for which I have paid you. I have no notion of vacating my hired lodgings, simply because you say, _go_. I shan't quarrel with you--I never quarrel with anybody. I'm as much your friend as ever; but, without the least wish to disoblige, I can't do this, positively I cannot. Is there anything else?"

I had not anticipated in the least the difficulty which thus encountered and upset our plans. I had so set my heart upon effecting the immediate retirement of our inauspicious inmate, that the disappointment literally stunned me for a moment. I, however, returned to the charge: I urged, and prayed, and almost besought him to give up his apartments, and to leave us. I offered to repay every farthing of the sum he had paid me--reserving nothing on account of the time he had already been with us. I suggested all the disadvantages of the house. I shifted my ground, and told him that my wife wanted the rooms; I pressed his gallantry--his good nature--his economy; in short, I assailed him upon every point--but in vain, he did not even take the trouble of repeating what he had said before--he neither relented, nor showed the least irritation, but simply said--

"I can't do this; here I am, and here I stay until the half-year has expired. You wanted a lodger, and you have got one--the quietest, least troublesome, least expensive person you could have; and though your house, servants, and furniture are none of the best, I don't care for that. I pursue my own poor business and enjoyments here entirely to my satisfaction."

Having thus spoken, he gave me a sort of nod, and closed the door.

So, instead of getting rid of him the next day, as we had hoped, we had nearly five months more of his company in expectancy; I hated, and my wife dreaded the prospect. She was literally miserable and panic-struck at her disappointment--and grew so nervous and wretched that I made up my mind to look out for lodgings for her and the children (subversive of all our schemes of retrenchment as such a step would be), and surrendering the house absolutely to Mr. Smith and the servants during the remainder of his term.

Circumstances, however, occurred to prevent our putting this plan in execution. My wife, meanwhile, was, if possible, more depressed and nervous every day. The servants seemed to sympathise in the dread and gloom which involved ourselves; the very children grew timid and spiritless, without knowing why--and the entire house was pervaded with an atmosphere of uncertainty and fear. A poorhouse or a dungeon would have been cheerful, compared with a dwelling haunted unceasingly with unearthly suspicions and alarms. I would have made any sacrifice short of ruin, to emancipate our household from the odious mental and moral thraldom which was invisibly established over us--overcasting us with strange anxieties and an undefined terror.

About this time my wife had a dream which troubled her much, although she could not explain its supposed significance satisfactorily by any of the ordinary rules of interpretation in such matters. The vision was as follows.

She dreamed that we were busily employed in carrying out our scheme of removal, and that I came into the parlour where she was making some arrangements, and, with rather an agitated manner, told her that the carriage had come for the children. She thought she went out to the hall, in consequence, holding little Fanny by one hand, and the boy--or, as we still called him, "baby,"--by the other, and feeling, as she did so, an unaccountable gloom, almost amounting to terror, steal over her. The children, too, seemed, she thought, frightened, and disposed to cry.

So close to the hall-door as to exclude the light, stood some kind of vehicle, of which she could see nothing but that its door was wide open, and the interior involved in total darkness. The children, she thought, shrunk back in great trepidation, and she addressed herself to induce them, by persuasion, to enter, telling them that they were only "going to their new home." So, in a while, little Fanny approached it; but, at the same instant, some person came swiftly up from behind, and, raising the little boy in his hands, said fiercely, "No, the baby first"; and placed him in the carriage. This person was our lodger, Mr. Smith, and was gone as soon as seen. My wife, even in her dream, could not act or speak; but as the child was lifted into the carriage-door, a man, whose face was full of beautiful tenderness and compassion, leaned forward from the carriage and received the little child, which, stretching his arms to the stranger, looked back with a strange smile upon his mother.

"He is safe with me, and I will deliver him to you when you come."

These words the man spoke, looking upon her, as he received him, and immediately the carriage-door shut, and the noise of its closing wakened my wife from her nightmare.

This dream troubled her very much, and even haunted my mind unpleasantly too. We agreed, however, not to speak of it to anybody, not to divulge any of our misgivings respecting the stranger. We were anxious that neither the children nor the servants should catch the contagion of those fears which had seized upon my poor little wife, and, if truth were spoken, upon myself in some degree also. But this precaution was, I believe, needless, for, as I said before, everybody under the same roof with Mr. Smith was, to a certain extent, affected with the same nervous gloom and apprehension.

And now commences a melancholy chapter in my life. My poor little Fanny was attacked with a cough which soon grew very violent, and after a time degenerated into a sharp attack of inflammation. We were seriously alarmed for her life, and nothing that care and medicine could effect was spared to save it. Her mother was indefatigable, and scarcely left her night or day; and, indeed, for some time, we all but despaired of her recovery.

One night, when she was at the worst, her poor mother, who had sat for many a melancholy hour listening, by her bedside, to those plaintive incoherences of delirium and moanings of fever, which have harrowed so many a fond heart, gained gradually from her very despair the courage which she had so long wanted, and knelt down at the side of her sick darling's bed to pray for her deliverance.

With clasped hands, in an agony of supplication, she prayed that God would, in his mercy, spare her little child--that, justly as she herself deserved the sorest chastisement his hand could inflict, he would yet deal patiently and tenderly with her in this one thing. She poured out her sorrows before the mercy-seat--she opened her heart, and declared her only hope to be in his pity; without which, she felt that her darling would only leave the bed where she was lying for her grave.

Exactly as she came to this part of her supplication, the child, who had grown, as it seemed, more and more restless, and moaned and muttered with increasing pain and irritation, on a sudden started upright in her bed, and, in a thrilling voice, cried--

"No! no!--the baby first."

The mysterious sentence which had secretly tormented her for so long, thus piercingly uttered by this delirious, and, perhaps, dying child, with what seemed a preternatural earnestness and strength, arrested her devotions, and froze her with a feeling akin to terror.

"Hush, hush, my darling!" said the poor mother, almost wildly, as she clasped the attenuated frame of the sick child in her arms; "hush, my darling; don't cry out so loudly--there--there--my own love."

The child did not appear to see or hear her, but sate up still with feverish cheeks, and bright unsteady eyes, while her dry lips were muttering inaudible words.

"Lie down, my sweet child--lie down, for your own mother," she said; "if you tire yourself, you can't grow well, and your poor mother will lose you."

At these words, the child suddenly cried out again, in precisely the same loud, strong voice--"No! no! the baby first, the baby first"--and immediately afterwards lay down, and fell, for the first time since her illness into a tranquil sleep.

My good little wife sate, crying bitterly by her bedside. The child was better--_that_ was, indeed, delightful. But then there was an omen in the words, thus echoed from her dream, which she dared not trust herself to interpret, and which yet had seized, with a grasp of iron, upon every fibre of her brain.

"Oh, Richard," she cried, as she threw her arms about my neck, "I am terrified at this horrible menace from the unseen world. Oh! poor, darling little baby, I shall lose you--I am sure I shall lose you. Comfort me, darling, and say he is not to die."

And so I did; and tasked all my powers of argument and persuasion to convince her how unsubstantial was the ground of her anxiety. The little boy was perfectly well, and, even were he to die before his sister that event might not occur for seventy years to come. I could not, however, conceal from myself that there was something odd and unpleasant in the coincidence; and my poor wife had grown so nervous and excitable, that a much less ominous conjecture would have sufficed to alarm her.

Meanwhile, the unaccountable terror which our lodger's presence inspired continued to increase. One of our maids gave us warning, solely from her dread of our queer inmate, and the strange accessories which haunted him. She said--and this was corroborated by her fellow-servant--that Mr. Smith seemed to have constantly a companion in his room; that although they never heard them speak, they continually and distinctly heard the tread of two persons walking up and down the room together, and described accurately the peculiar sound of a stick or crutch tapping upon the floor, which my own ears had heard. They also had seen the large, ill-conditioned cat I have mentioned, frequently steal in and out of the stranger's room; and observed that when our little girl was in greatest danger, the hateful animal was constantly writhing, fawning, and crawling about the door of the sick room after nightfall. They were thoroughly persuaded that this ill-omened beast was the foul fiend himself, and I confess I could not--sceptic as I was--bring myself absolutely to the belief that he was nothing more than a "harmless, necessary cat." These and similar reports--implicitly believed as they palpably were by those who made them--were certainly little calculated to allay the perturbation and alarm with which our household was filled.

The evenings had by this time shortened very much, and darkness often overtook us before we sate down to our early tea. It happened just at this period of which I have been speaking, after my little girl had begun decidedly to mend, that I was sitting in our dining-parlour, with my little boy fast asleep upon my knees, and thinking of I know not what, my wife having gone up stairs, as usual, to sit in the room with little Fanny. As I thus sate in what was to me, in effect, total solitude, darkness unperceived stole on us.

On a sudden, as I sate, with my elbow leaning upon the table, and my other arm round the sleeping child, I felt, as I thought, a cold current of air faintly blowing upon my forehead. I raised my head, and saw, as nearly as I could calculate, at the far end of the table on which my arm rested, two large green eyes confronting me. I could see no more, but instantly concluded they were those of the abominable cat. Yielding to an impulse of horror and abhorrence, I caught a water-croft that was close to my hand, and threw it full at it with all my force. I must have missed my object, for the shining eyes continued fixed for a second, and then glided still nearer to me, and then a little nearer still. The noise of the glass smashed with so much force upon the table called in the servant, who happened to be passing. She had a candle in her hand, and, perhaps, the light alarmed the odious beast, for as she came in it was gone.

I had had an undefined idea that its approach was somehow connected with a designed injury of some sort to the sleeping child. I could not be mistaken as to the fact that I had plainly seen the two broad, glaring, green eyes. Where the cursed animal had gone I had not observed: it might, indeed, easily have run out at the door as the servant opened it, but neither of us had seen it do so; and we were every one of us in such a state of nervous excitement, that even this incident was something in the catalogue of our ambiguous experiences.

It was a great happiness to see our darling little Fanny every day mending, and now quite out of danger: this was cheering and delightful. It was also something to know that more than two months of our lodger's term of occupation had already expired; and to realise, as we now could do, by anticipation, the unspeakable relief of his departure.

My wife strove hard to turn our dear child's recovery to good account for me; but the impressions of fear soon depart, and those of religious gratitude must be preceded by religious faith. All as yet was but as seed strewn upon the rock.

Little Fanny, though recovering rapidly, was still very weak, and her mother usually passed a considerable part of every evening in her bedroom--for the child was sometimes uneasy and restless at night. It happened at this period that, sitting as usual at Fanny's bedside, she witnessed an occurrence which agitated her not a little.

The child had been, as it seems, growing sleepy, and was lying listlessly, with eyes half open, apparently taking no note of what was passing. Suddenly, however, with an expression of the wildest terror, she drew up her limbs, and cowered in the bed's head, gazing at some object; which, judging from the motion of her eyes, must have been slowly advancing from the end of the room next the door.

The child made a low shuddering cry, as she grasped her mother's hand, and, with features white and tense with terror, slowly following with her eyes the noiseless course of some unseen spectre, shrinking more and more fearfully backward every moment.

"What is it? Where? What is it that frightens you, my darling?" asked the poor mother, who, thrilled with horror, looked in vain for the apparition which seemed to have all but bereft the child of reason.

"Stay with me--save me--keep it away--look, look at it--making signs to me--don't let it hurt me--it is angry--Oh! mamma, save me, save me!"

The child said this, all the time clinging to her with both her hands, in an ecstasy of panic.

"There--there, my darling," said my poor wife, "don't be afraid; there's nothing but me--your own mamma--and little baby in the room; nothing, my darling; nothing indeed."

"Mamma, mamma, don't move; don't go near him"; the child continued wildly. "It's only his back now; don't make him turn again; he's untying his handkerchief. Oh! baby, baby; he'll _kill_ baby! and he's lifting up those green things from his eyes; don't you see him doing it? Mamma, mamma, why does he come here? Oh, mamma, poor baby--poor little baby!"

She was looking with a terrified gaze at the little boy's bed, which lay directly opposite to her own, and in which he was sleeping calmly.

"Hush, hush, my darling child," said my wife, with difficulty restraining an hysterical burst of tears; "for God's sake don't speak so wildly, my own precious love--there, there--don't be frightened--there, darling, there."

"Oh! poor baby--poor little darling baby," the child continued as before; "will no one save him--tell that wicked man to go away--oh--there--why, mamma--don't--oh, sure you won't let him--don't--don't--he'll take the child's life--will you let him lie down that way on the bed--save poor little baby--oh, baby, baby, waken--his head is on your face."

As she said this she raised her voice to a cry of despairing terror which made the whole room ring again.

This cry, or rather yell, reached my ears as I sate reading in the parlour by myself, and fearing I knew not what, I rushed to the apartment; before I reached it, the sound had subsided into low but violent sobbing; and, just as I arrived at the threshold I heard, close at my feet, a fierce protracted growl, and something rubbing along the surbase. I was in the dark, but, with a feeling of mingled terror and fury, I stamped and struck at the abhorred brute with my feet, but in vain. The next moment I was in the room, and heard little Fanny, through her sobs, cry--

"Oh, poor baby is killed--that wicked man has killed him--he uncovered his face, and put it on him, and lay upon the bed and killed poor baby. I knew he came to kill him. Ah, papa, papa, why did you not come up before he went?--he is gone, he went away as soon as he killed our poor little darling baby."

I could not conceal my agitation, quite, and I said to my wife--

"Has he, Smith, been here?"

"No."

"What is it, then?"

"The child has seen _some_ one."

"Seen whom? Who? Who has been here?"

"I did not see it; but--but I am sure the child saw--that is, _thought_ she saw _him_;--the person you have named. Oh, God, in mercy deliver us! What shall I do--what shall I do!"

Thus saying, the dear little woman burst into tears, and crying, as if her heart would break, sobbed out an entreaty that I would look at baby; adding, that she herself had not courage to see whether her darling was sleeping or dead.

"Dead!" I exclaimed. "Tut, tut, my darling; you must not give way to such morbid fancies--he is very well, I see him breathing;" and so saying, I went over to the bed where our little boy was lying. He was slumbering; though it seemed to me very heavily, and his cheeks were flushed.

"Sleeping tranquilly, my darling--tranquilly, and deeply; and with a warm colour in his cheeks," I said, rearranging the coverlet, and retiring to my wife, who sate almost breathless whilst I was looking at our little boy.

"Thank God--thank God," she said quietly; and she wept again; and rising, came to his bedside.

"Yes, yes--alive; thank God; but it seems to me he is breathing very short, and with difficulty, and he looks--_does_ he not look hot and feverish? Yes, he _is_ very hot; feel his little hand--feel his neck; merciful heaven! he is burning."

It was, indeed, very true, that his skin was unnaturally dry and hot; his little pulse, too, was going at a fearful rate.

"I do think," said I--resolved to conceal the extent of my own apprehensions--"I do think that he is just a _little_ feverish; but he has often been much more so; and will, I dare say, in the morning, be perfectly well again. I dare say, but for little Fanny's _dream_, we should not have observed it at all."

"Oh, my darling, my darling, my darling!" sobbed the poor little woman, leaning over the bed, with her hands locked together, and looking the very picture of despair. "Oh, my darling, what has happened to you? I put you into your bed, looking so well and beautiful, this evening, and here you are, stricken with sickness, my own little love. Oh, you will not--you cannot, leave your poor mother!"

It was quite plain that she despaired of the child from the moment we had ascertained that it was unwell. As it happened, her presentiment was but too truly prophetic. The apothecary said the child's ailment was "suppressed small-pox"; the physician pronounced it "typhus." The only certainty about it was the issue--the child died.

To me few things appear so beautiful as a very young child in its shroud. The little innocent face looks so sublimely simple and confiding amongst the cold terrors of death--crimeless, and fearless, that little mortal has passed alone under the shadow, and explored the mystery of dissolution. There is death in its sublimest and purest image--no hatred, no hypocrisy, no suspicion, no care for the morrow ever darkened that little face; death has come lovingly upon it; there is nothing cruel, or harsh, in his victory. The yearnings of love, indeed, cannot be stifled; for the prattle, and smiles, and all the little world of thoughts that were so delightful, are gone for ever. Awe, too, will overcast us in its presence--for we are looking on death; but we do not fear for the little, lonely voyager--for the child has gone, simple and trusting, into the presence of its all-wise Father; and of such, we know, is the kingdom of heaven.

And so we parted from poor little baby. I and his poor old nurse drove in a mourning carriage, in which lay the little coffin, early in the morning, to the churchyard of ----. Sore, indeed, was my heart, as I followed that little coffin to the grave! Another burial had just concluded as we entered the churchyard, and the mourners stood in clusters round the grave, into which the sexton was now shovelling the mould.

As I stood, with head uncovered, listening to the sublime and touching service which our ritual prescribes, I found that a gentleman had drawn near also, and was standing at my elbow. I did not turn to look at him until the earth had closed over my darling boy; I then walked a little way apart, that I might be alone, and drying my eyes, sat down upon a tombstone, to let the confusion of my mind subside.

While I was thus lost in a sorrowful reverie, the gentleman who had stood near me at the grave was once more at my side. The face of the stranger, though I could not call it handsome, was very remarkable; its expression was the purest and noblest I could conceive, and it was made very beautiful by a look of such compassion as I never saw before.

"Why do you sorrow as one without hope?" he said, gently.

"I _have_ no hope," I answered.

"Nay, I think you have," he answered again; "and I am sure you will soon have more. That little child for which you grieve, has escaped the dangers and miseries of life; its body has perished; but he will receive in the end the crown of life. God has given him an early victory."

I know not what it was in him that rebuked my sullen pride, and humbled and saddened me, as I listened to this man. He was dressed in deep mourning, and looked more serene, noble, and sweet than any I had ever seen. He was young, too, as I have said, and his voice very clear and harmonious. He talked to me for a long time, and I listened to him with involuntary reverence. At last, however, he left me, saying he had often seen me walking into town, about the same hour that he used to go that way, and that if he saw me again he would walk with me, and so we might reason of these things together.

It was late when I returned to my home, now a house of mourning.

## PART II

Our home was one of sorrow and of fear. The child's death had stricken us with terror no less than grief. Referring it, as we both tacitly did, to the mysterious and fiendish agency of the abhorred being whom, in an evil hour, we had admitted into our house, we both viewed him with a degree and species of fear for which I can find no name.

I felt that some further calamity was impending. I could not hope that we were to be delivered from the presence of the malignant agent who haunted, rather than inhabited our home, without some additional proofs alike of his malice and his power.

My poor wife's presentiments were still more terrible and overpowering, though not more defined, than my own. She was never tranquil while our little girl was out of her sight; always dreading and expecting some new revelation of the evil influence which, as we were indeed both persuaded, had bereft our darling little boy of life. Against an hostility so unearthly and intangible there was no guarding, and the sense of helplessness intensified the misery of our situation. Tormented with doubts of the very basis of her religion, and recoiling from the ordeal of prayer with the strange horror with which the victim of hydrophobia repels the pure water, she no longer found the consolation which, had sorrow reached her in any other shape, she would have drawn from the healing influence of religion. We were both of us unhappy, dismayed, DEMON-STRICKEN.

Meanwhile, our lodger's habits continued precisely the same. If, indeed, the sounds which came from his apartments were to be trusted, he and his agents were more on the alert than ever. I can convey to you, good reader, no notion, even the faintest, of the dreadful sensation always more or less present to my mind, and sometimes with a reality which thrilled me almost to frenzy--the apprehension that I had admitted into my house the incarnate spirit of the dead or damned, to torment me and my family.

It was some nights after the burial of our dear little baby; we had not gone to bed until late, and I had slept, I suppose, some hours, when I was awakened by my wife, who clung to me with the energy of terror. She said nothing, but grasped and shook me with more than her natural strength. She had crept close to me, and was cowering with her head under the bedclothes.

The room was perfectly dark, as usual, for we burned no night-light; but from the side of the bed next her proceeded a voice as of one sitting there with his head within a foot of the curtains--and, merciful heavens! it was the voice of our lodger.

He was discoursing of the death of our baby, and inveighing, in the old mocking tone of hate and suppressed fury, against the justice, mercy, and goodness of God. He did this with a terrible plausibility of sophistry, and with a resolute emphasis and precision, which seemed to imply, "I have got something to tell you, and, whether you like it or like it not, I _will_ say out my say."

To pretend that I felt anger at his intrusion, or emotion of any sort, save the one sense of palsied terror, would be to depart from the truth. I lay, cold and breathless, as if frozen to death--unable to move, unable to utter a cry--with the voice of that demon pouring, in the dark, his undisguised blasphemies and temptations close into my ears. At last the dreadful voice ceased--whether the speaker went or stayed I could not tell--the silence, which he might be improving for the purpose of some hellish strategem, was to me more tremendous even than his speech.

We both lay awake, not daring to move or speak, scarcely even breathing, but clasping one another fast, until at length the welcome light of day streamed into the room through the opening door, as the servant came in to call us. I need not say that our nocturnal visitant had left us.

The magnanimous reader will, perhaps, pronounce that I ought to have pulled on my boots and inexpressibles with all available despatch, run to my lodger's bedroom, and kicked him forthwith downstairs, and the entire way moreover out to the public road, as some compensation for the scandalous affront put upon me and my wife by his impertinent visit. Now, at that time, I had no scruples against what are termed the laws of honour, was by no means deficient in "pluck," and gifted, moreover, with a somewhat excitable temper. Yet, I will honestly avow that, so far from courting a collision with the dreaded stranger, I would have recoiled at his very sight, and given my eyes to avoid him, such was the ascendancy which he had acquired over me, as well as everybody else in my household, in his own quiet, irresistible, hellish way.

The shuddering antipathy which our guest inspired did not rob his infernal homily of its effect. It was not a new or strange thing which he presented to our minds. There was an awful subtlety in the train of his suggestions. All that he had said had floated through my own mind before, without order, indeed, or shew of logic. From my own rebellious heart the same evil thoughts had risen, like pale apparitions hovering and lost in the fumes of a necromancer's cauldron. His was like the summing up of all this--a reflection of my own feelings and fancies--but reduced to an awful order and definiteness, and clothed with a sophistical form of argument. The effect of it was powerful. It revived and exaggerated these bad emotions--it methodised and justified them--and gave to impulses and impressions, vague and desultory before, something of the compactness of a system.

My misfortune, therefore, did not soften, it exasperated me. I regarded the Great Disposer of events as a persecutor of the human race, who took delight in their miseries. I asked why my innocent child had been smitten down into the grave?--and why my darling wife, whose first object, I knew, had ever been to serve and glorify her Maker, should have been thus tortured and desolated by the cruelest calamity which the malignity of a demon could have devised? I railed and blasphemed, and even in my agony defied God with the impotent rage and desperation of a devil, in his everlasting torment.

In my bitterness, I could not forbear speaking these impenitent repetitions of the language of our nightly visitant, even in the presence of my wife. She heard me with agony, almost with terror. I pitied and loved her too much not to respect even her weaknesses--for so I characterised her humble submission to the chastisements of heaven. But even while I spared her reverential sensitiveness, the spectacle of her patience but enhanced my own gloomy and impenitent rage.

I was walking into town in this evil mood, when I was overtaken by the gentleman whom I had spoken with in the churchyard on the morning when my little boy was buried. I call him _gentleman_, but I could not say _what_ was his rank--I never thought about it; there was a grace, a purity, a compassion, and a grandeur of intellect in his countenance, in his language, in his mien, that was beautiful and kinglike. I felt, in his company, a delightful awe, and an humbleness more gratifying than any elation of earthly pride.

He divined my state of feeling, but he said nothing harsh. He did not rebuke, but he reasoned with me--and oh! how mighty was that reasoning--without formality--without effort--as the flower grows and blossoms. Its process was in harmony with the successions of nature--gentle, spontaneous, irresistible.

At last he left me. I was grieved at his departure--I was wonder-stricken. His discourse had made me cry tears at once sweet and bitter; it had sounded depths I knew not of, and my heart was disquieted within me. Yet my trouble was happier than the resentful and defiant calm that had reigned within me before.

When I came home, I told my wife of my having met the same good, wise man I had first seen by the grave of my child. I recounted to her his discourse, and, as I brought it again to mind, my tears flowed afresh, and I was happy while I wept.

I now see that the calamity which bore at first such evil fruit, was good for me. It fixed my mind, however rebelliously, upon God, and it stirred up all the passions of my heart. Levity, inattention, and self-complacency are obstacles harder to be overcome than the violence of evil passions--the transition from hate is easier than from indifference, to love. A mighty change was making on my mind.

I need not particularise the occasions upon which I again met my friend, for so I knew him to be, nor detail the train of reasoning and feeling which in such interviews he followed out; it is enough to say, that he assiduously cultivated the good seed he had sown, and that his benignant teachings took deep root, and flourished in my soul, heretofore so barren.

One evening, having enjoyed on the morning of the same day another of those delightful and convincing conversations, I was returning on foot homeward; and as darkness had nearly closed, and the night threatened cold and fog, the footpaths were nearly deserted.

As I walked on, deeply absorbed in the discourse I had heard on the same morning, a person overtook me, and continued to walk, without much increasing the interval between us, a little in advance of me. There came upon me, at the same moment, an indefinable sinking of the heart, a strange and unaccountable fear. The pleasing topics of my meditations melted away, and gave place to a sense of danger, all the more unpleasant that it was vague and objectless. I looked up. What was that which moved before me? I stared--I faltered; my heart fluttered as if it would choke me, and then stood still. It was the peculiar and unmistakeable form of our lodger.

Exactly as I looked at him, he turned his head, and looked at me over his shoulder. His face was muffled as usual. I cannot have seen its features with any completeness, yet I felt that his look was one of fury. The next instant he was at my side; and my heart quailed within me--my limbs all but refused their office; yet the very emotions of terror, which might have overcome me, acted as a stimulus, and I quickened my pace.

"Hey! what a pious person! So I suppose you have learned at last that 'evil communications corrupt good manners'; and you are absolutely afraid of the old infidel, the old blasphemer, hey?"

I made him no answer; I was indeed too much agitated to speak.

"You'll make a good Christian, no doubt," he continued; "the independent man, who thinks for himself, reasons his way to his principles, and sticks fast to them, is sure to be true to whatever system he embraces. You have been so consistent a philosopher, that I am sure you will make a steady Christian. You're not the man to be led by the nose by a sophistical mumbler. _You_ could never be made the prey of a grasping proselytism; _you_ are not the sport of every whiff of doctrine, nor the facile slave of whatever superstition is last buzzed in your ear. No, no: you've got a masculine intellect, and think for yourself, hey?"

I was incapable of answering him. I quickened my pace to escape from his detested persecution; but he was close beside me still.

We walked on together thus for a time, during which I heard him muttering fast to himself, like a man under fierce and malignant excitement. We reached, at length, the gateway of my dwelling; and I turned the latch-key in the wicket, and entered the enclosure. As we stood together within, he turned full upon me, and confronting me with an aspect whose character I felt rather than saw, he said--

"And so you mean to be a Christian, after all! Now just reflect how very absurdly you are choosing. Leave the Bible to that class of fanatics who may hope to be saved under its system, and, in the name of common sense, study the Koran, or some less ascetic tome. Don't be gulled by a plausible slave, who wants nothing more than to multiply _professors_ of his theory. Why don't you _read_ the Bible, you miserable, puling poltroon, before you hug it as a treasure? Why don't you read it, and learn out of the mouth of the founder of Christianity, that there is one sin for which there is _no_ forgiveness--blasphemy against the Holy Ghost, hey?--and that sin I myself have heard you commit by the hour--in my presence--in my room. I have heard you commit it in our free discussions a dozen times. The Bible seals against you the lips of mercy. If _it_ be true, you are this moment as irrevocably damned as if you had died with those blasphemies on your lips."

Having thus spoken, he glided into the house. I followed slowly.

His words rang in my ears--I was stunned. What he had said I feared might be true. Giant despair felled me to the earth. He had recalled, and lighted up with a glare from the pit, remembrances with which I knew not how to cope. It was true I had spoken with daring impiety of subjects whose sacredness I now began to appreciate. With trembling hands I opened the Bible. I read and re-read the mysterious doom recorded by the Redeemer himself against blasphemers of the Holy Ghost--monsters set apart from the human race, and damned and dead, even while they live and walk upon the earth. I groaned--I wept. Henceforward the Bible, I thought, must be to me a dreadful record of despair. I dared not read it.

I will not weary you with all my mental agonies. My dear little wife did something toward relieving my mind, but it was reserved for the friend, to whose heavenly society I owed so much, to tranquillise it once more. He talked this time to me longer, and even more earnestly than before. I soon encountered him again. He expounded to me the ways of Providence, and showed me how needful sorrow was for every servant of God. How mercy was disguised in tribulation, and our best happiness came to us, like our children, in tears and wailing. He showed me that trials were sent to call us up, with a voice of preternatural power, from the mortal apathy of sin and the world. And then, again, in our new and better state, to prove our patience and our faith--

"The more trouble befalls you, the nearer is God to you. He visits you in sorrow--and sorrow, as well as joy, is a sign of his presence. If, then, other griefs overtake you, remember this--be patient, be faithful; and bless the name of God."

I returned home comforted and happy, although I felt assured that some further and sadder trial was before me.

Still our household was overcast by the same insurmountable dread of our tenant. The same strange habits characterised him, and the same unaccountable sounds disquieted us--an atmosphere of death and malice hovered about his door, and we all hated and feared to pass it.

Let me now tell, as well and briefly as I may, the dreadful circumstances of my last great trial. One morning, my wife being about her household affairs, and I on the point of starting for town, I went into the parlour for some letters which I was to take with me. I cannot easily describe my consternation when, on entering the room, I saw our lodger seated near the window, with our darling little girl upon his knee.

His back was toward the door, but I could plainly perceive that the respirator had been removed from his mouth, and that the odious green goggles were raised. He was sitting, as it seemed, absolutely without motion, and his face was advanced close to that of the child.

I stood looking at this group in a state of stupor for some seconds. He was, I suppose, conscious of my presence, for although he did not turn his head, or otherwise take any note of my arrival, he readjusted the muffler which usually covered his mouth, and lowered the clumsy spectacles to their proper place.

The child was sitting upon his knee as motionless as he himself, with a countenance white and rigid as that of a corpse, and from which every trace of meaning, except some vague character of terror, had fled, and staring with a fixed and dilated gaze into his face.

As it seemed, she did not perceive my presence. Her eyes were transfixed and fascinated. She did not even seem to me to breathe. Horror and anguish at last overcame my stupefaction.

"What--what is it?" I cried; "what ails my child, my darling child?"

"I'd be glad to know, myself," he replied, coolly; "it is certainly something very queer."

"What is it, darling?" I repeated, frantically, addressing the child.

"What is it?" he reiterated. "Why it's pretty plain, I should suppose, that the child is ill."

"Oh merciful God!" I cried, half furious, half terrified--"You have injured her--you have terrified her. Give me my child--give her to me."

These words I absolutely shouted, and stamped upon the floor in my horrid excitement.

"Pooh, pooh!" he said, with a sort of ugly sneer; "the child is nervous--you'll make her more so--be quiet and she'll probably find her tongue presently. I have had her on my knee some minutes, but the sweet bird could not tell what ails her."

"Let the child go," I shouted in a voice of thunder; "let her go, I say--let her go."

He took the passive, death-like child, and placed her standing by the window, and rising, he simply said--

"As soon as you grow cool, you are welcome to ask me what questions you like. The child is plainly ill. I should not wonder if she had seen something that frightened her."

Having thus spoken, he passed from the room. I felt as if I spoke, saw, and walked in a horrid dream. I seized the darling child in my arms, and bore her away to her mother.

"What is it--for mercy's sake what is the matter?" she cried, growing in an instant as pale as the poor child herself.

"I found that--that _demon_--in the parlour with the child on his lap, staring in her face. She is manifestly terrified."

"Oh! gracious God! she is lost--she is killed," cried the poor mother, frantically looking into the white, apathetic, meaningless face of the child.

"Fanny, darling Fanny, tell us if you are ill," I cried, pressing the little girl in terror to my heart.

"Tell your own mother, my darling," echoed my poor little wife. "Oh! darling, darling child, speak to your poor mother."

It was all in vain. Still the same dilated, imploring gaze--the same pale face--wild and dumb. We brought her to the open window--we gave her cold water to drink--we sprinkled it in her face. We sent for the apothecary, who lived hard by, and he arrived in a few moments, with a parcel of tranquillising medicines. These, however, were equally unavailing.

Hour after hour passed away. The darling child looked upon us as if she would have given the world to speak to us, or to weep, but she uttered no sound. Now and then she drew a long breath as though preparing to say something, but still she was mute. She often put her hand to her throat, as if there was some pain or obstruction there.

I never can, while I live, lose one line of that mournful and terrible portrait--the face of my stricken child. As hour after hour passed away, without bringing the smallest change or amendment, we grew both alarmed, and at length absolutely terrified for her safety.

We called in a physician toward night, and told him that we had reason to suspect that the child had somehow been frightened, and that in no other way could we at all account for the extraordinary condition in which he found her.

This was a man, I may as well observe, though I do not name him, of the highest eminence in his profession, and one in whose skill, from past personal experience, I had the best possible reasons for implicitly confiding.

He asked a multiplicity of questions, the answers to which seemed to baffle his attempts to arrive at a satisfactory diagnosis. There was something undoubtedly anomalous in the case, and I saw plainly that there were features in it which puzzled and perplexed him not a little.

At length, however, he wrote his prescription, and promised to return at nine o'clock. I remember there was something to be rubbed along her spine, and some medicines beside.

But these remedies were as entirely unavailing as the others. In a state of dismay and distraction we watched by the bed in which, in accordance with the physician's direction, we had placed her. The absolute changelessness of her condition filled us with despair. The day which had elapsed had not witnessed even a transitory variation in the dreadful character of her seizure. Any change, even a change for the worse, would have been better than this sluggish, hopeless monotony of suffering.

At the appointed hour the physician returned. He appeared disappointed, almost shocked, at the failure of his prescriptions. On feeling her pulse he declared that she must have a little wine. There had been a wonderful prostration of all the vital powers since he had seen her before. He evidently thought the case a strange and precarious one.

She was made to swallow the wine, and her pulse rallied for a time, but soon subsided again. I and the physician were standing by the fire, talking in whispers of the darling child's symptoms, and likelihood of recovery, when we were arrested in our conversation by a cry of anguish from the poor mother, who had never left the bedside of her little child, and this cry broke into bitter and convulsive weeping.

The poor little child had, on a sudden, stretched down her little hands and feet, and died. There is no mistaking the features of death: the filmy eye and dropt jaw once seen, are recognised whenever we meet them again. Yet, spite of our belief, we cling to hope; and the distracted mother called on the physician, in accents which might have moved a statue, to say that her darling was not dead, not quite dead--that something might still be done--that it could not be all over. Silently he satisfied himself that no throb of life still fluttered in that little frame.

"It is, indeed, all over," he said, in tones scarce above a whisper; and pressing my hand kindly, he said, "comfort your poor wife"; and so, after a momentary pause, he left the room.

This blow had smitten me with stunning suddenness. I looked at the dead child, and from her to her poor mother. Grief and pity were both swallowed up in transports of fury and detestation with which the presence in my house of the wretch who had wrought all this destruction and misery filled my soul. My heart swelled with ungovernable rage; for a moment my habitual fear of him was neutralised by the vehemence of these passions. I seized a candle in silence, and mounted the stairs. The sight of the accursed cat, flitting across the lobby, and the loneliness of the hour, made me hesitate for an instant. I had, however, gone so far, that shame sustained me. Overcoming a momentary thrill of dismay, and determined to repel and defy the influence that had so long awed me, I knocked sharply at the door, and, almost at the same instant, pushed it open, and entered our lodger's chamber.
He had had no candle in the room, and it was lighted only by the "darkness visible" that entered through the window. The candle which I held very imperfectly illuminated the large apartment; but I saw his spectral form floating, rather than walking, back and forward in front of the windows.

At sight of him, though I hated him more than ever, my instinctive fear returned. He confronted me, and drew nearer and nearer, without speaking. There was something indefinably fearful in the silent attraction which seemed to be drawing him to me. I could not help recoiling, little by little, as he came toward me, and with an effort I said--

"You know why I have come: the child--she's dead!"

"Dead--ha!--_dead_--is she?" he said, in his odious, mocking tone.

"Yes--dead!" I cried, with an excitement which chilled my very marrow with horror; "and _you_ have killed her, as you killed my other."

"How?--I killed her!--eh?--ha, ha!" he said, still edging nearer and nearer.

"Yes; I say you!" I shouted, trembling in every joint, but possessed by that unaccountable infatuation which has made men invoke, spite of themselves, their own destruction, and which I was powerless to resist--"deny it as you may, it is you who killed her--wretch!--FIEND!--no wonder she could not stand the breath and glare of HELL!"

"And you are one of those who believe that not a sparrow falls to the ground without your Creator's consent," he said, with icy sarcasm; "and this is a specimen of Christian resignation--hey? You charge his act upon a poor fellow like me, simply that you may cheat the devil, and rave and rebel against the decrees of heaven, under pretence of abusing me. The breath and flare of hell!--eh? You mean that I removed this and these (touching the covering of his mouth and eyes successively) as I _shall_ do now again, and show you there's no great harm in that."

There was a tone of menace in his concluding words not to be mistaken. "Murderer and liar from the beginning, as you are, I defy you!" I shouted, in a frenzy of hate and horror, stamping furiously on the floor.

As I said this, it seemed to me that he darkened and dilated before my eyes. My senses, thoughts, consciousness, grew horribly confused, as if some powerful, extraneous will, were seizing upon the functions of my brain. Whether I were to be mastered by death, or madness, or possession, I knew not; but hideous destruction of some sort was impending: all hung upon the moment, and I cried aloud, in my agony, an adjuration in the name of the three persons of the Trinity, that he should not torment me.

Stunned, bewildered, like a man recovered from a drunken fall, I stood, freezing and breathless, in the same spot, looking into the room, which wore, in my eyes, a strange, unearthly character. Mr. Smith was cowering darkly in the window, and, after a silence, spoke to me in a croaking, sulky tone, which was, however, unusually submissive.

"Don't it strike you as an odd procedure to break into a gentleman's apartment at such an hour, for the purpose of railing at him in the coarsest language? If you have any charge to make against me, do so; I invite inquiry and defy your worst. If you think you can bring home to me the smallest share of blame in this unlucky matter, call the coroner, and let his inquest examine and cross-examine me, and sift the matter--if, indeed, there is anything to _be_ sifted--to the bottom. Meanwhile, go you about your business, and leave me to mine. But I see how the wind sits; you want to get rid of me, and so you make the place odious to me. But it won't do; and if you take to making criminal charges against me, you had better look to yourself; for two can play at that game."

There was a suppressed whine in all this, which strangely contrasted with the cool and threatening tone of his previous conversation.

Without answering a word I hurried from the room, and scarcely felt secure, even when once more in the melancholy chamber, where my poor wife was weeping.

Miserable, horrible was the night that followed. The loss of our child was a calamity which we had not dared to think of. It had come, and with a suddenness enough to bereave me of reason. It seemed all unreal, all fantastic. It needed an effort to convince me, minute after minute, that the dreadful truth was so; and the old accustomed feeling that she was still alive, still running from room to room, and the expectation that I should hear her step and her voice, and see her entering at the door, would return. But still the sense of dismay, of having received some stunning, irreparable blow, remained behind; and then came the horrible effort, like that with which one rouses himself from a haunted sleep, the question, "What disaster is this that has befallen?"--answered, alas! but too easily, too terribly! Amidst all this was perpetually rising before my fancy the obscure, dilated figure of our lodger, as he had confronted me in his malign power that night. I dismissed the image with a shudder as often as it recurred; and even now, at this distance of time, I have felt more than I could well describe in the mere effort to fix my recollection upon its hated traits, while writing the passages I have just concluded.

This hateful scene I did not recount to my poor wife. Its horrors were too fresh upon me. I had not courage to trust myself with the agitating narrative; and so I sate beside her, with her hand locked in mine: I had no comfort to offer but the dear love I bore her.

At last, like a child, she cried herself to sleep--the dull, heavy slumber of worn-out grief. As for me, the agitation of my soul was too fearful and profound for repose. My eye accidentally rested on the holy volume, which lay upon the table open, as I had left it in the morning; and the first words which met my eye were these--"For our light affliction, which is but for a moment, worketh for us a far more exceeding and eternal weight of glory." This blessed sentence riveted my attention, and shed a stream of solemn joy upon my heart; and so the greater part of that mournful night, I continued to draw comfort and heavenly wisdom from the same inspired source.

Next day brought the odious incident, the visit of the undertaker--the carpentery, upholstery, and millinery of death. Why has not civilisation abolished these repulsive and shocking formalities? What has the poor corpse to do with frills, and pillows, and napkins, and all the equipage in which it rides on its last journey? There is no intrusion so jarring to the decent grief of surviving affection, no conceivable mummery more derisive of mortality.

In the room which we had been so long used to call "the nursery," now desolate and mute, the unclosed coffin lay, with our darling shrouded in it. Before we went to our rest at night we visited it. In the morning the lid was to close over that sweet face, and I was to see the child laid by her little brother. We looked upon the well-known and loved features, purified in the sublime serenity of death, for a long time, whispering to one another, among our sobs, how sweet and beautiful we thought she looked; and at length, weeping bitterly, we tore ourselves away.

We talked and wept for many hours, and at last, in sheer exhaustion, dropt asleep. My little wife awaked me, and said--

"I think they have come--the--the undertakers."

It was still dark, so I could not consult my watch; but they were to have arrived early, and as it was winter, and the nights long, the hour of their visit might well have arrived.

"What, darling, is your reason for thinking so?" I asked.

"I am sure I have heard them for some time in the nursery," she answered. "Oh! dear, dear little Fanny! Don't allow them to close the coffin until I have seen my darling once more."

I got up, and threw some clothes hastily about me. I opened the door and listened. A sound like a muffled knocking reached me from the nursery.

"Yes, my darling!" I said, "I think they have come. I will go and desire them to wait until you have seen her again."

And, so saying, I hastened from the room.

Our bedchamber lay at the end of a short corridor, opening from the lobby, at the head of the stairs, and the nursery was situated nearly at the end of a corresponding passage, which opened from the same lobby at the opposite side As I hurried along I distinctly heard the same sounds. The light of dawn had not yet appeared, but there was a strong moonlight shining through the windows. I thought the morning could hardly be so far advanced as we had at first supposed; but still, strangely as it now seems to me, suspecting nothing amiss, I walked on in noiseless, slippered feet, to the nursery-door. It stood half open; some one had unquestionably visited it since we had been there. I stepped forward, and entered. At the threshold horror arrested my advance.

The coffin was placed upon tressles at the further extremity of the chamber, with the foot of it nearly towards the door, and a large window at the side of it admitted the cold lustre of the moon full upon the apparatus of mortality, and the objects immediately about it.

At the foot of the coffin stood the ungainly form of our lodger. He seemed to be intently watching the face of the corpse, and was stooped a little, while with his hands he tapped sharply, from time to time at the sides of the coffin, like one who designs to awaken a slumberer. Perched upon the body of the child, and nuzzling among the grave-clothes, with a strange kind of ecstasy, was the detested brute, the cat I have so often mentioned.

The group thus revealed, I looked upon but for one instant; in the next I shouted, in absolute terror--

"In God's name! what are you doing?"

Our lodger shuffled away abruptly, as if disconcerted; but the ill-favoured cat, whisking round, stood like a demon sentinel upon the corpse, growling and hissing, with arched back and glaring eyes.

The lodger, turning abruptly toward me, motioned me to one side. Mechanically I obeyed his gesture, and he hurried hastily from the room.

Sick and dizzy, I returned to my own chamber. I confess I had not nerve to combat the infernal brute, which still held possession of the room, and so I left it undisturbed.

This incident I did not tell to my wife until some time afterwards; and I mention it here because it was, and is, in my mind associated with a painful circumstance which very soon afterwards came to light.
That morning I witnessed the burial of my darling child. Sore and desolate was my heart; but with infinite gratitude to the great controller of all events, I recognised in it a change which nothing but

the spirit of all good can effect. The love and fear of God had grown strong within me--in humbleness I bowed to his awful will--with a sincere trust I relied upon the goodness, the wisdom, and the mercy of him who had sent this great affliction. But a further incident connected with this very calamity was to test this trust and patience to the uttermost.

It was still early when I returned, having completed the last sad office. My wife, as I afterwards learned, still lay weeping upon her bed. But somebody awaited my return in the hall, and opened the door, anticipating my knock. This person was our lodger.

I was too much appalled by the sudden presentation of this abhorred spectre even to retreat, as my instinct would have directed, through the open door.

"I have been expecting your return," he said, "with the design of saying something which it might have profited you to learn, but now I apprehend it is too late. What a pity you are so violent and impatient; you would not have heard me, in all probability, this morning. You cannot think how cross-grained and intemperate you have grown since you became a saint--but that is your affair, not mine. You have buried your little daughter this morning. It requires a good deal of that new attribute of yours, _faith_, which judges all things by a rule of contraries, and can never see anything but kindness in the worst afflictions which malignity could devise, to discover benignity and mercy in the torturing calamity which has just punished you and your wife for _nothing_! But I fancy that it will be harder still when I tell you what I more than suspect--ha, ha. It would be really ridiculous, if it were not heart-rending; that your little girl has been actually buried _alive_; do you comprehend me?--alive. For, upon my life, I fancy she was not dead as she lay in her coffin."

I knew the wretch was exulting in the fresh anguish he had just inflicted. I know not how it was, but any announcement of _disaster_ from his lips, seemed to me to be necessarily true. Half-stifled with the dreadful emotions he had raised, palpitating between hope and terror, I rushed frantically back again, the way I had just come, running as fast as my speed could carry me, toward the, alas! distant burial-ground where my darling lay.

I stopped a cab slowly returning to town, at the corner of the lane, sprang into it, directed the man to drive to the church of ----, and promised him anything and everything for despatch. The man seemed amazed; doubtful, perhaps, whether he carried a maniac or a malefactor. Still he took his chance for the promised reward, and galloped his horse, while I, tortured with suspense, yelled my frantic incentives to further speed.

At last, in a space immeasurably short, but which to me was protracted almost beyond endurance, we reached the spot. I halloed to the sexton, who was now employed upon another grave, to follow me. I myself seized a mattock, and in obedience to my incoherent and agonised commands, he worked as he had never worked before. The crumbling mould flew swiftly to the upper soil--deeper and deeper, every moment, grew the narrow grave--at last I sobbed, "Thank God--thank God," as I saw the face of the coffin emerge; a few seconds more and it lay upon the sward beside me, and we both, with the edges of our spades, ripped up the lid.

_There_ was the corpse--but not the tranquil statue I had seen it last. Its knees were both raised, and one of its little hands drawn up and clenched near its throat, as if in a feeble but agonised struggle to force up the superincumbent mass. The eyes, that I had last seen closed, were now open, and the face no longer serenely pale, but livid and distorted.

I had time to see all in an instant; the whole scene reeled and darkened before me, and I swooned away.

When I came to myself, I found that I had been removed to the vestry-room. The open coffin was in the aisle of the church, surrounded by a curious crowd. A medical gentleman had examined the body carefully, and had pronounced life totally extinct. The trepidation and horror I experienced were indescribable. I felt like the murderer of my own child. Desperate as I was of any chance of its life, I dispatched messengers for no less than three of the most eminent physicians then practising in London. All concurred--the child was now as dead as any other, the oldest tenant of the churchyard.

Notwithstanding which, I would not permit the body to be reinterred for several days, until the symptoms of decay became unequivocal, and the most fantastic imagination could no longer cherish a doubt. This, however, I mention only parenthetically, as I hasten to the conclusion of my narrative. The circumstance which I have last described found its way to the public, and caused no small sensation at the time.

I drove part of the way home, and then discharged the cab, and walked the remainder. On my way, with an emotion of ecstasy I cannot describe, I met the good being to whom I owed so much. I ran to meet him, and felt as if I could throw myself at his feet, and kiss the very ground before him. I knew by his heavenly countenance he was come to speak comfort and healing to my heart.

With humbleness and gratitude, I drank in his sage and holy discourse. I need not follow the gracious and delightful exposition of God's revealed will and character with which he cheered and confirmed my faltering spirit. A solemn joy, a peace and trust, streamed on my heart. The wreck and desolation there, lost their bleak and ghastly character, like ruins illuminated by the mellow beams of a solemn summer sunset.

In this conversation, I told him what I had never revealed to any one before--the absolute terror, in all its stupendous and maddening amplitude, with which I regarded our ill-omened lodger, and my agonised anxiety to rid my house of him. My companion answered me--

"I know the person of whom you speak--he designs no good for you or any other. He, too, knows me, and I have intimated to him that he must now leave you, and visit you no more. Be firm and bold, trusting in God, through his Son, like a good soldier, and you will win the victory from a greater and even worse than he--the _unseen_ enemy of mankind. You need not see or speak with your evil tenant any more. Call to him from your hall, in the name of the Most Holy, to leave you bodily, with all that appertains to him, this evening. He knows that he must go, and will obey you. But leave the house as soon as may be yourself; you will scarce have peace in it. Your own remembrances will trouble you and _other minds have established associations within its walls and chambers too_."

These words sounded mysteriously in my ears.

Let me say here, before I bring my reminiscences to a close, a word or two about the house in which these detested scenes occurred, and which I did not long continue to inhabit. What I afterwards learned of it, seemed to supply in part a dim explanation of these words.

In a country village there is no difficulty in accounting for the tenacity with which the sinister character of a haunted tenement cleaves to it. Thin neighbourhoods are favourable to scandal; and in such localities the reputation of a house, like that of a woman, once blown upon, never quite recovers. In huge London, however, it is quite another matter; and, therefore, it was with some surprise that, five years after I had vacated the house in which the occurrences I have described took place, I learned that a respectable family who had taken it were obliged to give it up, on account of annoyances, for which they could not account, and all proceeding from the apartments formerly occupied by our "lodger." Among the sounds described were footsteps restlessly traversing the floor of that room, accompanied by the peculiar tapping of the crutch.

I was so anxious about this occurrence, that I contrived to have strict inquiries made into the matter. The result, however, added little to what I had at first learned--except, indeed, that our old friend, the cat, bore a part in the transaction as I suspected; for the servant, who had been placed to sleep in the room, complained that something bounded on and off, and ran to-and-fro along the foot of the bed, in the dark. The same servant, while in the room, in the broad daylight, had heard the sound of walking, and even the rustling of clothes near him, as of people passing and repassing; and, although he had never seen anything, he yet became so terrified that he would not remain in the house, and ultimately, in a short time, left his situation.

These sounds, attention having been called to them, were now incessantly observed--the measured walking up and down the room, the opening and closing of the door, and the teazing tap of the crutch--all these sounds were continually repeated, until at last, worn out, frightened, and worried, its occupants resolved on abandoning the house.

About four years since, having had occasion to visit the capital, I resolved on a ramble by Old Brompton, just to see if the house were still inhabited. I searched for it, however, in vain, and at length, with difficulty, ascertained its site, upon which now stood two small, staring, bran-new brick houses, with each a gay enclosure of flowers. Every trace of our old mansion, and, let us hope, of our "mysterious lodger," had entirely vanished.

Let me, however, return to my narrative where I left it.

Discoursing upon heavenly matters, my good and gracious friend accompanied me even within the outer gate of my own house. I asked him to come in and rest himself, but he would not; and before he turned to depart, he lifted up his hand, and blessed me and my household.

Having done this, he went away. My eyes followed him till he disappeared, and I turned to the house. My darling wife was standing at the window of the parlour. There was a seraphic smile on her face--pale, pure, and beautiful as death. She was gazing with an humble, heavenly earnestness on us. The parting blessing of the stranger shed a sweet and hallowed influence on my heart. I went into the parlour, to my darling: childless she was now; I had now need to be a tender companion to her.

She raised her arms in a sort of transport, with the same smile of gratitude and purity, and, throwing them round my neck, she said--

"I have seen him--it is he--the man that came with you to the door, and blessed us as he went away--is the same I saw in my dream--the same who took little baby in his arms, and said he would take care of him, and give him safely to me again."

More than a quarter of a century has glided away since then; other children have been given us by the good God--children who have been, from infancy to maturity, a pride and blessing to us. Sorrows and reverses, too, have occasionally visited us; yet, on the whole, we have been greatly blessed; prosperity has long since ended all the cares of the _res angusta domi_, and expanded our power of doing good to our fellow-creatures. God has given it; and God, we trust, directs its dispensation. In our children, and--would you think it?--our _grand_-children, too, the same beneficent God has given us objects that elicit and return all the delightful affections, and exchange the sweet converse that makes home and family dearer than aught else, save that blessed home where the Christian family shall meet at last.

The dear companion of my early love and sorrows still lives, blessed be Heaven! The evening tints of life have fallen upon her; but the dear remembrance of a first love, that never grew cold, makes her beauty changeless for me. As for your humble servant, he is considerably her senior, and looks it: time has stolen away his raven locks, and given him a _chevelure_ of snow instead. But, as I said before, I and my wife love, and, I believe, _admire_ one another more than ever; and I have often seen our elder children smile archly at one another, when they thought we did not observe them, thinking, no doubt, how like a pair of lovers we two were.

# SCHALKEN THE PAINTER (1851)

> _"For he is not a man as I am that we should come together; neither is there any that might lay his hand upon us both. Let him, therefore, take his rod away from me, and let not his fear terrify me."_

There exists, at this moment, in good preservation a remarkable work of Schalken's. The curious management of its lights constitutes, as usual in his pieces, the chief apparent merit of the picture. I say _apparent_, for in its subject, and not in its handling, however exquisite, consists its real value. The picture represents the interior of what might be a chamber in some antique religious building; and its foreground is occupied by a female figure, in a species of white robe, part of which is arranged so as to form a veil. The dress, however, is not that of any religious order. In her hand the figure bears a lamp, by which alone her figure and face are illuminated; and her features wear such an arch smile, as well becomes a pretty woman when practising some prankish roguery; in the background, and, excepting where the dim red light of an expiring fire serves to define the form, in total shadow, stands the figure of a man dressed in the old Flemish fashion, in an attitude of alarm, his hand being placed upon the hilt of his sword, which he appears to be in the act of drawing.

There are some pictures, which impress one, I know not how, with a conviction that they represent not the mere ideal shapes and combinations which have floated through the imagination of the artist, but scenes, faces, and situations which have actually existed. There is in that strange picture, something that stamps it as the representation of a reality.

And such in truth it is, for it faithfully records a remarkable and mysterious occurrence, and perpetuates, in the face of the female figure, which occupies the most prominent place in the design, an accurate portrait of Rose Velderkaust, the niece of Gerard Douw, the first, and, I believe, the only love of Godfrey Schalken. My great grandfather knew the painter well; and from Schalken himself he learned the fearful story of the painting, and from him too he ultimately received the picture itself as a bequest. The story and the picture have become heir-looms in my family, and having described the latter, I shall, if you please, attempt to relate the tradition which has descended with the canvas.

There are few forms on which the mantle of romance hangs more ungracefully than upon that of the uncouth Schalken--the boorish but most cunning worker in oils, whose pieces delight the critics of our day almost as much as his manners disgusted the refined of his own; and yet this man, so rude, so dogged, so slovenly, in the midst of his celebrity, had in his obscure, but happier days, played the hero in a wild romance of mystery and passion.

When Schalken studied under the immortal Gerard Douw, he was a very young man; and in spite of his phlegmatic temperament, he at once fell over head and ears in love with the beautiful niece of his wealthy master. Rose Velderkaust was still younger than he, having not yet attained her seventeenth year, and, if tradition speaks truth, possessed all the soft and dimpling charms of the fair, light-haired Flemish maidens. The young painter loved honestly and fervently. His frank adoration was rewarded. He declared his love, and extracted a faltering confession in return. He was the happiest and proudest painter in all Christendom. But there was somewhat to dash his elation; he was poor and undistinguished. He dared not ask old Gerard for the hand of his sweet ward. He must first win a reputation and a competence.

There were, therefore, many dread uncertainties and cold days before him; he had to fight his way against sore odds. But he had won the heart of dear Rose Velderkaust, and that was half the battle. It is needless to say his exertions were redoubled, and his lasting celebrity proves that his industry was not unrewarded by success.

These ardent labours, and worse still, the hopes that elevated and beguiled them, were however, destined to experience a sudden interruption--of a character so strange and mysterious as to baffle all inquiry and to throw over the events themselves a shadow of preternatural horror.

Schalken had one evening outstayed all his fellow-pupils, and still pursued his work in the deserted room. As the daylight was fast falling, he laid aside his colours, and applied himself to the completion of a sketch on which he had expressed extraordinary pains. It was a religious composition, and represented the temptations of a pot-bellied Saint Anthony. The young artist, however destitute of elevation, had, nevertheless, discernment enough to be dissatisfied with his own work, and many were the patient erasures and improvements which saint and devil underwent, yet all in vain. The large, old-fashioned room was silent, and, with the exception of himself, quite emptied of its usual inmates. An hour had thus passed away, nearly two, without any improved result. Daylight had already declined, and twilight was deepening into the darkness of night. The patience of the young painter was exhausted, and he stood before his unfinished production, angry and mortified, one hand buried in the folds of his long hair, and the other holding the piece of charcoal which had so ill-performed its office, and which he now rubbed, without much regard to the sable streaks it produced, with irritable pressure upon his ample Flemish inexpressibles. "Curse the subject!" said the young man aloud; "curse the picture, the devils, the saint--"

At this moment a short, sudden sniff uttered close beside him made the artist turn sharply round, and he now, for the first time, became aware that his labours had been overlooked by a stranger. Within about a yard and half, and rather behind him, there stood the figure of an elderly man in a cloak and broad-brimmed, conical hat; in his hand, which was protected with a heavy gauntlet-shaped glove, he carried a long ebony walking-stick, surmounted with what appeared, as it glittered dimly in the twilight, to be a massive head of gold, and upon his breast, through the folds of the cloak, there shone the links of a rich chain of the same metal. The room was so obscure that nothing further of the appearance of the figure could be ascertained, and his hat threw his features into profound shadow. It would not have been easy to conjecture the age of the intruder; but a quantity of dark hair escaping from beneath this sombre hat, as well as his firm and upright carriage served to indicate that his years could not yet exceed threescore, or thereabouts. There was an air of gravity and importance about the garb of the person, and something indescribably odd, I might say awful, in the perfect, stone-like stillness of the figure, that effectually checked the testy comment which had at once risen to the lips of the irritated artist. He, therefore, as soon as he had sufficiently recovered his surprise, asked the stranger, civilly, to be seated, and desired to know if he had any message to leave for his master.

"Tell Gerard Douw," said the unknown, without altering his attitude in the smallest degree, "that Minheer Vanderhausen, of Rotterdam, desires to speak with him on tomorrow evening at this hour, and if he please, in this room, upon matters of weight; that is all."

The stranger, having finished this message, turned abruptly, and, with a quick, but silent step quitted the room, before Schalken had time to say a word in reply. The young man felt a curiosity to see in what direction the burgher of Rotterdam would turn, on quitting the studio, and for that purpose he went directly to the window which commanded the door. A lobby of considerable extent intervened between the inner door of the painter's room and the street entrance, so that Schalken occupied the post of observation before the old man could possibly have reached the street. He watched in vain, however. There was no other mode of exit. Had the queer old man vanished, or was he lurking about the recesses of the lobby for some sinister purpose? This last suggestion filled the mind of Schalken with a vague uneasiness, which was so unaccountably intense as to make him alike afraid to remain in the room alone, and reluctant to pass through the lobby. However, with an effort which appeared very disproportioned to the occasion, he summoned resolution to leave the room, and, having locked the door and thrust the key in his pocket, without looking to the right or left, he traversed the passage which had so recently, perhaps still, contained the person of his mysterious visitant, scarcely venturing to breathe till he had arrived in the open street.

"Minheer Vanderhausen!" said Gerard Douw within himself, as the appointed hour approached, "Minheer Vanderhausen, of Rotterdam! I never heard of the man till yesterday. What can he want of me? A portrait, perhaps, to be painted; or a poor relation to be apprenticed; or a collection to be valued; or--pshaw! there's no one in Rotterdam to leave me a legacy. Well, whatever the business may be, we shall soon know it all."

It was now the close of day, and again every easel, except that of Schalken, was deserted. Gerard Douw was pacing the apartment with the restless step of impatient expectation, sometimes pausing to glance over the work of one of his absent pupils, but more frequently placing himself at the window, from whence he might observe the passengers who threaded the obscure by-street in which his studio was placed.

"Said you not, Godfrey," exclaimed Douw, after a long and fruitful gaze from his post of observation, and turning to Schalken, "that the hour he appointed was about seven by the clock of the Stadhouse?"

"It had just told seven when I first saw him, sir," answered the student.

"The hour is close at hand, then," said the master, consulting a horologe as large and as round as an orange. "Minheer Vanderhausen from Rotterdam--is it not so?"

"Such was the name."

"And an elderly man, richly clad?" pursued Douw, musingly.

"As well as I might see," replied his pupil; "he could not be young, nor yet very old, neither; and his dress was rich and grave, as might become a citizen of wealth and consideration."

At this moment the sonorous boom of the Stadhouse clock told, stroke after stroke, the hour of seven; the eyes of both master and student were directed to the door; and it was not until the last peal of the bell had ceased to vibrate, that Douw exclaimed----

"So, so; we shall have his worship presently, that is, if he means to keep his hour; if not, you may wait for him, Godfrey, if you court his acquaintance. But what, after all, if it should prove but a mummery got up by Vankarp, or some such wag? I wish you had run all risks, and cudgelled the old burgomaster soundly. I'd wager a dozen of Rhenish, his worship would have unmasked, and pleaded old acquaintance in a trice."

"Here he comes, sir," said Schalken, in a low monitory tone; and instantly, upon turning towards the door, Gerard Douw observed the same figure which had, on the day before, so unexpectedly greeted his pupil Schalken.

There was something in the air of the figure which at once satisfied the painter that there was no masquerading in the case, and that he really stood in the presence of a man of worship; and so, without hesitation, he doffed his cap, and courteously saluting the stranger, requested him to be seated. The visitor waved his hand slightly, as if in acknowledgment of the courtesy, but remained standing.

"I have the honour to see Minheer Vanderhausen of Rotterdam?" said Gerard Douw.

"The same," was the laconic reply of his visitor.

"I understand your worship desires to speak with me," continued Douw, "and I am here by appointment to wait your commands."

"Is that a man of trust?' said Vanderhausen, turning towards Schalken, who stood at a little distance behind his master.

"Certainly," replied Gerard.

"Then let him take this box, and get the nearest jeweller or goldsmith to value its contents, and let him return hither with a certificate of the valuation."

At the same time, he placed a small case about nine inches square in the hands of Gerard Douw, who was as much amazed at its weight as at the strange abruptness with which it was handed to him. In accordance with the wishes of the stranger, he delivered it into the hands of Schalken, and repeating his direction, despatched him upon the mission.

Schalken disposed his precious charge securely beneath the folds of his cloak, and rapidly traversing two or three narrow streets, he stopped at a corner house, the lower part of which was then occupied by the shop of a Jewish goldsmith. He entered the shop, and calling the little Hebrew into the obscurity of its back recesses, he proceeded to lay before him Vanderhausen's casket. On being examined by the light of a lamp, it appeared entirely cased with lead, the outer surface of which was much scraped and soiled, and nearly white with age. This having been partially removed, there appeared beneath a box of some hard wood; which also they forced open and after the removal of two or three folds of linen, they discovered its contents to be a mass of golden ingots, closely packed, and, as the Jew declared, of the most perfect quality. Every ingot underwent the scrutiny of the little Jew, who seemed to feel an epicurean delight in touching and testing these morsels of the glorious metal; and each one of them was replaced in its berth with the exclamation: "_Mein Gott_, how very perfect! not one grain of alloy--beautiful, beautiful!" The task was at length finished, and the Jew certified under his hand the value of the ingots submitted to his examination, to amount to many thousand rix-dollars. With the desired document in his pocket, and the rich box of gold carefully pressed under his arm, and concealed by his cloak, he retraced his way, and entering the studio, found his master and the stranger in close conference. Schalken had no sooner left the room, in order to execute the commission he had taken in charge, than Vanderhausen addressed Gerard Douw in the following terms:----

"I cannot tarry with you to-night more than a few minutes, and so I shall shortly tell you the matter upon which I come. You visited the town of Rotterdam some four months ago, and then I saw in the church of St. Lawrence your niece, Rose Velderkaust. I desire to marry her; and if I satisfy you that I am wealthier than any husband you can dream of for her, I expect that you will forward my suit with your authority. If you approve my proposal, you must close with it here and now, for I cannot wait for calculations and delays."

Gerard Douw was hugely astonished by the nature of Minheer Vanderhausen's communication, but he did not venture to express surprise; for besides the motives supplied by prudence and politeness, the painter experienced a kind of chill and oppression like that which is said to intervene when one is placed in unconscious proximity with the object of a natural antipathy--an undefined but overpowering sensation, while standing in the presence of the eccentric stranger, which made him very unwilling to say anything which might reasonably offend him.

"I have no doubt," said Gerard, after two or three prefatory hems, "that the alliance which you propose would prove alike advantageous and honourable to my niece; but you must be aware that she has a will of her own, and may not acquiesce in what _we_ may design for her advantage."

"Do not seek to deceive me, sir painter," said Vanderhausen; "you are her guardian--she is your ward--she is mine if _you_ like to make her so."

The man of Rotterdam moved forward a little as he spoke, and Gerard Douw, he scarce knew why, inwardly prayed for the speedy return of Schalken.

"I desire," said the mysterious gentleman, "to place in your hands at once an evidence of my wealth, and a security for my liberal dealing with your niece. The lad will return in a minute or two with a sum in value five times the fortune which she has a right to expect from her husband. This shall lie in your hands, together with her dowry, and you may apply the united sum as suits her interest best; it shall be all exclusively hers while she lives: is that liberal?"

Douw assented, and inwardly acknowledged that fortune had been extraordinarily kind to his niece; the stranger, he thought, must be both wealthy and generous, and such an offer was not to be despised, though made by a humourist, and one of no very prepossessing presence. Rose had no very high pretensions for she had but a modest dowry, which she owed entirely to the generosity of her uncle; neither had she any right to raise exceptions on the score of birth, for her own origin was far from splendid, and as the other objections, Gerald resolved, and indeed, by the usages of the time, was warranted in resolving, not to listen to them for a moment.
"Sir" said he, addressing the stranger, "your offer is liberal, and whatever hesitation I may feel in closing with it immediately, arises solely from my not having the honour of knowing anything of your family or station. Upon these points you can, of course, satisfy me without difficulty?'

"As to my respectability," said the stranger, drily, "you must take that for granted at present; pester me with no inquiries; you can discover nothing more about me than I choose to make known. You shall have sufficient security for my respectability--my word, if you are honourable: if you are sordid, my gold."

"A testy old gentleman," thought Douw, "he must have his own way; but, all things considered, I am not justified to declining his offer. I will not pledge myself unnecessarily, however."

"You will not pledge yourself unnecessarily," said Vanderhausen, strangely uttering the very words which had just floated through the mind of his companion; "but you will do so if it is necessary, I presume; and I will show you that I consider it indispensable. If the gold I mean to leave in your hands satisfy you, and if you don't wish my proposal to be at once withdrawn, you must, before I leave this room, write your name to this engagement."

Having thus spoken, he placed a paper in the hands of the master, the contents of which expressed an engagement entered into by Gerard Douw, to give to Wilken Vanderhausen of Rotterdam, in marriage, Rose Velderkaust, and so forth, within one week of the date thereof. While the painter was employed in reading this covenant, by the light of a twinkling oil lamp in the far wall of the room, Schalken, as we have stated, entered the studio, and having delivered the box and the valuation of the Jew, into the hands of the stranger, he was about to retire, when Vanderhausen called to him to wait; and, presenting the case and the certificate to Gerard Douw, he paused in silence until he had satisfied himself, by an inspection of both, respecting the value of the pledge left in his hands. At length he said----

"Are you content?"

The painter said he would fain have another day to consider.
"Not an hour," said the suitor, apathetically.

"Well then," said Douw, with a sore effort, "I am content, it is a bargain."

"Then sign at once," said Vanderhausen, "for I am weary."

At the same time he produced a small case of writing materials, and Gerard signed the important document.

"Let this youth witness the covenant," said the old man; and Godfrey Schalken unconsciously attested the instrument which for ever bereft him of his dear Rose Velderkaust.

The compact being thus completed, the strange visitor folded up the paper, and stowed it safely in an inner pocket.

"I will visit you to-morrow night at nine o'clock, at your own house, Gerard Douw, and will see the object of our contract;" and so saying Wilken Vanderhausen moved stiffly, but rapidly, out of the room.

Schalken, eager to resolve his doubts, had placed himself by the window, in order to watch the street entrance; but the experiment served only to support his suspicions, for the old man did not issue from the door. This was _very_ strange, odd, nay fearful. He and his master returned together, and talked but little on the way, for each had his own subjects of reflection, of anxiety, and of hope. Schalken, however, did not know the ruin which menaced his dearest projects.

Gerard Douw knew nothing of the attachment which had sprung up between his pupil and his niece; and even if he had, it is doubtful whether he would have regarded its existence as any serious obstruction to the wishes of Minheer Vanderhausen. Marriages were then and there matters of traffic and calculation; and it would have appeared as absurd in the eyes of the guardian to make a mutual attachment an essential element in a contract of the sort, as it would have been to draw up his bonds and receipts in the language of romance.

The painter, however, did not communicate to his niece the important step which he had taken in her behalf, a forebearance caused not by any anticipated opposition on her part, but solely by a ludicrous consciousness that if she were to ask him for a description of her destined bridegroom, he would be forced to confess that he had not once seen his face, and if called upon, would find it absolutely impossible to identify him. Upon the next day, Gerard Douw, after dinner, called his niece to him and having scanned her person with an air of satisfaction, he took her hand, and looking upon her pretty innocent face with a smile of kindness, he said:----

"Rose, my girl, that face of yours will make your fortune." Rose blushed and smiled. "Such faces and such tempers seldom go together, and when they do, the compound is a love charm, few heads or hearts can resist; trust me, you will soon be a bride, girl. But this is trifling, and I am pressed for time, so make ready the large room by eight o'clock to-night, and give directions for supper at nine. I expect a friend; and observe me, child, do you trick yourself out handsomely. I will not have him think us poor or sluttish."

With these words he left her, and took his way to the room in which his pupils worked.

When the evening closed in, Gerard called Schalken, who was about to take his departure to his own obscure and comfortless lodgings, and asked him to come home and sup with Rose and Vanderhausen. The invitation was, of course, accepted and Gerard Douw and his pupil soon found themselves in the handsome and, even then, antique chamber, which had been prepared for the reception of the stranger. A cheerful wood fire blazed in the hearth, a little at one side of which an old-fashioned table, which shone in the fire-light like burnished gold, was awaiting the supper, for which preparations were going forward; and ranged with exact regularity, stood the tall-backed chairs, whose ungracefulness was more than compensated by their comfort. The little party, consisting of Rose, her uncle, and the artist, awaited the arrival of the expected visitor with considerable impatience. Nine o'clock at length came, and with it a summons at the street door, which being speedily answered, was followed by a slow and emphatic tread upon the staircase; the steps moved heavily across the lobby, the door of the room in which the party we have described were assembled slowly opened, and there entered a figure which startled, almost appalled, the phlegmatic Dutchmen, and nearly made Rose scream with terror. It was the form, and arrayed in the garb of Minheer Vanderhausen; the air, the gait, the height were the same, but the features had never been seen by any of the party before. The stranger stopped at the door of the room, and displayed his form and face completely. He wore a dark-coloured cloth cloak, which was short and full, not falling quite to his knees; his legs were cased in dark purple silk stockings, and his shoes were adorned with roses of the same colour. The opening of the cloak in front showed the under-suit to consist of some very dark, perhaps sable material, and his hands were enclosed in a pair of heavy leather gloves, which ran up considerably above the wrist, in the manner of a gauntlet. In one hand he carried his walking-stick and his hat, which he had removed, and the other hung heavily by his side. A quantity of grizzled hair descended in long tresses from his head, and rested upon the plaits of a stiff ruff, which effectually concealed his neck. So far all was well; but the face!--all the flesh of the face was coloured with the bluish leaden hue, which is sometimes produced by metallic medicines, administered in excessive quantities; the eyes showed an undue proportion of muddy white, and had a certain indefinable character of insanity; the hue of the lips bearing the usual relation to that of the face, was, consequently, nearly black; and the entire character of the face was sensual, malignant, and even satanic. It was remarkable that the worshipful stranger suffered as little as possible of his flesh to appear, and that during his visit he did not once remove his gloves. Having stood for some moments at the door, Gerard Douw at length found breath and collectedness to bid him welcome, and with a mute inclination of the head, the stranger stepped forward into the room. There was something indescribably odd, even horrible, about all his motions, something undefinable, that was unnatural, unhuman; it was as if the limbs were guided and directed by a spirit unused to the management of bodily machinery. The stranger spoke hardly at all during his visit, which did not exceed half an hour; and the host himself could scarcely muster courage enough to utter the few necessary salutations and courtesies; and, indeed, such was the nervous terror which the presence of Vanderhausen inspired, that very little would have made all his entertainers fly in downright panic from the room. They had not so far lost all self-possession, however, as to fail to observe two strange peculiarities of their visitor. During his stay his eyelids did not once close, or, indeed, move in the slightest degree; and farther, there was a deathlike stillness in his whole person, owing to the absence of the heaving motion of the chest, caused by the process of respiration. These two peculiarities, though when told they may appear trifling, produced a very striking and unpleasant effect when seen and observed. Vanderhausen at length relieved the painter of Leyden of his inauspicious presence; and with no trifling sense of relief the little party heard the street door close after him.

"Dear uncle," said Rose, "what a frightful man! I would not see him again for the wealth of the States."

"Tush, foolish girl," said Douw, whose sensations were anything but comfortable. "A man may be as ugly as the devil, and yet, if his heart and actions are good, he is worth all the pretty-faced perfumed puppies that walk the Mall. Rose, my girl, it is very true he has not thy pretty face, but I know him to be wealthy and liberal; and were he ten times more ugly, these two virtues would be enough to counter balance all his deformity, and if not sufficient actually to alter the shape and hue of his features, at least enough to prevent one thinking them so much amiss."

"Do you know, uncle," said Rose, "when I saw him standing at the door, I could not get it out of my head that I saw the old painted wooden figure that used to frighten me so much in the Church of St. Laurence at Rotterdam."

Gerard laughed, though he could not help inwardly acknowledging the justness of the comparison. He was resolved, however, as far as he could, to check his niece's disposition to dilate upon the ugliness of her intended bridegroom, although he was not a little pleased, as well as puzzled, to observe that she appeared totally exempt from that mysterious dread of the stranger which, he could not disguise it from himself, considerably affected him, as also his pupil Godfrey Schalken.

Early on the next day there arrived, from various quarters of the town, rich presents of silks, velvets, jewellery, and so forth, for Rose; and also a packet directed to Gerard Douw, which on being opened, was found to contain a contract of marriage, formally drawn up, between Wilken Vanderhausen of the _Boom-quay_, in Rotterdam, and Rose Velderkaust of Leyden, niece to Gerard Douw, master in the art of painting, also of the same city; and containing engagements on the part of Vanderhausen to make settlements upon his bride, far more splendid than he had before led her guardian to believe likely, and which were to be secured to her use in the most unexceptionable manner possible--the money being placed in the hand of Gerard Douw himself.

I have no sentimental scenes to describe, no cruelty of guardians, no magnanimity of wards, no agonies, or transport of lovers. The record I have to make is one of sordidness, levity, and heartlessness. In less than a week after the first interview which we have just described, the contract of marriage was fulfilled, and Schalken saw the prize which he would have risked existence to secure, carried off in solemn pomp by his repulsive rival. For two or three days he absented himself from the school; he then returned and worked, if with less cheerfulness, with far more dogged resolution than before; the stimulus of love had given place to that of ambition. Months passed away, and, contrary to his expectation, and, indeed, to the direct promise of the parties, Gerard Douw heard nothing of his niece or her worshipful spouse. The interest of the money, which was to have been demanded in quarterly sums, lay unclaimed in his hands.

He began to grow extremely uneasy. Minheer Vanderhausen's direction in Rotterdam he was fully possessed of; after some irresolution he finally determined to journey thither--a trifling undertaking, and easily accomplished--and thus to satisfy himself of the safety and comfort of his ward, for whom he entertained an honest and strong affection. His search was in vain, however; no one in Rotterdam had ever heard of Minheer Vanderhausen. Gerard Douw left not a house in the _Boom-quay_ untried, but all in vain. No one could give him any information whatever touching the object of his inquiry, and he was obliged to return to Leyden nothing wiser and far more anxious, than when he had left it.

On his arrival he hastened to the establishment from which Vanderhausen had hired the lumbering, though, considering the times, most luxurious vehicle, which the bridal party had employed to convey them to Rotterdam. From the driver of this machine he learned, that having proceeded by slow stages, they had late in the evening approached
Rotterdam; but that before they entered the city, and while yet nearly a

mile from it, a small party of men, soberly clad, and after the old fashion, with peaked beards and moustaches, standing in the centre of the road, obstructed the further progress of the carriage. The driver reined in his horses, much fearing, from the obscurity of the hour, and the loneliness, of the road, that some mischief was intended. His fears were, however, somewhat allayed by his observing that these strange men carried a large litter, of an antique shape, and which they immediately set down upon the pavement, whereupon the bridegroom, having opened the coach-door from within, descended, and having assisted his bride to do likewise, led her, weeping bitterly, and wringing her hands, to the litter, which they both entered. It was then raised by the men who surrounded it, and speedily carried towards the city, and before it had proceeded very far, the darkness concealed it from the view of the Dutch coachman. In the inside of the vehicle he found a purse, whose contents more than thrice paid the hire of the carriage and man. He saw and could tell nothing more of Minheer Vanderhausen and his beautiful lady.

This mystery was a source of profound anxiety and even grief to Gerard Douw. There was evidently fraud in the dealing of Vanderhausen with him, though for what purpose committed he could not imagine. He greatly doubted how far it was possible for a man possessing such a countenance to be anything but a villain, and every day that passed without his hearing from or of his niece, instead of inducing him to forget his fears, on the contrary tended more and more to aggravate them. The loss of her cheerful society tended also to depress his spirits; and in order to dispel the gloom, which often crept upon his mind after his daily occupations were over, he was wont frequently to ask Schalken to accompany him home, and share his otherwise solitary supper.

One evening, the painter and his pupil were sitting by the fire, having accomplished a comfortable meal, and had yielded to the silent and delicious melancholy of digestion, when their ruminations were disturbed by a loud sound at the street door, as if occasioned by some person rushing and scrambling vehemently against it. A domestic had run without delay to ascertain the cause of the disturbance, and they heard him twice or thrice interrogate the applicant for admission, but without eliciting any other answer but a sustained reiteration of the sounds. They heard him then open the hall-door, and immediately there followed a light and rapid tread on the staircase. Schalken advanced towards the door. It opened before he reached it, and Rose rushed into the room. She looked wild, fierce and haggard with terror and exhaustion, but her dress surprised them as much as even her unexpected appearance. It consisted of a kind of white woollen wrapper, made close about the neck, and descending to the very ground. It was much deranged and travel-soiled. The poor creature had hardly entered the chamber when she fell senseless on the floor. With some difficulty they succeeded in reviving her, and on recovering her senses, she instantly exclaimed, in a tone of terror rather than mere impatience:----

"Wine! wine! quickly, or I'm lost!"

Astonished and almost scared at the strange agitation in which the call was made, they at once administered to her wishes, and she drank some wine with a haste and eagerness which surprised them. She had hardly swallowed it, when she exclaimed, with the same urgency:

"Food, for God's sake, food, at once, or I perish."

A considerable fragment of a roast joint was upon the table, and Schalken immediately began to cut some, but he was anticipated, for no sooner did she see it than she caught it, a more than mortal image of famine, and with her hands, and even with her teeth, she tore off the flesh, and swallowed it. When the paroxysm of hunger had been a little appeased, she appeared on a sudden overcome with shame, or it may have been that other more agitating thoughts overpowered and scared her, for she began to weep bitterly and to wring her hands.

"Oh, send for a minister of God," said she; "I am not safe till he comes; send for him speedily."

Gerard Douw despatched a messenger instantly, and prevailed on his niece to allow him to surrender his bed chamber to her use. He also persuaded her to retire to it at once to rest; her consent was extorted upon the condition that they would not leave her for a moment.

"Oh that the holy man were here," she said; "he can deliver me: the dead and the living can never be one: God has forbidden it."
With these mysterious words she surrendered herself to their guidance, and they proceeded to the chamber which Gerard Douw had assigned to her use.

"Do not, do not leave me for a moment," said she; "I am lost for ever if you do."

Gerard Douw's chamber was approached through a spacious apartment, which they were now about to enter. He and Schalken each carried a candle, so that a sufficiency of light was cast upon all surrounding objects. They were now entering the large chamber, which as I have said, communicated with Douw's apartment, when Rose suddenly stopped, and, in a whisper which thrilled them both with horror, she said:----

"Oh, God! he is here! he is here! See, see! there he goes!"

She pointed towards the door of the inner room, and Schalken thought he saw a shadowy and ill-defined form gliding into that apartment. He drew his sword, and, raising the candle so as to throw its light with increased distinctness upon the objects in the room, he entered the chamber into which the shadow had glided. No figure was there--nothing but the furniture which belonged to the room, and yet he could not be deceived as to the fact that something had moved before them into the chamber. A sickening dread came upon him, and the cold perspiration broke out in heavy drops upon his forehead; nor was he more composed, when he heard the increased urgency and agony of entreaty, with which Rose implored them not to leave her for a moment.

"I saw him," said she; "he's here. I cannot be deceived; I know him; he's by me; he is with me; he's in the room. Then, for God's sake, as you would save me, do not stir from beside me."

They at length prevailed upon her to lie down upon the bed, where she continued to urge them to stay by her. She frequently uttered incoherent sentences, repeating, again and again, "the dead and the living cannot be one: God has forbidden it." And then again, "Rest to the wakeful--sleep to the sleep-walkers." These and such mysterious and broken sentences, she continued to utter until the clergyman arrived. Gerard Douw began to fear, naturally enough, that terror or ill-treatment, had unsettled the poor girl's intellect, and he half suspected, by the suddenness of her appearance, the unseasonableness of the hour, and above all, from the wildness and terror of her manner, that she had made her escape from some place of confinement for lunatics, and was in imminent fear of pursuit. He resolved to summon medical advice as soon as the mind of his niece had been in some measure set at rest by the offices of the clergyman whose attendance she had so earnestly desired; and until this object had been attained, he did not venture to put any questions to her, which might possibly, by reviving painful or horrible recollections, increase her agitation. The clergyman soon arrived--a man of ascetic countenance and venerable age--one whom Gerard Douw respected very much, forasmuch as he was a veteran polemic, though one perhaps more dreaded as a combatant than beloved as a Christian--of pure morality, subtle brain, and frozen heart. He entered the chamber which communicated with that in which Rose reclined and immediately on his arrival, she requested him to pray for her, as for one who lay in the hands of Satan, and who could hope for deliverance only from heaven.

That you may distinctly understand all the circumstances of the event which I am going to describe, it is necessary to state the relative position of the parties who were engaged in it. The old clergyman and Schalken were in the anteroom of which I have already spoken; Rose lay in the inner chamber, the door of which was open; and by the side of the bed, at her urgent desire, stood her guardian; a candle burned in the bedchamber, and three were lighted in the outer apartment. The old man now cleared his voice as if about to commence, but before he had time to begin, a sudden gust of air blew out the candle which served to illuminate the room in which the poor girl lay, and she, with hurried alarm, exclaimed:----

"Godfrey, bring in another candle; the darkness is unsafe."

Gerard Douw forgetting for the moment her repeated injunctions, in the immediate impulse, stepped from the bedchamber into the other, in order to supply what she desired.

"Oh God! do not go, dear uncle," shrieked the unhappy girl--and at the same time she sprung from the bed, and darted after him, in order, by her grasp, to detain him. But the warning came too late, for scarcely had he passed the threshold, and hardly had his niece had time to utter the startling exclamation, when the door which divided the two rooms closed violently after him, as if swung by a strong blast of wind. Schalken and he both rushed to the door, but their united and desperate efforts could not avail so much as to shake it. Shriek after shriek burst from the inner chamber, with all the piercing loudness of despairing terror. Schalken and Douw applied every nerve to force open the door; but all in vain. There was no sound of struggling from within, but the screams seemed to increase in loudness, and at the same time they heard the bolts of the latticed window withdrawn, and the window itself grated upon the sill as if thrown open. One _last_ shriek, so long and piercing and agonized as to be scarcely human, swelled from the room, and suddenly there followed a death-like silence. A light step was heard crossing the floor, as if from the bed to the window; and almost at the same instant the door gave way, and, yielding to the pressure of the external applicants, nearly precipitated them into the room. It was empty. The window was open, and Schalken sprung to a chair and gazed out upon the street and canal below. He saw no form, but he saw, or thought he saw, the waters of the broad canal beneath settling ring after ring in heavy circles, as if a moment before disturbed by the submission of some ponderous body.

No trace of Rose was ever after found, nor was anything certain respecting her mysterious wooer discovered or even suspected--no clue whereby to trace the intricacies of the labyrinth and to arrive at its solution, presented itself. But an incident occurred, which, though it will not be received by our rational readers in lieu of evidence, produced nevertheless a strong and a lasting impression upon the mind of Schalken. Many years after the events which we have detailed, Schalken, then residing far away received an intimation of his father's death, and of his intended burial upon a fixed day in the church of Rotterdam. It was necessary that a very considerable journey should be performed by the funeral procession, which as it will be readily believed, was not very numerously attended. Schalken with difficulty arrived in Rotterdam late in the day upon which the funeral was appointed to take place. It had not then arrived. Evening closed in, and still it did not appear.

Schalken strolled down to the church; he found it open; notice of the arrival of the funeral had been given, and the vault in which the body was to be laid had been opened. The sexton, on seeing a well-dressed gentleman, whose object was to attend the expected obsequies, pacing the aisle of the church, hospitably invited him to share with him the comforts of a blazing fire, which, as was his custom in winter time upon such occasions, he had kindled in the hearth of a chamber in which he was accustomed to await the arrival of such grisly guests and which communicated, by a flight of steps, with the vault below. In this chamber, Schalken and his entertainer seated themselves; and the sexton, after some fruitless attempts to engage his guest in conversation, was obliged to apply himself to his tobacco-pipe and can, to solace his solitude. In spite of his grief and cares, the fatigues of a rapid journey of nearly forty hours gradually overcame the mind and body of Godfrey Schalken, and he sank into a deep sleep, from which he awakened by someone's shaking him gently by the shoulder. He first thought that the old sexton had called him, but _he_ was no longer in the room. He roused himself, and as soon as he could clearly see what was around him, he perceived a female form, clothed in a kind of light robe of white, part of which was so disposed as to form a veil, and in her hand she carried a lamp. She was moving rather away from him, in the direction of the flight of steps which conducted towards the vaults. Schalken felt a vague alarm at the sight of this figure and at the same time an irresistible impulse to follow its guidance. He followed it towards the vaults, but when it reached the head of the stairs, he paused; the figure paused also, and, turning gently round, displayed, by the light of the lamp it carried, the face and features of his first love, Rose Velderkaust. There was nothing horrible, or even sad, in the countenance. On the contrary, it wore the same arch smile which used to enchant the artist long before in his happy days. A feeling of awe and interest, too intense to be resisted, prompted him to follow the spectre, if spectre it were. She descended the stairs--he followed--and turning to the left, through a narrow passage, she led him, to his infinite surprise, into what appeared to be an old-fashioned Dutch apartment, such as the pictures of Gerard Douw have served to immortalize. Abundance of costly antique furniture was disposed about the room, and in one corner stood a four-post bed, with heavy black cloth curtains around it; the figure frequently turned towards him with the same arch smile; and when she came to the side of the bed, she drew the curtains, and, by the light of the lamp, which she held towards its contents, she disclosed to the horror-stricken painter, sitting bolt upright in the bed, the livid and demoniac form of Vanderhausen. Schalken had hardly seen him, when he fell senseless upon the floor, where he lay until discovered, on the next morning, by persons employed in closing the passages into the vaults. He was lying in a cell of considerable size, which had not been disturbed for a long time, and he had fallen beside a large coffin, which was supported upon small pillars, a security against the attacks of vermin.

To his dying day Schalken was satisfied of the reality of the vision which he had witnessed, and he has left behind him a curious evidence of the impression which it wrought upon his fancy, in a painting executed shortly after the event I have narrated, and which is valuable as exhibiting not only the peculiarities which have made Schalken's pictures sought after, but even more so as presenting a portrait of his early love, Rose Velderkaust, whose mysterious fate must always remain matter of speculation.

# GHOST STORIES OF CHAPELIZOD (1851)

Take my word for it, there is no such thing as an ancient village, especially if it has seen better days, unillustrated by its legends of terror. You might as well expect to find a decayed cheese without mites, or an old house without rats, as an antique and dilapidated town without an authentic population of goblins. Now, although this class of inhabitants are in nowise amenable to the police authorities, yet, as their demeanor directly affects the comforts of her Majesty's subjects, I cannot but regard it as a grave omission that the public have hitherto been left without any statistical returns of their numbers, activity, etc., etc. And I am persuaded that a Commission to inquire into and report upon the numerical strength, habits, haunts, etc., etc., of supernatural agents resident in Ireland, would be a great deal more innocent and entertaining than half the Commissions for which the country pays, and at least as instructive. This I say, more from a sense of duty, and to deliver my mind of a grave truth, than with any hope of seeing the suggestion adopted. But, I am sure, my readers will deplore with me that the comprehensive powers of belief, and apparently illimitable leisure, possessed by parliamentary commissions of inquiry, should never have been applied to the subject I have named, and that the collection of that species of information should be confided to the gratuitous and desultory labours of individuals, who, like myself, have other occupations to attend to. This, however, by the way.

Among the village outposts of Dublin, Chapelizod once held a considerable, if not a foremost rank. Without mentioning its connexion with the history of the great Kilmainham Preceptory of the Knights of St. John, it will be enough to remind the reader of its ancient and celebrated Castle, not one vestige of which now remains, and of the fact that it was for, we believe, some centuries, the summer residence of the Viceroys of Ireland. The circumstance of its being up, we believe, to the period at which that corps was disbanded, the headquarters of the Royal Irish Artillery, gave it also a consequence of an humbler, but not less substantial kind. With these advantages in its favour, it is not wonderful that the town exhibited at one time an air of substantial and semi-aristocratic prosperity unknown to Irish villages in modern times.

A broad street, with a well-paved footpath, and houses as lofty as were at that time to be found in the fashionable streets of Dublin; a goodly stone-fronted barrack; an ancient church, vaulted beneath, and with a tower clothed from its summit to its base with the richest ivy; an humble Roman Catholic chapel; a steep bridge spanning the Liffey, and a great old mill at the near end of it, were the principal features of the town. These, or at least most of them, remain still, but the greater part in a very changed and forlorn condition. Some of them indeed are superseded, though not obliterated by modern erections, such as the bridge, the chapel, and the church in part; the rest forsaken by the order who originally raised them, and delivered up to poverty, and in some cases to absolute decay.

The village lies in the lap of the rich and wooded valley of the Liffey, and is overlooked by the high grounds of the beautiful Phoenix Park on the one side, and by the ridge of the Palmerstown hills on the other. Its situation, therefore, is eminently picturesque; and factory-fronts and chimneys notwithstanding, it has, I think, even in its decay, a sort of melancholy picturesqueness of its own. Be that as it may, I mean to relate two or three stories of that sort which may be read with very good effect by a blazing fire on a shrewd winter's night, and are all directly connected with the altered and somewhat melancholy little town I have named. The first I shall relate concerns

## The Village Bully

About thirty years ago there lived in the town of Chapelizod an ill-conditioned fellow of herculean strength, well known throughout the neighbourhood by the title of Bully Larkin. In addition to his remarkable physical superiority, this fellow had acquired a degree of skill as a pugilist which alone would have made him formidable. As it was, he was the autocrat of the village, and carried not the sceptre in vain. Conscious of his superiority, and perfectly secure of impunity, he lorded it over his fellows in a spirit of cowardly and brutal insolence, which made him hated even more profoundly than he was feared.

Upon more than one occasion he had deliberately forced quarrels upon men whom he had singled out for the exhibition of his savage prowess; and in every encounter his over-matched antagonist had received an amount of "punishment" which edified and appalled the spectators, and in some instances left ineffaceable scars and lasting injuries after it.

Bully Larkin's pluck had never been fairly tried. For, owing to his prodigious superiority in weight, strength, and skill, his victories had always been certain and easy; and in proportion to the facility with which he uniformly smashed an antagonist, his pugnacity and insolence were inflamed. He thus became an odious nuisance in the neighbourhood, and the terror of every mother who had a son, and of every wife who had a husband who possessed a spirit to resent insult, or the smallest confidence in his own pugilistic capabilities.

Now it happened that there was a young fellow named Ned Moran--better known by the soubriquet of "Long Ned," from his slender, lathy proportions--at that time living in the town. He was, in truth, a mere lad, nineteen years of age, and fully twelve years younger than the stalwart bully. This, however, as the reader will see, secured for him no exemption from the dastardly provocations of the ill-conditioned pugilist. Long Ned, in an evil hour, had thrown eyes of affection upon a certain buxom damsel, who, notwithstanding Bully Larkin's amorous rivalry, inclined to reciprocate them.
I need not say how easily the spark of jealousy, once kindled, is blown into a flame, and how naturally, in a coarse and ungoverned nature, it explodes in acts of violence and outrage.

"The bully" watched his opportunity, and contrived to provoke Ned Moran, while drinking in a public-house with a party of friends, into an altercation, in the course of which he failed not to put such insults upon his rival as manhood could not tolerate. Long Ned, though a simple, good-natured sort of fellow, was by no means deficient in spirit, and retorted in a tone of defiance which edified the more timid, and gave his opponent the opportunity he secretly coveted.

Bully Larkin challenged the heroic youth, whose pretty face he had privately consigned to the mangling and bloody discipline he was himself so capable of administering. The quarrel, which he had himself contrived to get up, to a certain degree covered the ill blood and malignant premeditation which inspired his proceedings, and Long Ned, being full of generous ire and whiskey punch, accepted the gauge of battle on the instant. The whole party, accompanied by a mob of idle men and boys, and in short by all who could snatch a moment from the calls of business, proceeded in slow procession through the old gate into the Phoenix Park, and mounting the hill overlooking the town, selected near its summit a level spot on which to decide the quarrel.

The combatants stripped, and a child might have seen in the contrast presented by the slight, lank form and limbs of the lad, and the muscular and massive build of his veteran antagonist, how desperate was the chance of poor Ned Moran.

"Seconds" and "bottle-holders"--selected of course for their love of the game--were appointed, and "the fight" commenced.

I will not shock my readers with a description of the cool-blooded butchery that followed. The result of the combat was what anybody might have predicted. At the eleventh round, poor Ned refused to "give in"; the brawny pugilist, unhurt, in good wind, and pale with concentrated and as yet unslaked revenge, had the gratification of seeing his opponent seated upon his second's knee, unable to hold up his head, his left arm disabled; his face a bloody, swollen, and shapeless mass; his breast scarred and bloody, and his whole body panting and quivering with rage and exhaustion.

"Give in, Ned, my boy," cried more than one of the bystanders.

"Never, never," shrieked he, with a voice hoarse and choking.

Time being "up," his second placed him on his feet again. Blinded with his own blood, panting and staggering, he presented but a helpless mark for the blows of his stalwart opponent. It was plain that a touch would have been sufficient to throw him to the earth. But Larkin had no notion of letting him off so easily. He closed with him without striking a blow (the effect of which, prematurely dealt, would have been to bring him at once to the ground, and so put an end to the combat), and getting his battered and almost senseless head under his arm, fast in that peculiar "fix" known to the fancy pleasantly by the name of "chancery," he held him firmly, while with monotonous and brutal strokes he beat his fist, as it seemed, almost into his face. A cry of "shame" broke from the crowd, for it was plain that the beaten man was now insensible, and supported only by the herculean arm of the bully. The round and the fight ended by his hurling him upon the ground, falling upon him at the same time with his knee upon his chest.

The bully rose, wiping the perspiration from his white face with his blood-stained hands, but Ned lay stretched and motionless upon the grass. It was impossible to get him upon his legs for another round. So he was carried down, just as he was, to the pond which then lay close to the old Park gate, and his head and body were washed beside it. Contrary to the belief of all he was not dead. He was carried home, and after some months to a certain extent recovered. But he never held up his head again, and before the year was over he had died of consumption. Nobody could doubt how the disease had been induced, but there was no actual proof to connect the cause and effect, and the ruffian Larkin escaped the vengeance of the law. A strange retribution, however, awaited him.

After the death of Long Ned, he became less quarrelsome than before, but more sullen and reserved. Some said "he took it to heart," and others, that his conscience was not at ease about it. Be this as it may, however, his health did not suffer by reason of his presumed agitations, nor was his worldly prosperity marred by the blasting curses with which poor Moran's enraged mother pursued him; on the contrary he had rather risen in the world, and obtained regular and well-remunerated employment from the Chief Secretary's gardener, at the other side of the Park. He still lived in Chapelizod, whither, on the close of his day's work, he used to return across the Fifteen Acres.

It was about three years after the catastrophe we have mentioned, and late in the autumn, when, one night, contrary to his habit, he did not appear at the house where he lodged, neither had he been seen anywhere, during the evening, in the village. His hours of return had been so very regular, that his absence excited considerable surprise, though, of course, no actual alarm; and, at the usual hour, the house was closed for the night, and the absent lodger consigned to the mercy of the elements, and the care of his presiding star. Early in the morning, however, he was found lying in a state of utter helplessness upon the slope immediately overlooking the Chapelizod gate. He had been smitten with a paralytic stroke: his right side was dead; and it was many weeks before he had recovered his speech sufficiently to make himself at all understood.

He then made the following relation:--He had been detained, it appeared, later than usual, and darkness had closed before he commenced his homeward walk across the Park. It was a moonlit night, but masses of ragged clouds were slowly drifting across the heavens. He had not encountered a human figure, and no sounds but the softened rush of the wind sweeping through bushes and hollows met his ear. These wild and monotonous sounds, and the utter solitude which surrounded him, did not, however, excite any of those uneasy sensations which are ascribed to superstition, although he said he did feel depressed, or, in his own phraseology, "lonesome." Just as he crossed the brow of the hill which shelters the town of Chapelizod, the moon shone out for some moments with unclouded lustre, and his eye, which happened to wander by the shadowy enclosures which lay at the foot of the slope, was arrested by the sight of a human figure climbing, with all the haste of one pursued, over the churchyard wall, and running up the steep ascent directly towards him. Stories of "resurrectionists" crossed his recollection, as he observed this suspicious-looking figure. But he began, momentarily, to be aware with a sort of fearful instinct which he could not explain, that the running figure was directing his steps, with a sinister purpose, towards himself.

The form was that of a man with a loose coat about him, which, as he ran, he disengaged, and as well as Larkin could see, for the moon was again wading in clouds, threw from him. The figure thus advanced until within some two score yards of him, it arrested its speed, and approached with a loose, swaggering gait. The moon again shone out bright and clear, and, gracious God! what was the spectacle before him? He saw as distinctly as if he had been presented there in the flesh, Ned Moran, himself, stripped naked from the waist upward, as if for pugilistic combat, and drawing towards him in silence. Larkin would have shouted, prayed, cursed, fled across the Park, but he was absolutely powerless; the apparition stopped within a few steps, and leered on him with a ghastly mimicry of the defiant stare with which pugilists strive to cow one another before combat. For a time, which he could not so much as conjecture, he was held in the fascination of that unearthly gaze, and at last the thing, whatever it was, on a sudden swaggered close up to him with extended palms. With an impulse of horror, Larkin put out his hand to keep the figure off, and their palms touched--at least, so he believed--for a thrill of unspeakable agony, running through his arm, pervaded his entire frame, and he fell senseless to the earth.

Though Larkin lived for many years after, his punishment was terrible. He was incurably maimed; and being unable to work, he was forced, for existence, to beg alms of those who had once feared and flattered him. He suffered, too, increasingly, under his own horrible interpretation of the preternatural encounter which was the beginning of all his miseries. It was vain to endeavour to shake his faith in the reality of the apparition, and equally vain, as some compassionately did, to try to persuade him that the greeting with which his vision closed was intended, while inflicting a temporary trial, to signify a compensating reconciliation.

"No, no," he used to say, "all won't do. I know the meaning of it well enough; it is a challenge to meet him in the other world--in Hell, where I am going--that's what it means, and nothing else."

And so, miserable and refusing comfort, he lived on for some years, and then died, and was buried in the same narrow churchyard which contains the remains of his victim.

I need hardly say, how absolute was the faith of the honest inhabitants, at the time when I heard the story, in the reality of the preternatural summons which, through the portals of terror, sickness, and misery, had summoned Bully Larkin to his long, last home, and that, too, upon the very ground on which he had signalised the guiltiest triumph of his violent and vindictive career.

I recollect another story of the preternatural sort, which made no small sensation, some five-and-thirty years ago, among the good gossips of the town; and, with your leave, courteous reader, I shall relate it.

## The Sexton's Adventure

Those who remember Chapelizod a quarter of a century ago, or more, may possibly recollect the parish sexton. Bob Martin was held much in awe by truant boys who sauntered into the churchyard on Sundays, to read the tombstones, or play leap frog over them, or climb the ivy in search of bats or sparrows' nests, or peep into the mysterious aperture under the eastern window, which opened a dim perspective of descending steps losing themselves among profounder darkness, where lidless coffins gaped horribly among tattered velvet, bones, and dust, which time and mortality had strewn there. Of such horribly curious, and otherwise enterprising juveniles, Bob was, of course, the special scourge and terror. But terrible as was the official aspect of the sexton, and repugnant as his lank form, clothed in rusty, sable vesture, his small, frosty visage, suspicious grey eyes, and rusty, brown scratch-wig, might appear to all notions of genial frailty; it was yet true, that Bob Martin's severe morality sometimes nodded, and that Bacchus did not always solicit him in vain.

Bob had a curious mind, a memory well stored with "merry tales," and tales of terror. His profession familiarized him with graves and goblins, and his tastes with weddings, wassail, and sly frolics of all sorts. And as his personal recollections ran back nearly three score years into the perspective of the village history, his fund of local anecdote was copious, accurate, and edifying.

As his ecclesiastical revenues were by no means considerable, he was not unfrequently obliged, for the indulgence of his tastes, to arts which were, at the best, undignified.

He frequently invited himself when his entertainers had forgotten to do so; he dropped in accidentally upon small drinking parties of his acquaintance in public houses, and entertained them with stories, queer or terrible, from his inexhaustible reservoir, never scrupling to accept an acknowledgment in the shape of hot whiskey-punch, or whatever else was going.

There was at that time a certain atrabilious publican, called Philip Slaney, established in a shop nearly opposite the old turnpike. This man was not, when left to himself, immoderately given to drinking; but being naturally of a saturnine complexion, and his spirits constantly requiring a fillip, he acquired a prodigious liking for Bob Martin's company. The sexton's society, in fact, gradually became the solace of his existence, and he seemed to lose his constitutional melancholy in the fascination of his sly jokes and marvellous stories.

This intimacy did not redound to the prosperity or reputation of the convivial allies. Bob Martin drank a good deal more punch than was good for his health, or consistent with the character of an ecclesiastical functionary. Philip Slaney, too, was drawn into similar indulgences, for it was hard to resist the genial seductions of his gifted companion; and as he was obliged to pay for both, his purse was believed to have suffered even more than his head and liver.

Be this as it may, Bob Martin had the credit of having made a drunkard of "black Phil Slaney"--for by this cognomen was he distinguished; and Phil Slaney had also the reputation of having made the sexton, if possible, a "bigger bliggard" than ever. Under these circumstances, the accounts of the concern opposite the turnpike became somewhat entangled; and it came to pass one drowsy summer morning, the weather being at once sultry and cloudy, that Phil Slaney went into a small back parlour, where he kept his books, and which commanded, through its dirty window-panes, a full view of a dead wall, and having bolted the door, he took a loaded pistol, and clapping the muzzle in his mouth, blew the upper part of his skull through the ceiling.

This horrid catastrophe shocked Bob Martin extremely; and partly on this account, and partly because having been, on several late occasions, found at night in a state of abstraction, bordering on insensibility, upon the high road, he had been threatened with dismissal; and, as some said, partly also because of the difficulty of finding anybody to "treat" him as poor Phil Slaney used to do, he for a time forswore alcohol in all its combinations, and became an eminent example of temperance and sobriety.

Bob observed his good resolutions, greatly to the comfort of his wife, and the edification of the neighbourhood, with tolerable punctuality. He was seldom tipsy, and never drunk, and was greeted by the better part of society with all the honours of the prodigal son.

Now it happened, about a year after the grisly event we have mentioned, that the curate having received, by the post, due notice of a funeral to be consummated in the churchyard of Chapelizod, with certain instructions respecting the site of the grave, despatched a summons for Bob Martin, with a view to communicate to that functionary these official details.

It was a lowering autumn night: piles of lurid thunder-clouds, slowly rising from the earth, had loaded the sky with a solemn and boding canopy of storm. The growl of the distant thunder was heard afar off upon the dull, still air, and all nature seemed, as it were, hushed and cowering under the oppressive influence of the approaching tempest.

It was past nine o'clock when Bob, putting on his official coat of seedy black, prepared to attend his professional superior.

"Bobby, darlin'," said his wife, before she delivered the hat she held in her hand to his keeping, "sure you won't, Bobby, darlin'--you won't--you know what."

"I _don't_ know what," he retorted, smartly, grasping at his hat.

"You won't be throwing up the little finger, Bobby, acushla?" she said, evading his grasp.

"Arrah, why would I, woman? there, give me my hat, will you?"

"But won't you promise me, Bobby darlin'--won't you, alanna?"

"Ay, ay, to be sure I will--why not?--there, give me my hat, and let me go."

"Ay, but you're not promisin', Bobby, mavourneen; you're not promisin' all the time."

"Well, divil carry me if I drink a drop till I come back again," said the sexton, angrily; "will that do you? And _now_ will you give me my hat?"

"Here it is, darlin'," she said, "and God send you safe back."

And with this parting blessing she closed the door upon his retreating figure, for it was now quite dark, and resumed her knitting till his return, very much relieved; for she thought he had of late been oftener tipsy than was consistent with his thorough reformation, and feared the allurements of the half dozen "publics" which he had at that time to pass on his way to the other end of the town.

They were still open, and exhaled a delicious reek of whiskey, as Bob glided wistfully by them; but he stuck his hands in his pockets and looked the other way, whistling resolutely, and filling his mind with the image of the curate and anticipations of his coming fee. Thus he steered his morality safely through these rocks of offence, and reached the curate's lodging in safety.

He had, however, an unexpected sick call to attend, and was not at home, so that Bob Martin had to sit in the hall and amuse himself with the devil's tattoo until his return. This, unfortunately, was very long delayed, and it must have been fully twelve o'clock when Bob Martin set out upon his homeward way. By this time the storm had gathered to a pitchy darkness, the bellowing thunder was heard among the rocks and hollows of the Dublin mountains, and the pale, blue lightning shone upon the staring fronts of the houses.

By this time, too, every door was closed; but as Bob trudged homeward, his eye mechanically sought the public-house which had once belonged to Phil Slaney. A faint light was making its way through the shutters and the glass panes over the doorway, which made a sort of dull, foggy halo about the front of the house.

As Bob's eyes had become accustomed to the obscurity by this time, the light in question was quite sufficient to enable him to see a man in a sort of loose riding-coat seated upon a bench which, at that time, was fixed under the window of the house. He wore his hat very much over his eyes, and was smoking a long pipe. The outline of a glass and a quart bottle were also dimly traceable beside him; and a large horse saddled, but faintly discernible, was patiently awaiting his master's leisure.

There was something odd, no doubt, in the appearance of a traveller refreshing himself at such an hour in the open street; but the sexton accounted for it easily by supposing that, on the closing of the house for the night, he had taken what remained of his refection to the place where he was now discussing it al fresco.

At another time Bob might have saluted the stranger as he passed with a friendly "good night"; but, somehow, he was out of humour and in no genial mood, and was about passing without any courtesy of the sort, when the stranger, without taking the pipe from his mouth, raised the bottle, and with it beckoned him familiarly, while, with a sort of lurch of the head and shoulders, and at the same time shifting his seat to the end of the bench, he pantomimically invited him to share his seat and his cheer. There was a divine fragrance of whiskey about the spot, and Bob half relented; but he remembered his promise just as he began to waver, and said:

"No, I thank you, sir, I can't stop to-night."

The stranger beckoned with vehement welcome, and pointed to the vacant space on the seat beside him.

"I thank you for your polite offer," said Bob, "but it's what I'm too late as it is, and haven't time to spare, so I wish you a good night."

The traveller jingled the glass against the neck of the bottle, as if to intimate that he might at least swallow a dram without losing time. Bob was mentally quite of the same opinion; but, though his mouth watered, he remembered his promise, and shaking his head with incorruptible resolution, walked on.

The stranger, pipe in mouth, rose from his bench, the bottle in one hand, and the glass in the other, and followed at the sexton's heels, his dusky horse keeping close in his wake.

There was something suspicious and unaccountable in this importunity.

Bob quickened his pace, but the stranger followed close. The sexton began to feel queer, and turned about. His pursuer was behind, and still inviting him with impatient gestures to taste his liquor.

"I told you before," said Bob, who was both angry and frightened, "that I would not taste it, and that's enough. I don't want to have anything to say to you or your bottle; and in God's name," he added, more vehemently, observing that he was approaching still closer, "fall back and don't be tormenting me this way."

These words, as it seemed, incensed the stranger, for he shook the bottle with violent menace at Bob Martin; but, notwithstanding this gesture of defiance, he suffered the distance between them to increase. Bob, however, beheld him dogging him still in the distance, for his pipe shed a wonderful red glow, which duskily illuminated his entire figure like the lurid atmosphere of a meteor.

"I wish the devil had his own, my boy," muttered the excited sexton, "and I know well enough where you'd be."

The next time he looked over his shoulder, to his dismay he observed the importunate stranger as close as ever upon his track.
"Confound you," cried the man of skulls and shovels, almost beside himself with rage and horror, "what is it you want of me?"

The stranger appeared more confident, and kept wagging his head and extending both glass and bottle toward him as he drew near, and Bob Martin heard the horse snorting as it followed in the dark.

"Keep it to yourself, whatever it is, for there is neither grace nor luck about you," cried Bob Martin, freezing with terror; "leave me alone, will you."

And he fumbled in vain among the seething confusion of his ideas for a prayer or an exorcism. He quickened his pace almost to a run; he was now close to his own door, under the impending bank by the river side.

"Let me in, let me in, for God's sake; Molly, open the door," he cried, as he ran to the threshold, and leant his back against the plank. His pursuer confronted him upon the road; the pipe was no longer in his mouth, but the dusky red glow still lingered round him. He uttered some inarticulate cavernous sounds, which were wolfish and indescribable, while he seemed employed in pouring out a glass from the bottle.

The sexton kicked with all his force against the door, and cried at the same time with a despairing voice.

"In the name of God Almighty, once for all, leave me alone."

His pursuer furiously flung the contents of the bottle at Bob Martin; but instead of fluid it issued out in a stream of flame, which expanded and whirled round them, and for a moment they were both enveloped in a faint blaze; at the same instant a sudden gust whisked off the stranger's hat, and the sexton beheld that his skull was roofless. For an instant he beheld the gaping aperture, black and shattered, and then he fell senseless into his own doorway, which his affrighted wife had just unbarred.

I need hardly give my reader the key to this most intelligible and authentic narrative. The traveller was acknowledged by all to have been the spectre of the suicide, called up by the Evil One to tempt the convivial sexton into a violation of his promise, sealed, as it was, by an imprecation. Had he succeeded, no doubt the dusky steed, which Bob had seen saddled in attendance, was destined to have carried back a double burden to the place from whence he came.

As an attestation of the reality of this visitation, the old thorn tree which overhung the doorway was found in the morning to have been blasted with the infernal fires which had issued from the bottle, just as if a thunder-bolt had scorched it.

The moral of the above tale is upon the surface, apparent, and, so to speak, _self-acting_--a circumstance which happily obviates the necessity of our discussing it together. Taking our leave, therefore, of honest Bob Martin, who now sleeps soundly in the same solemn dormitory where, in his day, he made so many beds for others, I come to a legend of the

Royal Irish Artillery, whose headquarters were for so long a time in the town of Chapelizod. I don't mean to say that I cannot tell a great many more stories, equally authentic and marvellous, touching this old town; but as I may possibly have to perform a like office for other localities, and as Anthony Poplar is known, like Atropos, to carry a shears, wherewith to snip across all "yarns" which exceed reasonable bounds, I consider it, on the whole, safer to despatch the traditions of Chapelizod with one tale more.

Let me, however, first give it a name; for an author can no more despatch a tale without a title, than an apothecary can deliver his physic without a label. We shall, therefore, call it--

## The Spectre Lovers

There lived some fifteen years since in a small and ruinous house, little better than a hovel, an old woman who was reported to have considerably exceeded her eightieth year, and who rejoiced in the name of Alice, or popularly, Ally Moran. Her society was not much courted, for she was neither rich, nor, as the reader may suppose, beautiful. In addition to a lean cur and a cat she had one human companion, her grandson, Peter Brien, whom, with laudable good nature, she had supported from the period of his orphanage down to that of my story, which finds him in his twentieth year. Peter was a good-natured slob of a fellow, much more addicted to wrestling, dancing, and love-making, than to hard work, and fonder of whiskey-punch than good advice. His grandmother had a high opinion of his accomplishments, which indeed was but natural, and also of his genius, for Peter had of late years begun to apply his mind to politics; and as it was plain that he had a mortal hatred of honest labour, his grandmother predicted, like a true fortuneteller, that he was born to marry an heiress, and Peter himself (who had no mind to forego his freedom even on such terms) that he was destined to find a pot of gold. Upon one point both agreed, that being unfitted by the peculiar bias of his genius for work, he was to acquire the immense fortune to which his merits entitled him by means of a pure run of good luck. This solution of Peter's future had the double effect of reconciling both himself and his grandmother to his idle courses, and also of maintaining that even flow of hilarious spirits which made him everywhere welcome, and which was in truth the natural result of his consciousness of approaching affluence.

It happened one night that Peter had enjoyed himself to a very late hour with two or three choice spirits near Palmerstown. They had talked politics and love, sung songs, and told stories, and, above all, had swallowed, in the chastened disguise of punch, at least a pint of good whiskey, every man.

It was considerably past one o'clock when Peter bid his companions goodbye, with a sigh and a hiccough, and lighting his pipe set forth on his solitary homeward way.

The bridge of Chapelizod was pretty nearly the midway point of his night march, and from one cause or another his progress was rather slow, and it was past two o'clock by the time he found himself leaning over its old battlements, and looking up the river, over whose winding current and wooded banks the soft moonlight was falling.

The cold breeze that blew lightly down the stream was grateful to him. It cooled his throbbing head, and he drank it in at his hot lips. The scene, too, had, without his being well sensible of it, a secret fascination. The village was sunk in the profoundest slumber, not a mortal stirring, not a sound afloat, a soft haze covered it all, and the fairy moonlight hovered over the entire landscape.

In a state between rumination and rapture, Peter continued to lean over the battlements of the old bridge, and as he did so he saw, or fancied he saw, emerging one after another along the river bank in the little gardens and enclosures in the rear of the street of Chapelizod, the queerest little white-washed huts and cabins he had ever seen there before. They had not been there that evening when he passed the bridge on the way to his merry tryst. But the most remarkable thing about it was the odd way in which these quaint little cabins showed themselves. First he saw one or two of them just with the corner of his eye, and when he looked full at them, strange to say, they faded away and disappeared. Then another and another came in view, but all in the same coy way, just appearing and gone again before he could well fix his gaze upon them; in a little while, however, they began to bear a fuller gaze, and he found, as it seemed to himself, that he was able by an effort of attention to fix the vision for a longer and a longer time, and when they waxed faint and nearly vanished, he had the power of recalling them into light and substance, until at last their vacillating indistinctness became less and less, and they assumed a permanent place in the moonlit landscape.

"Be the hokey," said Peter, lost in amazement, and dropping his pipe into the river unconsciously, "them is the quarist bits iv mud cabins I ever seen, growing up like musharoons in the dew of an evening, and poppin' up here and down again there, and up again in another place, like so many white rabbits in a warren; and there they stand at last as firm and fast as if they were there from the Deluge; bedad it's enough to make a man a'most believe in the fairies."

This latter was a large concession from Peter, who was a bit of a free-thinker, and spoke contemptuously in his ordinary conversation of that class of agencies.

Having treated himself to a long last stare at these mysterious fabrics, Peter prepared to pursue his homeward way; having crossed the bridge and passed the mill, he arrived at the corner of the main-street of the little town, and casting a careless look up the Dublin road, his eye was arrested by a most unexpected spectacle.

This was no other than a column of foot soldiers, marching with perfect regularity towards the village, and headed by an officer on horseback. They were at the far side of the turnpike, which was closed; but much to his perplexity he perceived that they marched on through it without appearing to sustain the least check from that barrier.

On they came at a slow march; and what was most singular in the matter was, that they were drawing several cannons along with them; some held ropes, others spoked the wheels, and others again marched in front of the guns and behind them, with muskets shouldered, giving a stately character of parade and regularity to this, as it seemed to Peter, most unmilitary procedure.

It was owing either to some temporary defect in Peter's vision, or to some illusion attendant upon mist and moonlight, or perhaps to some other cause, that the whole procession had a certain waving and vapoury character which perplexed and tasked his eyes not a little. It was like the pictured pageant of a phantasmagoria reflected upon smoke. It was as if every breath disturbed it; sometimes it was blurred, sometimes obliterated; now here, now there. Sometimes, while the upper part was quite distinct, the legs of the column would nearly fade away or vanish outright, and then again they would come out into clear relief, marching on with measured tread, while the cocked hats and shoulders grew, as it were, transparent, and all but disappeared.

Notwithstanding these strange optical fluctuations, however, the column continued steadily to advance. Peter crossed the street from the corner near the old bridge, running on tip-toe, and with his body stooped to avoid observation, and took up a position upon the raised footpath in the shadow of the houses, where, as the soldiers kept the middle of the road, he calculated that he might, himself undetected, see them distinctly enough as they passed.

"What the div--, what on airth," he muttered, checking the irreligious ejaculation with which he was about to start, for certain queer misgivings were hovering about his heart, notwithstanding the factitious courage of the whiskey bottle. "What on airth is the manin' of all this? is it the French that's landed at last to give us a hand and help us in airnest to this blessed repale? If it is not them, I simply ask who the div--, I mane who on airth are they, for such sogers as them I never seen before in my born days?"

By this time the foremost of them were quite near, and truth to say they were the queerest soldiers he had ever seen in the course of his life. They wore long gaiters and leather breeches, three-cornered hats, bound with silver lace, long blue coats, with scarlet facings and linings, which latter were shewn by a fastening which held together the two opposite corners of the skirt behind; and in front the breasts were in like manner connected at a single point, where and below which they sloped back, disclosing a long-flapped waistcoat of snowy whiteness; they had very large, long cross-belts, and wore enormous pouches of white leather hung extraordinarily low, and on each of which a little silver star was glittering. But what struck him as most grotesque and outlandish in their costume was their extraordinary display of shirt-frill in front, and of ruffle about their wrists, and the strange manner in which their hair was frizzled out and powdered under their hats, and clubbed up into great rolls behind. But one of the party was mounted. He rode a tall white horse, with high action and arching neck; he had a snow-white feather in his three-cornered hat, and his coat was shimmering all over with a profusion of silver lace. From these circumstances Peter concluded that he must be the commander of the detachment, and examined him as he passed attentively. He was a slight, tall man, whose legs did not half fill his leather breeches, and he appeared to be at the wrong side of sixty. He had a shrunken, weather-beaten, mulberry-coloured face, carried a large black patch over one eye, and turned neither to the right nor to the left, but rode on at the head of his men, with a grim, military inflexibility.

The countenances of these soldiers, officers as well as men, seemed all full of trouble, and, so to speak, scared and wild. He watched in vain for a single contented or comely face. They had, one and all, a melancholy and hang-dog look; and as they passed by, Peter fancied that the air grew cold and thrilling.

He had seated himself upon a stone bench, from which, staring with all his might, he gazed upon the grotesque and noiseless procession as it filed by him. Noiseless it was; he could neither hear the jingle of accoutrements, the tread of feet, nor the rumble of the wheels; and when the old colonel turned his horse a little, and made as though he were giving the word of command, and a trumpeter, with a swollen blue nose and white feather fringe round his hat, who was walking beside him, turned about and put his bugle to his lips, still Peter heard nothing, although it was plain the sound had reached the soldiers, for they instantly changed their front to three abreast.

"Botheration!" muttered Peter, "is it deaf I'm growing?"

But that could not be, for he heard the sighing of the breeze and the rush of the neighbouring Liffey plain enough.

"Well," said he, in the same cautious key, "by the piper, this bangs Banagher fairly! It's either the Frinch army that's in it, come to take the town iv Chapelizod by surprise, an' makin' no noise for feard iv wakenin' the inhabitants; or else it's--it's--what it's--somethin' else. But, tundher-an-ouns, what's gone wid Fitzpatrick's shop across the way?"

The brown, dingy stone building at the opposite side of the street looked newer and cleaner than he had been used to see it; the front door of it stood open, and a sentry, in the same grotesque uniform, with shouldered musket, was pacing noiselessly to and fro before it. At the angle of this building, in like manner, a wide gate (of which Peter had no recollection whatever) stood open, before which, also, a similar sentry was gliding, and into this gateway the whole column gradually passed, and Peter finally lost sight of it.

"I'm not asleep; I'm not dhramin'," said he, rubbing his eyes, and stamping slightly on the pavement, to assure himself that he was wide awake. "It is a quare business, whatever it is; an' it's not alone that, but everything about town looks strange to me. There's Tresham's house new painted, bedad, an' them flowers in the windies! An' Delany's house, too, that had not a whole pane of glass in it this morning, and scarce a slate on the roof of it! It is not possible it's what it's dhrunk I am. Sure there's the big tree, and not a leaf of it changed since I passed, and the stars overhead, all right. I don't think it is in my eyes it is."

And so looking about him, and every moment finding or fancying new food for wonder, he walked along the pavement, intending, without further delay, to make his way home.

But his adventures for the night were not concluded. He had nearly reached the angle of the short land that leads up to the church, when for the first time he perceived that an officer, in the uniform he had just seen, was walking before, only a few yards in advance of him.

The officer was walking along at an easy, swinging gait, and carried his sword under his arm, and was looking down on the pavement with an air of reverie.

In the very fact that he seemed unconscious of Peter's presence, and disposed to keep his reflections to himself, there was something reassuring. Besides, the reader must please to remember that our hero had a quantum sufficit of good punch before his adventure commenced, and was thus fortified against those qualms and terrors under which, in a more reasonable state of mind, he might not impossibly have sunk.

The idea of the French invasion revived in full power in Peter's fuddled imagination, as he pursued the nonchalant swagger of the officer.

"Be the powers iv Moll Kelly, I'll ax him what it is," said Peter, with a sudden accession of rashness. "He may tell me or not, as he plases, but he can't be offinded, anyhow."

With this reflection having inspired himself, Peter cleared his voice and began--

"Captain!" said he, "I ax your pardon, captain, an' maybe you'd be so condescindin' to my ignorance as to tell me, if it's plasin' to yer honour, whether your honour is not a Frinchman, if it's plasin' to you."

This he asked, not thinking that, had it been as he suspected, not one word of his question in all probability would have been intelligible to the person he addressed. He was, however, understood, for the officer answered him in English, at the same time slackening his pace and moving a little to the side of the pathway, as if to invite his interrogator to take his place beside him.

"No; I am an Irishman," he answered.

"I humbly thank your honour," said Peter, drawing nearer--for the affability and the nativity of the officer encouraged him--"but maybe your honour is in the _sarvice_ of the King of France?"

"I serve the same King as you do," he answered, with a sorrowful significance which Peter did not comprehend at the time; and, interrogating in turn, he asked, "But what calls you forth at this hour of the day?"

"The _day,_ your honour!--the night, you mane."

"It was always our way to turn night into day, and we keep to it still," remarked the soldier. "But, no matter, come up here to my house; I have a job for you, if you wish to earn some money easily. I live here."

As he said this, he beckoned authoritatively to Peter, who followed almost mechanically at his heels, and they turned up a little lane near the old Roman Catholic chapel, at the end of which stood, in Peter's time, the ruins of a tall, stone-built house.

Like everything else in the town, it had suffered a metamorphosis. The stained and ragged walls were now erect, perfect, and covered with pebble-dash; window-panes glittered coldly in every window; the green hall-door had a bright brass knocker on it. Peter did not know whether to believe his previous or his present impressions; seeing is believing, and Peter could not dispute the reality of the scene. All the records of his memory seemed but the images of a tipsy dream. In a trance of astonishment and perplexity, therefore, he submitted himself to the chances of his adventure.

The door opened, the officer beckoned with a melancholy air of authority to Peter, and entered. Our hero followed him into a sort of hall, which was very dark, but he was guided by the steps of the soldier, and, in silence, they ascended the stairs. The moonlight, which shone in at the lobbies, showed an old, dark wainscoting, and a heavy, oak banister. They passed by closed doors at different landing-places, but all was dark and silent as, indeed, became that late hour of the night.

Now they ascended to the topmost floor. The captain paused for a minute at the nearest door, and, with a heavy groan, pushing it open, entered the room. Peter remained at the threshold. A slight female form in a sort of loose, white robe, and with a great deal of dark hair hanging loosely about her, was standing in the middle of the floor, with her back towards them.

The soldier stopped short before he reached her, and said, in a voice of great anguish, "Still the same, sweet bird--sweet bird! still the same." Whereupon, she turned suddenly, and threw her arms about the neck of the officer, with a gesture of fondness and despair, and her frame was agitated as if by a burst of sobs. He held her close to his breast in silence; and honest Peter felt a strange terror creep over him, as he witnessed these mysterious sorrows and endearments.

"To-night, to-night--and then ten years more--ten long years--another ten years."

The officer and the lady seemed to speak these words together; her voice mingled with his in a musical and fearful wail, like a distant summer wind, in the dead hour of night, wandering through ruins. Then he heard the officer say, alone, in a voice of anguish--

"Upon me be it all, for ever, sweet birdie, upon me."

And again they seemed to mourn together in the same soft and desolate wail, like sounds of grief heard from a great distance.

Peter was thrilled with horror, but he was also under a strange fascination; and an intense and dreadful curiosity held him fast.

The moon was shining obliquely into the room, and through the window Peter saw the familiar slopes of the Park, sleeping mistily under its shimmer. He could also see the furniture of the room with tolerable distinctness--the old balloon-backed chairs, a four-post bed in a sort of recess, and a rack against the wall, from which hung some military clothes and accoutrements; and the sight of all these homely objects reassured him somewhat, and he could not help feeling unspeakably curious to see the face of the girl whose long hair was streaming over the officer's epaulet.

Peter, accordingly, coughed, at first slightly, and afterward more loudly, to recall her from her reverie of grief; and, apparently, he succeeded; for she turned round, as did her companion, and both, standing hand in hand, gazed upon him fixedly. He thought he had never seen such large, strange eyes in all his life; and their gaze seemed to chill the very air around him, and arrest the pulses of his heart. An eternity of misery and remorse was in the shadowy faces that looked upon him.

If Peter had taken less whisky by a single thimbleful, it is probable that he would have lost heart altogether before these figures, which seemed every moment to assume a more marked and fearful, though hardly definable, contrast to ordinary human shapes.

"What is it you want with me?" he stammered.

"To bring my lost treasure to the churchyard," replied the lady, in a silvery voice of more than mortal desolation.

The word "treasure" revived the resolution of Peter, although a cold sweat was covering him, and his hair was bristling with horror; he believed, however, that he was on the brink of fortune, if he could but command nerve to brave the interview to its close.

"And where," he gasped, "is it hid--where will I find it?"

They both pointed to the sill of the window, through which the moon was shining at the far end of the room, and the soldier said--

"Under that stone."

Peter drew a long breath, and wiped the cold dew from his face, preparatory to passing to the window, where he expected to secure the reward of his protracted terrors. But looking steadfastly at the window, he saw the faint image of a new-born child sitting upon the sill in the moonlight, with its little arms stretched toward him, and a smile so heavenly as he never beheld before.

At sight of this, strange to say, his heart entirely failed him, he looked on the figures that stood near, and beheld them gazing on the infantine form with a smile so guilty and distorted, that he felt as if he were entering alive among the scenery of hell, and shuddering, he cried in an irrepressible agony of horror--

"I'll have nothing to say with you, and nothing to do with you; I don't know what yez are or what yez want iv me, but let me go this minute, every one of yez, in the name of God."

With these words there came a strange rumbling and sighing about Peter's ears; he lost sight of everything, and felt that peculiar and not unpleasant sensation of falling softly, that sometimes supervenes in sleep, ending in a dull shock. After that he had neither dream nor consciousness till he wakened, chill and stiff, stretched between two piles of old rubbish, among the black and roofless walls of the ruined house.

We need hardly mention that the village had put on its wonted air of neglect and decay, or that Peter looked around him in vain for traces of those novelties which had so puzzled and distracted him upon the previous night.

"Ay, ay," said his grandmother, removing her pipe, as he ended his description of the view from the bridge, "sure enough I remember myself, when I was a slip of a girl, these little white cabins among the gardens by the river side. The artillery sogers that was married, or had not room in the barracks, used to be in them, but they're all gone long ago.

"The Lord be merciful to us!" she resumed, when he had described the military procession, "It's often I seen the regiment marchin' into the town, jist as you saw it last night, acushla. Oh, voch, but it makes my heart sore to think iv them days; they were pleasant times, sure enough; but is not it terrible, avick, to think it's what it was the ghost of the rigiment you seen? The Lord betune us an' harm, for it was nothing else, as sure as I'm sittin' here."

When he mentioned the peculiar physiognomy and figure of the old officer who rode at the head of the regiment--

"That," said the old crone, dogmatically, "was ould Colonel Grimshaw, the

Lord presarve us! he's buried in the churchyard iv Chapelizod, and well I remember him, when I was a young thing, an' a cross ould floggin' fellow he was wid the men, an' a devil's boy among the girls--rest his soul!"

"Amen!" said Peter; "it's often I read his tombstone myself; but he's a long time dead."

"Sure, I tell you he died when I was no more nor a slip iv a girl--the Lord betune us and harm!"

"I'm afeard it is what I'm not long for this world myself, afther seeing such a sight as that," said Peter, fearfully.

"Nonsinse, avourneen," retorted his grandmother, indignantly, though she had herself misgivings on the subject; "sure there was Phil Doolan, the ferryman, that seen black Ann Scanlan in his own boat, and what harm ever kem of it?"

Peter proceeded with his narrative, but when he came to the description of the house, in which his adventure had had so sinister a conclusion, the old woman was at fault.

"I know the house and the ould walls well, an' I can remember the time there was a roof on it, and the doors an' windows in it, but it had a bad name about being haunted, but by who, or for what, I forget intirely."

"Did you ever hear was there goold or silver there?" he inquired.

"No, no, avick, don't be thinking about the likes; take a fool's advice, and never go next to near them ugly black walls again the longest day you have to live; an' I'd take my davy, it's what it's the same word the priest himself id be afther sayin' to you if you wor to ax his raverence consarnin' it, for it's plain to be seen it was nothing good you seen there, and there's neither luck nor grace about it."

Peter's adventure made no little noise in the neighbourhood, as the reader may well suppose; and a few evenings after it, being on an errand to old Major Vandeleur, who lived in a snug old-fashioned house, close by the river, under a perfect bower of ancient trees, he was called on to relate the story in the parlour.

The Major was, as I have said, an old man; he was small, lean, and upright, with a mahogany complexion, and a wooden inflexibility of face; he was a man, besides, of few words, and if _he_ was old, it follows plainly that his mother was older still. Nobody could guess or tell _how_ old, but it was admitted that her own generation had long passed away, and that she had not a competitor left. She had French blood in her veins, and although she did not retain her charms quite so well as Ninon de l'Enclos, she was in full possession of all her mental activity, and talked quite enough for herself and the Major.

"So, Peter," she said, "you have seen the dear, old Royal Irish again in the streets of Chapelizod. Make him a tumbler of punch, Frank; and Peter, sit down, and while you take it let us have the story."

Peter accordingly, seated, near the door, with a tumbler of the nectarian stimulant steaming beside him, proceeded with marvellous courage, considering they had no light but the uncertain glare of the fire, to relate with minute particularity his awful adventure. The old lady listened at first with a smile of good-natured incredulity; her cross-examination touching the drinking-bout at Palmerstown had been teazing, but as the narrative proceeded she became attentive, and at length absorbed, and once or twice she uttered ejaculations of pity or awe. When it was over, the old lady looked with a somewhat sad and stern abstraction on the table, patting her cat assiduously meanwhile, and then suddenly looking upon her son, the Major, she said--

"Frank, as sure as I live he has seen the wicked Captain Devereux."

The Major uttered an inarticulate expression of wonder.
"The house was precisely that he has described. I have told you the story often, as I heard it from your dear grandmother, about the poor young lady he ruined, and the dreadful suspicion about the little baby. _She_, poor thing, died in that house heart-broken, and you know he was shot shortly after in a duel."

This was the only light that Peter ever received respecting his adventure. It was supposed, however, that he still clung to the hope that treasure of some sort was hidden about the old house, for he was often seen lurking about its walls, and at last his fate overtook him, poor fellow, in the pursuit; for climbing near the summit one day, his holding gave way, and he fell upon the hard uneven ground, fracturing a leg and a rib, and after a short interval died, and he, like the other heroes of these true tales, lies buried in the little churchyard of Chapelizod.

# AN ACCOUNT OF SOME STRANGE DISTURBANCES IN AUNGIER STREET (1853)

It is not worth telling, this story of mine--at least, not worth writing. Told, indeed, as I have sometimes been called upon to tell it, to a circle of intelligent and eager faces, lighted up by a good after-dinner fire on a winter's evening, with a cold wind rising and wailing outside, and all snug and cosy within, it has gone off--though I say it, who should not--indifferent well. But it is a venture to do as you would have me. Pen, ink, and paper are cold vehicles for the marvellous, and a "reader" decidedly a more critical animal than a "listener." If, however, you can induce your friends to read it after nightfall, and when the fireside talk has run for a while on thrilling tales of shapeless terror; in short, if you will secure me the _mollia tempora fandi_, I will go to my work, and say my say, with better heart. Well, then, these conditions presupposed, I shall waste no more words, but tell you simply how it all happened.

My cousin (Tom Ludlow) and I studied medicine together. I think he would have succeeded, had he stuck to the profession; but he preferred the Church, poor fellow, and died early, a sacrifice to contagion, contracted in the noble discharge of his duties. For my present purpose, I say enough of his character when I mention that he was of a sedate but frank and cheerful nature; very exact in his observance of truth, and not by any means like myself--of an excitable or nervous temperament.

My Uncle Ludlow--Tom's father--while we were attending lectures, purchased three or four old houses in Aungier Street, one of which was unoccupied. _He_ resided in the country, and Tom proposed that we should take up our abode in the untenanted house, so long as it should continue unlet; a move which would accomplish the double end of settling us nearer alike to our lecture-rooms and to our amusements, and of relieving us from the weekly charge of rent for our lodgings.

Our furniture was very scant--our whole equipage remarkably modest and primitive; and, in short, our arrangements pretty nearly as simple as those of a bivouac. Our new plan was, therefore, executed almost as soon as conceived. The front drawing-room was our sitting-room. I had the bedroom over it, and Tom the back bedroom on the same floor, which nothing could have induced me to occupy.

The house, to begin with, was a very old one. It had been, I believe, newly fronted about fifty years before; but with this exception, it had nothing modern about it. The agent who bought it and looked into the titles for my uncle, told me that it was sold, along with much other forfeited property, at Chichester House, I think, in 1702; and had belonged to Sir Thomas Hacket, who was Lord Mayor of Dublin in James II.'s time. How old it was _then_, I can't say; but, at all events, it had seen years and changes enough to have contracted all that mysterious and saddened air, at once exciting and depressing, which belongs to most old mansions.

There had been very little done in the way of modernising details; and, perhaps, it was better so; for there was something queer and by-gone in the very walls and ceilings--in the shape of doors and windows--in the odd diagonal site of the chimney-pieces--in the beams and ponderous cornices--not to mention the singular solidity of all the woodwork, from the banisters to the window-frames, which hopelessly defied disguise, and would have emphatically proclaimed their antiquity through any conceivable amount of modern finery and varnish.

An effort had, indeed, been made, to the extent of papering the drawing-rooms; but somehow, the paper looked raw and out of keeping; and the old woman, who kept a little dirt-pie of a shop in the lane, and whose daughter--a girl of two and fifty--was our solitary handmaid, coming in at sunrise, and chastely receding again as soon as she had made all ready for tea in our state apartment;--this woman, I say, remembered it, when old Judge Horrocks (who, having earned the reputation of a particularly "hanging judge," ended by hanging himself, as the coroner's jury found, under an impulse of "temporary insanity," with a child's skipping-rope, over the massive old bannisters) resided there, entertaining good company, with fine venison and rare old port. In those halcyon days, the drawing-rooms were hung with gilded leather, and, I dare say, cut a good figure, for they were really spacious rooms.

The bedrooms were wainscoted, but the front one was not gloomy; and in it the cosiness of antiquity quite overcame its sombre associations. But the back bedroom, with its two queerly-placed melancholy windows, staring vacantly at the foot of the bed, and with the shadowy recess to be found in most old houses in Dublin, like a large ghostly closet, which, from congeniality of temperament, had amalgamated with the bedchamber, and dissolved the partition. At night-time, this "alcove"--as our "maid" was wont to call it--had, in my eyes, a specially sinister and suggestive character. Tom's distant and solitary candle glimmered vainly into its darkness. _There_ it was always overlooking him--always itself impenetrable. But this was only part of the effect. The whole room was, I can't tell how, repulsive to me. There was, I suppose, in its proportions and features, a latent discord--a certain mysterious and indescribable relation, which jarred indistinctly upon some secret sense of the fitting and the safe, and raised indefinable suspicions and apprehensions of the imagination. On the whole, as I began by saying, nothing could have induced me to pass a night alone in it.

I had never pretended to conceal from poor Tom my superstitious weakness; and he, on the other hand, most unaffectedly ridiculed my tremors. The sceptic was, however, destined to receive a lesson, as you shall hear.

We had not been very long in occupation of our respective dormitories, when I began to complain of uneasy nights and disturbed sleep. I was, I suppose, the more impatient under this annoyance, as I was usually a sound sleeper, and by no means prone to nightmares. It was now, however, my destiny, instead of enjoying my customary repose, every night to "sup full of horrors." After a preliminary course of disagreeable and frightful dreams, my troubles took a definite form, and the same vision, without an appreciable variation in a single detail, visited me at least (on an average) every second night in the week.

Now, this dream, nightmare, or infernal illusion--which you please--of which I was the miserable sport, was on this wise:----

I saw, or thought I saw, with the most abominable distinctness, although at the time in profound darkness, every article of furniture and accidental arrangement of the chamber in which I lay. This, as you know, is incidental to ordinary nightmare. Well, while in this clairvoyant condition, which seemed but the lighting up of the theatre in which was to be exhibited the monotonous tableau of horror, which made my nights insupportable, my attention invariably became, I know not why, fixed upon the windows opposite the foot of my bed; and, uniformly with the same effect, a sense of dreadful anticipation always took slow but sure possession of me. I became somehow conscious of a sort of horrid but undefined preparation going forward in some unknown quarter, and by some unknown agency, for my torment; and, after an interval, which always seemed to me of the same length, a picture suddenly flew up to the window, where it remained fixed, as if by an electrical attraction, and my discipline of horror then commenced, to last perhaps for hours. The picture thus mysteriously glued to the window-panes, was the portrait of an old man, in a crimson flowered silk dressing-gown, the folds of which I could now describe, with a countenance embodying a strange mixture of intellect, sensuality, and power, but withal sinister and full of malignant omen. His nose was hooked, like the beak of a vulture; his eyes large, grey, and prominent, and lighted up with a more than mortal cruelty and coldness. These features were surmounted by a crimson velvet cap, the hair that peeped from under which was white with age, while the eyebrows retained their original blackness. Well I remember every line, hue, and shadow of that stony countenance, and well I may! The gaze of this hellish visage was fixed upon me, and mine returned it with the inexplicable fascination of nightmare, for what appeared to me to be hours of agony. At last----

The cock he crew, away then flew

the fiend who had enslaved me through the awful watches of the night; and, harassed and nervous, I rose to the duties of the day.

I had--I can't say exactly why, but it may have been from the exquisite anguish and profound impressions of unearthly horror, with which this strange phantasmagoria was associated--an insurmountable antipathy to describing the exact nature of my nightly troubles to my friend and comrade. Generally, however, I told him that I was haunted by abominable dreams; and, true to the imputed materialism of medicine, we put our heads together to dispel my horrors, not by exorcism, but by a tonic.

I will do this tonic justice, and frankly admit that the accursed portrait began to intermit its visits under its influence. What of that? Was this singular apparition--as full of character as of terror--therefore the creature of my fancy, or the invention of my poor stomach? Was it, in short, _subjective_ (to borrow the technical slang of the day) and not the palpable aggression and intrusion of an external agent? That, good friend, as we will both admit, by no means follows. The evil spirit, who enthralled my senses in the shape of that portrait, may have been just as near me, just as energetic, just as malignant, though I saw him not. What means the whole moral code of revealed religion regarding the due keeping of our own bodies, soberness, temperance, etc.? here is an obvious connexion between the material and the invisible; the healthy tone of the system, and its unimpaired energy, may, for aught we can tell, guard us against influences which would otherwise render life itself terrific. The mesmerist and the electro-biologist will fail upon an average with nine patients out of ten--so may the evil spirit. Special conditions of the corporeal system are indispensable to the production of certain spiritual phenomena. The operation succeeds sometimes--sometimes fails--that is all.

I found afterwards that my would-be sceptical companion had his troubles too. But of these I knew nothing yet. One night, for a wonder, I was sleeping soundly, when I was roused by a step on the lobby outside my room, followed by the loud clang of what turned out to be a large brass candlestick, flung with all his force by poor Tom Ludlow over the banisters, and rattling with a rebound down the second flight of stairs; and almost concurrently with this, Tom burst open my door, and bounced into my room backwards, in a state of extraordinary agitation.

I had jumped out of bed and clutched him by the arm before I had any distinct idea of my own whereabouts. There we were--in our shirts--standing before the open door--staring through the great old banister opposite, at the lobby window, through which the sickly light of a clouded moon was gleaming.

"What's the matter, Tom? What's the matter with you? What the devil's the matter with you, Tom?" I demanded shaking him with nervous impatience.

He took a long breath before he answered me, and then it was not very coherently.

"It's nothing, nothing at all--did I speak?--what did I say?--where's the candle, Richard? It's dark; I--I had a candle!"

"Yes, dark enough," I said; "but what's the matter?--what _is_ it?--why don't you speak, Tom?--have you lost your wits?--what is the matter?"

"The matter?--oh, it is all over. It must have been a dream--nothing at all but a dream--don t you think so? It could not be anything more than a dream."

"Of _course_" said I, feeling uncommonly nervous, "it _was_ a dream."

"I thought," he said, ' there was a man in my room, and--and I jumped out of bed; and--and--where's the candle?"

"In your room, most likely," I said, "shall I go and bring it?"

"No; stay here--don't go; it's no matter--don't, I tell you; it was all a dream. Bolt the door, Dick; I'll stay here with you--I feel nervous. So, Dick, like a good fellow, light your candle and open the window--I am in a _shocking state_."

I did as he asked me, and robing himself like Granuaile in one of my blankets, he seated himself close beside my bed.

Every body knows how contagious is fear of all sorts, but more especially that particular kind of fear under which poor Tom was at that moment labouring. I would not have heard, nor I believe would he have recapitulated, just at that moment, for half the world, the details of the hideous vision which had so unmanned him.
"Don't mind telling me anything about your nonsensical dream, Tom," said I, affecting contempt, really in a panic; "let us talk about something else; but it is quite plain that this dirty old house disagrees with us both, and hang me if I stay here any longer, to be pestered with indigestion and--and--bad nights, so we may as well look out for lodgings--don't you think so?--at once."

Tom agreed, and, after an interval, said----

"I have been thinking, Richard, that it is a long time since I saw my father, and I have made up my mind to go down to-morrow and return in a day or two, and you can take rooms for us in the meantime."

I fancied that this resolution, obviously the result of the vision which had so profoundly scared him, would probably vanish next morning with the damps and shadows of night. But I was mistaken. Off went Tom at peep of day to the country, having agreed that so soon as I had secured suitable lodgings, I was to recall him by letter from his visit to my Uncle Ludlow.

Now, anxious as I was to change my quarters, it so happened, owing to a series of petty procrastinations and accidents, that nearly a week elapsed before my bargain was made and my letter of recall on the wing to Tom; and, in the meantime, a trifling adventure or two had occurred to your humble servant, which, absurd as they now appear, diminished by distance, did certainly at the time serve to whet my appetite for change considerably.

A night or two after the departure of my comrade, I was sitting by my bedroom fire, the door locked, and the ingredients of a tumbler of hot whisky-punch upon the crazy spider-table; for, as the best mode of keeping the

Black spirits and white,
Blue spirits and grey,

with which I was environed, at bay, I had adopted the practice recommended by the wisdom of my ancestors, and "kept my spirits up by pouring spirits down." I had thrown aside my volume of Anatomy, and was treating myself by way of a tonic, preparatory to my punch and bed, to half-a-dozen pages of the _Spectator_, when I heard a step on the flight of stairs descending from the attics. It was two o'clock, and the streets were as silent as a churchyard--the sounds were, therefore, perfectly distinct. There was a slow, heavy tread, characterised by the emphasis and deliberation of age, descending by the narrow staircase from above; and, what made the sound more singular, it was plain that the feet which produced it were perfectly bare, measuring the descent with something between a pound and a flop, very ugly to hear.

I knew quite well that my attendant had gone away many hours before, and that nobody but myself had any business in the house. It was quite plain also that the person who was coming down stairs had no intention whatever of concealing his movements; but, on the contrary, appeared disposed to make even more noise, and proceed more deliberately, than was at all necessary. When the step reached the foot of the stairs outside my room, it seemed to stop; and I expected every moment to see my door open spontaneously, and give admission to the original of my detested portrait. I was, however, relieved in a few seconds by hearing the descent renewed, just in the same manner, upon the staircase leading down to the drawing-rooms, and thence, after another pause, down the next flight, and so on to the hall, whence I heard no more.

Now, by the time the sound had ceased, I was wound up, as they say, to a very unpleasant pitch of excitement. I listened, but there was not a stir. I screwed up my courage to a decisive experiment--opened my door, and in a stentorian voice bawled over the banisters, "Who's there?" There was no answer but the ringing of my own voice through the empty old house,--no renewal of the movement; nothing, in short, to give my unpleasant sensations a definite direction. There is, I think, something most disagreeably disenchanting in the sound of one's own voice under such circumstances, exerted in solitude, and in vain. It redoubled my sense of isolation, and my misgivings increased on perceiving that the door, which I certainly thought I had left open, was closed behind me; in a vague alarm, lest my retreat should be cut off, I got again into my room as quickly as I could, where I remained in a state of imaginary blockade, and very uncomfortable indeed, till morning.

Next night brought no return of my barefooted fellow-lodger; but the night following, being in my bed, and in the dark--somewhere, I suppose, about the same hour as before, I distinctly heard the old fellow again descending from the garrets.

This time I had had my punch, and the _morale_ of the garrison was consequently excellent. I jumped out of bed, clutched the poker as I passed the expiring fire, and in a moment was upon the lobby. The sound had ceased by this time--the dark and chill were discouraging; and, guess my horror, when I saw, or thought I saw, a black monster, whether in the shape of a man or a bear I could not say, standing, with its back to the wall, on the lobby, facing me, with a pair of great greenish eyes shining dimly out. Now, I must be frank, and confess that the cupboard which displayed our plates and cups stood just there, though at the moment I did not recollect it. At the same time I must honestly say, that making every allowance for an excited imagination, I never could satisfy myself that I was made the dupe of my own fancy in this matter; for this apparition, after one or two shiftings of shape, as if in the act of incipient transformation, began, as it seemed on second thoughts, to advance upon me in its original form. From an instinct of terror rather than of courage, I hurled the poker, with all my force, at its head; and to the music of a horrid crash made my way into my room, and double-locked the door. Then, in a minute more, I heard the horrid bare feet walk down the stairs, till the sound ceased in the hall, as on the former occasion.

If the apparition of the night before was an ocular delusion of my fancy sporting with the dark outlines of our cupboard, and if its horrid eyes were nothing but a pair of inverted teacups, I had, at all events, the satisfaction of having launched the poker with admirable effect, and in true "fancy" phrase, "knocked its two daylights into one," as the commingled fragments of my tea-service testified. I did my best to gather comfort and courage from these evidences; but it would not do. And then what could I say of those horrid bare feet, and the regular tramp, tramp, tramp, which measured the distance of the entire staircase through the solitude of my haunted dwelling, and at an hour when no good influence was stirring? Confound it!--the whole affair was abominable. I was out of spirits, and dreaded the approach of night.

It came, ushered ominously in with a thunder-storm and dull torrents of depressing rain. Earlier than usual the streets grew silent; and by twelve o'clock nothing but the comfortless pattering of the rain was to be heard.

I made myself as snug as I could. I lighted _two_ candles instead of one. I forswore bed, and held myself in readiness for a sally, candle in hand; for, _coûte qui coûte_, I was resolved to _see_ the being, if visible at all, who troubled the nightly stillness of my mansion. I was fidgetty and nervous and tried in vain to interest myself with my books. I walked up and down my room, whistling in turn martial and hilarious music, and listening ever and anon for the dreaded noise. I sate down and stared at the square label on the solemn and reserved-looking black bottle, until "FLANAGAN & CO'S BEST OLD MALT WHISKY" grew into a sort of subdued accompaniment to all the fantastic and horrible speculations which chased one another through my brain.

Silence, meanwhile, grew more silent, and darkness darker. I listened in vain for the rumble of a vehicle, or the dull clamour of a distant row. There was nothing but the sound of a rising wind, which had succeeded the thunder-storm that had travelled over the Dublin mountains quite out of hearing. In the middle of this great city I began to feel myself alone with nature, and Heaven knows what beside. My courage was ebbing. Punch, however, which makes beasts of so many, made a man of me again--just in time to hear with tolerable nerve and firmness the lumpy, flabby, naked feet deliberately descending the stairs again.

I took a candle, not without a tremour. As I crossed the floor I tried to extemporise a prayer, but stopped short to listen, and never finished it. The steps continued. I confess I hesitated for some seconds at the door before I took heart of grace and opened it. When I peeped out the lobby was perfectly empty--there was no monster standing on the staircase; and as the detested sound ceased, I was reassured enough to venture forward nearly to the banisters. Horror of horrors! within a stair or two beneath the spot where I stood the unearthly tread smote the floor. My eye caught something in motion; it was about the size of Goliah's foot--it was grey, heavy, and flapped with a dead weight from one step to another. As I am alive, it was the most monstrous grey rat I ever beheld or imagined.
Shakespeare says--"Some men there are cannot abide a gaping pig, and some that are mad if they behold a cat." I went well-nigh out of my wits when I beheld this _rat_; for, laugh at me as you may, it fixed upon me, I thought, a perfectly human expression of malice; and, as it shuffled about and looked up into my face almost from between my feet, I saw, I could swear it--I felt it then, and know it now, the infernal gaze and the accursed countenance of my old friend in the portrait, transfused into the visage of the bloated vermin before me.

I bounced into my room again with a feeling of loathing and horror I cannot describe, and locked and bolted my door as if a lion had been at the other side. D--n him or _it_; curse the portrait and its original! I felt in my soul that the rat--yes, the _rat_, the RAT I had just seen, was that evil being in masquerade, and rambling through the house upon some infernal night lark.

Next morning I was early trudging through the miry streets; and, among other transactions, posted a peremptory note recalling Tom. On my return, however, I found a note from my absent "chum," announcing his intended return next day. I was doubly rejoiced at this, because I had succeeded in getting rooms; and because the change of scene and return of my comrade were rendered specially pleasant by the last night's half ridiculous half horrible adventure.

I slept extemporaneously in my new quarters in Digges' Street that night, and next morning returned for breakfast to the haunted mansion, where I was certain Tom would call immediately on his arrival.

I was quite right--he came; and almost his first question referred to the primary object of our change of residence.

"Thank God," he said with genuine fervour, on hearing that all was arranged. "On _your_ account I am delighted. As to myself, I assure you that no earthly consideration could have induced me ever again to pass a night in this disastrous old house."

"Confound the house!" I ejaculated, with a genuine mixture of fear and detestation, "we have not had a pleasant hour since we came to live here"; and so I went on, and related incidentally my adventure with the plethoric old rat.

"Well, if that were _all_," said my cousin, affecting to make light of the matter, "I don't think I should have minded it very much."

"Ay, but its eye--its countenance, my dear Tom," urged I; "if you had seen _that_, you would have felt it might be _anything_ but what it seemed."

"I inclined to think the best conjurer in such a case would be an able-bodied cat," he said, with a provoking chuckle.

"But let us hear your own adventure," I said tartly.

At this challenge he looked uneasily round him. I had poked up a very unpleasant recollection.

"You shall hear it, Dick; I'll tell it to you," he said. "Begad, sir, I should feel quite queer, though, telling it _here_, though we are too strong a body for ghosts to meddle with just now."

Though he spoke this like a joke, I think it was serious calculation. Our Hebe was in a corner of the room, packing our cracked delft tea and dinner-services in a basket. She soon suspended operations, and with mouth and eyes wide open became an absorbed listener. Tom's experiences were told nearly in these words:----

"I saw it three times, Dick--three distinct times; and I am perfectly certain it meant me some infernal harm. I was, I say, in danger--in _extreme_ danger; for, if nothing else had happened, my reason would most certainly have failed me, unless I had escaped so soon. Thank God. I _did_ escape.

"The first night of this hateful disturbance, I was lying in the attitude of sleep, in that lumbering old bed. I hate to think of it. I was really wide awake, though I had put out my candle, and was lying as quietly as if I had been asleep; and although accidentally restless, my thoughts were running in a cheerful and agreeable channel.

"I think it must have been two o'clock at least when I thought I heard a sound in that--that odious dark recess at the far end of the bedroom. It was as if someone was drawing a piece of cord slowly along the floor, lifting it up, and dropping it softly down again in coils. I sate up once or twice in my bed, but could see nothing, so I concluded it must be mice in the wainscot. I felt no emotion graver than curiosity, and after a few minutes ceased to observe it.

"While lying in this state, strange to say; without at first a suspicion of anything supernatural, on a sudden I saw an old man, rather stout and square, in a sort of roan-red dressing-gown, and with a black cap on his head, moving stiffly and slowly in a diagonal direction, from the recess, across the floor of the bedroom, passing my bed at the foot, and entering the lumber-closet at the left. He had something under his arm; his head hung a little at one side; and, merciful God! when I saw his face."

Tom stopped for a while, and then said----

"That awful countenance, which living or dying I never can forget, disclosed what he was. Without turning to the right or left, he passed beside me, and entered the closet by the bed's head.

"While this fearful and indescribable type of death and guilt was passing, I felt that I had no more power to speak or stir than if I had been myself a corpse. For hours after it had disappeared, I was too terrified and weak to move. As soon as daylight came, I took courage, and examined the room, and especially the course which the frightful intruder had seemed to take, but there was not a vestige to indicate anybody's having passed there; no sign of any disturbing agency visible among the lumber that strewed the floor of the closet.

"I now began to recover a little. I was fagged and exhausted, and at last, overpowered by a feverish sleep. I came down late; and finding you out of spirits, on account of your dreams about the portrait, whose _original_ I am now certain disclosed himself to me, I did not care to talk about the infernal vision. In fact, I was trying to persuade myself that the whole thing was an illusion, and I did not like to revive in their intensity the hated impressions of the past night--or to risk the constancy of my scepticism, by recounting the tale of my sufferings.

"It required some nerve, I can tell you, to go to my haunted chamber next night, and lie down quietly in the same bed," continued Tom. "I did so with a degree of trepidation, which, I am not ashamed to say, a very little matter would have sufficed to stimulate to downright panic. This night, however, passed off quietly enough, as also the next; and so too did two or three more. I grew more confident, and began to fancy that I believed in the theories of spectral illusions, with which I had at first vainly tried to impose upon my convictions.

"The apparition had been, indeed, altogether anomalous. It had crossed the room without any recognition of my presence: I had not disturbed _it_, and _it_ had no mission to _me_. What, then, was the imaginable use of its crossing the room in a visible shape at all? Of course it might have _been_ in the closet instead of _going_ there, as easily as it introduced itself into the recess without entering the chamber in a shape discernible by the senses. Besides, how the deuce _had_ I seen it? It was a dark night; I had no candle; there was no fire; and yet I saw it as distinctly, in colouring and outline, as ever I beheld human form! A cataleptic dream would explain it all; and I was determined that a dream it should be.

"One of the most remarkable phenomena connected with the practice of mendacity is the vast number of deliberate lies we tell ourselves, whom, of all persons, we can least expect to deceive. In all this, I need hardly tell you, Dick, I was simply lying to myself, and did not believe one word of the wretched humbug. Yet I went on, as men will do, like persevering charlatans and impostors, who tire people into credulity by the mere force of reiteration; so I hoped to win myself over at last to a comfortable scepticism about the ghost.

"He had not appeared a second time--that certainly was a comfort; and what, after all, did I care for him, and his queer old toggery and strange looks? Not a fig! I was nothing the worse for having seen him, and a good story the better. So I tumbled into bed, put out my candle, and, cheered by a loud drunken quarrel in the back lane, went fast asleep.

"From this deep slumber I awoke with a start. I knew I had had a horrible dream; but what it was I could not remember. My heart was thumping furiously; I felt bewildered and feverish; I sate up in the bed and looked about the room. A broad flood of moonlight came in through the curtainless window; everything was as I had last seen it; and though the domestic squabble in the back lane was, unhappily for me, allayed, I yet could hear a pleasant fellow singing, on his way home, the then popular comic ditty called, 'Murphy Delany.' Taking advantage of this diversion I lay down again, with my face towards the fireplace, and closing my eyes, did my best to think of nothing else but the song, which was every moment growing fainter in the distance:----

"'Twas Murphy Delany, so funny and frisky,
  Stept into a shebeen shop to get his skin full;
He reeled out again pretty well lined with whiskey,
  As fresh as a shamrock, as blind as a bull.

"The singer, whose condition I dare say resembled that of his hero, was soon too far off to regale my ears any more; and as his music died away, I myself sank into a doze, neither sound nor refreshing. Somehow the song had got into my head, and I went meandering on through the adventures of my respectable fellow-countryman, who, on emerging from the 'shebeen shop,' fell into a river, from which he was fished up to be 'sat upon' by a coroner's jury, who having learned from a 'horse-doctor' that he was 'dead as a door-nail, so there was an end,' returned their verdict accordingly, just as he returned to his senses, when an angry altercation and a pitched battle between the body and the coroner winds up the lay with due spirit and pleasantry.

"Through this ballad I continued with a weary monotony to plod, down to the very last line, and then _da capo_, and so on, in my uncomfortable half-sleep, for how long, I can't conjecture. I found myself at last, however, muttering, '_dead_ as a door-nail, so there was an end'; and something like another voice within me, seemed to say, very faintly, but sharply, 'dead! dead! _dead_! and may the Lord have mercy on your soul!' and instantaneously I was wide awake, and staring right before me from the pillow.

"Now--will you believe it, Dick?--I saw the same accursed figure standing full front, and gazing at me with its stony and fiendish countenance, not two yards from the bedside."

Tom stopped here, and wiped the perspiration from his face. I felt very queer. The girl was as pale as Tom; and, assembled as we were in the very scene of these adventures, we were all, I dare say, equally grateful for the clear daylight and the resuming bustle out of doors.

"For about three seconds only I saw it plainly; then it grew indistinct; but, for a long time, there was something like a column of dark vapour where it had been standing, between me and the wall; and I felt sure that he was still there. After a good while, this appearance went too. I took my clothes downstairs to the hall, and dressed there, with the door half open; then went out into the street, and walked about the town till morning, when I came back, in a miserable state of nervousness and exhaustion. I was such a fool, Dick, as to be ashamed to tell you how I came to be so upset. I thought you would laugh at me; especially as I had always talked philosophy, and treated _your_ ghosts with contempt. I concluded you would give me no quarter; and so kept my tale of horror to myself.

"Now, Dick, you will hardly believe me, when I assure you, that for many nights after this last experience, I did not go to my room at all. I used to sit up for a while in the drawing-room after you had gone up to your bed; and then steal down softly to the hall-door, let myself out, and sit in the 'Robin Hood' tavern until the last guest went off; and then I got through the night like a sentry, pacing the streets till morning.

"For more than a week I never slept in bed. I sometimes had a snooze on a form in the 'Robin Hood,' and sometimes a nap in a chair during the day; but regular sleep I had absolutely none.

"I was quite resolved that we should get into another house; but I could not bring myself to tell you the reason, and I somehow put it off from day to day, although my life was, during every hour of this procrastination, rendered as miserable as that of a felon with the constables on his track. I was growing absolutely ill from this wretched mode of life. "One afternoon I determined to enjoy an hour's sleep upon your bed. I hated mine; so that I had never, except in a stealthy visit every day to unmake it, lest Martha should discover the secret of my nightly absence, entered the ill-omened chamber.

"As ill-luck would have it, you had locked your bedroom, and taken away the key. I went into my own to unsettle the bedclothes, as usual, and give the bed the appearance of having been slept in. Now, a variety of circumstances concurred to bring about the dreadful scene through which I was that night to pass. In the first place, I was literally overpowered with fatigue, and longing for sleep; in the next place, the effect of this extreme exhaustion upon my nerves resembled that of a narcotic, and rendered me less susceptible than, perhaps, I should in any other condition have been, of the exciting fears which had become habitual to me. Then again, a little bit of the window was open, a pleasant freshness pervaded the room, and, to crown all, the cheerful sun of day was making the room quite pleasant. What was to prevent my enjoying an hour's nap _here_? The whole air was resonant with the cheerful hum of life, and the broad matter-of-fact light of day filled every corner of the room.

"I yielded--stifling my qualms--to the almost overpowering temptation; and merely throwing off my coat, and loosening my cravat, I lay down, limiting myself to _half_-an-hour's doze in the unwonted enjoyment of a feather bed, a coverlet, and a bolster.

"It was horribly insidious; and the demon, no doubt, marked my infatuated preparations. Dolt that I was, I fancied, with mind and body worn out for want of sleep, and an arrear of a full week's rest to my credit, that such measure as _half_-an-hour's sleep, in such a situation, was possible. My sleep was death-like, long, and dreamless.

"Without a start or fearful sensation of any kind, I waked gently, but completely. It was, as you have good reason to remember, long past midnight--I believe, about two o'clock. When sleep has been deep and long enough to satisfy nature thoroughly, one often wakens in this way, suddenly, tranquilly, and completely.

"There was a figure seated in that lumbering, old sofa-chair, near the fireplace. Its back was rather towards me, but I could not be mistaken; it turned slowly round, and, merciful heavens! there was the stony face, with its infernal lineaments of malignity and despair, gloating on me. There was now no doubt as to its consciousness of my presence, and the hellish malice with which it was animated, for it arose, and drew close to the bedside. There was a rope about its neck, and the other end, coiled up, it held stiffly in its hand.

"My good angel nerved me for this horrible crisis. I remained for some seconds transfixed by the gaze of this tremendous phantom. He came close to the bed, and appeared on the point of mounting upon it. The next instant I was upon the floor at the far side, and in a moment more was, I don't know how, upon the lobby.

"But the spell was not yet broken; the valley of the shadow of death was not yet traversed. The abhorred phantom was before me there; it was standing near the banisters, stooping a little, and with one end of the rope round its own neck, was poising a noose at the other, as if to throw over mine; and while engaged in this baleful pantomime, it wore a smile so sensual, so unspeakably dreadful, that my senses were nearly overpowered. I saw and remember nothing more, until I found myself in your room.

"I had a wonderful escape, Dick--there is no disputing _that_--an escape for which, while I live, I shall bless the mercy of heaven. No one can conceive or imagine what it is for flesh and blood to stand in the presence of such a thing, but one who has had the terrific experience. Dick, Dick, a shadow has passed over me--a chill has crossed my blood and marrow, and I will never be the same again--never, Dick--never!"

Our handmaid, a mature girl of two-and-fifty, as I have said, stayed her hand, as Tom's story proceeded, and by little and little drew near to us, with open mouth, and her brows contracted over her little, beady black eyes, till stealing a glance over her shoulder now and then, she established herself close behind us. During the relation, she had made various earnest comments, in an undertone; but these and her ejaculations, for the sake of brevity and simplicity, I have omitted in my narration. "It's often I heard tell of it," she now said, "but I never believed it rightly till now--though, indeed, why should not I? Does not my mother, down there in the lane, know quare stories, God bless us, beyant telling about it? But you ought not to have slept in the back bedroom. She was loath to let me be going in and out of that room even in the day time, let alone for any Christian to spend the night in it; for sure she says it was his own bedroom."

"_Whose_ own bedroom?" we asked, in a breath.

"Why, _his_--the ould Judge's--Judge Horrock's, to be sure, God rest his sowl"; and she looked fearfully round.

"Amen!" I muttered. "But did he die there?"

"Die there! No, not quite _there_," she said. "Shure, was not it over the banisters he hung himself, the ould sinner, God be merciful to us all? and was not it in the alcove they found the handles of the skipping-rope cut off and the knife where he was settling the cord, God bless us, to hang himself with? It was his housekeeper's daughter owned the rope, my mother often told me, and the child never throve after, and used to be starting up out of her sleep, and screeching in the night time, wid dhrames and frights that cum an her; and they said how it was the speerit of the ould Judge that was tormentin' her; and she used to be roaring and yelling out to hould back the big ould fellow with the crooked neck; and then she'd screech 'Oh, the master! the master! he's stampin' at me, and beckoning to me! Mother, darling, don't let me go!' And so the poor crathure died at last, and the docthers said it was wather on the brain, for it was all they could say."

"How long ago was all this?" I asked.

"Oh, then, how would I know?" she answered. "But it must be a wondherful long time ago, for the housekeeper was an ould woman, with a pipe in her mouth, and not a tooth left, and better nor eighty years ould when my mother was first married; and they said she was a rale buxom, fine-dressed woman when the ould Judge come to his end; an', indeed, my mother's not far from eighty years ould herself this day; and what made it worse for the unnatural ould villain, God rest his soul, to frighten the little girl out of the world the way he did, was what was mostly thought and believed by every one. My mother says how the poor little crathure was his own child; for he was by all accounts an ould villain every way, an' the hangin'est judge that ever was known in Ireland's ground."

"From what you said about the danger of sleeping in that bedroom," said I, "I suppose there were stories about the ghost having appeared there to others."

"Well, there was things said--quare things, surely," she answered, as it seemed, with some reluctance. "And why would not there? Sure was it not up in that same room he slept for more than twenty years? and was it not in the _alcove_ he got the rope ready that done his own business at last, the way he done many a betther man's in his lifetime?--and was not the body lying in the same bed after death, and put in the coffin there, too, and carried out to his grave from it in Pether's churchyard, after the coroner was done? But there was quare stories--my mother has them all--about how one Nicholas Spaight got into trouble on the head of it."

"And what did they say of this Nicholas Spaight?" I asked.

"Oh, for that matther, it's soon told," she answered.

And she certainly did relate a very strange story, which so piqued my curiosity, that I took occasion to visit the ancient lady, her mother, from whom I learned many very curious particulars. Indeed, I am tempted to tell the tale, but my fingers are weary, and I must defer it. But if you wish to hear it another time, I shall do my best.

When we had heard the strange tale I have _not_ told you, we put one or two further questions to her about the alleged spectral visitations, to which the house had, ever since the death of the wicked old Judge, been subjected.

"No one ever had luck in it," she told us. "There was always cross accidents, sudden deaths, and short times in it. The first that tuck, it was a family--I forget their name--but at any rate there was two young ladies and their papa. He was about sixty, and a stout healthy gentleman as you'd wish to see at that age. Well, he slept in that unlucky back bedroom; and, God between us an' harm! sure enough he was found dead one morning, half out of the bed, with his head as black as a sloe, and swelled like a puddin', hanging down near the floor. It was a fit, they said. He was as dead as a mackerel, and so _he_ could not say what it was; but the ould people was all sure that it was nothing at all but the ould Judge, God bless us! that frightened him out of his senses and his life together.

"Some time after there was a rich old maiden lady took the house. I don't know which room _she_ slept in, but she lived alone; and at any rate, one morning, the servants going down early to their work, found her sitting on the passage-stairs, shivering and talkin' to herself, quite mad; and never a word more could any of _them_ or her friends get from her ever afterwards but, 'Don't ask me to go, for I promised to wait for him.' They never made out from her who it was she meant by _him_, but of course those that knew all about the ould house were at no loss for the meaning of all that happened to her.

"Then afterwards, when the house was let out in lodgings, there was Micky Byrne that took the same room, with his wife and three little children; and sure I heard Mrs. Byrne myself telling how the children used to be lifted up in the bed at night, she could not see by what mains; and how they were starting and screeching every hour, just all as one as the housekeeper's little girl that died, till at last one night poor Micky had a dhrop in him, the way he used now and again; and what do you think in the middle of the night he thought he heard a noise on the stairs, and being in liquor, nothing less id do him but out he must go himself to see what was wrong. Well, after that, all she ever heard of him was himself sayin', 'Oh, God!' and a tumble that shook the very house; and there, sure enough, he was lying on the lower stairs, under the lobby, with his neck smashed double undher him, where he was flung over the banisters."

Then the handmaiden added----

"I'll go down to the lane, and send up Joe Gavvey to pack up the rest of the taythings, and bring all the things across to your new lodgings."

And so we all sallied out together, each of us breathing more freely, I have no doubt, as we crossed that ill-omened threshold for the last time.

Now, I may add thus much, in compliance with the immemorial usage of the realm of fiction, which sees the hero not only through his adventures, but fairly out of the world. You must have perceived that what the flesh, blood, and bone hero of romance proper is to the regular compounder of fiction, this old house of brick, wood, and mortar is to the humble recorder of this true tale. I, therefore, relate, as in duty bound, the catastrophe which ultimately befell it, which was simply this--that about two years subsequently to my story it was taken by a quack doctor, who called himself Baron Duhlstoerf, and filled the parlour windows with bottles of indescribable horrors preserved in brandy, and the newspapers with the usual grandiloquent and mendacious advertisements. This gentleman among his virtues did not reckon sobriety, and one night, being overcome with much wine, he set fire to his bed curtains, partially burned himself, and totally consumed the house. It was afterwards rebuilt, and for a time an undertaker established himself in the premises.

I have now told you my own and Tom's adventures, together with some valuable collateral particulars; and having acquitted myself of my engagement, I wish you a very good night, and pleasant dreams.

# ULTOR DE LACY: A LEGEND OF CAPPERCULLEN (1861)

## CHAPTER I

### The Jacobite's Legacy

In my youth I heard a great many Irish family traditions, more or less of a supernatural character, some of them very peculiar, and all, to a child at least, highly interesting. One of these I will now relate, though the translation to cold type from oral narrative, with all the aids of animated human voice and countenance, and the appropriate _mise-en-scène_ of the old-fashioned parlour fireside and its listening circle of excited faces, and, outside, the wintry blast and the moan of leafless boughs, with the occasional rattle of the clumsy old window-frame behind shutter and curtain, as the blast swept by, is at best a trying one.

About midway up the romantic glen of Cappercullen, near the point where the counties of Limerick, Clare, and Tipperary converge, upon the then sequestered and forest-bound range of the Slieve-Felim hills, there stood, in the reigns of the two earliest Georges, the picturesque and massive remains of one of the finest of the Anglo-Irish castles of Munster--perhaps of Ireland.

It crowned the precipitous edge of the wooded glen, itself half-buried among the wild forest that covered that long and solitary range. There was no human habitation within a circle of many miles, except the half-dozen hovels and the small thatched chapel composing the little village of Murroa, which lay at the foot of the glen among the straggling skirts of the noble forest.

Its remoteness and difficulty of access saved it from demolition. It was worth nobody's while to pull down and remove the ponderous and clumsy oak, much less the masonry or flagged roofing of the pile. Whatever would pay the cost of removal had been long since carried away. The rest was abandoned to time--the destroyer.

The hereditary owners of this noble building and of a wide territory in the contiguous counties I have named, were English--the De Lacys--long naturalized in Ireland. They had acquired at least this portion of their estate in the reign of Henry VIII. and held it, with some vicissitudes, down to the establishment of the revolution in Ireland, when they suffered attainder, and, like other great families of that period, underwent a final eclipse.

The De Lacy of that day retired to France, and held a brief command in the Irish Brigade, interrupted by sickness. He retired, became a poor hanger-on of the Court of St. Germains, and died early in the eighteenth century--as well as I remember, 1705--leaving an only son, hardly twelve years old, called by the strange but significant name of Ultor.

At this point commences the marvellous ingredient of my tale.

When his father was dying, he had him to his bedside, with no one by except his confessor; and having told him, first, that on reaching the age of twenty-one, he was to lay claim to a certain small estate in the county of Clare, in Ireland, in right of his mother--the title-deeds of which he gave him--and next, having enjoined him not to marry before the age of thirty, on the ground that earlier marriages destroyed the spirit and the power of enterprise, and would incapacitate him from the accomplishment of his destiny--the restoration of his family--he then went on to open to the child a matter which so terrified him that he cried lamentably, trembling all over, clinging to the priest's gown with one hand and to his father's cold wrist with the other, and imploring him, with screams of horror, to desist from his communication.

But the priest, impressed, no doubt, himself, with its necessity, compelled him to listen. And then his father showed him a small picture, from which also the child turned with shrieks, until similarly constrained to look. They did not let him go until he had carefully conned the features, and was able to tell them, from memory, the colour of the eyes and hair, and the fashion and hues of the dress. Then his father gave him a black box containing this portrait, which was a full-length miniature, about nine inches long, painted very finely in oils, as smooth as enamel, and folded above it a sheet of paper, written over in a careful and very legible hand.

The deeds and this black box constituted the most important legacy bequeathed to his only child by the ruined Jacobite, and he deposited them in the hands of the priest, in trust, till his boy, Ultor, should have attained to an age to understand their value, and to keep them securely.

When this scene was ended, the dying exile's mind, I suppose, was relieved, for he spoke cheerily, and said he believed he would recover; and they soothed the crying child, and his father kissed him, and gave him a little silver coin to buy fruit with; and so they sent him off with another boy for a walk, and when he came back his father was dead.

He remained in France under the care of this ecclesiastic until he had attained the age of twenty-one, when he repaired to Ireland, and his title being unaffected by his father's attainder, he easily made good his claim to the small estate in the county of Clare.

There he settled, making a dismal and solitary tour now and then of the vast territories which had once been his father's, and nursing those gloomy and impatient thoughts which befitted the enterprises to which he was devoted.

Occasionally he visited Paris, that common centre of English, Irish, and Scottish disaffection; and there, when a little past thirty, he married the daughter of another ruined Irish house. His bride returned with him to the melancholy seclusion of their Munster residence, where she bore him in succession two daughters--Alice, the elder, dark-eyed and dark-haired, grave and sensible--Una, four years younger, with large blue eyes and long and beautiful golden hair.

Their poor mother was, I believe, naturally a lighthearted, sociable, high-spirited little creature; and her gay and childish nature pined in the isolation and gloom of her lot. At all events she died young, and the children were left to the sole care of their melancholy and embittered father. In process of time the girls grew up, tradition says, beautiful. The elder was designed for a convent, the younger her father hoped to mate as nobly as her high blood and splendid beauty seemed to promise, if only the great game on which he had resolved to stake all succeeded.

# CHAPTER II

## The Fairies in the Castle

The Rebellion of '45 came, and Ultor de Lacy was one of the few Irishmen implicated treasonably in that daring and romantic insurrection. Of course there were warrants out against him, but he was not to be found. The young ladies, indeed, remained as heretofore in their father's lonely house in Clare; but whether he had crossed the water or was still in Ireland was for some time unknown, even to them. In due course he was attainted, and his little estate forfeited. It was a miserable catastrophe--a tremendous and beggarly waking up from a life-long dream of returning principality.

In due course the officers of the crown came down to take possession, and it behoved the young ladies to flit. Happily for them the ecclesiastic I have mentioned was not quite so confident as their father, of his winning back the magnificent patrimony of his ancestors; and by his advice the daughters had been secured twenty pounds a year each, under the marriage settlement of their parents, which was all that stood between this proud house and literal destitution.

Late one evening, as some little boys from the village were returning from a ramble through the dark and devious glen of Cappercullen, with their pockets laden with nuts and "frahans," to their amazement and even terror they saw a light streaming redly from the narrow window of one of the towers overhanging the precipice among the ivy and the lofty branches, across the glen, already dim in the shadows of the deepening night.

"Look--look--look--'tis the Phooka's tower!" was the general cry, in the vernacular Irish, and a universal scamper commenced.

The bed of the glen, strewn with great fragments of rock, among which rose the tall stems of ancient trees, and overgrown with a tangled copse, was at the best no favourable ground for a run. Now it was dark; and, terrible work breaking through brambles and hazels and tumbling over rocks. Little Shaeen Mull Ryan, the last of the panic rout, screaming to his mates to wait for him--saw a whitish figure emerge from the thicket at the base of the stone flight of steps that descended the side of the glen, close by the castle-wall, intercepting his flight, and a discordant male voice shrieked----

"I have you!"

At the same time the boy, with a cry of terror, tripped and tumbled; and felt himself roughly caught by the arm, and hauled to his feet with a shake.

A wild yell from the child, and a volley of terror and entreaty followed.

"Who is it, Larry; what's the matter?" cried a voice, high in air, from the turret window, The words floated down through the trees, clear and sweet as the low notes of a flute.

"Only a child, my lady; a boy."

"Is he hurt?"

"Are you hurted?" demanded the whitish man, who held him fast, and repeated the question in Irish; but the child only kept blubbering and crying for mercy, with his hands clasped, and trying to drop on his knees.

Larry's strong old hand held him up. He _was_ hurt, and bleeding from over his eye.

"Just a trifle hurted, my lady!"

"Bring him up here."

Shaeen Mull Ryan gave himself over. He was among "the good people," who he knew would keep him prisoner for ever and a day. There was no good in resisting. He grew bewildered, and yielded himself passively to his fate, and emerged from the glen on the platform above; his captor's knotted old hand still on his arm, and looked round on the tall mysterious trees, and the gray front of the castle, revealed in the imperfect moonlight, as upon the scenery of a dream.

The old man who, with thin wiry legs, walked by his side, in a dingy white coat, and blue facings, and great pewter buttons, with his silver gray hair escaping from under his battered three-cocked hat; and his shrewd puckered resolute face, in which the boy could read no promise of sympathy, showing so white and phantom-like in the moonlight, was, as he thought, the incarnate ideal of a fairy.

This figure led him in silence under the great arched gateway, and across the grass-grown court, to the door in the far angle of the building; and so, in the dark, round and round, up a stone screw stair, and with a short turn into a large room, with a fire of turf and wood, burning on its long unused hearth, over which hung a pot, and about it an old woman with a great wooden spoon was busy. An iron candlestick supported their solitary candle; and about the floor of the room, as well as on the table and chairs, lay a litter of all sorts of things; piles of old faded hangings, boxes, trunks, clothes, pewter-plates, and cups; and I know not what more.

But what instantly engaged the fearful gaze of the boy were the figures of two ladies; red drugget cloaks they had on, like the peasant girls of Munster and Connaught, and the rest of their dress was pretty much in keeping. But they had the grand air, the refined expression and beauty, and above all, the serene air of command that belong to people of a higher rank.

The elder, with black hair and full brown eyes, sat writing at the deal table on which the candle stood, and raised her dark gaze to the boy as he came in. The other, with her hood thrown back, beautiful and _riant_, with a flood of wavy golden hair, and great blue eyes, and with something kind, and arch, and strange in her countenance, struck him as the most wonderful beauty he could have imagined.

They questioned the man in a language strange to the child. It was not English, for he had a smattering of that, and the man's story seemed to amuse them. The two young ladies exchanged a glance, and smiled mysteriously. He was more convinced than ever that he was among the good people. The younger stepped gaily forward and said----

"Do you know who _I_ am, my little man? Well, I'm the fairy Una, and this is my palace; and that fairy you see there (pointing to the dark lady, who was looking out something in a box), is my sister and family physician, the Lady Graveairs; and these (glancing at the old man and woman), are some of my courtiers; and I'm considering now what I shall do with _you_, whether I shall send you to-night to Lough Guir, riding on a rush, to make my compliments to the Earl of Desmond in his enchanted castle; or, straight to your bed, two thousand miles under ground, among the gnomes; or to prison in that little corner of the moon you see through the window--with the man-in-the-moon for your gaoler, for thrice three hundred years and a day! There, don't cry. You only see how serious a thing it is for you, little boys, to come so near my castle. Now, for this once, I'll let you go. But, henceforward, any boys I, or my people, may find within half a mile round my castle, shall belong to me for life, and never behold their home or their people more."

And she sang a little air and chased mystically half a dozen steps before him, holding out her cloak with her pretty fingers, and courtesying very low, to his indescribable alarm.

Then, with a little laugh, she said----

"My little man, we must mend your head."

And so they washed his scratch, and the elder one applied a plaister to it. And she of the great blue eyes took out of her pocket a little French box of bon-bons and emptied it into his hand, and she said----

"You need not be afraid to eat these--they are very good--and I'll send my fairy, Blanc-et-bleu, to set you free. Take him (she addressed Larry), and let him go, with a solemn charge."

The elder, with a grave and affectionate smile, said, looking on the fairy----

"Brave, dear, wild Una! nothing can ever quell your gaiety of heart."

And Una kissed her merrily on the cheek.

So the oak door of the room again opened, and Shaeen, with his conductor, descended the stair. He walked with the scared boy in grim silence near half way down the wild hill-side toward Murroa, and then he stopped, and said in Irish----

"You never saw the fairies before, my fine fellow, and 'tisn't often those who once set eyes on us return to tell it. Whoever comes nearer, night or day, than this stone," and he tapped it with the end of his cane, "will never see his home again, for we'll keep him till the day of judgment; goodnight, little gossoon--and away with you."

So these young ladies, Alice and Una, with two old servants, by their father's direction, had taken up their abode in a portion of that side of the old castle which overhung the glen; and with the furniture and hangings they had removed from their late residence, and with the aid of glass in the casements and some other indispensable repairs, and a thorough airing, they made the rooms they had selected just habitable, as a rude and temporary shelter.

## CHAPTER III

## The Priest's Adventures in the Glen

At first, of course, they saw or heard little of their father. In general, however, they knew that his plan was to procure some employment in France, and to remove them there. Their present strange abode was only an adventure and an episode, and they believed that any day they might receive instructions to commence their journey.

After a little while the pursuit relaxed. The government, I believe, did not care, provided he did not obtrude himself, what became of him, or where he concealed himself. At all events, the local authorities showed no disposition to hunt him down. The young ladies' charges on the little forfeited property were paid without any dispute, and no vexatious inquiries were raised as to what had become of the furniture and other personal property which had been carried away from the forfeited house.

The haunted reputation of the castle--for in those days, in matters of the marvellous, the oldest were children--secured the little family in the seclusion they coveted. Once, or sometimes twice a week, old Laurence, with a shaggy little pony, made a secret expedition to the city of Limerick, starting before dawn, and returning under the cover of the night, with his purchases. There was beside an occasional sly moonlit visit from the old parish priest, and a midnight mass in the old castle for the little outlawed congregation.

As the alarm and inquiry subsided, their father made them, now and then, a brief and stealthy visit. At first these were but of a night's duration, and with great precaution; but gradually they were extended and less guarded. Still he was, as the phrase is in Munster, "on his keeping." He had firearms always by his bed, and had arranged places of concealment in the castle in the event of a surprise. But no attempt nor any disposition to molest him appearing, he grew more at ease, if not more cheerful.

It came, at last, that he would sometimes stay so long as two whole months at a time, and then depart as suddenly and mysteriously as he came. I suppose he had always some promising plot on hand, and his head full of ingenious treason, and lived on the sickly and exciting dietary of hope deferred.

Was there a poetical justice in this, that the little _ménage_ thus secretly established, in the solitary and timeworn pile, should have themselves experienced, but from causes not so easily explicable, those very supernatural perturbations which they had themselves essayed to inspire?

The interruption of the old priest's secret visits was the earliest consequence of the mysterious interference which now began to display itself. One night, having left his cob in care of his old sacristan in the little village, he trudged on foot along the winding pathway, among the gray rocks and ferns that threaded the glen, intending a ghostly visit to the fair recluses of the castle, and he lost his way in this strange fashion.

There was moonlight, indeed, but it was little more than quarter-moon, and a long train of funereal clouds were sailing slowly across the sky--so that, faint and wan as it was, the light seldom shone full out, and was often hidden for a minute or two altogether. When he reached the point in the glen where the castle-stairs were wont to be, he could see nothing of them, and above, no trace of the castle-towers. So, puzzled somewhat, he pursued his way up the ravine, wondering how his walk had become so unusually protracted and fatiguing.

At last, sure enough, he saw the castle as plain as could be, and a lonely streak of candle-light issuing from the tower, just as usual, when his visit was expected. But he could not find the stair; and had to clamber among the rocks and copse-wood the best way he could. But when he emerged at top, there was nothing but the bare heath. Then the clouds stole over the moon again, and he moved along with hesitation and difficulty, and once more he saw the outline of the castle against the sky, quite sharp and clear. But this time it proved to be a great battlemented mass of cloud on the horizon. In a few minutes more he was quite close, all of a sudden, to the great front, rising gray and dim in the feeble light, and not till he could have struck it with his good oak "wattle" did he discover it to be only one of those wild, gray frontages of living rock that rise here and there in picturesque tiers along the slopes of those solitary mountains. And so, till dawn, pursuing this mirage of the castle, through pools and among ravines, he wore out a night of miserable misadventure and fatigue.

Another night, riding up the glen, so far as the level way at bottom would allow, and intending to make his nag fast at his customary tree, he heard on a sudden a horrid shriek at top of the steep rocks above his head, and something--a gigantic human form, it seemed--came tumbling and bounding headlong down through the rocks, and fell with a fearful impetus just before his horse's hoofs and there lay like a huge palpitating carcass. The horse was scared, as, indeed, was his rider, too, and more so when this apparently lifeless thing sprang up to his legs, and throwing his arms apart to bar their further progress, advanced his white and gigantic face towards them. Then the horse started about, with a snort of terror, nearly unseating the priest, and broke away into a furious and uncontrollable gallop.

I need not recount all the strange and various misadventures which the honest priest sustained in his endeavours to visit the castle, and its isolated tenants. They were enough to wear out his resolution, and frighten him into submission. And so at last these spiritual visits quite ceased; and fearing to awaken inquiry and suspicion, he thought it only prudent to abstain from attempting them in the daytime.

So the young ladies of the castle were more alone than ever. Their father, whose visits were frequently of long duration, had of late ceased altogether to speak of their contemplated departure for France, grew angry at any allusion to it, and they feared, had abandoned the plan altogether.

# CHAPTER IV

## The Light in the Bell Tower

Shortly after the discontinuance of the priest's visits, old Laurence, one night, to his surprise, saw light issuing from a window in the Bell Tower. It was at first only a tremulous red ray, visible only for a few minutes, which seemed to pass from the room, through whose window it escaped upon the courtyard of the castle, and so to lose itself. This tower and casement were in the angle of the building, exactly confronting that in which the little outlawed family had taken up their quarters.

The whole family were troubled at the appearance of this dull red ray from the chamber in the Bell Tower. Nobody knew what to make of it. But Laurence, who had campaigned in Italy with his old master, the young ladies' grandfather--"the heavens be his bed this night!"--was resolved to see it out, and took his great horse-pistols with him, and ascended to the corridor leading to the tower. But his search was vain.

This light left a sense of great uneasiness among the inmates, and most certainly it was not pleasant to suspect the establishment of an independent and possibly dangerous lodger or even colony, within the walls of the same old building.

The light very soon appeared again, steadier and somewhat brighter, in the same chamber. Again old Laurence buckled on his armour, swearing ominously to himself, and this time bent in earnest upon conflict. The young ladies watched in thrilling suspense from the great window in _their_ stronghold, looking diagonally across the court. But as Laurence, who had entered the massive range of buildings opposite, might be supposed to be approaching the chamber from which this ill-omened glare proceeded, it steadily waned, finally disappearing altogether, just a few seconds before his voice was heard shouting from the arched window to know which way the light had gone.

This lighting up of the great chamber of the Bell Tower grew at last to be of frequent and almost continual recurrence. It was, there, long ago, in times of trouble and danger, that the De Lacys of those evil days used to sit in feudal judgment upon captive adversaries, and, as tradition alleged, often gave them no more time for shrift and prayer, than it needed to mount to the battlement of the turret over-head, from which they were forthwith hung by the necks, for a caveat and admonition to all evil disposed persons viewing the same from the country beneath.

Old Laurence observed these mysterious glimmerings with an evil and an anxious eye, and many and various were the stratagems he tried, but in vain, to surprise the audacious intruders. It is, however, I believe, a fact that no phenomenon, no matter how startling at first, if prosecuted with tolerable regularity, and unattended with any new circumstances of terror, will very long continue to excite alarm or even wonder.

So the family came to acquiesce in this mysterious light. No harm accompanied it. Old Laurence, as he smoked his lonely pipe in the grass-grown courtyard, would cast a disturbed glance at it, as it softly glowed out through the darking aperture, and mutter a prayer or an oath. But he had given over the chase as a hopeless business. And Peggy Sullivan, the old dame of all work, when, by chance, for she never willingly looked toward the haunted quarter, she caught the faint reflection of its dull effulgence with the corner of her eye, would sign herself with the cross or fumble at her beads, and deeper furrows would gather in her forehead, and her face grow ashen and perturbed. And this was not mended by the levity with which the young ladies, with whom the spectre had lost his influence, familiarity, as usual, breeding contempt, had come to talk, and even to jest, about it.

## CHAPTER V

### The Man with the Claret Mark

But as the former excitement flagged, old Peggy Sullivan produced a new one; for she solemnly avowed that she had seen a thin-faced man, with an ugly red mark all over the side of his cheek, looking out of the same window, just at sunset, before the young ladies returned from their evening walk.

This sounded in their ears like an old woman's dream, but still it was an excitement, jocular in the morning, and just, perhaps, a little fearful as night overspread the vast and desolate building, but still, not wholly unpleasant. This little flicker of credulity suddenly, however, blazed up into the full light of conviction.

Old Laurence, who was not given to dreaming, and had a cool, hard head, and an eye like a hawk, saw the same figure, just about the same hour, when the last level gleam of sunset was tinting the summits of the towers and the tops of the tall trees that surrounded them.

He had just entered the court from the great gate, when he heard all at once the hard peculiar twitter of alarm which sparrows make when a cat or a hawk invades their safety, rising all round from the thick ivy that overclimbed the wall on his left, and raising his eyes listlessly, he saw, with a sort of shock, a thin, ungainly man, standing with his legs crossed, in the recess of the window from which the light was wont to issue, leaning with his elbows on the stone mullion, and looking down with a sort of sickly sneer, his hollow yellow cheeks being deeply stained on one side with what is called a "claret-mark."

"I have you at last, you villain!" cried Larry, in a strange rage and panic: "drop down out of that on the grass here, and give yourself up, or I'll shoot you."

The threat was backed with an oath, and he drew from his coat pocket the long holster pistol he was wont to carry, and covered his man cleverly. "I give you while I count ten--one-two-three-four. If you draw back, I'll fire, mind; five-six--you'd better be lively--seven-eight-nine--one chance more; will you come down? Then take it--ten!"

Bang went the pistol. The sinister stranger was hardly fifteen feet removed from him, and Larry was a dead shot. But this time he made a scandalous miss, for the shot knocked a little white dust from the stone wall a full yard at one side; and the fellow never shifted his negligent posture or qualified his sardonic smile during the procedure.

Larry was mortified and angry.

"You'll not get off this time, my tulip!" he said with a grin, exchanging the smoking weapon for the loaded pistol in reserve.

"What are you pistolling, Larry?" said a familiar voice close by his elbow, and he saw his master, accompanied by a handsome young man in a cloak.

"That villain, your honour, in the window, there."

"Why there's nobody there, Larry," said De Lacy, with a laugh, though that was no common indulgence with him.

As Larry gazed, the figure somehow dissolved and broke up without receding. A hanging tuft of yellow and red ivy nodded queerly in place of the face, some broken and discoloured masonry in perspective took up the outline and colouring of the arms and figure, and two imperfect red and yellow lichen streaks carried on the curved tracing of the long spindle shanks. Larry blessed himself, and drew his hand across his damp forehead, over his bewildered eyes, and could not speak for a minute. It was all some devilish trick; he could take his oath he saw every feature in the fellow's face, the lace and buttons of his cloak and doublet, and even his long finger nails and thin yellow fingers that overhung the cross-shaft of the window, where there was now nothing but a rusty stain left.

The young gentleman who had arrived with De Lacy, stayed that night and shared with great apparent relish the homely fare of the family. He was a gay and gallant Frenchman, and the beauty of the younger lady, and her pleasantry and spirit, seemed to make his hours pass but too swiftly, and the moment of parting sad.

When he had departed early in the morning, Ultor De Lacy had a long talk with his elder daughter, while the younger was busy with her early dairy task, for among their retainers this _proles generosa_ reckoned a "kind" little Kerry cow.

He told her that he had visited France since he had been last at Cappercullen, and how good and gracious their sovereign had been, and how he had arranged a noble alliance for her sister Una. The young gentleman was of high blood, and though not rich, had, nevertheless, his acres and his _nom de terre_, besides a captain's rank in the army. He was, in short, the very gentleman with whom they had parted only that morning. On what special business he was now in Ireland there was no necessity that he should speak; but being here he had brought him hither to present him to his daughter, and found that the impression she had made was quite what was desirable.

"You, you know, dear Alice, are promised to a conventual life. Had it been otherwise--"

He hesitated for a moment.

"You are right, dear father," she said, kissing his hand, "I _am_ so promised, and no earthly tie or allurement has power to draw me from that holy engagement."

"Well," he said, returning her caress, "I do not mean to urge you upon that point. It must not, however, be until Una's marriage has taken place. That cannot be, for many good reasons, sooner than this time twelve months; we shall then exchange this strange and barbarous abode for Paris, where are many eligible convents, in which are entertained as sisters some of the noblest ladies of France; and there, too, in Una's marriage will be continued, though not the name, at all events the blood, the lineage, and the title which, so sure as justice ultimately governs the course of human events, will be again established, powerful and honoured in this country, the scene of their ancient glory and transitory misfortunes. Meanwhile, we must not mention this engagement to Una. Here she runs no risk of being sought or won; but the mere knowledge that her hand was absolutely pledged, might excite a capricious opposition and repining such as neither I nor you would like to see; therefore be secret."

The same evening he took Alice with him for a ramble round the castle wall, while they talked of grave matters, and he as usual allowed her a dim and doubtful view of some of those cloud-built castles in which he habitually dwelt, and among which his jaded hopes revived.

They were walking upon a pleasant short sward of darkest green, on one side overhung by the gray castle walls, and on the other by the forest trees that here and there closely approached it, when precisely as they turned the angle of the Bell Tower, they were encountered by a person walking directly towards them. The sight of a stranger, with the exception of the one visitor introduced by her father, was in this place so absolutely unprecedented, that Alice was amazed and affrighted to such a degree that for a moment she stood stock-still.

But there was more in this apparition to excite unpleasant emotions, than the mere circumstance of its unexpectedness. The figure was very strange, being that of a tall, lean, ungainly man, dressed in a dingy suit, somewhat of a Spanish fashion, with a brown laced cloak, and faded red stockings. He had long lank legs, long arms, hands, and fingers, and a very long sickly face, with a drooping nose, and a sly, sarcastic leer, and a great purplish stain over-spreading more than half of one cheek.

As he strode past, he touched his cap with his thin, discoloured fingers, and an ugly side glance, and disappeared round the corner. The eyes of father and daughter followed him in silence.

Ultor De Lacy seemed first absolutely terror-stricken, and then suddenly inflamed with ungovernable fury. He dropped his cane on the ground, drew his rapier, and, without wasting a thought on his daughter, pursued.

He just had a glimpse of the retreating figure as it disappeared round the far angle. The plume, and the lank hair, the point of the rapier-scabbard, the flutter of the skirt of the cloak, and one red stocking and heel; and this was the last he saw of him.

When Alice reached his side, his drawn sword still in his hand, he was in a state of abject agitation.

"Thank Heaven, he's gone!" she exclaimed.

"He's gone," echoed Ultor, with a strange glare.

"And you are safe," she added, clasping his hand.

He sighed a great sigh.

"And you don't think he's coming back?"

"He!--who?"

"The stranger who passed us but now. Do you know him, father?"

"Yes--and--no, child--I know him not--and yet I know him too well. Would to heaven we could leave this accursed haunt tonight. Cursed be the stupid malice that first provoked this horrible feud, which no sacrifice and misery can appease, and no exorcism can quell or even suspend. The wretch has come from afar with a sure instinct to devour my last hope--to dog us into our last retreat--and to blast with his triumph the very dust and ruins of our house. What ails that stupid priest that he has given over his visits? Are _my_ children to be left without mass or confession--the sacraments which _guard_ as well as save--because he once loses his way in a mist, or mistakes a streak of foam in the brook for a dead man's face? D--n him!"

"See, Alice, if he won't come," he resumed, "you must only _write_ your confession to him in full--you and Una. Laurence is trusty, and will carry it--and we'll get the bishop's--or, if need be, the Pope's leave for him to give you absolution. I'll move heaven and earth, but you _shall_ have the sacraments, poor children!--and see him. I've been a wild fellow in my youth, and never pretended to sanctity; but I know there's but one safe way--and--and--keep you each a bit of this--(he opened a small silver box)--about you while you stay here--fold and sew it up reverently in a bit of the old psaltery parchment and wear it next your hearts--'tis a fragment of the consecrated wafer--and will help, with the saints' protection, to guard you from harm--and be strict in fasts, and constant in prayer--_I_ can do nothing--nor devise any help. The curse has fallen, indeed, on me and mine."

And Alice, saw, in silence, the tears of despair roll down his pale and agitated face.

This adventure was also a secret, and Una was to hear nothing of it.

## CHAPTER VI

## Voices

Now Una, nobody knew why, began to lose spirit, and to grow pale. Her fun and frolic were quite gone! Even her songs ceased. She was silent with her sister, and loved solitude better. She said she was well, and quite happy, and could in no wise be got to account for the lamentable change that had stolen over her. She had grown odd too, and obstinate in trifles; and strangely reserved and cold.

Alice was very unhappy in consequence. What was the cause of this estrangement--had she offended her, and how? But Una had never before borne resentment for an hour. What could have altered her entire nature so? Could it be the shadow and chill of coming insanity?

Once or twice, when her sister urged her with tears and entreaties to disclose the secret of her changed spirits and demeanour, she seemed to listen with a sort of silent wonder and suspicion, and then she looked for a moment full upon her, and seemed on the very point of revealing all. But the earnest dilated gaze stole downward to the floor, and subsided into an odd wily smile, and she began to whisper to herself, and the smile and the whisper were both a mystery to Alice.
She and Alice slept in the same bedroom--a chamber in a projecting tower--which on their arrival, when poor Una was so merry, they had hung round with old tapestry, and decorated fantastically according to their skill and frolic. One night, as they went to bed, Una said, as if speaking to herself----

"'Tis my last night in this room--I shall sleep no more with Alice."

"And what has poor Alice done, Una, to deserve your strange unkindness?"

Una looked on her curiously, and half frightened, and then the odd smile stole over her face like a gleam of moonlight.

"My poor Alice, what have you to do with it?" she whispered.

"And why do you talk of sleeping no more with me?" said Alice.

"Why? Alice dear--no why--no reason--only a knowledge that it must be so, or Una will die."

"Die, Una darling!--what can you mean?"

"Yes, sweet Alice, die, indeed. We must all die some time, you know, or--or undergo a change; and my time is near--_very_ near--unless I sleep apart from you."

"Indeed, Una, sweetheart, I think you _are_ ill, but not near death."

"Una knows what you think, wise Alice--but she's not mad--on the contrary, she's wiser than other folks."

"She's sadder and stranger too," said Alice, tenderly.

"Knowledge is sorrow," answered Una, and she looked across the room

through her golden hair which she was combing--and through the window, beyond which lay the tops of the great trees, and the still foliage of the glen in the misty moonlight.
"'Tis enough, Alice dear; it must be so. The bed must move hence, or Una's bed will be low enough ere long. See, it shan't be far though, only into that small room."

She pointed to an inner room or closet opening from that in which they lay. The walls of the building were hugely thick, and there were double doors of oak between the chambers, and Alice thought, with a sigh, how completely separated they were going to be.

However she offered no opposition. The change was made, and the girls for the first time since childhood lay in separate chambers. A few nights afterwards Alice awoke late in the night from a dreadful dream, in which the sinister figure which she and her father had encountered in their ramble round the castle walls, bore a principal part.

When she awoke there were still in her ears the sounds which had mingled in her dream. They were the notes of a deep, ringing, bass voice rising from the glen beneath the castle walls--something between humming and singing--listlessly unequal and intermittent, like the melody of a man whiling away the hours over his work. While she was wondering at this unwonted minstrelsy, there came a silence, and--could she believe her ears?--it certainly was Una's clear low contralto--softly singing a bar or two from the window. Then once more silence--and then again the strange manly voice, faintly chaunting from the leafy abyss.

With a strange wild feeling of suspicion and terror, Alice glided to the window. The moon who sees so many things, and keeps all secrets, with her cold impenetrable smile, was high in the sky. But Alice saw the red flicker of a candle from Una's window, and, she thought, the shadow of her head against the deep side wall of its recess. Then this was gone, and there were no more sights or sounds that night.

As they sate at breakfast, the small birds were singing merrily from among the sun-tipped foliage.

"I love this music," said Alice, unusually pale and sad; "it comes with the pleasant light of morning. I remember, Una, when you used to sing, like those gay birds, in the fresh beams of the morning; that was in the old time, when Una kept no secret from poor Alice."

"And Una knows what her sage Alice means; but there are other birds, silent all day long, and, they say, the sweetest too, that love to sing by _night_ alone."

So things went on--the elder girl pained and melancholy--the younger silent, changed, and unaccountable.

A little while after this, very late one night, on awaking, Alice heard a conversation being carried on in her sister's room. There seemed to be no disguise about it. She could not distinguish the words, indeed, the walls being some six feet thick, and two great oak doors intercepting. But Una's clear voice, and the deep bell-like tones of the unknown, made up the dialogue.

Alice sprung from her bed, threw her clothes about her, and tried to enter her sister's room; but the inner door was bolted. The voices ceased to speak as she knocked, and Una opened it, and stood before her in her nightdress, candle in hand.

"Una--Una, darling, as you hope for peace, tell me who is here?" cried frightened Alice, with her trembling arms about her neck.

Una drew back, with her large innocent blue eyes fixed full upon her.

"Come in, Alice," she said, coldly.

And in came Alice, with a fearful glance around. There was no hiding place there; a chair, a table, a little bedstead, and two or three pegs in the wall to hang clothes on; a narrow window, with two iron bars across; no hearth or chimney--nothing but bare walls.

Alice looked round in amazement, and her eyes glanced with painful inquiry into those of her sister. Una smiled one of her peculiar sidelong smiles, and said----

"Strange dreams! I've been dreaming--so has Alice. She hears and sees Una's dreams, and wonders--and well she may."

And she kissed her sister's cheek with a cold kiss, and lay down in her little bed, her slender hand under her head, and spoke no more.

Alice, not knowing what to think, went back to hers.

About this time Ultor De Lacy returned. He heard his elder daughter's strange narrative with marked uneasiness, and his agitation seemed to grow rather than subside. He enjoined her, however, not to mention it to the old servant, nor in presence of anybody she might chance to see, but only to him and to the priest, if he could be persuaded to resume his duty and return. The trial, however, such as it was, could not endure very long; matters had turned out favourably. The union of his younger daughter might be accomplished within a few months, and in eight or nine weeks they should be on their way to Paris.

A night or two after her father's arrival, Alice, in the dead of the night, heard the well-known strange deep voice speaking softly, as it seemed, close to her own window on the outside; and Una's voice, clear and tender, spoke in answer. She hurried to her own casement, and pushed it open, kneeling in the deep embrasure, and looking with a stealthy and affrighted gaze towards her sister's window. As she crossed the floor the voices subsided, and she saw a light withdrawn from within. The moonbeams slanted bright and clear on the whole side of the castle overlooking the glen, and she plainly beheld the shadow of a man projected on the wall as on a screen.

This black shadow recalled with a horrid thrill the outline and fashion of the figure in the Spanish dress. There were the cap and mantle, the rapier, the long thin limbs and sinister angularity. It was so thrown obliquely that the hands reached to the window-sill, and the feet stretched and stretched, longer and longer as she looked, toward the ground, and disappeared in the general darkness; and the rest, with a sudden flicker, shot downwards, as shadows will on the sudden movement of a light, and was lost in one gigantic leap down the castle wall.

"I do not know whether I dream or wake when I hear and see these sights; but I will ask my father to sit up with me, and we _two_ surely cannot be mistaken. May the holy saints keep and guard us!" And in her terror she buried her head under the bed-clothes, and whispered her prayers for an hour.

# CHAPTER VII

## Una's Love

"I have been with Father Denis," said De Lacy, next day, "and he will come to-morrow; and, thank Heaven! you may both make your confession and hear mass, and my mind will be at rest; and you'll find poor Una happier and more like herself."

But 'tween cup and lip there's many a slip. The priest was not destined to hear poor Una's shrift. When she bid her sister goodnight she looked on her with her large, cold, wild eyes, till something of her old human affections seemed to gather there, and they slowly filled with tears, which dropped one after the other on her homely dress as she gazed in her sister's face.

Alice, delighted, sprang up, and clasped her arms about her neck. "My own darling treasure,'tis all over; you love your poor Alice again, and will be happier than ever."

But while she held her in her embrace Una's eyes were turned towards the window, and her lips apart, and Alice felt instinctively that her thoughts were already far away.

"Hark!--listen!--hush!" and Una, with her delighted gaze fixed, as if she saw far away beyond the castle wall, the trees, the glen, and the night's dark curtain, held her hand raised near her ear, and waved her head slightly in time, as it seemed, to music that reached not Alice's ear, and smiled her strange pleased smile, and then the smile slowly faded away, leaving that sly suspicious light behind it which somehow scared her sister with an uncertain sense of danger; and she sang in tones so sweet and low that it seemed but a reverie of a song, recalling, as Alice fancied, the strain to which she had just listened in that strange ecstasy, the plaintive and beautiful Irish ballad, "Shule, shule, shule, aroon," the midnight summons of the outlawed Irish soldier to his darling to follow him.

Alice had slept little the night before. She was now overpowered with fatigue; and leaving her candle burning by her bedside, she fell into a deep sleep. From this she awoke suddenly, and completely, as will sometimes happen without any apparent cause, and she saw Una come into the room. She had a little purse of embroidery--her own work--in her hand; and she stole lightly to the bedside, with her peculiar oblique smile, and evidently thinking that her sister was asleep.

Alice was thrilled with a strange terror, and did not speak or move; and her sister slipped her hand softly under her bolster, and withdrew it. Then Una stood for while by the hearth, and stretched her hand up to the mantelpiece, from which she took a little bit of chalk, and Alice thought she saw her place it in the fingers of a long yellow hand that was stealthily introduced from her own chamber-door to receive it; and Una paused in the dark recess of the door, and smiled over her shoulder toward her sister, and then glided into her room, closing the doors.

Almost freezing with terror, Alice rose and glided after her, and stood in her chamber, screaming----

"Una, Una, in heaven's name what troubles you?"

But Una seemed to have been sound asleep in her bed, and raised herself with a start, and looking upon her with a peevish surprise, said----

"What does Alice seek here?"

"You were in my room, Una, dear; you seem disturbed and troubled."

"Dreams, Alice. My dreams crossing your brain; only dreams--dreams. Get you to bed, and sleep."

And to bed she went, but _not_ to sleep. She lay awake more than an hour; and then Una emerged once more from her room. This time she was fully dressed, and had her cloak and thick shoes on, as their rattle on the floor plainly discovered. She had a little bundle tied up in a handkerchief in her hand, and her hood was drawn about her head; and thus equipped, as it seemed, for a journey, she came and stood at the foot of Alice's bed, and stared on her with a look so soulless and terrible that her senses almost forsook her. Then she turned and went back into her own chamber.

She may have returned; but Alice thought not--at least she did not see her. But she lay in great excitement and perturbation; and was terrified, about an hour later, by a knock at her chamber door--not that opening into Una's room, but upon the little passage from the stone screw staircase. She sprang from her bed; but the door was secured on the inside, and she felt relieved. The knock was repeated, and she heard some one laughing softly on the outside.

The morning came at last; that dreadful night was over. But Una! Where was Una?

Alice never saw her more. On the head of her empty bed were traced in chalk the words--Ultor De Lacy, Ultor O'Donnell. And Alice found beneath her own pillow the little purse of embroidery she had seen in Una's hand. It was her little parting token, and bore the simple legend--"Una's love!"

De Lacy's rage and horror were boundless. He charged the priest, in frantic language, with having exposed his child, by his cowardice and neglect, to the machinations of the Fiend, and raved and blasphemed like a man demented.

It is said that he procured a solemn exorcism to be performed, in the hope of disenthralling and recovering his daughter. Several times, it is alleged, she was seen by the old servants. Once on a sweet summer morning, in the window of the tower, she was perceived combing her beautiful golden tresses, and holding a little mirror in her hand; and first, when she saw herself discovered, she looked affrighted, and then smiled, her slanting, cunning smile. Sometimes, too, in the glen, by moonlight, it was said belated villagers had met her, always startled first, and then smiling, generally singing snatches of old Irish ballads, that seemed to bear a sort of dim resemblance to her melancholy fate. The apparition has long ceased. But it is said that now and again, perhaps once in two or three years, late on a summer night, you may hear--but faint and far away in the recesses of the glen--the sweet, sad notes of Una's voice, singing those plaintive melodies. This, too, of course, in time will cease, and all be forgotten.

# CHAPTER VIII

## Sister Agnes and the Portrait

When Ultor De Lacy died, his daughter Alice found among his effects a small box, containing a portrait such as I have described. When she looked on it, she recoiled in horror. There, in the plenitude of its sinister peculiarities, was faithfully portrayed the phantom which lived with a vivid and horrible accuracy in her remembrance. Folded in the same box was a brief narrative, stating that, "A.D. 1601, in the month of December, Walter De Lacy, of Cappercullen, made many prisoners at the ford of Ownhey, or Abington, of Irish and Spanish soldiers, flying from the great overthrow of the rebel powers at Kinsale, and among the number one Roderic O'Donnell, an arch traitor, and near kinsman to that other O'Donnell who led the rebels; who, claiming kindred through his mother to De Lacy, sued for his life with instant and miserable entreaty, and offered great ransom, but was by De Lacy, through great zeal for the queen, as some thought, cruelly put to death. When he went to the tower-top, where was the gallows, finding himself in extremity, and no hope of mercy, he swore that though he could work them no evil before his death, yet that he would devote himself thereafter to blast the greatness of the De Lacys, and never leave them till his work was done. He hath been seen often since, and always for that family perniciously, insomuch that it hath been the custom to show to young children of that lineage the picture of the said O'Donnell, in little, taken among his few valuables, to prevent their being misled by him unawares, so that he should not have his will, who by devilish wiles and hell-born cunning, hath steadfastly sought the ruin of that ancient house, and especially to leave that _stemma generosum_ destitute of issue for the transmission of their pure blood and worshipful name."

Old Miss Croker, of Ross House, who was near seventy in the year 1821, when she related this story to me, had seen and conversed with Alice De Lacy, a professed nun, under the name of Sister Agnes, in a religious house in King-street, in Dublin, founded by the famous Duchess of Tyrconnell, and had the narrative from her own lips. I thought the tale worth preserving, and have no more to say.

# AN AUTHENTIC NARRATIVE OF A HAUNTED HOUSE (1862)

[The Editor of the UNIVERSITY MAGAZINE submits the following very remarkable statement, with every detail of which he has been for some years acquainted, upon the ground that it affords the most authentic and ample relation of a series of marvellous phenoma, in nowise connected with what is technically termed "spiritualism," which he has anywhere met with. All the persons--and there are many of them living--upon whose separate evidence some parts, and upon whose united testimony others, of this most singular recital depend, are, in their several walks of life, respectable, and such as would in any matter of judicial investigation be deemed wholly unexceptionable witnesses. There is not an incident here recorded which would not have been distinctly deposed to on oath had any necessity existed, by the persons who severally, and some of them in great fear, related their own distinct experiences. The Editor begs most pointedly to meet _in limine_ the suspicion, that he is elaborating a trick, or vouching for another ghost of Mrs. Veal. As a mere story the narrative is valueless: its sole claim to attention is its absolute truth. For the good faith of its relator he pledges his own and the character of this Magazine. With the Editor's concurrence, the name of the watering-place, and some special circumstances in no essential way bearing upon the peculiar character of the story, but which might have indicated the locality, and possibly annoyed persons interested in house property there, have been suppressed by the narrator. Not the slightest liberty has been taken with the narrative, which is presented precisely in the terms in which the writer of it, who employs throughout the first person, would, if need were, fix it in the form of an affidavit.]

Within the last eight years--the precise date I purposely omit--I I was ordered by my physician, my health being in an unsatisfactory state, to change my residence to one upon the sea-coast; and accordingly, I took a house for a year in a fashionable watering-place, at a moderate distance from the city in which I had previously resided, and connected with it by a railway.

Winter was setting in when my removal thither was decided upon; but there was nothing whatever dismal or depressing in the change. The house I had taken was to all appearance, and in point of convenience, too, quite a modern one. It formed one in a cheerful row, with small gardens in front, facing the sea, and commanding sea air and sea views in perfection. In the rear it had coach-house and stable, and between them and the house a considerable grass-plot, with some flower-beds, interposed.

Our family consisted of my wife and myself, with three children, the eldest about nine years old, she and the next in age being girls; and the youngest, between six and seven, a boy. To these were added six servants, whom, although for certain reasons I decline giving their real names, I shall indicate, for the sake of clearness, by arbitrary ones. There was a nurse, Mrs. Southerland; a nursery-maid, Ellen Page; the cook, Mrs. Greenwood; and the housemaid, Ellen Faith; a butler, whom I shall call Smith, and his son, James, about two-and-twenty.

We came out to take possession at about seven o'clock in the evening; every thing was comfortable and cheery; good fires lighted, the rooms neat and airy, and a general air of preparation and comfort, highly conducive to good spirits and pleasant anticipations.

The sitting-rooms were large and cheerful, and they and the bed-rooms more than ordinarily lofty, the kitchen and servants' rooms, on the same level, were well and comfortably furnished, and had, like the rest of the house, an air of recent painting and fitting up, and a completely modern character, which imparted a very cheerful air of cleanliness and convenience.

There had been just enough of the fuss of settling agreeably to occupy us, and to give a pleasant turn to our thoughts after we had retired to our rooms. Being an invalid, I had a small bed to myself--resigning the four-poster to my wife. The candle was extinguished, but a night-light was burning. I was coming up stairs, and she, already in bed, had just dismissed her maid, when we were both startled by a wild scream from her room; I found her in a state of the extremest agitation and terror. She insisted that she had seen an unnaturally tall figure come beside her bed and stand there. The light was too faint to enable her to define any thing respecting this apparition, beyond the fact of her having most distinctly seen such a shape, colourless from the insufficiency of the light to disclose more than its dark outline.

We both endeavoured to re-assure her. The room once more looked so cheerful in the candlelight, that we were quite uninfluenced by the contagion of her terrors. The movements and voices of the servants down stairs still getting things into their places and completing our comfortable arrangements, had also their effect in steeling us against any such influence, and we set the whole thing down as a dream, or an imperfectly-seen outline of the bed-curtains. When, however, we were alone, my wife reiterated, still in great agitation, her clear assertion that she had most positively seen, being at the time as completely awake as ever she was, precisely what she had described to us. And in this conviction she continued perfectly firm.

A day or two after this, it came out that our servants were under an apprehension that, somehow or other, thieves had established a secret mode of access to the lower part of the house. The butler, Smith, had seen an ill-looking woman in his room on the first night of our arrival; and he and other servants constantly saw, for many days subsequently, glimpses of a retreating figure, which corresponded with that so seen by him, passing through a passage which led to a back area in which were some coal-vaults.

This figure was seen always in the act of retreating, its back turned, generally getting round the corner of the passage into the area, in a stealthy and hurried way, and, when closely followed, imperfectly seen again entering one of the coal-vaults, and when pursued into it, nowhere to be found.

The idea of any thing supernatural in the matter had, strange to say, not yet entered the mind of any one of the servants. They had heard some stories of smugglers having secret passages into houses, and using their means of access for purposes of pillage, or with a view to frighten superstitious people out of houses which they needed for their own objects, and a suspicion of similar practices here, caused them extreme uneasiness. The apparent anxiety also manifested by this retreating figure to escape observation, and her always appearing to make her egress at the same point, favoured this romantic hypothesis. The men, however, made a most careful examination of the back area, and of the coal-vaults, with a view to discover some mode of egress, but entirely without success. On the contrary, the result was, so far as it went, subversive of the theory; solid masonry met them on every hand.

I called the man, Smith, up, to hear from his own lips the particulars of what he had seen; and certainly his report was very curious. I give it as literally as my memory enables me:----

His son slept in the same room, and was sound asleep; but he lay awake, as men sometimes will on a change of bed, and having many things on his mind. He was lying with his face towards the wall, but observing a light and some little stir in the room, he turned round in his bed, and saw the figure of a woman, squalid, and ragged in dress; her figure rather low and broad; as well as I recollect, she had something--either a cloak or shawl--on, and wore a bonnet. Her back was turned, and she appeared to be searching or rummaging for something on the floor, and, without appearing to observe him, she turned in doing so towards him. The light, which was more like the intense glow of a coal, as he described it, being of a deep red colour, proceeded from the hollow of her hand, which she held beside her head, and he saw her perfectly distinctly. She appeared middle-aged, was deeply pitted with the smallpox, and blind of one eye. His phrase in describing her general appearance was, that she was "a miserable, poor-looking creature."

He was under the impression that she must be the woman who had been left by the proprietor in charge of the house, and who had that evening, after having given up the keys, remained for some little time with the female servants. He coughed, therefore, to apprize her of his presence, and turned again towards the wall. When he again looked round she and the light were gone; and odd as was her method of lighting herself in her search, the circumstances excited neither uneasiness nor curiosity in his mind, until he discovered next morning that the woman in question had left the house long before he had gone to his bed.
I examined the man very closely as to the appearance of the person who had visited him, and the result was what I have described. It struck me as an odd thing, that even then, considering how prone to superstition persons in his rank of life usually are, he did not seem to suspect any thing supernatural in the occurrence; and, on the contrary, was thoroughly persuaded that his visitant was a living person, who had got into the house by some hidden entrance.

On Sunday, on his return from his place of worship, he told me that, when the service was ended, and the congregation making their way slowly out, he saw the very woman in the crowd, and kept his eye upon her for several minutes, but such was the crush, that all his efforts to reach her were unavailing, and when he got into the open street she was gone. He was quite positive as to his having distinctly seen her, however, for several minutes, and scouted the possibility of any mistake as to identity; and fully impressed with the substantial and living reality of his visitant, he was very much provoked at her having escaped him. He made inquiries also in the neighbourhood, but could procure no information, nor hear of any other persons having seen any woman corresponding with his visitant.

The cook and the housemaid occupied a bed-room on the kitchen floor. It had whitewashed walls, and they were actually terrified by the appearance of the shadow of a woman passing and repassing across the side wall opposite to their beds. They suspected that this had been going on much longer than they were aware, for its presence was discovered by a sort of accident, its movements happening to take a direction in distinct contrariety to theirs.

This shadow always moved upon one particular wall, returning after short intervals, and causing them extreme terror. They placed the candle, as the most obvious specific, so close to the infested wall, that the flame all but touched it; and believed for some time that they had effectually got rid of this annoyance; but one night, notwithstanding this arrangement of the light, the shadow returned, passing and repassing, as heretofore, upon the same wall, although their only candle was burning within an inch of it, and it was obvious that no substance capable of casting such a shadow could have interposed; and, indeed, as they described it, the shadow seemed to have no sort of relation to the position of the light, and appeared, as I have said, in manifest defiance of the laws of optics.

I ought to mention that the housemaid was a particularly fearless sort of person, as well as a very honest one; and her companion, the cook, a scrupulously religious woman, and both agreed in every particular in their relation of what occurred.

Meanwhile, the nursery was not without its annoyances, though as yet of a comparatively trivial kind. Sometimes, at night, the handle of the door was turned hurriedly as if by a person trying to come in, and at others a knocking was made at it. These sounds occurred after the children had settled to sleep, and while the nurse still remained awake. Whenever she called to know "who is there," the sounds ceased; but several times, and particularly at first, she was under the impression that they were caused by her mistress, who had come to see the children, and thus impressed she had got up and opened the door, expecting to see her, but discovering only darkness, and receiving no answer to her inquiries.

With respect to this nurse, I must mention that I believe no more perfectly trustworthy servant was ever employed in her capacity; and, in addition to her integrity, she was remarkably gifted with sound common sense.

One morning, I think about three or four weeks after our arrival, I was sitting at the parlour window which looked to the front, when I saw the little iron door which admitted into the small garden that lay between the window where I was sitting and the public road, pushed open by a woman who so exactly answered the description given by Smith of the woman who had visited his room on the night of his arrival as instantaneously to impress me with the conviction that she must be the identical person. She was a square, short woman, dressed in soiled and tattered clothes, scarred and pitted with small-pox, and blind of an eye. She stepped hurriedly into the little enclosure, and peered from a distance of a few yards into the room where I was sitting. I felt that now was the moment to clear the matter up; but there was something stealthy in the manner and look of the woman which convinced me that I must not appear to notice her until her retreat was fairly cut off. Unfortunately, I was suffering from a lame foot, and could not reach the bell as quickly as I wished. I made all the haste I could, and rang violently to bring up the servant Smith. In the short interval that intervened, I observed the woman from the window, who having in a leisurely way, and with a kind of scrutiny, looked along the front windows of the house, passed quickly out again, closing the gate after her, and followed a lady who was walking along the footpath at a quick pace, as if with the intention of begging from her. The moment the man entered I told him--"the blind woman you described to me has this instant followed a lady in that direction, try to overtake her." He was, if possible, more eager than I in the chase, but returned in a short time after a vain pursuit, very hot, and utterly disappointed. And, thereafter, we saw her face no more.

All this time, and up to the period of our leaving the house, which was not for two or three months later, there occurred at intervals the only phenomenon in the entire series having any resemblance to what we hear described of "Spiritualism." This was a knocking, like a soft hammering with a wooden mallet, as it seemed in the timbers between the bedroom ceilings and the roof. It had this special peculiarity, that it was always rythmical, and, I think, invariably, the emphasis upon the last stroke. It would sound rapidly "one, two, three, _four_--one, two, three, _four_;" or "one, two, _three_--one, two, _three_," and sometimes "one, _two_--one, _two_," &c., and this, with intervals and resumptions, monotonously for hours at a time.

At first this caused my wife, who was a good deal confined to her bed, much annoyance; and we sent to our neighbours to inquire if any hammering or carpentering was going on in their houses but were informed that nothing of the sort was taking place. I have myself heard it frequently, always in the same inaccessible part of the house, and with the same monotonous emphasis. One odd thing about it was, that on my wife's calling out, as she used to do when it became more than usually troublesome, "stop that noise," it was invariably arrested for a longer or shorter time.

Of course none of these occurrences were ever mentioned in hearing of the children. They would have been, no doubt, like most children, greatly terrified had they heard any thing of the matter, and known that their elders were unable to account for what was passing; and their fears would have made them wretched and troublesome.

They used to play for some hours every day in the back garden--the house forming one end of this oblong inclosure, the stable and coach-house the other, and two parallel walls of considerable height the sides. Here, as it afforded a perfectly safe playground, they were frequently left quite to themselves; and in talking over their days' adventures, as children will, they happened to mention a woman, or rather the woman, for they had long grown familiar with her appearance, whom they used to see in the garden while they were at play. They assumed that she came in and went out at the stable door, but they never actually saw her enter or depart. They merely saw a figure--that of a very poor woman, soiled and ragged--near the stable wall, stooping over the ground, and apparently grubbing in the loose clay in search of something. She did not disturb, or appear to observe them; and they left her in undisturbed possession of her nook of ground. When seen it was always in the same spot, and similarly occupied; and the description they gave of her general appearance--for they never saw her face--corresponded with that of the one-eyed woman whom Smith, and subsequently as it seemed, I had seen.

The other man, James, who looked after a mare which I had purchased for the purpose of riding exercise, had, like every one else in the house, his little trouble to report, though it was not much. The stall in which, as the most comfortable, it was decided to place her, she peremptorily declined to enter. Though a very docile and gentle little animal, there was no getting her into it. She would snort and rear, and, in fact, do or suffer any thing rather than set her hoof in it. He was fain, therefore, to place her in another. And on several occasions he found her there, exhibiting all the equine symptoms of extreme fear. Like the rest of us, however, this man was not troubled in the particular case with any superstitious qualms. The mare had evidently been frightened; and he was puzzled to find out how, or by whom, for the stable was well-secured, and had, I am nearly certain, a lock-up yard outside.

One morning I was greeted with the intelligence that robbers had certainly got into the house in the night; and that one of them had actually been seen in the nursery. The witness, I found, was my eldest child, then, as I have said, about nine years of age. Having awoke in the night, and lain awake for some time in her bed, she heard the handle of the door turn, and a person whom she distinctly saw--for it was a light night, and the window-shutters unclosed--but whom she had never seen before, stepped in on tiptoe, and with an appearance of great caution. He was a rather small man, with a very red face; he wore an oddly cut frock coat, the collar of which stood up, and trousers, rough and wide, like those of a sailor, turned up at the ankles, and either short boots or clumsy shoes, covered with mud. This man listened beside the nurse's bed, which stood next the door, as if to satisfy himself that she was sleeping soundly; and having done so for some seconds, he began to move cautiously in a diagonal line, across the room to the chimney-piece, where he stood for a while, and so resumed his tiptoe walk, skirting the wall, until he reached a chest of drawers, some of which were open, and into which he looked, and began to rummage in a hurried way, as the child supposed, making search for something worth taking away. He then passed on to the window, where was a dressing-table, at which he also stopped, turning over the things upon it, and standing for some time at the window as if looking out, and then resuming his walk by the side wall opposite to that by which he had moved up to the window, he returned in the same way toward the nurse's bed, so as to reach it at the foot. With its side to the end wall, in which was the door, was placed the little bed in which lay my eldest child, who watched his proceedings with the extremest terror. As he drew near she instinctively moved herself in the bed, with her head and shoulders to the wall, drawing up her feet; but he passed by without appearing to observe, or, at least, to care for her presence. Immediately after the nurse turned in her bed as if about to waken; and when the child, who had drawn the clothes about her head, again ventured to peep out, the man was gone.

The child had no idea of her having seen any thing more formidable than a thief. With the prowling, cautious, and noiseless manner of proceeding common to such marauders, the air and movements of the man whom she had seen entirely corresponded. And on hearing her perfectly distinct and consistent account, I could myself arrive at no other conclusion than that a stranger had actually got into the house. I had, therefore, in the first instance, a most careful examination made to discover any traces of an entrance having been made by any window into the house. The doors had been found barred and locked as usual; but no sign of any thing of the sort was discernible. I then had the various articles--plate, wearing apparel, books, &c., counted; and after having conned over and reckoned up every thing, it became quite clear that nothing whatever had been removed from the house, nor was there the slightest indication of any thing having been so much as disturbed there. I must here state that this child was remarkably clear, intelligent, and observant; and that her description of the man, and of all that had occurred, was most exact, and as detailed as the want of perfect light rendered possible.

I felt assured that an entrance had actually been effected into the house, though for what purpose was not easily to be conjectured. The man, Smith, was equally confident upon this point; and his theory was that the object was simply to frighten us out of the house by making us believe it haunted; and he was more than ever anxious and on the alert to discover the conspirators. It often since appeared to me odd. Every year, indeed, more odd, as this cumulative case of the marvellous becomes to my mind more and more inexplicable--that underlying my sense of mystery and puzzle, was all along the quiet assumption that all these occurrences were one way or another referable to natural causes. I could not account for them, indeed, myself; but during the whole period I inhabited that house, I never once felt, though much alone, and often up very late at night, any of those tremors and thrills which every one has at times experienced when situation and the hour are favourable. Except the cook and housemaid, who were plagued with the shadow I mentioned crossing and recrossing upon the bedroom wall, we all, without exception, experienced the same strange sense of security, and regarded these phenomena rather with a perplexed sort of interest and curiosity, than with any more unpleasant sensations.

The knockings which I have mentioned at the nursery door, preceded generally by the sound of a step on the lobby, meanwhile continued. At that time (for my wife, like myself, was an invalid) two eminent physicians, who came out occasionally by rail, were attending us. These gentlemen were at first only amused, but ultimately interested, and very much puzzled by the occurrences which we described. One of them, at last, recommended that a candle should be kept burning upon the lobby. It was in fact a recurrence to an old woman's recipe against ghosts--of course it might be serviceable, too, against impostors; at all events, seeming, as I have said, very much interested and puzzled, he advised it, and it was tried. We fancied that it was successful; for there was an interval of quiet for, I think, three or four nights. But after that, the noises--the footsteps on the lobby--the knocking at the door, and the turning of the handle recommenced in full force, notwithstanding the light upon the table outside; and these particular phenomena became only more perplexing than ever.

The alarm of robbers and smugglers gradually subsided after a week or two; but we were again to hear news from the nursery. Our second little girl, then between seven and eight years of age, saw in the night time--she alone being awake--a young woman, with black, or very dark hair, which hung loose, and with a black cloak on, standing near the middle of the floor, opposite the hearthstone, and fronting the foot of her bed. She appeared quite unobservant of the children and nurse sleeping in the room. She was very pale, and looked, the child said, both "sorry and frightened," and with something very peculiar and terrible about her eyes, which made the child conclude that she was dead. She was looking, not at, but in the direction of the child's bed, and there was a dark streak across her throat, like a scar with blood upon it. This figure was not motionless; but once or twice turned slowly, and without appearing to be conscious of the presence of the child, or the other occupants of the room, like a person in vacancy or abstraction. There was on this occasion a night-light burning in the chamber; and the child saw, or thought she saw, all these particulars with the most perfect distinctness. She got her head under the bed-clothes; and although a good many years have passed since then, she cannot recall the spectacle without feelings of peculiar horror.

One day, when the children were playing in the back garden, I asked them to point out to me the spot where they were accustomed to see the woman who occasionally showed herself as I have described, near the stable wall. There was no division of opinion as to this precise point, which they indicated in the most distinct and confident way. I suggested that, perhaps, something might be hidden there in the ground; and advised them digging a hole there with their little spades, to try for it. Accordingly, to work they went, and by my return in the evening they had grubbed up a piece of a jawbone, with several teeth in it. The bone was very much decayed, and ready to crumble to pieces, but the teeth were quite sound. I could not tell whether they were human grinders; but I showed the fossil to one of the physicians I have mentioned, who came out the next evening, and he pronounced them human teeth. The same conclusion was come to a day or two later by the other medical man. It appears to me now, on reviewing the whole matter, almost unaccountable that, with such evidence before me, I should not have got in a labourer, and had the spot effectually dug and searched. I can only say, that so it was. I was quite satisfied of the moral truth of every word that had been related to me, and which I have here set down with scrupulous accuracy. But I experienced an apathy, for which neither then nor afterwards did I quite know how to account. I had a vague, but immovable impression that the whole affair was referable to natural agencies. It was not until some time after we had left the house, which, by-the-by, we afterwards found had had the reputation of being haunted before we had come to live in it, that on reconsideration I discovered the serious difficulty of accounting satisfactorily for all that had occurred upon ordinary principles. A great deal we might arbitrarily set down to imagination. But even in so doing there was, _in limine_, the oddity, not to say improbability, of so many different persons having nearly simultaneously suffered from different spectral and other illusions during the short period for which we had occupied that house, who never before, nor so far as we learned, afterwards were troubled by any fears or fancies of the sort. There were other things, too, not to be so accounted for. The odd knockings in the roof I frequently heard myself.

There were also, which I before forgot to mention, in the daytime, rappings at the doors of the sitting-rooms, which constantly deceived us; and it was not till our "come in" was unanswered, and the hall or passage outside the door was discovered to be empty, that we learned that whatever else caused them, human hands did not. All the persons who reported having seen the different persons or appearances here described by me, were just as confident of having literally and distinctly seen them, as

I was of having seen the hard-featured woman with the blind eye, so remarkably corresponding with Smith's description.

About a week after the discovery of the teeth, which were found, I think, about two feet under the ground, a friend, much advanced in years, and who remembered the town in which we had now taken up our abode, for a very long time, happened to pay us a visit. He good-humouredly pooh-poohed the whole thing; but at the same time was evidently curious about it. "We might construct a sort of story," said I (I am giving, of course, the substance and purport, not the exact words, of our dialogue), "and assign to each of the three figures who appeared their respective parts in some dreadful tragedy enacted in this house. The male figure represents the murderer; the ill-looking, one-eyed woman his accomplice, who, we will suppose, buried the body where she is now so often seen grubbing in the earth, and where the human teeth and jawbone have so lately been disinterred; and the young woman with dishevelled tresses, and black cloak, and the bloody scar across her throat, their victim. A difficulty, however, which I cannot get over, exists in the cheerfulness, the great publicity, and the evident very recent date of the house." "Why, as to that," said he, "the house is _not_ modern; it and those beside it formed an old government store, altered and fitted up recently as you see. I remember it well in my young days, fifty years ago, before the town had grown out in this direction, and a more entirely lonely spot, or one more fitted for the commission of a secret crime, could not have been imagined."

I have nothing to add, for very soon after this my physician pronounced a longer stay unnecessary for my health, and we took our departure for another place of abode. I may add, that although I have resided for considerable periods in many other houses, I never experienced any annoyances of a similar kind elsewhere; neither have I made (stupid dog! you will say), any inquiries respecting either the antecedents or subsequent history of the house in which we made so disturbed a sojourn. I was content with what I knew, and have here related as clearly as I could, and I think it a very pretty puzzle as it stands.

[Thus ends the statement, which we abandon to the ingenuity of our readers, having ourselves no satisfactory explanation to suggest; and simply repeating the assurance with which we prefaced it, namely, that we can vouch for the perfect good faith and the accuracy of the narrator.--E.D.U.M.]

# WICKED CAPTAIN WALSHAWE, OF WAULING (1869)

## CHAPTER I.

_Peg O'Neill Pays the Captain's Debts_

A very odd thing happened to my uncle, Mr. Watson, of Haddlestone; and to enable you to understand it, I must begin at the beginning.

In the year 1822, Mr. James Walshawe, more commonly known as Captain Walshawe, died at the age of eighty-one years. The Captain in his early days, and so long as health and strength permitted, was a scamp of the active, intriguing sort; and spent his days and nights in sowing his wild oats, of which he seemed to have an inexhaustible stock. The harvest of this tillage was plentifully interspersed with thorns, nettles, and thistles, which stung the husbandman unpleasantly, and did not enrich him.

Captain Walshawe was very well known in the neighborhood of Wauling, and very generally avoided there. A "captain" by courtesy, for he had never reached that rank in the army list. He had quitted the service in 1766, at the age of twenty-five; immediately previous to which period his debts had grown so troublesome, that he was induced to extricate himself by running away with and marrying an heiress.

Though not so wealthy quite as he had imagined, she proved a very comfortable investment for what remained of his shattered affections; and he lived and enjoyed himself very much in his old way, upon her income, getting into no end of scrapes and scandals, and a good deal of debt and money trouble.

When he married his wife, he was quartered in Ireland, at Clonmel, where was a nunnery, in which, as pensioner, resided Miss O'Neill, or as she was called in the country, Peg O'Neill--the heiress of whom I have spoken.

Her situation was the only ingredient of romance in the affair, for the young lady was decidedly plain, though good-humoured looking, with that style of features which is termed _potato_; and in figure she was a little too plump, and rather short. But she was impressible; and the handsome young English Lieutenant was too much for her monastic tendencies, and she eloped.

In England there are traditions of Irish fortune-hunters, and in Ireland of English. The fact is, it was the vagrant class of each country that chiefly visited the other in old times; and a handsome vagabond, whether at home or abroad, I suppose, made the most of his face, which was also his fortune.

At all events, he carried off the fair one from the sanctuary; and for some sufficient reason, I suppose, they took up their abode at Wauling, in Lancashire.

Here the gallant captain amused himself after his fashion, sometimes running up, of course on business, to London. I believe few wives have ever cried more in a given time than did that poor, dumpy, potato-faced heiress, who got over the nunnery garden wall, and jumped into the handsome Captain's arms, for love.

He spent her income, frightened her out of her wits with oaths and threats, and broke her heart.

Latterly she shut herself up pretty nearly altogether in her room. She had an old, rather grim, Irish servant-woman in attendance upon her. This domestic was tall, lean, and religious, and the Captain knew instinctively she hated him; and he hated her in return, often threatened to put her out of the house, and sometimes even to kick her out of the window. And whenever a wet day confined him to the house, or the stable, and he grew tired of smoking, he would begin to swear and curse at her for a _diddled_ old mischief-maker, that could never be easy, and was always troubling the house with her cursed stories, and so forth.

But years passed away, and old Molly Doyle remained still in her original position. Perhaps he thought that there must be somebody there, and that he was not, after all, very likely to change for the better.

# CHAPTER II

## _The Blessed Candle_

He tolerated another intrusion, too, and thought himself a paragon of patience and easy good nature for so doing. A Roman Catholic clergyman, in a long black frock, with a low standing collar, and a little white muslin fillet round his neck--tall, sallow, with blue chin, and dark steady eyes--used to glide up and down the stairs, and through the passages; and the Captain sometimes met him in one place and sometimes in another. But by a caprice incident to such tempers he treated this cleric exceptionally, and even with a surly sort of courtesy, though he grumbled about his visits behind his back.

I do not know that he had a great deal of moral courage, and the ecclesiastic looked severe and self-possessed; and somehow he thought he had no good opinion of him, and if a natural occasion were offered, might say extremely unpleasant things, and hard to be answered.

Well the time came at last, when poor Peg O'Neill--in an evil hour Mrs. James Walshawe--must cry, and quake, and pray her last. The doctor came from Penlynden, and was just as vague as usual, but more gloomy, and for about a week came and went oftener. The cleric in the long black frock was also daily there. And at last came that last sacrament in the gates of death, when the sinner is traversing those dread steps that never can be retraced; when the face is turned for ever from life, and we see a receding shape, and hear a voice already irrevocably in the land of spirits.
So the poor lady died, and some people said the Captain "felt it very much." I don't think he did. But he was not very well just then, and looked the part of mourner and penitent to admiration--being seedy and sick. He drank a great deal of brandy and water that night, and called in Farmer Dobbs, for want of better company, to drink with him; and told him all his grievances, and how happy he and "the poor lady up-stairs" might have been, had it not been for liars, and pick-thanks, and tale-bearers, and the like, who came between them--meaning Molly Doyle--whom, as he waxed eloquent over his liquor, he came at last to curse and rail at by name, with more than his

accustomed freedom. And he described his own natural character and amiability in such moving terms, that he wept maudlin tears of sensibility over his theme; and when Dobbs was gone, drank some more grog, and took to railing and cursing again by himself; and then mounted the stairs unsteadily, to see "what the devil Doyle and the other ---- old witches were about in poor Peg's room."

When he pushed open the door, he found some half-dozen crones, chiefly Irish, from the neighbouring town of Hackleton, sitting over tea and snuff, etc., with candles lighted round the corpse, which was arrayed in a strangely cut robe of brown serge. She had secretly belonged to some order--I think the Carmelite, but I am not certain--and wore the habit in her coffin.

"What the d---- are you doing with my wife?" cried the Captain, rather thickly. "How dare you dress her up in this ---- trumpery, you--you cheating old witch; and what's that candle doing in her hand?"

I think he was a little startled, for the spectacle was grisly enough. The dead lady was arrayed in this strange brown robe, and in her rigid fingers, as in a socket, with the large wooden beads and cross wound round it, burned a wax candle, shedding its white light over the sharp features of the corpse. Moll Doyle was not to be put down by the Captain, whom she hated, and accordingly, in her phrase, "he got as good as he gave." And the Captain's wrath waxed fiercer, and he chucked the wax taper from the dead hand, and was on the point of flinging it at the old serving-woman's head.

"The holy candle, you sinner!" cried she.
"I've a mind to make you eat it, you beast," cried the Captain.

But I think he had not known before what it was, for he subsided a little sulkily, and he stuffed his hand with the candle (quite extinct by this time) into his pocket, and said he--

"You know devilish well you had no business going on with y-y-your d---- _witch_-craft about my poor wife, without my leave--you do--and you'll please take off that d---- brown pinafore, and get her decently into her coffin, and I'll pitch your devil's waxlight into the sink."

And the Captain stalked out of the room.

"An' now her poor sowl's in prison, you wretch, be the mains o' ye; an' may yer own be shut into the wick o' that same candle, till it's burned out, ye savage."

"I'd have you ducked for a witch, for two-pence," roared the Captain up the staircase, with his hand on the banisters, standing on the lobby. But the door of the chamber of death clapped angrily, and he went down to the parlour, where he examined the holy candle for a while, with a tipsy gravity, and then with something of that reverential feeling for the symbolic, which is not uncommon in rakes and scamps, he thoughtfully locked it up in a press, where were accumulated all sorts of obsolete rubbish--soiled packs of cards, disused tobacco pipes, broken powder flasks, his military sword, and a dusky bundle of the "Flash Songster," and other questionable literature.

He did not trouble the dead lady's room any more. Being a volatile man it is probable that more cheerful plans and occupations began to entertain his fancy.

## CHAPTER III

### _My Uncle Watson Visits Wauling_

So the poor lady was buried decently, and Captain Walshawe reigned alone for many years at Wauling. He was too shrewd and too experienced by this time to run violently down the steep hill that leads to ruin. So there was a method in his madness; and after a widowed career of more than forty years, he, too, died at last with some guineas in his purse.

Forty years and upwards is a great _edax rerum_, and a wonderful chemical power. It acted forcibly upon the gay Captain Walshawe. Gout supervened, and was no more conducive to temper than to enjoyment, and made his elegant hands lumpy at all the small joints, and turned them slowly into crippled claws. He grew stout when his exercise was interfered with, and ultimately almost corpulent. He suffered from what Mr. Holloway calls "bad legs," and was wheeled about in a great leathern-backed chair, and his infirmities went on accumulating with his years.

I am sorry to say, I never heard that he repented, or turned his thoughts seriously to the future. On the contrary, his talk grew fouler, and his fun ran upon his favourite sins, and his temper waxed more truculent. But he did not sink into dotage. Considering his bodily infirmities, his energies and his malignities, which were many and active, were marvellously little abated by time. So he went on to the close. When his temper was stirred, he cursed and swore in a way that made decent people tremble. It was a word and a blow with him; the latter, luckily, not very sure now. But he would seize his crutch and make a swoop or a pound at the offender, or shy his medicine-bottle, or his tumbler, at his head.

It was a peculiarity of Captain Walshawe, that he, by this time, hated nearly everybody. My uncle, Mr. Watson, of Haddlestone, was cousin to the Captain, and his heir-at-law. But my uncle had lent him money on mortgage of his estates, and there had been a treaty to sell, and terms and a price were agreed upon, in "articles" which the lawyers said were still in force.

I think the ill-conditioned Captain bore him a grudge for being richer than he, and would have liked to do him an ill turn. But it did not lie in his way; at least while he was living.

My uncle Watson was a Methodist, and what they call a "classleader"; and, on the whole, a very good man. He was now near fifty--grave, as beseemed his profession--somewhat dry--and a little severe, perhaps--but a just man.

A letter from the Penlynden doctor reached him at Haddlestone, announcing the death of the wicked old Captain; and suggesting his attendance at the funeral, and the expediency of his being on the spot to look after things at Wauling. The reasonableness of this striking my good uncle, he made his journey to the old house in Lancashire incontinently, and reached it in time for the funeral.

My uncle, whose traditions of the Captain were derived from his mother, who remembered him in his slim, handsome youth--in shorts, cocked-hat and lace, was amazed at the bulk of the coffin which contained his mortal remains; but the lid being already screwed down, he did not see the face of the bloated old sinner.

## CHAPTER IV

### _In the Parlour_

What I relate, I had from the lips of my uncle, who was a truthful man, and not prone to fancies.

The day turning out awfully rainy and tempestuous, he persuaded the doctor and the attorney to remain for the night at Wauling.

There was no will--the attorney was sure of that; for the Captain's enmities were perpetually shifting, and he could never quite make up his mind, as to how best to give effect to a malignity whose direction was constantly being modified. He had had instructions for drawing a will a dozen times over. But the process had always been arrested by the intending testator.

Search being made, no will was found. The papers, indeed, were all right, with one important exception: the leases were nowhere to be seen. There were special circumstances connected with several of the principal tenancies on the estate--unnecessary here to detail--which rendered the loss of these documents one of very serious moment, and even of very obvious danger.

My uncle, therefore, searched strenuously. The attorney was at his elbow, and the doctor helped with a suggestion now and then. The old serving-man seemed an honest deaf creature, and really knew nothing.

My uncle Watson was very much perturbed. He fancied--but this possibly was only fancy--that he had detected for a moment a queer look in the attorney's face; and from that instant it became fixed in his mind that he knew all about the leases. Mr. Watson expounded that evening in the parlour to the doctor, the attorney, and the deaf servant.

Ananias and Sapphira figured in the foreground; and the awful nature of fraud and theft, of tampering in anywise with the plain rule of honesty in matters pertaining to estates, etc., were pointedly dwelt upon; and then came a long and strenuous prayer, in which he entreated with fervour and aplomb that the hard heart of the sinner who had abstracted the leases might be softened or broken in such a way as to lead to their restitution; or that, if he continued reserved and contumacious, it might at least be the will of Heaven to bring him to public justice and the documents to light. The fact is, that he was praying all this time at the attorney.

When these religious exercises were over, the visitors retired to their rooms, and my Uncle Watson wrote two or three pressing letters by the fire. When his task was done, it had grown late; the candles were flaring in their sockets, and all in bed, and, I suppose, asleep, but he.

The fire was nearly out, he chilly, and the flame of the candles throbbing strangely in their sockets, shed alternate glare and shadow round the old wainscoted room and its quaint furniture. Outside were all the wild thunder and piping of the storm; and the rattling of distant windows sounded through the passages, and down the stairs, like angry people astir in the house.

My Uncle Watson belonged to a sect who by no means rejected the supernatural, and whose founder, on the contrary, has sanctioned ghosts in the most emphatic way. He was glad therefore to remember, that in prosecuting his search that day, he had seen some six inches of wax candle in the press in the parlour; for he had no fancy to be overtaken by darkness in his present situation. He had no time to lose; and taking the bunch of keys--of which he was now master--he soon fitted the lock, and secured the candle--a treasure in his circumstances; and lighting it, he stuffed it into the socket of one of the expiring candles, and extinguishing the other, he looked round the room in the steady light reassured. At the same moment, an unusual violent gust of the storm blew a handful of gravel against the parlour window, with a sharp rattle that startled him in the midst of the roar and hubbub; and the flame of the candle itself was agitated by the air.

# CHAPTER V

## _The Bed-Chamber_

My uncle walked up to bed, guarding his candle with his hand, for the lobby windows were rattling furiously, and he disliked the idea of being left in the dark more than ever.

His bedroom was comfortable, though old-fashioned. He shut and bolted the door. There was a tall looking-glass opposite the foot of his four-poster, on the dressing-table between the windows. He tried to make the curtains meet, but they would not draw; and like many a gentleman in a like perplexity, he did not possess a pin, nor was there one in the huge pincushion beneath the glass.
He turned the face of the mirror away therefore, so that its back was presented to the bed, pulled the curtains together, and placed a chair against them, to prevent their falling open again. There was a good fire, and a reinforcement of round coal and wood inside the fender. So he piled it up to ensure a cheerful blaze through the night, and placing a little black mahogany table, with the legs of a satyr, beside the bed, and his candle upon it, he got between the sheets, and laid his red nightcapped head upon his pillow, and disposed himself to sleep.

The first thing that made him uncomfortable was a sound at the foot of his bed, quite distinct in a momentary lull of the storm. It was only the gentle rustle and rush of the curtains, which fell open again; and as his eyes opened, he saw them resuming their perpendicular dependence, and sat up in his bed almost expecting to see something uncanny in the aperture.

There was nothing, however, but the dressing-table, and other dark furniture, and the window-curtains faintly undulating in the violence of the storm. He did not care to get up, therefore--the fire being bright and cheery--to replace the curtains by a chair, in the position in which he had left them, anticipating possibly a new recurrence of the relapse which had startled him from his incipient doze.

So he got to sleep in a little while again, but he was disturbed by a sound, as he fancied, at the table on which stood the candle. He could not say what it was, only that he wakened with a start, and lying so in some amaze, he did distinctly hear a sound which startled him a good deal, though there was nothing necessarily supernatural in it. He described it as resembling what would occur if you fancied a thinnish table-leaf, with a convex warp in it, depressed the reverse way, and suddenly with a spring recovering its natural convexity. It was a loud, sudden thump, which made the heavy candlestick jump, and there was an end, except that my uncle did not get again into a doze for ten minutes at least.

The next time he awoke, it was in that odd, serene way that sometimes occurs. We open our eyes, we know not why, quite placidly, and are on the instant wide awake. He had had a nap of some duration this time, for his candle-flame was fluttering and flaring, _in articulo_, in the silver socket. But the fire was still bright and cheery; so he popped the extinguisher on the socket, and almost at the same time there came a tap at his door, and a sort of crescendo "hush-sh-sh!" Once more my uncle was sitting up, scared and perturbed, in his bed. He recollected, however, that he had bolted his door; and such inveterate materialists are we in the midst of our spiritualism, that this reassured him, and he breathed a deep sigh, and began to grow tranquil. But after a rest of a minute or two, there came a louder and sharper knock at his door; so that instinctively he called out, "Who's there?" in a loud, stern key. There was no sort of response, however. The nervous effect of the start subsided; and I think my uncle must have remembered how constantly, especially on a stormy night, these creaks or cracks which simulate all manner of goblin noises, make themselves naturally audible.

## CHAPTER VI

### _The Extinguisher Is Lifted_

After a while, then, he lay down with his back turned toward that side of the bed at which was the door, and his face toward the table on which stood the massive old candlestick, capped with its extinguisher, and in that position he closed his eyes. But sleep would not revisit them. All kinds of queer fancies began to trouble him--some of them I remember.

He felt the point of a finger, he averred, pressed most distinctly on the tip of his great toe, as if a living hand were between his sheets, and making a sort of signal of attention or silence. Then again he felt something as large as a rat make a sudden bounce in the middle of his bolster, just under his head. Then a voice said "Oh!" very gently, close at the back of his head. All these things he felt certain of, and yet investigation led to nothing. He felt odd little cramps stealing now and then about him; and then, on a sudden, the middle finger of his right hand was plucked backwards, with a light playful jerk that frightened him awfully.
Meanwhile the storm kept singing, and howling, and ha-ha-hooing hoarsely among the limbs of the old trees and the chimney-pots; and my Uncle Watson, although he prayed and meditated as was his wont when he lay awake, felt his heart throb excitedly, and sometimes thought he was beset with evil spirits, and at others that he was in the early stage of a fever.

He resolutely kept his eyes closed, however, and, like St. Paul's shipwrecked companions, wished for the day. At last another little doze seems to have stolen upon his senses, for he awoke quietly and completely as before--opening his eyes all at once, and seeing everything as if he had not slept for a moment.

The fire was still blazing redly--nothing uncertain in the light--the massive silver candlestick, topped with its tall extinguisher, stood on the centre of the black mahogany table as before; and, looking by what seemed a sort of accident to the apex of this, he beheld something which made him quite misdoubt the evidence of his eyes.

He saw the extinguisher lifted by a tiny hand, from beneath, and a small human face, no bigger than a thumb-nail, with nicely proportioned features, peep from beneath it. In this Lilliputian countenance was such a ghastly consternation as horrified my uncle unspeakably. Out came a little foot then and there, and a pair of wee legs, in short silk stockings and buckled shoes, then the rest of the figure; and, with the arms holding about the socket, the little legs stretched and stretched, hanging about the stem of the candlestick till the feet reached the base, and so down the satyr-like leg of the table, till they reached the floor, extending elastically, and strangely enlarging in all proportions as they approached the ground, where the feet and buckles were those of a well-shaped, full grown man, and the figure tapering upward until it dwindled to its original fairy dimensions at the top, like an object seen in some strangely curved mirror.

Standing upon the floor he expanded, my amazed uncle could not tell how, into his proper proportions; and stood pretty nearly in profile at the bedside, a handsome and elegantly shaped young man, in a bygone military costume, with a small laced, three-cocked hat and plume on his head, but looking like a man going to be hanged--in unspeakable despair.

He stepped lightly to the hearth, and turned for a few seconds very dejectedly with his back toward the bed and the mantel-piece, and he saw the hilt of his rapier glittering in the firelight; and then walking across the room he placed himself at the dressing-table, visible through the divided curtains at the foot of the bed. The fire was blazing still so brightly that my uncle saw him as distinctly as if half a dozen candles were burning.

## CHAPTER VII

### _The Visitation Culminates_

The looking-glass was an old-fashioned piece of furniture, and had a drawer beneath it. My uncle had searched it carefully for the papers in the daytime; but the silent figure pulled the drawer quite out, pressed a spring at the side, disclosing a false receptable behind it, and from this he drew a parcel of papers tied together with pink tape.

All this time my uncle was staring at him in a horrified state, neither winking nor breathing, and the apparition had not once given the smallest intimation of consciousness that a living person was in the same room. But now, for the first time, it turned its livid stare full upon my uncle with a hateful smile of significance, lifting up the little parcel of papers between his slender finger and thumb. Then he made a long, cunning wink at him, and seemed to blow out one of his cheeks in a burlesque grimace, which, but for the horrific circumstances, would have been ludicrous. My uncle could not tell whether this was really an intentional distortion or only one of those horrid ripples and deflections which were constantly disturbing the proportions of the figure, as if it were seen through some unequal and perverting medium.

The figure now approached the bed, seeming to grow exhausted and malignant as it did so. My uncle's terror nearly culminated at this point, for he believed it was drawing near him with an evil purpose. But it was not so; for the soldier, over whom twenty years seemed to have passed in his brief transit to the dressing-table and back again, threw himself into a great high-backed arm-chair of stuffed leather at the far side of the fire, and placed his heels on the fender. His feet and legs seemed indistinctly to swell, and swathings showed themselves round them, and they grew into something enormous, and the upper figure swayed and shaped itself into corresponding proportions, a great mass of corpulence, with a cadaverous and malignant face, and the furrows of a great old age, and colourless glassy eyes; and with these changes, which came indefinitely but rapidly as those of a sunset cloud, the fine regimentals faded away, and a loose, gray, woollen drapery, somehow, was there in its stead; and all seemed to be stained and rotten, for swarms of worms seemed creeping in and out, while the figure grew paler and paler, till my uncle, who liked his pipe, and employed the simile naturally, said the whole effigy grew to the colour of tobacco ashes, and the clusters of worms into little wriggling knots of sparks such as we see running over the residuum of a burnt sheet of paper. And so with the strong draught caused by the fire, and the current of air from the window, which was rattling in the storm, the feet seemed to be drawn into the fire-place, and the whole figure, light as ashes, floated away with them, and disappeared with a whisk up the capacious old chimney.

It seemed to my uncle that the fire suddenly darkened and the air grew icy cold, and there came an awful roar and riot of tempest, which shook the old house from top to base, and sounded like the yelling of a blood-thirsty mob on receiving a new and long-expected victim.

Good Uncle Watson used to say, "I have been in many situations of fear and danger in the course of my life, but never did I pray with so much agony before or since; for then, as now, it was clear beyond a cavil that I had actually beheld the phantom of an evil spirit."

## CONCLUSION

Now there are two curious circumstances to be observed in this relation of my uncle's, who was, as I have said, a perfectly veracious man.

First--The wax candle which he took from the press in the parlour and burnt at his bedside on that horrible night was unquestionably, according to the testimony of the old deaf servant, who had been fifty years at Wauling, that identical piece of "holy candle" which had stood in the fingers of the poor lady's corpse, and concerning which the old Irish crone, long since dead, had delivered the curious curse I have mentioned against the Captain.

Secondly--Behind the drawer under the looking-glass, he did actually discover a second but secret drawer, in which were concealed the identical papers which he had suspected the attorney of having made away with. There were circumstances, too, afterwards disclosed which convinced my uncle that the old man had deposited them there preparatory to burning them, which he had nearly made up his mind to do.

Now, a very remarkable ingredient in this tale of my Uncle Watson was this, that so far as my father, who had never seen Captain Walshawe in the course of his life, could gather, the phantom had exhibited a horrible and grotesque, but unmistakeable resemblance to that defunct scamp in the various stages of his long life.

Wauling was sold in the year 1837, and the old house shortly after pulled down, and a new one built nearer to the river. I often wonder whether it was rumoured to be haunted, and, if so, what stories were current about it. It was a commodious and stanch old house, and withal rather handsome; and its demolition was certainly suspicious.

# THE CHILD THAT WENT WITH THE FAIRIES (1870)

Eastward of the old city of Limerick, about ten Irish miles under the range of mountains known as the Slieveelim hills, famous as having afforded Sarsfield a shelter among their rocks and hollows, when he crossed them in his gallant descent upon the cannon and ammunition of King William, on its way to the beleaguering army, there runs a very old and narrow road. It connects the Limerick road to Tipperary with the old road from Limerick to Dublin, and runs by bog and pasture, hill and hollow, straw-thatched village, and roofless castle, not far from twenty miles.

Skirting the healthy mountains of which I have spoken, at one part it becomes singularly lonely. For more than three Irish miles it traverses a deserted country. A wide, black bog, level as a lake, skirted with copse, spreads at the left, as you journey northward, and the long and irregular line of mountain rises at the right, clothed in heath, broken with lines of grey rock that resemble the bold and irregular outlines of fortifications, and riven with many a gully, expanding here and there into rocky and wooded glens, which open as they approach the road.

A scanty pasturage, on which browsed a few scattered sheep or kine, skirts this solitary road for some miles, and under shelter of a hillock, and of two or three great ash-trees, stood, not many years ago, the little thatched cabin of a widow named Mary Ryan.

Poor was this widow in a land of poverty. The thatch had acquired the grey tint and sunken outlines, that show how the alternations of rain and sun have told upon that perishable shelter.

But whatever other dangers threatened, there was one well provided against by the care of other times. Round the cabin stood half a dozen mountain ashes, as the rowans, inimical to witches, are there called. On the worn planks of the door were nailed two horse-shoes, and over the lintel and spreading along the thatch, grew, luxuriant, patches of that ancient cure for many maladies, and prophylactic against the machinations of the evil one, the house-leek. Descending into the doorway, in the _chiaroscuro_ of the interior, when your eye grew sufficiently accustomed to that dim light, you might discover, hanging at the head of the widow's wooden-roofed bed, her beads and a phial of holy water.

Here certainly were defences and bulwarks against the intrusion of that unearthly and evil power, of whose vicinity this solitary family were constantly reminded by the outline of Lisnavoura, that lonely hillhaunt of the "Good people," as the fairies are called euphemistically, whose strangely dome-like summit rose not half a mile away, looking like an outwork of the long line of mountain that sweeps by it.

It was at the fall of the leaf, and an autumnal sunset threw the lengthening shadow of haunted Lisnavoura, close in front of the solitary little cabin, over the undulating slopes and sides of Slieveelim. The birds were singing among the branches in the thinning leaves of the melancholy ash-trees that grew at the roadside in front of the door. The widow's three younger children were playing on the road, and their voices mingled with the evening song of the birds. Their elder sister, Nell, was "within in the house," as their phrase is, seeing after the boiling of the potatoes for supper.

Their mother had gone down to the bog, to carry up a hamper of turf on her back. It is, or was at least, a charitable custom--and if not disused, long may it continue--for the wealthier people when cutting their turf and stacking it in the bog, to make a smaller stack for the behoof of the poor, who were welcome to take from it so long as it lasted, and thus the potato pot was kept boiling, and hearth warm that would have been cold enough but for that good-natured bounty, through wintry months.

Moll Ryan trudged up the steep "bohereen" whose banks were overgrown with thorn and brambles, and stooping under her burden, re-entered her door, where her dark-haired daughter Nell met her with a welcome, and relieved her of her hamper.

Moll Ryan looked round with a sigh of relief, and drying her forehead, uttered the Munster ejaculation:

"Eiah, wisha! It's tired I am with it, God bless it. And where's the craythurs, Nell?"

"Playin' out on the road, mother; didn't ye see them and you comin' up?"

"No; there was no one before me on the road," she said, uneasily; "not a soul, Nell; and why didn't ye keep an eye on them?"

"Well, they're in the haggard, playin' there, or round by the back o' the house. Will I call them in?"

"Do so, good girl, in the name o' God. The hens is comin' home, see, and the sun was just down over Knockdoulah, an' I comin' up."

So out ran tall, dark-haired Nell, and standing on the road, looked up and down it; but not a sign of her two little brothers, Con and Bill, or her little sister, Peg, could she see. She called them; but no answer came from the little haggard, fenced with straggling bushes. She listened, but the sound of their voices was missing. Over the stile, and behind the house she ran--but there all was silent and deserted.

She looked down toward the bog, as far as she could see; but they did not appear. Again she listened--but in vain. At first she had felt angry, but now a different feeling overcame her, and she grew pale. With an undefined boding she looked toward the heathy boss of Lisnavoura, now darkening into the deepest purple against the flaming sky of sunset.

Again she listened with a sinking heart, and heard nothing but the farewell twitter and whistle of the birds in the bushes around. How many stories had she listened to by the winter hearth, of children stolen by the fairies, at nightfall, in lonely places! With this fear she knew her mother was haunted.

No one in the country round gathered her little flock about her so early as this frightened widow, and no door "in the seven parishes" was barred so early.

Sufficiently fearful, as all young people in that part of the world are of such dreaded and subtle agents, Nell was even more than usually afraid of them, for her terrors were infected and redoubled by her mother's. She was looking towards Lisnavoura in a trance of fear, and crossed herself again and again, and whispered prayer after prayer. She was interrupted by her mother's voice on the road calling her loudly. She answered, and ran round to the front of the cabin, where she found her standing.

"And where in the world's the craythurs--did ye see sight o' them anywhere?" cried Mrs. Ryan, as the girl came over the stile.

"Arrah! mother, 'tis only what they're run down the road a bit. We'll see them this minute coming back. It's like goats they are, climbin' here and runnin' there; an' if I had them here, in my hand, maybe I wouldn't give them a hiding all round."

"May the Lord forgive you, Nell! the childhers gone. They're took, and not a soul near us, and Father Tom three miles away! And what'll I do, or who's to help us this night? Oh, wirristhru, wirristhru! The craythurs is gone!"

"Whisht, mother, be aisy: don't ye see them comin' up?"

And then she shouted in menacing accents, waving her arm, and beckoning the children, who were seen approaching on the road, which some little way off made a slight dip, which had concealed them. They were approaching from the westward, and from the direction of the dreaded hill of Lisnavoura.

But there were only two of the children, and one of them, the little girl, was crying. Their mother and sister hurried forward to meet them, more alarmed than ever.

"Where is Billy--where is he?" cried the mother, nearly breathless, so soon as she was within hearing.

"He's gone--they took him away; but they said he'll come back again," answered little Con, with the dark brown hair.

"He's gone away with the grand ladies," blubbered the little girl.

"What ladies--where? Oh, Leum, asthora! My darlin', are you gone away at last? Where is he? Who took him? What ladies are you talkin' about?

What way did he go?" she cried in distraction.

"I couldn't see where he went, mother; 'twas like as if he was going to Lisnavoura."

With a wild exclamation the distracted woman ran on towards the hill alone, clapping her hands, and crying aloud the name of her lost child.

Scared and horrified, Nell, not daring to follow, gazed after her, and burst into tears; and the other children raised high their lamentations in shrill rivalry.

Twilight was deepening. It was long past the time when they were usually barred securely within their habitation. Nell led the younger children into the cabin, and made them sit down by the turf fire, while she stood in the open door, watching in great fear for the return of her mother.

After a long while they did see their mother return. She came in and sat down by the fire, and cried as if her heart would break.

"Will I bar the doore, mother?" asked Nell.

"Ay, do--didn't I lose enough, this night, without lavin' the doore open, for more o' yez to go; but first take an' sprinkle a dust o' the holy waters over ye, acuishla, and bring it here till I throw a taste iv it over myself and the craythurs; an' I wondher, Nell, you'd forget to do the like yourself, lettin' the craythurs out so near nightfall. Come here and sit on my knees, asthora, come to me, mavourneen, and hould me fast, in the name o' God, and I'll hould you fast that none can take yez from me, and tell me all about it, and what it was--the Lord between us and harm--an' how it happened, and who was in it."

And the door being barred, the two children, sometimes speaking together, often interrupting one another, often interrupted by their mother, managed to tell this strange story, which I had better relate connectedly and in my own language.

The Widow Ryan's three children were playing, as I have said, upon the narrow old road in front of her door. Little Bill or Leum, about five years old, with golden hair and large blue eyes, was a very pretty boy, with all the clear tints of healthy childhood, and that gaze of earnest simplicity which belongs not to town children of the same age. His little sister Peg, about a year older, and his brother Con, a little more than a year elder than she, made up the little group.

Under the great old ash-trees, whose last leaves were falling at their feet, in the light of an October sunset, they were playing with the hilarity and eagerness of rustic children, clamouring together, and their faces were turned toward the west and storied hill of Lisnavoura.

Suddenly a startling voice with a screech called to them from behind, ordering them to get out of the way, and turning, they saw a sight, such as they never beheld before. It was a carriage drawn by four horses that were pawing and snorting, in impatience, as it just pulled up. The children were almost under their feet, and scrambled to the side of the road next their own door.

This carriage and all its appointments were old-fashioned and gorgeous, and presented to the children, who had never seen anything finer than a turf car, and once, an old chaise that passed that way from Killaloe, a spectacle perfectly dazzling.

Here was antique splendour. The harness and trappings were scarlet, and blazing with gold. The horses were huge, and snow white, with great manes, that as they tossed and shook them in the air, seemed to stream and float sometimes longer and sometimes shorter, like so much smoke--their tails were long, and tied up in bows of broad scarlet and gold ribbon. The coach itself was glowing with colours, gilded and emblazoned. There were footmen in gay liveries, and three-cocked hats, like the coachman's; but he had a great wig, like a judge's, and their hair was frizzed out and powdered, and a long thick "pigtail," with a bow to it, hung down the back of each.

All these servants were diminutive, and ludicrously out of proportion with the enormous horses of the equipage, and had sharp, sallow features, and small, restless fiery eyes, and faces of cunning and malice that chilled the children. The little coachman was scowling and showing his white fangs under his cocked hat, and his little blazing beads of eyes were quivering with fury in their sockets as he whirled his whip round and round over their heads, till the lash of it looked like a streak of fire in the evening sun, and sounded like the cry of a legion of "fillapoueeks" in the air.

"Stop the princess on the highway!" cried the coachman, in a piercing treble.

"Stop the princess on the highway!" piped each footman in turn, scowling over his shoulder down on the children, and grinding his keen teeth.

The children were so frightened they could only gape and turn white in their panic. But a very sweet voice from the open window of the carriage reassured them, and arrested the attack of the lackeys.

A beautiful and "very grand-looking" lady was smiling from it on them, and they all felt pleased in the strange light of that smile.

"The boy with the golden hair, I think," said the lady, bending her large and wonderfully clear eyes on little Leum.

The upper sides of the carriage were chiefly of glass, so that the children could see another woman inside, whom they did not like so well.

This was a black woman, with a wonderfully long neck, hung round with many strings of large variously-coloured beads, and on her head was a sort of turban of silk striped with all the colours of the rainbow, and fixed in it was a golden star.

This black woman had a face as thin almost as a death's-head, with high cheekbones, and great goggle eyes, the whites of which, as well as her wide range of teeth, showed in brilliant contrast with her skin, as she looked over the beautiful lady's shoulder, and whispered something in her ear.

"Yes; the boy with the golden hair, I think," repeated the lady.

And her voice sounded sweet as a silver bell in the children's ears, and her smile beguiled them like the light of an enchanted lamp, as she leaned from the window with a look of ineffable fondness on the golden-haired boy, with the large blue eyes; insomuch that little Billy, looking up, smiled in return with a wondering fondness, and when she stooped down, and stretched her jewelled arms towards him, he stretched his little hands up, and how they touched the other children did not know; but, saying, "Come and give me a kiss, my darling," she raised him, and he seemed to ascend in her small fingers as lightly as a feather, and she held him in her lap and covered him with kisses.

Nothing daunted, the other children would have been only too happy to change places with their favoured little brother. There was only one thing that was unpleasant, and a little frightened them, and that was the black woman, who stood and stretched forward, in the carriage as before. She gathered a rich silk and gold handkerchief that was in her fingers up to her lips, and seemed to thrust ever so much of it, fold after fold, into her capacious mouth, as they thought to smother her laughter, with which she seemed convulsed, for she was shaking and quivering, as it seemed, with suppressed merriment; but her eyes, which remained uncovered, looked angrier than they had ever seen eyes look before.

But the lady was so beautiful they looked on her instead, and she continued to caress and kiss the little boy on her knee; and smiling at the other children she held up a large russet apple in her fingers, and the carriage began to move slowly on, and with a nod inviting them to take the fruit, she dropped it on the road from the window; it rolled some way beside the wheels, they following, and then she dropped another, and then another, and so on. And the same thing happened to all; for just as either of the children who ran beside had caught the rolling apple, somehow it slipt into a hole or ran into a ditch, and looking up they saw the lady drop another from the window, and so the chase was taken up and continued till they got, hardly knowing how far they had gone, to the old cross-road that leads to Owney. It seemed that there the horses' hoofs and carriage wheels rolled up a wonderful dust, which being caught in one of those eddies that whirl the dust up into a column, on the calmest day, enveloped the children for a moment, and passed whirling on towards Lisnavoura, the carriage, as they fancied, driving in the centre of it; but suddenly it subsided, the straws and leaves floated to the ground, the dust dissipated itself, but the white horses and the lackeys, the gilded carriage, the lady and their little golden-haired brother were gone.

At the same moment suddenly the upper rim of the clear setting sun disappeared behind the hill of Knockdoula, and it was twilight. Each child felt the transition like a shock--and the sight of the rounded summit of Lisnavoura, now closely overhanging them, struck them with a new fear.

They screamed their brother's name after him, but their cries were lost in the vacant air. At the same time they thought they heard a hollow voice say, close to them, "Go home."

Looking round and seeing no one, they were scared, and hand in hand--the little girl crying wildly, and the boy white as ashes, from fear, they trotted homeward, at their best speed, to tell, as we have seen, their strange story.

Molly Ryan never more saw her darling. But something of the lost little boy was seen by his former playmates.
Sometimes when their mother was away earning a trifle at haymaking, and Nelly washing the potatoes for their dinner, or "beatling" clothes in the little stream that flows in the hollow close by, they saw the pretty face of little Billy peeping in archly at the door, and smiling silently at them, and as they ran to embrace him, with cries of delight, he drew back, still smiling archly, and when they got out into the open day, he was gone, and they could see no trace of him anywhere.

This happened often, with slight variations in the circumstances of the visit. Sometimes he would peep for a longer time, sometimes for a shorter time, sometimes his little hand would come in, and, with bended finger, beckon them to follow; but always he was smiling with the same arch look and wary silence--and always he was gone when they reached the door. Gradually these visits grew less and less frequent, and in about eight months they ceased altogether, and little Billy, irretrievably lost, took rank in their memories with the dead.

One wintry morning, nearly a year and a half after his disappearance, their mother having set out for Limerick soon after cockcrow, to sell some fowls at the market, the little girl, lying by the side of her elder sister, who was fast asleep, just at the grey of the morning heard the latch lifted softly, and saw little Billy enter and close the door gently after him. There was light enough to see that he was barefoot and ragged, and looked pale and famished. He went straight to the fire, and cowered over the turf embers, and rubbed his hands slowly, and seemed to shiver as he gathered the smouldering turf together.

The little girl clutched her sister in terror and whispered, "Waken, Nelly, waken; here's Billy come back!"

Nelly slept soundly on, but the little boy, whose hands were extended close over the coals, turned and looked toward the bed, it seemed to her, in fear, and she saw the glare of the embers reflected on his thin cheek as he turned toward her. He rose and went, on tiptoe, quickly to the door, in silence, and let himself out as softly as he had come in.

After that, the little boy was never seen any more by any one of his kindred.

"Fairy doctors," as the dealers in the preternatural, who in such cases were called in, are termed, did all that in them lay--but in vain. Father Tom came down, and tried what holier rites could do, but equally without result. So little Billy was dead to mother, brother, and sisters; but no grave received him. Others whom affection cherished, lay in holy ground, in the old churchyard of Abington, with headstone to mark the spot over which the survivor might kneel and say a kind prayer for the peace of the departed soul. But there was no landmark to show where little Billy was hidden from their loving eyes, unless it was in the old hill of Lisnavoura, that cast its long shadow at sunset before the cabin-door; or that, white and filmy in the moonlight, in later years, would occupy his brother's gaze as he returned from fair or market, and draw from him a sigh and a prayer for the little brother he had lost so long ago, and was never to see again.

# THE VISION OF TOM CHUFF
## (1870)

At the edge of melancholy Catstean Moor, in the north of England, with half-a-dozen ancient poplar-trees with rugged and hoary stems around, one smashed across the middle by a flash of lightning thirty summers before, and all by their great height dwarfing the abode near which they stand, there squats a rude stone house, with a thick chimney, a kitchen and bedroom on the ground-floor, and a loft, accessible by a ladder, under the shingle roof, divided into two rooms.

Its owner was a man of ill repute. Tom Chuff was his name. A shock-headed, broad-shouldered, powerful man, though somewhat short, with lowering brows and a sullen eye. He was a poacher, and hardly made an ostensible pretence of earning his bread by any honest industry. He was a drunkard. He beat his wife, and led his children a life of terror and lamentation, when he was at home. It was a blessing to his frightened little family when he absented himself, as he sometimes did, for a week or more together.

On the night I speak of he knocked at the door with his cudgel at about eight o'clock. It was winter, and the night was very dark. Had the summons been that of a bogie from the moor, the inmates of this small house could hardly have heard it with greater terror.

His wife unbarred the door in fear and haste. Her hunchbacked sister stood by the hearth, staring toward the threshold. The children cowered behind.

Tom Chuff entered with his cudgel in his hand, without speaking, and threw himself into a chair opposite the fire. He had been away two or three days. He looked haggard, and his eyes were bloodshot. They knew he had been drinking.

Tom raked and knocked the peat fire with his stick, and thrust his feet close to it. He signed towards the little dresser, and nodded to his wife, and she knew he wanted a cup, which in silence she gave him. He pulled a bottle of gin from his coat-pocket, and nearly filling the teacup, drank off the dram at a few gulps.

He usually refreshed himself with two or three drams of this kind before beating the inmates of his house. His three little children, cowering in a corner, eyed him from under a table, as Jack did the ogre in the nursery tale. His wife, Nell, standing behind a chair, which she was ready to snatch up to meet the blow of the cudgel, which might be levelled at her at any moment, never took her eyes off him; and hunchbacked Mary showed the whites of a large pair of eyes, similarly employed, as she stood against the oaken press, her dark face hardly distinguishable in the distance from the brown panel behind it.

Tom Chuff was at his third dram, and had not yet spoken a word since his entrance, and the suspense was growing dreadful, when, on a sudden, he leaned back in his rude seat, the cudgel slipped from his hand, a change and a death-like pallor came over his face.

For a while they all stared on; such was their fear of him, they dared not speak or move, lest it should prove to have been but a doze, and Tom should wake up and proceed forthwith to gratify his temper and exercise his cudgel.

In a very little time, however, things began to look so odd, that they ventured, his wife and Mary, to exchange glances full of doubt and wonder. He hung so much over the side of the chair, that if it had not been one of cyclopean clumsiness and weight, he would have borne it to the floor. A leaden tint was darkening the pallor of his face. They were becoming alarmed, and finally braving everything his wife timidly said, "Tom!" and then more sharply repeated it, and finally cried the appellative loudly, and again and again, with the terrified accompaniment, "He's dying--he's dying!" her voice rising to a scream, as she found that neither it nor her plucks and shakings of him by the shoulder had the slightest effect in recalling him from his torpor.

And now from sheer terror of a new kind the children added their shrilly piping to the talk and cries of their seniors; and if anything could have called Tom up from his lethargy, it might have been the piercing chorus that made the rude chamber of the poacher's habitation ring again. But Tom continued unmoved, deaf, and stirless.

His wife sent Mary down to the village, hardly a quarter of a mile away, to implore of the doctor, for whose family she did duty as laundress, to come down and look at her husband, who seemed to be dying.

The doctor, who was a good-natured fellow, arrived. With his hat still on, he looked at Tom, examined him, and when he found that the emetic he had brought with him, on conjecture from Mary's description, did not act, and that his lancet brought no blood, and that he felt a pulseless wrist, he shook his head, and inwardly thought:

"What the plague is the woman crying for? Could she have desired a greater blessing for her children and herself than the very thing that has happened?"

Tom, in fact, seemed quite gone. At his lips no breath was perceptible. The doctor could discover no pulse. His hands and feet were cold, and the chill was stealing up into his body.

The doctor, after a stay of twenty minutes, had buttoned up his great-coat again and pulled down his hat, and told Mrs. Chuff that there was no use in his remaining any longer, when, all of a sudden, a little rill of blood began to trickle from the lancet-cut in Tom Chuffs temple.

"That's very odd," said the doctor. "Let us wait a little."

I must describe now the sensations which Tom Chuff had experienced.

With his elbows on his knees, and his chin upon his hands, he was staring into the embers, with his gin beside him, when suddenly a swimming came in his head, he lost sight of the fire, and a sound like one stroke of a loud church bell smote his brain.

Then he heard a confused humming, and the leaden weight of his head held him backward as he sank in his chair, and consciousness quite forsook him.

When he came to himself he felt chilled, and was leaning against a huge leafless tree. The night was moonless, and when he looked up he thought he had never seen stars so large and bright, or sky so black. The stars, too, seemed to blink down with longer intervals of darkness, and fiercer and more dazzling emergence, and something, he vaguely thought, of the character of silent menace and fury.

He had a confused recollection of having come there, or rather of having been carried along, as if on men's shoulders, with a sort of rushing motion. But it was utterly indistinct; the imperfect recollection simply of a sensation. He had seen or heard nothing on his way.

He looked round. There was not a sign of a living creature near. And he began with a sense of awe to recognise the place.

The tree against which he had been leaning was one of the noble old beeches that surround at irregular intervals the churchyard of Shackleton, which spreads its green and wavy lap on the edge of the Moor of Catstean, at the opposite side of which stands the rude cottage in which he had just lost consciousness. It was six miles or more across the moor to his habitation, and the black expanse lay before him, disappearing dismally in the darkness. So that, looking straight before him, sky and land blended together in an undistinguishable and awful blank.

There was a silence quite unnatural over the place. The distant murmur of the brook, which he knew so well, was dead; not a whisper in the leaves about him; the air, earth, everything about and above was indescribably still; and he experienced that quaking of the heart that seems to portend the approach of something awful. He would have set out upon his return across the moor, had he not an undefined presentiment that he was waylaid by something he dared not pass.

The old grey church and tower of Shackleton stood like a shadow in the rear. His eye had grown accustomed to the obscurity, and he could just trace its outline. There were no comforting associations in his mind connected with it; nothing but menace and misgiving. His early training in his lawless calling was connected with this very spot. Here his father used to meet two other poachers, and bring his son, then but a boy, with him.

Under the church porch, towards morning, they used to divide the game they had taken, and take account of the sales they had made on the previous day, and make partition of the money, and drink their gin. It was here he had taken his early lessons in drinking, cursing, and lawlessness. His father's grave was hardly eight steps from the spot where he stood. In his present state of awful dejection, no scene on earth could have so helped to heighten his fear.

There was one object close by which added to his gloom. About a yard away, in rear of the tree, behind himself, and extending to his left, was an open grave, the mould and rubbish piled on the other side. At the head of this grave stood the beech-tree; its columnar stem rose like a huge monumental pillar. He knew every line and crease on its smooth surface. The initial letters of his own name, cut in its bark long ago, had spread out and wrinkled like the grotesque capitals of a fanciful engraver, and now with a sinister significance overlooked the open grave, as if answering his mental question, "Who for is t' grave cut?"

He felt still a little stunned, and there was a faint tremor in his joints that disinclined him to exert himself; and, further, he had a vague apprehension that take what direction he might, there was danger around him worse than that of staying where he was.

On a sudden the stars began to blink more fiercely, a faint wild light overspread for a minute the bleak landscape, and he saw approaching from the moor a figure at a kind of swinging trot, with now and then a zig-zag hop or two, such as men accustomed to cross such places make, to avoid the patches of slob or quag that meet them here and there. This figure resembled his father's, and like him, whistled through his finger by way of signal as he approached; but the whistle sounded not now shrilly and sharp, as in old times, but immensely far away, and seemed to sing strangely through Tom's head. From habit or from fear, in answer to the signal, Tom whistled as he used to do five-and-twenty years ago and more, although he was already chilled with an unearthly fear.

Like his father, too, the figure held up the bag that was in his left hand as he drew near, when it was his custom to call out to him what was in it. It did not reassure the watcher, you may be certain, when a shout unnaturally faint reached him, as the phantom dangled the bag in the air, and he heard with a faint distinctness the words, "Tom Chuff's soul!"

Scarcely fifty yards away from the low churchyard fence at which Tom was standing, there was a wider chasm in the peat, which there threw up a growth of reeds and bulrushes, among which, as the old poacher used to do on a sudden alarm, the approaching figure suddenly cast itself down.

From the same patch of tall reeds and rushes emerged instantaneously what he at first mistook for the same figure creeping on all-fours, but what he soon perceived to be an enormous black dog with a rough coat like a bear's, which at first sniffed about, and then started towards him in what seemed to be a sportive amble, bouncing this way and that, but as it drew near it displayed a pair of fearful eyes that glowed like live coals, and emitted from the monstrous expanse of its jaws a terrifying growl.

This beast seemed on the point of seizing him, and Tom recoiled in panic and fell into the open grave behind him. The edge which he caught as he tumbled gave way, and down he went, expecting almost at the same instant to reach the bottom. But never was such a fall! Bottomless seemed the abyss! Down, down, down, with immeasurable and still increasing speed, through utter darkness, with hair streaming straight upward, breathless, he shot with a rush of air against him, the force of which whirled up his very arms, second after second, minute after minute, through the chasm downward he flew, the icy perspiration of horror covering his body, and suddenly, as he expected to be dashed into annihilation, his descent was in an instant arrested with a tremendous shock, which, however, did not deprive him of consciousness even for a moment. He looked about him. The place resembled a smoke-stained cavern or catacomb, the roof of which, except for a ribbed arch here and there faintly visible, was lost in darkness. From several rude passages, like the galleries of a gigantic mine, which opened from this centre chamber, was very dimly emitted a dull glow as of charcoal, which was the only light by which he could imperfectly discern the objects immediately about him.

What seemed like a projecting piece of the rock, at the corner of one of these murky entrances, moved on a sudden, and proved to be a human figure, that beckoned to him. He approached, and saw his father. He could barely recognise him, he was so monstrously altered.

"I've been looking for you, Tom. Welcome home, lad; come along to your place."

Tom's heart sank as he heard these words, which were spoken in a hollow and, he thought, derisive voice that made him tremble. But he could not help accompanying the wicked spirit, who led him into a place, in passing which he heard, as it were from within the rock, deadful cries and appeals for mercy.

"What is this?" said he.

"Never mind."

"Who are they?"

"New-comers, like yourself, lad," answered his father apathetically. "They give over that work in time, finding it is no use."

"What shall I do?" said Tom, in an agony.

"It's all one."

"But what shall I do?" reiterated Tom, quivering in every joint and nerve.

"Grin and bear it, I suppose."
"For God's sake, if ever you cared for me, as I am your own child, let me out of this!"

"There's no way out."

"If there's a way in there's a way out, and for Heaven's sake let me out of this."

But the dreadful figure made no further answer, and glided backwards by his shoulder to the rear; and others appeared in view, each with a faint red halo round it, staring on him with frightful eyes, images, all in hideous variety, of eternal fury or derision. He was growing mad, it seemed, under the stare of so many eyes, increasing in number and drawing closer every moment, and at the same time myriads and myriads of voices were calling him by his name, some far away, some near, some from one point, some from another, some from behind, close to his ears. These cries were increased in rapidity and multitude, and mingled with laughter, with flitting blasphemies, with broken insults and mockeries, succeeded and obliterated by others, before he could half catch their meaning.

All this time, in proportion to the rapidity and urgency of these dreadful sights and sounds, the epilepsy of terror was creeping up to his brain, and with a long and dreadful scream he lost consciousness.

When he recovered his senses, he found himself in a small stone chamber, vaulted above, and with a ponderous door. A single point of light in the wall, with a strange brilliancy illuminated this cell.

Seated opposite to him was a venerable man with a snowy beard of immense length; an image of awful purity and severity. He was dressed in a coarse robe, with three large keys suspensed from his girdle. He might have filled one's idea of an ancient porter of a city gate; such spiritual cities, I should say, as John Bunyan loved to describe.

This old man's eyes were brilliant and awful, and fixed on him as they were, Tom Chuff felt himself helplessly in his power. At length he spoke:

"The command is given to let you forth for one trial more. But if you are found again drinking with the drunken, and beating your fellow-servants, you shall return through the door by which you came, and go out no more."

With these words the old man took him by the wrist and led him through the first door, and then unlocking one that stood in the cavern outside, he struck Tom Chuff sharply on the shoulder, and the door shut behind him with a sound that boomed peal after peal of thunder near and far away, and all round and above, till it rolled off gradually into silence. It was totally dark, but there was a fanning of fresh cool air that overpowered him. He felt that he was in the upper world again.

In a few minutes he began to hear voices which he knew, and first a faint point of light appeared before his eyes, and gradually he saw the flame of the candle, and, after that, the familiar faces of his wife and children, and he heard them faintly when they spoke to him, although he was as yet unable to answer.

He also saw the doctor, like an isolated figure in the dark, and heard him say:

"There, now, you have him back. He'll do, I think."

His first words, when he could speak and saw clearly all about him, and felt the blood on his neck and shirt, were:

"Wife, forgie me. I'm a changed man. Send for't sir."

Which last phrase means, "Send for the clergyman."

When the vicar came and entered the little bedroom where the scared poacher, whose soul had died within him, was lying, still sick and weak, in his bed, and with a spirit that was prostrate with terror, Tom Chuff feebly beckoned the rest from the room, and, the door being closed, the good parson heard the strange confession, and with equal amazement the man's earnest and agitated vows of amendment, and his helpless appeals to him for support and counsel.
These, of course, were kindly met; and the visits of the rector, for some time, were frequent.

One day, when he took Tom Chuff's hand on bidding him good-bye, the sick man held it still, and said:

"Ye'r vicar o' Shackleton, sir, and if I sud dee, ye'll promise me a'e thing, as I a promised ye a many. I a said I'll never gie wife, nor barn, nor folk o' no sort, skelp nor sizzup more, and ye'll know o' me no more among the sipers. Nor never will Tom draw trigger, nor set a snare again, but in an honest way, and after that ye'll no make it a bootless bene for me, but bein', as I say, vicar o' Shackleton, and able to do as ye list, ye'll no let them bury me within twenty good yerd-wands measure o' the a'd beech trees that's round the churchyard of Shackleton."

"I see; you would have your grave, when your time really comes, a good way from the place where lay the grave you dreamed of."

"That's jest it. I'd lie at the bottom o' a marl-pit liefer! And I'd be laid in anither churchyard just to be shut o' my fear o' that, but that a' my kinsfolk is buried beyond in Shackleton, and ye'll gie me yer promise, and no break yer word."

"I do promise, certainly. I'm not likely to outlive you; but, if I should, and still be vicar of Shackleton, you shall be buried somewhere as near the middle of the churchyard as we can find space."

"That'll do."

And so content they parted.

The effect of the vision upon Tom Chuff was powerful, and promised to be lasting. With a sore effort he exchanged his life of desultory adventure and comparative idleness for one of regular industry. He gave up drinking; he was as kind as an originally surly nature would allow to his wife and family; he went to church; in fine weather they crossed the moor to Shackleton Church; the vicar said he came there to look at the scenery of his vision, and to fortify his good resolutions by the reminder.

Impressions upon the imagination, however, are but transitory, and a bad man acting under fear is not a free agent; his real character does not appear. But as the images of the imagination fade, and the action of fear abates, the essential qualities of the man reassert themselves.

So, after a time, Tom Chuff began to grow weary of his new life; he grew lazy, and people began to say that he was catching hares, and pursuing his old contraband way of life, under the rose.

He came home one hard night, with signs of the bottle in his thick speech and violent temper. Next day he was sorry, or frightened, at all events repentant, and for a week or more something of the old horror returned, and he was once more on his good behaviour. But in a little time came a relapse, and another repentance, and then a relapse again, and gradually the return of old habits and the flooding in of all his old way of life, with more violence and gloom, in proportion as the man was alarmed and exasperated by the remembrance of his despised, but terrible, warning.

With the old life returned the misery of the cottage. The smiles, which had begun to appear with the unwonted sunshine, were seen no more. Instead, returned to his poor wife's face the old pale and heartbroken look. The cottage lost its neat and cheerful air, and the melancholy of neglect was visible. Sometimes at night were overheard, by a chance passer-by, cries and sobs from that ill-omened dwelling. Tom Chuff was now often drunk, and not very often at home, except when he came in to sweep away his poor wife's earnings.

Tom had long lost sight of the honest old parson. There was shame mixed with his degradation. He had grace enough left when he saw the thin figure of "t' sir" walking along the road to turn out of his way and avoid meeting him. The clergyman shook his head, and sometimes groaned, when his name was mentioned. His horror and regret were more for the poor wife than for the relapsed sinner, for her case was pitiable indeed.

Her brother, Jack Everton, coming over from Hexley, having heard stories of all this, determined to beat Tom, for his ill-treatment of his sister, within an inch of his life. Luckily, perhaps, for all concerned, Tom happened to be away upon one of his long excursions, and poor Nell besought her brother, in extremity of terror, not to interpose between them. So he took his leave and went home muttering and sulky.

Now it happened a few months later that Nelly Chuff fell sick. She had been ailing, as heartbroken people do, for a good while. But now the end had come.

There was a coroner's inquest when she died, for the doctor had doubts as to whether a blow had not, at least, hastened her death. Nothing certain, however, came of the inquiry. Tom Chuff had left his home more than two days before his wife's death. He was absent upon his lawless business still when the coroner had held his quest.

Jack Everton came over from Hexley to attend the dismal obsequies of his sister. He was more incensed than ever with the wicked husband, who, one way or other, had hastened Nelly's death. The inquest had closed early in the day. The husband had not appeared.

An occasional companion--perhaps I ought to say accomplice--of Chuff's happened to turn up. He had left him on the borders of Westmoreland, and said he would probably be home next day. But Everton affected not to believe it. Perhaps it was to Tom Chuff, he suggested, a secret satisfaction to crown the history of his bad married life with the scandal of his absence from the funeral of his neglected and abused wife.

Everton had taken on himself the direction of the melancholy preparations. He had ordered a grave to be opened for his sister beside her mother's, in Shackleton churchyard, at the other side of the moor. For the purpose, as I have said, of marking the callous neglect of her husband, he determined that the funeral should take place that night. His brother Dick had accompanied him, and they and his sister, with Mary and the children, and a couple of the neighbours, formed the humble cortège. Jack Everton said he would wait behind, on the chance of Tom Chuff coming in time, that he might tell him what had happened, and make him cross the moor with him to meet the funeral. His real object, I think, was to inflict upon the villain the drubbing he had so long wished to give him. Anyhow, he was resolved, by crossing the moor, to reach the churchyard in time to anticipate the arrival of the funeral, and to have a few words with the vicar, clerk, and sexton, all old friends of his, for the parish of Shackleton was the place of his birth and early recollections.

But Tom Chuff did not appear at his house that night. In surly mood, and without a shilling in his pocket, he was making his way homeward. His bottle of gin, his last investment, half emptied, with its neck protruding, as usual on such returns, was in his coat-pocket.

His way home lay across the moor of Catstean, and the point at which he best knew the passage was from the churchyard of Shackleton. He vaulted the low wall that forms its boundary, and strode across the graves, and over many a flat, half-buried tombstone, toward the side of the churchyard next Catstean Moor.

The old church of Shackleton and its tower rose, close at his right, like a black shadow against the sky. It was a moonless night, but clear. By this time he had reached the low boundary wall, at the other side, that overlooks the wide expanse of Catstean Moor. He stood by one of the huge old beech-trees, and leaned his back to its smooth trunk. Had he ever seen the sky look so black, and the stars shine out and blink so vividly? There was a deathlike silence over the scene, like the hush that precedes thunder in sultry weather. The expanse before him was lost in utter blackness. A strange quaking unnerved his heart. It was the sky and scenery of his vision! The same horror and misgiving. The same invincible fear of venturing from the spot where he stood. He would have prayed if he dared. His sinking heart demanded a restorative of some sort, and he grasped the bottle in his coat-pocket. Turning to his left, as he did so, he saw the piled-up mould of an open grave that gaped with its head close to the base of the great tree against which he was leaning.

He stood aghast. His dream was returning and slowly enveloping him. Everything he saw was weaving itself into the texture of his vision. The chill of horror stole over him.

A faint whistle came shrill and clear over the moor, and he saw a figure approaching at a swinging trot, with a zig-zag course, hopping now here and now there, as men do over a surface where one has need to choose their steps. Through the jungle of reeds and bulrushes in the foreground this figure advanced; and with the same unaccountable impulse that had coerced him in his dream, he answered the whistle of the advancing figure.

On that signal it directed its course straight toward him. It mounted the low wall, and, standing there, looked into the graveyard.

"Who med answer?" challenged the new-comer from his post of observation.

"Me," answered Tom.

"Who are you?" repeated the man upon the wall.

"Tom Chuff; and who's this grave cut for?" He answered in a savage tone, to cover the secret shudder of his panic.

"I'll tell you that, ye villain!" answered the stranger, descending from the wall, "I a' looked for you far and near, and waited long, and now you're found at last."

Not knowing what to make of the figure that advanced upon him, Tom Chuff recoiled, stumbled, and fell backward into the open grave. He caught at the sides as he fell, but without retarding his fall.

An hour later, when lights came with the coffin, the corpse of Tom Chuff was found at the bottom of the grave. He had fallen direct upon his head, and his neck was broken. His death must have been simultaneous with his fall. Thus far his dream was accomplished.

It was his brother-in-law who had crossed the moor and approached the churchyard of Shackleton, exactly in the line which the image of his father had seemed to take in his strange vision. Fortunately for Jack Everton, the sexton and clerk of Shackleton church were, unseen by him, crossing the churchyard toward the grave of Nelly Chuff, just as Tom the poacher stumbled and fell. Suspicion of direct violence would otherwise have inevitably attached to the exasperated brother. As it was, the catastrophe was followed by no legal consequences.

The good vicar kept his word, and the grave of Tom Chuff is still pointed out by the old inhabitants of Shackleton pretty nearly in the centre of the churchyard. This conscientious compliance with the entreaty of the panic-stricken man as to the place of his sepulture gave a horrible and mocking emphasis to the strange combination by which fate had defeated his precaution, and fixed the place of his death.

The story was for many a year, and we believe still is, told round many a cottage hearth, and though it appeals to what many would term superstition, it yet sounded, in the ears of a rude and simple audience, a thrilling, and let us hope, not altogether fruitless homily.

# STORIES OF LOUGH GUIR
## (1870)

When the present writer was a boy of twelve or thirteen, he first made the acquaintance of Miss Anne Baily, of Lough Guir, in the county of Limerick. She and her sister were the last representatives at that place, of an extremely good old name in the county. They were both what is termed "old maids," and at that time past sixty. But never were old ladies more hospitable, lively, and kind, especially to young people. They were both remarkably agreeable and clever. Like all old county ladies of their time, they were great genealogists, and could recount the origin, generations, and intermarriages, of every county family of note.

These ladies were visited at their house at Lough Guir by Mr. Crofton Croker; and are, I think, mentioned, by name, in the second series of his fairy legends; the series in which (probably communicated by Miss Anne Baily), he recounts some of the picturesque traditions of those beautiful lakes--lakes, I should no longer say, for the smaller and prettier has since been drained, and gave up from its depths some long lost and very interesting relics.

In their drawing-room stood a curious relic of another sort: old enough, too, though belonging to a much more modern period. It was the ancient stirrup cup of the hospitable house of Lough Guir. Crofton Croker has preserved a sketch of this curious glass. I have often had it in my hand. It had a short stem; and the cup part, having the bottom rounded, rose cylindrically, and, being of a capacity to contain a whole bottle of claret, and almost as narrow as an old-fashioned ale glass, was tall to a degree that filled me with wonder. As it obliged the rider to extend his arm as he raised the glass, it must have tried a tipsy man, sitting in the saddle, pretty severely. The wonder was that the marvellous tall glass had come down to our times without a crack.

There was another glass worthy of remark in the same drawing-room. It was gigantic, and shaped conically, like one of those old-fashioned jelly glasses which used to be seen upon the shelves of confectioners. It was engraved round the rim with the words, "The glorious, pious, and immortal memory"; and on grand occasions, was filled to the brim, and after the manner of a loving cup, made the circuit of the Whig guests, who owed all to the hero whose memory its legend invoked.

It was now but the transparent phantom of those solemn convivialities of a generation, who lived, as it were, within hearing of the cannon and shoutings of those stirring times. When I saw it, this glass had long retired from politics and carousals, and stood peacefully on a little table in the drawing-room, where ladies' hands replenished it with fair water, and crowned it daily with flowers from the garden.

Miss Anne Baily's conversation ran oftener than her sister's upon the legendary and supernatural; she told her stories with the sympathy, the colour, and the mysterious air which contribute so powerfully to effect, and never wearied of answering questions about the old castle, and amusing her young audience with fascinating little glimpses of old adventure and bygone days. My memory retains the picture of my early friend very distinctly. A slim straight figure, above the middle height; a general likeness to the full-length portrait of that delightful Countess d'Aulnois, to whom we all owe our earliest and most brilliant glimpses of fairy-land; something of her gravely-pleasant countenance, plain, but refined and ladylike, with that kindly mystery in her side-long glance and uplifted finger, which indicated the approaching climax of a tale of wonder.

Lough Guir is a kind of centre of the operations of the Munster fairies. When a child is stolen by the "good people," Lough Guir is conjectured to be the place of its unearthly transmutation from the human to the fairy state. And beneath its waters lie enchanted, the grand old castle of the Desmonds, the great earl himself, his beautiful young countess, and all the retinue that surrounded him in the years of his splendour, and at the moment of his catastrophe.

Here, too, are historic associations. The huge square tower that rises at one side of the stable-yard close to the old house, to a height that amazed my young eyes, though robbed of its battlements and one story, was a stronghold of the last rebellious Earl of Desmond, and is specially mentioned in that delightful old folio, the _Hibernia Pacata_, as having, with its Irish garrison on the battlements, defied the army of the lord deputy, then marching by upon the summits of the overhanging hills. The house, built under shelter of this stronghold of the once proud and turbulent Desmonds, is old, but snug, with a multitude of small low rooms, such as I have seen in houses of the same age in Shropshire and the neighbouring English counties.

The hills that overhang the lakes appeared to me, in my young days (and I have not seen them since), to be clothed with a short soft verdure, of a hue so dark and vivid as I had never seen before.

In one of the lakes is a small island, rocky and wooded, which is believed by the peasantry to represent the top of the highest tower of the castle which sank, under a spell, to the bottom. In certain states of the atmosphere, I have heard educated people say, when in a boat you have reached a certain distance, the island appears to rise some feet from the water, its rocks assume the appearance of masonry, and the whole circuit presents very much the effect of the battlements of a castle rising above the surface of the lake.

This was Miss Anne Baily's story of the submersion of this lost castle:

## The Magician Earl

It is well known that the great Earl of Desmond, though history pretends to dispose of him differently, lives to this hour enchanted in his castle, with all his household, at the bottom of the lake.

There was not, in his day, in all the world, so accomplished a magician as he. His fairest castle stood upon an island in the lake, and to this he brought his young and beautiful bride, whom he loved but too well; for she prevailed upon his folly to risk all to gratify her imperious caprice.

They had not been long in this beautiful castle, when she one day presented herself in the chamber in which her husband studied his forbidden art, and there implored him to exhibit before her some of the wonders of his evil science. He resisted long; but her entreaties, tears, and wheedlings were at length too much for him and he consented.

But before beginning those astonishing transformations with which he was about to amaze her, he explained to her the awful conditions and dangers of the experiment.

Alone in this vast apartment, the walls of which were lapped, far below, by the lake whose dark waters lay waiting to swallow them, she must witness a certain series of frightful phenomena, which once commenced, he could neither abridge nor mitigate; and if throughout their ghastly succession she spoke one word, or uttered one exclamation, the castle and all that it contained would in one instant subside to the bottom of the lake, there to remain, under the servitude of a strong spell, for ages.

The dauntless curiosity of the lady having prevailed, and the oaken door of the study being locked and barred, the fatal experiments commenced.

Muttering a spell, as he stood before her, feathers sprouted thickly over him, his face became contracted and hooked, a cadaverous smell filled the air, and, with heavy winnowing wings, a gigantic vulture rose in his stead, and swept round and round the room, as if on the point of pouncing upon her.

The lady commanded herself through this trial, and instantly another began.

The bird alighted near the door, and in less than a minute changed, she saw not how, into a horribly deformed and dwarfish hag: who, with yellow skin hanging about her face and enormous eyes, swung herself on crutches toward the lady, her mouth foaming with fury, and her grimaces and contortions becoming more and more hideous every moment, till she rolled with a yell on the floor, in a horrible convulsion, at the lady's feet, and then changed into a huge serpent, with crest erect, and quivering tongue. Suddenly, as it seemed on the point of darting at her, she saw her husband in its stead, standing pale before her, and, with his finger on his lip, enforcing the continued necessity of silence. He then placed himself at his length on the floor, and began to stretch himself out and out, longer and longer, until his head nearly reached to one end of the vast room, and his feet to the other.

This horror overcame her. The ill-starred lady uttered a wild scream, whereupon the castle and all that was within it, sank in a moment to the bottom of the lake.

But, once in every seven years, by night, the Earl of Desmond and his retinue emerge, and cross the lake, in shadowy cavalcade. His white horse is shod with silver. On that one night, the earl may ride till daybreak, and it behoves him to make good use of his time; for, until the silver shoes of his steed be worn through, the spell that holds him and his beneath the lake, will retain its power.

When I (Miss Anne Baily) was a child, there was still living a man named Teigue O'Neill, who had a strange story to tell.

He was a smith, and his forge stood on the brow of the hill, overlooking the lake, on a lonely part of the road to Cahir Conlish. One bright moonlight night, he was working very late, and quite alone. The clink of his hammer, and the wavering glow reflected through the open door on the bushes at the other side of the narrow road, were the only tokens that told of life and vigil for miles around.

In one of the pauses of his work, he heard the ring of many hoofs ascending the steep road that passed his forge, and, standing in this doorway, he was just in time to see a gentleman, on a white horse, who was dressed in a fashion the like of which the smith had never seen before. This man was accompanied and followed by a mounted retinue, as strangely dressed as he.

They seemed, by the clang and clatter that announced their approach, to be riding up the hill at a hard hurry-scurry gallop; but the pace abated as they drew near, and the rider of the white horse who, from his grave and lordly air, he assumed to be a man of rank, and accustomed to command, drew bridle and came to a halt before the smith's door.

He did not speak, and all his train were silent, but he beckoned to the smith, and pointed down to one of his horse's hoofs.

Teigue stooped and raised it, and held it just long enough to see that it was shod with a silver shoe; which, in one place, he said, was worn as thin as a shilling. Instantaneously, his situation was made apparent to him by this sign, and he recoiled with a terrified prayer. The lordly rider, with a look of pain and fury, struck at him suddenly, with something that whistled in the air like a whip; and an icy streak seemed to traverse his body as if he had been cut through with a leaf of steel. But he was without scathe or scar, as he afterwards found. At the same moment he saw the whole cavalcade break into a gallop and disappear down the hill, with a momentary hurtling in the air, like the flight of a volley of cannon shot.

Here had been the earl himself. He had tried one of his accustomed stratagems to lead the smith to speak to him. For it is well known that either for the purpose of abridging or of mitigating his period of enchantment, he seeks to lead people to accost him. But what, in the event of his succeeding, would befall the person whom he had thus ensnared, no one knows.

## Moll Rial's Adventure

When Miss Anne Baily was a child, Moll Rial was an old woman. She had lived all her days with the Bailys of Lough Guir; in and about whose house, as was the Irish custom of those days, were a troop of bare-footed country girls, scullery maids, or laundresses, or employed about the poultry yard, or running of errands.

Among these was Moll Rial, then a stout good-humoured lass, with little to think of, and nothing to fret about. She was once washing clothes by the process known universally in Munster as beetling. The washer stands up to her ankles in water, in which she has immersed the clothes, which she lays in that state on a great flat stone, and smacks with lusty strokes of an instrument which bears a rude resemblance to a cricket bat, only shorter, broader, and light enough to be wielded freely with one hand. Thus, they smack the dripping clothes, turning them over and over, sousing them in the water, and replacing them on the same stone, to undergo a repetition of the process, until they are thoroughly washed.

Moll Rial was plying her "beetle" at the margin of the lake, close under the old house and castle. It was between eight and nine o'clock on a fine summer morning, everything looked bright and beautiful. Though quite alone, and though she could not see even the windows of the house (hidden from her view by the irregular ascent and some interposing bushes), her loneliness was not depressing.

Standing up from her work, she saw a gentleman walking slowly down the slope toward her. He was a "grand-looking" gentleman, arrayed in a flowered silk dressing-gown, with a cap of velvet on his head; and as he stepped toward her, in his slippered feet, he showed a very handsome leg. He was smiling graciously as he approached, and drawing a ring from his finger with an air of gracious meaning, which seemed to imply that he wished to make her a present, he raised it in his fingers with a pleased look, and placed it on the flat stones beside the clothes she had been beetling so industriously.

He drew back a little, and continued to look at her with an encouraging smile, which seemed to say: "You have earned your reward; you must not be afraid to take it."

The girl fancied that this was some gentleman who had arrived, as often happened in those hospitable and haphazard times, late and unexpectedly the night before, and who was now taking a little indolent ramble before breakfast.

Moll Rial was a little shy, and more so at having been discovered by so grand a gentleman with her petticoats gathered a little high about her bare shins. She looked down, therefore, upon the water at her feet, and then she saw a ripple of blood, and then another, ring after ring, coming and going to and from her feet. She cried out the sacred name in horror, and, lifting her eyes, the courtly gentleman was gone, but the blood-rings about her feet spread with the speed of light over the surface of the lake, which for a moment glowed like one vast estuary of blood.

Here was the earl once again, and Moll Rial declared that if it had not been for that frightful transformation of the water she would have spoken to him next minute, and would thus have passed under a spell, perhaps as direful as his own.

# The Banshee

So old a Munster family as the Bailys, of Lough Guir, could not fail to have their attendant banshee. Everyone attached to the family knew this well, and could cite evidences of that unearthly distinction. I heard Miss Baily relate the only experience she had personally had of that wild spiritual sympathy.

She said that, being then young, she and Miss Susan undertook a long attendance upon the sick bed of their sister, Miss Kitty, whom I have heard remembered among her contemporaries as the merriest and most entertaining of human beings. This light-hearted young lady was dying of consumption. The sad duties of such attendance being divided among many sisters, as there then were, the night watches devolved upon the two ladies I have named: I think, as being the eldest.

It is not improbable that these long and melancholy vigils, lowering the spirits and exciting the nervous system, prepared them for illusions. At all events, one night at dead of night, Miss Baily and her sister, sitting in the dying lady's room, heard such sweet and melancholy music as they had never heard before. It seemed to them like distant cathedral music. The room of the dying girl had its windows toward the yard, and the old castle stood near, and full in sight. The music was not in the house, but seemed to come from the yard, or beyond it. Miss Anne Baily took a candle, and went down the back stairs. She opened the back door, and, standing there, heard the same faint but solemn harmony, and could not tell whether it most resembled the distant music of instruments, or a choir of voices. It seemed to come through the windows of the old castle, high in the air. But when she approached the tower, the music, she thought, came from above the house, at the other side of the yard; and thus perplexed, and at last frightened, she returned.

This aerial music both she and her sister, Miss Susan Baily, avowed that they distinctly heard, and for a long time. Of the fact she was clear, and she spoke of it with great awe.

# The Governess's Dream

This lady, one morning, with a grave countenance that indicated something weighty upon her mind, told her pupils that she had, on the night before, had a very remarkable dream.

The first room you enter in the old castle, having reached the foot of the spiral stone stair, is a large hall, dim and lofty, having only a small window or two, set high in deep recesses in the wall. When I saw the castle many years ago, a portion of this capacious chamber was used as a store for the turf laid in to last the year.

Her dream placed her, alone, in this room, and there entered a grave-looking man, having something very remarkable in his countenance: which impressed her, as a fine portrait sometimes will, with a haunting sense of character and individuality.

In his hand this man carried a wand, about the length of an ordinary walking cane. He told her to observe and remember its length, and to mark well the measurements he was about to make, the result of which she was to communicate to Mr. Baily of Lough Guir.

From a certain point in the wall, with this wand, he measured along the floor, at right angles with the wall, a certain number of its lengths, which he counted aloud; and then, in the same way, from the adjoining wall he measured a certain number of its lengths, which he also counted distinctly. He then told her that at the point where these two lines met, at a depth of a certain number of feet which he also told her, treasure lay buried. And so the dream broke up, and her remarkable visitant vanished.

She took the girls with her to the old castle, where, having cut a switch to the length represented to her in her dream, she measured the distances, and ascertained, as she supposed, the point on the floor beneath which the treasure lay. The same day she related her dream to Mr. Baily. But he treated it laughingly, and took no step in consequence.

Some time after this, she again saw, in a dream, the same remarkable-looking man, who repeated his message, and appeared displeased. But the dream was treated by Mr. Baily as before.

The same dream occurred again, and the children became so clamorous to have the castle floor explored, with pick and shovel, at the point indicated by the thrice-seen messenger, that at length Mr. Baily consented, and the floor was opened, and a trench was sunk at the spot which the governess had pointed out.

Miss Anne Baily, and nearly all the members of the family, her father included, were present at this operation. As the workmen approached the depth described in the vision, the interest and suspense of all increased; and when the iron implements met the solid resistance of a broad flagstone, which returned a cavernous sound to the stroke, the excitement of all present rose to its acme.

With some difficulty the flag was raised, and a chamber of stone work, large enough to receive a moderately-sized crock or pit, was disclosed. Alas! it was empty. But in the earth at the bottom of it, Miss Baily said, she herself saw, as every other bystander plainly did, the circular impression of a vessel: which had stood there, as the mark seemed to indicate, for a very long time.

Both the Miss Bailys were strong in their belief hereafterwards, that the treasure which they were convinced had actually been deposited there, had been removed by some more trusting and active listener than their father had proved.

This same governess remained with them to the time of her death, which occurred some years later, under the following circumstances as extraordinary as her dream.

## The Earl's Hall

The good governess had a particular liking for the old castle, and when lessons were over, would take her book or her work into a large room in the ancient building, called the Earl's Hall. Here she caused a table and chair to be placed for her use, and in the chiaroscuro would so sit at her favourite occupations, with just a little ray of subdued light, admitted through one of the glassless windows above her, and falling upon her table.

The Earl's Hall is entered by a narrow-arched door, opening close to the winding stair. It is a very large and gloomy room, pretty nearly square, with a lofty vaulted ceiling, and a stone floor. Being situated high in the castle, the walls of which are immensely thick, and the windows very small and few, the silence that reigns here is like that of a subterranean cavern. You hear nothing in this solitude, except perhaps twice in a day, the twitter of a swallow in one of the small windows high in the wall.

This good lady having one day retired to her accustomed solitude, was missed from the house at her wonted hour of return. This in a country house, such as Irish houses were in those days, excited little surprise, and no harm. But when the dinner hour came, which was then, in country houses, five o'clock, and the governess had not appeared, some of her young friends, it being not yet winter, and sufficient light remaining to guide them through the gloom of the dim ascent and passages, mounted the old stone stair to the level of the Earl's Hall, gaily calling to her as they approached.

There was no answer. On the stone floor, outside the door of the Earl's Hall, to their horror, they found her lying insensible. By the usual means she was restored to consciousness; but she continued very ill, and was conveyed to the house, where she took to her bed.

It was there and then that she related what had occurred to her. She had placed herself, as usual, at her little work table, and had been either working or reading--I forget which--for some time, and felt in her usual health and serene spirits. Raising her eyes, and looking towards the door, she saw a horrible-looking little man enter. He was dressed in red, was very short, had a singularly dark face, and a most atrocious countenance. Having walked some steps into the room, with his eyes fixed on her, he stopped, and beckoning to her to follow, moved back toward the door. About half way, again he stopped once more and turned. She was so terrified that she sat staring at the apparition without moving or speaking. Seeing that she had not obeyed him, his face became more frightful and menacing, and as it underwent this change, he raised his hand and stamped on the floor. Gesture, look, and all, expressed diabolical fury. Through sheer extremity of terror she did rise, and, as he turned again, followed him a step or two in the direction of the door. He again stopped, and with the same mute menace, compelled her again to follow him.

She reached the narrow stone doorway of the Earl's Hall, through which he had passed; from the threshold she saw him standing a little way off, with his eyes still fixed on her. Again he signed to her, and began to move along the short passage that leads to the winding stair. But instead of following him further, she fell on the floor in a fit.

The poor lady was thoroughly persuaded that she was not long to survive this vision, and her foreboding proved true. From her bed she never rose. Fever and delirium supervened in a few days and she died. Of course it is possible that fever, already approaching, had touched her brain when she was visited by the phantom, and that it had no external existence.

# GREEN TEA (1871)

## PROLOGUE

### Martin Hesselius, the German Physician

Though carefully educated in medicine and surgery, I have never practised either. The study of each continues, nevertheless, to interest me profoundly. Neither idleness nor caprice caused my secession from the honourable calling which I had just entered. The cause was a very trifling scratch inflicted by a dissecting knife. This trifle cost me the loss of two fingers, amputated promptly, and the more painful loss of my health, for I have never been quite well since, and have seldom been twelve months together in the same place.

In my wanderings I became acquainted with Dr. Martin Hesselius, a wanderer like myself, like me a physician, and like me an enthusiast in his profession. Unlike me in this, that his wanderings were voluntary, and he a man, if not of fortune, as we estimate fortune in England, at least in what our forefathers used to term "easy circumstances." He was an old man when I first saw him; nearly five-and-thirty years my senior.

In Dr. Martin Hesselius, I found my master. His knowledge was immense, his grasp of a case was an intuition. He was the very man to inspire a young enthusiast, like me, with awe and delight. My admiration has stood the test of time and survived the separation of death. I am sure it was well-founded.

For nearly twenty years I acted as his medical secretary. His immense collection of papers he has left in my care, to be arranged, indexed and bound. His treatment of some of these cases is curious. He writes in two distinct characters. He describes what he saw and heard as an intelligent layman might, and when in this style of narrative he had seen the patient either through his own hall-door, to the light of day, or through the gates of darkness to the caverns of the dead, he returns upon the narrative, and in the terms of his art and with all the force and originality of genius, proceeds to the work of analysis, diagnosis and illustration.

Here and there a case strikes me as of a kind to amuse or horrify a lay reader with an interest quite different from the peculiar one which it may possess for an expert. With slight modifications, chiefly of language, and of course a change of names, I copy the following. The narrator is Dr. Martin Hesselius. I find it among the voluminous notes of cases which he made during a tour in England about sixty-four years ago.

It is related in series of letters to his friend Professor Van Loo of Leyden. The professor was not a physician, but a chemist, and a man who read history and metaphysics and medicine, and had, in his day, written a play.

The narrative is therefore, if somewhat less valuable as a medical record, necessarily written in a manner more likely to interest an unlearned reader.

These letters, from a memorandum attached, appear to have been returnedon the death of the professor, in 1819, to Dr. Hesselius. They are written, some in English, some in French, but the greater part in German. I am a faithful, though I am conscious, by no means a graceful translator, and although here and there I omit some passages, and shorten others, and disguise names, I have interpolated nothing.

# CHAPTER I

## Dr. Hesselius Relates How He Met the Rev. Mr. Jennings

The Rev. Mr. Jennings is tall and thin. He is middle-aged, and dresses with a natty, old-fashioned, high-church precision. He is naturally a little stately, but not at all stiff. His features, without being handsome, are well formed, and their expression extremely kind, but also shy.

I met him one evening at Lady Mary Heyduke's. The modesty and benevolence of his countenance are extremely prepossessing.

We were but a small party, and he joined agreeably enough in the conversation, He seems to enjoy listening very much more than contributing to the talk; but what he says is always to the purpose and well said. He is a great favourite of Lady Mary's, who it seems, consults him upon many things, and thinks him the most happy and blessed person on earth. Little knows she about him.

The Rev. Mr. Jennings is a bachelor, and has, they say sixty thousand pounds in the funds. He is a charitable man. He is most anxious to be actively employed in his sacred profession, and yet though always tolerably well elsewhere, when he goes down to his vicarage in Warwickshire, to engage in the actual duties of his sacred calling, his health soon fails him, and in a very strange way. So says Lady Mary.

There is no doubt that Mr. Jennings' health does break down in, generally, a sudden and mysterious way, sometimes in the very act of officiating in his old and pretty church at Kenlis. It may be his heart, it may be his brain. But so it has happened three or four times, or oftener, that after proceeding a certain way in the service, he has on a sudden stopped short, and after a silence, apparently quite unable to resume, he has fallen into solitary, inaudible prayer, his hands and his eyes uplifted, and then pale as death, and in the agitation of a strange shame and horror, descended trembling, and got into the vestry-room, leaving his congregation, without explanation, to themselves. This occurred when his curate was absent. When he goes down to Kenlis now, he always takes care to provide a clergyman to share his duty, and to supply his place on the instant should he become thus suddenly incapacitated.

When Mr. Jennings breaks down quite, and beats a retreat from the vicarage, and returns to London, where, in a dark street off Piccadilly, he inhabits a very narrow house, Lady Mary says that he is always perfectly well. I have my own opinion about that. There are degrees of course. We shall see.

Mr. Jennings is a perfectly gentlemanlike man. People, however, remark something odd. There is an impression a little ambiguous. One thing which certainly contributes to it, people I think don't remember; or, perhaps, distinctly remark. But I did, almost immediately. Mr. Jennings has a way of looking sidelong upon the carpet, as if his eye followed the movements of something there. This, of course, is not always. It occurs now and then. But often enough to give a certain oddity, as I have said, to his manner, and in this glance travelling along the floor there is something both shy and anxious.

A medical philosopher, as you are good enough to call me, elaborating theories by the aid of cases sought out by himself, and by him watched and scrutinised with more time at command, and consequently infinitely more minuteness than the ordinary practitioner can afford, falls insensibly into habits of observation, which accompany him everywhere, and are exercised, as some people would say, impertinently, upon every subject that presents itself with the least likelihood of rewarding inquiry.

There was a promise of this kind in the slight, timid, kindly, but reserved gentleman, whom I met for the first time at this agreeable little evening gathering. I observed, of course, more than I here set down; but I reserve all that borders on the technical for a strictly scientific paper.

I may remark, that when I here speak of medical science, I do so, as I hope some day to see it more generally understood, in a much more comprehensive sense than its generally material treatment would warrant. I believe the entire natural world is but the ultimate expression of that spiritual world from which, and in which alone, it has its life. I believe that the essential man is a spirit, that the spirit is an organised substance, but as different in point of material from what we ordinarily understand by matter, as light or electricity is; that the material body is, in the most literal sense, a vesture, and death consequently no interruption of the living man's existence, but simply his extrication from the natural body--a process which commences at the moment of what we term death, and the completion of which, at furthest a few days later, is the resurrection "in power."

The person who weighs the consequences of these positions will probably see their practical bearing upon medical science. This is, however, by no means the proper place for displaying the proofs and discussing the consequences of this too generally unrecognized state of facts.

In pursuance of my habit, I was covertly observing Mr. Jennings, with all my caution--I think he perceived it--and I saw plainly that he was as cautiously observing me. Lady Mary happening to address me by my name, as Dr. Hesselius, I saw that he glanced at me more sharply, and then became thoughtful for a few minutes.

After this, as I conversed with a gentleman at the other end of the room, I saw him look at me more steadily, and with an interest which I thought I understood. I then saw him take an opportunity of chatting with Lady Mary, and was, as one always is, perfectly aware of being the subject of a distant inquiry and answer.

This tall clergyman approached me by-and-by; and in a little time we had got into conversation. When two people, who like reading, and know books and places, having travelled, wish to discourse, it is very strange if they can't find topics. It was not accident that brought him near me, and led him into conversation. He knew German and had read my Essays on Metaphysical Medicine which suggest more than they actually say.

This courteous man, gentle, shy, plainly a man of thought and reading, who moving and talking among us, was not altogether of us, and whom I already suspected of leading a life whose transactions and alarms were carefully concealed, with an impenetrable reserve from, not only the world, but his best beloved friends--was cautiously weighing in his own mind the idea of taking a certain step with regard to me.

I penetrated his thoughts without his being aware of it, and was careful to say nothing which could betray to his sensitive vigilance my suspicions respecting his position, or my surmises about his plans respecting myself.

We chatted upon indifferent subjects for a time but at last he said:

"I was very much interested by some papers of yours, Dr. Hesselius, upon what you term Metaphysical Medicine--I read them in German, ten or twelve years ago--have they been translated?"

"No, I'm sure they have not--I should have heard. They would have asked my leave, I think."

"I asked the publishers here, a few months ago, to get the book for me in the original German; but they tell me it is out of print."

"So it is, and has been for some years; but it flatters me as an author to find that you have not forgotten my little book, although," I added, laughing, "ten or twelve years is a considerable time to have managed without it; but I suppose you have been turning the subject over again in your mind, or something has happened lately to revive your interest in it."

At this remark, accompanied by a glance of inquiry, a sudden embarrassment disturbed Mr. Jennings, analogous to that which makes a young lady blush and look foolish. He dropped his eyes, and folded his hands together uneasily, and looked oddly, and you would have said, guiltily, for a moment.

I helped him out of his awkwardness in the best way, by appearing not to observe it, and going straight on, I said: "Those revivals of interest in a subject happen to me often; one book suggests another, and often sends me back a wild-goose chase over an interval of twenty years. But if you still care to possess a copy, I shall be only too happy to provide you; I have still got two or three by me--and if you allow me to present one I shall be very much honoured."

"You are very good indeed," he said, quite at his ease again, in a moment: "I almost despaired--I don't know how to thank you."

"Pray don't say a word; the thing is really so little worth that I am only ashamed of having offered it, and if you thank me any more I shall throw it into the fire in a fit of modesty."

Mr. Jennings laughed. He inquired where I was staying in London, and after a little more conversation on a variety of subjects, he took his departure.

# CHAPTER II

## The Doctor Questions Lady Mary and She Answers

"I like your vicar so much, Lady Mary," said I, as soon as he was gone. "He has read, travelled, and thought, and having also suffered, he ought to be an accomplished companion."

"So he is, and, better still, he is a really good man," said she. "His advice is invaluable about my schools, and all my little undertakings at Dawlbridge, and he's so painstaking, he takes so much trouble--you have no idea--wherever he thinks he can be of use: he's so good-natured and so sensible."

"It is pleasant to hear so good an account of his neighbourly virtues. I can only testify to his being an agreeable and gentle companion, and in addition to what you have told me, I think I can tell you two or three things about him," said I.
"Really!"

"Yes, to begin with, he's unmarried."

"Yes, that's right--go on."

"He has been writing, that is he _was_, but for two or three years perhaps, he has not gone on with his work, and the book was upon some rather abstract subject--perhaps theology."

"Well, he was writing a book, as you say; I'm not quite sure what it was about, but only that it was nothing that I cared for; very likely you are right, and he certainly did stop--yes."

"And although he only drank a little coffee here to-night, he likes tea, at least, did like it extravagantly."

"Yes, that's _quite_ true."

"He drank green tea, a good deal, didn't he?" I pursued.

"Well, that's very odd! Green tea was a subject on which we used almost to quarrel."

"But he has quite given that up," said I.

"So he has."

"And, now, one more fact. His mother or his father, did you know them?"

"Yes, both; his father is only ten years dead, and their place is near Dawlbridge. We knew them very well," she answered.

"Well, either his mother or his father--I should rather think his father, saw a ghost," said I.

"Well, you really are a conjurer, Dr. Hesselius."

"Conjurer or no, haven't I said right?" I answered merrily.
"You certainly have, and it _was_ his father: he was a silent, whimsical man, and he used to bore my father about his dreams, and at last he told him a story about a ghost he had seen and talked with, and a very odd story it was. I remember it particularly, because I was so afraid of him. This story was long before he died--when I was quite a child--and his ways were so silent and moping, and he used to drop in sometimes, in the dusk, when I was alone in the drawing-room, and I used to fancy there were ghosts about him."

I smiled and nodded.

"And now, having established my character as a conjurer, I think I must say good-night," said I.

"But how _did_ you find it out?"

"By the planets, of course, as the gipsies do," I answered, and so, gaily we said good-night.

Next morning I sent the little book he had been inquiring after, and a note to Mr. Jennings, and on returning late that evening, I found that he had called at my lodgings, and left his card. He asked whether I was at home, and asked at what hour he would be most likely to find me.

Does he intend opening his case, and consulting me "professionally," as they say? I hope so. I have already conceived a theory about him. It is supported by Lady Mary's answers to my parting questions. I should like much to ascertain from his own lips. But what can I do consistently with good breeding to invite a confession? Nothing. I rather think he meditates one. At all events, my dear Van L., I shan't make myself difficult of access; I mean to return his visit tomorrow. It will be only civil in return for his politeness, to ask to see him. Perhaps something may come of it. Whether much, little, or nothing, my dear Van L., you shall hear.

# CHAPTER III

## Dr. Hesselius Picks Up Something in Latin Books

Well, I have called at Blank Street.

On inquiring at the door, the servant told me that Mr. Jennings was engaged very particularly with a gentleman, a clergyman from Kenlis, his parish in the country. Intending to reserve my privilege, and to call again, I merely intimated that I should try another time, and had turned to go, when the servant begged my pardon, and asked me, looking at me little more attentively than well-bred persons of his order usually do, whether I was Dr. Hesselius; and, on learning that I was, he said, "Perhaps then, sir, you would allow me to mention it to Mr. Jennings, for I am sure he wishes to see you."

The servant returned in a moment, with a message from Mr. Jennings, asking me to go into his study, which was in effect his back drawing-room, promising to be with me in a very few minutes.

This was really a study--almost a library. The room was lofty, with two tall slender windows, and rich dark curtains. It was much larger than I had expected, and stored with books on every side, from the floor to the ceiling. The upper carpet--for to my tread it felt that there were two or three--was a Turkey carpet. My steps fell noiselessly. The bookcases standing out, placed the windows, particularly narrow ones, in deep recesses. The effect of the room was, although extremely comfortable, and even luxurious, decidedly gloomy, and aided by the silence, almost oppressive. Perhaps, however, I ought to have allowed something for association. My mind had connected peculiar ideas with Mr. Jennings. I stepped into this perfectly silent room, of a very silent house, with a peculiar foreboding; and its darkness, and solemn clothing of books, for except where two narrow looking-glasses were set in the wall, they were everywhere, helped this somber feeling.

While awaiting Mr. Jennings' arrival, I amused myself by looking into some of the books with which his shelves were laden. Not among these, but immediately under them, with their backs upward, on the floor, I lighted upon a complete set of Swedenborg's "Arcana Caelestia," in the original Latin, a very fine folio set, bound in the natty livery which theology affects, pure vellum, namely, gold letters, and carmine edges. There were paper markers in several of these volumes, I raised and placed them, one after the other, upon the table, and opening where these papers were placed, I read in the solemn Latin phraseology, a series of sentences indicated by a pencilled line at the margin. Of these I copy here a few, translating them into English.

"When man's interior sight is opened, which is that of his spirit, then there appear the things of another life, which cannot possibly be made visible to the bodily sight."...

"By the internal sight it has been granted me to see the things that are in the other life, more clearly than I see those that are in the world. From these considerations, it is evident that external vision exists from interior vision, and this from a vision still more interior, and so on."...

"There are with every man at least two evil spirits."...

"With wicked genii there is also a fluent speech, but harsh and grating. There is also among them a speech which is not fluent, wherein the dissent of the thoughts is perceived as something secretly creeping along within it."

"The evil spirits associated with man are, indeed from the hells, but when with man they are not then in hell, but are taken out thence. The place where they then are, is in the midst between heaven and hell, and is called the world of spirits--when the evil spirits who are with man, are in that world, they are not in any infernal torment, but in every thought and affection of man, and so, in all that the man himself enjoys. But when they are remitted into their hell, they return to their former state."...

"If evil spirits could perceive that they were associated with man, and yet that they were spirits separate from him, and if they could flow in into the things of his body, they would attempt by a thousand means to destroy him; for they hate man with a deadly hatred."...

"Knowing, therefore, that I was a man in the body, they were continually striving to destroy me, not as to the body only, but especially as to the soul; for to destroy any man or spirit is the very delight of the life of all who are in hell; but I have been continually protected by the Lord. Hence it appears how dangerous it is for man to be in a living consort with spirits, unless he be in the good of faith."...

"Nothing is more carefully guarded from the knowledge of associate spirits than their being thus conjoint with a man, for if they knew it they would speak to him, with the intention to destroy him."...

"The delight of hell is to do evil to man, and to hasten his eternal ruin."

A long note, written with a very sharp and fine pencil, in Mr. Jennings' neat hand, at the foot of the page, caught my eye. Expecting his criticism upon the text, I read a word or two, and stopped, for it was something quite different, and began with these words, _Deus misereatur mei_--"May God compassionate me." Thus warned of its private nature, I averted my eyes, and shut the book, replacing all the volumes as I had found them, except one which interested me, and in which, as men studious and solitary in their habits will do, I grew so absorbed as to take no cognisance of the outer world, nor to remember where I was.

I was reading some pages which refer to "representatives" and "correspondents," in the technical language of Swedenborg, and had arrived at a passage, the substance of which is, that evil spirits, when seen by other eyes than those of their infernal associates, present themselves, by "correspondence," in the shape of the beast (_fera_) which represents their particular lust and life, in aspect direful and atrocious. This is a long passage, and particularises a number of those bestial forms.

# CHAPTER IV

## Four Eyes Were Reading the Passage

I was running the head of my pencil-case along the line as I read it, and something caused me to raise my eyes.

Directly before me was one of the mirrors I have mentioned, in which I saw reflected the tall shape of my friend, Mr. Jennings, leaning over my shoulder, and reading the page at which I was busy, and with a face so dark and wild that I should hardly have known him.

I turned and rose. He stood erect also, and with an effort laughed a little, saying:

"I came in and asked you how you did, but without succeeding in awaking you from your book; so I could not restrain my curiosity, and very impertinently, I'm afraid, peeped over your shoulder. This is not your first time of looking into those pages. You have looked into Swedenborg, no doubt, long ago?"

"Oh dear, yes! I owe Swedenborg a great deal; you will discover traces of him in the little book on Metaphysical Medicine, which you were so good as to remember."

Although my friend affected a gaiety of manner, there was a slight flush in his face, and I could perceive that he was inwardly much perturbed.

"I'm scarcely yet qualified, I know so little of Swedenborg. I've only had them a fortnight," he answered, "and I think they are rather likely to make a solitary man nervous--that is, judging from the very little I have read--I don't say that they have made me so," he laughed; "and I'm so very much obliged for the book. I hope you got my note?"

I made all proper acknowledgments and modest disclaimers.

"I never read a book that I go with, so entirely, as that of yours," he continued. "I saw at once there is more in it than is quite unfolded. Do you know Dr. Harley?" he asked, rather abruptly.

In passing, the editor remarks that the physician here named was one of the most eminent who had ever practised in England.

I did, having had letters to him, and had experienced from him great courtesy and considerable assistance during my visit to England.

"I think that man one of the very greatest fools I ever met in my life," said Mr. Jennings.

This was the first time I had ever heard him say a sharp thing of anybody, and such a term applied to so high a name a little startled me.

"Really! and in what way?" I asked.

"In his profession," he answered.

I smiled.

"I mean this," he said: "he seems to me, one half, blind--I mean one half of all he looks at is dark--preternaturally bright and vivid all the rest; and the worst of it is, it seems _wilful_. I can't get him--I mean he won't--I've had some experience of him as a physician, but I look on him as, in that sense, no better than a paralytic mind, an intellect half dead. I'll tell you--I know I shall some time--all about it," he said, with a little agitation. "You stay some months longer in England. If I should be out of town during your stay for a little time, would you allow me to trouble you with a letter?"

"I should be only too happy," I assured him.

"Very good of you. I am so utterly dissatisfied with Harley."

"A little leaning to the materialistic school," I said.

"A _mere_ materialist," he corrected me; "you can't think how that sort of thing worries one who knows better. You won't tell any one--any of my friends you know--that I am hippish; now, for instance, no one knows—not even Lady Mary--that I have seen Dr. Harley, or any other doctor. So pray don't mention it; and, if I should have any threatening of an attack, you'll kindly let me write, or, should I be in town, have a little talk with you."

I was full of conjecture, and unconsciously I found I had fixed my eyes gravely on him, for he lowered his for a moment, and he said:

"I see you think I might as well tell you now, or else you are forming a conjecture; but you may as well give it up. If you were guessing all the rest of your life, you will never hit on it."

He shook his head smiling, and over that wintry sunshine a black cloud suddenly came down, and he drew his breath in, through his teeth as men do in pain.

"Sorry, of course, to learn that you apprehend occasion to consult any of us; but, command me when and how you like, and I need not assure you that your confidence is sacred."

He then talked of quite other things, and in a comparatively cheerful way and after a little time, I took my leave.

# CHAPTER V

## Dr. Hesselius is Summoned to Richmond

We parted cheerfully, but he was not cheerful, nor was I. There are certain expressions of that powerful organ of spirit--the human face--which, although I have seen them often, and possess a doctor's nerve, yet disturb me profoundly. One look of Mr. Jennings haunted me. It had seized my imagination with so dismal a power that I changed my plans for the evening, and went to the opera, feeling that I wanted a change of ideas.

I heard nothing of or from him for two or three days, when a note in his hand reached me. It was cheerful, and full of hope. He said that he had been for some little time so much better--quite well, in fact--that he was going to make a little experiment, and run down for a month or so to his parish, to try whether a little work might not quite set him up. There was in it a fervent religious expression of gratitude for his restoration, as he now almost hoped he might call it.

A day or two later I saw Lady Mary, who repeated what his note had announced, and told me that he was actually in Warwickshire, having resumed his clerical duties at Kenlis; and she added, "I begin to think that he is really perfectly well, and that there never was anything the matter, more than nerves and fancy; we are all nervous, but I fancy there is nothing like a little hard work for that kind of weakness, and he has made up his mind to try it. I should not be surprised if he did not come back for a year."

Notwithstanding all this confidence, only two days later I had this note, dated from his house off Piccadilly:

> Dear Sir,--I have returned disappointed. If I should feel at all able to see you, I shall write to ask you kindly to call. At present, I am too low, and, in fact, simply unable to say all I wish to say. Pray don't mention my name to my friends. I can see no one. By-and-by, please God, you shall hear from me. I mean to take a run into Shropshire, where some of my people are. God bless you! May we, on my return, meet more happily than I can now write.

About a week after this I saw Lady Mary at her own house, the last person, she said, left in town, and just on the wing for Brighton, for the London season was quite over. She told me that she had heard from Mr. Jenning's niece, Martha, in Shropshire. There was nothing to be gathered from her letter, more than that he was low and nervous. In those words, of which healthy people think so lightly, what a world of suffering is sometimes hidden!

Nearly five weeks had passed without any further news of Mr. Jennings. At the end of that time I received a note from him. He wrote:

"I have been in the country, and have had change of air, change of scene, change of faces, change of everything--and in everything--but _myself_. I have made up my mind, so far as the most irresolute creature on earth can do it, to tell my case fully to you. If your engagements will permit, pray come to me to-day, to-morrow, or the next day; but, pray defer as little as possible. You know not how much I need help. I have a quiet house at Richmond, where I now am. Perhaps you can manage to come to dinner, or to luncheon, or even to tea. You shall have no trouble in finding me out. The servant at Blank Street, who takes this note, will have a carriage at your door at any hour you please; and I am always to be found. You will say that I ought not to be alone. I have tried everything. Come and see."

I called up the servant, and decided on going out the same evening, which accordingly I did.

He would have been much better in a lodging-house, or hotel, I thought, as I drove up through a short double row of sombre elms to a very old-fashioned brick house, darkened by the foliage of these trees, which overtopped, and nearly surrounded it. It was a perverse choice, for nothing could be imagined more triste and silent. The house, I found, belonged to him. He had stayed for a day or two in town, and, finding it for some cause insupportable, had come out here, probably because being furnished and his own, he was relieved of the thought and delay of selection, by coming here.

The sun had already set, and the red reflected light of the western sky illuminated the scene with the peculiar effect with which we are all familiar. The hall seemed very dark, but, getting to the back drawing-room, whose windows command the west, I was again in the same dusky light.

I sat down, looking out upon the richly-wooded landscape that glowed in the grand and melancholy light which was every moment fading. The corners of the room were already dark; all was growing dim, and the gloom was insensibly toning my mind, already prepared for what was sinister. I was waiting alone for his arrival, which soon took place. The door communicating with the front room opened, and the tall figure of Mr. Jennings, faintly seen in the ruddy twilight, came, with quiet stealthy steps, into the room.

We shook hands, and, taking a chair to the window, where there was still light enough to enable us to see each other's faces, he sat down beside me, and, placing his hand upon my arm, with scarcely a word of preface began his narrative.

# CHAPTER VI

## How Mr. Jennings Met His Companion

The faint glow of the west, the pomp of the then lonely woods of Richmond, were before us, behind and about us the darkening room, and on the stony face of the sufferer--for the character of his face, though still gentle and sweet, was changed--rested that dim, odd glow which seems to descend and produce, where it touches, lights, sudden though faint, which are lost, almost without gradation, in darkness. The silence, too, was utter: not a distant wheel, or bark, or whistle from without; and within the depressing stillness of an invalid bachelor's house.

I guessed well the nature, though not even vaguely the particulars of the revelations I was about to receive, from that fixed face of suffering that so oddly flushed stood out, like a portrait of Schalken's, before its background of darkness.

"It began," he said, "on the 15th of October, three years and eleven weeks ago, and two days--I keep very accurate count, for every day is torment. If I leave anywhere a chasm in my narrative tell me.

"About four years ago I began a work, which had cost me very much thought and reading. It was upon the religious metaphysics of the ancients."

"I know," said I, "the actual religion of educated and thinking paganism, quite apart from symbolic worship? A wide and very interesting field."

"Yes, but not good for the mind--the Christian mind, I mean. Paganism is all bound together in essential unity, and, with evil sympathy, their religion involves their art, and both their manners, and the subject is a degrading fascination and the Nemesis sure. God forgive me!

"I wrote a great deal; I wrote late at night. I was always thinking on the subject, walking about, wherever I was, everywhere. It thoroughly infected me. You are to remember that all the material ideas connected with it were more or less of the beautiful, the subject itself delightfully interesting, and I, then, without a care."

He sighed heavily.

"I believe, that every one who sets about writing in earnest does his work, as a friend of mine phrased it, _on_ something--tea, or coffee, or tobacco. I suppose there is a material waste that must be hourly supplied in such occupations, or that we should grow too abstracted, and the mind, as it were, pass out of the body, unless it were reminded often enough of the connection by actual sensation. At all events, I felt the want, and I supplied it. Tea was my companion--at first the ordinary black tea, made in the usual way, not too strong: but I drank a good deal, and increased its strength as I went on. I never experienced an uncomfortable symptom from it. I began to take a little green tea. I found the effect pleasanter, it cleared and intensified the power of thought so, I had come to take it frequently, but not stronger than one might take it for pleasure. I wrote a great deal out here, it was so quiet, and in this room. I used to sit up very late, and it became a habit with me to sip my tea--green tea--every now and then as my work proceeded. I had a little kettle on my table, that swung over a lamp, and made tea two or three times between eleven o'clock and two or three in the morning, my hours of going to bed. I used to go into town every day. I was not a monk, and, although I spent an hour or two in a library, hunting up authorities and looking out lights upon my theme, I was in no morbid state as far as I can judge. I met my friends pretty much as usual and enjoyed their society, and, on the whole, existence had never been, I think, so pleasant before.

"I had met with a man who had some odd old books, German editions in mediaeval Latin, and I was only too happy to be permitted access to them. This obliging person's books were in the City, a very out-of-the-way part of it. I had rather out-stayed my intended hour, and, on coming out, seeing no cab near, I was tempted to get into the omnibus which used to drive past this house. It was darker than this by the time the 'bus had reached an old house, you may have remarked, with four poplars at each side of the door, and there the last passenger but myself got out. We drove along rather faster. It was twilight now. I leaned back in my corner next the door ruminating pleasantly.

"The interior of the omnibus was nearly dark. I had observed in the corner opposite to me at the other side, and at the end next the horses,

two small circular reflections, as it seemed to me of a reddish light. They were about two inches apart, and about the size of those small brass buttons that yachting men used to put upon their jackets. I began to speculate, as listless men will, upon this trifle, as it seemed. From what centre did that faint but deep red light come, and from what--glass beads, buttons, toy decorations--was it reflected? We were lumbering along gently, having nearly a mile still to go. I had not solved the puzzle, and it became in another minute more odd, for these two luminous points, with a sudden jerk, descended nearer and nearer the floor, keeping still their relative distance and horizontal position, and then, as suddenly, they rose to the level of the seat on which I was sitting
and I saw them no more.

"My curiosity was now really excited, and, before I had time to think, I saw again these two dull lamps, again together near the floor; again they disappeared, and again in their old corner I saw them.

"So, keeping my eyes upon them, I edged quietly up my own side, towards the end at which I still saw these tiny discs of red.

"There was very little light in the 'bus. It was nearly dark. I leaned forward to aid my endeavour to discover what these little circles really were. They shifted position a little as I did so. I began now to perceive an outline of something black, and I soon saw, with tolerable distinctness, the outline of a small black monkey, pushing its face forward in mimicry to meet mine; those were its eyes, and I now dimly saw its teeth grinning at me.

"I drew back, not knowing whether it might not meditate a spring. I fancied that one of the passengers had forgot this ugly pet, and wishing to ascertain something of its temper, though not caring to trust my fingers to it, I poked my umbrella softly towards it. It remained immovable--up to it--_through_ it. For through it, and back and forward it passed, without the slightest resistance.

"I can't, in the least, convey to you the kind of horror that I felt. When I had ascertained that the thing was an illusion, as I then supposed, there came a misgiving about myself and a terror that fascinated me in impotence to remove my gaze from the eyes of the brute for some moments. As I looked, it made a little skip back, quite into the corner, and I, in a panic, found myself at the door, having put my head out, drawing deep breaths of the outer air, and staring at the lights and tress we were passing, too glad to reassure myself of reality.

"I stopped the 'bus and got out. I perceived the man look oddly at me as I paid him. I dare say there was something unusual in my looks and manner, for I had never felt so strangely before."

# CHAPTER VII

## The Journey: First Stage

"When the omnibus drove on, and I was alone upon the road, I looked carefully round to ascertain whether the monkey had followed me. To my indescribable relief I saw it nowhere. I can't describe easily what a shock I had received, and my sense of genuine gratitude on finding myself, as I supposed, quite rid of it.

"I had got out a little before we reached this house, two or three hundred steps. A brick wall runs along the footpath, and inside the wall is a hedge of yew, or some dark evergreen of that kind, and within that again the row of fine trees which you may have remarked as you came.

"This brick wall is about as high as my shoulder, and happening to raise my eyes I saw the monkey, with that stooping gait, on all fours, walking or creeping, close beside me, on top of the wall. I stopped, looking at it with a feeling of loathing and horror. As I stopped so did it. It sat up on the wall with its long hands on its knees looking at me. There was not light enough to see it much more than in outline, nor was it dark enough to bring the peculiar light of its eyes into strong relief. I still saw, however, that red foggy light plainly enough. It did not show its teeth, nor exhibit any sign of irritation, but seemed jaded and sulky, and was observing me steadily.

"I drew back into the middle of the road. It was an unconscious recoil, and there I stood, still looking at it. It did not move.

"With an instinctive determination to try something--anything, I turned about and walked briskly towards town with askance look, all the time, watching the movements of the beast. It crept swiftly along the wall, at exactly my pace.

"Where the wall ends, near the turn of the road, it came down, and with a wiry spring or two brought itself close to my feet, and continued to keep up with me, as I quickened my pace. It was at my left side, so close to my leg that I felt every moment as if I should tread upon it.

"The road was quite deserted and silent, and it was darker every moment. I stopped dismayed and bewildered, turning as I did so, the other way--I mean, towards this house, away from which I had been walking. When I stood still, the monkey drew back to a distance of, I suppose, about five or six yards, and remained stationary, watching me.

"I had been more agitated than I have said. I had read, of course, as everyone has, something about 'spectral illusions,' as you physicians term the phenomena of such cases. I considered my situation, and looked my misfortune in the face.

"These affections, I had read, are sometimes transitory and sometimes obstinate. I had read of cases in which the appearance, at first harmless, had, step by step, degenerated into something direful and insupportable, and ended by wearing its victim out. Still as I stood there, but for my bestial companion, quite alone, I tried to comfort myself by repeating again and again the assurance, 'the thing is purely disease, a well-known physical affection, as distinctly as small-pox or neuralgia. Doctors are all agreed on that, philosophy demonstrates it. I must not be a fool. I've been sitting up too late, and I daresay my digestion is quite wrong, and, with God's help, I shall be all right, and this is but a symptom of nervous dyspepsia.' Did I believe all this? Not one word of it, no more than any other miserable being ever did who is once seized and riveted in this satanic captivity. Against my convictions, I might say my knowledge, I was simply bullying myself into a false courage.

"I now walked homeward. I had only a few hundred yards to go. I had forced myself into a sort of resignation, but I had not got over the sickening shock and the flurry of the first certainty of my misfortune.

"I made up my mind to pass the night at home. The brute moved close beside me, and I fancied there was the sort of anxious drawing toward the house, which one sees in tired horses or dogs, sometimes as they come toward home. "I was afraid to go into town, I was afraid of any one's seeing and recognizing me. I was conscious of an irrepressible agitation in my manner. Also, I was afraid of any violent change in my habits, such as going to a place of amusement, or walking from home in order to fatigue myself. At the hall door it waited till I mounted the steps, and when the door was opened entered with me.

"I drank no tea that night. I got cigars and some brandy and water. My idea was that I should act upon my material system, and by living for a while in sensation apart from thought, send myself forcibly, as it were, into a new groove. I came up here to this drawing-room. I sat just here. The monkey then got upon a small table that then stood _there_. It looked dazed and languid. An irrepressible uneasiness as to its movements kept my eyes always upon it. Its eyes were half closed, but I could see them glow. It was looking steadily at me. In all situations, at all hours, it is awake and looking at me. That never changes.

"I shall not continue in detail my narrative of this particular night. I shall describe, rather, the phenomena of the first year, which never varied, essentially. I shall describe the monkey as it appeared in daylight. In the dark, as you shall presently hear, there are peculiarities. It is a small monkey, perfectly black. It had only one peculiarity--a character of malignity--unfathomable malignity. During the first year it looked sullen and sick. But this character of intense malice and vigilance was always underlying that surly languor. During all that time it acted as if on a plan of giving me as little trouble as was consistent with watching me. Its eyes were never off me. I have never lost sight of it, except in my sleep, light or dark, day or night, since it came here, excepting when it withdraws for some weeks at a time, unaccountably.

"In total dark it is visible as in daylight. I do not mean merely its eyes. It is _all_ visible distinctly in a halo that resembles a glow of red embers, and which accompanies it in all its movements.

"When it leaves me for a time, it is always at night, in the dark, and in the same way. It grows at first uneasy, and then furious, and then advances towards me, grinning and shaking, its paws clenched, and, at the same time, there comes the appearance of fire in the grate. I never have any fire. I can't sleep in the room where there is any, and it draws nearer and nearer to the chimney, quivering, it seems, with rage, and when its fury rises to the highest pitch, it springs into the grate, and up the chimney, and I see it no more.

"When first this happened, I thought I was released. I was now a new man. A day passed--a night--and no return, and a blessed week--a week--another week. I was always on my knees, Dr. Hesselius, always, thanking God and praying. A whole month passed of liberty, but on a sudden, it was with me again."

# CHAPTER VIII

## The Second Stage

"It was with me, and the malice which before was torpid under a sullen exterior, was now active. It was perfectly unchanged in every other respect. This new energy was apparent in its activity and its looks, and soon in other ways.

"For a time, you will understand, the change was shown only in an increased vivacity, and an air of menace, as if it were always brooding over some atrocious plan. Its eyes, as before, were never off me."

"Is it here now?" I asked.

"No," he replied, "it has been absent exactly a fortnight and a day--fifteen days. It has sometimes been away so long as nearly two months, once for three. Its absence always exceeds a fortnight, although it may be but by a single day. Fifteen days having past since I saw it last, it may return now at any moment."

"Is its return," I asked, "accompanied by any peculiar manifestation?" "Nothing--no," he said. "It is simply with me again. On lifting my eyes from a book, or turning my head, I see it, as usual, looking at me, and then it remains, as before, for its appointed time. I have never told so much and so minutely before to any one."

I perceived that he was agitated, and looking like death, and he repeatedly applied his handkerchief to his forehead; I suggested that he might be tired, and told him that I would call, with pleasure, in the morning, but he said:

"No, if you don't mind hearing it all now. I have got so far, and I should prefer making one effort of it. When I spoke to Dr. Harley, I had nothing like so much to tell. You are a philosophic physician. You give spirit its proper rank. If this thing is real--"

He paused looking at me with agitated inquiry.

"We can discuss it by-and-by, and very fully. I will give you all I think," I answered, after an interval.

"Well--very well. If it is anything real, I say, it is prevailing, little by little, and drawing me more interiorly into hell. Optic nerves, he talked of. Ah! well--there are other nerves of communication. May God Almighty help me! You shall hear.

"Its power of action, I tell you, had increased. Its malice became, in a way, aggressive. About two years ago, some questions that were pending between me and the bishop having been settled, I went down to my parish in Warwickshire, anxious to find occupation in my profession. I was not prepared for what happened, although I have since thought I might have apprehended something like it. The reason of my saying so is this--"

He was beginning to speak with a great deal more effort and reluctance, and sighed often, and seemed at times nearly overcome. But at this time his manner was not agitated. It was more like that of a sinking patient, who has given himself up.

"Yes, but I will first tell you about Kenlis, my parish.
"It was with me when I left this place for Dawlbridge. It was my silent travelling companion, and it remained with me at the vicarage. When I entered on the discharge of my duties, another change took place. The thing exhibited an atrocious determination to thwart me. It was with me in the church--in the reading-desk--in the pulpit--within the communion rails. At last, it reached this extremity, that while I was reading to the congregation, it would spring upon the book and squat there, so that I was unable to see the page. This happened more than once.

"I left Dawlbridge for a time. I placed myself in Dr. Harley's hands. I did everything he told me. He gave my case a great deal of thought. It interested him, I think. He seemed successful. For nearly three months I was perfectly free from a return. I began to think I was safe. With his full assent I returned to Dawlbridge.

"I travelled in a chaise. I was in good spirits. I was more--I was happy and grateful. I was returning, as I thought, delivered from a dreadful hallucination, to the scene of duties which I longed to enter upon. It was a beautiful sunny evening, everything looked serene and cheerful, and I was delighted. I remember looking out of the window to see the spire of my church at Kenlis among the trees, at the point where one has the earliest view of it. It is exactly where the little stream that bounds the parish passes under the road by a culvert, and where it emerges at the road-side, a stone with an old inscription is placed. As we passed this point, I drew my head in and sat down, and in the corner of the chaise was the monkey.

"For a moment I felt faint, and then quite wild with despair and horror. I called to the driver, and got out, and sat down at the road-side, and prayed to God silently for mercy. A despairing resignation supervened. My companion was with me as I re-entered the vicarage. The same persecution followed. After a short struggle I submitted, and soon I left the place.

"I told you," he said, "that the beast has before this become in certain ways aggressive. I will explain a little. It seemed to be actuated by intense and increasing fury, whenever I said my prayers, or even meditated prayer. It amounted at last to a dreadful interruption. You will ask, how could a silent immaterial phantom effect that? It was thus, whenever I meditated praying; It was always before me, and nearer and nearer.

"It used to spring on a table, on the back of a chair, on the chimney-piece, and slowly to swing itself from side to side, looking at me all the time. There is in its motion an indefinable power to dissipate thought, and to contract one's attention to that monotony, till the ideas shrink, as it were, to a point, and at last to nothing--and unless I had started up, and shook off the catalepsy I have felt as if my mind were on the point of losing itself. There are other ways," he sighed heavily; "thus, for instance, while I pray with my eyes closed, it comes closer and closer, and I see it. I know it is not to be accounted for physically, but I do actually see it, though my lids are dosed, and so it rocks my mind, as it were, and overpowers me, and I am obliged to rise from my knees. If you had ever yourself known this, you would be acquainted with desperation."

# CHAPTER IX

## The Third Stage

"I see, Dr. Hesselius, that you don't lose one word of my statement. I need not ask you to listen specially to what I am now going to tell you. They talk of the optic nerves, and of spectral illusions, as if the organ of sight was the only point assailable by the influences that have fastened upon me--I know better. For two years in my direful case that limitation prevailed. But as food is taken in softly at the lips, and then brought under the teeth, as the tip of the little finger caught in a mill crank will draw in the hand, and the arm, and the whole body, so the miserable mortal who has been once caught firmly by the end of the finest fibre of his nerve, is drawn in and in, by the enormous machinery of hell, until he is as I am. Yes, Doctor, as _I_ am, for a while I talk to you, and implore relief, I feel that my prayer is for the impossible, and my pleading with the inexorable." I endeavoured to calm his visibly increasing agitation, and told him that he must not despair.

While we talked the night had overtaken us. The filmy moonlight was wide over the scene which the window commanded, and I said:

"Perhaps you would prefer having candles. This light, you know, is odd. I should wish you, as much as possible, under your usual conditions while I make my diagnosis, shall I call it--otherwise I don't care."

"All lights are the same to me," he said; "except when I read or write, I care not if night were perpetual. I am going to tell you what happened about a year ago. The thing began to speak to me."

"Speak! How do you mean--speak as a man does, do you mean?"

"Yes; speak in words and consecutive sentences, with perfect coherence and articulation; but there is a peculiarity. It is not like the tone of a human voice. It is not by my ears it reaches me--it comes like a singing through my head.

"This faculty, the power of speaking to me, will be my undoing. It won't let me pray, it interrupts me with dreadful blasphemies. I dare not go on, I could not. Oh! Doctor, can the skill, and thought, and prayers of man avail me nothing!"

"You must promise me, my dear sir, not to trouble yourself with unnecessarily exciting thoughts; confine yourself strictly to the narrative of _facts_; and recollect, above all, that even if the thing that infests you be, you seem to suppose a reality with an actual independent life and will, yet it can have no power to hurt you, unless it be given from above: its access to your senses depends mainly upon your physical condition--this is, under God, your comfort and reliance: we are all alike environed. It is only that in your case, the _'paries,'_ the veil of the flesh, the screen, is a little out of repair, and sights and sounds are transmitted. We must enter on a new course, sir,--be encouraged. I'll give to-night to the careful consideration of the whole case."
"You are very good, sir; you think it worth trying, you don't give me quite up; but, sir, you don't know, it is gaining such an influence over me: it orders me about, it is such a tyrant, and I'm growing so helpless. May God deliver me!"

"It orders you about--of course you mean by speech?"

"Yes, yes; it is always urging me to crimes, to injure others, or myself. You see, Doctor, the situation is urgent, it is indeed. When I was in Shropshire, a few weeks ago" (Mr. Jennings was speaking rapidly and trembling now, holding my arm with one hand, and looking in my face), "I went out one day with a party of friends for a walk: my persecutor, I tell you, was with me at the time. I lagged behind the rest: the country near the Dee, you know, is beautiful. Our path happened to lie near a coal mine, and at the verge of the wood is a perpendicular shaft, they say, a hundred and fifty feet deep. My niece had remained behind with me--she knows, of course nothing of the nature of my sufferings. She knew, however, that I had been ill, and was low, and she remained to prevent my being quite alone. As we loitered slowly on together, the brute that accompanied me was urging me to throw myself down the shaft. I tell you now--oh, sir, think of it!--the one consideration that saved me from that hideous death was the fear lest the shock of witnessing the occurrence should be too much for the poor girl. I asked her to go on and walk with her friends, saying that I could go no further. She made excuses, and the more I urged her the firmer she became. She looked doubtful and frightened. I suppose there was something in my looks or manner that alarmed her; but she would not go, and that literally saved me. You had no idea, sir, that a living man could be made so abject a slave of Satan," he said, with a ghastly groan and a shudder.

There was a pause here, and I said, "You _were_ preserved nevertheless. It was the act of God. You are in His hands and in the power of no other being: be therefore confident for the future."

# CHAPTER X

## Home

I made him have candles lighted, and saw the room looking cheery and inhabited before I left him. I told him that he must regard his illness strictly as one dependent on physical, though _subtle_ physical causes. I told him that he had evidence of God's care and love in the deliverance which he had just described, and that I had perceived with pain that he seemed to regard its peculiar features as indicating that he had been delivered over to spiritual reprobation. Than such a conclusion nothing could be, I insisted, less warranted; and not only so, but more contrary to facts, as disclosed in his mysterious deliverance from that murderous influence during his Shropshire excursion. First, his niece had been retained by his side without his intending to keep her near him; and, secondly, there had been infused into his mind an irresistible repugnance to execute the dreadful suggestion in her presence.

As I reasoned this point with him, Mr. Jennings wept. He seemed comforted. One promise I exacted, which was that should the monkey at any time return, I should be sent for immediately; and, repeating my assurance that I would give neither time nor thought to any other subject until I had thoroughly investigated his case, and that to-morrow he should hear the result, I took my leave.

Before getting into the carriage I told the servant that his master was far from well, and that he should make a point of frequently looking into his room. My own arrangements I made with a view to being quite secure from interruption.

I merely called at my lodgings, and with a travelling-desk and carpet-bag, set off in a hackney carriage for an inn about two miles out of town, called "The Horns," a very quiet and comfortable house, with good thick walls. And there I resolved, without the possibility of intrusion or distraction, to devote some hours of the night, in my comfortable sitting-room, to Mr. Jennings' case, and so much of the morning as it might require.

(There occurs here a careful note of Dr. Hesselius' opinion upon the case, and of the habits, dietary, and medicines which he prescribed. It is curious--some persons would say mystical. But, on the whole, I doubt whether it would sufficiently interest a reader of the kind I am likely to meet with, to warrant its being here reprinted. The whole letter was plainly written at the inn where he had hid himself for the occasion. The next letter is dated from his town lodgings.)

I left town for the inn where I slept last night at half-past nine, and did not arrive at my room in town until one o'clock this afternoon. I found a letter in Mr. Jennings' hand upon my table. It had not come by post, and, on inquiry, I learned that Mr. Jennings' servant had brought it, and on learning that I was not to return until to-day, and that no one could tell him my address, he seemed very uncomfortable, and said his orders from his master were that that he was not to return without an answer.

I opened the letter and read:

> DEAR DR. HESSELIUS.--It is here. You had not been an hour gone when it returned. It is speaking. It knows all that has happened. It knows everything--it knows you, and is frantic and atrocious. It reviles. I send you this. It knows every word I have written--I

write. This I promised, and I therefore write, but I fear very confused, very incoherently. I am so interrupted, disturbed.

Ever yours, sincerely yours,
Robert Lynder Jennings.

"When did this come?" I asked.

"About eleven last night: the man was here again, and has been here three times to-day. The last time is about an hour since."

Thus answered, and with the notes I had made upon his case in my pocket, I was in a few minutes driving towards Richmond, to see Mr. Jennings.

I by no means, as you perceive, despaired of Mr. Jennings' case. He had himself remembered and applied, though quite in a mistaken way, the principle which I lay down in my Metaphysical Medicine, and which governs all such cases. I was about to apply it in earnest. I was profoundly interested, and very anxious to see and examine him while the "enemy" was actually present.

I drove up to the sombre house, and ran up the steps, and knocked. The door, in a little time, was opened by a tall woman in black silk. She looked ill, and as if she had been crying. She curtseyed, and heard my question, but she did not answer. She turned her face away, extending her hand towards two men who were coming down-stairs; and thus having, as it were, tacitly made me over to them, she passed through a side-door hastily and shut it.

The man who was nearest the hall, I at once accosted, but being now close to him, I was shocked to see that both his hands were covered with blood.

I drew back a little, and the man, passing downstairs, merely said in a low tone, "Here's the servant, sir."

The servant had stopped on the stairs, confounded and dumb at seeing me. He was rubbing his hands in a handkerchief, and it was steeped in blood.

"Jones, what is it? what has happened?" I asked, while a sickening suspicion overpowered me.

The man asked me to come up to the lobby. I was beside him in a moment, and, frowning and pallid, with contracted eyes, he told me the horror which I already half guessed.

His master had made away with himself.

I went upstairs with him to the room--what I saw there I won't tell you. He had cut his throat with his razor. It was a frightful gash. The two men had laid him on the bed, and composed his limbs. It had happened, as the immense pool of blood on the floor declared, at some distance between the bed and the window. There was carpet round his bed, and a carpet under his dressing-table, but none on the rest of the floor, for the man said he did not like a carpet on his bedroom. In this sombre and now terrible room, one of the great elms that darkened the house was slowly moving the shadow of one of its great boughs upon this dreadful floor.

I beckoned to the servant, and we went downstairs together. I turned off the hall into an old-fashioned panelled room, and there standing, I heard all the servant had to tell. It was not a great deal.

"I concluded, sir, from your words, and looks, sir, as you left last night, that you thought my master was seriously ill. I thought it might be that you were afraid of a fit or something. So I attended very close to your directions. He sat up late, till past three o'clock. He was not writing or reading. He was talking a great deal to himself, but that was nothing unusual. At about that hour I assisted him to undress, and left him in his slippers and dressing-gown. I went back softly in about half-an-hour. He was in his bed, quite undressed, and a pair of candles lighted on the table beside his bed. He was leaning on his elbow, and looking out at the other side of the bed when I came in. I asked him if he wanted anything, and he said No.

"I don't know whether it was what you said to me, sir, or something a little unusual about him, but I was uneasy, uncommon uneasy about him last night.

"In another half hour, or it might be a little more, I went up again. I did not hear him talking as before. I opened the door a little. The candles were both out, which was not usual. I had a bedroom candle, and I let the light in, a little bit, looking softly round. I saw him sitting in that chair beside the dressing-table with his clothes on again. He turned round and looked at me. I thought it strange he should get up and dress, and put out the candles to sit in the dark, that way. But I only asked him again if I could do anything for him. He said, No, rather sharp, I thought. I asked him if I might light the candles, and he said, 'Do as you like, Jones.' So I lighted them, and I lingered about the room, and he said, 'Tell me truth, Jones; why did you come again--you did not hear anyone cursing?' 'No, sir,' I said, wondering what he could mean.

"'No,' said he, after me, 'of course, no;' and I said to him, 'Wouldn't it be well, sir, you went to bed? It's just five o'clock;' and he said nothing, but, 'Very likely; good-night, Jones.' So I went, sir, but in less than an hour I came again. The door was fast, and he heard me, and called as I thought from the bed to know what I wanted, and he desired me not to disturb him again. I lay down and slept for a little. It must have been between six and seven when I went up again. The door was still fast, and he made no answer, so I did not like to disturb him, and thinking he was asleep, I left him till nine. It was his custom to ring when he wished me to come, and I had no particular hour for calling him. I tapped very gently, and getting no answer, I stayed away a good while, supposing he was getting some rest then. It was not till eleven o'clock I grew really uncomfortable about him--for at the latest he was never, that I could remember, later than half-past ten. I got no answer. I knocked and called, and still no answer. So not being able to force the door, I called Thomas from the stables, and together we forced it, and found him in the shocking way you saw."

Jones had no more to tell. Poor Mr. Jennings was very gentle, and very kind. All his people were fond of him. I could see that the servant was very much moved.

So, dejected and agitated, I passed from that terrible house, and its dark canopy of elms, and I hope I shall never see it more. While I write to you I feel like a man who has but half waked from a frightful and monotonous dream. My memory rejects the picture with incredulity and horror. Yet I know it is true. It is the story of the process of a poison, a poison which excites the reciprocal action of spirit and nerve, and paralyses the tissue that separates those cognate functions of the senses, the external and the interior. Thus we find strange bed-fellows, and the mortal and immortal prematurely make acquaintance.

# CONCLUSION

## A Word for Those Who Suffer

My dear Van L----, you have suffered from an affection similar to that which I have just described. You twice complained of a return of it.

Who, under God, cured you? Your humble servant, Martin Hesselius. Let me rather adopt the more emphasised piety of a certain good old French surgeon of three hundred years ago: "I treated, and God cured you."

Come, my friend, you are not to be hippish. Let me tell you a fact.

I have met with, and treated, as my book shows, fifty-seven cases of this kind of vision, which I term indifferently "sublimated," "precocious," and "interior."

There is another class of affections which are truly termed--though commonly confounded with those which I describe--spectral illusions. These latter I look upon as being no less simply curable than a cold in the head or a trifling dyspepsia.

It is those which rank in the first category that test our promptitude of thought. Fifty-seven such cases have I encountered, neither more nor less. And in how many of these have I failed? In no one single instance.

There is no one affliction of mortality more easily and certainly reducible, with a little patience, and a rational confidence in the physician. With these simple conditions, I look upon the cure as absolutely certain.

You are to remember that I had not even commenced to treat Mr. Jennings' case. I have not any doubt that I should have cured him perfectly in eighteen months, or possibly it might have extended to two years. Some cases are very rapidly curable, others extremely tedious. Every intelligent physician who will give thought and diligence to the task, will effect a cure.

You know my tract on "The Cardinal Functions of the Brain." I there, by the evidence of innumerable facts, prove, as I think, the high probability of a circulation arterial and venous in its mechanism, through the nerves. Of this system, thus considered, the brain is the heart. The fluid, which is propagated hence through one class of nerves, returns in an altered state through another, and the nature of that fluid is spiritual, though not immaterial, any more than, as I before remarked, light or electricity are so.

By various abuses, among which the habitual use of such agents as green tea is one, this fluid may be affected as to its quality, but it is more frequently disturbed as to equilibrium. This fluid being that which we have in common with spirits, a congestion found upon the masses of brain or nerve, connected with the interior sense, forms a surface unduly exposed, on which disembodied spirits may operate: communication is thus more or less effectually established. Between this brain circulation and the heart circulation there is an intimate sympathy. The seat, or rather the instrument of exterior vision, is the eye. The seat of interior vision is the nervous tissue and brain, immediately about and above the eyebrow. You remember how effectually I dissipated your pictures by the simple application of iced eau-de-cologne. Few cases, however, can be treated exactly alike with anything like rapid success. Cold acts powerfully as a repellant of the nervous fluid. Long enough continued it will even produce that permanent insensibility which we call numbness, and a little longer, muscular as well as sensational paralysis.

I have not, I repeat, the slightest doubt that I should have first dimmed and ultimately sealed that inner eye which Mr. Jennings had inadvertently opened. The same senses are opened in delirium tremens, and entirely shut up again when the overaction of the cerebral heart, and the prodigious nervous congestions that attend it, are terminated by a decided change in the state of the body. It is by acting steadily upon the body, by a simple process, that this result is produced--and inevitably produced--I have never yet failed. Poor Mr. Jennings made away with himself. But that catastrophe was the result of a totally different malady, which, as it were, projected itself upon the disease which was established. His case was in the distinctive manner a complication, and the complaint under which he really succumbed, was hereditary suicidal mania. Poor Mr. Jennings I cannot call a patient of mine, for I had not even begun to treat his case, and he had not yet given me, I am convinced, his full and unreserved confidence. If the patient do not array himself on the side of the disease, his cure is certain.

# MADAM CROWL'S GHOST (1871)

Twenty years have passed since you last saw Mrs. Jolliffe's tall slim figure. She is now past seventy, and can't have many mile-stones more to count on the journey that will bring her to her long home. The hair has grown white as snow, that is parted under her cap, over her shrewd, but kindly face. But her figure is still straight, and her step light and active.

She has taken of late years to the care of adult invalids, having surrendered to younger hands the little people who inhabit cradles, and crawl on all-fours. Those who remember that good-natured face among the earliest that emerge from the darkness of non-entity, and who owe to their first lessons in the accomplishment of walking, and a delighted appreciation of their first babblings and earliest teeth, have "spired up" into tall lads and lasses, now. Some of them shew streaks of white by this time, in brown locks, "the bonny gouden" hair, that she was so proud to brush and shew to admiring mothers, who are seen no more on the green of Golden Friars, and whose names are traced now on the flat grey stones in the church-yard.

So the time is ripening some, and searing others; and the saddening and tender sunset hour has come; and it is evening with the kind old north-country dame, who nursed pretty Laura Mildmay, who now steppinginto the room, smiles so gladly, and throws her arms round the old woman's neck, and kisses her twice.

"Now, this is so lucky!" said Mrs. Jenner, "you have just come in time to hear a story."

"Really! That's delightful."

"Na, na, od wite it! no story, ouer true for that, I sid it a wi my aan eyen. But the barn here, would not like, at these hours, just goin' to her bed, to hear tell of freets and boggarts."
"Ghosts? The very thing of all others I should most likely to hear of."

"Well, dear," said Mrs. Jenner, "if you are not afraid, sit ye down here, with us."

"She was just going to tell me all about her first engagement to attend a dying old woman," says Mrs. Jenner, "and of the ghost she saw there. Now, Mrs. Jolliffe, make your tea first, and then begin."

The good woman obeyed, and having prepared a cup of that companionable nectar, she sipped a little, drew her brows slightly together to collect her thoughts, and then looked up with a wondrous solemn face to begin.

Good Mrs. Jenner, and the pretty girl, each gazed with eyes of solemn expectation in the face of the old woman, who seemed to gather awe from the recollections she was summoning.

The old room was a good scene for such a narrative, with the oak-wainscoting, quaint, and clumsy furniture, the heavy beams that crossed its ceiling, and the tall four-post bed, with dark curtains, within which you might imagine what shadows you please.

Mrs. Jolliffe cleared her voice, rolled her eyes slowly round, and began her tale in these words:--

MADAM CROWL'S GHOST

"I'm an ald woman now, and I was but thirteen, my last birthday, the night I came to Applewale House. My aunt was the housekeeper there, and a sort o' one-horse carriage was down at Lexhoe waitin' to take me and my box up to Applewale.

"I was a bit frightened by the time I got to Lexhoe, and when I saw the carriage and horse, I wished myself back again with my mother at Hazelden. I was crying when I got into the 'shay'--that's what we used to call it--and old John Mulbery that drove it, and was a good-natured fellow, bought me a handful of apples at the Golden Lion to cheer me up a bit; and he told me that there was a currant-cake, and tea, and pork-chops, waiting for me, all hot, in my aunt's room at the great house. It was a fine moonlight night, and I eat the apples, lookin' out o' the shay winda.

"It's a shame for gentlemen to frighten a poor foolish child like I was. I sometimes think it might be tricks. There was two on 'em on the tap o' the coach beside me. And they began to question me after nightfall, when the moon rose, where I was going to. Well, I told them it was to wait on Dame Arabella Crowl, of Applewale House, near by Lexhoe.

"'Ho, then,' says one of them, 'you'll not be long there!'

"And I looked at him as much as to say 'Why not?' for I had spoken out when I told them where I was goin', as if 'twas something clever I hed to say.

"'Because,' says he, 'and don't you for your life tell no one, only watch her and see--she's possessed by the devil, and more an half a ghost. Have you got a Bible?'

"'Yes, sir,' says I. For my mother put my little Bible in my box, and I knew it was there: and by the same token, though the print's too small for my ald eyes, I have it in my press to this hour.

"As I looked up at him saying 'Yes, sir,' I thought I saw him winkin' at his friend; but I could not be sure.

"'Well,' says he, 'be sure you put it under your bolster every night, it will keep the ald girl's claws aff ye.'

"And I got such a fright when he said that, you wouldn't fancy! And I'd a liked to ask him a lot about the ald lady, but I was too shy, and he and his friend began talkin' together about their own consarns, and dowly enough I got down, as I told ye, at Lexhoe. My heart sank as I drove into the dark avenue. The trees stand very thick and big, as ald as the ald house almost, and four people, with their arms out and finger-tips touchin', barely girds round some of them.

"Well my neck was stretched out o' the winda, looking for the first view o' the great house; and all at once we pulled up in front of it.

"A great white-and-black house it is, wi' great black beams across and right up it, and gables lookin' out, as white as a sheet, to the moon, and the shadows o' the trees, two or three up and down in front, you could count the leaves on them, and all the little diamond-shaped winda-panes, glimmering on the great hall winda, and great shutters, in the old fashion, hinged on the wall outside, boulted across all the rest o' the windas in front, for there was but three or four servants, and the old lady in the house, and most o' t' rooms was locked up.

"My heart was in my mouth when I sid the journey was over, and this the great house afoore me, and I sa near my aunt that I never sid till noo, and Dame Crowl, that I was come to wait upon, and was afeard on already.

"My aunt kissed me in the hall, and brought me to her room. She was tall and thin, wi' a pale face and black eyes, and long thin hands wi' black mittins on. She was past fifty, and her word was short; but her word was law. I hev no complaints to make of her; but she was a hard woman, and I think she would hev bin kinder to me if I had bin her sister's child in place of her brother's. But all that's o' no consequence noo.

"The squire--his name was Mr. Chevenix Crowl, he was Dame Crowl's grandson--came down there, by way of seeing that the old lady was well treated, about twice or thrice in the year. I sid him but twice all the time I was at Applewale House.

"I can't say but she was well taken care of, notwithstanding; but that was because my aunt and Meg Wyvern, that was her maid, had a conscience, and did their duty by her.

"Mrs. Wyvern--Meg Wyvern my aunt called her to herself, and Mrs. Wyvern to me--was a fat, jolly lass of fifty, a good height and a good breadth, always good-humoured and walked slow. She had fine wages, but she was a bit stingy, and kept all her fine clothes under lock and key, and wore, mostly, a twilled chocolate cotton, wi' red, and yellow, and green sprigs and balls on it, and it lasted wonderful.

"She never gave me nout, not the vally o' a brass thimble, all the time I was there; but she was good-humoured, and always laughin', and she talked no end o' proas over her tea; and, seeing me sa sackless and dowly, she roused me up wi' her laughin' and stories; and I think I liked her better than my aunt--children is so taken wi' a bit o' fun or a story--though my aunt was very good to me, but a hard woman about some things, and silent always.

"My aunt took me into her bed-chamber, that I might rest myself a bit while she was settin' the tea in her room. But first, she patted me on the shouther, and said I was a tall lass o' my years, and had spired up well, and asked me if I could do plain work and stitchin'; and she looked in my face, and said I was like my father, her brother, that was dead and gone, and she hoped I was a better Christian, and wad na du a' that lids (would not do anything of that sort).

"It was a hard sayin' the first time I set foot in her room, I thought.

"When I went into the next room, the housekeeper's room--very comfortable, yak (oak) all round--there was a fine fire blazin' away, wi' coal, and peat, and wood, all in a low together, and tea on the table, and hot cake, and smokin' meat; and there was Mrs. Wyvern, fat, jolly, and talkin' away, more in an hour than my aunt would in a year.

"While I was still at my tea my aunt went up-stairs to see Madam Crowl.

"'She's agone up to see that old Judith Squailes is awake,' says Mrs. Wyvern. 'Judith sits with Madam Crowl when me and Mrs. Shutters'--that was my aunt's name--'is away. She's a troublesome old lady. Ye'll hev to be sharp wi' her, or she'll be into the fire, or out o' t' winda. She goes on wires, she does, old though she be.'

"'How old, ma'am?' says I.

"'Ninety-three her last birthday, and that's eight months gone,' says she; and she laughed. 'And don't be askin' questions about her before your aunt--mind, I tell ye; just take her as you find her, and that's all.'

"'And what's to be my business about her, please, ma'am?' says I.

"'About the old lady? Well,' says she, 'your aunt, Mrs. Shutters, will tell you that; but I suppose you'll hev to sit in the room with your work, and see she's at no mischief, and let her amuse herself with her things on the table, and get her her food or drink as she calls for it, and keep her out o' mischief, and ring the bell hard if she's troublesome.'

"'Is she deaf, ma'am?'

"'No, nor blind,' says she; 'as sharp as a needle, but she's gone quite aupy, and can't remember nout rightly; and Jack the Giant Killer, or Goody Twoshoes will please her as well as the king's court, or the affairs of the nation.'

"'And what did the little girl go away for, ma'am, that went on Friday last? My aunt wrote to my mother she was to go.'

"'Yes; she's gone.'

"'What for?' says I again.

"'She didn't answer Mrs. Shutters, I do suppose,' says she. 'I don't know. Don't be talkin'; your aunt can't abide a talkin' child.'

"'And please, ma'am, is the old lady well in health?' says I.

"'It ain't no harm to ask that,' says she. 'She's torflin a bit lately, but better this week past, and I dare say she'll last out her hundred years yet. Hish! Here's your aunt coming down the passage.'

"In comes my aunt, and begins talkin' to Mrs. Wyvern, and I, beginnin' to feel more comfortable and at home like, was walkin' about the room lookin' at this thing and at that. There was pretty old china things on the cupboard, and pictures again the wall; and there was a door open in the wainscot, and I sees a queer old leathern jacket, wi' straps and buckles to it, and sleeves as long as the bed-post hangin' up inside.

"'What's that you're at, child?' says my aunt, sharp enough, turning about when I thought she least minded. 'What's that in your hand?'

"'This, ma'am?' says I, turning about with the leathern jacket. 'I don't know what it is, ma'am.'

"Pale as she was, the red came up in her cheeks, and her eyes flashed wi' anger, and I think only she had half a dozen steps to take, between her and me, she'd a gev me a sizzup. But she did gie me a shake by the shouther, and she plucked the thing out o' my hand, and says she, 'While ever you stay here, don't ye meddle wi' nout that don't belong to ye', and she hung it up on the pin that was there, and shut the door wi' a bang and locked it fast.

"Mrs. Wyvern was liftin' up her hands and laughin' all this time, quietly, in her chair, rolling herself a bit in it, as she used when she was kinkin'.

"The tears was in my eyes, and she winked at my aunt, and says she, dryin' her own eyes that was wet wi' the laughin', 'Tut, the child meant no harm--come here to me, child. It's only a pair o' crutches for lame ducks, and ask us no questions mind, and we'll tell ye no lies; and come here and sit down, and drink a mug o' beer before ye go to your bed.'

"My room, mind ye, was upstairs, next to the old lady's, and Mrs. Wyvern's bed was near hers in her room, and I was to be ready at call, if need should be.

"The old lady was in one of her tantrums that night and part of the day before. She used to take fits o' the sulks. Sometimes she would not let them dress her, and at other times she would not let them take her clothes off. She was a great beauty, they said, in her day. But there was no one about Applewale that remembered her in her prime. And she was dreadful fond o' dress, and had thick silks, and stiff satins, and velvets, and laces, and all sorts, enough to set up seven shops at the least. All her dresses was old-fashioned and queer, but worth a fortune.

"Well, I went to my bed. I lay for a while awake; for a' things was new to me; and I think the tea was in my nerves, too, for I wasn't used to it, except now and then on a holiday, or the like. And I heard Mrs. Wyvern talkin', and I listened with my hand to my ear; but I could not hear Mrs. Crowl, and I don't think she said a word.

"There was great care took of her. The people at Applewale knew that when she died they would every one get the sack; and their situations was well paid and easy.

"The doctor came twice a week to see the old lady, and you may be sure they all did as he bid them. One thing was the same every time; they were never to cross or frump her, any way, but to humour and please her in everything.

"So she lay in her clothes all that night, and next day, not a word she said, and I was at my needlework all that day, in my own room, except when I went down to my dinner.

"I would a liked to see the ald lady, and even to hear her speak. But she might as well a' bin in Lunnon a' the time for me.

"When I had my dinner my aunt sent me out for a walk for an hour. I was glad when I came back, the trees was so big, and the place so dark and lonesome, and 'twas a cloudy day, and I cried a deal, thinkin' of home, while I was walkin' alone there. That evening, the candles bein' alight, I was sittin' in my room, and the door was open into Madam Crowl's chamber, where my aunt was. It was, then, for the first time I heard what I suppose was the ald lady talking.

"It was a queer noise like, I couldn't well say which, a bird, or a beast, only it had a bleatin' sound in it, and was very small.

"I pricked my ears to hear all I could. But I could not make out one word she said. And my aunt answered:

"'The evil one can't hurt no one, ma'am, bout the Lord permits.'

"Then the same queer voice from the bed says something more that I couldn't make head nor tail on.

"And my aunt med answer again: 'Let them pull faces, ma'am, and say what they will; if the Lord be for us, who can be against us?'

"I kept listenin' with my ear turned to the door, holdin' my breath, but not another word or sound came in from the room. In about twenty minutes, as I was sittin' by the table, lookin' at the pictures in the old Aesop's Fables, I was aware o' something moving at the door, and lookin' up I sid my aunt's face lookin' in at the door, and her hand raised.

"'Hish!' says she, very soft, and comes over to me on tiptoe, and she says in a whisper: 'Thank God, she's asleep at last, and don't ye make no noise till I come back, for I'm goin' down to take my cup o' tea, and I'll be back i' noo--me and Mrs. Wyvern, and she'll be sleepin' in the room, and you can run down when we come up, and Judith will gie ye yaur supper in my room.'

"And with that she goes.

"I kep' looking at the picture-book, as before, listenin' every noo and then, but there was no sound, not a breath, that I could hear; an' I began whisperin' to the pictures and talkin' to myself to keep my heart up, for I was growin' feared in that big room.

"And at last up I got, and began walkin' about the room, lookin' at this and peepin' at that, to amuse my mind, ye'll understand. And at last what sud I do but peeps into Madam Crowl's bedchamber.

"A grand chamber it was, wi' a great four-poster, wi' flowered silk curtains as tall as the ceilin', and foldin' down on the floor, and drawn close all round. There was a lookin'-glass, the biggest I ever sid before, and the room was a blaze o' light. I counted twenty-two wax candles, all alight. Such was her fancy, and no one dared say her nay.

"I listened at the door, and gaped and wondered all round. When I heard there was not a breath, and did not see so much as a stir in the curtains, I took heart, and walked into the room on tiptoe, and looked round again. Then I takes a keek at myself in the big glass; and at last it came in my head, 'Why couldn't I ha' a keek at the ald lady herself in the bed?

"Ye'd think me a fule if ye knew half how I longed to see Dame Crowl, and I thought to myself if I didn't peep now I might wait many a day before I got so gude a chance again.

"Well, my dear, I came to the side o' the bed, the curtains bein' close, and my heart a'most failed me. But I took courage, and I slips my finger in between the thick curtains, and then my hand. So I waits a bit, but all was still as death. So, softly, softly I draws the curtain, and there, sure enough, I sid before me, stretched out like the painted lady on the tomb-stean in Lexhoe Church, the famous Dame Crowl, of Applewale House. There she was, dressed out. You never sid the like in they days. Satin and silk, and scarlet and green, and gold and pint lace; by Jen! 'twas a sight! A big powdered wig, half as high as herself, was a-top o' her head, and, wow!--was ever such wrinkles?--and her old baggy throat all powdered white, and her cheeks rouged, and mouse-skin eyebrows, that Mrs. Wyvern used to stick on, and there she lay proud and stark, wi' a pair o' clocked silk hose on, and heels to her shoon as tall as nine-pins. Lawk! But her nose was crooked and thin, and half the whites o' her eyes was open. She used to stand, dressed as she was, gigglin' and dribblin' before the lookin'-glass, wi' a fan in her hand and a big nosegay in her bodice.

Her wrinkled little hands was stretched down by her sides, and such long nails, all cut into points, I never sid in my days. Could it even a bin the fashion for grit fowk to wear their fingernails so?

"Well, I think ye'd a-bin frightened yourself if ye'd a sid such a sight. I couldn't let go the curtain, nor move an inch, nor take my eyes off her; my very heart stood still. And in an instant she opens her eyes and up she sits, and spins herself round, and down wi' her, wi' a clack on her two tall heels on the floor, facin' me, ogglin' in my face wi' her two great glassy eyes, and a wicked simper wi' her wrinkled lips, and lang fause teeth.

"Well, a corpse is a natural thing; but this was the dreadfullest sight I ever sid. She had her fingers straight out pointin' at me, and her back was crooked, round again wi' age. Says she:

"'Ye little limb! what for did ye say I killed the boy? I'll tickle ye till ye're stiff!'

"If I'd a thought an instant, I'd a turned about and run. But I couldn't take my eyes off her, and I backed from her as soon as I could; and she came clatterin' after like a thing on wires, with her fingers pointing to my throat, and she makin' all the time a sound with her tongue like zizz-zizz-zizz.

"I kept backin' and backin' as quick as I could, and her fingers was only a few inches away from my throat, and I felt I'd lose my wits if she touched me.

"I went back this way, right into the corner, and I gev a yellock, ye'd think saul and body was partin', and that minute my aunt, from the door, calls out wi' a blare, and the ald lady turns round on her, and I turns about, and ran through my room, and down the stairs, as hard as my legs could carry me.

"I cried hearty, I can tell you, when I got down to the housekeeper's room. Mrs. Wyvern laughed a deal when I told her what happened. But she changed her key when she heard the ald lady's words.

"'Say them again,' says she.

"So I told her.

"'Ye little limb! What for did ye say I killed the boy? I'll tickle ye till ye're stiff.'

"'And did ye say she killed a boy?' says she.

"'Not I, ma'am,' says I.

"Judith was always up with me, after that, when the two elder women was away from her. I would a jumped out at winda, rather than stay alone in the same room wi' her.

"It was about a week after, as well as I can remember, Mrs. Wyvern, one day when me and her was alone, told me a thing about Madam Crowl that I did not know before.

"She being young and a great beauty, full seventy year before, had married Squire Crowl, of Applewale. But he was a widower, and had a son about nine years old.

"There never was tale or tidings of this boy after one mornin'. No one could say where he went to. He was allowed too much liberty, and used to be off in the morning, one day, to the keeper's cottage and breakfast wi' him, and away to the warren, and not home, mayhap, till evening; and another time down to the lake, and bathe there, and spend the day fishin' there, or paddlin' about in the boat. Well, no one could say what was gone wi' him; only this, that his hat was found by the lake, under a haathorn that grows thar to this day, and 'twas thought he was drowned bathin'. And the squire's son, by his second marriage, with this Madam Crowl that lived sa dreadful lang, came in far the estates. It was his son, the ald lady's grandson, Squire Chevenix Crowl, that owned the estates at the time I came to Applewale.

"There was a deal o' talk lang before my aunt's time about it; and 'twas said the step-mother knew more than she was like to let out. And she managed her husband, the ald squire, wi' her white-heft and flatteries. And as the boy was never seen more, in course of time the thing died out of fowks' minds.

"I'm goin' to tell ye noo about what I sid wi' my own een.
"I was not there six months, and it was winter time, when the ald lady took her last sickness.

"The doctor was afeard she might a took a fit o' madness, as she did fifteen years befoore, and was buckled up, many a time, in a strait-waistcoat, which was the very leathern jerkin I sid in the closet, off my aunt's room.

"Well, she didn't. She pined, and windered, and went off, torflin', torflin', quiet enough, till a day or two before her flittin', and then she took to rabblin', and sometimes skirlin' in the bed, ye'd think a robber had a knife to her throat, and she used to work out o' the bed, and not being strong enough, then, to walk or stand, she'd fall on the flure, wi' her ald wizened hands stretched before her face, and skirlin' still for mercy.

"Ye may guess I didn't go into the room, and I used to be shiverin' in my bed wi' fear, at her skirlin' and scrafflin' on the flure, and blarin' out words that id make your skin turn blue.

"My aunt, and Mrs. Wyvern, and Judith Squailes, and a woman from Lexhoe, was always about her. At last she took fits, and they wore her out.

"T' sir was there, and prayed for her; but she was past praying with. I suppose it was right, but none could think there was much good in it, and sa at lang last she made her flittin', and a' was over, and old Dame Crowl was shrouded and coffined, and Squire Chevenix was wrote for. But he was away in France, and the delay was sa lang, that t' sir and doctor both agreed it would not du to keep her langer out o' her place, and no one cared but just them two, and my aunt and the rest o' us, from Applewale, to go to the buryin'. So the old lady of Applewale was laid in the vault under Lexhoe Church; and we lived up at the great house till such time as the squire should come to tell his will about us, and pay off such as he chose to discharge.

"I was put into another room, two doors away from what was Dame Crowl's chamber, after her death, and this thing happened the night before Squire Chevenix came to Applewale.

"The room I was in now was a large square chamber, covered wi' yak pannels, but unfurnished except for my bed, which had no curtains to it, and a chair and a table, or so, that looked nothing at all in such a big room. And the big looking-glass, that the old lady used to keek into and admire herself from head to heel, now that there was na mair o' that wark, was put out of the way, and stood against the wall in my room, for there was shiftin' o' many things in her chamber ye may suppose, when she came to be coffined.

"The news had come that day that the squire was to be down next morning at Applewale; and not sorry was I, for I thought I was sure to be sent home again to my mother. And right glad was I, and I was thinkin' of a' at hame, and my sister Janet, and the kitten and the pymag, and Trimmer the tike, and all the rest, and I got sa fidgetty, I couldn't sleep, and the clock struck twelve, and me wide awake, and the room as dark as pick. My back was turned to the door, and my eyes toward the wall opposite.

"Well, it could na be a full quarter past twelve, when I sees a lightin' on the wall befcore me, as if something took fire behind, and the shadas o' the bed, and the chair, and my gown, that was hangin' from the wall, was dancin' up and down on the ceilin' beams and the yak pannels; and I turns my head ower my shouther quick, thinkin' something must a gone a' fire.

"And what sud I see, by Jen! but the likeness o' the ald beldame, bedizened out in her satins and velvets, on her dead body, simperin', wi' her eyes as wide as saucers, and her face like the fiend himself. 'Twas a red light that rose about her in a fuffin low, as if her dress round her feet was blazin'. She was drivin' on right for me, wi' her ald shrivelled hands crooked as if she was goin' to claw me. I could not stir, but she passed me straight by, wi' a blast o' cald air, and I sid her, at the wall, in the alcove as my aunt used to call it, which was a recess where the state bed used to stand in ald times wi' a door open wide, and her hands gropin' in at somethin' was there. I never sid that door befcore. And she turned round to me, like a thing on a pivot, flyrin', and all at once the room was dark, and I standin' at the far side o' the bed; I don't know how I got there, and I found my tongue at last, and if I did na blare a yellock, rennin' down the gallery and almost pulled Mrs. Wyvern's door off t' hooks, and frighted her half out o' wits.

"Ye may guess I did na sleep that night; and wi' the first light, down wi' me to my aunt, as fast as my two legs cud carry me.

"Well my aunt did na frump or flite me, as I thought she would, but she held me by the hand, and locked hard in my face all the time. And she telt me not to be feared; and says she:

"'Hed the appearance a key in its hand?'

"'Yes,' says I, bringin' it to mind, 'a big key in a queer brass handle.'

"'Stop a bit,' says she, lettin' go ma hand, and openin' the cupboard-door. 'Was it like this?' says she, takin' one out in her fingers, and showing it to me, with a dark look in my face.

"'That was it,' says I, quick enough.

"'Are ye sure?' she says, turnin' it round.

"'Sart,' says I, and I felt like I was gain' to faint when I sid it.

"'Well, that will do, child,' says she, saftly thinkin', and she locked it up again.

"'The squire himself will be here today, before twelve o'clock, and ye must tell him all about it,' says she, thinkin', 'and I suppose I'll be leavin' soon, and so the best thing for the present is, that ye should go home this afternoon, and I'll look out another place for you when I can.'

"Fain was I, ye may guess, at that word.

"My aunt packed up my things for me, and the three pounds that was due to me, to bring home, and Squire Crowl himself came down to Applewale that day, a handsome man, about thirty years ald. It was the second time I sid him. But this was the first time he spoke to me.

"My aunt talked wi' him in the housekeeper's room, and I don't know what they said. I was a bit feared on the squire, he bein' a great gentleman down in Lexhoe, and I darn't go near till I was called. And says he, smilin':

"'What's a' this ye a sen, child? it mun be a dream, for ye know there's na sic a thing as a bo or a freet in a' the world. But whatever it was, ma little maid, sit ye down and tell all about it from first to last.'

"Well, so soon as I made an end, he thought a bit, and says he to my aunt:

"'I mind the place well. In old Sir Olivur's time lame Wyndel told me there was a door in that recess, to the left, where the lassie dreamed she saw my grandmother open it. He was past eighty when he told me that, and I but a boy. It's twenty year sen. The plate and jewels used to be kept there, long ago, before the iron closet was made in the arras chamber, and he told me the key had a brass handle, and this ye say was found in the bottom o' the kist where she kept her old fans. Now, would not it be a queer thing if we found some spoons or diamonds forgot there? Ye mun come up wi' us, lassie, and point to the very spot.'

"Loth was I, and my heart in my mouth, and fast I held by my aunt's hand as I stept into that awsome room, and showed them both how she came and passed me by, and the spot where she stood, and where the door seemed to open.

"There was an ald empty press against the wall then, and shoving it aside, sure enough there was the tracing of a door in the wainscot, and a keyhole stopped with wood, and planed across as smooth as the rest, and the joining of the door all stopped wi' putty the colour o' yak, and, but for the hinges that showed a bit when the press was shoved aside, ye would not consayt there was a door there at all.

"'Ha!' says he, wi' a queer smile, 'this looks like it.'
"It took some minutes wi' a small chisel and hammer to pick the bit o' wood out o' the keyhole. The key fitted, sure enough, and, wi' a strang twist and a lang skreak, the boult went back and he pulled the door open.

"There was another door inside, stranger than the first, but the lacks was gone, and it opened easy. Inside was a narrow floor and walls and vault o' brick; we could not see what was in it, for 'twas dark as pick.

"When my aunt had lighted the candle, the squire held it up and stept in.

"My aunt stood on tiptoe tryin' to look over his shouther, and I did na see nout.

"'Ha! ha!' says the squire, steppin' backward. 'What's that? Gi' ma the poker--quick!' says he to my aunt. And as she went to the hearth I peeps beside his arm, and I sid squat down in the far corner a monkey or a flayin' on the chest, or else the maist shrivelled up, wizzened ald wife that ever was sen on yearth.

"'By Jen!' says my aunt, as puttin' the poker in his hand, she keeked by his shouther, and sid the ill-favoured thing, 'hae a care, sir, what ye're doin'. Back wi' ye, and shut to the door!'

"But in place o' that he steps in saftly, wi' the poker pointed like a swoord, and he gies it a poke, and down it a' tumbles together, head and a', in a heap o' bayans and dust, little meyar an' a hatful.

"'Twas the bayans o' a child; a' the rest went to dust at a touch. They said nout for a while, but he turns round the skull, as it lay on the floor.

"Young as I was, I consayted I knew well enough what they was thinkin' on.

"'A dead cat!' says he, pushin' back and blowin' out the can'le, and shuttin' to the door. 'We'll come back, you and me, Mrs. Shutters, and look on the shelves by-and-bye. I've other matters first to speak to ye about; and this little girl's goin' hame, ye say. She has her wages, and I mun mak' her a present,' says he, pattin' my shouther wi' his hand.

"And he did gimma a goud pound and I went aff to Lexhoe about an hour after, and sa hame by the stage-coach, and fain was I to be at hame again; and I never sid Dame Crowl o' Applewale, God be thanked, either in appearance or in dream, at-efter. But when I was grown to be a woman, my aunt spent a day and night wi' me at Littleham, and she telt me there was no doubt it was the poor little boy that was missing sa lang sen, that was shut up to die thar in the dark by that wicked beldame, whar his skirls, or his prayers, or his thumpin' cud na be heard, and his hat was left by the water's edge, whoever did it, to mak' belief he was drowned. The clothes, at the first touch, a' ran into a snuff o' dust in the cell whar the bayans was found. But there was a handful o' jet buttons, and a knife with a green heft, together wi' a couple o' pennies the poor little fella had in his pocket, I suppose, when he was decoyed in thar, and sid his last o' the light. And there was, amang the squire's papers, a copy o' the notice that was prented after he was lost, when the ald squire thought he might 'a run away, or bin took by gipsies, and it said he had a green-hefted knife wi' him, and that his buttons were o' cut jet. Sa that is a' I hev to say consarnin' ald Dame Crowl, o' Applewale House."

# THE DEAD SEXTON (1871)

The sunsets were red, the nights were long, and the weather pleasantly frosty; and Christmas, the glorious herald of the New Year, was at hand, when an event--still recounted by winter firesides, with a horror made delightful by the mellowing influence of years--occurred in the beautiful little town of Golden Friars, and signalized, as the scene of its catastrophe, the old inn known throughout a wide region of the Northumbrian counties as the George and Dragon.

Toby Crooke, the sexton, was lying dead in the old coach-house in the inn yard. The body had been discovered, only half an hour before this story begins, under strange circumstances, and in a place where it might have lain the better part of a week undisturbed; and a dreadful suspicion astounded the village of Golden Friars.

A wintry sunset was glaring through a gorge of the western mountains, turning into fire the twigs of the leafless elms, and all the tiny blades of grass on the green by which the quaint little town is surrounded. It is built of light, grey stone, with steep gables and slender chimneys rising with airy lightness from the level sward by the margin of the beautiful lake, and backed by the grand amphitheatre of the fells at the other side, whose snowy peaks show faintly against the sky, tinged with the vaporous red of the western light. As you descend towards the margin of the lake, and see Golden Friars, its taper chimneys and slender gables, its curious old inn and gorgeous sign, and over all the graceful tower and spire of the ancient church, at this hour or by moonlight, in the solemn grandeur and stillness of the natural scenery that surrounds it, it stands before you like a fairy town.

Toby Crooke, the lank sexton, now fifty or upwards, had passed an hour or two with some village cronies, over a solemn pot of purl, in the kitchen of that cosy hostelry, the night before. He generally turned in there at about seven o'clock, and heard the news. This contented him: for he talked little, and looked always surly.

Many things are now raked up and talked over about him.

In early youth, he had been a bit of a scamp. He broke his indentures, and ran away from his master, the tanner of Bryemere; he had got into fifty bad scrapes and out again; and, just as the little world of Golden Friars had come to the conclusion that it would be well for all parties--except, perhaps, himself--and a happy riddance for his afflicted mother, if he were sunk, with a gross of quart pots about his neck, in the bottom of the lake in which the grey gables, the elms, and the towering fells of Golden Friars are mirrored, he suddenly returned, a reformed man at the ripe age of forty.

For twelve years he had disappeared, and no one knew what had become of him. Then, suddenly, as I say, he reappeared at Golden Friars--a very black and silent man, sedate and orderly. His mother was dead and buried; but the "prodigal son" was received good-naturedly. The good vicar, Doctor Jenner, reported to his wife:

"His hard heart has been softened, dear Dolly. I saw him dry his eyes, poor fellow, at the sermon yesterday."

"I don't wonder, Hugh darling. I know the part--'There is joy in Heaven.' I am sure it was--wasn't it? It was quite beautiful. I almost cried myself."

The Vicar laughed gently, and stooped over her chair and kissed her, and patted her cheek fondly.

"You think too well of your old man's sermons," he said. "I preach, you see, Dolly, very much to the _poor_. If _they_ understand me, I am pretty sure everyone else must; and I think that my simple style goes more home to both feelings and conscience--"

"You ought to have told me of his crying before. You _are_ so eloquent," exclaimed Dolly Jenner. "No one preaches like my man. I have never heard such sermons."
Not many, we may be sure; for the good lady had not heard more than six from any other divine for the last twenty years.

The personages of Golden Friars talked Toby Crooke over on his return. Doctor Lincote said:

"He must have led a hard life; he had _dried in_ so, and got a good deal of hard muscle; and he rather fancied he had been soldiering--he stood like a soldier; and the mark over his right eye looked like a gunshot."

People might wonder how he could have survived a gunshot over the eye; but was not Lincote a doctor--and an army doctor to boot--when he was young; and who, in Golden Friars, could dispute with him on points of surgery? And I believe the truth is, that this mark had been really made by a pistol bullet.

Mr. Jarlcot, the attorney, would "go bail" he had picked up some sense in his travels; and honest Turnbull, the host of the George and Dragon, said heartily:

"We must look out something for him to put his hand to. _Now's_ the time to make a man of him."

The end of it was that he became, among other things, the sexton of Golden Friars.

He was a punctual sexton. He meddled with no other person's business; but he was a silent man, and by no means popular. He was reserved in company; and he used to walk alone by the shore of the lake, while other fellows played at fives or skittles; and when he visited the kitchen of the George, he had his liquor to himself, and in the midst of the general talk was a saturnine listener. There was something sinister in this man's face; and when things went wrong with him, he could look dangerous enough.

There were whispered stories in Golden Friars about Toby Crooke. Nobody could say how they got there. Nothing is more mysterious than the spread of rumour. It is like a vial poured on the air. It travels, like an epidemic, on the sightless currents of the atmosphere, or by the laws of a telluric influence equally intangible. These stories treated, though darkly, of the long period of his absence from his native village; but they took no well-defined shape, and no one could refer them to any authentic source.

The Vicar's charity was of the kind that thinketh no evil; and in such cases he always insisted on proof. Crooke was, of course, undisturbed in his office.

On the evening before the tragedy came to light--trifles are always remembered after the catastrophe--a boy, returning along the margin of the mere, passed him by seated on a prostrate trunk of a tree, under the "bield" of a rock, counting silver money. His lean body and limbs were bent together, his knees were up to his chin, and his long fingers were telling the coins over hurriedly in the hollow of his other hand. He glanced at the boy, as the old English saying is, like "the devil looking over Lincoln." But a black and sour look from Mr. Crooke, who never had a smile for a child nor a greeting for a wayfarer, was nothing strange.

Toby Crooke lived in the grey stone house, cold and narrow, that stands near the church porch, with the window of its staircase looking out into the churchyard, where so much of his labour, for many a day, had been expended. The greater part of this house was untenanted.

The old woman who was in charge of it slept in a settle-bed, among broken stools, old sacks, rotten chests and other rattle-traps, in the small room at the rear of the house, floored with tiles.

At what time of the night she could not tell, she awoke, and saw a man, with his hat on, in her room. He had a candle in his hand, which he shaded with his coat from her eye; his back was towards her, and he was rummaging in the drawer in which she usually kept her money.

Having got her quarter's pension of two pounds that day, however, she had placed it, folded in a rag, in the corner of her tea caddy, and locked it up in the "eat-malison" or cupboard.

She was frightened when she saw the figure in her room, and she could not tell whether her visitor might not have made his entrance from the contiguous churchyard. So, sitting bolt upright in her bed, her grey hair almost lifting her kerchief off her head, and all over in "a fit o' t' creepins," as she expressed it, she demanded:

"In God's name, what want ye thar?"

"Whar's the peppermint ye used to hev by ye, woman? I'm bad wi' an inward pain."

"It's all gane a month sin'," she answered; and offered to make him a "het" drink if he'd get to his room.

But he said:

"Never mind, I'll try a mouthful o' gin."

And, turning on his heel, he left her.

In the morning the sexton was gone. Not only in his lodging was there no account of him, but, when inquiry began to be extended, nowhere in the village of Golden Friars could he be found.

Still he might have gone off, on business of his own, to some distant village, before the town was stirring; and the sexton had no near kindred to trouble their heads about him. People, therefore, were willing to wait, and take his return ultimately for granted.

At three o'clock the good Vicar, standing at his hall door, looking across the lake towards the noble fells that rise, steep and furrowed, from that beautiful mere, saw two men approaching across the green, in a straight line, from a boat that was moored at the water's edge. They were carrying between them something which, though not very large, seemed ponderous.

"Ye'll ken this, sir," said one of the boatmen as they set down, almost at his feet, a small church bell, such as in old-fashioned chimes yields the treble notes.
"This won't be less nor five stean. I ween it's fra' the church steeple yon."

"What! one of our church bells?" ejaculated the Vicar--for a moment lost in horrible amazement. "Oh, no!--_no_, that can't possibly be! Where did you find it?"

He had found the boat, in the morning, moored about fifty yards from her moorings where he had left it the night before, and could not think how that came to pass; and now, as he and his partner were about to take their oars, they discovered this bell in the bottom of the boat, under a bit of canvas, also the sexton's pick and spade--"tom-spey'ad," they termed that peculiar, broad-bladed implement.

"Very extraordinary! We must try whether there is a bell missing from the tower," said the Vicar, getting into a fuss. "Has Crooke come back yet? Does anyone know where he is?"

The sexton had not yet turned up.

"That's odd--that's provoking,' said the Vicar. "However, my key will let us in. Place the bell in the hall while I get it; and then we can see what all this means."

To the church, accordingly, they went, the Vicar leading the way, with his own key in his hand. He turned it in the lock, and stood in the shadow of the ground porch, and shut the door.

A sack, half full, lay on the ground, with open mouth, a piece of cord lying beside it. Something clanked within it as one of the men shoved it aside with his clumsy shoe.

The Vicar opened the church door and peeped in. The dusky glow from the western sky, entering through a narrow window, illuminated the shafts and arches, the old oak carvings, and the discoloured monuments, with the melancholy glare of a dying fire.

The Vicar withdrew his head and closed the door. The gloom of the porch was deeper than ever as, stooping, he entered the narrow door that opened at the foot of the winding stair that leads to the first loft; from which a rude ladder-stair of wood, some five and twenty feet in height, mounts through a trap to the ringers' loft.

Up the narrow stairs the Vicar climbed, followed by his attendants, to the first loft. It was very dark: a narrow bow-slit in the thick wall admitted the only light they had to guide them. The ivy leaves, seen from the deep shadow, flashed and flickered redly, and the sparrows twittered among them.

"Will one of you be so good as to go up and count the bells, and see if they are all right?" said the Vicar. "There should be--"

"Agoy! what's that?" exclaimed one of the men, recoiling from the foot of the ladder.

"By Jen!" ejaculated the other, in equal surprise.

"Good gracious!" gasped the Vicar, who, seeing indistinctly a dark mass lying on the floor, had stooped to examine it, and placed his hand upon a cold, dead face.

The men drew the body into the streak of light that traversed the floor.

It was the corpse of Toby Crooke! There was a frightful scar across his forehead.

The alarm was given. Doctor Lincote, and Mr. Jarlcot, and Turnbull, of the George and Dragon, were on the spot immediately; and many curious and horrified spectators of minor importance.

The first thing ascertained was that the man must have been many hours dead. The next was that his skull was fractured, across the forehead, by an awful blow. The next was that his neck was broken.

His hat was found on the floor, where he had probably laid it, with his handkerchief in it. The mystery now began to clear a little; for a bell--one of the chime hung in the tower--was found where it had rolled to, against the wall, with blood and hair on the rim of it, which corresponded with the grizzly fracture across the front of his head.

The sack that lay in the vestibule was examined, and found to contain all the church plate; a silver salver that had disappeared, about a month before, from Dr. Lincote's store of valuables; the Vicar's gold pencil-case, which he thought he had forgot in the vestry book; silver spoons, and various other contributions, levied from time to time off a dozen different households, the mysterious disappearance of which spoils had, of late years, begun to make the honest little community uncomfortable. Two bells had been taken down from the chime; and now the shrewd part of the assemblage, putting things together, began to comprehend the nefarious plans of the sexton, who lay mangled and dead on the floor of the tower, where only two days ago he had tolled the holy bell to call the good Christians of Golden Friars to worship.

The body was carried into the yard of the George and Dragon and laid in the old coach-house; and the townsfolk came grouping in to have a peep at the corpse, and stood round, looking darkly, and talking as low as if they were in a church.

The Vicar, in gaiters and slightly shovel hat, stood erect, as one in a little circle of notables--the doctor, the attorney, Sir Geoffrey Mardykes, who happened to be in the town, and Turnbull, the host--in the centre of the paved yard, they having made an inspection of the body, at which troops of the village stragglers, to-ing and fro-ing, were gaping and frowning as they whispered their horrible conjectures.

"What d'ye think o' that?" said Tom Scales, the old hostler of the George, looking pale, with a stern, faint smile on his lips, as he and Dick Linklin sauntered out of the coach-house together.

"The deaul will hev his ain noo," answered Dick, in his friend's ear. "T' sexton's got a craigthraw like he gav' the lass over the clints of Scarsdale; ye mind what the ald soger telt us when he hid his face in the kitchen of the George here? By Jen! I'll ne'er forget that story."

"I ween 'twas all true enough," replied the hostler; "and the sizzup he gav' the sleepin' man wi' t' poker across the forehead. See whar the edge o' t' bell took him, and smashed his ain, the self-same lids. By ma sang, I wonder the deaul did na carry awa' his corpse i' the night, as he did wi' Tam Lunder's at Mooltern Mill."

"Hout, man, who ever sid t' deaul inside o' a church?"

"The corpse is ill-faur'd enew to scare Satan himsel', for that matter; though it's true what you say. Ay, ye're reet tul a trippet, thar; for Beelzebub dar'n't show his snout inside the church, not the length o' the black o' my nail."

While this discussion was going on, the gentlefolk who were talking the matter over in the centre of the yard had dispatched a message for the coroner all the way to the town of Hextan.

The last tint of sunset was fading from the sky by this time; so, of course, there was no thought of an inquest earlier than next day.

In the meantime it was horribly clear that the sexton had intended to rob the church of its plate, and had lost his life in the attempt to carry the second bell, as we have seen, down the worn ladder of the tower. He had tumbled backwards and broken his neck upon the floor of the loft; and the heavy bell, in its fall, descended with its edge across his forehead.

Never was a man more completely killed by a double catastrophe, in a moment.

The bells and the contents of the sack, it was surmised, he meant to have conveyed across the lake that night, and with the help of his spade and pick to have buried them in Cloustеd Forest, and returned, after an absence of but a few hours--as he easily might--before morning, unmissed and unobserved. He would no doubt, having secured his booty, have made such arrangements as would have made it appear that the church had been broken into. He would, of course, have taken all measures to divert suspicion from himself, and have watched a suitable opportunity to repossess himself of the buried treasure and dispose of it in safety.

And now came out, into sharp relief, all the stories that had, one way or other, stolen after him into the town. Old Mrs. Pullen fainted when she saw him, and told Doctor Lincote, after, that she thought he was the highwayman who fired the shot that killed the coachman the night they were robbed on Hounslow Heath. There were the stories also told by the wayfaring old soldier with the wooden leg, and fifty others, up to this more than half disregarded, but which now seized on the popular belief with a startling grasp.

The fleeting light soon expired, and twilight was succeeded by the early night.

The inn yard gradually became quiet; and the dead sexton lay alone, in the dark, on his back, locked up in the old coach-house, the key of which was safe in the pocket of Tom Scales, the trusty old hostler of the George.

It was about eight o'clock, and the hostler, standing alone on the road in the front of the open door of the George and Dragon, had just smoked his pipe out. A bright moon hung in the frosty sky. The fells rose from the opposite edge of the lake like phantom mountains. The air was stirless. Through the boughs and sprays of the leafless elms no sigh or motion, however hushed, was audible. Not a ripple glimmered on the lake, which at one point only reflected the brilliant moon from its dark blue expanse like burnished steel. The road that runs by the inn door, along the margin of the lake, shone dazzlingly white.

White as ghosts, among the dark holly and juniper, stood the tall piers of the Vicar's gate, and their great stone balls, like heads, overlooking the same road, a few hundred yards up the lake, to the left. The early little town of Golden Friars was quiet by this time. Except for the townsfolk who were now collected in the kitchen of the inn itself, no inhabitant was now outside his own threshold.

Tom Scales was thinking of turning in. He was beginning to fell a little queer. He was thinking of the sexton, and could not get the fixed features of the dead man out of his head, when he heard the sharp though distant ring of a horse's hoof upon the frozen road. Tom's instinct apprized him of the approach of a guest to the George and Dragon. His experienced ear told him that the horseman was approaching by the Dardale road, which, after crossing that wide and dismal moss, passes the southern fells by Dunner Cleugh and finally enters the town of Golden Friars by joining the Mardykes road, at the edge of the lake, close to the gate of the Vicar's house.

A clump of tall trees stood at this point; but the moon shone full upon the road and cast their shadow backward.

The hoofs were plainly coming at a gallop, with a hollow rattle. The horseman was a long time in appearing. Tom wondered how he had heard the sound--so sharply frosty as the air was--so very far away.

He was right in his guess. The visitor was coming over the mountainous road from Dardale Moss; and he now saw a horseman, who must have turned the corner of the Vicar's house at the moment when his eye was wearied; for when he saw him for the first time he was advancing, in the hazy moonlight, like the shadow of a cavalier, at a gallop, upon the level strip of road that skirts the margin of the mere, between the George and the Vicar's piers.

The hostler had not long to wonder why the rider pushed his beast at so furious a pace, and how he came to have heard him, as he now calculated, at least three miles away. A very few moments sufficed to bring horse and rider to the inn door.

It was a powerful black horse, something like the great Irish hunter that figured a hundred years ago, and would carry sixteen stone with ease across country. It would have made a grand charger. Not a hair turned. It snorted, it pawed, it arched its neck; then threw back its ears and down its head, and looked ready to lash, and then to rear; and seemed impatient to be off again, and incapable of standing quiet for a moment.

The rider got down

As light as shadow falls.

But he was a tall, sinewy figure. He wore a cape or short mantle, a cocked hat, and a pair of jack-boots, such as held their ground in some primitive corners of England almost to the close of the last century.

"Take him, lad," said he to old Scales. "You need not walk or wisp him--he never sweats or tires. Give him his oats, and let him take his own time to eat them. House!" cried the stranger--in the old-fashioned form of summons which still lingered, at that time, in out-of-the-way places--in a deep and piercing voice.

As Tom Scales led the horse away to the stables it turned its head towards its master with a short, shill neigh.

"About _your_ business, old gentleman--we must not go too fast," the stranger cried back again to his horse, with a laugh as harsh and piercing; and he strode into the house.

The hostler led this horse into the inn yard. In passing, it sidled up to the coach-house gate, within which lay the dead sexton--snorted, pawed and lowered its head suddenly, with ear close to the plank, as if listening for a sound from within; then uttered again the same short, piercing neigh.

The hostler was chilled at this mysterious coquetry with the dead. He liked the brute less and less every minute.

In the meantime, its master had proceeded.

"I'll go to the inn kitchen," he said, in his startling bass, to the drawer who met him in the passage.

And on he went, as if he had known the place all his days: not seeming to hurry himself--stepping leisurely, the servant thought--but gliding on at such a rate, nevertheless, that he had passed his guide and was in the kitchen of the George before the drawer had got much more than half-way to it. A roaring fire of dry wood, peat and coal lighted up this snug but spacious apartment--flashing on pots and pans, and dressers high-piled with pewter plates and dishes; and making the uncertain shadows of the long "hanks" of onions and many a flitch and ham, depending from the ceiling, dance on its glowing surface.

The doctor and the attorney, even Sir Geoffrey Mardykes, did not disdain on this occasion to take chairs and smoke their pipes by the kitchen fire, where they were in the thick of the gossip and discussion excited by the terrible event.

The tall stranger entered uninvited.

He looked like a gaunt, athletic Spaniard of forty, burned half black in the sun, with a bony, flattened nose. A pair of fierce black eyes were just visible under the edge of his hat; and his mouth seemed divided, beneath the moustache, by the deep scar of a hare-lip.

Sir Geoffrey Mardykes and the host of the George, aided by the doctor and the attorney, were discussing and arranging, for the third or fourth time, their theories about the death and the probable plans of Toby Crooke, when the stranger entered.

The new-comer lifted his hat, with a sort of smile, for a moment from his black head.

"What do you call this place, gentlemen?" asked the stranger.

"The town of Golden Friars, sir," answered the doctor politely.

"The George and Dragon, sir: Anthony Turnbull, at your service," answered mine host, with a solemn bow, at the same moment--so that the two voices went together, as if the doctor and the innkeeper were singing a catch.

"The George and the Dragon," repeated the horseman, expanding his long hands over the fire which he had approached. "Saint George, King George, the Dragon, the Devil: it is a very grand idol, that outside your door, sir. You catch all sorts of worshippers--courtiers, fanatics, scamps: all's fish, eh? Everybody welcome, provided he drinks like one. Suppose you brew a bowl or two of punch. I'll stand it. How many are we? _Here_--count, and let us have enough. Gentlemen, I mean to spend the night here, and my horse is in the stable. What holiday, fun, or fair has got so many pleasant faces together? When I last called here--for, now I bethink me, I have seen the place before--you all looked sad. It was on a Sunday, that dismalest of holidays; and it would have been positively melancholy only that your sexton--that saint upon earth--Mr. Crooke, was here." He was looking round, over his shoulder, and added: "Ha! don't I see him there?"

Frightened a good deal were some of the company. All gaped in the direction in which, with a nod, he turned his eyes.

"He's _not_ thar--he _can't_ be thar--we _see_ he's not thar," said Turnbull, as dogmatically as old Joe Willet might have delivered himself--for he did not care that the George should earn the reputation of a haunted house. "He's met an accident, sir: he's dead--he's elsewhere--and therefore can't be here."

Upon this the company entertained the stranger with the narrative--which they made easy by a division of labour, two or three generally speaking at a time, and no one being permitted to finish a second sentence without finding himself corrected and supplanted.

"The man's in Heaven, so sure as you're not," said the traveller so soon as the story was ended. "What! he was fiddling with the church bell, was he, and d----d for that--eh? Landlord, get us some drink. A sexton d----d for pulling down a church bell he has been pulling at for ten years!"

"You came, sir, by the Dardale-road, I believe?" said the doctor (village folk are curious). "A dismal moss is Dardale Moss, sir; and a bleak clim' up the fells on t' other side."

"I say 'Yes' to all--from Dardale Moss, as black as pitch and as rotten as the grave, up that zigzag wall you call a road, that looks like chalk in the moonlight, through Dunner Cleugh, as dark as a coal-pit, and down here to the George and the Dragon, where you have a roaring fire, wise men, good punch--here it is--and a corpse in your coach-house. Where the carcase is, there will the eagles be gathered together. Come, landlord, ladle out the nectar. Drink, gentlemen--drink, all. Brew another bowl at the bar. How divinely it stinks of alcohol!

I hope you like it, gentlemen: it smells all over of spices, like a mummy. Drink, friends. Ladle, landlord. Drink, all. Serve it out."

The guest fumbled in his pocket, and produced three guineas, which he slipped into Turnbull's fat palm.

"Let punch flow till that's out. I'm an old friend of the house. I call here, back and forward. I know you well, Turnbull, though you don't recognize me."

"You have the advantage of me, sir," said Mr. Turnbull, looking hard on that dark and sinister countenance--which, or the like of which, he could have sworn he had never seen before in his life. But he liked the weight and colour of his guineas, as he dropped them into his pocket. "I hope you will find yourself comfortable while you stay."

"You have given me a bedroom?"

"Yes, sir--the cedar chamber."

"I know it--the very thing. No--no punch for me. By and by, perhaps."

The talk went on, but the stranger had grown silent. He had seated himself on an oak bench by the fire, towards which he extended his feet and hands with seeming enjoyment; his cocked hat being, however, a little over his face.

Gradually the company began to thin. Sir Geoffrey Mardykes was the first to go; then some of the humbler townsfolk. The last bowl of punch was on its last legs. The stranger walked into the passage and said to the drawer:

"Fetch me a lantern. I must see my nag. Light it--hey! That will do. No--you need not come."

The gaunt traveller took it from the man's hand and strode along the passage to the door of the stableyard, which he opened and passed out.

Tom Scales, standing on the pavement, was looking through the stable window at the horses when the stranger plucked his shirtsleeve. With an inward shock the hostler found himself alone in presence of the very person he had been thinking of.

"I say--they tell me you have something to look at in there"--he pointed with his thumb at the old coach-house door. "Let us have a peep."

Tom Scales happened to be at that moment in a state of mind highly favourable to anyone in search of a submissive instrument. He was in great perplexity, and even perturbation. He suffered the stranger to lead him to the coach-house gate.

"You must come in and hold the lantern," said he. "I'll pay you handsomely."

The old hostler applied his key and removed the padlock.

"What are you afraid of? Step in and throw the light on his face," said the stranger grimly. "Throw open the lantern: stand _there_. Stoop over him a little--he won't bite you. Steady, or you may pass the night with him!"

* * * * *

In the meantime the company at the George had dispersed; and, shortly after, Anthony Turnbull--who, like a good landlord, was always last in bed, and first up, in his house--was taking, alone, his last look round the kitchen before making his final visit to the stable-yard, when Tom Scales tottered into the kitchen, looking like death, his hair standing upright; and he sat down on an oak chair, all in a tremble, wiped his forehead with his hand, and, instead of speaking, heaved a great sigh or two.

It was not till after he had swallowed a dram of brandy that he found his voice, and said:

"We've the deaul himsel' in t' house! By Jen! ye'd best send fo t' sir" (the clergyman). "Happen he'll tak him in hand wi' holy writ, and send him elsewhidder deftly. Lord atween us and harm! I'm a sinfu' man. I tell ye, Mr. Turnbull, I dar' n't stop in t' George to-night under the same roof wi' him."

"Ye mean the ra-beyoned, black-feyaced lad, wi' the brocken neb? Why, that's a gentleman wi' a pocket ful o' guineas, man, and a horse worth fifty pounds!"

"That horse is no better nor his rider. The nags that were in the stable wi' him, they all tuk the creepins, and sweated like rain down a thack. I tuk them all out o' that, away from him, into the hack-stable, and I thocht I cud never get them past him. But that's not all. When I was keekin inta t' winda at the nags, he comes behint me and claps his claw on ma shouther, and he gars me gang wi' him, and open the aad coach-house door, and haad the cannle for him, till he pearked into the deed man't feyace; and, as God's my judge, I sid the corpse open its eyes and wark its mouth, like a man smoorin' and strivin' to talk. I cudna move or say a word, though I felt my hair rising on my heed; but at lang-last I gev a yelloch, and say I, 'La! what is that?' And he himsel' looked round on me, like the devil he is; and, wi' a skirl o' a laugh, he strikes the lantern out o' my hand. When I cum to myself we were outside the coach-house door. The moon was shinin' in, ad I cud see the corpse stretched on the table whar we left it; and he kicked the door to wi' a purr o' his foot. 'Lock it,' says he; and so I did. And here's the key for ye--tak it yoursel', sir. He offer'd me money: he said he'd mak me a rich man if I'd sell him the corpse, and help him awa' wi' it."

"Hout, man! What cud he want o' t' corpse? He's not doctor, to do a' that lids. He was takin' a rise out o' ye, lad," said Turnbull.

"Na, na--he wants the corpse. There's summat you a' me can't tell he wants to do wi' 't; and he'd liefer get it wi' sin and thievin', and the damage of my soul. He's one of them freytens a boo or a dobbies off Dardale Moss, that's always astir wi' the like after nightfall; unless--Lord save us!--he be the deaul himsel.'"

"Whar is he noo?" asked the landlord, who was growing uncomfortable.

"He spang'd up the back stair to his room. I wonder you didn't hear him trampin' like a wild horse; and he clapt his door that the house shook again--but Lord knows whar he is noo. Let us gang awa's up to the Vicar's, and gan _him_ come down, and talk wi' him."

"Hoity toity, man--you're too easy scared," said the landlord, pale enough by this time. "'Twould be a fine thing, truly, to send abroad that the house was haunted by the deaul himsel'! Why, 'twould be the ruin o' the George. You're sure ye locked the door on the corpse?"

"Aye, sir--sartain."

"Come wi' me, Tom--we'll gi' a last look round the yard."

So, side by side, with many a jealous look right and left, and over their shoulders, they went in silence. On entering the old-fashioned quadrangle, surrounded by stables and other offices--built in the antique cagework fashion--they stopped for a while under the shadow of the inn gable, and looked round the yard, and listened. All was silent--nothing stirring.

The stable lantern was lighted; and with it in his hand Tony Turnbull, holding Tom Scales by the shoulder, advanced. He hauled Tom after him for a step or two; then stood still and shoved him before him for a step or two more; and thus cautiously--as a pair of skirmishers under fire--they approached the coach-house door.

"There, ye see--all safe," whispered Tom, pointing to the lock, which hung--distinct in the moonlight--in its place. "Cum back, I say!"

"Cum on, say I!" retorted the landlord valorously. "It would never do to allow any tricks to be played with the chap in there"--he pointed to the coachhouse door.

"The coroner here in the morning, and never a corpse to sit on!" He unlocked the padlock with these words, having handed the lantern to Tom. "Here, keck in, Tom," he continued; "ye hev the lantern--and see if all's as ye left it."

"Not me--na, not for the George and a' that's in it!" said Tom, with a shudder, sternly, as he took a step backward.

"What the--what are ye afraid on? Gi' me the lantern--it is all one: _I_ will."

And cautiously, little by little, he opened the door; and, holding the lantern over his head in the narrow slit, he peeped in--frowning and pale--with one eye, as if he expected something to fly in his face. He closed the door without speaking, and locked it again.

"As safe as a thief in a mill," he whispered with a nod to his companion. And at that moment a harsh laugh overhead broke the silence startlingly, and set all the poultry in the yard gabbling.

"Thar he be!" said Tom, clutching the landlord's arm--"in the winda--see!"

The window of the cedar-room, up two pair of stairs, was open; and in the shadow a darker outline was visible of a man, with his elbows on the window-stone, looking down upon them.

"Look at his eyes--like two live coals!" gasped Tom.

The landlord could not see all this so sharply, being confused, and not so long-sighted as Tom.

"Time, sir," called Tony Turnbull, turning cold as he thought he saw a pair of eyes shining down redly at him--"time for honest folk to be in their beds, and asleep!"

"As sound as your sexton!" said the jeering voice from above.

"Come out of this," whispered the landlord fiercely to his hostler, plucking him hard by the sleeve.
They got into the house, and shut the door.

"I wish we were shot of him," said the landlord, with something like a groan, as he leaned against the wall of the passage. "I'll sit up, anyhow--and, Tom, you'll sit wi' me. Cum into the gun-room. No one shall steal the dead man out of my yard while I can draw a trigger."

The gun-room in the George is about twelve feet square. It projects into the stable-yard and commands a full view of the old coach-house; and, through a narrow side window, a flanking view of the back door of the inn, through which the yard is reached.

Tony Turnbull took down the blunderbuss--which was the great ordnance of the house--and loaded it with a stiff charge of pistol bullets.

He put on a great-coat which hung there, and was his covering when he went out at night, to shoot wild ducks. Tom made himself comfortable likewise. They then sat down at the window, which was open, looking into the yard, the opposite side of which was white in the brilliant moonlight.

The landlord laid the blunderbuss across his knees, and stared into the yard. His comrade stared also. The door of the gun-room was locked; so they felt tolerably secure.

An hour passed; nothing had occurred. Another. The clock struck one. The shadows had shifted a little; but still the moon shone full on the old coach-house, and the stable where the guest's horse stood.

Turnbull thought he heard a step on the back-stair. Tom was watching the back-door through the side window, with eyes glazing with the intensity of his stare. Anthony Turnbull, holding his breath, listened at the room door. It was a false alarm.

When he came back to the window looking into the yard:

"Hish! Look thar!" said he in a vehement whisper.

From the shadow at the left they saw the figure of the gaunt horseman, in short cloak and jack-boots, emerge. He pushed open the stable door, and led out his powerful black horse. He walked it across the front of the building till he reached the old coach-house door; and there, with its bridle on its neck, he left it standing, while he stalked to the yard gate; and, dealing it a kick with his heel, it sprang back with the rebound, shaking from top to bottom, and stood open. The stranger returned to the side of his horse; and the door which secured the corpse of the dead sexton seemed to swing slowly open of itself as he entered, and returned with the corpse in his arms, and swung it across the shoulders of the horse, and instantly sprang into the saddle.

"Fire!" shouted Tom, and bang went the blunderbuss with a stunning crack. A thousand sparrows' wings winnowed through the air from the thick ivy. The watch-dog yelled a furious bark. There was a strange ring and whistle in the air. The blunderbuss had burst to shivers right down to the very breech. The recoil rolled the inn-keeper upon his back on the floor, and Tom Scales was flung against the side of the recess of the window, which had saved him from a tumble as violent. In this position they heard the searing laugh of the departing horseman, and saw him ride out of the gate with his ghastly burden.

* * * * *

Perhaps some of my readers, like myself, have heard this story told by Roger Turnbull, now host of the George and Dragon, the grandson of the very Tony who then swayed the spigot and keys of that inn, in the identical kitchen of which the fiend treated so many of the neighbours to punch.

* * * * *

What infernal object was subserved by the possession of the dead villain's body, I have not learned. But a very curious story, in which a vampire resuscitation of Crooke the sexton figures, may throw a light upon this part of the tale.

The result of Turnbull's shot at the disappearing fiend certainly justifies old Andrew Moreton's dictum, which is thus expressed in his curious "History of Apparitions' : "I warn rash brands who, pretending not to fear the devil, are for using the ordinary violences with him, which affect one man from another--or with an apparition, in which they may be sure to receive some mischief. I knew one fired a gun at an apparition and the gun burst in a hundred pieces in his hand; another struck at an apparition with a sword, and broke his sword in pieces and wounded his hand grievously; and 'tis next to madness for anyone to go that way to work with any spirit, be it angel or be it devil."

# LAURA SILVER BELL (1872)

In the five Northumbrian counties you will scarcely find so bleak, ugly, and yet, in a savage way, so picturesque a moor as Dardale Moss. The moor itself spreads north, south, east, and west, a great undulating sea of black peat and heath.

What we may term its shores are wooded wildly with birch, hazel, and dwarf-oak. No towering mountains surround it, but here and there you have a rocky knoll rising among the trees, and many a wooded promontory of the same pretty, because utterly wild, forest, running out into its dark level.

Habitations are thinly scattered in this barren territory, and a full mile away from the meanest was the stone cottage of Mother Carke.

Let not my southern reader who associates ideas of comfort with the term "cottage" mistake. This thing is built of shingle, with low walls. Its thatch is hollow; the peat-smoke curls stingily from its stunted chimney. It is worthy of its savage surroundings.

The primitive neighbours remark that no rowan-tree grows near, nor holly, nor bracken, and no horseshoe is nailed on the door.

Not far from the birches and hazels that straggle about the rude wall of the little enclosure, on the contrary, they say, you may discover the broom and the rag-wort, in which witches mysteriously delight. But this is perhaps a scandal.

Mall Carke was for many a year the _sage femme_ of this wild domain. She has renounced practice, however, for some years; and now, under the rose, she dabbles, it is thought, in the black art, in which she has always been secretly skilled, tells fortunes, practises charms, and in popular esteem is little better than a witch.

Mother Carke has been away to the town of Willarden, to sell knit stockings, and is returning to her rude dwelling by Dardale Moss. To her right, as far away as the eye can reach, the moor stretches. The narrow track she has followed here tops a gentle upland, and at her left a sort of jungle of dwarf-cak and brushwood approaches its edge. The sun is sinking blood-red in the west. His disk has touched the broad black level of the moor and his parting beams glare athwart the gaunt figure of the old beldame, as she strides homeward stick in hand, and bring into relief the folds of her mantle, which gleam like the draperies of a bronze image in the light of a fire. For a few moments this light floods the air--tree, gorse, rock, and bracken glare; and then it is out, and gray twilight over everything.

All is still and sombre. At this hour the simple traffic of the thinly-peopled country is over, and nothing can be more solitary.

From this jungle, nevertheless, through which the mists of evening are already creeping, she sees a gigantic man approaching her.

In that poor and primitive country robbery is a crime unknown. She, therefore, has no fears for her pound of tea, and pint of gin, and sixteen shillings in silver which she is bringing home in her pocket. But there is something that would have frighted another woman about this man.

He is gaunt, sombre, bony, dirty, and dressed in a black suit which a beggar would hardly care to pick out of the dust.

This ill-looking man nodded to her as he stepped on the road.

"I don't know you," she said.

He nodded again.

"I never sid ye neyawheere," she exclaimed sternly.

"Fine evening, Mother Carke," he says, and holds his snuff-box toward her.

She widened the distance between them by a step or so, and said again sternly and pale,

"I hev nowt to say to thee, whoe'er thou beest."

"You know Laura Silver Bell?"

"That's a byneyam; the lass's neyam is Laura Lew," she answered, looking straight before her.

"One name's as good as another for one that was never christened, mother."

"How know ye that?" she asked grimly; for it is a received opinion in that part of the world that the fairies have power over those who have never been baptised.

The stranger turned on her a malignant smile.

"There is a young lord in love with her," the stranger says, "and I'm that lord. Have her at your house to-morrow night at eight o'clock, and you must stick cross pins through the candle, as you have done for many a one before, to bring her lover thither by ten, and her fortune's made. And take this for your trouble."

He extended his long finger and thumb toward her, with a guinea temptingly displayed.

"I have nowt to do wi' thee. I nivver sid thee afoore. Git thee awa'! I earned nea goold o' thee, and I'll tak' nane. Awa' wi' thee, or I'll find ane that will mak' thee!"

The old woman had stopped, and was quivering in every limb as she thus spoke.

He looked very angry. Sulkily he turned away at her words, and strode slowly toward the wood from which he had come; and as he approached it, he seemed to her to grow taller and taller, and stalked into it as high as a tree.

"I conceited there would come something o't", she said to herself. "Farmer Lew must git it done nesht Sunda'. The a'ad awpy!"

Old Farmer Lew was one of that sect who insist that baptism shall be but once administered, and not until the Christian candidate had attained to adult years. The girl had indeed for some time been of an age not only, according to this theory, to be baptised, but if need be to be married.

Her story was a sad little romance. A lady some seventeen years before had come down and paid Farmer Lew for two rooms in his house. She told him that her husband would follow her in a fortnight, and that he was in the mean time delayed by business in Liverpool.

In ten days after her arrival her baby was born, Mall Carke acting as _sage femme_ on the occasion; and on the evening of that day the poor young mother died. No husband came; no wedding-ring, they said, was on her finger. About fifty pounds was found in her desk, which Farmer Lew, who was a kind old fellow and had lost his two children, put in bank for the little girl, and resolved to keep her until a rightful owner should step forward to claim her.

They found half-a-dozen love-letters signed "Francis," and calling the dead woman "Laura."

So Farmer Lew called the little girl Laura; and her _sobriquet_ of "Silver Bell" was derived from a tiny silver bell, once gilt, which was found among her poor mother's little treasures after her death, and which the child wore on a ribbon round her neck.

Thus, being very pretty and merry, she grew up as a North-country farmer's daughter; and the old man, as she needed more looking after, grew older and less able to take care of her; so she was, in fact, very nearly her own mistress, and did pretty much in all things as she liked.

Old Mall Carke, by some caprice for which no one could account, cherished an affection for the girl, who saw her often, and paid her many a small fee in exchange for the secret indications of the future.

It was too late when Mother Carke reached her home to look for a visit from Laura Silver Bell that day.

About three o'clock next afternoon, Mother Carke was sitting knitting, with her glasses on, outside her door on the stone bench, when she saw the pretty girl mount lightly to the top of the stile at her left under the birch, against the silver stem of which she leaned her slender hand, and called,

"Mall, Mall! Mother Carke, are ye alane all by yersel'?"

"Ay, Laura lass, we can be clooas enoo, if ye want a word wi' me," says the old woman, rising, with a mysterious nod, and beckoning her stiffly with her long fingers.

The girl was, assuredly, pretty enough for a "lord" to fall in love with. Only look at her. A profusion of brown rippling hair, parted low in the middle of her forehead, almost touched her eyebrows, and made the pretty oval of her face, by the breadth of that rich line, more marked. What a pretty little nose! what scarlet lips, and large, dark, long-fringed eyes!

Her face is transparently tinged with those clear Murillo tints which appear in deeper dyes on her wrists and the backs of her hands. These are the beautiful gipsy-tints with which the sun dyes young skins so richly.

The old woman eyes all this, and her pretty figure, so round and slender, and her shapely little feet, cased in the thick shoes that can't hide their comely proportions, as she stands on the top of the stile. But it is with a dark and saturnine aspect.

"Come, lass, what stand ye for atoppa t' wall, whar folk may chance to see thee? I hev a thing to tell thee, lass."

She beckoned her again.

"An' I hev a thing to tell _thee_, Mall."

"Come hidder," said the old woman peremptorily.

"But ye munna gie me the creepin's" (make me tremble). "I winna look again into the glass o' water, mind ye."

The old woman smiled grimly, and changed her tone.

"Now, hunny, git tha down, and let ma see thy canny feyace," and she beckoned her again.

Laura Silver Bell did get down, and stepped lightly toward the door of the old woman's dwelling.

"Tak this," said the girl, unfolding a piece of bacon from her apron, "and I hev a silver sixpence to gie thee, when I'm gaen away heyam."

They entered the dark kitchen of the cottage, and the old woman stood by the door, lest their conference should be lighted on by surprise.

"Afoore ye begin," said Mother Carke (I soften her patois), "I mun tell ye there's ill folk watchin' ye. What's auld Farmer Lew about, he doesna get t' sir" (the clergyman) "to baptise thee? If he lets Sunda' next pass, I'm afeared ye'll never be sprinkled nor signed wi' cross, while there's a sky aboon us."

"Agoy!" exclaims the girl, "who's lookin' after me?"

"A big black fella, as high as the kipples, came out o' the wood near Deadman's Grike, just after the sun gaed down yester e'en; I knew weel what he was, for his feet ne'er touched the road while he made as if he walked beside me. And he wanted to gie me snuff first, and I wouldna hev that; and then he offered me a gowden guinea, but I was no sic awpy, and to bring you here to-night, and cross the candle wi' pins, to call your lover in. And he said he's a great lord, and in luve wi' thee."

"And you refused him?'
"Well for thee I did, lass," says Mother Carke.

"Why, it's every word true!" cries the girl vehemently, starting to her feet, for she had seated herself on the great oak chest.

"True, lass? Come, say what ye mean," demanded Mall Carke, with a dark and searching gaze.

"Last night I was coming heyam from the wake, wi' auld farmer Dykes and his wife and his daughter Nell, and when we came to the stile, I bid them good-night, and we parted."

"And ye came by the path alone in the night-time, did ye?" exclaimed old Mall Carke sternly.

"I wasna afeared, I don't know why; the path heyam leads down by the wa'as o' auld Hawarth Castle."

"I knaa it weel, and a dowly path it is; ye'll keep indoors o' nights for a while, or ye'll rue it. What saw ye?"

"No freetin, mother; nowt I was feared on."

"Ye heard a voice callin' yer neyame?"

"I heard nowt that was dow, but the hullyhoo in the auld castle wa's," answered the pretty girl. "I heard nor sid nowt that's dow, but mickle that's conny and gladsome. I heard singin' and laughin' a long way off, I consaited; and I stopped a bit to listen. Then I walked on a step or two, and there, sure enough in the Pie-Mag field, under the castle wa's, not twenty steps away, I sid a grand company; silks and satins, and men wi' velvet coats, wi' gowd-lace striped over them, and ladies wi' necklaces that would dazzle ye, and fans as big as griddles; and powdered footmen, like what the shirra hed behind his coach, only these was ten times as grand."

"It was full moon last night," said the old woman.

"Sa bright 'twould blind ye to look at it," said the girl.
"Never an ill sight but the deaul finds a light," quoth the old woman. "There's a rinnin brook thar--you were at this side, and they at that; did they try to mak ye cross over?"

"Agoy! didn't they? Nowt but civility and kindness, though. But ye mun let me tell it my own way. They was talkin' and laughin', and eatin', and drinkin' out o' long glasses and goud cups, seated on the grass, and music was playin'; and I keekin' behind a bush at all the grand doin's; and up they gits to dance; and says a tall fella I didna see afoore, 'Ye mun step across, and dance wi' a young lord that's faan in luv wi' thee, and that's mysel',' and sure enow I keeked at him under my lashes and a conny lad he is, to my teyaste, though he be dressed in black, wi' sword and sash, velvet twice as fine as they sells in the shop at Gouden Friars; and keekin' at me again fra the corners o' his een. And the same fella telt me he was mad in luv wi' me, and his fadder was there, and his sister, and they came all the way from Catstean Castle to see me that night; and that's t' other side o' Gouden Friars."

"Come, lass, yer no mafflin; tell me true. What was he like? Was his feyace grimed wi' sut? a tall fella wi' wide shouthers, and lukt like an ill-thing, wi' black clothes amaist in rags?"

"His feyace was long, but weel-faured, and darker nor a gipsy; and his clothes were black and grand, and made o' velvet, and he said he was the young lord himsel'; and he lukt like it."

"That will be the same fella I sid at Deadman's Grike," said Mall Carke, with an anxious frown.

"Hoot, mudder! how cud that be?" cried the lass, with a toss of her pretty head and a smile of scorn. But the fortune-teller made no answer, and the girl went on with her story.

"When they began to dance," continued Laura Silver Bell, "he urged me again, but I wudna step o'er; 'twas partly pride, coz I wasna dressed fine enough, and partly contrairiness, or something, but gaa I wudna, not a fut. No but I more nor half wished it a' the time."

"Weel for thee thou dudstna cross the brook."

"Hoity-toity, why not?"

"Keep at heyame after nightfall, and don't ye be walking by yersel' by daylight or any light lang lonesome ways, till after ye're baptised," said Mall Carke.

"I'm like to be married first."

"Tak care _that_ marriage won't hang i' the bell-ropes," said Mother Carke.

"Leave me alane for that. The young lord said he was maist daft wi' luv o' me. He wanted to gie me a conny ring wi' a beautiful stone in it. But, drat it, I was sic an awpy I wudna tak it, and he a young lord!"

"Lord, indeed! are ye daft or dreamin'? Those fine folk, what were they? I'll tell ye. Dobies and fairies; and if ye don't du as yer bid, they'll tak ye, and ye'll never get out o' their hands again while grass grows," said the old woman grimly.

"Od wite it!" replies the girl impatiently, "who's daft or dreamin' noo? I'd a bin dead wi' fear, if 'twas any such thing. It cudna be;

all was sa luvesome, and bonny, and shaply."

"Weel, and what do ye want o' me, lass?" asked the old woman sharply.

"I want to know--here's t' sixpence--what I sud du," said the young lass. "'Twud be a pity to lose such a marrow, hey?"

"Say yer prayers, lass; _I_ can't help ye," says the old woman darkly. "If ye gaa wi' _the_ people, ye'll never come back. Ye munna talk wi' them, nor eat wi' them, nor drink wi' them, nor tak a pin's-worth by way o' gift fra them--mark weel what I say--or ye're _lost!_"

The girl looked down, plainly much vexed.

The old woman stared at her with a mysterious frown steadily, for a few seconds.

"Tell me, lass, and tell me true, are ye in luve wi' that lad?"

"What for sud I?" said the girl with a careless toss of her head, and blushing up to her very temples.

"I see how it is," said the old woman, with a groan, and repeated the words, sadly thinking; and walked out of the door a step or two, and looked jealously round. "The lass is witched, the lass is witched!"

"Did ye see him since?" asked Mother Carke, returning.

The girl was still embarrassed; and now she spoke in a lower tone, and seemed subdued.

"I thought I sid him as I came here, walkin' beside me among the trees; but I consait it was only the trees themsels that lukt like rinnin' one behind another, as I walked on."

"I can tell thee nowt, lass, but what I telt ye afoore," answered the old woman peremptorily. "Get ye heyame, and don't delay on the way; and say yer prayers as ye gaa; and let none but good thoughts come nigh ye; and put nayer foot autside the door-steyan again till ye gaa to be christened; and get that done a Sunda' next."

And with this charge, given with grizzly earnestness, she saw her over the stile, and stood upon it watching her retreat, until the trees quite hid her and her path from view.

The sky grew cloudy and thunderous, and the air darkened rapidly, as the girl, a little frightened by Mall Carke's view of the case, walked homeward by the lonely path among the trees.

A black cat, which had walked close by her--for these creatures sometimes take a ramble in search of their prey among the woods and thickets--crept from under the hollow of an oak, and was again with her. It seemed to her to grow bigger and bigger as the darkness deepened, and its green eyes glared as large as halfpennies in her affrighted vision as the thunder came booming along the heights from the Willarden-road.

She tried to drive it away; but it growled and hissed awfully, and set up its back as if it would spring at her, and finally it skipped up into a tree, where they grew thickest at each side of her path, and accompanied her, high over head, hopping from bough to bough as if meditating a pounce upon her shoulders. Her fancy being full of strange thoughts, she was frightened, and she fancied that it was haunting her steps, and destined to undergo some hideous transformation, the moment she ceased to guard her path with prayers.

She was frightened for a while after she got home. The dark looks of Mother Carke were always before her eyes, and a secret dread prevented her passing the threshold of her home again that night.

Next day it was different. She had got rid of the awe with which Mother Carke had inspired her. She could not get the tall dark-featured lord, in the black velvet dress, out of her head. He had "taken her fancy"; she was growing to love him. She could think of nothing else.

Bessie Hennock, a neighbour's daughter, came to see her that day, and proposed a walk toward the ruins of Hawarth Castle, to gather "blaebirries." So off the two girls went together.

In the thicket, along the slopes near the ivied walls of Hawarth Castle, the companions began to fill their baskets. Hours passed. The sun was sinking near the west, and Laura Silver Bell had not come home.

Over the hatch of the farm-house door the maids leant ever and anon with outstretched necks, watching for a sign of the girl's return, and wondering, as the shadows lengthened, what had become of her.

At last, just as the rosy sunset gilding began to overspread the landscape, Bessie Hennock, weeping into her apron, made her appearance without her companion.

Her account of their adventures was curious.

I will relate the substance of it more connectedly than her agitation would allow her to give it, and without the disguise of the rude Northumbrian dialect.

The girl said, that, as they got along together among the brambles that grow beside the brook that bounds the Pie-Mag field, she on a sudden saw a very tall big-boned man, with an ill-favoured smirched face, and dressed in worn and rusty black, standing at the other side of a little stream. She was frightened; and while looking at this dirty, wicked, starved figure, Laura Silver Bell touched her, gazing at the same tall scarecrow, but with a countenance full of confusion and even rapture. She was peeping through the bush behind which she stood, and with a sigh she said:

"Is na that a conny lad? Agoy! See his bonny velvet clothes, his sword and sash; that's a lord, I can tell ye; and weel I know who he follows, who he luves, and who he'll wed."

Bessie Hennock thought her companion daft.

"See how luvesome he luks!" whispered Laura.

Bessie looked again, and saw him gazing at her companion with a malignant smile, and at the same time he beckoned her to approach.

"Darrat ta! gaa not near him! he'll wring thy neck!" gasped Bessie in great fear, as she saw Laura step forward with a look of beautiful bashfulness and joy.

She took the hand he stretched across the stream, more for love of the hand than any need of help, and in a moment was across and by his side, and his long arm about her waist.

"Fares te weel, Bessie, I'm gain my ways," she called, leaning her head to his shoulder; "and tell gud Fadder Lew I'm gain my ways to be happy, and may be, at lang last, I'll see him again."

And with a farewell wave of her hand, she went away with her dismal partner; and Laura Silver Bell was never more seen at home, or among the "coppies" and "wickwoods," the bonny fields and bosky hollows, by Dardale Moss.

Bessie Hennock followed them for a time.

She crossed the brook, and though they seemed to move slowly enough, she was obliged to run to keep them in view; and she all the time cried to her continually, "Come back, come back, bonnie Laurie!" until, getting over a bank, she was met by a white-faced old man, and so frightened was she, that she thought she fainted outright. At all events, she did not come to herself until the birds were singing their vespers in the amber light of sunset, and the day was over.

No trace of the direction of the girl's flight was ever discovered. Weeks and months passed, and more than a year.

At the end of that time, one of Mall Carke's goats died, as she suspected, by the envious practices of a rival witch who lived at the far end of Dardale Moss.

All alone in her stone cabin the old woman had prepared her charm to ascertain the author of her misfortune.

The heart of the dead animal, stuck all over with pins, was burnt in the fire; the windows, doors, and every other aperture of the house being first carefully stopped. After the heart, thus prepared with suitable incantations, is consumed in the fire, the first person who comes to the door or passes by it is the offending magician.

Mother Carke completed these lonely rites at dead of night. It was a dark night, with the glimmer of the stars only, and a melancholy night-wind was soughing through the scattered woods that spread around.

After a long and dead silence, there came a heavy thump at the door, and a deep voice called her by name.

She was startled, for she expected no man's voice; and peeping from the window, she saw, in the dim light, a coach and four horses, with gold-laced footmen, and coachman in wig and cocked hat, turned out as if for a state occasion.

She unbarred the door; and a tall gentleman, dressed in black, waiting at the threshold, entreated her, as the only _sage femme_ within reach, to come in the coach and attend Lady Lairdale, who was about to give birth to a baby, promising her handsome payment.

Lady Lairdale! She had never heard of her.

"How far away is it?"

"Twelve miles on the old road to Golden Friars."

Her avarice is roused, and she steps into the coach. The footman claps-to the door; the glass jingles with the sound of a laugh. The tall dark-faced gentleman in black is seated opposite; they are driving at a furious pace; they have turned out of the road into a narrower one, dark with thicker and loftier forest than she was accustomed to. She grows anxious; for she knows every road and by-path in the country round, and she has never seen this one.

He encourages her. The moon has risen above the edge of the horizon, and she sees a noble old castle. Its summit of tower, watchtower and battlement, glimmers faintly in the moonlight. This is their destination.

She feels on a sudden all but overpowered by sleep; but although she nods, she is quite conscious of the continued motion, which has become even rougher.

She makes an effort, and rouses herself. What has become of the coach, the castle, the servants? Nothing but the strange forest remains the same.

She is jolting along on a rude hurdle, seated on rushes, and a tall, big-boned man, in rags, sits in front, kicking with his heel the ill-favoured beast that pulls them along, every bone of which sticks out, and holding the halter which serves for reins. They stop at the door of a miserable building of loose stone, with a thatch so sunk and rotten, that the roof-tree and couples protrude in crooked corners, like the bones of the wretched horse, with enormous head and ears, that dragged them to the door.

The long gaunt man gets down, his sinister face grimed like his hands.

It was the same grimy giant who had accosted her on the lonely road near Deadman's Grike. But she feels that she "must go through with it" now, and she follows him into the house.

Two rushlights were burning in the large and miserable room, and on a coarse ragged bed lay a woman groaning piteously.

"That's Lady Lairdale," says the gaunt dark man, who then began to stride up and down the room rolling his head, stamping furiously, and thumping one hand on the palm of the other, and talking and laughing in the corners, where there was no one visible to hear or to answer.

Old Mall Carke recognized in the faded half-starved creature who lay on the bed, as dark now and grimy as the man, and looking as if she had never in her life washed hands or face, the once blithe and pretty Laura Lew.

The hideous being who was her mate continued in the same odd fluctuations of fury, grief, and merriment; and whenever she uttered a groan, he parodied it with another, as Mother Carke thought, in saturnine derision.

At length he strode into another room, and banged the door after him.

In due time the poor woman's pains were over, and a daughter was born.

Such an imp! with long pointed ears, flat nose, and enormous restless eyes and mouth. It instantly began to yell and talk in some unknown language, at the noise of which the father looked into the room, and told the _sage femme_ that she should not go unrewarded.

The sick woman seized the moment of his absence to say in the ear of Mall Carke:

"If ye had not been at ill work tonight, he could not hev fetched ye. Tak no more now than your rightful fee, or he'll keep ye here."

At this moment he returned with a bag of gold and silver coins, which he emptied on the table, and told her to help herself.

She took four shillings, which was her primitive fee, neither more nor less; and all his urgency could not prevail with her to take a farthing more. He looked so terrible at her refusal, that she rushed out of the house.

He ran after her.

"You'll take your money with you," he roared, snatching up the bag, still half full, and flung it after her.

It lighted on her shoulder; and partly from the blow, partly from terror, she fell to the ground; and when she came to herself, it was morning, and she was lying across her own door-stone.

It is said that she never more told fortune or practised spell. And though all that happened sixty years ago and more, Laura Silver Bell, wise folk think, is still living, and will so continue till the day of doom among the fairies.

# DICKON THE DEVIL (1872)

About thirty years ago I was selected by two rich old maids to visit a property in that part of Lancashire which lies near the famous forest of Pendle, with which Mr. Ainsworth's "Lancashire Witches" has made us so pleasantly familiar. My business was to make partition of a small property, including a house and demesne, to which they had a long time before succeeded as co-heiresses.

The last forty miles of my journey I was obliged to post, chiefly by cross-roads, little known, and less frequented, and presenting scenery often extremely interesting and pretty. The picturesqueness of the landscape was enhanced by the season, the beginning of September, at which I was travelling.

I had never been in this part of the world before; I am told it is now a great deal less wild, and, consequently, less beautiful.

At the inn where I had stopped for a relay of horses and some dinner--for it was then past five o'clock--I found the host, a hale old fellow of five-and-sixty, as he told me, a man of easy and garrulous benevolence, willing to accommodate his guests with any amount of talk, which the slightest tap sufficed to set flowing, on any subject you pleased.

I was curious to learn something about Barwyke, which was the name of the demesne and house I was going to. As there was no inn within some miles of it, I had written to the steward to put me up there, the best way he could, for a night.

The host of the "Three Nuns," which was the sign under which he entertained wayfarers, had not a great deal to tell. It was twenty years, or more, since old Squire Bowes died, and no one had lived in the Hall ever since, except the gardener and his wife.

"Tom Wyndsour will be as old a man as myself; but he's a bit taller, and not so much in flesh, quite," said the fat innkeeper.

"But there were stories about the house," I repeated, "that they said, prevented tenants from coming into it?"

"Old wives' tales; many years ago, that will be, sir; I forget 'em; I forget 'em all. Oh yes, there always will be, when a house is left so; foolish folk will always be talkin'; but I hadn't heard a word about it this twenty year."

It was vain trying to pump him; the old landlord of the "Three Nuns," for some reason, did not choose to tell tales of Barwyke Hall, if he really did, as I suspected, remember them.

I paid my reckoning, and resumed my journey, well pleased with the good cheer of that old-world inn, but a little disappointed.

We had been driving for more than an hour, when we began to cross a wild common; and I knew that, this passed, a quarter of an hour would bring me to the door of Barwyke Hall.

The peat and furze were pretty soon left behind; we were again in the wooded scenery that I enjoyed so much, so entirely natural and pretty, and so little disturbed by traffic of any kind. I was looking from the chaise-window, and soon detected the object of which, for some time, my eye had been in search. Barwyke Hall was a large, quaint house, of that cage-work fashion known as "black-and-white," in which the bars and angles of an oak framework contrast, black as ebony, with the white plaster that overspreads the masonry built into its interstices. This steep-roofed Elizabethan house stood in the midst of park-like grounds of no great extent, but rendered imposing by the noble stature of the old trees that now cast their lengthening shadows eastward over the sward, from the declining sun.

The park-wall was grey with age, and in many places laden with ivy. In deep grey shadow, that contrasted with the dim fires of evening reflected on the foliage above it, in a gentle hollow, stretched a lake that looked cold and black, and seemed, as it were, to skulk from observation with a guilty knowledge.

I had forgot that there was a lake at Barwyke; but the moment this caught my eye, like the cold polish of a snake in the shadow, my instinct seemed to recognize something dangerous, and I knew that the lake was connected, I could not remember how, with the story I had heard of this place in my boyhood.

I drove up a grass-grown avenue, under the boughs of these noble trees, whose foliage, dyed in autumnal red and yellow, returned the beams of the western sun gorgeously.

We drew up at the door. I got out, and had a good look at the front of the house; it was a large and melancholy mansion, with signs of long neglect upon it; great wooden shutters, in the old fashion, were barred, outside, across the windows; grass, and even nettles, were growing thick on the courtyard, and a thin moss streaked the timber beams; the plaster was discoloured by time and weather, and bore great russet and yellow stains. The gloom was increased by several grand old trees that crowded close about the house.

I mounted the steps, and looked round; the dark lake lay near me now, a little to the left. It was not large; it may have covered some ten or twelve acres; but it added to the melancholy of the scene. Near the centre of it was a small island, with two old ash trees, leaning toward each other, their pensive images reflected in the stirless water. The only cheery influence in this scene of antiquity, solitude, and neglect was that the house and landscape were warmed with the ruddy western beams. I knocked, and my summons resounded hollow and ungenial in my ear; and the bell, from far away, returned a deep-mouthed and surly ring, as if it resented being roused from a score years' slumber.

A light-limbed, jolly-looking old fellow, in a barracan jacket and gaiters, with a smile of welcome, and a very sharp, red nose, that seemed to promise good cheer, opened the door with a promptitude that indicated a hospitable expectation of my arrival.

There was but little light in the hall, and that little lost itself in darkness in the background. It was very spacious and lofty, with a gallery running round it, which, when the door was open, was visible at two or three points. Almost in the dark my new acquaintance led me across this wide hall into the room destined for my reception. It was spacious, and wainscoted up to the ceiling. The furniture of this capacious chamber was old-fashioned and clumsy. There were curtains still to the windows, and a piece of Turkey carpet lay upon the floor; those windows were two in number, looking out, through the trunks of the trees close to the house, upon the lake. It needed all the fire, and all the pleasant associations of my entertainer's red nose, to light up this melancholy chamber. A door at its farther end admitted to the room that was prepared for my sleeping apartment. It was wainscoted, like the other. It had a four-post bed, with heavy tapestry curtains, and in other respects was furnished in the same old-world and ponderous style as the other room. Its window, like those of that apartment, looked out upon the lake.

Sombre and sad as these rooms were, they were yet scrupulously clean. I had nothing to complain of; but the effect was rather dispiriting. Having given some directions about supper--a pleasant incident to look forward to--and made a rapid toilet, I called on my friend with the gaiters and red nose (Tom Wyndsour) whose occupation was that of a "bailiff," or under-steward, of the property, to accompany me, as we had still an hour or so of sun and twilight, in a walk over the grounds.

It was a sweet autumn evening, and my guide, a hardy old fellow, strode at a pace that tasked me to keep up with.

Among clumps of trees at the northern boundary of the demesne we lighted upon the little antique parish church. I was looking down upon it, from an eminence, and the park-wall interposed; but a little way down was a stile affording access to the road, and by this we approached the iron gate of the churchyard. I saw the church door open; the sexton was replacing his pick, shovel, and spade, with which he had just been digging a grave in the churchyard, in their little repository under the stone stair of the tower. He was a polite, shrewd little hunchback, who was very happy to show me over the church. Among the monuments was one that interested me; it was erected to commemorate the very Squire Bowes from whom my two old maids had inherited the house and estate of Barwyke. It spoke of him in terms of grandiloquent eulogy, and informed the Christian reader that he had died, in the bosom of the Church of England, at the age of seventy-one.

I read this inscription by the parting beams of the setting sun, which disappeared behind the horizon just as we passed out from under the porch.

"Twenty years since the Squire died," said I, reflecting as I loitered still in the churchyard.

"Ay, sir; 'twill be twenty year the ninth o' last month."

"And a very good old gentleman?"

"Good-natured enough, and an easy gentleman he was, sir; I don't think while he lived he ever hurt a fly," acquiesced Tom Wyndsour. "It ain't always easy sayin' what's in 'em though, and what they may take or turn to afterwards; and some o' them sort, I think, goes mad."

"You don't think he was out of his mind?" I asked.

"He? La! no; not he, sir; a bit lazy, mayhap, like other old fellows; but a knew devilish well what he was about."

Tom Wyndsour's account was a little enigmatical; but, like old Squire Bowes, I was "a bit lazy" that evening, and asked no more questions about him.

We got over the stile upon the narrow road that skirts the churchyard. It is overhung by elms more than a hundred years old, and in the twilight, which now prevailed, was growing very dark. As side-by-side we walked along this road, hemmed in by two loose stone-like walls, something running towards us in a zig-zag line passed us at a wild pace, with a sound like a frightened laugh or a shudder, and I saw, as it passed, that it was a human figure. I may confess now, that I was a little startled. The dress of this figure was, in part, white: I know I mistook it at first for a white horse coming down the road at a gallop. Tom Wyndsour turned about and looked after the retreating figure.

"He'll be on his travels to-night," he said, in a low tone. "Easy served with a bed, _that_ lad be; six foot o' dry peat or heath, or a nook in a dry ditch. That lad hasn't slept once in a house this twenty year, and never will while grass grows."

"Is he mad?" I asked.

"Something that way, sir; he's an idiot, an awpy; we call him 'Dickon the devil,' because the devil's almost the only word that's ever in his mouth."

It struck me that this idiot was in some way connected with the story of old Squire Bowes.

"Queer things are told of him, I dare say?" I suggested.

"More or less, sir; more or less. Queer stories, some."

"Twenty years since he slept in a house? That's about the time the Squire died," I continued.

"So it will be, sir; and not very long after."

"You must tell me all about that, Tom, to-night, when I can hear it comfortably, after supper."

Tom did not seem to like my invitation; and looking straight before him as we trudged on, he said,

"You see, sir, the house has been quiet, and nout's been troubling folk inside the walls or out, all round the woods of Barwyke, this ten year, or more; and my old woman, down there, is clear against talking about such matters, and thinks it best--and so do I--to let sleepin' dogs be."

He dropped his voice towards the close of the sentence, and nodded significantly.

We soon reached a point where he unlocked a wicket in the park wall, by which we entered the grounds of Barwyke once more.

The twilight deepening over the landscape, the huge and solemn trees, and the distant outline of the haunted house, exercised a sombre influence on me, which, together with the fatigue of a day of travel, and the brisk walk we had had, disinclined me to interrupt the silence in which my companion now indulged.

A certain air of comparative comfort, on our arrival, in great measure dissipated the gloom that was stealing over me. Although it was by no means a cold night, I was very glad to see some wood blazing in the grate; and a pair of candles aiding the light of the fire, made the room look cheerful. A small table, with a very white cloth, and preparations for supper, was also a very agreeable object.

I should have liked very well, under these influences, to have listened to Tom Wyndsour's story; but after supper I grew too sleepy to attempt to lead him to the subject; and after yawning for a time, I found there was no use in contending against my drowsiness, so I betook myself to my bedroom, and by ten o'clock was fast asleep.

What interruption I experienced that night I shall tell you presently. It was not much, but it was very odd.

By next night I had completed my work at Barwyke. From early morning till then I was so incessantly occupied and hard-worked, that I had not time to think over the singular occurrence to which I have just referred. Behold me, however, at length once more seated at my little supper-table, having ended a comfortable meal. It had been a sultry day, and I had thrown one of the large windows up as high as it would go. I was sitting near it, with my brandy and water at my elbow, looking out into the dark. There was no moon, and the trees that are grouped about the house make the darkness round it supernaturally profound on such nights.

"Tom," said I, so soon as the jug of hot punch I had supplied him with began to exercise its genial and communicative influence; "you must tell me who beside your wife and you and myself slept in the house last night."

Tom, sitting near the door, set down his tumbler, and looked at me askance, while you might count seven, without speaking a word.

"Who else slept in the house?" he repeated, very deliberately. "Not a living soul, sir"; and he looked hard at me, still evidently expecting something more.

"That _is_ very odd," I said returning his stare, and feeling really a little odd. "You are sure _you_ were not in my room last night?"

"Not till I came to call you, sir, this morning; _I_ can make oath of that."

"Well," said I, "there was some one there, _I_ can make oath of that. I was so tired I could not make up my mind to get up; but I was waked by a sound that I thought was some one flinging down the two tin boxes in which my papers were locked up violently on the floor. I heard a slow step on the ground, and there was light in the room, although I remembered having put out my candle. I thought it must have been you, who had come in for my clothes, and upset the boxes by accident. Whoever it was, he went out and the light with him. I was about to settle again, when, the curtain being a little open at the foot of the bed, I saw a light on the wall opposite; such as a candle from outside would cast if the door were very cautiously opening. I started up in the bed, drew the side curtain, and saw that the door _was_ opening, and admitting light from outside. It is close, you know, to the head of the bed. A hand was holding on the edge of the door and pushing it open; not a bit like yours; a very singular hand. Let me look at yours."

He extended it for my inspection.

"Oh no; there's nothing wrong with your hand. This was differently shaped; fatter; and the middle finger was stunted, and shorter than the rest, looking as if it had once been broken, and the nail was crooked like a claw. I called out 'Who's there?' and the light and the hand were withdrawn, and I saw and heard no more of my visitor."

"So sure as you're a living man, that was him!" exclaimed Tom Wyndsour, his very nose growing pale, and his eyes almost starting out of his head.

"Who?" I asked.

"Old Squire Bowes; 'twas _his_ hand you saw; the Lord a' mercy on us!" answered Tom. "The broken finger, and the nail bent like a hoop. Well for you, sir, he didn't come back when you called, that time. You came here about them Miss Dymock's business, and he never meant they should have a foot o' ground in Barwyke; and he was making a will to give it away quite different, when death took him short. He never was uncivil to no one; but he couldn't abide them ladies. My mind misgave me when I heard 'twas about their business you were coming; and now you see how it is; he'll be at his old tricks again!"

With some pressure and a little more punch, I induced Tom Wyndsour to explain his mysterious allusions by recounting the occurrences which followed the old Squire's death.

"Squire Bowes of Barwyke died without making a will, as you know," said Tom. "And all the folk round were sorry; that is to say, sir, as sorry as folk will be for an old man that has seen a long tale of years, and has no right to grumble that death has knocked an hour too soon at his door. The Squire was well liked; he was never in a passion, or said a hard word; and he would not hurt a fly; and that made what happened after his decease the more surprising.

"The first thing these ladies did, when they got the property, was to buy stock for the park.

"It was not wise, in any case, to graze the land on their own account. But they little knew all they had to contend with.

"Before long something went wrong with the cattle; first one, and then another, took sick and died, and so on, till the loss began to grow heavy. Then, queer stories, little by little, began to be told. It was said, first by one, then by another, that Squire Bowes was seen, about evening time, walking, just as he used to do when he was alive, among the old trees, leaning on his stick; and, sometimes when he came up with the cattle, he would stop and lay his hand kindly like on the back of one of them; and that one was sure to fall sick next day, and die soon after.

"No one ever met him in the park, or in the woods, or ever saw him, except a good distance off. But they knew his gait and his figure well, and the clothes he used to wear; and they could tell the beast he laid his hand on by its colour--white, dun, or black; and that beast was sure to sicken and die. The neighbours grew shy of taking the path over the park; and no one liked to walk in the woods, or come inside the bounds of Barwyke: and the cattle went on sickening and dying as before.

"At that time there was one Thomas Pyke; he had been a groom to the old Squire; and he was in care of the place, and was the only one that used to sleep in the house.

"Tom was vexed, hearing these stories; which he did not believe the half on 'em; and more especial as he could not get man or boy to herd the cattle; all being afeared. So he wrote to Matlock in Derbyshire, for his brother, Richard Pyke, a clever lad, and one that knew nout o' the story of the old Squire walking.

"Dick came; and the cattle was better; folk said they could still see the old Squire, sometimes, walking, as before, in openings of the wood, with his stick in his hand; but he was shy of coming nigh the cattle, whatever his reason might be, since Dickon Pyke came; and he used to stand a long bit off, looking at them, with no more stir in him than a trunk o' one of the old trees, for an hour at a time, till the shape melted away, little by little, like the smoke of a fire that burns out.

"Tom Pyke and his brother Dickon, being the only living souls in the house, lay in the big bed in the servants' room, the house being fast barred and locked, one night in November.

"Tom was lying next the wall, and he told me, as wide awake as ever he was at noonday. His brother Dickon lay outside, and was sound asleep.

"Well, as Tom lay thinking, with his eyes turned toward the door, it opens slowly, and who should come in but old Squire Bowes, his face lookin' as dead as he was in his coffin.

"Tom's very breath left his body; he could not take his eyes off him; and he felt the hair rising up on his head.

"The Squire came to the side of the bed, and put his arms under Dickon, and lifted the boy--in a dead sleep all the time--and carried him out so, at the door.

"Such was the appearance, to Tom Pyke's eyes, and he was ready to swear to it, anywhere.

"When this happened, the light, wherever it came from, all on a sudden went out, and Tom could not see his own hand before him.

"More dead than alive, he lay till daylight.

"Sure enough his brother Dickon was gone. No sign of him could he discover about the house; and with some trouble he got a couple of the neighbours to help him to search the woods and grounds. Not a sign of him anywhere.

"At last one of them thought of the island in the lake; the little boat was moored to the old post at the water's edge. In they got, though with small hope of finding him there. Find him, nevertheless, they did, sitting under the big ash tree, quite out of his wits; and to all their questions he answered nothing but one cry--'Bowes, the devil! See him; see him; Bowes, the devil!' An idiot they found him; and so he will be till God sets all things right. No one could ever get him to sleep under roof-tree more. He wanders from house to house while daylight lasts; and no one cares to lock the harmless creature in the workhouse. And folk would rather not meet him after nightfall, for they think where he is there may be worse things near."

A silence followed Tom's story. He and I were alone in that large room; I was sitting near the open window, looking into the dark night air. I fancied I saw something white move across it; and I heard a sound like low talking that swelled into a discordant shriek--"Hoo-oo-oo! Bowes, the devil! Over your shoulder. Hoo-oo-oo! ha! ha! ha!" I started up, and saw, by the light of the candle with which Tom strode to the window, the wild eyes and blighted face of the idiot, as, with a sudden change of mood, he drew off, whispering and tittering to himself, and holding up his long fingers, and looking at the tips like a "hand of glory."

Tom pulled down the window. The story and its epilogue were over. I confess I was rather glad when I heard the sound of the horses' hoofs on the court-yard, a few minutes later; and still gladder when, having bidden Tom a kind farewell, I had left the neglected house of Barwyke a mile behind me.

# CARMILLA (1872)

## PROLOGUE

Upon a paper attached to the Narrative which follows, Doctor Hesselius has written a rather elaborate note, which he accompanies with a reference to his Essay on the strange subject which the MS. illuminates.

This mysterious subject he treats, in that Essay, with his usual learning and acumen, and with remarkable directness and condensation. It will form but one volume of the series of that extraordinary man's collected papers.

As I publish the case, in this volume, simply to interest the "laity," I shall forestall the intelligent lady, who relates it, in nothing; and after due consideration, I have determined, therefore, to abstain from presenting any précis of the learned Doctor's reasoning, or extract from his statement on a subject which he describes as "involving, not improbably, some of the profoundest arcana of our dual existence, and its intermediates."

I was anxious on discovering this paper, to reopen the correspondence commenced by Doctor Hesselius, so many years before, with a person so clever and careful as his informant seems to have been. Much to my regret, however, I found that she had died in the interval.

She, probably, could have added little to the Narrative which she communicates in the following pages, with, so far as I can pronounce, such conscientious particularity.

# I.
# An Early Fright

In Styria, we, though by no means magnificent people, inhabit a castle, or schloss. A small income, in that part of the world, goes a great way. Eight or nine hundred a year does wonders. Scantily enough ours would have answered among wealthy people at home. My father is English, and I bear an English name, although I never saw England. But here, in this lonely and primitive place, where everything is so marvelously cheap, I really don't see how ever so much more money would at all materially add to our comforts, or even luxuries.

My father was in the Austrian service, and retired upon a pension and his patrimony, and purchased this feudal residence, and the small estate on which it stands, a bargain.

Nothing can be more picturesque or solitary. It stands on a slight eminence in a forest. The road, very old and narrow, passes in front of its drawbridge, never raised in my time, and its moat, stocked with perch, and sailed over by many swans, and floating on its surface white fleets of water lilies.

Over all this the schloss shows its many-windowed front; its towers, and its Gothic chapel.

The forest opens in an irregular and very picturesque glade before its gate, and at the right a steep Gothic bridge carries the road over a stream that winds in deep shadow through the wood. I have said that this is a very lonely place. Judge whether I say truth. Looking from the hall door towards the road, the forest in which our castle stands extends fifteen miles to the right, and twelve to the left. The nearest inhabited village is about seven of your English miles to the left. The nearest inhabited schloss of any historic associations, is that of old General Spielsdorf, nearly twenty miles away to the right.

I have said "the nearest _inhabited_ village," because there is, only three miles westward, that is to say in the direction of General Spielsdorf's schloss, a ruined village, with its quaint little church, now roofless, in the aisle of which are the moldering tombs of the proud family of Karnstein, now extinct, who once owned the equally desolate chateau which, in the thick of the forest, overlooks the silent ruins of the town.

Respecting the cause of the desertion of this striking and melancholy spot, there is a legend which I shall relate to you another time.

I must tell you now, how very small is the party who constitute the inhabitants of our castle. I don't include servants, or those dependents who occupy rooms in the buildings attached to the schloss. Listen, and wonder! My father, who is the kindest man on earth, but growing old; and I, at the date of my story, only nineteen. Eight years have passed since then.

I and my father constituted the family at the schloss. My mother, a Styrian lady, died in my infancy, but I had a good-natured governess, who had been with me from, I might almost say, my infancy. I could not remember the time when her fat, benignant face was not a familiar picture in my memory.

This was Madame Perrodon, a native of Berne, whose care and good nature now in part supplied to me the loss of my mother, whom I do not even remember, so early I lost her. She made a third at our little dinner party. There was a fourth, Mademoiselle De Lafontaine, a lady such as you term, I believe, a "finishing governess." She spoke French and German, Madame Perrodon French and broken English, to which my father and I added English, which, partly to prevent its becoming a lost language among us, and partly from patriotic motives, we spoke every day. The consequence was a Babel, at which strangers used to laugh, and which I shall make no attempt to reproduce in this narrative. And there were two or three young lady friends besides, pretty nearly of my own age, who were occasional visitors, for longer or shorter terms; and these visits I sometimes returned.

These were our regular social resources; but of course there were chance visits from "neighbors" of only five or six leagues distance. My life was, notwithstanding, rather a solitary one, I can assure you.

My gouvernantes had just so much control over me as you might conjecture such sage persons would have in the case of a rather spoiled girl, whose only parent allowed her pretty nearly her own way in everything.

The first occurrence in my existence, which produced a terrible impression upon my mind, which, in fact, never has been effaced, was one of the very earliest incidents of my life which I can recollect. Some people will think it so trifling that it should not be recorded here. You will see, however, by-and-by, why I mention it. The nursery, as it was called, though I had it all to myself, was a large room in the upper story of the castle, with a steep oak roof. I can't have been more than six years old, when one night I awoke, and looking round the room from my bed, failed to see the nursery maid. Neither was my nurse there; and I thought myself alone. I was not frightened, for I was one of those happy children who are studiously kept in ignorance of ghost stories, of fairy tales, and of all such lore as makes us cover up our heads when the door cracks suddenly, or the flicker of an expiring candle makes the shadow of a bedpost dance upon the wall, nearer to our faces. I was vexed and insulted at finding myself, as I conceived, neglected, and I began to whimper, preparatory to a hearty bout of roaring; when to my surprise, I saw a solemn, but very pretty face looking at me from the side of the bed. It was that of a young lady who was kneeling, with her hands under the coverlet. I looked at her with a kind of pleased wonder, and ceased whimpering. She caressed me with her hands, and lay down beside me on the bed, and drew me towards her, smiling; I felt immediately delightfully soothed, and fell asleep again. I was wakened by a sensation as if two needles ran into my breast very deep at the same moment, and I cried loudly. The lady started back, with her eyes fixed on me, and then slipped down upon the floor, and, as I thought, hid herself under the bed.

I was now for the first time frightened, and I yelled with all my might and main. Nurse, nursery maid, housekeeper, all came running in, and hearing my story, they made light of it, soothing me all they could meanwhile. But, child as I was, I could perceive that their faces were pale with an unwonted look of anxiety, and I saw them look under the bed, and about the room, and peep under tables and pluck open cupboards; and the housekeeper whispered to the nurse: "Lay your hand along that hollow in the bed; someone _did_ lie there, so sure as you did not; the place is still warm."

I remember the nursery maid petting me, and all three examining my chest, where I told them I felt the puncture, and pronouncing that there was no sign visible that any such thing had happened to me.

The housekeeper and the two other servants who were in charge of the nursery, remained sitting up all night; and from that time a servant always sat up in the nursery until I was about fourteen.

I was very nervous for a long time after this. A doctor was called in, he was pallid and elderly. How well I remember his long saturnine face, slightly pitted with smallpox, and his chestnut wig. For a good while, every second day, he came and gave me medicine, which of course I hated.

The morning after I saw this apparition I was in a state of terror, and could not bear to be left alone, daylight though it was, for a moment.

I remember my father coming up and standing at the bedside, and talking cheerfully, and asking the nurse a number of questions, and laughing very heartily at one of the answers; and patting me on the shoulder, and kissing me, and telling me not to be frightened, that it was nothing but a dream and could not hurt me.

But I was not comforted, for I knew the visit of the strange woman was _not_ a dream; and I was _awfully_ frightened.

I was a little consoled by the nursery maid's assuring me that it was she who had come and looked at me, and lain down beside me in the bed, and that I must have been half-dreaming not to have known her face. But this, though supported by the nurse, did not quite satisfy me.

I remembered, in the course of that day, a venerable old man, in a black cassock, coming into the room with the nurse and housekeeper, and talking a little to them, and very kindly to me; his face was very sweet and gentle, and he told me they were going to pray, and joined my hands together, and desired me to say, softly, while they were praying, "Lord hear all good prayers for us, for Jesus' sake." I think these were the very words, for I often repeated them to myself, and my nurse used for years to make me say them in my prayers.

I remembered so well the thoughtful sweet face of that white-haired old man, in his black cassock, as he stood in that rude, lofty, brown room, with the clumsy furniture of a fashion three hundred years old about him, and the scanty light entering its shadowy atmosphere through the small lattice. He kneeled, and the three women with him, and he prayed aloud with an earnest quavering voice for, what appeared to me, a long time. I forget all my life preceding that event, and for some time after it is all obscure also, but the scenes I have just described stand out vivid as the isolated pictures of the phantasmagoria surrounded by darkness.

## II.
## A Guest

I am now going to tell you something so strange that it will require all your faith in my veracity to believe my story. It is not only true, nevertheless, but truth of which I have been an eyewitness.

It was a sweet summer evening, and my father asked me, as he sometimes did, to take a little ramble with him along that beautiful forest vista which I have mentioned as lying in front of the schloss.

"General Spielsdorf cannot come to us so soon as I had hoped," said my father, as we pursued our walk.

He was to have paid us a visit of some weeks, and we had expected his arrival next day. He was to have brought with him a young lady, his niece and ward, Mademoiselle Rheinfeldt, whom I had never seen, but whom I had heard described as a very charming girl, and in whose society I had promised myself many happy days. I was more disappointed than a young lady living in a town, or a bustling neighborhood can possibly imagine. This visit, and the new acquaintance it promised, had furnished my day dream for many weeks.

"And how soon does he come?" I asked.

"Not till autumn. Not for two months, I dare say," he answered. "And I am very glad now, dear, that you never knew Mademoiselle Rheinfeldt."

"And why?" I asked, both mortified and curious.

"Because the poor young lady is dead," he replied. "I quite forgot I had not told you, but you were not in the room when I received the General's letter this evening."

I was very much shocked. General Spielsdorf had mentioned in his first letter, six or seven weeks before, that she was not so well as he would wish her, but there was nothing to suggest the remotest suspicion of danger.

"Here is the General's letter," he said, handing it to me. "I am afraid he is in great affliction; the letter appears to me to have been written very nearly in distraction."

We sat down on a rude bench, under a group of magnificent lime trees. The sun was setting with all its melancholy splendor behind the sylvan horizon, and the stream that flows beside our home, and passes under the steep old bridge I have mentioned, wound through many a group of noble trees, almost at our feet, reflecting in its current the fading crimson of the sky. General Spielsdorf's letter was so extraordinary, so vehement, and in some places so self-contradictory, that I read it twice over—the second time aloud to my father—and was still unable to account for it, except by supposing that grief had unsettled his mind.

It said "I have lost my darling daughter, for as such I loved her. During the last days of dear Bertha's illness I was not able to write to you. Before then I had no idea of her danger. I have lost her, and now learn _all_, too late. She died in the peace of innocence, and in the glorious hope of a blessed futurity. The fiend who betrayed our infatuated hospitality has done it all. I thought I was receiving into my house innocence, gaiety, a charming companion for my lost Bertha. Heavens! what a fool have I been!

I thank God my child died without a suspicion of the cause of her sufferings. She is gone without so much as conjecturing the nature of her illness, and the accursed passion of the agent of all this misery. I devote my remaining days to tracking and extinguishing a monster. I am told I may hope to accomplish my righteous and merciful purpose. At present there is scarcely a gleam of light to guide me. I curse my conceited incredulity, my despicable affectation of superiority, my blindness, my obstinacy—all—too late. I cannot write or talk collectedly now. I am distracted. So soon as I shall have a little recovered, I mean to devote myself for a time to enquiry, which may possibly lead me as far as Vienna. Some time in the autumn, two months hence, or earlier if I live, I will see you—that is, if you permit me; I will then tell you all that I scarce dare put upon paper now. Farewell. Pray for me, dear friend."

In these terms ended this strange letter. Though I had never seen Bertha Rheinfeldt my eyes filled with tears at the sudden intelligence; I was startled, as well as profoundly disappointed.

The sun had now set, and it was twilight by the time I had returned the General's letter to my father.

It was a soft clear evening, and we loitered, speculating upon the possible meanings of the violent and incoherent sentences which I had just been reading. We had nearly a mile to walk before reaching the road that passes the schloss in front, and by that time the moon was shining brilliantly. At the drawbridge we met Madame Perrodon and Mademoiselle De Lafontaine, who had come out, without their bonnets, to enjoy the exquisite moonlight. We heard their voices gabbling in animated dialogue as we approached. We joined them at the drawbridge, and turned about to admire with them the beautiful scene.

The glade through which we had just walked lay before us. At our left the narrow road wound away under clumps of lordly trees, and was lost to sight amid the thickening forest. At the right the same road crosses the steep and picturesque bridge, near which stands a ruined tower which once guarded that pass; and beyond the bridge an abrupt eminence rises, covered with trees, and showing in the shadows some grey ivy-clustered rocks.

Over the sward and low grounds a thin film of mist was stealing like smoke, marking the distances with a transparent veil; and here and there we could see the river faintly flashing in the moonlight.

No softer, sweeter scene could be imagined. The news I had just heard made it melancholy; but nothing could disturb its character of profound serenity, and the enchanted glory and vagueness of the prospect.

My father, who enjoyed the picturesque, and I, stood looking in silence over the expanse beneath us. The two good governesses, standing a little way behind us, discoursed upon the scene, and were eloquent upon the moon.

Madame Perrodon was fat, middle-aged, and romantic, and talked and sighed poetically. Mademoiselle De Lafontaine—in right of her father who was a German, assumed to be psychological, metaphysical, and something of a mystic—now declared that when the moon shone with a light so intense it was well known that it indicated a special spiritual activity. The effect of the full moon in such a state of brilliancy was manifold. It acted on dreams, it acted on lunacy, it acted on nervous people, it had marvelous physical influences connected with life. Mademoiselle related that her cousin, who was mate of a merchant ship, having taken a nap on deck on such a night, lying on his back, with his face full in the light on the moon, had wakened, after a dream of an old woman clawing him by the cheek, with his features horribly drawn to one side; and his countenance had never quite recovered its equilibrium. "The moon, this night," she said, "is full of idyllic and magnetic influence—and see, when you look behind you at the front of the schloss how all its windows flash and twinkle with that silvery splendor, as if unseen hands had lighted up the rooms to receive fairy guests."

There are indolent styles of the spirits in which, indisposed to talk ourselves, the talk of others is pleasant to our listless ears; and I gazed on, pleased with the tinkle of the ladies' conversation.

"I have got into one of my moping moods tonight," said my father, after a silence, and quoting Shakespeare, whom, by way of keeping up our English, he used to read aloud, he said:

"'In truth I know not why I am so sad.
It wearies me: you say it wearies you;
But how I got it—came by it.'

"I forget the rest. But I feel as if some great misfortune were hanging over us. I suppose the poor General's afflicted letter has had something to do with it."

At this moment the unwonted sound of carriage wheels and many hoofs upon the road, arrested our attention.

They seemed to be approaching from the high ground overlooking the bridge, and very soon the equipage emerged from that point. Two horsemen first crossed the bridge, then came a carriage drawn by four horses, and two men rode behind.

It seemed to be the traveling carriage of a person of rank; and we were all immediately absorbed in watching that very unusual spectacle. It became, in a few moments, greatly more interesting, for just as the carriage had passed the summit of the steep bridge, one of the leaders, taking fright, communicated his panic to the rest, and after a plunge or two, the whole team broke into a wild gallop together, and dashing between the horsemen who rode in front, came thundering along the road towards us with the speed of a hurricane.

The excitement of the scene was made more painful by the clear, long-drawn screams of a female voice from the carriage window.

We all advanced in curiosity and horror; me rather in silence, the rest with various ejaculations of terror.

Our suspense did not last long. Just before you reach the castle drawbridge, on the route they were coming, there stands by the roadside a magnificent lime tree, on the other stands an ancient stone cross, at sight of which the horses, now going at a pace that was perfectly frightful, swerved so as to bring the wheel over the projecting roots of the tree.

I knew what was coming. I covered my eyes, unable to see it out, and turned my head away; at the same moment I heard a cry from my lady friends, who had gone on a little.

Curiosity opened my eyes, and I saw a scene of utter confusion. Two of the horses were on the ground, the carriage lay upon its side with two wheels in the air; the men were busy removing the traces, and a lady with a commanding air and figure had got out, and stood with clasped hands, raising the handkerchief that was in them every now and then to her eyes.

Through the carriage door was now lifted a young lady, who appeared to be lifeless. My dear old father was already beside the elder lady, with his hat in his hand, evidently tendering his aid and the resources of his schloss. The lady did not appear to hear him, or to have eyes for anything but the slender girl who was being placed against the slope of the bank.

I approached; the young lady was apparently stunned, but she was certainly not dead. My father, who piqued himself on being something of a physician, had just had his fingers on her wrist and assured the lady, who declared herself her mother, that her pulse, though faint and irregular, was undoubtedly still distinguishable. The lady clasped her hands and looked upward, as if in a momentary transport of gratitude; but immediately she broke out again in that theatrical way which is, I believe, natural to some people. She was what is called a fine looking woman for her time of life, and must have been handsome; she was tall, but not thin, and dressed in black velvet, and looked rather pale, but with a proud and commanding countenance, though now agitated strangely.

"Who was ever being so born to calamity?" I heard her say, with clasped hands, as I came up. "Here am I, on a journey of life and death, in prosecuting which to lose an hour is possibly to lose all. My child will not have recovered sufficiently to resume her route for who can say how long. I must leave her: I cannot, dare not, delay. How far on, sir, can you tell, is the nearest village? I must leave her there; and shall not see my darling, or even hear of her till my return, three months hence."

I plucked my father by the coat, and whispered earnestly in his ear: "Oh! papa, pray ask her to let her stay with us—it would be so delightful. Do, pray."

"If Madame will entrust her child to the care of my daughter, and of her good gouvernante, Madame Perrodon, and permit her to remain as our guest, under my charge, until her return, it will confer a distinction and an obligation upon us, and we shall treat her with all the care and devotion which so sacred a trust deserves."

"I cannot do that, sir, it would be to task your kindness and chivalry too cruelly," said the lady, distractedly.

"It would, on the contrary, be to confer on us a very great kindness at the moment when we most need it. My daughter has just been disappointed by a cruel misfortune, in a visit from which she had long anticipated a great deal of happiness. If you confide this young lady to our care it will be her best consolation. The nearest village on your route is distant, and affords no such inn as you could think of placing your daughter at; you cannot allow her to continue her journey for any considerable distance without danger. If, as you say, you cannot suspend your journey, you must part with her tonight, and nowhere could you do so with more honest assurances of care and tenderness than here."

There was something in this lady's air and appearance so distinguished and even imposing, and in her manner so engaging, as to impress one, quite apart from the dignity of her equipage, with a conviction that she was a person of consequence.

By this time the carriage was replaced in its upright position, and the horses, quite tractable, in the traces again.

The lady threw on her daughter a glance which I fancied was not quite so affectionate as one might have anticipated from the beginning of the scene; then she beckoned slightly to my father, and withdrew two or three steps with him out of hearing; and talked to him with a fixed and stern countenance, not at all like that with which she had hitherto spoken.

I was filled with wonder that my father did not seem to perceive the change, and also unspeakably curious to learn what it could be that she was speaking, almost in his ear, with so much earnestness and rapidity.

Two or three minutes at most I think she remained thus employed, then she turned, and a few steps brought her to where her daughter lay, supported by Madame Perrodon. She kneeled beside her for a moment and whispered, as Madame supposed, a little benediction in her ear; then hastily kissing her she stepped into her carriage, the door was closed, the footmen in stately liveries jumped up behind, the outriders spurred on, the postilions cracked their whips, the horses plunged and broke suddenly into a furious canter that threatened soon again to become a gallop, and the carriage whirled away, followed at the same rapid pace by the two horsemen in the rear.

# III.
# We Compare Notes

We followed the _cortege_ with our eyes until it was swiftly lost to sight in the misty wood; and the very sound of the hoofs and the wheels died away in the silent night air.

Nothing remained to assure us that the adventure had not been an illusion of a moment but the young lady, who just at that moment opened her eyes. I could not see, for her face was turned from me, but she raised her head, evidently looking about her, and I heard a very sweet voice ask complainingly, "Where is mamma?"

Our good Madame Perrodon answered tenderly, and added some comfortable assurances.

I then heard her ask:

"Where am I? What is this place?" and after that she said, "I don't see the carriage; and Matska, where is she?"

Madame answered all her questions in so far as she understood them; and gradually the young lady remembered how the misadventure came about, and was glad to hear that no one in, or in attendance on, the carriage was hurt; and on learning that her mamma had left her here, till her return in about three months, she wept.

I was going to add my consolations to those of Madame Perrodon when Mademoiselle De Lafontaine placed her hand upon my arm, saying:

"Don't approach, one at a time is as much as she can at present converse with; a very little excitement would possibly overpower her now." As soon as she is comfortably in bed, I thought, I will run up to her room and see her.

My father in the meantime had sent a servant on horseback for the physician, who lived about two leagues away; and a bedroom was being prepared for the young lady's reception.

The stranger now rose, and leaning on Madame's arm, walked slowly over the drawbridge and into the castle gate.

In the hall, servants waited to receive her, and she was conducted forthwith to her room. The room we usually sat in as our drawing room is long, having four windows, that looked over the moat and drawbridge, upon the forest scene I have just described.

It is furnished in old carved oak, with large carved cabinets, and the chairs are cushioned with crimson Utrecht velvet. The walls are covered with tapestry, and surrounded with great gold frames, the figures being as large as life, in ancient and very curious costume, and the subjects represented are hunting, hawking, and generally festive. It is not too stately to be extremely comfortable; and here we had our tea, for with his usual patriotic leanings he insisted that the national beverage should make its appearance regularly with our coffee and chocolate.

We sat here this night, and with candles lighted, were talking over the adventure of the evening.

Madame Perrodon and Mademoiselle De Lafontaine were both of our party. The young stranger had hardly lain down in her bed when she sank into a deep sleep; and those ladies had left her in the care of a servant.

"How do you like our guest?" I asked, as soon as Madame entered. "Tell me all about her?"

"I like her extremely," answered Madame, "she is, I almost think, the prettiest creature I ever saw; about your age, and so gentle and nice."

"She is absolutely beautiful," threw in Mademoiselle, who had peeped for a moment into the stranger's room. "And such a sweet voice!" added Madame Perrodon.

"Did you remark a woman in the carriage, after it was set up again, who did not get out," inquired Mademoiselle, "but only looked from the window?"

"No, we had not seen her."

Then she described a hideous black woman, with a sort of colored turban on her head, and who was gazing all the time from the carriage window, nodding and grinning derisively towards the ladies, with gleaming eyes and large white eyeballs, and her teeth set as if in fury.

"Did you remark what an ill-looking pack of men the servants were?" asked Madame.

"Yes," said my father, who had just come in, "ugly, hang-dog looking fellows as ever I beheld in my life. I hope they mayn't rob the poor lady in the forest. They are clever rogues, however; they got everything to rights in a minute."

"I dare say they are worn out with too long traveling," said Madame.

"Besides looking wicked, their faces were so strangely lean, and dark, and sullen. I am very curious, I own; but I dare say the young lady will tell you all about it tomorrow, if she is sufficiently recovered."

"I don't think she will," said my father, with a mysterious smile, and a little nod of his head, as if he knew more about it than he cared to tell us.

This made us all the more inquisitive as to what had passed between him and the lady in the black velvet, in the brief but earnest interview that had immediately preceded her departure.

We were scarcely alone, when I entreated him to tell me. He did not need much pressing.

"There is no particular reason why I should not tell you. She expressed a reluctance to trouble us with the care of her daughter, saying she was in delicate health, and nervous, but not subject to any kind of seizure—she volunteered that—nor to any illusion; being, in fact, perfectly sane."

"How very odd to say all that!" I interpolated. "It was so unnecessary."

"At all events it _was_ said," he laughed, "and as you wish to know all that passed, which was indeed very little, I tell you. She then said, 'I am making a long journey of _vital_ importance—she emphasized the word—rapid and secret; I shall return for my child in three months; in the meantime, she will be silent as to who we are, whence we come, and whither we are traveling.' That is all she said. She spoke very pure French. When she said the word 'secret,' she paused for a few seconds, looking sternly, her eyes fixed on mine. I fancy she makes a great point of that. You saw how quickly she was gone. I hope I have not done a very foolish thing, in taking charge of the young lady."

For my part, I was delighted. I was longing to see and talk to her; and only waiting till the doctor should give me leave. You, who live in towns, can have no idea how great an event the introduction of a new friend is, in such a solitude as surrounded us.

The doctor did not arrive till nearly one o'clock; but I could no more have gone to my bed and slept, than I could have overtaken, on foot, the carriage in which the princess in black velvet had driven away.

When the physician came down to the drawing room, it was to report very favorably upon his patient. She was now sitting up, her pulse quite regular, apparently perfectly well. She had sustained no injury, and the little shock to her nerves had passed away quite harmlessly. There could be no harm certainly in my seeing her, if we both wished it; and, with this permission I sent, forthwith, to know whether she would allow me to visit her for a few minutes in her room.

The servant returned immediately to say that she desired nothing more.

You may be sure I was not long in availing myself of this permission. Our visitor lay in one of the handsomest rooms in the schloss. It was, perhaps, a little stately. There was a somber piece of tapestry opposite the foot of the bed, representing Cleopatra with the asps to her bosom; and other solemn classic scenes were displayed, a little faded, upon the other walls. But there was gold carving, and rich and varied color enough in the other decorations of the room, to more than redeem the gloom of the old tapestry.

There were candles at the bedside. She was sitting up; her slender pretty figure enveloped in the soft silk dressing gown, embroidered with flowers, and lined with thick quilted silk, which her mother had thrown over her feet as she lay upon the ground.

What was it that, as I reached the bedside and had just begun my little greeting, struck me dumb in a moment, and made me recoil a step or two from before her? I will tell you.

I saw the very face which had visited me in my childhood at night, which remained so fixed in my memory, and on which I had for so many years so often ruminated with horror, when no one suspected of what I was thinking.

It was pretty, even beautiful; and when I first beheld it, wore the same melancholy expression.

But this almost instantly lighted into a strange fixed smile of recognition.

There was a silence of fully a minute, and then at length she spoke; I could not.

"How wonderful!" she exclaimed. "Twelve years ago, I saw your face in a dream, and it has haunted me ever since."

"Wonderful indeed!" I repeated, overcoming with an effort the horror that had for a time suspended my utterances. "Twelve years ago, in vision or reality, I certainly saw you. I could not forget your face. It has remained before my eyes ever since."

Her smile had softened. Whatever I had fancied strange in it, was gone, and it and her dimpling cheeks were now delightfully pretty and intelligent.

I felt reassured, and continued more in the vein which hospitality indicated, to bid her welcome, and to tell her how much pleasure her accidental arrival had given us all, and especially what a happiness it was to me.

I took her hand as I spoke. I was a little shy, as lonely people are, but the situation made me eloquent, and even bold. She pressed my hand, she laid hers upon it, and her eyes glowed, as, looking hastily into mine, she smiled again, and blushed.

She answered my welcome very prettily. I sat down beside her, still wondering; and she said:

"I must tell you my vision about you; it is so very strange that you and I should have had, each of the other so vivid a dream, that each should have seen, I you and you me, looking as we do now, when of course we both were mere children. I was a child, about six years old, and I awoke from a confused and troubled dream, and found myself in a room, unlike my nursery, wainscoted clumsily in some dark wood, and with cupboards and bedsteads, and chairs, and benches placed about it. The beds were, I thought, all empty, and the room itself without anyone but myself in it; and I, after looking about me for some time, and admiring especially an iron candlestick with two branches, which I should certainly know again, crept under one of the beds to reach the window; but as I got from under the bed, I heard someone crying; and looking up, while I was still upon my knees, I saw you—most assuredly you—as I see you now; a beautiful young lady, with golden hair and large blue eyes, and lips—your lips—you as you are here.

"Your looks won me; I climbed on the bed and put my arms about you, and I think we both fell asleep. I was aroused by a scream; you were sitting up screaming. I was frightened, and slipped down upon the ground, and, it seemed to me, lost consciousness for a moment; and when I came to myself, I was again in my nursery at home. Your face I have never forgotten since. I could not be misled by mere resemblance. _You are_ the lady whom I saw then."

It was now my turn to relate my corresponding vision, which I did, to the undisguised wonder of my new acquaintance.

"I don't know which should be most afraid of the other," she said, again smiling—"If you were less pretty I think I should be very much afraid of you, but being as you are, and you and I both so young, I feel only that I have made your acquaintance twelve years ago, and have already a right to your intimacy; at all events it does seem as if we were destined, from our earliest childhood, to be friends. I wonder whether you feel as strangely drawn towards me as I do to you; I have never had a friend—shall I find one now?" She sighed, and her fine dark eyes gazed passionately on me.

Now the truth is, I felt rather unaccountably towards the beautiful stranger. I did feel, as she said, "drawn towards her," but there was also something of repulsion. In this ambiguous feeling, however, the sense of attraction immensely prevailed. She interested and won me; she was so beautiful and so indescribably engaging.

I perceived now something of languor and exhaustion stealing over her, and hastened to bid her good night.

"The doctor thinks," I added, "that you ought to have a maid to sit up with you tonight; one of ours is waiting, and you will find her a very useful and quiet creature."

"How kind of you, but I could not sleep, I never could with an attendant in the room. I shan't require any assistance—and, shall I confess my weakness, I am haunted with a terror of robbers. Our house was robbed once, and two servants murdered, so I always lock my door. It has become a habit—and you look so kind I know you will forgive me. I see there is a key in the lock."

She held me close in her pretty arms for a moment and whispered in my ear, "Good night, darling, it is very hard to part with you, but good night; tomorrow, but not early, I shall see you again."

She sank back on the pillow with a sigh, and her fine eyes followed me with a fond and melancholy gaze, and she murmured again "Good night, dear friend."

Young people like, and even love, on impulse. I was flattered by the evident, though as yet undeserved, fondness she showed me. I liked the confidence with which she at once received me. She was determined that we should be very near friends.

Next day came and we met again. I was delighted with my companion; that is to say, in many respects.

Her looks lost nothing in daylight—she was certainly the most beautiful creature I had ever seen, and the unpleasant remembrance of the face presented in my early dream, had lost the effect of the first unexpected recognition.

She confessed that she had experienced a similar shock on seeing me, and precisely the same faint antipathy that had mingled with my admiration of her. We now laughed together over our momentary horrors.

# IV.
# Her Habits—A Saunter

I told you that I was charmed with her in most particulars.

There were some that did not please me so well.

She was above the middle height of women. I shall begin by describing her.

She was slender, and wonderfully graceful. Except that her movements were languid—very languid—indeed, there was nothing in her appearance to indicate an invalid. Her complexion was rich and brilliant; her features were small and beautifully formed; her eyes large, dark, and lustrous; her hair was quite wonderful, I never saw hair so magnificently thick and long when it was down about her shoulders; I have often placed my hands under it, and laughed with wonder at its weight. It was exquisitely fine and soft, and in color a rich very dark brown, with something of gold. I loved to let it down, tumbling with its own weight, as, in her room, she lay back in her chair talking in her sweet low voice, I used to fold and braid it, and spread it out and play with it. Heavens! If I had but known all!

I said there were particulars which did not please me. I have told you that her confidence won me the first night I saw her; but I found that she exercised with respect to herself, her mother, her history, everything in fact connected with her life, plans, and people, an ever wakeful reserve. I dare say I was unreasonable, perhaps I was wrong; I dare say I ought to have respected the solemn injunction laid upon my father by the stately lady in black velvet. But curiosity is a restless and unscrupulous passion, and no one girl can endure, with patience, that hers should be baffled by another. What harm could it do anyone to tell me what I so ardently desired to know? Had she no trust in my good sense or honor? Why would she not believe me when I assured her, so solemnly, that I would not divulge one syllable of what she told me to any mortal breathing.

There was a coldness, it seemed to me, beyond her years, in her smiling melancholy persistent refusal to afford me the least ray of light.

I cannot say we quarreled upon this point, for she would not quarrel upon any. It was, of course, very unfair of me to press her, very ill-bred, but I really could not help it; and I might just as well have let it alone.

What she did tell me amounted, in my unconscionable estimation—to nothing.

It was all summed up in three very vague disclosures:

First—Her name was Carmilla.

Second—Her family was very ancient and noble.

Third—Her home lay in the direction of the west.

She would not tell me the name of her family, nor their armorial bearings, nor the name of their estate, nor even that of the country they lived in.

You are not to suppose that I worried her incessantly on these subjects. I watched opportunity, and rather insinuated than urged my inquiries. Once or twice, indeed, I did attack her more directly. But no matter what my tactics, utter failure was invariably the result. Reproaches and caresses were all lost upon her. But I must add this, that her evasion was conducted with so pretty a melancholy and deprecation, with so many, and even passionate declarations of her liking for me, and trust in my honor, and with so many promises that I should at last know all, that I could not find it in my heart long to be offended with her.

She used to place her pretty arms about my neck, draw me to her, and laying her cheek to mine, murmur with her lips near my ear, "Dearest, your little heart is wounded; think me not cruel because I obey the irresistible law of my strength and weakness; if your dear heart is wounded, my wild heart bleeds with yours. In the rapture of my enormous humiliation I live in your warm life, and you shall die—die, sweetly die—into mine. I cannot help it; as I draw near to you, you, in your turn, will draw near to others, and learn the rapture of that cruelty, which yet is love; so, for a while, seek to know no more of me and mine, but trust me with all your loving spirit."

And when she had spoken such a rhapsody, she would press me more closely in her trembling embrace, and her lips in soft kisses gently glow upon my cheek.

Her agitations and her language were unintelligible to me.

From these foolish embraces, which were not of very frequent occurrence, I must allow, I used to wish to extricate myself; but my energies seemed to fail me. Her murmured words sounded like a lullaby in my ear, and soothed my resistance into a trance, from which I only seemed to recover myself when she withdrew her arms.

In these mysterious moods I did not like her. I experienced a strange tumultuous excitement that was pleasurable, ever and anon, mingled with a vague sense of fear and disgust. I had no distinct thoughts about her while such scenes lasted, but I was conscious of a love growing into adoration, and also of abhorrence. This I know is paradox, but I can make no other attempt to explain the feeling.

I now write, after an interval of more than ten years, with a trembling hand, with a confused and horrible recollection of certain occurrences and situations, in the ordeal through which I was unconsciously passing; though with a vivid and very sharp remembrance of the main current of my story.

But, I suspect, in all lives there are certain emotional scenes, those in which our passions have been most wildly and terribly roused, that are of all others the most vaguely and dimly remembered.

Sometimes after an hour of apathy, my strange and beautiful companion would take my hand and hold it with a fond pressure, renewed again and again; blushing softly, gazing in my face with languid and burning eyes, and breathing so fast that her dress rose and fell with the tumultuous respiration. It was like the ardor of a lover; it embarrassed me; it was hateful and yet over-powering; and with gloating eyes she drew me to her, and her hot lips traveled along my cheek in kisses; and she would whisper, almost in sobs, "You are mine, you _shall_ be mine, you and I are one for ever." Then she had thrown herself back in her chair, with her small hands over her eyes, leaving me trembling.

"Are we related," I used to ask; "what can you mean by all this? I remind you perhaps of someone whom you love; but you must not, I hate it; I don't know you—I don't know myself when you look so and talk so."

She used to sigh at my vehemence, then turn away and drop my hand. Respecting these very extraordinary manifestations I strove in vain to form any satisfactory theory—I could not refer them to affectation or trick. It was unmistakably the momentary breaking out of suppressed instinct and emotion. Was she, notwithstanding her mother's volunteered denial, subject to brief visitations of insanity; or was there here a disguise and a romance? I had read in old storybooks of such things. What if a boyish lover had found his way into the house, and sought to prosecute his suit in masquerade, with the assistance of a clever old adventuress. But there were many things against this hypothesis, highly interesting as it was to my vanity.

I could boast of no little attentions such as masculine gallantry delights to offer. Between these passionate moments there were long intervals of commonplace, of gaiety, of brooding melancholy, during which, except that I detected her eyes so full of melancholy fire, following me, at times I might have been as nothing to her. Except in these brief periods of mysterious excitement her ways were girlish; and there was always a languor about her, quite incompatible with a masculine system in a state of health.

In some respects her habits were odd. Perhaps not so singular in the opinion of a town lady like you, as they appeared to us rustic people. She used to come down very late, generally not till one o'clock, she would then take a cup of chocolate, but eat nothing; we then went out for a walk, which was a mere saunter, and she seemed, almost immediately, exhausted, and either returned to the schloss or sat on one of the benches that were placed, here and there, among the trees. This was a bodily languor in which her mind did not sympathize. She was always an animated talker, and very intelligent.

She sometimes alluded for a moment to her own home, or mentioned an adventure or situation, or an early recollection, which indicated a people of strange manners, and described customs of which we knew nothing. I gathered from these chance hints that her native country was much more remote than I had at first fancied.

As we sat thus one afternoon under the trees a funeral passed us by. It was that of a pretty young girl, whom I had often seen, the daughter of one of the rangers of the forest. The poor man was walking behind the coffin of his darling; she was his only child, and he looked quite heartbroken.

Peasants walking two-and-two came behind, they were singing a funeral hymn.

I rose to mark my respect as they passed, and joined in the hymn they were very sweetly singing.

My companion shook me a little roughly, and I turned surprised.

She said brusquely, "Don't you perceive how discordant that is?"

"I think it very sweet, on the contrary," I answered, vexed at the interruption, and very uncomfortable, lest the people who composed the little procession should observe and resent what was passing.

I resumed, therefore, instantly, and was again interrupted. "You pierce my ears," said Carmilla, almost angrily, and stopping her ears with her tiny fingers. "Besides, how can you tell that your religion and mine are the same; your forms wound me, and I hate funerals. What a fuss! Why you must die—_everyone_ must die; and all are happier when they do. Come home."

"My father has gone on with the clergyman to the churchyard. I thought you knew she was to be buried today."

"She? I don't trouble my head about peasants. I don't know who she is," answered Carmilla, with a flash from her fine eyes.

"She is the poor girl who fancied she saw a ghost a fortnight ago, and has been dying ever since, till yesterday, when she expired."

"Tell me nothing about ghosts. I shan't sleep tonight if you do."

"I hope there is no plague or fever coming; all this looks very like it," I continued. "The swineherd's young wife died only a week ago, and she thought something seized her by the throat as she lay in her bed, and nearly strangled her. Papa says such horrible fancies do accompany some forms of fever. She was quite well the day before. She sank afterwards, and died before a week."

"Well, _her_ funeral is over, I hope, and _her_ hymn sung; and our ears shan't be tortured with that discord and jargon. It has made me nervous. Sit down here, beside me; sit close; hold my hand; press it hard-hard-harder."

We had moved a little back, and had come to another seat.

She sat down. Her face underwent a change that alarmed and even terrified me for a moment. It darkened, and became horribly livid; her teeth and hands were clenched, and she frowned and compressed her lips, while she stared down upon the ground at her feet, and trembled all over with a continued shudder as irrepressible as ague. All her energies seemed strained to suppress a fit, with which she was then breathlessly tugging; and at length a low convulsive cry of suffering broke from her, and gradually the hysteria subsided. "There! That comes of strangling people with hymns!" she said at last. "Hold me, hold me still. It is passing away."

And so gradually it did; and perhaps to dissipate the somber impression which the spectacle had left upon me, she became unusually animated and chatty; and so we got home.

This was the first time I had seen her exhibit any definable symptoms of that delicacy of health which her mother had spoken of. It was the first time, also, I had seen her exhibit anything like temper.

Both passed away like a summer cloud; and never but once afterwards did I witness on her part a momentary sign of anger. I will tell you how it happened.

She and I were looking out of one of the long drawing room windows, when there entered the courtyard, over the drawbridge, a figure of a wanderer whom I knew very well. He used to visit the schloss generally twice a year.

It was the figure of a hunchback, with the sharp lean features that generally accompany deformity. He wore a pointed black beard, and he was smiling from ear to ear, showing his white fangs. He was dressed in buff, black, and scarlet, and crossed with more straps and belts than I could count, from which hung all manner of things. Behind, he carried a magic lantern, and two boxes, which I well knew, in one of which was a salamander, and in the other a mandrake. These monsters used to make my father laugh. They were compounded of parts of monkeys, parrots, squirrels, fish, and hedgehogs, dried and stitched together with great neatness and startling effect. He had a fiddle, a box of conjuring apparatus, a pair of foils and masks attached to his belt, several other mysterious cases dangling about him, and a black staff with copper ferrules in his hand. His companion was a rough spare dog, that followed at his heels, but stopped short, suspiciously at the drawbridge, and in a little while began to howl dismally.

In the meantime, the mountebank, standing in the midst of the courtyard, raised his grotesque hat, and made us a very ceremonious bow, paying his compliments very volubly in execrable French, and German not much better.

Then, disengaging his fiddle, he began to scrape a lively air to which he sang with a merry discord, dancing with ludicrous airs and activity, that made me laugh, in spite of the dog's howling.

Then he advanced to the window with many smiles and salutations, and his hat in his left hand, his fiddle under his arm, and with a fluency that never took breath, he gabbled a long advertisement of all his accomplishments, and the resources of the various arts which he placed at our service, and the curiosities and entertainments which it was in his power, at our bidding, to display.

"Will your ladyships be pleased to buy an amulet against the oupire, which is going like the wolf, I hear, through these woods," he said dropping his hat on the pavement. "They are dying of it right and left and here is a charm that never fails; only pinned to the pillow, and you may laugh in his face."

These charms consisted of oblong slips of vellum, with cabalistic ciphers and diagrams upon them. Carmilla instantly purchased one, and so did I.

He was looking up, and we were smiling down upon him, amused; at least, I can answer for myself. His piercing black eye, as he looked up in our faces, seemed to detect something that fixed for a moment his curiosity,

In an instant he unrolled a leather case, full of all manner of odd little steel instruments.

"See here, my lady," he said, displaying it, and addressing me, "I profess, among other things less useful, the art of dentistry. Plague take the dog!" he interpolated. "Silence, beast! He howls so that your ladyships can scarcely hear a word. Your noble friend, the young lady at your right, has the sharpest tooth,—long, thin, pointed, like an awl, like a needle; ha, ha! With my sharp and long sight, as I look up, I have seen it distinctly; now if it happens to hurt the young lady, and I think it must, here am I, here are my file, my punch, my nippers; I will make it round and blunt, if her ladyship pleases; no longer the tooth of a fish, but of a beautiful young lady as she is. Hey? Is the young lady displeased? Have I been too bold? Have I offended her?"

The young lady, indeed, looked very angry as she drew back from the window.

"How dares that mountebank insult us so? Where is your father? I shall demand redress from him. My father would have had the wretch tied up to the pump, and flogged with a cart whip, and burnt to the bones with the cattle brand!"

She retired from the window a step or two, and sat down, and had hardly lost sight of the offender, when her wrath subsided as suddenly as it had risen, and she gradually recovered her usual tone, and seemed to forget the little hunchback and his follies.

My father was out of spirits that evening. On coming in he told us that there had been another case very similar to the two fatal ones which had lately occurred. The sister of a young peasant on his estate, only a mile away, was very ill, had been, as she described it, attacked very nearly in the same way, and was now slowly but steadily sinking.

"All this," said my father, "is strictly referable to natural causes. These poor people infect one another with their superstitions, and so repeat in imagination the images of terror that have infested their neighbors."

"But that very circumstance frightens one horribly," said Carmilla.

"How so?" inquired my father.

"I am so afraid of fancying I see such things; I think it would be as bad as reality."

"We are in God's hands: nothing can happen without his permission, and all will end well for those who love him. He is our faithful creator; He has made us all, and will take care of us."

"Creator! _Nature!_" said the young lady in answer to my gentle father. "And this disease that invades the country is natural. Nature. All things proceed from Nature—don't they? All things in the heaven, in the earth, and under the earth, act and live as Nature ordains? I think so."

"The doctor said he would come here today," said my father, after a silence. "I want to know what he thinks about it, and what he thinks we had better do."

"Doctors never did me any good," said Carmilla.

"Then you have been ill?" I asked.

"More ill than ever you were," she answered.

"Long ago?"

"Yes, a long time. I suffered from this very illness; but I forget all but my pain and weakness, and they were not so bad as are suffered in other diseases." "You were very young then?"

"I dare say, let us talk no more of it. You would not wound a friend?"

She looked languidly in my eyes, and passed her arm round my waist lovingly, and led me out of the room. My father was busy over some papers near the window.

"Why does your papa like to frighten us?" said the pretty girl with a sigh and a little shudder.

"He doesn't, dear Carmilla, it is the very furthest thing from his mind."

"Are you afraid, dearest?"

"I should be very much if I fancied there was any real danger of my being attacked as those poor people were."

"You are afraid to die?"

"Yes, every one is."

"But to die as lovers may—to die together, so that they may live together.

Girls are caterpillars while they live in the world, to be finally butterflies when the summer comes; but in the meantime there are grubs and larvae, don't you see—each with their peculiar propensities, necessities and structure. So says Monsieur Buffon, in his big book, in the next room."

Later in the day the doctor came, and was closeted with papa for some time.

He was a skilful man, of sixty and upwards, he wore powder, and shaved his pale face as smooth as a pumpkin. He and papa emerged from the room together, and I heard papa laugh, and say as they came out:
"Well, I do wonder at a wise man like you. What do you say to hippogriffs and dragons?"

The doctor was smiling, and made answer, shaking his head—

"Nevertheless life and death are mysterious states, and we know little of the resources of either."

And so they walked on, and I heard no more. I did not then know what the doctor had been broaching, but I think I guess it now.

## V.
## A Wonderful Likeness

This evening there arrived from Gratz the grave, dark-faced son of the picture cleaner, with a horse and cart laden with two large packing cases, having many pictures in each. It was a journey of ten leagues, and whenever a messenger arrived at the schloss from our little capital of Gratz, we used to crowd about him in the hall, to hear the news.

This arrival created in our secluded quarters quite a sensation. The cases remained in the hall, and the messenger was taken charge of by the servants till he had eaten his supper. Then with assistants, and armed with hammer, ripping chisel, and turnscrew, he met us in the hall, where we had assembled to witness the unpacking of the cases.

Carmilla sat looking listlessly on, while one after the other the old pictures, nearly all portraits, which had undergone the process of renovation, were brought to light. My mother was of an old Hungarian family, and most of these pictures, which were about to be restored to their places, had come to us through her.

My father had a list in his hand, from which he read, as the artist rummaged out the corresponding numbers. I don't know that the pictures were very good, but they were, undoubtedly, very old, and some of them very curious also. They had, for the most part, the merit of being now seen by me, I may say, for the first time; for the smoke and dust of
time had all but obliterated them.

"There is a picture that I have not seen yet," said my father. "In one corner, at the top of it, is the name, as well as I could read, 'Marcia Karnstein,' and the date '1698'; and I am curious to see how it has turned out."

I remembered it; it was a small picture, about a foot and a half high, and nearly square, without a frame; but it was so blackened by age that I could not make it out.

The artist now produced it, with evident pride. It was quite beautiful; it was startling; it seemed to live. It was the effigy of Carmilla!

"Carmilla, dear, here is an absolute miracle. Here you are, living, smiling, ready to speak, in this picture. Isn't it beautiful, Papa? And see, even the little mole on her throat."

My father laughed, and said "Certainly it is a wonderful likeness," but he looked away, and to my surprise seemed but little struck by it, and went on talking to the picture cleaner, who was also something of an artist, and discoursed with intelligence about the portraits or other works, which his art had just brought into light and color, while I was more and more lost in wonder the more I looked at the picture.

"Will you let me hang this picture in my room, papa?" I asked.

"Certainly, dear," said he, smiling, "I'm very glad you think it so like.

It must be prettier even than I thought it, if it is."

The young lady did not acknowledge this pretty speech, did not seem to hear it. She was leaning back in her seat, her fine eyes under their long lashes gazing on me in contemplation, and she smiled in a kind of rapture.

"And now you can read quite plainly the name that is written in the corner.

It is not Marcia; it looks as if it was done in gold. The name is Mircalla, Countess Karnstein, and this is a little coronet over and underneath A.D.

1698. I am descended from the Karnsteins; that is, mamma was."

"Ah!" said the lady, languidly, "so am I, I think, a very long descent, very ancient. Are there any Karnsteins living now?"

"None who bear the name, I believe. The family were ruined, I believe, in some civil wars, long ago, but the ruins of the castle are only about three miles away."

"How interesting!" she said, languidly. "But see what beautiful moonlight!" She glanced through the hall door, which stood a little open. "Suppose you take a little ramble round the court, and look down at the road and river."

"It is so like the night you came to us," I said.

She sighed; smiling.

She rose, and each with her arm about the other's waist, we walked out upon the pavement.

In silence, slowly we walked down to the drawbridge, where the beautiful landscape opened before us.

"And so you were thinking of the night I came here?" she almost whispered.

"Are you glad I came?"

"Delighted, dear Carmilla," I answered.
"And you asked for the picture you think like me, to hang in your room," she murmured with a sigh, as she drew her arm closer about my waist, and let her pretty head sink upon my shoulder. "How romantic you are, Carmilla," I said. "Whenever you tell me your story, it will be made up chiefly of some one great romance."

She kissed me silently.

"I am sure, Carmilla, you have been in love; that there is, at this moment, an affair of the heart going on."

"I have been in love with no one, and never shall," she whispered, "unless it should be with you."

How beautiful she looked in the moonlight!

Shy and strange was the look with which she quickly hid her face in my neck and hair, with tumultuous sighs, that seemed almost to sob, and pressed in mine a hand that trembled.

Her soft cheek was glowing against mine. "Darling, darling," she murmured, "I live in you; and you would die for me, I love you so."

I started from her.

She was gazing on me with eyes from which all fire, all meaning had flown, and a face colorless and apathetic.

"Is there a chill in the air, dear?" she said drowsily. "I almost shiver; have I been dreaming? Let us come in. Come; come; come in."

"You look ill, Carmilla; a little faint. You certainly must take some wine," I said.

"Yes. I will. I'm better now. I shall be quite well in a few minutes. Yes, do give me a little wine," answered Carmilla, as we approached the door.

"Let us look again for a moment; it is the last time, perhaps, I shall see the moonlight with you."

"How do you feel now, dear Carmilla? Are you really better?" I asked.

I was beginning to take alarm, lest she should have been stricken with the strange epidemic that they said had invaded the country about us.

"Papa would be grieved beyond measure," I added, "if he thought you were ever so little ill, without immediately letting us know. We have a very skilful doctor near us, the physician who was with papa today."

"I'm sure he is. I know how kind you all are; but, dear child, I am quite well again. There is nothing ever wrong with me, but a little weakness.

People say I am languid; I am incapable of exertion; I can scarcely walk as far as a child of three years old: and every now and then the little strength I have falters, and I become as you have just seen me. But after all I am very easily set up again; in a moment I am perfectly myself. See how I have recovered."

So, indeed, she had; and she and I talked a great deal, and very animated she was; and the remainder of that evening passed without any recurrence of what I called her infatuations. I mean her crazy talk and looks, which embarrassed, and even frightened me.

But there occurred that night an event which gave my thoughts quite a new turn, and seemed to startle even Carmilla's languid nature into momentary energy.

## VI.
## A Very Strange Agony

When we got into the drawing room, and had sat down to our coffee and chocolate, although Carmilla did not take any, she seemed quite herself again, and Madame, and Mademoiselle De Lafontaine, joined us, and made a little card party, in the course of which papa came in for what he called his "dish of tea."

When the game was over he sat down beside Carmilla on the sofa, and asked her, a little anxiously, whether she had heard from her mother since her arrival.

She answered "No."

He then asked whether she knew where a letter would reach her at present.

"I cannot tell," she answered ambiguously, "but I have been thinking of leaving you; you have been already too hospitable and too kind to me. I have given you an infinity of trouble, and I should wish to take a carriage tomorrow, and post in pursuit of her; I know where I shall ultimately find her, although I dare not yet tell you."

"But you must not dream of any such thing," exclaimed my father, to my great relief. "We can't afford to lose you so, and I won't consent to your leaving us, except under the care of your mother, who was so good as to consent to your remaining with us till she should herself return. I should be quite happy if I knew that you heard from her: but this evening the accounts of the progress of the mysterious disease that has invaded our neighborhood, grow even more alarming; and my beautiful guest, I do feel the responsibility, unaided by advice from your mother, very much. But I shall do my best; and one thing is certain, that you must not think of leaving us without her distinct direction to that effect. We should suffer too much in parting from you to consent to it easily." "Thank you, sir, a thousand times for your hospitality," she answered, smiling bashfully. "You have all been too kind to me; I have seldom been so happy in all my life before, as in your beautiful chateau, under your care, and in the society of your dear daughter."

So he gallantly, in his old-fashioned way, kissed her hand, smiling and pleased at her little speech.

I accompanied Carmilla as usual to her room, and sat and chatted with her while she was preparing for bed.

"Do you think," I said at length, "that you will ever confide fully in me?"

She turned round smiling, but made no answer, only continued to smile on me.

"You won't answer that?" I said. "You can't answer pleasantly; I ought not to have asked you."

"You were quite right to ask me that, or anything. You do not know how dear you are to me, or you could not think any confidence too great to look for.

But I am under vows, no nun half so awfully, and I dare not tell my story yet, even to you. The time is very near when you shall know everything. You will think me cruel, very selfish, but love is always selfish; the more ardent the more selfish. How jealous I am you cannot know. You must come with me, loving me, to death; or else hate me and still come with me. and _hating_ me through death and after. There is no such word as indifference in my apathetic nature."

"Now, Carmilla, you are going to talk your wild nonsense again," I said hastily.

"Not I, silly little fool as I am, and full of whims and fancies; for your sake I'll talk like a sage. Were you ever at a ball?"

"No; how you do run on. What is it like? How charming it must be."
"I almost forget, it is years ago."

I laughed.

"You are not so old. Your first ball can hardly be forgotten yet."

"I remember everything about it—with an effort. I see it all, as divers see what is going on above them, through a medium, dense, rippling, but transparent. There occurred that night what has confused the picture, and made its colours faint. I was all but assassinated in my bed, wounded here," she touched her breast, "and never was the same since."

"Were you near dying?"

"Yes, very—a cruel love—strange love, that would have taken my life. Love will have its sacrifices. No sacrifice without blood. Let us go to sleep now; I feel so lazy. How can I get up just now and lock my door?"

She was lying with her tiny hands buried in her rich wavy hair, under her cheek, her little head upon the pillow, and her glittering eyes followed me wherever I moved, with a kind of shy smile that I could not decipher.

I bid her good night, and crept from the room with an uncomfortable sensation.

I often wondered whether our pretty guest ever said her prayers. I certainly had never seen her upon her knees. In the morning she never came down until long after our family prayers were over, and at night she never left the drawing room to attend our brief evening prayers in the hall.

If it had not been that it had casually come out in one of our careless talks that she had been baptised, I should have doubted her being a Christian. Religion was a subject on which I had never heard her speak a word. If I had known the world better, this particular neglect or antipathy would not have so much surprised me.

The precautions of nervous people are infectious, and persons of a like temperament are pretty sure, after a time, to imitate them. I had adopted Carmilla's habit of locking her bedroom door, having taken into my head all her whimsical alarms about midnight invaders and prowling assassins. I had also adopted her precaution of making a brief search through her room, to satisfy herself that no lurking assassin or robber was "ensconced."

These wise measures taken, I got into my bed and fell asleep. A light was burning in my room. This was an old habit, of very early date, and which nothing could have tempted me to dispense with.

Thus fortifed I might take my rest in peace. But dreams come through stone walls, light up dark rooms, or darken light ones, and their persons make their exits and their entrances as they please, and laugh at locksmiths.

I had a dream that night that was the beginning of a very strange agony.

I cannot call it a nightmare, for I was quite conscious of being asleep.

But I was equally conscious of being in my room, and lying in bed, precisely as I actually was. I saw, or fancied I saw, the room and its furniture just as I had seen it last, except that it was very dark, and I saw something moving round the foot of the bed, which at first I could not accurately distinguish. But I soon saw that it was a sooty-black animal that resembled a monstrous cat. It appeared to me about four or five feet long for it measured fully the length of the hearthrug as it passed over it; and it continued to-ing and fro-ing with the lithe, sinister restlessness of a beast in a cage. I could not cry out, although as you may suppose, I was terrified. Its pace was growing faster, and the room rapidly darker and darker, and at length so dark that I could no longer see anything of it but its eyes. I felt it spring lightly on the bed. The two broad eyes approached my face, and suddenly I felt a stinging pain as if two large needles darted, an inch or two apart, deep into my breast. I waked with a scream. The room was lighted by the candle that burnt there all through the night, and I saw a female figure standing at the foot of the bed, a little at the right side. It was in a dark loose dress, and its hair was down and covered its shoulders. A block of stone could not have been more still. There was not the slightest stir of respiration. As I stared at it, the figure appeared to have changed its place, and was now nearer the door; then, close to it, the door opened, and it passed out.

I was now relieved, and able to breathe and move. My first thought was that Carmilla had been playing me a trick, and that I had forgotten to secure my door. I hastened to it, and found it locked as usual on the inside. I was afraid to open it—I was horrified. I sprang into my bed and covered my head up in the bedclothes, and lay there more dead than alive till morning.

## VII.
## Descending

It would be vain my attempting to tell you the horror with which, even now, I recall the occurrence of that night. It was no such transitory terror as a dream leaves behind it. It seemed to deepen by time, and communicated itself to the room and the very furniture that had encompassed the apparition.

I could not bear next day to be alone for a moment. I should have told papa, but for two opposite reasons. At one time I thought he would laugh at my story, and I could not bear its being treated as a jest; and at another I thought he might fancy that I had been attacked by the mysterious complaint which had invaded our neighborhood. I had myself no misgiving of the kind, and as he had been rather an invalid for some time, I was afraid of alarming him.

I was comfortable enough with my good-natured companions, Madame Perrodon, and the vivacious Mademoiselle Lafontaine. They both perceived that I was out of spirits and nervous, and at length I told them what lay so heavy at my heart. Mademoiselle laughed, but I fancied that Madame Perrodon looked anxious.

"By-the-by," said Mademoiselle, laughing, "the long lime tree walk, behind Carmilla's bedroom window, is haunted!"

"Nonsense!" exclaimed Madame, who probably thought the theme rather inopportune, "and who tells that story, my dear?"

"Martin says that he came up twice, when the old yard gate was being repaired, before sunrise, and twice saw the same female figure walking down the lime tree avenue."

"So he well might, as long as there are cows to milk in the river fields," said Madame.

"I daresay; but Martin chooses to be frightened, and never did I see fool more frightened."

"You must not say a word about it to Carmilla, because she can see down that walk from her room window," I interposed, "and she is, if possible, a greater coward than I."

Carmilla came down rather later than usual that day.

"I was so frightened last night," she said, so soon as were together, "and I am sure I should have seen something dreadful if it had not been for that charm I bought from the poor little hunchback whom I called such hard names. I had a dream of something black coming round my bed, and I awoke in a perfect horror, and I really thought, for some seconds, I saw a dark figure near the chimneypiece, but I felt under my pillow for my charm, and the moment my fingers touched it, the figure disappeared, and I felt quite certain, only that I had it by me, that something frightful would have made its appearance, and, perhaps, throttled me, as it did those poor people we heard of.

"Well, listen to me," I began, and recounted my adventure, at the recital of which she appeared horrified.

"And had you the charm near you?" she asked, earnestly.

"No, I had dropped it into a china vase in the drawing room, but I shall certainly take it with me tonight, as you have so much faith in it."

At this distance of time I cannot tell you, or even understand, how I overcame my horror so effectually as to lie alone in my room that night. I remember distinctly that I pinned the charm to my pillow. I fell asleep almost immediately, and slept even more soundly than usual all night.

Next night I passed as well. My sleep was delightfully deep and dreamless.

But I wakened with a sense of lassitude and melancholy, which, however, did not exceed a degree that was almost luxurious.

"Well, I told you so," said Carmilla, when I described my quiet sleep, "I had such delightful sleep myself last night; I pinned the charm to the breast of my nightdress. It was too far away the night before. I am quite sure it was all fancy, except the dreams. I used to think that evil spirits made dreams, but our doctor told me it is no such thing. Only a fever passing by, or some other malady, as they often do, he said, knocks at the door, and not being able to get in, passes on, with that alarm."

"And what do you think the charm is?" said I.

"It has been fumigated or immersed in some drug, and is an antidote against the malaria," she answered.

"Then it acts only on the body?"

"Certainly; you don't suppose that evil spirits are frightened by bits of ribbon, or the perfumes of a druggist's shop? No, these complaints, wandering in the air, begin by trying the nerves, and so infect the brain, but before they can seize upon you, the antidote repels them. That I am sure is what the charm has done for us. It is nothing magical, it is simply natural.

I should have been happier if I could have quite agreed with Carmilla, but I did my best, and the impression was a little losing its force.

For some nights I slept profoundly; but still every morning I felt the same lassitude, and a languor weighed upon me all day. I felt myself a changed girl. A strange melancholy was stealing over me, a melancholy that I would not have interrupted. Dim thoughts of death began to open, and an idea that I was slowly sinking took gentle, and, somehow, not unwelcome, possession of me. If it was sad, the tone of mind which this induced was also sweet.

Whatever it might be, my soul acquiesced in it.

I would not admit that I was ill, I would not consent to tell my papa, or to have the doctor sent for.

Carmilla became more devoted to me than ever, and her strange paroxysms of languid adoration more frequent. She used to gloat on me with increasing ardor the more my strength and spirits waned. This always shocked me like a momentary glare of insanity.

Without knowing it, I was now in a pretty advanced stage of the strangest illness under which mortal ever suffered. There was an unaccountable fascination in its earlier symptoms that more than reconciled me to the incapacitating effect of that stage of the malady. This fascination increased for a time, until it reached a certain point, when gradually a sense of the horrible mingled itself with it, deepening, as you shall hear, until it discolored and perverted the whole state of my life.

The first change I experienced was rather agreeable. It was very near the turning point from which began the descent of Avernus.

Certain vague and strange sensations visited me in my sleep. The prevailing one was of that pleasant, peculiar cold thrill which we feel in bathing, when we move against the current of a river. This was soon accompanied by dreams that seemed interminable, and were so vague that I could never recollect their scenery and persons, or any one connected portion of their action. But they left an awful impression, and a sense of exhaustion, as if I had passed through a long period of great mental exertion and danger.

After all these dreams there remained on waking a remembrance of having been in a place very nearly dark, and of having spoken to people whom I could not see; and especially of one clear voice, of a female's, very deep, that spoke as if at a distance, slowly, and producing always the same sensation of indescribable solemnity and fear. Sometimes there came a sensation as if a hand was drawn softly along my cheek and neck. Sometimes it was as if warm lips kissed me, and longer and longer and more lovingly as they reached my throat, but there the caress fixed itself. My heart beat faster, my breathing rose and fell rapidly and full drawn; a sobbing, that rose into a sense of strangulation, supervened, and turned into a dreadful convulsion, in which my senses left me and I became unconscious.

It was now three weeks since the commencement of this unaccountable state.

My sufferings had, during the last week, told upon my appearance. I had grown pale, my eyes were dilated and darkened underneath, and the languor which I had long felt began to display itself in my countenance.

My father asked me often whether I was ill; but, with an obstinacy which now seems to me unaccountable, I persisted in assuring him that I was quite well.

In a sense this was true. I had no pain, I could complain of no bodily derangement. My complaint seemed to be one of the imagination, or the nerves, and, horrible as my sufferings were, I kept them, with a morbid reserve, very nearly to myself.

It could not be that terrible complaint which the peasants called the oupire, for I had now been suffering for three weeks, and they were seldom ill for much more than three days, when death put an end to their miseries.

Carmilla complained of dreams and feverish sensations, but by no means of so alarming a kind as mine. I say that mine were extremely alarming. Had I been capable of comprehending my condition, I would have invoked aid and advice on my knees. The narcotic of an unsuspected influence was acting upon me, and my perceptions were benumbed.

I am going to tell you now of a dream that led immediately to an odd discovery.

One night, instead of the voice I was accustomed to hear in the dark, I heard one, sweet and tender, and at the same time terrible, which said,

“Your mother warns you to beware of the assassin.” At the same time a light unexpectedly sprang up, and I saw Carmilla, standing, near the foot of my bed, in her white nightdress, bathed, from her chin to her feet, in one great stain of blood.

I wakened with a shriek, possessed with the one idea that Carmilla was being murdered. I remember springing from my bed, and my next recollection is that of standing on the lobby, crying for help.

Madame and Mademoiselle came scurrying out of their rooms in alarm; a lamp burned always on the lobby, and seeing me, they soon learned the cause of my terror.

I insisted on our knocking at Carmilla's door. Our knocking was unanswered.

It soon became a pounding and an uproar. We shrieked her name, but all was vain.

We all grew frightened, for the door was locked. We hurried back, in panic, to my room. There we rang the bell long and furiously. If my father's room had been at that side of the house, we would have called him up at once to our aid. But, alas! he was quite out of hearing, and to reach him involved an excursion for which we none of us had courage.

Servants, however, soon came running up the stairs; I had got on my dressing gown and slippers meanwhile, and my companions were already similarly furnished. Recognizing the voices of the servants on the lobby, we sallied out together; and having renewed, as fruitlessly, our summons at Carmilla's door, I ordered the men to force the lock. They did so, and we stood, holding our lights aloft, in the doorway, and so stared into the room.

We called her by name; but there was still no reply. We looked round the room. Everything was undisturbed. It was exactly in the state in which I had left it on bidding her good night. But Carmilla was gone.

## VIII.
## Search

At sight of the room, perfectly undisturbed except for our violent entrance, we began to cool a little, and soon recovered our senses sufficiently to dismiss the men. It had struck Mademoiselle that possibly Carmilla had been wakened by the uproar at her door, and in her first panic had jumped from her bed, and hid herself in a press, or behind a curtain, from which she could not, of course, emerge until the majordomo and his myrmidons had withdrawn. We now recommenced our search, and began to call her name again.

It was all to no purpose. Our perplexity and agitation increased. We examined the windows, but they were secured. I implored of Carmilla, if she had concealed herself, to play this cruel trick no longer—to come out and to end our anxieties. It was all useless. I was by this time convinced that she was not in the room, nor in the dressing room, the door of which was still locked on this side. She could not have passed it. I was utterly puzzled. Had Carmilla discovered one of those secret passages which the old housekeeper said were known to exist in the schloss, although the tradition of their exact situation had been lost? A little time would, no doubt, explain all—utterly perplexed as, for the present, we were.

It was past four o'clock, and I preferred passing the remaining hours of darkness in Madame's room. Daylight brought no solution of the difficulty.

The whole household, with my father at its head, was in a state of agitation next morning. Every part of the chateau was searched. The grounds were explored. No trace of the missing lady could be discovered. The stream was about to be dragged; my father was in distraction; what a tale to have to tell the poor girl's mother on her return. I, too, was almost beside myself, though my grief was quite of a different kind.

The morning was passed in alarm and excitement. It was now one o'clock, and still no tidings. I ran up to Carmilla's room, and found her standing at her dressing table. I was astounded. I could not believe my eyes. She beckoned me to her with her pretty finger, in silence. Her face expressed extreme fear.

I ran to her in an ecstasy of joy; I kissed and embraced her again and again. I ran to the bell and rang it vehemently, to bring others to the spot who might at once relieve my father's anxiety.

"Dear Carmilla, what has become of you all this time? We have been in agonies of anxiety about you," I exclaimed. "Where have you been? How did you come back?"

"Last night has been a night of wonders," she said.

"For mercy's sake, explain all you can."

"It was past two last night," she said, "when I went to sleep as usual in my bed, with my doors locked, that of the dressing room, and that opening upon the gallery. My sleep was uninterrupted, and, so far as I know, dreamless; but I woke just now on the sofa in the dressing room there, and I found the door between the rooms open, and the other door forced. How could all this have happened without my being wakened? It must have been accompanied with a great deal of noise, and I am particularly easily wakened; and how could I have been carried out of my bed without my sleep having been interrupted, I whom the slightest stir startles?"

By this time, Madame, Mademoiselle, my father, and a number of the servants were in the room. Carmilla was, of course, overwhelmed with inquiries, congratulations, and welcomes. She had but one story to tell, and seemed the least able of all the party to suggest any way of accounting for what had happened.

My father took a turn up and down the room, thinking. I saw Carmilla's eye follow him for a moment with a sly, dark glance.

When my father had sent the servants away, Mademoiselle having gone in search of a little bottle of valerian and salvolatile, and there being no one now in the room with Carmilla, except my father, Madame, and myself, he came to her thoughtfully, took her hand very kindly, led her to the sofa, and sat down beside her.

"Will you forgive me, my dear, if I risk a conjecture, and ask a question?"

"Who can have a better right?" she said. "Ask what you please, and I will tell you everything. But my story is simply one of bewilderment and darkness. I know absolutely nothing. Put any question you please, but you know, of course, the limitations mamma has placed me under."

"Perfectly, my dear child. I need not approach the topics on which she desires our silence. Now, the marvel of last night consists in your having been removed from your bed and your room, without being wakened, and this removal having occurred apparently while the windows were still secured, and the two doors locked upon the inside. I will tell you my theory and ask you a question."

Carmilla was leaning on her hand dejectedly; Madame and I were listening breathlessly.

"Now, my question is this. Have you ever been suspected of walking in your sleep?"

"Never, since I was very young indeed."

"But you did walk in your sleep when you were young?"

"Yes; I know I did. I have been told so often by my old nurse."

My father smiled and nodded.

"Well, what has happened is this. You got up in your sleep, unlocked the door, not leaving the key, as usual, in the lock, but taking it out and locking it on the outside; you again took the key out, and carried it away with you to some one of the five-and-twenty rooms on this floor, or perhaps upstairs or downstairs. There are so many rooms and closets, so much heavy furniture, and such accumulations of lumber, that it would require a week to search this old house thoroughly. Do you see, now, what I mean?"

"I do, but not all," she answered.

"And how, papa, do you account for her finding herself on the sofa in the dressing room, which we had searched so carefully?"

"She came there after you had searched it, still in her sleep, and at last awoke spontaneously, and was as much surprised to find herself where she was as any one else. I wish all mysteries were as easily and innocently explained as yours, Carmilla," he said, laughing. "And so we may congratulate ourselves on the certainty that the most natural explanation of the occurrence is one that involves no drugging, no tampering with locks, no burglars, or poisoners, or witches—nothing that need alarm Carmilla, or anyone else, for our safety."

Carmilla was looking charmingly. Nothing could be more beautiful than
her tints. Her beauty was, I think, enhanced by that graceful languor that was peculiar to her. I think my father was silently contrasting her looks with mine, for he said:

"I wish my poor Laura was looking more like herself"; and he sighed.

So our alarms were happily ended, and Carmilla restored to her friends.

## IX.
## The Doctor

As Carmilla would not hear of an attendant sleeping in her room, my father arranged that a servant should sleep outside her door, so that she would not attempt to make another such excursion without being arrested at her own door.

That night passed quietly; and next morning early, the doctor, whom my father had sent for without telling me a word about it, arrived to see me.

Madame accompanied me to the library; and there the grave little doctor, with white hair and spectacles, whom I mentioned before, was waiting to receive me.

I told him my story, and as I proceeded he grew graver and graver.

We were standing, he and I, in the recess of one of the windows, facing one another. When my statement was over, he leaned with his shoulders against the wall, and with his eyes fixed on me earnestly, with an interest in which was a dash of horror.

After a minute's reflection, he asked Madame if he could see my father.

He was sent for accordingly, and as he entered, smiling, he said:

"I dare say, doctor, you are going to tell me that I am an old fool for having brought you here; I hope I am."

But his smile faded into shadow as the doctor, with a very grave face, beckoned him to him.

He and the doctor talked for some time in the same recess where I had just conferred with the physician. It seemed an earnest and argumentative conversation. The room is very large, and I and Madame stood together, burning with curiosity, at the farther end. Not a word could we hear, however, for they spoke in a very low tone, and the deep recess of the window quite concealed the doctor from view, and very nearly my father, whose foot, arm, and shoulder only could we see; and the voices were, I suppose, all the less audible for the sort of closet which the thick wall and window formed.

After a time my father's face looked into the room; it was pale, thoughtful, and, I fancied, agitated.

"Laura, dear, come here for a moment. Madame, we shan't trouble you, the doctor says, at present."

Accordingly I approached, for the first time a little alarmed; for, although I felt very weak, I did not feel ill; and strength, one always fancies, is a thing that may be picked up when we please.

My father held out his hand to me, as I drew near, but he was looking at the doctor, and he said:

"It certainly is very odd; I don't understand it quite. Laura, come here, dear; now attend to Doctor Spielsberg, and recollect yourself."

"You mentioned a sensation like that of two needles piercing the skin, somewhere about your neck, on the night when you experienced your first horrible dream. Is there still any soreness?"

"None at all," I answered.

"Can you indicate with your finger about the point at which you think this occurred?"

"Very little below my throat—here," I answered.

I wore a morning dress, which covered the place I pointed to.

"Now you can satisfy yourself," said the doctor. "You won't mind your papa's lowering your dress a very little. It is necessary, to detect a symptom of the complaint under which you have been suffering."

I acquiesced. It was only an inch or two below the edge of my collar.

"God bless me!—so it is," exclaimed my father, growing pale.

"You see it now with your own eyes," said the doctor, with a gloomy triumph.

"What is it?" I exclaimed, beginning to be frightened.

"Nothing, my dear young lady, but a small blue spot, about the size of the tip of your little finger; and now," he continued, turning to papa, "the question is what is best to be done?"

Is there any danger?"I urged, in great trepidation.

"I trust not, my dear," answered the doctor. "I don't see why you should not recover. I don't see why you should not begin immediately to get better. That is the point at which the sense of strangulation begins?"

"Yes," I answered.

"And—recollect as well as you can—the same point was a kind of center of that thrill which you described just now, like the current of a cold stream running against you?"

"It may have been; I think it was."

"Ay, you see?" he added, turning to my father. "Shall I say a word to Madame?"

"Certainly," said my father.

He called Madame to him, and said:

"I find my young friend here far from well. It won't be of any great consequence, I hope; but it will be necessary that some steps be taken, which I will explain by-and-by; but in the meantime, Madame, you will be so good as not to let Miss Laura be alone for one moment. That is the only direction I need give for the present. It is indispensable."

"We may rely upon your kindness, Madame, I know," added my father.

Madame satisfied him eagerly.

"And you, dear Laura, I know you will observe the doctor's direction."

"I shall have to ask your opinion upon another patient, whose symptoms slightly resemble those of my daughter, that have just been detailed to you—very much milder in degree, but I believe quite of the same sort. She is a young lady—our guest; but as you say you will be passing this way again this evening, you can't do better than take your supper here, and you can then see her. She does not come down till the afternoon."

"I thank you," said the doctor. "I shall be with you, then, at about seven this evening."

And then they repeated their directions to me and to Madame, and with this parting charge my father left us, and walked out with the doctor; and I saw them pacing together up and down between the road and the moat, on the grassy platform in front of the castle, evidently absorbed in earnest conversation.

The doctor did not return. I saw him mount his horse there, take his leave, and ride away eastward through the forest.

Nearly at the same time I saw the man arrive from Dranfield with the letters, and dismount and hand the bag to my father.

In the meantime, Madame and I were both busy, lost in conjecture as to the reasons of the singular and earnest direction which the doctor and my father had concurred in imposing. Madame, as she afterwards told me, was afraid the doctor apprehended a sudden seizure, and that, without prompt assistance, I might either lose my life in a fit, or at least be seriously hurt.

The interpretation did not strike me; and I fancied, perhaps luckily for my nerves, that the arrangement was prescribed simply to secure a companion, who would prevent my taking too much exercise, or eating unripe fruit, or doing any of the fifty foolish things to which young people are supposed to be prone.

About half an hour after my father came in—he had a letter in his hand—and said:

"This letter had been delayed; it is from General Spielsdorf. He might have been here yesterday, he may not come till tomorrow or he may be here today."

He put the open letter into my hand; but he did not look pleased, as he used when a guest, especially one so much loved as the General, was coming.

On the contrary, he looked as if he wished him at the bottom of the Red Sea. There was plainly something on his mind which he did not choose to divulge.

"Papa, darling, will you tell me this?" said I, suddenly laying my hand on his arm, and looking, I am sure, imploringly in his face.

"Perhaps," he answered, smoothing my hair caressingly over my eyes.

"Does the doctor think me very ill?"

"No, dear; he thinks, if right steps are taken, you will be quite well again, at least, on the high road to a complete recovery, in a day or two," he answered, a little dryly. "I wish our good friend, the General, had chosen any other time; that is, I wish you had been perfectly well to receive him."

"But do tell me, papa," I insisted, "what does he think is the matter with me?"

"Nothing; you must not plague me with questions," he answered, with more irritation than I ever remember him to have displayed before; and seeing that I looked wounded, I suppose, he kissed me, and added, "You shall know all about it in a day or two; that is, all that I know. In the meantime you are not to trouble your head about it."

He turned and left the room, but came back before I had done wondering and puzzling over the oddity of all this; it was merely to say that he was going to Karnstein, and had ordered the carriage to be ready at twelve, and that I and Madame should accompany him; he was going to see the priest who lived near those picturesque grounds, upon business, and as Carmilla had never seen them, she could follow, when she came down, with Mademoiselle, who would bring materials for what you call a picnic, which might be laid for us in the ruined castle.

At twelve o'clock, accordingly, I was ready, and not long after, my father, Madame and I set out upon our projected drive.

Passing the drawbridge we turn to the right, and follow the road over the steep Gothic bridge, westward, to reach the deserted village and ruined castle of Karnstein.

No sylvan drive can be fancied prettier. The ground breaks into gentle hills and hollows, all clothed with beautiful wood, totally destitute of the comparative formality which artificial planting and early culture and pruning impart.

The irregularities of the ground often lead the road out of its course, and cause it to wind beautifully round the sides of broken hollows and the steeper sides of the hills, among varieties of ground almost inexhaustible.

Turning one of these points, we suddenly encountered our old friend, the General, riding towards us, attended by a mounted servant. His portmanteaus were following in a hired wagon, such as we term a cart.

The General dismounted as we pulled up, and, after the usual greetings, was easily persuaded to accept the vacant seat in the carriage and send his horse on with his servant to the schloss.

# X.
# Bereaved

It was about ten months since we had last seen him: but that time had sufficed to make an alteration of years in his appearance. He had grown thinner; something of gloom and anxiety had taken the place of that cordial serenity which used to characterize his features. His dark blue eyes, always penetrating, now gleamed with a sterner light from under his shaggy grey eyebrows. It was not such a change as grief alone usually induces, and angrier passions seemed to have had their share in bringing it about.

We had not long resumed our drive, when the General began to talk, with his usual soldierly directness, of the bereavement, as he termed it, which he had sustained in the death of his beloved niece and ward; and he then broke out in a tone of intense bitterness and fury, inveighing against the "hellish arts" to which she had fallen a victim, and expressing, with more exasperation than piety, his wonder that Heaven should tolerate so monstrous an indulgence of the lusts and malignity of hell.

My father, who saw at once that something very extraordinary had befallen, asked him, if not too painful to him, to detail the circumstances which he thought justified the strong terms in which he expressed himself.

"I should tell you all with pleasure," said the General, "but you would not believe me."

"Why should I not?" he asked.
"Because," he answered testily, "you believe in nothing but what consists with your own prejudices and illusions. I remember when I was like you, but I have learned better."

"Try me," said my father; "I am not such a dogmatist as you suppose.

Besides which, I very well know that you generally require proof for what you believe, and am, therefore, very strongly predisposed to respect your conclusions."

"You are right in supposing that I have not been led lightly into a belief in the marvelous—for what I have experienced is marvelous—and I have been forced by extraordinary evidence to credit that which ran counter, diametrically, to all my theories. I have been made the dupe of a preternatural conspiracy."

Notwithstanding his professions of confidence in the General's penetration, I saw my father, at this point, glance at the General, with, as I thought, a marked suspicion of his sanity.

The General did not see it, luckily. He was looking gloomily and curiously into the glades and vistas of the woods that were opening before us.

"You are going to the Ruins of Karnstein?" he said. "Yes, it is a lucky coincidence; do you know I was going to ask you to bring me there to inspect them. I have a special object in exploring. There is a ruined chapel, ain't there, with a great many tombs of that extinct family?"

"So there are—highly interesting," said my father. "I hope you are thinking of claiming the title and estates?"

My father said this gaily, but the General did not recollect the laugh, or even the smile, which courtesy exacts for a friend's joke; on the contrary, he looked grave and even fierce, ruminating on a matter that stirred his anger and horror.

"Something very different," he said, gruffly. "I mean to unearth some of those fine people. I hope, by God's blessing, to accomplish a pious sacrilege here, which will relieve our earth of certain monsters, and enable honest people to sleep in their beds without being assailed by murderers. I have strange things to tell you, my dear friend, such as I myself would have scouted as incredible a few months since."

My father looked at him again, but this time not with a glance of suspicion—with an eye, rather, of keen intelligence and alarm.

"The house of Karnstein," he said, "has been long extinct: a hundred years at least. My dear wife was maternally descended from the Karnsteins. But the name and title have long ceased to exist. The castle is a ruin; the very village is deserted; it is fifty years since the smoke of a chimney was seen there; not a roof left."

"Quite true. I have heard a great deal about that since I last saw you; a great deal that will astonish you. But I had better relate everything in the order in which it occurred," said the General. "You saw my dear ward—my child, I may call her. No creature could have been more beautiful, and only three months ago none more blooming."

"Yes, poor thing! when I saw her last she certainly was quite lovely," said my father. "I was grieved and shocked more than I can tell you, my dear friend; I knew what a blow it was to you."

He took the General's hand, and they exchanged a kind pressure. Tears gathered in the old soldier's eyes. He did not seek to conceal them. He said:

"We have been very old friends; I knew you would feel for me, childless as I am. She had become an object of very near interest to me, and repaid my care by an affection that cheered my home and made my life happy. That is all gone. The years that remain to me on earth may not be very long; but by God's mercy I hope to accomplish a service to mankind before I die, and to subserve the vengeance of Heaven upon the fiends who have murdered my poor child in the spring of her hopes and beauty!"

"You said, just now, that you intended relating everything as it occurred," said my father. "Pray do; I assure you that it is not mere curiosity that prompts me."

By this time we had reached the point at which the Drunstall road, by which the General had come, diverges from the road which we were traveling to Karnstein.

"How far is it to the ruins?" inquired the General, looking anxiously forward.

"About half a league," answered my father. "Pray let us hear the story you were so good as to promise."

# XI.
# The Story

With all my heart," said the General, with an effort; and after a short pause in which to arrange his subject, he commenced one of the strangest narratives I ever heard.

"My dear child was looking forward with great pleasure to the visit you had been so good as to arrange for her to your charming daughter." Here he made me a gallant but melancholy bow. "In the meantime we had an invitation to my old friend the Count Carlsfeld, whose schloss is about six leagues to the other side of Karnstein. It was to attend the series of fetes which, you remember, were given by him in honor of his illustrious visitor, the Grand Duke Charles."

"Yes; and very splendid, I believe, they were," said my father.

"Princely! But then his hospitalities are quite regal. He has Aladdin's lamp. The night from which my sorrow dates was devoted to a magnificentmasquerade. The grounds were thrown open, the trees hung with colored lamps. There was such a display of fireworks as Paris itself had never witnessed. And such music—music, you know, is my weakness—such ravishing music! The finest instrumental band, perhaps, in the world, and the finest singers who could be collected from all the great operas in Europe. As you wandered through these fantastically illuminated grounds, the moon-lighted chateau throwing a rosy light from its long rows of windows, you would suddenly hear these ravishing voices stealing from the silence of some grove, or rising from boats upon the lake. I felt myself, as I looked and listened, carried back into the romance and poetry of my early youth.

"When the fireworks were ended, and the ball beginning, we returned to the noble suite of rooms that were thrown open to the dancers. A masked ball, you know, is a beautiful sight; but so brilliant a spectacle of the kind I never saw before.

"It was a very aristocratic assembly. I was myself almost the only 'nobody' present.

"My dear child was looking quite beautiful. She wore no mask. Her excitement and delight added an unspeakable charm to her features, always lovely. I remarked a young lady, dressed magnificently, but wearing a mask, who appeared to me to be observing my ward with extraordinary interest. I had seen her, earlier in the evening, in the great hall, and again, for a few minutes, walking near us, on the terrace under the castle windows, similarly employed. A lady, also masked, richly and gravely dressed, and with a stately air, like a person of rank, accompanied her as a chaperon.

Had the young lady not worn a mask, I could, of course, have been much more certain upon the question whether she was really watching my poor darling.

I am now well assured that she was.

"We were now in one of the salons. My poor dear child had been dancing, and was resting a little in one of the chairs near the door; I was standing near. The two ladies I have mentioned had approached and the younger took the chair next my ward; while her companion stood beside me, and for a little time addressed herself, in a low tone, to her charge. "Availing herself of the privilege of her mask, she turned to me, and in the tone of an old friend, and calling me by my name, opened a conversation with me, which piqued my curiosity a good deal. She referred to many scenes where she had met me—at Court, and at distinguished houses. She alluded to little incidents which I had long ceased to think of, but which, I found, had only lain in abeyance in my memory, for they instantly started into life at her touch.

"I became more and more curious to ascertain who she was, every moment. She parried my attempts to discover very adroitly and pleasantly. The knowledge she showed of many passages in my life seemed to me all but unaccountable; and she appeared to take a not unnatural pleasure in foiling my curiosity, and in seeing me flounder in my eager perplexity, from one conjecture to another.

"In the meantime the young lady, whom her mother called by the odd name of Millarca, when she once or twice addressed her, had, with the same ease and grace, got into conversation with my ward.

"She introduced herself by saying that her mother was a very old acquaintance of mine. She spoke of the agreeable audacity which a mask rendered practicable; she talked like a friend; she admired her dress, and insinuated very prettily her admiration of her beauty. She amused her with laughing criticisms upon the people who crowded the ballroom, and laughed at my poor child's fun. She was very witty and lively when she pleased, and after a time they had grown very good friends, and the young stranger lowered her mask, displaying a remarkably beautiful face. I had never seen it before, neither had my dear child. But though it was new to us, the features were so engaging, as well as lovely, that it was impossible not to feel the attraction powerfully. My poor girl did so. I never saw anyone more taken with another at first sight, unless, indeed, it was the stranger herself, who seemed quite to have lost her heart to her.

"In the meantime, availing myself of the license of a masquerade, I put not a few questions to the elder lady.

"'You have puzzled me utterly,' I said, laughing. 'Is that not enough?

Won't you, now, consent to stand on equal terms, and do me the kindness to remove your mask?'

"'Can any request be more unreasonable?' she replied. 'Ask a lady to yield an advantage! Beside, how do you know you should recognize me? Years make changes.'

"'As you see,' I said, with a bow, and, I suppose, a rather melancholy little laugh.

"'As philosophers tell us,' she said; 'and how do you know that a sight of my face would help you?'

"'I should take chance for that,' I answered. 'It is vain trying to make yourself out an old woman; your figure betrays you.'

"'Years, nevertheless, have passed since I saw you, rather since you saw me, for that is what I am considering. Millarca, there, is my daughter; I cannot then be young, even in the opinion of people whom time has taught to be indulgent, and I may not like to be compared with what you remember me.

You have no mask to remove. You can offer me nothing in exchange.'

"'My petition is to your pity, to remove it.'

"'And mine to yours, to let it stay where it is,' she replied.

"'Well, then, at least you will tell me whether you are French or German; you speak both languages so perfectly.'

"'I don't think I shall tell you that, General; you intend a surprise, and are meditating the particular point of attack.'

"'At all events, you won't deny this,' I said, 'that being honored by your permission to converse, I ought to know how to address you. Shall I say Madame la Comtesse?'

"She laughed, and she would, no doubt, have met me with another evasion—if, indeed, I can treat any occurrence in an interview every circumstance of which was prearranged, as I now believe, with the profoundest cunning, as liable to be modified by accident.

"'As to that,' she began; but she was interrupted, almost as she opened her lips, by a gentleman, dressed in black, who looked particularly elegant and distinguished, with this drawback, that his face was the most deadly pale I ever saw, except in death. He was in no masquerade—in the plain evening dress of a gentleman; and he said, without a smile, but with a courtly and unusually low bow:—

"'Will Madame la Comtesse permit me to say a very few words which may interest her?'

"The lady turned quickly to him, and touched her lip in token of silence; she then said to me, 'Keep my place for me, General; I shall return when I have said a few words.'

"And with this injunction, playfully given, she walked a little aside with the gentleman in black, and talked for some minutes, apparently very earnestly. They then walked away slowly together in the crowd, and I lost them for some minutes.

"I spent the interval in cudgeling my brains for a conjecture as to the identity of the lady who seemed to remember me so kindly, and I was thinking of turning about and joining in the conversation between my pretty ward and the Countess's daughter, and trying whether, by the time she returned, I might not have a surprise in store for her, by having her name, title, chateau, and estates at my fingers' ends. But at this moment she returned, accompanied by the pale man in black, who said:

"'I shall return and inform Madame la Comtesse when her carriage is at the door.'

"He withdrew with a bow."

## XII.
## A Petition

"'Then we are to lose Madame la Comtesse, but I hope only for a few hours,' I said, with a low bow.

"'It may be that only, or it may be a few weeks. It was very unlucky his speaking to me just now as he did. Do you now know me?'

"I assured her I did not.

"'You shall know me,' she said, 'but not at present. We are older and better friends than, perhaps, you suspect. I cannot yet declare myself. I shall in three weeks pass your beautiful schloss, about which I have been making enquiries. I shall then look in upon you for an hour or two, and renew a friendship which I never think of without a thousand pleasant recollections. This moment a piece of news has reached me like a thunderbolt. I must set out now, and travel by a devious route, nearly a hundred miles, with all the dispatch I can possibly make. My perplexities multiply. I am only deterred by the compulsory reserve I practice as to my name from making a very singular request of you. My poor child has not quite recovered her strength. Her horse fell with her, at a hunt which she had ridden out to witness, her nerves have not yet recovered the shock, and our physician says that she must on no account exert herself for some time to come. We came here, in consequence, by very easy stages—hardly six leagues a day. I must now travel day and night, on a mission of life and death—a mission the critical and momentous nature of which I shall be able to explain to you when we meet, as I hope we shall, in a few weeks, without the necessity of any concealment.'

"She went on to make her petition, and it was in the tone of a person from whom such a request amounted to conferring, rather than seeking a favor.

This was only in manner, and, as it seemed, quite unconsciously. Than the terms in which it was expressed, nothing could be more deprecatory. It was simply that I would consent to take charge of her daughter during her absence.

"This was, all things considered, a strange, not to say, an audacious request. She in some sort disarmed me, by stating and admitting everything that could be urged against it, and throwing herself entirely upon my chivalry. At the same moment, by a fatality that seems to have predetermined all that happened, my poor child came to my side, and, in an undertone, besought me to invite her new friend, Millarca, to pay us a visit. She had just been sounding her, and thought, if her mamma would allow her, she would like it extremely.

"At another time I should have told her to wait a little, until, at least, we knew who they were. But I had not a moment to think in. The two ladies assailed me together, and I must confess the refined and beautiful face of the young lady, about which there was something extremely engaging, as well as the elegance and fire of high birth, determined me; and, quite overpowered, I submitted, and undertook, too easily, the care of the young lady, whom her mother called Millarca.

"The Countess beckoned to her daughter, who listened with grave attention while she told her, in general terms, how suddenly and peremptorily she had been summoned, and also of the arrangement she had made for her under my care, adding that I was one of her earliest and most valued friends.

"I made, of course, such speeches as the case seemed to call for, and found myself, on reflection, in a position which I did not half like.

"The gentleman in black returned, and very ceremoniously conducted the lady from the room.

"The demeanor of this gentleman was such as to impress me with the conviction that the Countess was a lady of very much more importance than her modest title alone might have led me to assume.

"Her last charge to me was that no attempt was to be made to learn more about her than I might have already guessed, until her return. Our distinguished host, whose guest she was, knew her reasons.

"'But here,' she said, 'neither I nor my daughter could safely remain for more than a day. I removed my mask imprudently for a moment, about an hour ago, and, too late, I fancied you saw me. So I resolved to seek an opportunity of talking a little to you. Had I found that you had seen me, I would have thrown myself on your high sense of honor to keep my secret some weeks. As it is, I am satisfied that you did not see me; but if you now suspect, or, on reflection, should suspect, who I am, I commit myself, in like manner, entirely to your honor. My daughter will observe the same secrecy, and I well know that you will, from time to time, remind her, lest she should thoughtlessly disclose it.'

"She whispered a few words to her daughter, kissed her hurriedly twice, and went away, accompanied by the pale gentleman in black, and disappeared in the crowd.

"'In the next room,' said Millarca, 'there is a window that looks upon the hall door. I should like to see the last of mamma, and to kiss my hand to her.'

"We assented, of course, and accompanied her to the window. We looked out, and saw a handsome old-fashioned carriage, with a troop of couriers and footmen. We saw the slim figure of the pale gentleman in black, as he held a thick velvet cloak, and placed it about her shoulders and threw the hood over her head. She nodded to him, and just touched his hand with hers. He bowed low repeatedly as the door closed, and the carriage began to move.

"'She is gone,' said Millarca, with a sigh.

"'She is gone,' I repeated to myself, for the first time—in the hurried moments that had elapsed since my consent—reflecting upon the folly of my act.

"'She did not look up,' said the young lady, plaintively.

"'The Countess had taken off her mask, perhaps, and did not care to show her face,' I said; 'and she could not know that you were in the window.'

"She sighed, and looked in my face. She was so beautiful that I relented. I was sorry I had for a moment repented of my hospitality, and I determined to make her amends for the unavowed churlishness of my reception.

"The young lady, replacing her mask, joined my ward in persuading me to return to the grounds, where the concert was soon to be renewed. We did so, and walked up and down the terrace that lies under the castle windows.

Millarca became very intimate with us, and amused us with lively descriptions and stories of most of the great people whom we saw upon the terrace. I liked her more and more every minute. Her gossip without being ill-natured, was extremely diverting to me, who had been so long out of the great world. I thought what life she would give to our sometimes lonely evenings at home.

"This ball was not over until the morning sun had almost reached the horizon. It pleased the Grand Duke to dance till then, so loyal people could not go away, or think of bed.

"We had just got through a crowded saloon, when my ward asked me what had become of Millarca. I thought she had been by her side, and she fancied she was by mine. The fact was, we had lost her.

"All my efforts to find her were vain. I feared that she had mistaken, in the confusion of a momentary separation from us, other people for her new friends, and had, possibly, pursued and lost them in the extensive grounds which were thrown open to us.

"Now, in its full force, I recognized a new folly in my having undertaken the charge of a young lady without so much as knowing her name; and fettered as I was by promises, of the reasons for imposing which I knew nothing, I could not even point my inquiries by saying that the missing young lady was the daughter of the Countess who had taken her departure a few hours before. "Morning broke. It was clear daylight before I gave up my search. It was not till near two o'clock next day that we heard anything of my missing charge.

"At about that time a servant knocked at my niece's door, to say that he had been earnestly requested by a young lady, who appeared to be in great distress, to make out where she could find the General Baron Spielsdorf and the young lady his daughter, in whose charge she had been left by her mother.

"There could be no doubt, notwithstanding the slight inaccuracy, that our young friend had turned up; and so she had. Would to heaven we had lost her!

"She told my poor child a story to account for her having failed to recover us for so long. Very late, she said, she had got to the housekeeper's bedroom in despair of finding us, and had then fallen into a deep sleep which, long as it was, had hardly sufficed to recruit her strength after the fatigues of the ball.

"That day Millarca came home with us. I was only too happy, after all, to have secured so charming a companion for my dear girl."

## XIII.
## The Woodman

"There soon, however, appeared some drawbacks. In the first place, Millarca complained of extreme languor—the weakness that remained after her late illness—and she never emerged from her room till the afternoon was pretty far advanced. In the next place, it was accidentally discovered, although she always locked her door on the inside, and never disturbed the key from its place till she admitted the maid to assist at her toilet, that she was undoubtedly sometimes absent from her room in the very early morning, and at various times later in the day, before she wished it to be understood that she was stirring. She was repeatedly seen from the windows of the schloss, in the first faint grey of the morning, walking through the trees, in an easterly direction, and looking like a person in a trance. This convinced me that she walked in her sleep. But this hypothesis did not solve the puzzle. How did she pass out from her room, leaving the door locked on the inside? How did she escape from the house without unbarring door or window?

"In the midst of my perplexities, an anxiety of a far more urgent kind presented itself.

"My dear child began to lose her looks and health, and that in a manner so mysterious, and even horrible, that I became thoroughly frightened.

"She was at first visited by appalling dreams; then, as she fancied, by a specter, sometimes resembling Millarca, sometimes in the shape of a beast, indistinctly seen, walking round the foot of her bed, from side to side.

Lastly came sensations. One, not unpleasant, but very peculiar, she said, resembled the flow of an icy stream against her breast. At a later time, she felt something like a pair of large needles pierce her, a little below the throat, with a very sharp pain. A few nights after, followed a gradual and convulsive sense of strangulation; then came unconsciousness."

I could hear distinctly every word the kind old General was saying, because by this time we were driving upon the short grass that spreads on either side of the road as you approach the roofless village which had not shown the smoke of a chimney for more than half a century.

You may guess how strangely I felt as I heard my own symptoms so exactly described in those which had been experienced by the poor girl who, but for the catastrophe which followed, would have been at that moment a visitor at my father's chateau. You may suppose, also, how I felt as I heard him detail habits and mysterious peculiarities which were, in fact, those of our beautiful guest, Carmilla!

A vista opened in the forest; we were on a sudden under the chimneys and gables of the ruined village, and the towers and battlements of the dismantled castle, round which gigantic trees are grouped, overhung us from a slight eminence.

In a frightened dream I got down from the carriage, and in silence, for we had each abundant matter for thinking; we soon mounted the ascent, and were among the spacious chambers, winding stairs, and dark corridors of the castle.

"And this was once the palatial residence of the Karnsteins!" said the old General at length, as from a great window he looked out across the village, and saw the wide, undulating expanse of forest. "It was a bad family, and here its bloodstained annals were written," he continued. "It is hard that they should, after death, continue to plague the human race with their atrocious lusts. That is the chapel of the Karnsteins, down there."

He pointed down to the grey walls of the Gothic building partly visible through the foliage, a little way down the steep. "And I hear the axe of a woodman," he added, "busy among the trees that surround it; he possibly may give us the information of which I am in search, and point out the grave of Mircalla, Countess of Karnstein. These rustics preserve the local traditions of great families, whose stories die out among the rich and titled so soon as the families themselves become extinct."

"We have a portrait, at home, of Mircalla, the Countess Karnstein; should you like to see it?" asked my father.

"Time enough, dear friend," replied the General. "I believe that I have seen the original; and one motive which has led me to you earlier than I at first intended, was to explore the chapel which we are now approaching."

"What! see the Countess Mircalla," exclaimed my father; "why, she has been dead more than a century!"

"Not so dead as you fancy, I am told," answered the General.
"I confess, General, you puzzle me utterly," replied my father, looking at him, I fancied, for a moment with a return of the suspicion I detected before. But although there was anger and detestation, at times, in the old General's manner, there was nothing flighty.

"There remains to me," he said, as we passed under the heavy arch of the Gothic church—for its dimensions would have justified its being so styled—"but one object which can interest me during the few years that remain to me on earth, and that is to wreak on her the vengeance which, I thank God, may still be accomplished by a mortal arm."

"What vengeance can you mean?" asked my father, in increasing amazement.

"I mean, to decapitate the monster," he answered, with a fierce flush, and a stamp that echoed mournfully through the hollow ruin, and his clenched hand was at the same moment raised, as if it grasped the handle of an axe, while he shook it ferociously in the air.

"What?" exclaimed my father, more than ever bewildered.

"To strike her head off."

"Cut her head off!"

"Aye, with a hatchet, with a spade, or with anything that can cleave through her murderous throat. You shall hear," he answered, trembling with rage. And hurrying forward he said:

"That beam will answer for a seat; your dear child is fatigued; let her be seated, and I will, in a few sentences, close my dreadful story."

The squared block of wood, which lay on the grass-grown pavement of the chapel, formed a bench on which I was very glad to seat myself, and in the meantime the General called to the woodman, who had been removing some boughs which leaned upon the old walls; and, axe in hand, the hardy old fellow stood before us.

He could not tell us anything of these monuments; but there was an old man, he said, a ranger of this forest, at present sojourning in the house of the priest, about two miles away, who could point out every monument of the old Karnstein family; and, for a trifle, he undertook to bring him back with him, if we would lend him one of our horses, in little more than half an hour.

"Have you been long employed about this forest?" asked my father of the old man.

"I have been a woodman here," he answered in his patois, "under the forester, all my days; so has my father before me, and so on, as many generations as I can count up. I could show you the very house in the village here, in which my ancestors lived."

"How came the village to be deserted?" asked the General.

"It was troubled by revenants, sir; several were tracked to their graves, there detected by the usual tests, and extinguished in the usual way, by decapitation, by the stake, and by burning; but not until many of the villagers were killed.

"But after all these proceedings according to law," he continued—"so many graves opened, and so many vampires deprived of their horrible animation—the village was not relieved. But a Moravian nobleman, who happened to be traveling this way, heard how matters were, and being skilled—as many people are in his country—in such affairs, he offered to deliver the village from its tormentor. He did so thus: There being a bright moon that night, he ascended, shortly after sunset, the towers of the chapel here, from whence he could distinctly see the churchyard beneath him; you can see it from that window. From this point he watched until he saw the vampire come out of his grave, and place near it the linen clothes in which he had been folded, and then glide away towards the village to plague its inhabitants.

"The stranger, having seen all this, came down from the steeple, took the linen wrappings of the vampire, and carried them up to the top of the tower, which he again mounted. When the vampire returned from his prowlings and missed his clothes, he cried furiously to the Moravian, whom he saw at the summit of the tower, and who, in reply, beckoned him to ascend and take them. Whereupon the vampire, accepting his invitation, began to climb the steeple, and so soon as he had reached the battlements, the Moravian, with a stroke of his sword, clove his skull in twain, hurling him down to the churchyard, whither, descending by the winding stairs, the stranger followed and cut his head off, and next day delivered it and the body to the villagers, who duly impaled and burnt them.

"This Moravian nobleman had authority from the then head of the family to remove the tomb of Mircalla, Countess Karnstein, which he did effectually, so that in a little while its site was quite forgotten."

"Can you point out where it stood?" asked the General, eagerly.

The forester shook his head, and smiled.

"Not a soul living could tell you that now," he said; "besides, they say her body was removed; but no one is sure of that either."

Having thus spoken, as time pressed, he dropped his axe and departed, leaving us to hear the remainder of the General's strange story.

## XIV.
## The Meeting

"My beloved child," he resumed, "was now growing rapidly worse. The physician who attended her had failed to produce the slightest impression on her disease, for such I then supposed it to be. He saw my alarm, and suggested a consultation. I called in an abler physician, from Gratz.

Several days elapsed before he arrived. He was a good and pious, as well as a learned man. Having seen my poor ward together, they withdrew to my library to confer and discuss. I, from the adjoining room, where I awaited their summons, heard these two gentlemen's voices raised in something sharper than a strictly philosophical discussion. I knocked at the door and entered. I found the old physician from Gratz
maintaining his theory. His rival was combating it with undisguised ridicule, accompanied with bursts of laughter. This unseemly manifestation subsided and the altercation ended on my entrance.

"'Sir,' said my first physician,'my learned brother seems to think that you want a conjuror, and not a doctor.'

"'Pardon me,' said the old physician from Gratz, looking displeased, 'I shall state my own view of the case in my own way another time. I grieve, Monsieur le General, that by my skill and science I can be of no use.

Before I go I shall do myself the honor to suggest something to you.'

"He seemed thoughtful, and sat down at a table and began to write.

Profoundly disappointed, I made my bow, and as I turned to go, the other doctor pointed over his shoulder to his companion who was writing, and then, with a shrug, significantly touched his forehead.

"This consultation, then, left me precisely where I was. I walked out into the grounds, all but distracted. The doctor from Gratz, in ten or fifteen minutes, overtook me. He apologized for having followed me, but said that he could not conscientiously take his leave without a few words more. He told me that he could not be mistaken; no natural disease exhibited the same symptoms; and that death was already very near. There remained, however, a day, or possibly two, of life. If the fatal seizure were at once arrested, with great care and skill her strength might possibly return. But all hung now upon the confines of the irrevocable. One more assault might extinguish the last spark of vitality which is, every moment, ready to die.

"'And what is the nature of the seizure you speak of?' I entreated.

"'I have stated all fully in this note, which I place in your hands upon the distinct condition that you send for the nearest clergyman, and open my letter in his presence, and on no account read it till he is with you; you would despise it else, and it is a matter of life and death. Should the priest fail you, then, indeed, you may read it.'

"He asked me, before taking his leave finally, whether I would wish to see a man curiously learned upon the very subject, which, after I had read his letter, would probably interest me above all others, and he urged me earnestly to invite him to visit him there; and so took his leave.

"The ecclesiastic was absent, and I read the letter by myself. At another time, or in another case, it might have excited my ridicule. But into what quackeries will not people rush for a last chance, where all accustomed means have failed, and the life of a beloved object is at stake?

"Nothing, you will say, could be more absurd than the learned man's letter.

It was monstrous enough to have consigned him to a madhouse. He said that the patient was suffering from the visits of a vampire! The punctures which she described as having occurred near the throat, were, he insisted, the insertion of those two long, thin, and sharp teeth which, it is well known, are peculiar to vampires; and there could be no doubt, he added, as to the well-defined presence of the small livid mark which all concurred in describing as that induced by the demon's lips, and every symptom described by the sufferer was in exact conformity with those recorded in every case of a similar visitation.

"Being myself wholly skeptical as to the existence of any such portent as the vampire, the supernatural theory of the good doctor furnished, in my opinion, but another instance of learning and intelligence oddly associated with some one hallucination. I was so miserable, however, that, rather than try nothing, I acted upon the instructions of the letter.

"I concealed myself in the dark dressing room, that opened upon the poor patient's room, in which a candle was burning, and watched there till she was fast asleep. I stood at the door, peeping through the small crevice, my sword laid on the table beside me, as my directions prescribed, until, a little after one, I saw a large black object, very ill-defined, crawl, as it seemed to me, over the foot of the bed, and swiftly spread itself up to the poor girl's throat, where it swelled, in a moment, into a great, palpitating mass.

"For a few moments I had stood petrified. I now sprang forward, with my sword in my hand. The black creature suddenly contracted towards the foot of the bed, glided over it, and, standing on the floor about a yard below the foot of the bed, with a glare of skulking ferocity and horror fixed on me, I saw Millarca. Speculating I know not what, I struck at her instantly with my sword; but I saw her standing near the door, unscathed. Horrified, I pursued, and struck again. She was gone; and my sword flew to shivers against the door.

"I can't describe to you all that passed on that horrible night. The whole house was up and stirring. The specter Millarca was gone. But her victim was sinking fast, and before the morning dawned, she died."

The old General was agitated. We did not speak to him. My father walked to some little distance, and began reading the inscriptions on the tombstones; and thus occupied, he strolled into the door of a side chapel to prosecute his researches. The General leaned against the wall, dried his eyes, and sighed heavily. I was relieved on hearing the voices of Carmilla and Madame, who were at that moment approaching. The voices died away.

In this solitude, having just listened to so strange a story, connected, as it was, with the great and titled dead, whose monuments were moldering among the dust and ivy round us, and every incident of which bore so awfully upon my own mysterious case—in this haunted spot, darkened by the towering foliage that rose on every side, dense and high above its noiseless walls—a horror began to steal over me, and my heart sank as I thought that my friends were, after all, not about to enter and disturb this triste and ominous scene.

The old General's eyes were fixed on the ground, as he leaned with his hand upon the basement of a shattered monument.

Under a narrow, arched doorway, surmounted by one of those demoniacal grotesques in which the cynical and ghastly fancy of old Gothic carving delights, I saw very gladly the beautiful face and figure of Carmilla enter the shadowy chapel.

I was just about to rise and speak, and nodded smiling, in answer to her peculiarly engaging smile; when with a cry, the old man by my side caught up the woodman's hatchet, and started forward. On seeing him a brutalized change came over her features. It was an instantaneous and horrible transformation, as she made a crouching step backwards. Before I could utter a scream, he struck at her with all his force, but she dived under his blow, and unscathed, caught him in her tiny grasp by the wrist. He struggled for a moment to release his arm, but his hand opened, the axe fell to the ground, and the girl was gone.

He staggered against the wall. His grey hair stood upon his head, and a moisture shone over his face, as if he were at the point of death.

The frightful scene had passed in a moment. The first thing I recollect after, is Madame standing before me, and impatiently repeating again and again, the question, "Where is Mademoiselle Carmilla?"

I answered at length, "I don't know—I can't tell—she went there," and I pointed to the door through which Madame had just entered; "only a minute or two since."

"But I have been standing there, in the passage, ever since Mademoiselle Carmilla entered; and she did not return."

She then began to call "Carmilla," through every door and passage and from the windows, but no answer came.

"She called herself Carmilla?" asked the General, still agitated.

"Carmilla, yes," I answered.

"Aye," he said; "that is Millarca. That is the same person who long ago was called Mircalla, Countess Karnstein. Depart from this accursed ground, my poor child, as quickly as you can. Drive to the clergyman's house, and stay there till we come. Begone! May you never behold Carmilla more; you will not find her here."

## XV.
## Ordeal and Execution

As he spoke one of the strangest looking men I ever beheld entered the chapel at the door through which Carmilla had made her entrance and her exit. He was tall, narrow-chested, stooping, with high shoulders, and dressed in black. His face was brown and dried in with deep furrows; he wore an oddly-shaped hat with a broad leaf. His hair, long and grizzled, hung on his shoulders. He wore a pair of gold spectacles, and walked slowly, with an odd shambling gait, with his face sometimes turned up to the sky, and sometimes bowed down towards the ground, seemed to wear a perpetual smile; his long thin arms were swinging, and his lank hands, in old black gloves ever so much too wide for them, waving and gesticulating in utter abstraction.

"The very man!" exclaimed the General, advancing with manifest delight. "My dear Baron, how happy I am to see you, I had no hope of meeting you so soon." He signed to my father, who had by this time returned, and leading the fantastic old gentleman, whom he called the Baron to meet him. He introduced him formally, and they at once entered into earnest conversation. The stranger took a roll of paper from his pocket, and spread it on the worn surface of a tomb that stood by. He had a pencil case in his fingers, with which he traced imaginary lines from point to point on the paper, which from their often glancing from it, together, at certain points of the building, I concluded to be a plan of the chapel. He accompanied, what I may term, his lecture, with occasional readings from a dirty little book, whose yellow leaves were closely written over.

They sauntered together down the side aisle, opposite to the spot where I was standing, conversing as they went; then they began measuring distances by paces, and finally they all stood together, facing a piece of the sidewall, which they began to examine with great minuteness; pulling off the ivy that clung over it, and rapping the plaster with the ends of their sticks, scraping here, and knocking there. At length they ascertained the existence of a broad marble tablet, with letters carved in relief upon it.

With the assistance of the woodman, who soon returned, a monumental inscription, and carved escutcheon, were disclosed. They proved to be those of the long lost monument of Mircalla, Countess Karnstein.

The old General, though not I fear given to the praying mood, raised his hands and eyes to heaven, in mute thanksgiving for some moments.

"Tomorrow," I heard him say; "the commissioner will be here, and the Inquisition will be held according to law."

Then turning to the old man with the gold spectacles, whom I have described, he shook him warmly by both hands and said:

"Baron, how can I thank you? How can we all thank you? You will have delivered this region from a plague that has scourged its inhabitants for more than a century. The horrible enemy, thank God, is at last tracked."

My father led the stranger aside, and the General followed. I know that he had led them out of hearing, that he might relate my case, and I saw them glance often quickly at me, as the discussion proceeded.

My father came to me, kissed me again and again, and leading me from the chapel, said:

"It is time to return, but before we go home, we must add to our party the good priest, who lives but a little way from this; and persuade him to accompany us to the schloss."

In this quest we were successful: and I was glad, being unspeakably fatigued when we reached home. But my satisfaction was changed to dismay, on discovering that there were no tidings of Carmilla. Of the scene that had occurred in the ruined chapel, no explanation was offered to me, and it was clear that it was a secret which my father for the present determined to keep from me.

The sinister absence of Carmilla made the remembrance of the scene more horrible to me. The arrangements for the night were singular. Two servants, and Madame were to sit up in my room that night; and the ecclesiastic with my father kept watch in the adjoining dressing room.

The priest had performed certain solemn rites that night, the purport of which I did not understand any more than I comprehended the reason of this extraordinary precaution taken for my safety during sleep.

I saw all clearly a few days later.

The disappearance of Carmilla was followed by the discontinuance of my nightly sufferings.

You have heard, no doubt, of the appalling superstition that prevails in Upper and Lower Styria, in Moravia, Silesia, in Turkish Serbia, in Poland, even in Russia; the superstition, so we must call it, of the Vampire.

If human testimony, taken with every care and solemnity, judicially, before commissions innumerable, each consisting of many members, all chosen for integrity and intelligence, and constituting reports more voluminous perhaps than exist upon any one other class of cases, is worth anything, it is difficult to deny, or even to doubt the existence of such a phenomenon as the Vampire.

For my part I have heard no theory by which to explain what I myself have witnessed and experienced, other than that supplied by the ancient and well-attested belief of the country.

The next day the formal proceedings took place in the Chapel of Karnstein.

The grave of the Countess Mircalla was opened; and the General and my father recognized each his perfidious and beautiful guest, in the face now disclosed to view. The features, though a hundred and fifty years had passed since her funeral, were tinted with the warmth of life. Her eyes were open; no cadaverous smell exhaled from the coffin. The two medical men, one officially present, the other on the part of the promoter of the inquiry, attested the marvelous fact that there was a faint but appreciable respiration, and a corresponding action of the heart. The limbs were perfectly flexible, the flesh elastic; and the leaden coffin floated with blood, in which to a depth of seven inches, the body lay immersed.

Here then, were all the admitted signs and proofs of vampirism. The body, therefore, in accordance with the ancient practice, was raised, and a sharp stake driven through the heart of the vampire, who uttered a piercing shriek at the moment, in all respects such as might escape from a living person in the last agony. Then the head was struck off, and a torrent of blood flowed from the severed neck. The body and head was next placed on a pile of wood, and reduced to ashes, which were thrown upon the river and borne away, and that territory has never since been plagued by the visits of a vampire.

My father has a copy of the report of the Imperial Commission, with the signatures of all who were present at these proceedings, attached in verification of the statement. It is from this official paper that I have summarized my account of this last shocking scene.

## XVI.
## Conclusion

I write all this you suppose with composure. But far from it; I cannot think of it without agitation. Nothing but your earnest desire so repeatedly expressed, could have induced me to sit down to a task that has unstrung my nerves for months to come, and reinduced a shadow of the unspeakable horror which years after my deliverance continued to make my days and nights dreadful, and solitude insupportably terrific.

Let me add a word or two about that quaint Baron Vordenburg, to whose curious lore we were indebted for the discovery of the Countess

Mircalla's grave.

He had taken up his abode in Gratz, where, living upon a mere pittance, which was all that remained to him of the once princely estates of his family, in Upper Styria, he devoted himself to the minute and laborious investigation of the marvelously authenticated tradition of Vampirism. He had at his fingers' ends all the great and little works upon the subject.

"Magia Posthuma," "Phlegon de Mirabilibus," "Augustinus de cura pro Mortuis," "Philosophicae et Christianae Cogitationes de Vampiris," by John Christofer Herenberg; and a thousand others, among which I remember only a few of those which he lent to my father. He had a voluminous digest of all the judicial cases, from which he had extracted a system of principles that appear to govern—some always, and others occasionally only—the condition of the vampire. I may mention, in passing, that the deadly pallor attributed to that sort of revenants, is a mere melodramatic fiction. They present, in the grave, and when they show themselves in human society, the appearance of healthy life. When disclosed to light in their coffins, they exhibit all the symptoms that are enumerated as those which proved the vampire-life of the long-dead Countess Karnstein.

How they escape from their graves and return to them for certain hours every day, without displacing the clay or leaving any trace of disturbance in the state of the coffin or the cerements, has always been admitted to be utterly inexplicable. The amphibious existence of the vampire is sustained by daily renewed slumber in the grave. Its horrible lust for living blood supplies the vigor of its waking existence. The vampire is prone to be fascinated with an engrossing vehemence, resembling the passion of love, by particular persons. In pursuit of these it will exercise inexhaustible patience and stratagem, for access to a particular object may be obstructed in a hundred ways. It will never desist until it has satiated its passion, and drained the very life of its coveted victim. But it will, in these cases, husband and protract its murderous enjoyment with the refinement of an epicure, and heighten it by the gradual approaches of an artful courtship. In these cases it seems to yearn for something like sympathy and consent. In ordinary ones it goes direct to its object, overpowers with violence, and strangles and exhausts often at a single feast.

The vampire is, apparently, subject, in certain situations, to special conditions. In the particular instance of which I have given you a relation, Mircalla seemed to be limited to a name which, if not her real one, should at least reproduce, without the omission or addition of a single letter, those, as we say, anagrammatically, which compose it.

Carmilla did this; so did Millarca.

My father related to the Baron Vordenburg, who remained with us for two or three weeks after the expulsion of Carmilla, the story about the Moravian nobleman and the vampire at Karnstein churchyard, and then he asked the Baron how he had discovered the exact position of the long-concealed tomb of the Countess Mircalla? The Baron's grotesque features puckered up into a mysterious smile; he looked down, still smiling on his worn spectacle case and fumbled with it. Then looking up, he said:

"I have many journals, and other papers, written by that remarkable man; the most curious among them is one treating of the visit of which you speak, to Karnstein. The tradition, of course, discolors and distorts a little. He might have been termed a Moravian nobleman, for he had changed his abode to that territory, and was, beside, a noble. But he was, in truth, a native of Upper Styria. It is enough to say that in very early youth he had been a passionate and favored lover of the beautiful Mircalla, Countess Karnstein. Her early death plunged him into inconsolable grief. It is the nature of vampires to increase and multiply, but according to an ascertained and ghostly law.

"Assume, at starting, a territory perfectly free from that pest. How does it begin, and how does it multiply itself? I will tell you. A person, more or less wicked, puts an end to himself. A suicide, under certain circumstances, becomes a vampire. That specter visits living people in their slumbers; they die, and almost invariably, in the grave, develop into vampires. This happened in the case of the beautiful Mircalla, who was haunted by one of those demons. My ancestor, Vordenburg, whose title I still bear, soon discovered this, and in the course of the studies to which he devoted himself, learned a great deal more.

"Among other things, he concluded that suspicion of vampirism would probably fall, sooner or later, upon the dead Countess, who in life had been his idol. He conceived a horror, be she what she might, of her remains being profaned by the outrage of a posthumous execution. He has left a curious paper to prove that the vampire, on its expulsion from its amphibious existence, is projected into a far more horrible life; and he resolved to save his once beloved Mircalla from this.

"He adopted the stratagem of a journey here, a pretended removal of her remains, and a real obliteration of her monument. When age had stolen upon him, and from the vale of years, he looked back on the scenes he was leaving, he considered, in a different spirit, what he had done, and a horror took possession of him. He made the tracings and notes which have guided me to the very spot, and drew up a confession of the deception that he had practiced. If he had intended any further action in this matter, death prevented him; and the hand of a remote descendant has, too late for many, directed the pursuit to the lair of the beast."

We talked a little more, and among other things he said was this:

"One sign of the vampire is the power of the hand. The slender hand of Mircalla closed like a vice of steel on the General's wrist when he raised the hatchet to strike. But its power is not confined to its grasp; it leaves a numbness in the limb it seizes, which is slowly, if ever, recovered from."

The following Spring my father took me a tour through Italy. We remained away for more than a year. It was long before the terror of recent events subsided; and to this hour the image of Carmilla returns to memory with ambiguous alternations—sometimes the playful, languid, beautiful girl; sometimes the writhing fiend I saw in the ruined church; and often from a reverie I have started, fancying I heard the light step of Carmilla at the drawing room door.

# MR. JUSTICE HARBOTTLE (1872)

## PROLOGUE

On this case Doctor Hesselius has inscribed nothing more than the words, "Harman's Report," and a simple reference to his own extraordinary Essay on "The Interior Sense, and the Conditions of the Opening thereof."

The reference is to Vol. I., Section 317, Note Z^{a}. The note to which reference is thus made, simply says: "There are two accounts of the remarkable case of the Honourable Mr. Justice Harbottle, one furnished to me by Mrs. Trimmer, of Tunbridge Wells (June, 1805); the other at a much later date, by Anthony Harman, Esq. I much prefer the former; in the first place, because it is minute and detailed, and written, it seems to me, with more caution and knowledge; and in the next, because the letters from Dr. Hedstone, which are embodied in it, furnish matter of the highest value to a right apprehension of the nature of the case. It was one of the best declared cases of an opening of the interior sense, which I have met with. It was affected too, by the phenomenon, which occurs so frequently as to indicate a law of these eccentric conditions; that is to say, it exhibited what I may term, the contagious character of this sort of intrusion of the spirit-world upon the proper domain of matter. So soon as the spirit-action has established itself in the case of one patient, its developed energy begins to radiate, more or less effectually, upon others. The interior vision of the child was opened; as was, also, that of its mother, Mrs. Pyneweck; and both the interior vision and hearing of the scullery-maid, were opened on the same occasion. After-appearances are the result of the law explained in Vol. II., Section 17 to 49. The common centre of association, simultaneously recalled, unites, or _re_unites, as the case may be, for a period measured, as we see, in Section 37. The _maximum_ will extend to days, the _minimum_ is little more than a second. We see the operation of this principle perfectly displayed, in certain cases of lunacy, of epilepsy, of catalepsy, and of mania, of a peculiar and painful character, though unattended by incapacity of business."

The memorandum of the case of Judge Harbottle, which was written by Mrs. Trimmer, of Tunbridge Wells, which Doctor Hesselius thought the better of the two, I have been unable to discover among his papers. I found in his escritoire a note to the effect that he had lent the Report of Judge Harbottle's case, written by Mrs. Trimmer, to Dr. F. Heyne. To that learned and able gentleman accordingly I wrote, and received from him, in his reply, which was full of alarms and regrets, on account of the uncertain safety of that "valuable MS.," a line written long since by Dr. Hesselius, which completely exonerated him, inasmuch as it acknowledged the safe return of the papers. The narrative of Mr. Harman, is therefore, the only one available for this collection. The late Dr. Hesselius, in another passage of the note that I have cited, says, "As to the facts (non-medical) of the case, the narrative of Mr. Harman exactly tallies with that furnished by Mrs. Trimmer." The strictly scientific view of the case would scarcely interest the popular reader; and, possibly, for the purposes of this selection, I should, even had I both papers to choose between, have preferred that of Mr. Harman, which is given, in full, in the following pages.

# CHAPTER I

## The Judge's House

Thirty years ago, an elderly man, to whom I paid quarterly a small annuity charged on some property of mine, came on the quarter-day to receive it. He was a dry, sad, quiet man, who had known better days, and had always maintained an unexceptionable character. No better authority could be imagined for a ghost story.

He told me one, though with a manifest reluctance; he was drawn into the narration by his choosing to explain what I should not have remarked, that he had called two days earlier than that week after the strict day of payment, which he had usually allowed to elapse. His reason was a sudden determination to change his lodgings, and the consequent necessity of paying his rent a little before it was due.

He lodged in a dark street in Westminster, in a spacious old house, very warm, being wainscoted from top to bottom, and furnished with no undue abundance of windows, and those fitted with thick sashes and small panes.

This house was, as the bills upon the windows testified, offered to be sold or let. But no one seemed to care to look at it.

A thin matron, in rusty black silk, very taciturn, with large, steady, alarmed eyes, that seemed to look in your face, to read what you might have seen in the dark rooms and passages through which you had passed, was in charge of it, with a solitary "maid-of-all-work" under her command. My poor friend had taken lodgings in this house, on account of their extraordinary cheapness. He had occupied them for nearly a year without the slightest disturbance, and was the only tenant, under rent, in the house. He had two rooms; a sitting-room and a bed-room with a closet opening from it, in which he kept his books and papers locked up. He had gone to his bed, having also locked the outer door. Unable to sleep, he had lighted a candle, and after having read for a time, had laid the book beside him. He heard the old clock at the stairhead strike one; and very shortly after, to his alarm, he saw the closet-door, which he thought he had locked, open stealthily, and a slight dark man, particularly sinister, and somewhere about fifty, dressed in mourning of a very antique fashion, such a suit as we see in Hogarth, entered the room on tip-toe. He was followed by an elder man, stout, and blotched with scurvy, and whose features, fixed as a corpse's, were stamped with dreadful force with a character of sensuality and villany.

This old man wore a flowered silk dressing-gown and ruffles, and he remarked a gold ring on his finger, and on his head a cap of velvet, such as, in the days of perukes, gentlemen wore in undress.

This direful old man carried in his ringed and ruffled hand a coil of rope; and these two figures crossed the floor diagonally, passing the foot of his bed, from the closet door at the farther end of the room, at the left, near the window, to the door opening upon the lobby, close to the bed's head, at his right.

He did not attempt to describe his sensations as these figures passed so near him. He merely said, that so far from sleeping in that room again, no consideration the world could offer would induce him so much as to enter it again alone, even in the daylight. He found both doors, that of the closet, and that of the room opening upon the lobby, in the morning fast locked as he had left them before going to bed.

In answer to a question of mine, he said that neither appeared the least conscious of his presence. They did not seem to glide, but walked as living men do, but without any sound, and he felt a vibration on the floor as they crossed it. He so obviously suffered from speaking about the apparitions, that I asked him no more questions.

There were in his description, however, certain coincidences so very singular, as to induce me, by that very post, to write to a friend much my senior, then living in a remote part of England, for the information which I knew he could give me. He had himself more than once pointed out that old house to my attention, and told me, though very briefly, the strange story which I now asked him to give me in greater detail.

His answer satisfied me; and the following pages convey its substance.

Your letter (he wrote) tells me you desire some particulars about the closing years of the life of Mr. Justice Harbottle, one of the judges of the Court of Common Pleas. You refer, of course, to the extraordinary occurrences that made that period of his life long after a theme for "winter tales" and metaphysical speculation. I happen to know perhaps more than any other man living of those mysterious particulars.

The old family mansion, when I revisited London, more than thirty years ago, I examined for the last time. During the years that have passed since then, I hear that improvement, with its preliminary demolitions, has been doing wonders for the quarter of Westminster in which it stood. If I were quite certain that the house had been taken down, I should have no difficulty about naming the street in which it stood. As what I have to tell, however, is not likely to improve its letting value, and as I should not care to get into trouble, I prefer being silent on that particular point.

How old the house was, I can't tell. People said it was built by Roger Harbottle, a Turkey merchant, in the reign of King James I. I am not a good opinion upon such questions; but having been in it, though in its forlorn and deserted state, I can tell you in a general way what it was like. It was built of dark-red brick, and the door and windows were faced with stone that had turned yellow by time. It receded some feet from the line of the other houses in the street; and it had a florid and fanciful rail of iron about the broad steps that invited your ascent to the hall-door, in which were fixed, under a file of lamps among scrolls and twisted leaves, two immense "extinguishers," like the conical caps of fairies, into which, in old times, the footmen used to thrust their flambeaux when their chairs or coaches had set down their great people, in the hall or at the steps, as the case might be. That hall is panelled up to the ceiling, and has a large fire-place. Two or three stately old rooms open from it at each side. The windows of these are tall, with many small panes. Passing through the arch at the back of the hall, you come upon the wide and heavy well-staircase. There is a back staircase also. The mansion is large, and has not as much light, by any means, in proportion to its extent, as modern houses enjoy. When I saw it, it had long been untenanted, and had the gloomy reputation beside of a haunted house. Cobwebs floated from the ceilings or spanned the corners of the cornices, and dust lay thick over everything. The windows were stained with the dust and rain of fifty years, and darkness had thus grown darker.

When I made it my first visit, it was in company with my father, when I was still a boy, in the year 1808. I was about twelve years old, and my imagination impressible, as it always is at that age. I looked about me with great awe. I was here in the very centre and scene of those occurrences which I had heard recounted at the fireside at home, with so delightful a horror.

My father was an old bachelor of nearly sixty when he married. He had, when a child, seen Judge Harbottle on the bench in his robes and wig a dozen times at least before his death, which took place in 1748, and his appearance made a powerful and unpleasant impression, not only on his imagination, but upon his nerves.

The Judge was at that time a man of some sixty-seven years. He had a great mulberry-coloured face, a big, carbuncled nose, fierce eyes, and a grim and brutal mouth. My father, who was young at the time, thought it the most formidable face he had ever seen; for there were evidences of intellectual power in the formation and lines of the forehead. His voice was loud and harsh, and gave effect to the sarcasm which was his habitual weapon on the bench.

This old gentleman had the reputation of being about the wickedest man in England. Even on the bench he now and then showed his scorn of opinion. He had carried cases his own way, it was said, in spite of counsel, authorities, and even of juries, by a sort of cajolery, violence, and bamboozling, that somehow confused and overpowered resistance. He had never actually committed himself; he was too cunning to do that. He had the character of being, however, a dangerous and unscrupulous judge; but his character did not trouble him. The associates he chose for his hours of relaxation cared as little as he did about it.

# CHAPTER II

## Mr. Peters

One night during the session of 1746 this old Judge went down in his chair to wait in one of the rooms of the House of Lords for the result of a division in which he and his order were interested.

This over, he was about to return to his house close by, in his chair; but the night had become so soft and fine that he changed his mind, sent it home empty, and with two footmen, each with a flambeau, set out on foot in preference. Gout had made him rather a slow pedestrian. It took him some time to get through the two or three streets he had to pass before reaching his house.

In one of those narrow streets of tall houses, perfectly silent at that hour, he overtook, slowly as he was walking, a very singular-looking old gentleman.

He had a bottle-green coat on, with a cape to it, and large stone buttons, a broad-leafed low-crowned hat, from under which a big powdered wig escaped; he stooped very much, and supported his bending knees with the aid of a crutch-handled cane, and so shuffled and tottered along painfully.

"I ask your pardon, sir," said this old man, in a very quavering voice, as the burly Judge came up with him, and he extended his hand feebly towards his arm.

Mr. Justice Harbottle saw that the man was by no means poorly dressed, and his manner that of a gentleman.
The Judge stopped short, and said, in his harsh peremptory tones, "Well, sir, how can I serve you?"

"Can you direct me to Judge Harbottle's house? I have some intelligence of the very last importance to communicate to him."

"Can you tell it before witnesses?" asked the Judge.

"By no means; it must reach _his_ ear only," quavered the old man earnestly.

"If that be so, sir, you have only to accompany me a few steps farther to reach my house, and obtain a private audience; for I am Judge Harbottle."

With this invitation the infirm gentleman in the white wig complied very readily; and in another minute the stranger stood in what was then termed the front parlour of the Judge's house, _tête-à-tête_ with that shrewd and dangerous functionary.

He had to sit down, being very much exhausted, and unable for a little time to speak; and then he had a fit of coughing, and after that a fit of gasping; and thus two or three minutes passed, during which the Judge dropped his roquelaure on an arm-chair, and threw his cocked-hat over that.

The venerable pedestrian in the white wig quickly recovered his voice. With closed doors they remained together for some time.

There were guests waiting in the drawing-rooms, and the sound of men's voices laughing, and then of a female voice singing to a harpsichord, were heard distinctly in the hall over the stairs; for old Judge Harbottle had arranged one of his dubious jollifications, such as might well make the hair of godly men's heads stand upright for that night.

This old gentleman in the powdered white wig, that rested on his stooped shoulders, must have had something to say that interested the Judge very much; for he would not have parted on easy terms with the ten minutes and upwards which that conference filched from the sort of revelry in which he most delighted, and in which he was the roaring king, and in some sort the tyrant also, of his company.

The footman who showed the aged gentleman out observed that the Judge's mulberry-coloured face, pimples and all, were bleached to a dingy yellow, and there was the abstraction of agitated thought in his manner, as he bid the stranger good-night. The servant saw that the conversation had been of serious import, and that the Judge was frightened.

Instead of stumping upstairs forthwith to his scandalous hilarities, his profane company, and his great china bowl of punch--the identical bowl from which a bygone Bishop of London, good easy man, had baptised this Judge's grandfather, now clinking round the rim with silver ladles, and hung with scrolls of lemon-peel--instead, I say, of stumping and clambering up the great staircase to the cavern of his Circean enchantment, he stood with his big nose flattened against the window-pane, watching the progress of the feeble old man, who clung stiffly to the iron rail as he got down, step by step, to the pavement.

The hall-door had hardly closed, when the old Judge was in the hall bawling hasty orders, with such stimulating expletives as old colonels under excitement sometimes indulge in now-a-days, with a stamp or two of his big foot, and a waving of his clenched fist in the air. He commanded the footman to overtake the old gentleman in the white wig, to offer him his protection on his way home, and in no case to show his face again without having ascertained where he lodged, and who he was, and all about him.

"By ---, sirrah! if you fail me in this, you doff my livery to-night!"

Forth bounced the stalwart footman, with his heavy cane under his arm, and skipped down the steps, and looked up and down the street after the singular figure, so easy to recognize.

What were his adventures I shall not tell you just now.

The old man, in the conference to which he had been admitted in that stately panelled room, had just told the Judge a very strange story. He might be himself a conspirator; he might possibly be crazed; or possibly his whole story was straight and true.

The aged gentleman in the bottle-green coat, in finding himself alone with Mr. Justice Harbottle, had become agitated. He said,

"There is, perhaps you are not aware, my lord, a prisoner in Shrewsbury jail, charged with having forged a bill of exchange for a hundred and twenty pounds, and his name is Lewis Pyneweck, a grocer of that town."

"Is there?" says the Judge, who knew well that there was.

"Yes, my lord," says the old man.

"Then you had better say nothing to affect this case. If you do, by ---, I'll commit you! for I'm to try it," says the judge, with his terrible look and tone.

"I am not going to do anything of the kind, my lord; of him or his case I know nothing, and care nothing. But a fact has come to my knowledge which it behoves you to well consider."

"And what may that fact be?" inquired the Judge; "I'm in haste, sir, and beg you will use dispatch."

"It has come to my knowledge, my lord, that a secret tribunal is in process of formation, the object of which is to take cognisance of the conduct of the judges; and first, of _your_ conduct, my lord; it is a wicked conspiracy."

"Who are of it?" demands the Judge.

"I know not a single name as yet. I know but the fact, my lord; it is most certainly true."

"I'll have you before the Privy Council, sir," says the Judge.

"That is what I most desire; but not for a day or two, my lord."

"And why so?"
"I have not as yet a single name, as I told your lordship; but I expect to have a list of the most forward men in it, and some other papers connected with the plot, in two or three days."

"You said one or two just now."

"About that time, my lord."

"Is this a Jacobite plot?"

"In the main I think it is, my lord."

"Why, then, it is political. I have tried no State prisoners, nor am like to try any such. How, then, doth it concern me?"

"From what I can gather, my lord, there are those in it who desire private revenges upon certain judges."

"What do they call their cabal?"

"The High Court of Appeal, my lord."

"Who are you, sir? What is your name?"

"Hugh Peters, my lord."

"That should be a Whig name?"

"It is, my lord." "Where do you lodge, Mr. Peters?"

"In Thames Street, my lord, over against the sign of the 'Three Kings.'"

"'Three Kings?' Take care one be not too many for you, Mr. Peters! How come you, an honest Whig, as you say, to be privy to a Jacobite plot? Answer me that."

"My lord, a person in whom I take an interest has been seduced to take a part in it; and being frightened at the unexpected wickedness of their plans, he is resolved to become an informer for the Crown."
"He resolves like a wise man, sir. What does he say of the persons? Who are in the plot? Doth he know them?"

"Only two, my lord; but he will be introduced to the club in a few days, and he will then have a list, and more exact information of their plans, and above all of their oaths, and their hours and places of meeting, with which he wishes to be acquainted before they can have any suspicions of his intentions. And being so informed, to whom, think you, my lord, had he best go then?"

"To the king's attorney-general straight. But you say this concerns me, sir, in particular? How about this prisoner, Lewis Pyneweck? Is he one of them?"

"I can't tell, my lord; but for some reason, it is thought your lordship will be well advised if you try him not. For if you do, it is feared 'twill shorten your days."

"So far as I can learn, Mr. Peters, this business smells pretty strong of blood and treason. The king's attorney-general will know how to deal with it. When shall I see you again, sir?"

"If you give me leave, my lord, either before your lordship's court sits, or after it rises, to-morrow. I should like to come and tell your lordship what has passed."

"Do so, Mr. Peters, at nine o'clock to-morrow morning. And see you play me no trick, sir, in this matter; if you do, by ---, sir, I'll lay you by the heels!"

"You need fear no trick from me, my lord; had I not wished to serve you, and acquit my own conscience, I never would have come all this way to talk with your lordship."

"I'm willing to believe you, Mr. Peters; I'm willing to believe you, sir."

And upon this they parted.

"He has either painted his face, or he is consumedly sick," thought the old Judge.

The light had shown more effectually upon his features as he turned to leave the room with a low bow, and they looked, he fancied, unnaturally chalky.

"D--- him!" said the Judge ungraciously, as he began to scale the stairs: "he has half-spoiled my supper."

But if he had, no one but the Judge himself perceived it, and the evidence was all, as any one might perceive, the other way.

# CHAPTER III

## Lewis Pyneweck

In the meantime the footman dispatched in pursuit of Mr. Peters speedily overtook that feeble gentleman. The old man stopped when he heard the sound of pursuing steps, but any alarms that may have crossed his mind seemed to disappear on his recognizing the livery. He very gratefully accepted the proffered assistance, and placed his tremulous arm within the servant's for support. They had not gone far, however, when the old man stopped suddenly, saying,

"Dear me! as I live, I have dropped it. You heard it fall. My eyes, I fear, won't serve me, and I'm unable to stoop low enough; but if _you_ will look, you shall have half the find. It is a guinea; I carried it in my glove."

The street was silent and deserted. The footman had hardly descended to what he termed his "hunkers," and begun to search the pavement about the spot which the old man indicated, when Mr. Peters, who seemed very much exhausted, and breathed with difficulty, struck him a violent blow, from above, over the back of the head with a heavy instrument, and then another; and leaving him bleeding and senseless in the gutter, ran like a lamplighter down a lane to the right, and was gone.

When an hour later, the watchman brought the man in livery home, still stupid and covered with blood, Judge Harbottle cursed his servant roundly, swore he was drunk, threatened him with an indictment for taking bribes to betray his master, and cheered him with a perspective of the broad street leading from the Old Bailey to Tyburn, the cart's tail, and the hangman's lash.

Notwithstanding this demonstration, the Judge was pleased. It was a disguised "affidavit man," or footpad, no doubt, who had been employed to frighten him. The trick had fallen through.

A "court of appeal," such as the false Hugh Peters had indicated, with assassination for its sanction, would be an uncomfortable institution for a "hanging judge" like the Honourable Justice Harbottle. That sarcastic and ferocious administrator of the criminal code of England, at that time a rather pharisaical, bloody and heinous system of justice, had reasons of his own for choosing to try that very Lewis Pyneweck, on whose behalf this audacious trick was devised. Try him he would. No man living should take that morsel out of his mouth.

Of Lewis Pyneweck, of course, so far as the outer world could see, he knew nothing. He would try him after his fashion, without fear, favour, or affection.

But did he not remember a certain thin man, dressed in mourning, in whose house, in Shrewsbury, the Judge's lodgings used to be, until a scandal of ill-treating his wife came suddenly to light? A grocer with a demure look, a soft step, and a lean face as dark as mahogany, with a nose sharp and long, standing ever so little awry, and a pair of dark steady brown eyes under thinly-traced black brows--a man whose thin lips wore always a faint unpleasant smile.

Had not that scoundrel an account to settle with the Judge? had he not been troublesome lately? and was not his name Lewis Pyneweck, some time grocer in Shrewsbury, and now prisoner in the jail of that town?

The reader may take it, if he pleases, as a sign that Judge Harbottle was a good Christian, that he suffered nothing ever from remorse. That was undoubtedly true. He had, nevertheless, done this grocer, forger, what you will, some five or six years before, a grievous wrong; but it was not that, but a possible scandal, and possible complications, that troubled the learned Judge now.

Did he not, as a lawyer, know, that to bring a man from his shop to the dock, the chances must be at least ninety-nine out of a hundred that he is guilty?

A weak man like his learned brother Withershins was not a judge to keep the high-roads safe, and make crime tremble. Old Judge Harbottle was the man to make the evil-disposed quiver, and to refresh the world with showers of wicked blood, and thus save the innocent, to the refrain of the ancient saw he loved to quote:

Foolish pity<br>
Ruins a city.

In hanging that fellow he could not be wrong. The eye of a man accustomed to look upon the dock could not fail to read "villain" written sharp and clear in his plotting face. Of course he would try him, and no one else should.

A saucy-looking woman, still handsome, in a mob-cap gay with blue ribbons, in a saque of flowered silk, with lace and rings on, much too fine for the Judge's housekeeper, which nevertheless she was, peeped into his study next morning, and, seeing the Judge alone, stepped in.

"Here's another letter from him, come by the post this morning. Can't you do nothing for him?" she said wheedlingly, with her arm over his neck, and her delicate finger and thumb fiddling with the lobe of his purple ear.

"I'll try," said Judge Harbottle, not raising his eyes from the paper he was reading.

"I knew you'd do what I asked you," she said.

The Judge clapt his gouty claw over his heart, and made her an ironical bow.

"What," she asked, "will you do?"

"Hang him," said the Judge with a chuckle.

"You don't mean to; no, you don't, my little man," said she, surveying herself in a mirror on the wall.

"I'm d----d but I think you're falling in love with your husband at last!" said Judge Harbottle.

"I'm blest but I think you're growing jealous of him," replied the lady with a laugh. "But no; he was always a bad one to me; I've done with him long ago."

"And he with you, by George! When he took your fortune, and your spoons, and your ear-rings, he had all he wanted of you. He drove you from his house; and when he discovered you had made yourself comfortable, and found a good situation, he'd have taken your guineas, and your silver, and your ear-rings over again, and then allowed you half-a-dozen years more to make a new harvest for his mill. You don't wish him good; if you say you do, you lie."

She laughed a wicked, saucy laugh, and gave the terrible Rhadamanthus a playful tap on the chops.

"He wants me to send him money to fee a counsellor," she said, while her eyes wandered over the pictures on the wall, and back again to the looking-glass; and certainly she did not look as if his jeopardy troubled her very much.

"Confound his impudence, the _scoundrel_!" thundered the old Judge, throwing himself back in his chair, as he used to do _in furore_ on the bench, and the lines of his mouth looked brutal, and his eyes ready to leap from their sockets. "If you answer his letter from my house to please yourself, you'll write your next from somebody else's to please me. You understand, my pretty witch, I'll not be pestered. Come, no pouting; whimpering won't do. You don't care a brass farthing for the villain, body or soul. You came here but to make a row. You are one of Mother Carey's chickens; and where you come, the storm is up. Get you gone, baggage! get you _gone_!" he repeated, with a stamp; for a knock at the hall-door made her instantaneous disappearance indispensable.

I need hardly say that the venerable Hugh Peters did not appear again. The Judge never mentioned him. But oddly enough, considering how he laughed to scorn the weak invention which he had blown into dust at the very first puff, his white-wigged visitor and the conference in the dark front parlour were often in his memory.

His shrewd eye told him that allowing for change of tints and such disguises as the playhouse affords every night, the features of this false old man, who had turned out too hard for his tall footman, were identical with those of Lewis Pyneweck.

Judge Harbottle made his registrar call upon the crown solicitor, and tell him that there was a man in town who bore a wonderful resemblance to a prisoner in Shrewsbury jail named Lewis Pyneweck, and to make inquiry through the post forthwith whether any one was personating

Pyneweck in prison and whether he had thus or otherwise made his escape.

The prisoner was safe, however, and no question as to his identity.

## CHAPTER IV

### Interruption in Court

In due time Judge Harbottle went circuit; and in due time the judges were in Shrewsbury. News travelled slowly in those days, and newspapers, like the wagons and stage coaches, took matters easily. Mrs. Pyneweck, in the Judge's house, with a diminished household--the greater part of the Judge's servants having gone with him, for he had given up riding circuit, and travelled in his coach in state--kept house rather solitarily at home.

In spite of quarrels, in spite of mutual injuries--some of them, inflicted by herself, enormous--in spite of a married life of spited bickerings--a life in which there seemed no love or liking or forbearance, for years--now that Pyneweck stood in near danger of death, something like remorse came suddenly upon her. She knew that in Shrewsbury were transacting the scenes which were to determine his fate. She knew she did not love him; but she could not have supposed, even a fortnight before, that the hour of suspense could have affected her so powerfully.

She knew the day on which the trial was expected to take place. She could not get it out of her head for a minute; she felt faint as it drew towards evening.

Two or three days passed; and then she knew that the trial must be over by this time. There were floods between London and Shrewsbury, and news was long delayed. She wished the floods would last forever. It was dreadful waiting to hear; dreadful to know that the event was over, and that she could not hear till self-willed rivers subsided; dreadful to know that they must subside and the news come at last.

She had some vague trust in the Judge's good nature, and much in the resources of chance and accident. She had contrived to send the money he wanted. He would not be without legal advice and energetic and skilled support.

At last the news did come--a long arrear all in a gush: a letter from a female friend in Shrewsbury; a return of the sentences, sent up for the Judge; and most important, because most easily got at, being told with great aplomb and brevity, the long-deferred intelligence of the Shrewsbury Assizes in the _Morning Advertiser_. Like an impatient reader of a novel, who reads the last page first, she read with dizzy eyes the list of the executions.

Two were respited, seven were hanged; and in that capital catalogue was this line:

"Lewis Pyneweck--forgery."

She had to read it a half-a-dozen times over before she was sure she understood it. Here was the paragraph:

> _Sentence, Death--7._
>
> Executed accordingly, on Friday the 13th instant, to wit:
>
> Thomas Primer, _alias_ Duck--highway robbery. Flora Guy--stealing to the value of 11s. 6d. Arthur Pounden--burglary. Matilda Mummery--riot. Lewis Pyneweck--forgery, bill of exchange.

And when she reached this, she read it over and over, feeling very cold and sick.

This buxom housekeeper was known in the house as Mrs. Carwell—Carwell being her maiden name, which she had resumed.

No one in the house except its master knew her history. Her introduction had been managed craftily. No one suspected that it had been concerted between her and the old reprobate in scarlet and ermine.

Flora Carwell ran up the stairs now, and snatched her little girl, hardly seven years of age, whom she met on the lobby, hurriedly up in her arms, and carried her into her bedroom, without well knowing what she was doing, and sat down, placing the child before her. She was not able to speak. She held the child before her, and looked in the little girl's wondering face, and burst into tears of horror.

She thought the Judge could have saved him. I daresay he could. For a time she was furious with him, and hugged and kissed her bewildered little girl, who returned her gaze with large round eyes.

That little girl had lost her father, and knew nothing of the matter. She had always been told that her father was dead long ago.

A woman, coarse, uneducated, vain, and violent, does not reason, or even feel, very distinctly; but in these tears of consternation were mingling a self-upbraiding. She felt afraid of that little child.

But Mrs. Carwell was a person who lived not upon sentiment, but upon beef and pudding; she consoled herself with punch; she did not trouble herself long even with resentments; she was a gross and material person, and could not mourn over the irrevocable for more than a limited number of hours, even if she would.

Judge Harbottle was soon in London again. Except the gout, this savage old epicurean never knew a day's sickness. He laughed, and coaxed, and bullied away the young woman's faint upbraidings, and in a little time Lewis Pyneweck troubled her no more; and the Judge secretly chuckled over the perfectly fair removal of a bore, who might have grown little by little into something very like a tyrant.

It was the lot of the Judge whose adventures I am now recounting to try criminal cases at the Old Bailey shortly after his return. He had commenced his charge to the jury in a case of forgery, and was, after his wont, thundering dead against the prisoner, with many a hard aggravation and cynical gibe, when suddenly all died away in silence, and, instead of looking at the jury, the eloquent Judge was gaping at some person in the body of the court.

Among the persons of small importance who stand and listen at the sides was one tall enough to show with a little prominence; a slight mean figure, dressed in seedy black, lean and dark of visage. He had just handed a letter to the crier, before he caught the Judge's eye.

That Judge descried, to his amazement, the features of Lewis Pyneweck.

He had the usual faint thin-lipped smile; and with his blue chin raised in air, and as it seemed quite unconscious of the distinguished notice he has attracted, he was stretching his low cravat with his crooked fingers, while he slowly turned his head from side to side--a process which enabled the Judge to see distinctly a stripe of swollen blue round his neck, which indicated, he thought, the grip of the rope.

This man, with a few others, had got a footing on a step, from which he could better see the court. He now stepped down, and the Judge lost sight of him.

His lordship signed energetically with his hand in the direction in which this man had vanished. He turned to the tipstaff. His first effort to speak ended in a gasp. He cleared his throat, and told the astounded official to arrest that man who had interrupted the court.

"He's but this moment gone down _there_. Bring him in custody before me, within ten minutes' time, or I'll strip your gown from your shoulders and fine the sheriff!" he thundered, while his eyes flashed round the court in search of the functionary.

Attorneys, counsellors, idle spectators, gazed in the direction in which Mr. Justice Harbottle had shaken his gnarled old hand. They compared notes. Not one had seen any one making a disturbance. They asked one another if the Judge was losing his head.

Nothing came of the search. His lordship concluded his charge a great deal more tamely; and when the jury retired, he stared round the court with a wandering mind, and looked as if he would not have given sixpence to see the prisoner hanged.

# CHAPTER V

## Caleb Searcher

The Judge had received the letter; had he known from whom it came, he would no doubt have read it instantaneously. As it was he simply read the direction:

_To the Honourable
The Lord Justice
Elijah Harbottle,
One of his Majesty's Justices of the
Honourable Court of Common Pleas._

It remained forgotten in his pocket till he reached home.

When he pulled out that and others from the capacious pocket of his coat, it had its turn, as he sat in his library in his thick silk dressing-gown; and then he found its contents to be a closely-written letter, in a clerk's hand, and an enclosure in "secretary hand," as I believe the angular scrivinary of law-writings in those days was termed, engrossed on a bit of parchment about the size of this page. The letter said:

MR. JUSTICE HARBOTTLE,--MY LORD,

I am ordered by the High Court of Appeal to acquaint your lordship, in order to your better preparing yourself for your trial, that a true bill hath been sent down, and the indictment lieth against your lordship for the murder of one Lewis Pyneweck of Shrewsbury, citizen, wrongfully executed for the forgery of a bill of exchange, on the ----th day of ---- last, by reason of the wilful perversion of the evidence, and the undue pressure put upon the jury, together with the illegal admission of evidence by your lordship, well knowing the same to be illegal, by all which the promoter of the prosecution of the said indictment, before the High Court of Appeal, hath lost his life.

And the trial of the said indictment, I am farther ordered to acquaint your lordship, is fixed for the both day of ---- next ensuing, by the right honourable the Lord Chief Justice Twofold, of the court aforesaid, to wit, the High Court of Appeal, on which day it will most certainly take place. And I am farther to acquaint your lordship, to prevent any surprise or miscarriage, that your case stands first for the said day, and that the said High Court of Appeal sits day and night, and never rises; and herewith, by order of the said court, I furnish your lordship with a copy (extract) of the record in this case, except of the indictment, whereof, notwithstanding, the substance and effect is supplied to your lordship in this Notice. And farther I am to inform you, that in case the jury then to try your lordship should find you guilty, the right honourable the Lord Chief Justice will, in passing sentence of death upon you, fix the day of execution for the 10th day of ----, being one calendar month from the day of your trial.

It was signed by
CALEB SEARCHER,
Officer of the Crown Solicitor in the Kingdom of Life and Death.

The Judge glanced through the parchment.

"'Sblood! Do they think a man like me is to be bamboozled by their buffoonery?"

The Judge's coarse features were wrung into one of his sneers; but he was pale. Possibly, after all, there was a conspiracy on foot. It was queer. Did they mean to pistol him in his carriage? or did they only aim at frightening him?

Judge Harbottle had more than enough of animal courage. He was not afraid of highwaymen, and he had fought more than his share of duels, being a foul-mouthed advocate while he held briefs at the bar. No one questioned his fighting qualities. But with respect to this particular case of Pyneweck, he lived in a house of glass. Was there not his pretty, dark-eyed, over-dressed housekeeper, Mrs. Flora Carwell? Very easy for people who knew Shrewsbury to identify Mrs. Pyneweck, if once put upon the scent; and had he not stormed and worked hard in that case? Had he not made it hard sailing for the prisoner? Did he not know very well what the bar thought of it? It would be the worst scandal that ever blasted Judge.

So much there was intimidating in the matter but nothing more. The Judge was a little bit gloomy for a day or two after, and more testy with every one than usual.

He locked up the papers; and about a week after he asked his housekeeper, one day, in the library:

"Had your husband never a brother?"

Mrs. Carwell squalled on this sudden introduction of the funereal topic, and cried exemplary "piggins full," as the Judge used pleasantly to say. But he was in no mood for trifling now, and he said sternly:

"Come, madam! this wearies me. Do it another time; and give me an answer to my question." So she did.

Pyneweck had no brother living. He once had one; but he died in Jamaica.

"How do you know he is dead?" asked the Judge.

"Because he told me so."

"Not the dead man."

"Pyneweck told me so."

"Is that all?" sneered the Judge.

He pondered this matter; and time went on. The Judge was growing a little morose, and less enjoying. The subject struck nearer to his thoughts than he fancied it could have done. But so it is with most undivulged vexations, and there was no one to whom he could tell this one.

It was now the ninth; and Mr Justice Harbottle was glad. He knew nothing would come of it. Still it bothered him; and to-morrow would see it well over.

[What of the paper I have cited? No one saw it during his life; no one, after his death. He spoke of it to Dr. Hedstone; and what purported to be "a copy," in the old Judge's handwriting, was found. The original was nowhere. Was it a copy of an illusion, incident to brain disease? Such is my belief.]

# CHAPTER VI

## Arrested

Judge Harbottle went this night to the play at Drury Lane. He was one of the old fellows who care nothing for late hours, and occasional knocking about in pursuit of pleasure. He had appointed with two cronies of Lincoln's Inn to come home in his coach with him to sup after the play.

They were not in his box, but were to meet him near the entrance, and get into his carriage there; and Mr. Justice Harbottle, who hated waiting, was looking a little impatiently from the window.

The Judge yawned.

He told the footman to watch for Counsellor Thavies and Counsellor Beller, who were coming; and, with another yawn, he laid his cocked hat on his knees, closed his eyes, leaned back in his corner, wrapped his mantle closer about him, and began to think of pretty Mrs. Abington.

And being a man who could sleep like a sailor, at a moment's notice, he was thinking of taking a nap. Those fellows had no business to keep a judge waiting.

He heard their voices now. Those rake-hell counsellors were laughing, and bantering, and sparring after their wont. The carriage swayed and jerked, as one got in, and then again as the other followed. The door clapped, and the coach was now jogging and rumbling over the pavement. The Judge was a little bit sulky. He did not care to sit up and open his eyes. Let them suppose he was asleep. He heard them laugh with more malice than good-humour, he thought, as they observed it. He would give them a d----d hard knock or two when they got to his door, and till then he would counterfeit his nap.

The clocks were chiming twelve. Beller and Thavies were silent as tombstones. They were generally loquacious and merry rascals.

The Judge suddenly felt himself roughly seized and thrust from his corner into the middle of the seat, and opening his eyes, instantly he found himself between his two companions.

Before he could blurt out the oath that was at his lips, he saw that they were two strangers--evil-looking fellows, each with a pistol in his hand, and dressed like Bow Street officers.

The Judge clutched at the check-string. The coach pulled up. He stared about him. They were not among houses; but through the windows, under a broad moonlight, he saw a black moor stretching lifelessly from right to left, with rotting trees, pointing fantastic branches in the air, standing here and there in groups, as if they held up their arms and twigs like fingers, in horrible glee at the Judge's coming.

A footman came to the window. He knew his long face and sunken eyes. He knew it was Dingly Chuff, fifteen years ago a footman in his service, whom he had turned off at a moment's notice, in a burst of jealousy, and indicted for a missing spoon. The man had died in prison of the jail-fever.

The Judge drew back in utter amazement. His armed companions signed mutely; and they were again gliding over this unknown moor.
The bloated and gouty old man, in his horror considered the question of resistance. But his athletic days were long over. This moor was a desert. There was no help to be had. He was in the hands of strange servants, even if his recognition turned out to be a delusion, and they were under the command of his captors. There was nothing for it but submission, for the present.

Suddenly the coach was brought nearly to a standstill, so that the prisoner saw an ominous sight from the window.

It was a gigantic gallows beside the road; it stood three-sided, and from each of its three broad beams at top depended in chains some eight or ten bodies, from several of which the cere-clothes had dropped away, leaving the skeletons swinging lightly by their chains. A tall ladder reached to the summit of the structure, and on the peat beneath lay bones.

On top of the dark transverse beam facing the road, from which, as from the other two completing the triangle of death, dangled a row of these unfortunates in chains, a hangman, with a pipe in his mouth, much as we see him in the famous print of the "Idle Apprentice," though here his perch was ever so much higher, was reclining at his ease and listlessly shying bones, from a little heap at his elbow, at the skeletons that hung round, bringing down now a rib or two, now a hand, now half a leg. A long-sighted man could have discerned that he was a dark fellow, lean; and from continually looking down on the earth from the elevation over which, in another sense, he always hung, his nose, his lips, his chin were pendulous and loose, and drawn down into a monstrous grotesque.

This fellow took his pipe from his mouth on seeing the coach, stood up, and cut some solemn capers high on his beam, and shook a new rope in the air, crying with a voice high and distant as the caw of a raven hovering over a gibbet, "A robe for Judge Harbottle!"

The coach was now driving on at its old swift pace.

So high a gallows as that, the Judge had never, even in his most hilarious moments, dreamed of. He thought, he must be raving. And the dead footman! He shook his ears and strained his eyelids; but if he was dreaming, he was unable to awake himself.

There was no good in threatening these scoundrels. A _brutum fulmen_ might bring a real one on his head.

Any submission to get out of their hands; and then heaven and earth he would move to unearth and hunt them down.

Suddenly they drove round a corner of a vast white building, and under a _porte-cochère_.

# CHAPTER VII

## Chief-Justice Twofold

The Judge found himself in a corridor lighted with dingy oil lamps, the walls of bare stone; it looked like a passage in a prison. His guards placed him in the hands of other people. Here and there he saw bony and gigantic soldiers passing to and fro, with muskets over their shoulders. They looked straight before them, grinding their teeth, in bleak fury, with no noise but the clank of their shoes. He saw these by glimpses, round corners, and at the ends of passages, but he did not actually pass them by.

And now, passing under a narrow doorway, he found himself in the dock, confronting a judge in his scarlet robes, in a large court-house. There was nothing to elevate this Temple of Themis above its vulgar kind elsewhere. Dingy enough it looked, in spite of candles lighted in decent abundance. A case had just closed, and the last juror's back was seen escaping through the door in the wall of the jury-box. There were some dozen barristers, some fiddling with pen and ink, others buried in briefs, some beckoning, with the plumes of their pens, to their attorneys, of whom there were no lack; there were clerks to-ing and fro-ing, and the officers of the court, and the registrar, who was handing up a paper to the judge; and the tipstaff, who was presenting a note at the end of his wand to a king's counsel over the heads of the crowd between. If this was the High Court of Appeal, which never rose day or night, it might account for the pale and jaded aspect of everybody in it. An air of indescribable gloom hung upon the pallid features of all the people here; no one ever smiled; all looked more or less secretly suffering.

"The King against Elijah Harbottle!" shouted the officer.

"Is the appellant Lewis Pyneweck in court?" asked Chief-Justice Twofold, in a voice of thunder, that shook the woodwork of the court, and boomed down the corridors.

Up stood Pyneweck from his place at the table.

"Arraign the prisoner!" roared the Chief: and Judge Harbottle felt the panels of the dock round him, and the floor, and the rails quiver in the vibrations of that tremendous voice.

The prisoner, _in limine_, objected to this pretended court, as being a sham, and non-existent in point of law; and then, that, even if it were a court constituted by law (the Judge was growing dazed), it had not and could not have any jurisdiction to try him for his conduct on the bench.

Whereupon the chief-justice laughed suddenly, and every one in court, turning round upon the prisoner, laughed also, till the laugh grew and roared all round like a deafening acclamation; he saw nothing but glittering eyes and teeth, a universal stare and grin; but though all the voices laughed, not a single face of all those that concentrated their gaze upon him looked like a laughing face. The mirth subsided as suddenly as it began.

The indictment was read. Judge Harbottle actually pleaded! He pleaded "Not Guilty." A jury were sworn. The trial proceeded. Judge Harbottle was bewildered. This could not be real. He must be either mad, or _going_ mad, he thought.

One thing could not fail to strike even him. This Chief-Justice Twofold, who was knocking him about at every turn with sneer and gibe, and roaring him down with his tremendous voice, was a dilated effigy of himself; an image of Mr. Justice Harbottle, at least double his size, and with all his fierce colouring, and his ferocity of eye and visage, enhanced awfully.

Nothing the prisoner could argue, cite, or state, was permitted to retard for a moment the march of the case towards its catastrophe.

The chief-justice seemed to feel his power over the jury, and to exult and riot in the display of it. He glared at them, he nodded to them; he seemed to have established an understanding with them. The lights were faint in that part of the court. The jurors were mere shadows, sitting in rows; the prisoner could see a dozen pair of white eyes shining, coldly, out of the darkness; and whenever the judge in his charge, which was contemptuously brief, nodded and grinned and gibed, the prisoner could see, in the obscurity, by the dip of all these rows of eyes together, that the jury nodded in acquiescence.

And now the charge was over, the huge chief-justice leaned back panting and gloating on the prisoner. Every one in the court turned about, and gazed with steadfast hatred on the man in the dock. From the jury-box where the twelve sworn brethren were whispering together, a sound in the general stillness like a prolonged "hiss-s-s!" was heard; and then, in answer to the challenge of the officer, "How say you, gentlemen of the jury, guilty or not guilty?" came in a melancholy voice the finding, "Guilty."

The place seemed to the eyes of the prisoner to grow gradually darker and darker, till he could discern nothing distinctly but the lumen of the eyes that were turned upon him from every bench and side and corner and gallery of the building. The prisoner doubtless thought that he had quite enough to say, and conclusive, why sentence of death should not be pronounced upon him; but the lord chief-justice puffed it contemptuously away, like so much smoke, and proceeded to pass sentence of death upon the prisoner, having named the tenth of the ensuing month for his execution.

Before he had recovered the stun of this ominous farce, in obedience to the mandate, "Remove the prisoner," he was led from the dock. The lamps seemed all to have gone out, and there were stoves and charcoal-fires here and there, that threw a faint crimson light on the walls of the corridors through which he passed. The stones that composed them looked now enormous, cracked and unhewn.

He came into a vaulted smithy, where two men, naked to the waist, with heads like bulls, round shoulders, and the arms of giants, were welding red-hot chains together with hammers that pelted like thunderbolts.

They looked on the prisoner with fierce red eyes, and rested on their hammers for a minute; and said the elder to his companion, "Take out Elijah Harbottle's gyves;" and with a pincers he plucked the end which lay dazzling in the fire from the furnace.

"One end locks," said he, taking the cool end of the iron in one hand, while with the grip of a vice he seized the leg of the Judge, and locked the ring round his ankle. "The other," he said with a grin, "is welded."

The iron band that was to form the ring for the other leg lay still red hot upon the stone floor, with briliant sparks sporting up and down its surface.

His companion, in his gigantic hands, seized the old Judge's other leg, and pressed his foot immovably to the stone floor; while his senior, in a twinkling, with a masterly application of pincers and hammer, sped the glowing bar around his ankle so tight that the skin and sinews smoked and bubbled again, and old Judge Harbottle uttered a yell that seemed to chill the very stones, and make the iron chains quiver on the wall.

Chains, vaults, smiths, and smithy all vanished in a moment; but the pain continued. Mr. Justice Harbottle was suffering torture all round the ankle on which the infernal smiths had just been operating.

His friends, Thavies and Beller, were startled by the Judge's roar in the midst of their elegant trifling about a marriage _à-la-mode_ case which was going on. The Judge was in panic as well as pain. The street lamps and the light of his own hall door restored him.
"I'm very bad," growled he between his set teeth; "my foot's blazing. Who was he that hurt my foot? 'Tis the gout--'tis the gout!" he said, awaking completely. "How many hours have we been coming from the playhouse? 'Sblood, what has happened on the way? I've slept half the night!"

There had been no hitch or delay, and they had driven home at a good pace.

The Judge, however, was in gout; he was feverish too; and the attack, though very short, was sharp; and when, in about a fortnight, it subsided, his ferocious joviality did not return. He could not get this dream, as he chose to call it, out of his head.

# CHAPTER VIII

## Somebody Has Got Into the House

People remarked that the Judge was in the vapours. His doctor said he should go for a fortnight to Buxton.

Whenever the Judge fell into a brown study, he was always conning over the terms of the sentence pronounced upon him in his vision--"in one calendar month from the date of this day;" and then the usual form, "and you shall be hanged by the neck till you are dead," etc. "That will be the 10th--I'm not much in the way of being hanged. I know what stuff dreams are, and I laugh at them; but this is continually in my thoughts, as if it forecast misfortune of some sort. I wish the day my dream gave me were passed and over. I wish I were well purged of my gout. I wish I were as I used to be. 'Tis nothing but vapours, nothing but a maggot." The copy of the parchment and letter which had announced his trial with many a snort and sneer he would read over and over again, and the scenery and people of his dream would rise about him in places the most unlikely, and steal him in a moment from all that surrounded him into a world of shadows.

The Judge had lost his iron energy and banter. He was growing taciturn and morose. The Bar remarked the change, as well they might. His friends thought him ill. The doctor said he was troubled with hypochondria, and that his gout was still lurking in his system, and ordered him to that ancient haunt of crutches and chalk-stones, Buxton.

The Judge's spirits were very low; he was frightened about himself; and he described to his housekeeper, having sent for her to his study to drink a dish of tea, his strange dream in his drive home from Drury Lane Playhouse. He was sinking into the state of nervous dejection in which men lose their faith in orthodox advice, and in despair consult quacks, astrologers, and nursery storytellers. Could such a dream mean that he was to have a fit, and so die on the both? She did not think so. On the contrary, it was certain some good luck must happen on that day.

The Judge kindled; and for the first time for many days, he looked for a minute or two like himself, and he tapped her on the cheek with the hand that was not in flannel.

"Odsbud! odsheart! you dear rogue! I had forgot. There is young Tom--yellow Tom, my nephew, you know, lies sick at Harrogate; why shouldn't he go that day as well as another, and if he does, I get an estate by it? Why, lookee, I asked Doctor Hedstone yesterday if I was like to take a fit any time, and he laughed, and swore I was the last man in town to go off that way."

The Judge sent most of his servants down to Buxton to make his lodgings and all things comfortable for him. He was to follow in a day or two.

It was now the 9th; and the next day well over, he might laugh at his visions and auguries.

On the evening of the 9th, Dr. Hedstone's footman knocked at the Judge's door. The Doctor ran up the dusky stairs to the drawing-room. It was a March evening, near the hour of sunset, with an east wind whistling sharply through the chimney-stacks. A wood fire blazed cheerily on the hearth. And Judge Harbottle, in what was then called a brigadier-wig, with his red roquelaure on, helped the glowing effect of the darkened chamber, which looked red all over like a room on fire.

The Judge had his feet on a stool, and his huge grim purple face confronted the fire, and seemed to pant and swell, as the blaze alternately spread upward and collapsed. He had fallen again among his blue devils, and was thinking of retiring from the Bench, and of fifty other gloomy things.

But the Doctor, who was an energetic son of Aesculapius, would listen to no croaking, told the Judge he was full of gout, and in his present condition no judge even of his own case, but promised him leave to pronounce on all those melancholy questions, a fortnight later.

In the meantime the Judge must be very careful. He was overcharged with gout, and he must not provoke an attack, till the waters of Buxton should do that office for him, in their own salutary way.

The Doctor did not think him perhaps quite so well as he pretended, for he told him he wanted rest, and would be better if he went forthwith to his bed.

Mr. Gerningham, his valet, assisted him, and gave him his drops; and the Judge told him to wait in his bedroom till he should go to sleep.

Three persons that night had specially odd stories to tell.

The housekeeper had got rid of the trouble of amusing her little girl at this anxious time, by giving her leave to run about the sitting-rooms and look at the pictures and china, on the usual condition of touching nothing. It was not until the last gleam of sunset had for some time faded, and the twilight had so deepened that she could no longer discern the colours on the china figures on the chimneypiece or in the cabinets, that the child returned to the housekeeper's room to find her mother.

To her she related, after some prattle about the china, and the pictures, and the Judge's two grand wigs in the dressing-room off the library, an adventure of an extraordinary kind.
In the hall was placed, as was customary in those times, the sedan-chair which the master of the house occasionally used, covered with stamped leather, and studded with gilt nails, and with its red silk blinds down. In this case, the doors of this old-fashioned conveyance were locked, the windows up, and, as I said, the blinds down, but not so closely that the curious child could not peep underneath one of them, and see into the interior.

A parting beam from the setting sun, admitted through the window of a back room, shot obliquely through the open door, and lighting on the chair, shone with a dull transparency through the crimson blind.

To her surprise, the child saw in the shadow a thin man, dressed in black, seated in it; he had sharp dark features; his nose, she fancied, a little awry, and his brown eyes were looking straight before him; his hand was on his thigh, and he stirred no more than the waxen figure she had seen at Southwark fair.

A child is so often lectured for asking questions, and on the propriety of silence, and the superior wisdom of its elders, that it accepts most things at last in good faith; and the little girl acquiesced respectfully in the occupation of the chair by this mahogany-faced person as being all right and proper.

It was not until she asked her mother who this man was, and observed her scared face as she questioned her more minutely upon the appearance of the stranger, that she began to understand that she had seen something unaccountable.

Mrs. Carwell took the key of the chair from its nail over the footman's shelf, and led the child by the hand up to the hall, having a lighted candle in her other hand. She stopped at a distance from the chair, and placed the candlestick in the child's hand.

"Peep in, Margery, again, and try if there's anything there," she whispered; "hold the candle near the blind so as to throw its light through the curtain."

The child peeped, this time with a very solemn face, and intimated at once that he was gone.

"Look again, and be sure," urged her mother.

The little girl was quite certain; and Mrs. Carwell, with her mob-cap of lace and cherry-coloured ribbons, and her dark brown hair, not yet powdered, over a very pale face, unlocked the door, looked in, and beheld emptiness.

"All a mistake, child, you see."

"_There!_ ma'am! see there! He's gone round the corner," said the child.

"Where?" said Mrs. Carwell, stepping backward a step.

"Into that room."

"Tut, child! 'twas the shadow," cried Mrs. Carwell, angrily, because she was frightened. "I moved the candle." But she clutched one of the poles of the chair, which leant against the wall in the corner, and pounded the floor furiously with one end of it, being afraid to pass the open door the child had pointed to.

The cook and two kitchen-maids came running upstairs, not knowing what to make of this unwonted alarm.

They all searched the room; but it was still and empty, and no sign of any one's having been there.

Some people may suppose that the direction given to her thoughts by this odd little incident will account for a very strange illusion which Mrs. Carwell herself experienced about two hours later.

# CHAPTER IX

## The Judge Leaves His House

Mrs. Flora Carwell was going up the great staircase with a posset for the Judge in a china bowl, on a little silver tray.

Across the top of the well-staircase there runs a massive oak rail; and, raising her eyes accidentally, she saw an extremely odd-looking stranger, slim and long, leaning carelessly over with a pipe between his finger and thumb. Nose, lips, and chin seemed all to droop downward into extraordinary length, as he leant his odd peering face over the banister. In his other hand he held a coil of rope, one end of which escaped from under his elbow and hung over the rail.

Mrs. Carwell, who had no suspicion at the moment, that he was not a real person, and fancied that he was some one employed in cording the Judge's luggage, called to know what he was doing there.

Instead of answering, he turned about, and walked across the lobby, at about the same leisurely pace at which she was ascending, and entered a room, into which she followed him. It was an uncarpeted and unfurnished chamber. An open trunk lay upon the floor empty, and beside it the coil of rope; but except herself there her. Perhaps, when she was able to think it over, it was a relief to was no one in the room.

Mrs. Carwell was very much frightened, and now concluded that the child must have seen the same ghost that had just appeared to believe so; for the face, figure, and dress described by the child were awfully like Pyneweck; and this certainly was not he.

Very much scared and very hysterical, Mrs. Carwell ran down to her room, afraid to look over her shoulder, and got some companions about her, and wept, and talked, and drank more than one cordial, and talked and wept again, and so on, until, in those early days, it was ten o'clock, and time to go to bed. A scullery maid remained up finishing some of her scouring and "scalding" for some time after the other servants--who, as I said, were few in number--that night had got to their beds. This was a low-browed, broad-faced, intrepid wench with black hair, who did not "vally a ghost not a button," and treated the housekeeper's hysterics with measureless scorn.

The old house was quiet now. It was near twelve o'clock, no sounds were audible except the muffled wailing of the wintry winds, piping high among the roofs and chimneys, or rumbling at intervals, in under gusts, through the narrow channels of the street.

The spacious solitudes of the kitchen level were awfully dark, and this sceptical kitchen-wench was the only person now up and about the house. She hummed tunes to herself, for a time; and then stopped and listened; and then resumed her work again. At last, she was destined to be more terrified than even was the housekeeper.

There was a back kitchen in this house, and from this she heard, as if coming from below its foundations, a sound like heavy strokes, that seemed to shake the earth beneath her feet. Sometimes a dozen in sequence, at regular intervals; sometimes fewer. She walked out softly into the passage, and was surprised to see a dusky glow issuing from this room, as if from a charcoal fire.

The room seemed thick with smoke.

Looking in she very dimly beheld a monstrous figure, over a furnace, beating with a mighty hammer the rings and rivets of a chain.

The strokes, swift and heavy as they looked, sounded hollow and distant. The man stopped, and pointed to something on the floor, that, through the smoky haze, looked, the thought, like a dead body. She remarked no more; but the servants in the room close by, startled from their sleep by a hideous scream, found her in a swoon on the flags, close to the door, where she had just witnessed this ghastly vision.

Startled by the girl's incoherent asseverations that she had seen the Judge's corpse on the floor, two servants having first searched the lower part of the house, went rather frightened up-stairs to inquire whether their master was well. They found him, not in his bed, but in his room. He had a table with candles burning at his bedside, and was getting on his clothes again; and he swore and cursed at them roundly in his old style, telling them that he had business, and that he would discharge on the spot any scoundrel who should dare to disturb him again.

So the invalid was left to his quietude.

In the morning it was rumored here and there in the street that the Judge was dead. A servant was sent from the house three doors away, by Counsellor Traverse, to inquire at Judge Harbottle's hall door.

The servant who opened it was pale and reserved, and would only say that the Judge was ill. He had had a dangerous accident; Doctor Hedstone had been with him at seven o'clock in the morning.

There were averted looks, short answers, pale and frowning faces, and all the usual signs that there was a secret that sat heavily upon their minds and the time for disclosing which had not yet come. That time would arrive when the coroner had arrived, and the mortal scandal that had befallen the house could be no longer hidden. For that morning Mr. Justice Harbottle had been found hanging by the neck from the banister at the top of the great staircase, and quite dead.

There was not the smallest sign of any struggle or resistance. There had not been heard a cry or any other noise in the slightest degree indicative of violence. There was medical evidence to show that, in his atrabilious state, it was quite on the cards that he might have made away with himself. The jury found accordingly that it was a case of suicide. But to those who were acquainted with the strange story which Judge Harbottle had related to at least two persons, the fact that the catastrophe occurred on the morning of March 10th seemed a startling coincidence.

A few days after, the pomp of a great funeral attended him to the grave; and so, in the language of Scripture, "the rich man died, and was buried."

# THE WATCHER (1894)

It is now more than fifty years since the occurrences which I am about to relate caused a strange sensation in the gay society of Dublin. The fashionable world, however, is no recorder of traditions; the memory of selfishness seldom reaches far; and the events which occasionally disturb the polite monotony of its pleasant and heartless progress, however stamped with the characters of misery and horror, scarcely outlive the gossip of a season, and (except, perhaps, in the remembrance of a few more directly interested in the consequences of the catastrophe) are in a little time lost to the recollection of all. The appetite for scandal, or for horror, has been sated; the incident can yield no more of interest or novelty; curiosity, frustrated by impenetrable mystery, gives over the pursuit in despair; the tale has ceased to be new, grows stale and flat; and so, in a few years, inquiry subsides into indifference.

Somewhere about the year 1794, the younger brother of a certain baronet, whom I shall call Sir James Barton, returned to Dublin. He had served in the navy with some distinction, having commanded one of his Majesty's frigates during the greater part of the American war. Captain Barton was now apparently some two or three-and-forty years of age. He was an intelligent and agreeable companion, when he chose it, though generally reserved, and occasionally even moody. In society, however, he deported himself as a man of the world and a gentleman. He had not contracted any of the noisy brusqueness sometimes acquired at sea; on the contrary, his manners were remarkably easy, quiet, and even polished. He was in person about the middle size, and somewhat strongly formed; his countenance was marked with the lines of thought, and on the whole wore an expression of gravity and even of melancholy. Being, however, as we have said, a man of perfect breeding, as well as of affluent circumstances and good family, he had, of course, ready access to the best society of the metropolis, without the necessity of any other credentials. In his personal habits Captain Barton was economical. He occupied lodgings in one of the then fashionable streets in the south side of the town, kept but one horse and one servant, and though a reputed free-thinker, he lived an orderly and moral life, indulging neither in gaming, drinking, nor any other vicious pursuit, living very much to himself, without forming any intimacies, or choosing any companions, and appearing to mix in gay society rather for the sake of its bustle and distraction, than for any opportunities which it offered of interchanging either thoughts or feelings with its votaries. Barton was therefore pronounced a saving, prudent, unsocial sort of a fellow, who bid fair to maintain his celibacy alike against stratagem and assault, and was likely to live to a good old age, die rich and leave his money to a hospital.

It was soon apparent, however, that the nature of Captain Barton's plans had been totally misconceived. A young lady, whom we shall call Miss Montague, was at this time introduced into the fashionable world of Dublin by her aunt, the Dowager Lady Rochdale. Miss Montague was decidedly pretty and accomplished, and having some natural cleverness, and a great deal of gaiety, became for a while the reigning toast. Her popularity, however, gained her, for a time, nothing more than that unsubstantial admiration which, however pleasant as an incense to vanity, is by no means necessarily antecedent to matrimony, for, unhappily for the young lady in question, it was an understood thing, that, beyond her personal attractions, she had no kind of earthly provision. Such being the state of affairs, it will readily be believed that no little surprise was consequent upon the appearance of Captain Barton as the avowed lover of the penniless Miss Montague.

His suit prospered, as might have been expected, and in a short time it was confidentially communicated by old Lady Rochdale to each of her hundred and fifty particular friends in succession, that Captain Barton had actually tendered proposals of marriage, with her approbation, to her niece, Miss Montague, who had, moreover, accepted the offer of his hand, conditionally upon the consent of her father, who was then upon his homeward voyage from India, and expected in two or three months at furthest. About his consent there could be no doubt. The delay, therefore, was one merely of form; they were looked upon as absolutely engaged, and Lady Rochdale, with a vigour of old-fashioned decorum with which her niece would, no doubt, gladly have dispensed, withdrew her thenceforward from all further participation in the gaieties of the town. Captain Barton was a constant visitor as well as a frequent guest at the house, and was permitted all the privileges and intimacy which a betrothed suitor is usually accorded. Such was the relation of parties, when the mysterious circumstances which darken this narrative with inexplicable melancholy first began to unfold themselves.

Lady Rochdale resided in a handsome mansion at the north side of Dublin, and Captain Barton's lodgings, as we have already said, were situated at the south. The distance intervening was considerable, and it was Captain Barton's habit generally to walk home without an attendant, as often as he passed the evening with the old lady and her fair charge. His shortest way in such nocturnal walks lay, for a considerable space, through a line of streets which had as yet been merely laid out, and little more than the foundations of the houses constructed. One night, shortly after his engagement with Miss Montague had commenced, he happened to remain unusually late, in company only with her and Lady Rochdale. The conversation had turned upon the evidences of revelation, which he had disputed with the callous scepticism of a confirmed infidel. What were called "French principles" had, in those days, found their way a good deal into fashionable society, especially that portion of it which professed allegiance to Whiggism, and neither the old lady nor her charge was so perfectly free from the taint as to look upon Captain Barton's views as any serious objection to the proposed union. The discussion had degenerated into one upon the supernatural and the marvellous, in which he had pursued precisely the same line of argument and ridicule. In all this, it is but true to state, Captain Barton was guilty of no affectation; the doctrines upon which he insisted were, in reality, but too truly the basis of his own fixed belief, if so it might be called; and perhaps not the least strange of the many strange circumstances connected with this narrative, was the fact that the subject of the fearful influences we are about to describe was himself, from the deliberate conviction of years, an utter disbeliever in what are usually termed preternatural agencies.

It was considerably past midnight when Mr. Barton took his leave, and set out upon his solitary walk homeward. He rapidly reached the lonely road, with its unfinished dwarf walls tracing the foundations of the projected rows of houses on either side. The moon was shining mistily, and its imperfect light made the road he trod but additionally dreary; that utter silence, which has in it something indefinably exciting, reigned there, and made the sound of his steps, which alone broke it, unnaturally loud and distinct. He had proceeded thus some way, when on a sudden he heard other footsteps, pattering at a measured pace, and, as it seemed, about two score steps behind him. The suspicion of being dogged is at all times unpleasant; it is, however, especially so in a spot so desolate and lonely: and this suspicion became so strong in the mind of Captain Barton, that he abruptly turned about to confront his pursuers, but, though there was quite sufficient moonlight to disclose any object upon the road he had traversed, no form of any kind was visible.

The steps he had heard could not have been the reverberation of his own, for he stamped his foot upon the ground, and walked briskly up and down, in the vain attempt to wake an echo. Though by no means a fanciful person, he was at last compelled to charge the sounds upon his imagination, and treat them as an illusion. Thus satisfying himself, he resumed his walk, and before he had proceeded a dozen paces, the mysterious footfalls were again audible from behind, and this time, as if with the special design of showing that the sounds were not the responses of an echo, the steps sometimes slackened nearly to a halt, and sometimes hurried for six or eight strides to a run, and again abated to a walk.

Captain Barton, as before, turned suddenly round, and with the same result; no object was visible above the deserted level of the road. He walked back over the same ground, determined that, whatever might have been the cause of the sounds which had so disconcerted him, it should not escape his search; the endeavour, however, was unrewarded. In spite of all his scepticism, he felt something like a superstitious fear stealing fast upon him, and, with these unwonted and uncomfortable sensations, he once more turned and pursued his way. There was no repetition of these haunting sounds, until he had reached the point where he had last stopped to retrace his steps. Here they were resumed, and with sudden starts of running, which threatened to bring the unseen pursuer close up to the alarmed pedestrian. Captain Barton arrested his course as formerly; the unaccountable nature of the occurrence filled him with vague and almost horrible sensations, and, yielding to the excitement he felt gaining upon him, he shouted, sternly, "Who goes there?" The sound of one's own voice, thus exerted, in utter solitude, and followed by total silence, has in it something unpleasantly exciting, and he felt a degree of nervousness which, perhaps, from no cause had he ever known before. To the very end of this solitary street the steps pursued him, and it required a strong effort of stubborn pride on his part to resist the impulse that prompted him every moment to run for safety at the top of his speed. It was not until he had reached his lodging, and sat by his own fireside, that he felt sufficiently reassured to arrange and reconsider in his own mind the occurrences which had so discomposed him: so little a matter, after all, is sufficient to upset the pride of scepticism, and vindicate the old simple laws of nature within us.

Mr. Barton was next morning sitting at a late breakfast, reflecting upon the incidents of the previous night, with more of inquisitiveness than awe--so speedily do gloomy impressions upon the fancy disappear under the cheerful influences of day--when a letter just delivered by the postman was placed upon the table before him. There was nothing remarkable in the address of this missive, except that it was written in a hand which he did not know--perhaps it was disguised--for the tall narrow characters were sloped backward; and with the self-inflicted suspense which we so often see practised in such cases, he puzzled over the inscription for a full minute before he broke the seal. When he did so, he read the following words, written in the same hand:--

"Mr. Barton, late Captain of the _Dolphin_, is warned of _danger_. He will do wisely to avoid ---- Street--(here the locality of his last night's adventure was named)--if he walks there as usual, he will meet with something bad. Let him take warning, once for all, for he has good reason to dread

"THE WATCHER."

Captain Barton read and re-read this strange effusion; in every light and in every direction he turned it over and over. He examined the paper on which it was written, and closely scrutinized the handwriting. Defeated here, he turned to the seal; it was nothing but a patch of wax, upon which the accidental impression of a coarse thumb was imperfectly visible. There was not the slightest mark, no clue or indication of any kind, to lead him to even a guess as to its possible origin. The writer's object seemed a friendly one, and yet he subscribed himself as one whom he had "good reason to dread." Altogether, the letter, its author, and its real purpose, were to him an inexplicable puzzle, and one, moreover, unpleasantly suggestive, in his mind, of associations connected with the last night's adventure.

In obedience to some feeling--perhaps of pride--Mr. Barton did not communicate, even to his intended bride, the occurrences which we have just detailed. Trifling as they might appear, they had in reality most disagreeably affected his imagination, and he cared not to disclose, even to the young lady in question, what she might possibly look upon as evidences of weakness. The letter might very well be but a hoax, and the mysterious footfall but a delusion of his fancy. But although he affected to treat the whole affair as unworthy of a thought, it yet haunted him pertinaciously, tormenting him with perplexing doubts, and depressing him with undefined apprehensions. Certain it is, that for a considerable time afterwards he carefully avoided the street indicated in the letter as the scene of danger.

It was not until about a week after the receipt of the letter which I have transcribed, that anything further occurred to remind Captain Barton of its contents, or to counteract the gradual disappearance from his mind of the disagreeable impressions which he had then received. He was returning one night, after the interval I have stated, from the theatre, which was then situated in Crow Street, and having there handed Miss Montague and Lady Rochdale into their carriage, he loitered for some time with two or three acquaintances. With these, however, he parted close to the College, and pursued his way alone. It was now about one o'clock, and the streets were quite deserted. During the whole of his walk with the companions from whom he had just parted, he had been at times painfully aware of the sound of steps, as it seemed, dogging them on their way. Once or twice he had looked back, in the uneasy anticipation that he was again about to experience the same mysterious annoyances which had so much disconcerted him a week before, and earnestly hoping that he might _see_ some form from whom the sounds might naturally proceed. But the street was deserted; no form was visible. Proceeding now quite alone upon his homeward way, he grew really nervous and uncomfortable, as he became sensible, with increased distinctness, of the well-known and now absolutely dreaded sounds.

By the side of the dead wall which bounded the College Park, the sounds followed, recommencing almost simultaneously with his own steps. The same unequal pace, sometimes slow, sometimes, for a score yards or so, quickened to a run, was audible from behind him. Again and again he turned, quickly and stealthily he glanced over his shoulder almost at every half-dozen steps; but no one was visible. The horrors of this intangible and unseen persecution became gradually all but intolerable; and when at last he reached his home his nerves were strung to such a pitch of excitement that he could not rest, and did not attempt even to lie down until after the daylight had broken.

He was awakened by a knock at his chamber-door, and his servant entering, handed him several letters which had just been received by the early post. One among them instantly arrested his attention; a single glance at the direction aroused him thoroughly. He at once recognized its character, and read as follows:--

"You may as well think, Captain Barton, to escape from your own shadow as from me; do what you may, I will see you as often as I please, and you shall see me, for I do not want to hide myself, as you fancy. Do not let it trouble your rest, Captain Barton; for, with a _good conscience_, what need you fear from the eye of

"THE WATCHER?"

It is scarcely necessary to dwell upon the feelings elicited by a perusal of this strange communication. Captain Barton was observed to be unusually absent and out of spirits for several days afterwards; but no one divined the cause. Whatever he might think as to the phantom steps which followed him, there could be no possible illusion about the letters he had received; and, to say the least of it, their immediate sequence upon the mysterious sounds which had haunted him was an odd coincidence. The whole circumstance, in his own mind, was vaguely and instinctively connected with certain passages in his past life, which, of all others, he hated to remember.

It so happened that just about this time, in addition to his approaching nuptials, Captain Barton had fortunately, perhaps, for himself, some business of an engrossing kind connected with the adjustment of a large and long-litigated claim upon certain properties. The hurry and excitement of business had its natural effect in gradually dispelling the marked gloom which had for a time occasionally oppressed him, and in a little while his spirits had entirely resumed their accustomed tone.

During all this period, however, he was occasionally dismayed by indistinct and half-heard repetitions of the same annoyance, and that in lonely places, in the day time as well as after nightfall. These renewals of the strange impressions from which he had suffered so much were, however, desultory and faint, insomuch that often he really could not, to his own satisfaction, distinguish between them and the mere suggestions of an excited imagination. One evening he walked down to the House of Commons with a Mr. Norcott, a Member. As they walked down together he was observed to become absent and silent, and to a degree so marked as scarcely to consist with good breeding; and this, in one who was obviously in all his habits so perfectly a gentleman, seemed to argue the pressure of some urgent and absorbing anxiety. It was afterwards known that, during the whole of that walk, he had heard the well-known footsteps dogging him as he proceeded. This, however, was the last time he suffered from this phase of the persecution of which he was already the anxious victim. A new and a very different one was about to be presented.

Of the new series of impressions which were afterwards gradually to work out his destiny, that evening disclosed the first; and but for its relation to the train of events which followed, the incident would scarcely have been remembered by any one. As they were walking in at the passage, a man (of whom his friend could afterwards remember only that he was short in stature, looked like a foreigner, and wore a kind of travelling-cap) walked very rapidly, and, as if under some fierce excitement, directly towards them, muttering to himself fast and vehemently the while. This odd-looking person proceeded straight toward Barton, who was foremost, and halted, regarding him for a moment or two with a look of menace and fury almost maniacal; and then turning about as abruptly, he walked before them at the same agitated pace, and disappeared by a side passage. Norcott distinctly remembered being a good deal shocked at the countenance and bearing of this man, which indeed irresistibly impressed him with an undefined sense of danger, such as he never felt before or since from the presence of anything human; but these sensations were far from amounting to anything so disconcerting as to flurry or excite him--he had seen only a singularly evil countenance, agitated, as it seemed, with the excitement of madness. He was absolutely astonished, however, at the effect of this apparition upon Captain Barton. He knew him to be a man of proved courage and coolness in real danger, a circumstance which made his conduct upon this occasion the more conspicuously odd. He recoiled a step or two as the stranger advanced, and clutched his companion's arm in silence, with a spasm of agony or terror; and then, as the figure disappeared, shoving him roughly back, he followed it for a few paces, stopped in great disorder, and sat down upon a form. A countenance more ghastly and haggard it was impossible to fancy.

"For God's sake, Barton, what is the matter?" said Norcott, really alarmed at his friend's appearance. "You're not hurt, are you? nor unwell? What is it?"

"What did he say? I did not hear it. What was it?" asked Barton, wholly disregarding the question.

"Tut, tut, nonsense!" said Norcott, greatly surprised; "who cares what the fellow said? You are unwell, Barton, decidedly unwell; let me call a coach."

"Unwell! Yes, no, not exactly unwell," he said, evidently making an effort to recover his self-possession; "but, to say the truth, I am fatigued, a little overworked, and perhaps over anxious. You know I have been in Chancery, and the winding up of a suit is always a nervous affair. I have felt uncomfortable all this evening; but I am better now. Come, come, shall we go on?"

"No, no. Take my advice, Barton, and go home; you really do need rest; you are looking absolutely ill. I really do insist on your allowing me to see you home," replied his companion.

It was obvious that Barton was not himself disinclined to be persuaded. He accordingly took his leave, politely declining his friend's offered escort. Notwithstanding the few commonplace regrets which Norcott had expressed, it was plain that he was just as little deceived as Barton himself by the extempore plea of illness with which he had accounted for the strange exhibition, and that he even then suspected some lurking mystery in the matter.

Norcott called next day at Barton's lodgings, to inquire for him, and learned from the servant that he had not left his room since his return the night before; but that he was not seriously indisposed, and hoped to be out again in a few days. That evening he sent for Doctor Richards, then in large and fashionable practice in Dublin, and their interview was, it is said, an odd one.

He entered into a detail of his own symptoms in an abstracted and desultory kind of way, which seemed to argue a strange want of interest in his own cure, and, at all events, made it manifest that there was some topic engaging his mind of more engrossing importance than his present ailment. He complained of occasional palpitations, and headache. Doctor Richards asked him, among other questions, whether there was any irritating circumstance or anxiety to account for it. This he denied quickly and peevishly; and the physician thereupon declared his opinion, that there was nothing amiss except some slight derangement of the digestion, for which he accordingly wrote a prescription, and was about to withdraw, when Mr. Barton, with the air of a man who suddenly recollects a topic which had nearly escaped him, recalled him.

"I beg your pardon, doctor, but I had really almost forgot; will you permit me to ask you two or three medical questions?--rather odd ones, perhaps, but as a wager depends upon their solution, you will, I hope, excuse my unreasonableness."

The physician readily undertook to satisfy the inquirer.

Barton seemed to have some difficulty about opening the proposed interrogatories, for he was silent for a minute, then walked to his book-case and returned as he had gone; at last he sat down, and said,--

"You'll think them very childish questions, but I can't recover my wager without a decision; so I must put them. I want to know first about lock-jaw. If a man actually has had that complaint, and appears to have died of it--so that in fact a physician of average skill pronounces him actually dead--may he, after all, recover?"

Doctor Richards smiled, and shook his head.

"But--but a blunder may be made," resumed Barton. "Suppose an ignorant pretender to medical skill; may _he_ be so deceived by any stage of the complaint, as to mistake what is only a part of the progress of the disease, for death itself?"

"No one who had ever seen death," answered he, "could mistake it in the case of lock-jaw."

Barton mused for a few minutes. "I am going to ask you a question, perhaps still more childish; but first tell me, are not the regulations of foreign hospitals, such as those of, let us say, Lisbon, very lax and bungling? May not all kinds of blunders and slips occur in their entries of names, and so forth?"

Doctor Richards professed his inability to answer that query.

"Well, then, doctor, here is the last of my questions. You will probably laugh at it; but it must out nevertheless. Is there any disease, in all the range of human maladies, which would have the effect of perceptibly contracting the stature, and the whole frame--causing the man to shrink in all his proportions, and yet to preserve his exact resemblance to himself in every particular--with the one exception, his height and bulk; _any_ disease, mark, no matter how rare, how little believed in, generally, which could possibly result in producing such an effect?"

The physician replied with a smile, and a very decided negative.

"Tell me, then," said Barton, abruptly, "if a man be in reasonable fear of assault from a lunatic who is at large, can he not procure a warrant for his arrest and detention?"

"Really, that is more a lawyer's question than one in my way," replied Doctor Richards; "but I believe, on applying to a magistrate, such a course would be directed."

The physician then took his leave; but, just as he reached the hall-door, remembered that he had left his cane upstairs, and returned. His reappearance was awkward, for a piece of paper, which he recognized as his own prescription, was slowly burning upon the fire, and Barton sitting close by with an expression of settled gloom and dismay. Doctor Richards had too much tact to appear to observe what presented itself; but he had seen quite enough to assure him that the mind, and not the body, of Captain Barton was in reality the seat of his sufferings.

A few days afterwards, the following advertisement appeared in the Dublin newspapers:--

"If Sylvester Yelland, formerly a foremast man on board his Majesty's frigate _Dolphin_, or his nearest of kin, will apply to Mr. Robery Smith, solicitor, at his office, Dame Street, he or they may hear of something greatly to his or their advantage. Admission may be had at any hour up to twelve o'clock at night for the next fortnight, should parties desire to avoid observation; and the strictest secrecy, as to all communications intended to be confidential, shall be honourably observed."

The _Dolphin_, as we have mentioned, was the vessel which Captain Barton had commanded; and this circumstance, connected with the extraordinary exertions made by the circulation of hand-bills, etc., as well as by repeated advertisements, to secure for this strange notice the utmost possible publicity, suggested to Doctor Richards the idea that Captain Barton's extreme uneasiness was somehow connected with the individual to whom the advertisement was addressed, and he himself the author of it. This, however, it is needless to add, was no more than a conjecture. No information whatsoever, as to the real purpose of the advertisement itself, was divulged by the agent, nor yet any hint as to who his employer might be.

Mr. Barton, although he had latterly begun to earn for himself the character of a hypochondriac, was yet very far from deserving it. Though by no means lively, he had yet, naturally, what are termed "even spirits," and was not subject to continual depressions. He soon, therefore, began to return to his former habits; and one of the earliest symptoms of this healthier tone of spirits was his appearing at a grand dinner of the Freemasons, of which worthy fraternity he was himself a brother. Barton, who had been at first gloomy and abstracted, drank much more freely than was his wont--possibly with the purpose of dispelling his own secret anxieties--and under the influence of good wine, and pleasant company, became gradually (unlike his usual self) talkative, and even noisy. It was under this unwonted excitement that he left his company at about half-past ten o'clock; and as conviviality is a strong incentive to gallantry, it occurred to him to proceed forthwith to Lady Rochdale's, and pass the remainder of the evening with her and his destined bride.

Accordingly, he was soon at ---- Street, and chatting gaily with the ladies. It is not to be supposed that Captain Barton had exceeded the limits which propriety prescribes to good fellowship; he had merely taken enough of wine to raise his spirits, without, however, in the least degree unsteadying his mind, or affecting his manners. With this undue elevation of spirits had supervened an entire oblivion or contempt of those undefined apprehensions which had for so long weighed upon his mind, and to a certain extent estranged him from society; but as the night wore away, and his artificial gaiety began to flag, these painful feelings gradually intruded themselves again, and he grew abstracted and anxious as heretofore. He took his leave at length, with an unpleasant foreboding of some coming mischief, and with a mind haunted with a thousand mysterious apprehensions, such as, even while he acutely felt their pressure, he, nevertheless, inwardly strove, or affected to contemn.

It was his proud defiance of what he considered to be his own weakness which prompted him upon this occasion to the course which brought about the adventure which we are now about to relate. Mr. Barton might have easily called a coach, but he was conscious that his strong inclination to do so proceeded from no cause other than what he desperately persisted in representing to himself to be his own superstitious tremors. He might also have returned home by a route different from that against which he had been warned by his mysterious correspondent; but for the same reason he dismissed this idea also, and with a dogged and half desperate resolution to force matters to a crisis of some kind, to see if there were any reality in the causes of his former suffering, and if not, satisfactorily to bring their delusiveness to the proof, he determined to follow precisely the course which he had trodden upon the night so painfully memorable in his own mind as that on which his strange persecution had commenced. Though, sooth to say, the pilot who for the first time steers his vessel under the muzzles of a hostile battery never felt his resolution more severely tasked than did Captain Barton, as he breathlessly pursued this solitary path; a path which, spite of every effort of scepticism and reason, he felt to be, as respected _him_, infested by a malignant influence.

He pursued his way steadily and rapidly, scarcely breathing from intensity of suspense; he, however, was troubled by no renewal of the dreaded footsteps, and was beginning to feel a return of confidence, as, more than three-fourths of the way being accomplished with impunity, he approached the long line of twinkling oil lamps which indicated the frequented streets. This feeling of self-congratulation was, however, but momentary. The report of a musket at some two hundred yards behind him, and the whistle of a bullet close to his head, disagreeably and startlingly dispelled it. His first impulse was to retrace his steps in pursuit of the assassin; but the road on either side was, as we have said, embarrassed by the foundations of a street, beyond which extended waste fields, full of rubbish and neglected lime and brick kilns, and all now as utterly silent as though no sound had ever disturbed their dark and unsightly solitude. The futility of attempting, single-handed, under such circumstances, a search for the murderer, was apparent, especially as no further sound whatever was audible to direct his pursuit.

With the tumultuous sensations of one whose life had just been exposed to a murderous attempt, and whose escape has been the narrowest possible, Captain Barton turned, and without, however, quickening his pace actually to a run, hurriedly pursued his way. He had turned, as we have said, after a pause of a few seconds, and had just commenced his rapid retreat, when on a sudden he met the well-remembered little man in the fur cap. The encounter was but momentary. The figure was walking at the same exaggerated pace, and with the same strange air of menace as before; and as it passed him, he thought he heard it say, in a furious whisper, "Still alive, still alive!"

The state of Mr. Barton's spirits began now to work a corresponding alteration in his health and looks, and to such a degree that it was impossible that the change should escape general remark. For some reasons, known but to himself, he took no step whatsoever to bring the attempt upon his life, which he had so narrowly escaped, under the notice of the authorities; on the contrary, he kept it jealously to himself; and it was not for many weeks after the occurrence that he mentioned it, and then in strict confidence to a gentleman, the torments of his mind at last compelled him to consult a friend.

Spite of his blue devils, however, poor Barton, having no satisfactory reason to render to the public for any undue remissness in the attentions which his relation to Miss Montague required, was obliged to exert himself, and present to the world a confident and cheerful bearing. The true source of his sufferings, and every circumstance connected with them, he guarded with a reserve so jealous, that it seemed dictated by at least a suspicion that the origin of his strange persecution was known to himself, and that it was of a nature which, upon his own account, he could not or dare not disclose.

The mind thus turned in upon itself, and constantly occupied with a haunting anxiety which it dared not reveal, or confide to any human breast, became daily more excited; and, of course, more vividly impressible, by a system of attack which operated through the nervous system; and in this state he was destined to sustain, with increasing frequency, the stealthy visitations of that apparition, which from the first had seemed to possess so unearthly and terrible a hold upon his imagination.

* * * * *

It was about this time that Captain Barton called upon the then celebrated preacher, Doctor Macklin, with whom he had a slight acquaintance; and an extraordinary conversation ensued. The divine was seated in his chambers in college, surrounded with works upon his favourite pursuit and deep in theology, when Barton was announced. There was something at once embarrassed and excited in his manner, which, along with his wan and haggard countenance, impressed the student with the unpleasant consciousness that his visitor must have recently suffered terribly indeed to account for an alteration so striking, so shocking.

After the usual interchange of polite greeting, and a few commonplace remarks, Captain Barton, who obviously perceived the surprise which his visit had excited, and which Doctor Macklin was unable wholly to conceal, interrupted a brief pause by remarking,--

"This is a strange call, Doctor Macklin, perhaps scarcely warranted by an acquaintance so slight as mine with you. I should not, under ordinary circumstances, have ventured to disturb you, but my visit is neither an idle nor impertinent intrusion. I am sure you will not so account it, when--"

Doctor Macklin interrupted him with assurances, such as good breeding suggested, and Barton resumed,--

"I am come to task your patience by asking your advice. When I say your patience, I might, indeed, say more; I might have said your humanity, your compassion; for I have been, and am a great sufferer."

"My dear sir," replied the churchman, "it will, indeed, afford me infinite gratification if I can give you comfort in any distress of mind, but--but--"

"I know what you would say," resumed Barton, quickly. "I am an unbeliever, and, therefore, incapable of deriving help from religion, but don't take that for granted. At least you must not assume that, however unsettled my convictions may be, I do not feel a deep, a very deep, interest in the subject. Circumstances have lately forced it upon my attention in such a way as to compel me to review the whole question in a more candid and teachable spirit, I believe, than I ever studied it in before."

"Your difficulties, I take it for granted, refer to the evidences of revelation," suggested the clergyman.

"Why--no--yes; in fact I am ashamed to say I have not considered even my objections sufficiently to state them connectedly; but--but there is one subject on which I feel a peculiar interest."

He paused again, and Doctor Macklin pressed him to proceed.

"The fact is," said Barton, "whatever may be my uncertainty as to the authenticity of what we are taught to call revelation, of one fact I am deeply and horribly convinced: that there does exist beyond this a spiritual world--a system whose workings are generally in mercy hidden from us--a system which may be, and which is sometimes, partially and terribly revealed. I am sure, I know," continued Barton, with increasing excitement, "there is a God--a dreadful God--and that retribution follows guilt. In ways, the most mysterious and stupendous; by agencies, the most inexplicable and terrific; there is a spiritual system--great Heavens, how frightfully I have been convinced!--a system malignant, and inexorable, and omnipotent, under whose persecutions I am, and have been, suffering the torments of the damned!--yes, sir--yes--the fires and frenzy of hell!"

As Barton continued, his agitation became so vehement that the divine was shocked and even alarmed. The wild and excited rapidity with which he spoke, and, above all, the indefinable horror which stamped his features, afforded a contrast to his ordinary cool and unimpassioned self-possession, striking and painful in the last degree.

"My dear sir," said Doctor Macklin, after a brief pause, "I fear you have been suffering much, indeed; but I venture to predict that the depression under which you labour will be found to originate in purely physical causes, and that with a change of air and the aid of a few tonics, your spirits will return, and the tone of your mind be once more cheerful and tranquil as heretofore. There was, after all, more truth than we are quite willing to admit in the classic theories which assigned the undue predominance of any one affection of the mind to the undue action or torpidity of one or other of our bodily organs. Believe me, that a little attention to diet, exercise, and the other essentials of health, under competent direction, will make you as much yourself as you can wish."

"Doctor Macklin," said Barton, with something like a shudder, "I _cannot_ delude myself with such a hope. I have no hope to cling to but one, and that is, that by some other spiritual agency more potent than that which tortures me, _it_ may be combated, and I delivered. If this may not be, I am lost--now and for ever lost."

"But, Mr. Barton, you must remember," urged his companion, "that others have suffered as you have done, and--"

"No, no, no," interrupted he with irritability; "no, sir, I am not a credulous--far from a superstitious man. I have been, perhaps, too much the reverse--too sceptical, too slow of belief; but unless I were one whom no amount of evidence could convince, unless I were to contemn the repeated, the _perpetual_ evidence of my own senses, I am now--now at last constrained to believe I have no escape from the conviction, the overwhelming certainty, that I am haunted and dogged, go where I may, by--by a Demon."

There was an almost preternatural energy of horror in Barton's face, as, with its damp and death-like lineaments turned towards his companion, he thus delivered himself.

"God help you, my poor friend!" said Doctor Macklin, much shocked. "God help you; for, indeed, you _are_ a sufferer, however your sufferings may have been caused."

"Ay, ay, God help me," echoed Barton sternly; "but _will_ He help me? will He help me?"

"Pray to Him; pray in an humble and trusting spirit," said he.
"Pray, pray," echoed he again; "I can't pray; I could as easily move a mountain by an effort of my will. I have not belief enough to pray; there is something within me that will not pray. You prescribe impossibilities--literal impossibilities."

"You will not find it so, if you will but try," said Doctor Macklin.

"Try! I _have_ tried, and the attempt only fills me with confusion and terror. I have tried in vain, and more than in vain. The awful, unutterable idea of eternity and infinity oppresses and maddens my brain, whenever my mind approaches the contemplation of the Creator; I recoil from the effort, scared, confounded, terrified. I tell you, Doctor Macklin, if I am to be saved, it must be by other means. The idea of the Creator is to me intolerable; my mind cannot support it."

"Say, then, my dear sir," urged he, "say how you would have me serve you. What you would learn of me. What can I do or say to relieve you?"

"Listen to me first," replied Captain Barton, with a subdued air, and an evident effort to suppress his excitement; "listen to me while I detail the circumstances of the terrible persecution under which my life has become all but intolerable--a persecution which has made me fear _death_ and the world beyond the grave as much as I have grown to hate existence."

Barton then proceeded to relate the circumstances which we have already detailed, and then continued,--

"This has now become habitual--an accustomed thing. I do not mean the actual seeing him in the flesh; thank God, _that_ at least is not permitted daily. Thank God, from the unutterable horrors of that visitation I have been mercifully allowed intervals of repose, though none of security; but from the consciousness that a malignant spirit is following and watching me wherever I go, I have never, for a single instant, a temporary respite: I am pursued with blasphemies, cries of despair, and appalling hatred; I hear those dreadful sounds called after me as I turn the corners of streets; they come in the night-time while I sit in my chamber alone; they haunt me everywhere, charging me with hideous crimes, and--great God!--threatening me with coming vengeance and eternal misery! Hush! do you hear _that_?" he cried, with a horrible smile of triumph. "There--there, will that convince you?"

The clergyman felt the chillness of horror irresistibly steal over him, while, during the wail of a sudden gust of wind, he heard, or fancied he heard, the half articulate sounds of rage and derision mingling in their sough.

"Well, what do you think of _that_?" at length Barton cried, drawing a long breath through his teeth.

"I heard the wind," said Doctor Macklin; "what should I think of it? What is there remarkable about it?"

"The prince of the powers of the air," muttered Barton, with a shudder.

"Tut, tut! my dear sir!" said the student, with an effort to reassure himself; for though it was broad daylight, there was nevertheless something disagreeably contagious in the nervous excitement under which his visitor so obviously suffered. "You must not give way to those wild fancies: you must resist those impulses of the imagination."

"Ay, ay; 'resist the devil, and he will flee from thee,'" said Barton, in the same tone; "but _how_ resist him? Ay, there it is: there is the rub. What--_what_ am I to do? What _can_ I do?"

"My dear sir, this is fancy," said the man of folios; "you are your own tormentor."

"No, no, sir; fancy has no part in it," answered Barton, somewhat sternly. "Fancy, forsooth! Was it that made _you_, as well as me, hear, but this moment, those appalling accents of hell? Fancy, indeed! No, no."

"But you have seen this person frequently," said the ecclesiastic; "why have you not accosted or secured him? Is it not somewhat precipitate, to say no more, to assume, as you have done, the existence of preternatural agency, when, after all, everything may be easily accountable, if only proper means were taken to sift the matter."

"There are circumstances connected with this--this _appearance_," said Barton, "which it were needless to disclose, but which to _me_ are proofs of its horrible and unearthly nature. I know that the being who haunts me is not _man_. I say I _know_ this; I could prove it to your own conviction." He paused for a minute, and then added, "And as to accosting it, I dare not--I could not! When I see it I am powerless; I stand in the gaze of death, in the triumphant presence of preterhuman power and malignity; my strength, and faculties, and memory all forsake me. Oh, God! I fear, sir, you know not what you speak of. Mercy, mercy! heaven have pity on me!"

He leaned his elbow on the table, and passed his hand across his eyes, as if to exclude some image of horror, muttering the last words of the sentence he had just concluded, again and again.

"Dr. Macklin," he said, abruptly raising himself, and looking full upon the clergyman with an imploring eye, "I know you will do for me whatever may be done. You know now fully the circumstances and the nature of the mysterious agency of which I am the victim. I tell you I cannot help myself; I cannot hope to escape; I am utterly passive. I conjure you, then, to weigh my case well, and if anything may be done for me by vicarious supplication, by the intercession of the good, or by any aid or influence whatsoever, I implore of you, I adjure you in the name of the Most High, give me the benefit of that influence, deliver me from the body of this death! Strive for me; pity me! I know you will; you cannot refuse this; it is the purpose and object of my visit. Send me away with some hope, however little--some faint hope of ultimate deliverance, and I will nerve myself to endure, from hour to hour, the hideous dream into which my existence is transformed."

Doctor Macklin assured him that all he could do was to pray earnestly for him, and that so much he would not fail to do. They parted with a hurried and melancholy valediction. Barton hastened to the carriage which awaited him at the door, drew the blinds, and drove away, while Dr. Macklin returned to his chamber, to ruminate at leisure upon the strange interview which had just interrupted his studies.

It was not to be expected that Captain Barton's changed and eccentric habits should long escape remark and discussion. Various were the theories suggested to account for it. Some attributed the alteration to the pressure of secret pecuniary embarrassments; others to a repugnance to fulfil an engagement into which he was presumed to have too precipitately entered; and others, again, to the supposed incipiency of mental disease, which latter, indeed, was the most plausible, as well as the most generally received, of the hypotheses circulated in the gossip of the day.

From the very commencement of this change, at first so gradual in its advances, Miss Montague had, of course, been aware of it. The intimacy involved in their peculiar relation, as well as the near interest which it inspired, afforded, in her case, alike opportunity and motive for the successful exercise of that keen and penetrating observation peculiar to the sex. His visits became, at length, so interrupted, and his manner, while they lasted, so abstracted, strange, and agitated, that Lady Rochdale, after hinting her anxiety and her suspicions more than once, at length distinctly stated her anxiety, and pressed for an explanation. The explanation was given, and although its nature at first relieved the worst solicitudes of the old lady and her niece, yet the circumstances which attended it, and the really dreadful consequences which it obviously threatened as regarded the spirits, and, indeed, the reason, of the now wretched man who made the strange declaration, were enough, upon a little reflection, to fill their minds with perturbation and alarm.

General Montague, the young lady's father, at length arrived. He had himself slightly known Barton, some ten or twelve years previously, and being aware of his fortune and connections, was disposed to regard him as an unexceptionable and indeed a most desirable match for his daughter. He laughed at the story of Barton's supernatural visitations, and lost not a moment in calling upon his intended son-in-law.

"My dear Barton," he continued gaily, after a little conversation, "my sister tells me that you are a victim to blue devils in quite a new and original shape." Barton changed countenance, and sighed profoundly.

"Come, come; I protest this will never do," continued the General; "you are more like a man on his way to the gallows than to the altar. These devils have made quite a saint of you."

Barton made an effort to change the conversation.

"No, no, it won't do," said his visitor, laughing; "I am resolved to say out what I have to say about this magnificent mock mystery of yours. Come, you must not be angry; but, really, it is too bad to see you, at your time of life, absolutely frightened into good behaviour, like a naughty child, by a bugaboo, and, as far as I can learn, a very particularly contemptible one. Seriously, though, my dear Barton, I have been a good deal annoyed at what they tell me; but, at the same time, thoroughly convinced that there is nothing in the matter that may not be cleared up, with just a little attention and management, within a week at furthest."

"Ah, General, you do not know--" he began.

"Yes, but I do know quite enough to warrant my confidence," interrupted the soldier. "I know that all your annoyance proceeds from the occasional appearance of a certain little man in a cap and great-coat, with a red vest and bad countenance, who follows you about, and pops upon you at the corners of lanes, and throws you into ague fits. Now, my dear fellow, I'll make it my business to _catch_ this mischievous little mountebank, and either beat him into a jelly with my own hands, or have him whipped through the town at the cart's tail."

"If _you_ knew what I know," said Barton, with gloomy agitation, "you would speak very differently. Don't imagine that I am so weak and foolish as to assume, without proof the most overwhelming, the conclusion to which I have been forced. The proofs are here, locked up here." As he spoke, he tapped upon his breast, and with an anxious sigh continued to walk up and down the room.

"Well, well, Barton," said his visitor, "I'll wager a rump and a dozen I collar the ghost, and convince yourself before many days are over." He was running on in the same strain when he was suddenly arrested, and not a little shocked, by observing Barton, who had approached the window, stagger slowly back, like one who had received a stunning blow--his arm feebly extended towards the street, his face and his very lips white as ashes--while he uttered, "There--there--there!"

General Montague started mechanically to his feet, and, from the window of the drawing-room, saw a figure corresponding, as well as his hurry would permit him to discern, with the description of the person whose appearance so constantly and dreadfully disturbed the repose of his friend. The figure was just turning from the rails of the area upon which it had been leaning, and without waiting to see more, the old gentleman snatched his cane and hat, and rushed down the stairs and into the street, in the furious hope of securing the person, and punishing the audacity of the mysterious stranger. He looked around him, but in vain, for any trace of the form he had himself distinctly beheld. He ran breathlessly to the nearest corner, expecting to see from thence the retreating figure, but no such form was visible. Back and forward, from crossing to crossing, he ran at fault, and it was not until the curious gaze and laughing countenances of the passers-by reminded him of the absurdity of his pursuit, that he checked his hurried pace, lowered his walking-cane from the menacing altitude which he had mechanically given it, adjusted his hat, and walked composedly back again, inwardly vexed and flurried. He found Barton pale and trembling in every joint; they both remained silent, though under emotions very different. At last Barton whispered, "You saw it?"

"It!--him--someone--you mean--to be sure I did," replied Montague, testily. "But where is the good or the harm of seeing him? The fellow runs like a lamplighter. I wanted to _catch_ him, but he had stolen away before I could reach the hall door. However, it is no great matter; next time, I dare say, I'll do better; and, egad, if I once come within reach of him, I'll introduce his shoulders to the weight of my cane, in a way to make him cry _peccavi_."

Notwithstanding General Montague's undertakings and exhortations, however, Barton continued to suffer from the self-same unexplained cause. Go how, when, or where he would, he was still constantly dogged or confronted by the hateful being who had established over him so

dreadful and mysterious an influence; nowhere, and at no time, was he secure against the odious appearance which haunted him with such diabolical perseverance. His depression, misery, and excitement became more settled and alarming every day, and the mental agonies that ceaselessly preyed upon him began at last so sensibly to affect his general health, that Lady Rochdale and General Montague succeeded (without, indeed, much difficulty) in persuading him to try a short tour on the Continent, in the hope that an entire change of scene would, at all events, have the effect of breaking through the influences of local association, which the more sceptical of his friends assumed to be by no means inoperative in suggesting and perpetuating what they conceived to be a mere form of nervous illusion. General Montague, moreover, was persuaded that the figure which haunted his intended son-in-law was by no means the creation of his own imagination, but, on the contrary, a substantial form of flesh and blood, animated by a spiteful and obstinate resolution, perhaps with some murderous object in perspective, to watch and follow the unfortunate gentleman. Even this hypothesis was not a very pleasant one; yet it was plain that if Barton could once be convinced that there was nothing preternatural in the phenomenon, which he had hitherto regarded in that light, the affair would lose all its terrors in his eyes, and wholly cease to exercise upon his health and spirits the baneful influence which it had hitherto done. He therefore reasoned, that if the annoyance were actually escaped from by mere change of scene, it obviously could not have originated in any
supernatural agency.

Yielding to their persuasions, Barton left Dublin for England, accompanied by General Montague. They posted rapidly to London, and thence to Dover, whence they took the packet with a fair wind for Calais. The General's confidence in the result of the expedition on Barton's spirits had risen day by day since their departure from the shores of Ireland; for, to the inexpressible relief and delight of the latter, he had not, since then, so much as even once fancied a repetition of those impressions which had, when at home, drawn him gradually down to the very abyss of horror and despair. This exemption from what he had begun to regard as the inevitable condition of his existence, and the sense of security which began to pervade his mind, were inexpressibly delightful; and in the exultation of what he considered his deliverance, he indulged in a thousand happy anticipations for a future into which so lately he had hardly dared to look. In short, both he and his companion secretly congratulated themselves upon the termination of that persecution which had been to

its immediate victim a source of such unspeakable agony.
It was a beautiful day, and a crowd of idlers stood upon the jetty to receive the packet, and enjoy the bustle of the new arrivals. Montague walked a few paces in advance of his friend, and as he made his way through the crowd, a little man touched his arm, and said to him, in a broad provincial _patois_,--

"Monsieur is walking too fast; he will lose his sick comrade in the throng, for, by my faith, the poor gentleman seems to be fainting."

Montague turned quickly, and observed that Barton did indeed look deadly pale. He hastened to his side.

"My poor fellow, are you ill?" he asked anxiously.

The question was unheeded, and twice repeated, ere Barton stammered,--

"I saw him--by ----, I saw him!"

"_Him!_--who?--where?--when did you see him?--where is he?" cried Montague, looking around him.

"I saw him--but he is gone," repeated Barton, faintly.

"But where--where? For God's sake, speak," urged Montague, vehemently.

"It is but this moment--_here_," said he.

"But what did he look like?--what had he on?--what did he wear?--quick, quick," urged his excited companion, ready to dart among the crowd, and collar the delinquent on the spot.

"He touched your arm--he spoke to you--he pointed to me. God be merciful to me, there is no escape!" said Barton, in the low, subdued tones of intense despair.

Montague had already bustled away in all the flurry of mingled hope and indignation; but though the singular _personnel_ of the stranger who had accosted him was vividly and perfectly impressed upon his recollection, he failed to discover among the crowd even the slightest resemblance to him. After a fruitless search, in which he enlisted the services of several of the bystanders, who aided all the more zealously as they believed he had been robbed, he at length, out of breath and baffled, gave over the attempt.

"Ah, my friend, it won't do," said Barton, with the faint voice and bewildered, ghastly look of one who has been stunned by some mortal shock; "there is no use in contending with it; whatever it is, the dreadful association between me and it is now established; I shall never escape--never, never!"

"Nonsense, nonsense, my dear fellow; don't talk so," said Montague, with something at once of irritation and dismay; "you must not; never mind, I say--never mind, we'll jockey the scoundrel yet."

It was, however, but lost labour to endeavour henceforward to inspire Barton with one ray of hope; he became utterly desponding. This intangible and, as it seemed, utterly inadequate influence was fast destroying his energies of intellect, character, and health. His first object was now to return to Ireland, there, as he believed, and now almost hoped, speedily to die.

To Ireland, accordingly, he came, and one of the first faces he saw upon the shore was again that of his implacable and dreaded persecutor. Barton seemed at last to have lost not only all enjoyment and every hope in existence, but all independence of will besides. He now submitted himself passively to the management of the friends most nearly interested in his welfare. With the apathy of entire despair, he implicitly assented to whatever measures they suggested and advised; and, as a last resource, it was determined to remove him to a house of Lady Rochdale's in the neighbourhood of Clontarf, where, with the advice of his medical attendant (who persisted in his opinion that the whole train of impressions resulted merely from some nervous derangement) it was resolved that he was to confine himself strictly to the house, and to make use only of those apartments which commanded a view of an enclosed yard, the gates of which were to be kept jealously locked. These precautions would at least secure him against the casual appearance of any living form which his excited imagination might possibly confound with the spectre which, as it was contended, his fancy recognized in every figure that bore even a distant or general resemblance to the traits with which he had at first invested it. A month or six weeks' absolute seclusion under these conditions, it was hoped, might, by interrupting the series of these terrible impressions, gradually dispel the predisposing apprehension, and effectually break up the associations which had confirmed the supposed disease, and rendered recovery hopeless. Cheerful society and that of his friends was to be constantly supplied, and on the whole, very sanguine expectations were indulged in, that under this treatment the obstinate hypochondria of the patient might at length give way.

Accompanied, therefore, by Lady Rochdale, General Montague, and his daughter--his own affianced bride--poor Barton, himself never daring to cherish a hope of his ultimate emancipation from the strange horrors under which his life was literally wasting away, took possession of the apartments whose situation protected him against the dreadful intrusions from which he shrank with such unutterable terror.

After a little time, a steady persistence in this system began to manifest its results in a very marked though gradual improvement alike in the health and spirits of the invalid. Not, indeed, that anything at all approaching to complete recovery was yet discernible. On the contrary, to those who had not seen him since the commencement of his strange sufferings, such an alteration would have been apparent as might well have shocked them. The improvement, however, such as it was, was welcomed with gratitude and delight, especially by the poor young lady, whom her attachment to him, as well as her now singularly painful position, consequent on his mysterious and protracted illness, rendered an object of pity scarcely one degree less to be commiserated than himself.

A week passed--a fortnight--a month--and yet no recurrence of the hated visitation had agitated and terrified him as before. The treatment had, so far, been followed by complete success. The chain of association had been broken. The constant pressure upon the overtasked spirits had been removed, and, under these comparatively favourable circumstances, the sense of social community with the world about him, and something of human interest, if not of enjoyment, began to reanimate his mind.

It was about this time that Lady Rochdale, who, like most old ladies of the day, was deep in family receipts, and a great pretender to medical science, being engaged in the concoction of certain unpalatable mixtures of marvellous virtue, despatched her own maid to the kitchen garden with a list of herbs which were there to be carefully culled and brought back to her for the purpose stated. The hand-maiden, however, returned with her task scarce half-completed, and a good deal flurried and alarmed. Her mode of accounting for her precipitate retreat and evident agitation was odd, and to the old lady unpleasantly startling.

It appeared that she had repaired to the kitchen garden, pursuant to her mistress's directions, and had there begun to make the specified selection among the rank and neglected herbs which crowded one corner of the enclosure, and while engaged in this pleasant labour she carelessly sang a fragment of an old song, as she said, "to keep herself company." She was, however, interrupted by a sort of mocking echo of the air she was singing; and looking up, she saw through the old thorn hedge, which surrounded the garden, a singularly ill-looking, little man, whose countenance wore the stamp of menace and malignity, standing close to her at the other side of the hawthorn screen. She described herself as utterly unable to move or speak, while he charged her with a message for Captain Barton, the substance of which she distinctly remembered to have been to the effect that he, Captain Barton, must come abroad as usual, and show himself to his friends out of doors, or else prepare for a visit in his own chamber. On concluding this brief message, the stranger had, with a threatening air, got down into the outer ditch, and seizing the hawthorn stems in his hands, seemed on the point of climbing through the fence, a feat which might have been accomplished without much difficulty. Without, of course, awaiting this result, the girl, throwing down her treasures of thyme and rosemary, had turned and run, with the swiftness of terror, to the house. Lady Rochdale commanded her, on pain of instant dismissal, to observe an absolute silence respecting all that portion of the incident which related to Captain Barton; and, at the same time, directed instant search to be made by her men in the garden and fields adjacent. This measure, however, was attended with the usual unsuccess, and filled with fearful and indefinable misgivings, Lady Rochdale communicated the incident to her brother. The story, however, until long afterwards, went no further, and of course it was jealously guarded from Barton, who continued to mend, though slowly and imperfectly.

Barton now began to walk occasionally in the courtyard which we have mentioned, and which, being surrounded by a high wall, commanded no view beyond its own extent. Here he, therefore, considered himself perfectly secure; and, but for a careless violation of orders by one of the grooms, he might have enjoyed, at least for some time longer, his much-prized immunity. Opening upon the public road, this yard was entered by a wooden gate, with a wicket in it, which was further defended by an iron gate upon the outside. Strict orders had been given to keep them carefully locked; but, in spite of these, it had happened that one day, as Barton was slowly pacing this narrow enclosure, in his accustomed walk, and reaching the further extremity, was turning to retrace his steps, he saw the boarded wicket ajar, and the face of his tormentor immovably looking at him through the iron bars. For a few seconds he stood riveted to the earth, breathless and bloodless, in the fascination of that dreaded gaze, and then fell helplessly upon the pavement.

There was he found a few minutes afterwards, and conveyed to his room, the apartment which he was never afterwards to leave alive. Henceforward, a marked and unaccountable change was observable in the tone of his mind. Captain Barton was now no longer the excited and despairing man he had been before; a strange alteration had passed upon him, an unearthly tranquillity reigned in his mind; it was the anticipated stillness of the grave.

"Montague, my friend, this struggle is nearly ended now," he said, tranquilly, but with a look of fixed and fearful awe. "I have, at last, some comfort from that world of spirits, from which my _punishment_ has come. I know now that my sufferings will be soon over."

Montague pressed him to speak on.

"Yes," said he, in a softened voice, "my punishment is nearly ended. From sorrow perhaps I shall never, in time or eternity, escape; but my _agony_ is almost over. Comfort has been revealed to me, and what remains of my allotted struggle I will bear with submission, even with hope."

"I am glad to hear you speak so tranquilly, my dear fellow," said Montague; "peace and cheerfulness of mind are all you need to make you what you were."

"No, no, I never can be that," said he, mournfully. "I am no longer fit for life. I am soon to die: I do not shrink from death as I did. I am to see _him_ but once again, and then all is ended."

"He said so, then?" suggested Montague.

"_He?_ No, no; good tidings could scarcely come through him; and these were good and welcome; and they came so solemnly and sweetly, with unutterable love and melancholy, such as I could not, without saying more than is needful or fitting, of other long-past scenes and persons, fully explain to you." As Barton said this he shed tears.

"Come, come," said Montague, mistaking the source of his emotions, "you must not give way. What is it, after all, but a pack of dreams and nonsense; or, at worst, the practices of a scheming rascal that enjoys his power of playing upon your nerves, and loves to exert it; a sneaking vagabond that owes you a grudge, and pays it off this way, not daring to try a more manly one."

"A grudge, indeed, he owes me; you say rightly," said Barton, with a sullen shudder; "a grudge as you call it. Oh, God! when the justice of heaven permits the Evil One to carry out a scheme of vengeance, when its execution is committed to the lost and frightful victim of sin, who owes his own ruin to the man, the very man, whom he is commissioned to pursue; then, indeed, the torments and terrors of hell are anticipated on earth. But heaven has dealt mercifully with me: hope has opened to me at last; and if death could come without the dreadful sight I am doomed to see, I would gladly close my eyes this moment upon the world. But though death is welcome, I shrink with an agony you cannot understand; a maddening agony, an actual frenzy of terror, from the last encounter with that--that DEMON, who has drawn me thus to the verge of the chasm, and who is himself to plunge me down. I am to see him again, once more, but under circumstances unutterably more terrific than ever."

As Barton thus spoke, he trembled so violently that Montague was really alarmed at the extremity of his sudden agitation, and hastened to lead him back to the topic which had before seemed to exert so tranquillizing an effect upon his mind.

"It was not a dream," he said, after a time; "I was in a different state, I felt differently and strangely; and yet it was all as real, as clear and vivid, as what I now see and hear; it was a reality."

"And what _did_ you see and hear?" urged his companion.

"When I awakened from the swoon I fell into on seeing _him_," said Barton, continuing, as if he had not heard the question, "it was slowly, very slowly; I was reclining by the margin of a broad lake, surrounded by misty hills, and a soft, melancholy, rose-coloured light illuminated it all. It was indescribably sad and lonely, and yet more beautiful than any earthly scene. My head was leaning on the lap of a girl, and she was singing a strange and wondrous song, that told, I know not how, whether by words or harmony, of all my life, all that is past, and all that is still to come. And with the song the old feelings that I thought had perished within me came back, and tears flowed from my eyes, partly for the song and its mysterious beauty, and partly for the unearthly sweetness of her voice; yet I know the voice, oh! how well; and I was spell-bound as I listened and looked at the strange and solitary scene, without stirring, almost without breathing, and, alas! alas! without turning my eyes toward the face that I knew was near me, so sweetly powerful was the enchantment that held me. And so, slowly and softly, the song and scene grew fainter, and ever fainter, to my senses, till all was dark and still again. And then I wakened to this world, as you saw, comforted, for I knew that I was forgiven much." Barton wept again long and bitterly.

From this time, as we have said, the prevailing tone of his mind was one of profound and tranquil melancholy. This, however, was not without its interruptions. He was thoroughly impressed with the conviction that he was to experience another and a final visitation, illimitably transcending in horror all he had before experienced. From this anticipated and unknown agony he often shrunk in such paroxysms of abject terror and distraction, as filled the whole household with dismay and superstitious panic. Even those among them who affected to discredit the supposition of preternatural agency in the matter, were often in their secret souls visited during the darkness and solitude of night with qualms and apprehensions which they would not have readily confessed; and none of them attempted to dissuade Barton from the resolution on which he now systematically acted, of shutting himself up in his own apartment. The window-blinds of this room were kept jealously down; and his own man was seldom out of his presence, day or night, his bed being placed in the same chamber.

This man was an attached and respectable servant; and his duties, in addition to those ordinarily imposed upon _valets_, but which Barton's independent habits generally dispensed with, were to attend carefully to the simple precautions by means of which his master hoped to exclude the dreaded intrusion of the "Watcher," as the strange letter he had at first received had designated his persecutor. And, in addition to attending to these arrangements, which consisted merely in anticipating the possibility of his master's being, through any unscreened window or opened door, exposed to the dreaded influence, the valet was never to suffer him to be for one moment alone: total solitude, even for a minute, had become to him now almost as intolerable as the idea of going abroad into the public ways; it was an instinctive anticipation of what was coming.

It is needless to say, that, under these mysterious and horrible circumstances, no steps were taken toward the fulfilment of that engagement into which he had entered. There was quite disparity enough in point of years, and indeed of habits, between the young lady and Captain Barton, to have precluded anything like very vehement or romantic attachment on her part. Though grieved and anxious, therefore, she was very far from being heart-broken; a circumstance which, for the sentimental purposes of our tale, is much to be deplored. But truth must be told, especially in a narrative whose chief, if not only, pretensions to interest consist in a rigid adherence to facts, or what are so reported to have been.

Miss Montague, nevertheless, devoted much of her time to a patient but fruitless attempt to cheer the unhappy invalid. She read for him, and conversed with him; but it was apparent that whatever exertions he made, the endeavour to escape from the one constant and ever-present fear that preyed upon him was utterly and miserably unavailing.

Young ladies, as all the world knows, are much given to the cultivation of pets; and among those who shared the favour of Miss Montague was a fine old owl, which the gardener, who caught him napping among the ivy of a ruined stable, had dutifully presented to that young lady.

The caprice which regulates such preferences was manifested in the extravagant favour with which this grim and ill-favoured bird was at once distinguished by his mistress; and, trifling as this whimsical circumstance may seem, I am forced to mention it, inasmuch as it is connected, oddly enough, with the concluding scene of the story. Barton, so far from sharing in this liking for the new favourite, regarded it from the first with an antipathy as violent as it was utterly unaccountable. Its very vicinity was insupportable to him. He seemed to hate and dread it with a vehemence absolutely laughable, and to those who have never witnessed the exhibition of antipathies of this kind, his dread would seem all but incredible.

With these few words of preliminary explanation, I shall proceed to state the particulars of the last scene in this strange series of incidents. It was almost two o'clock one winter's night, and Barton was, as usual at that hour, in his bed; the servant we have mentioned occupied a smaller bed in the same room, and a candle was burning. The man was on a sudden aroused by his master, who said,--

"I can't get it out of my head that that accursed bird has escaped somehow, and is lurking in some corner of the room. I have been dreaming of him. Get up, Smith, and look about; search for him. Such hateful dreams!"

The servant rose, and examined the chamber, and while engaged in so doing, he heard the well-known sound, more like a long-drawn gasp than a hiss, with which these birds from their secret haunts affright the quiet of the night. This ghostly indication of its proximity, for the sound proceeded from the passage upon which Barton's chamber-door opened, determined the search of the servant, who, opening the door, proceeded a step or two forward for the purpose of driving the bird away. He had, however, hardly entered the lobby, when the door behind him slowly swung to under the impulse, as it seemed, of some gentle current of air; but as immediately over the door there was a kind of window, intended in the daytime to aid in lighting the passage, and through which the rays of the candle were then issuing, the valet could see quite enough for his purpose. As he advanced he heard his master (who, lying in a well-curtained bed had not, as it seemed, perceived his exit from the room) call him by name, and direct him to place the candle on the table by his bed. The servant, who was now some way in the long passage, did not like to raise his voice for the purpose of replying, lest he should startle the sleeping inmates of the house, began to walk hurriedly and softly back again, when, to his amazement, he heard a voice in the interior of the chamber answering calmly, and the man actually saw, through the window which over-topped the door, that the light was slowly shifting, as if carried across the chamber in answer to his master's call. Palsied by a feeling akin to terror, yet not unmingled with a horrible curiosity, he stood breathless and listening at the threshold, unable to summon resolution to push open the door and enter. Then came a rustling of the curtains, and a sound like that of one who in a low voice hushes a child to rest, in the midst of which he heard Barton say, in a tone of stifled horror--"Oh, God--oh, my God!" and repeat the same exclamation several times. Then ensued a silence, which again was broken by the same strange soothing sound; and at last there burst forth, in one swelling peal, a yell of agony so appalling and hideous, that, under some impulse of ungovernable horror, the man rushed to the door, and with his whole strength strove to force it open. Whether it was that, in his agitation, he had himself but imperfectly turned the handle, or that the door was really secured upon the inside, he failed to effect an entrance; and as he tugged and pushed, yell after yell rang louder and wilder through the chamber, accompanied all the while by the same hushing sounds. Actually freezing with terror, and scarce knowing what he did, the man turned and ran down the passage, wringing his hands in the extremity of horror and irresolution. At the stair-head he was encountered by General Montague, scared and eager, and just as they met the fearful sounds had ceased.

"What is it?--who--where is your master?" said Montague, with the incoherence of extreme agitation. "Has anything--for God's sake, is anything wrong?"

"Lord have mercy on us, it's all over," said the man, staring wildly towards his master's chamber. "He's dead, sir; I'm sure he's dead."

Without waiting for inquiry or explanation, Montague, closely followed by the servant, hurried to the chamber-door, turned the handle, and pushed it open. As the door yielded to his pressure, the ill-omened bird of which the servant had been in search, uttering its spectral warning, started suddenly from the far side of the bed, and flying through the doorway close over their heads, and extinguishing, in its passage, the candle which Montague carried, crashed through the skylight that overlooked the lobby, and sailed away into the darkness of the outer space.

"There it is, God bless us!" whispered the man, after a breathless pause.

"Curse that bird!" muttered the general, startled by the suddenness of the apparition, and unable to conceal his discomposure.

"The candle was moved," said the man, after another breathless pause; "see, they put it by the bed!"

"Draw the curtains, fellow, and don't stand gaping there," whispered Montague, sternly.

The man hesitated.

"Hold this, then," said Montague, impatiently, thrusting the candlestick into the servant's hand; and himself advancing to the bedside, he drew the curtains apart. The light of the candle, which was still burning at the bedside, fell upon a figure huddled together, and half upright, at the head of the bed. It seemed as though it had shrunk back as far as the solid panelling would allow, and the hands were still clutched in the bed-clothes.

"Barton, Barton, Barton!" cried the general, with a strange mixture of awe and vehemence.

He took the candle, and held it so that it shone full upon his face. The features were fixed, stern and white; the jaw was fallen, and the sightless eyes, still open, gazed vacantly forward toward the front of the bed.

"God Almighty, he's dead!" muttered the general, as he looked upon this fearful spectacle. They both continued to gaze upon it in silence for a minute or more. "And cold, too," said Montague, withdrawing his hand from that of the dead man.

"And see, see; may I never have life, sir," added the man, after another pause, with a shudder, "but there was something else on the bed with him! Look there--look there; see that, sir!"

As the man thus spoke, he pointed to a deep indenture, as if caused by a heavy pressure, near the foot of the bed.

Montague was silent.

"Come, sir, come away, for God's sake!" whispered the man, drawing close up to him, and holding fast by his arm, while he glanced fearfully round; "what good can be done here now?--come away, for God's sake!"

At this moment they heard the steps of more than one approaching, and Montague, hastily desiring the servant to arrest their progress, endeavoured to loose the rigid grip with which the fingers of the dead man were clutched in the bed-clothes, and drew, as well as he was able, the awful figure into a reclining posture. Then closing the curtains carefully upon it, he hastened himself to meet those who were approaching.

* * * * *

It is needless to follow the personages so slightly connected with this narrative into the events of their after lives; it is enough for us to remark that no clue to the solution of these mysterious occurrences was ever afterwards discovered; and so long an interval having now passed, it is scarcely to be expected that time can throw any new light upon their inexplicable obscurity. Until the secrets of the earth shall be no longer hidden these transactions must remain shrouded in mystery.

The only occurrence in Captain Barton's former life to which reference was ever made, as having any possible connection with the sufferings with which his existence closed, and which he himself seemed to regard as working out a retribution for some grievous sin of his past life, was a circumstance which not for several years after his death was brought to light. The nature of this disclosure was painful to his relatives and discreditable to his memory.

It appeared, then, that some eight years before Captain Barton's final return to Dublin, he had formed, in the town of Plymouth, a guilty attachment, the object of which was the daughter of one of the ship's crew under his command. The father had visited the frailty of his unhappy child with extreme harshness, and even brutality, and it was said that she had died heart-broken. Presuming upon Barton's implication in her guilt, this man had conducted himself towards him with marked insolence, and Barton resented this--and what he resented with still more exasperated bitterness, his treatment of the unfortunate girl—by a systematic exercise of those terrible and arbitrary severities with which the regulations of the navy arm those who are responsible for its discipline. The man had at length made his escape, while the vessel was in port at Lisbon, but died, as it was said, in an hospital in that town, of the wounds inflicted in one of his recent and sanguinary punishments.

Whether these circumstances in reality bear or not upon the occurrences of Barton's after-life, it is of course impossible to say. It seems, however, more than probable that they were, at least in his own mind, closely associated with them. But however the truth may be as to the origin and motives of this mysterious persecution, there can be no doubt that, with respect to the agencies by which it was accomplished, absolute and impenetrable mystery is like to prevail until the day of doom.

# PASSAGE IN THE SECRET HISTORY OF AN IRISH COUNTESS (1894)

The following paper is written in a female hand, and was no doubt communicated to my much regretted friend by the lady whose early history it serves to illustrate, the Countess D----. She is no more--she long since died, a childless and a widowed wife, and, as her letter sadly predicts, none survive to whom the publication of this narrative can prove "injurious, or even painful." Strange! two powerful and wealthy families, that in which she was born, and that into which she had married, are utterly extinct.

To those who know anything of the history of Irish families, as they were less than a century ago, the facts which immediately follow will at once suggest the names of the principal actors; and to others their publication would be useless--to us, possibly, if not probably injurious. I have therefore altered such of the names as might, if stated, get us into difficulty; others, belonging to minor characters in the strange story, I have left untouched.

* * * * *

MY DEAR FRIEND,--You have asked me to furnish you with a detail of the strange events which marked my early history, and I have, without hesitation, applied myself to the task, knowing that, while I live, a kind consideration for my feelings will prevent you giving publicity to the statement; and conscious that, when I am no more, there will not survive one to whom the narrative can prove injurious, or even painful.

My mother died when I was quite an infant, and of her I have no recollection, even the faintest. By her death, my education and habits were left solely to the guidance of my surviving parent; and, so far as a stern attention to my religious instruction, and an active anxiety evinced by his procuring for me the best masters to perfect me in those accomplishments which my station and wealth might seem to require, could avail, he amply discharged the task.

My father was what is called an oddity, and his treatment of me, though uniformly kind, flowed less from affection and tenderness than from a sense of obligation and duty. Indeed, I seldom even spoke to him except at meal-times, and then his manner was silent and abrupt; his leisure hours, which were many, were passed either in his study or in solitary walks; in short, he seemed to take no further interest in my happiness or improvement than a conscientious regard to the discharge of his own duty would seem to claim.

Shortly before my birth, a circumstance had occurred which had contributed much to form and to confirm my father's secluded habits--it was the fact that a suspicion of murder had fallen upon his younger brother, a suspicion not sufficiently definite to lead to an indictment, yet strong enough to ruin him in public opinion.

This disgraceful and dreadful doubt cast upon the family name my father felt deeply and bitterly, and not the less so that he himself was thoroughly convinced of his brother's innocence. The sincerity and strength of this impression he shortly afterwards proved in a manner which produced the dark events which follow. Before, however, I enter upon the statement of them, I ought to relate the circumstances which had awakened the suspicion; inasmuch as they are in themselves somewhat curious, and, in their effects, most intimately connected with my after history.

My uncle, Sir Arthur T----n, was a gay and extravagant man, and, among other vices, was ruinously addicted to gaming; this unfortunate propensity, even after his fortune had suffered so severely as to render inevitable a reduction in his expenses by no means inconsiderable, nevertheless continued to actuate him, almost to the exclusion of all other pursuits. He was a proud, or rather a vain man, and could not bear to make the diminution of his income a matter of gratulation and triumph to those with whom he had hitherto competed; and the consequence was that he frequented no longer the expensive haunts of dissipation, and retired from the gay world, leaving his coterie to discover his reasons as best they might.
He did not, however, forego his favourite vice, for, though he could not worship his divinity in the costly temples where it was formerly his wont to take his stand, yet he found it very possible to bring about him a sufficient number of the votaries of chance to answer all his ends.
The consequence was that Carrickleigh, which was the name of my uncle's residence, was never without one or more of such reckless visitors.

It happened that upon one occasion he was visited by one Hugh Tisdall—a gentleman of loose habits but of considerable wealth--who had, in early youth, travelled with my uncle upon the Continent. The period of his visit was winter, and, consequently, the house was nearly deserted except by its regular inmates; Mr. Tisdall was therefore highly acceptable, particularly as my uncle was aware that his visitor's tastes accorded exactly with his own.

Both parties seemed determined to avail themselves of their suitability during the brief stay which Mr. Tisdall had promised; the consequence was that they shut themselves up in Sir Arthur's private room for nearly all the day and the greater part of the night, during the space of nearly a week. At the end of this period the servant having one morning, as usual, knocked at Mr. Tisdall's bedroom door repeatedly, received no answer, and, upon attempting to enter, found that it was locked. This appeared suspicious, and the inmates of the house having been alarmed, the door was forced open, and, on proceeding to the bed, they found the body of its occupant perfectly lifeless, and hanging half-way out, the head downwards, and near the floor. One deep wound had been inflicted upon the temple, apparently with some blunt instrument, which had penetrated the brain; and another blow less effective, probably the first aimed, had grazed the head, removing some of the scalp, but leaving the skull untouched. The door had been double-locked upon the inside, in evidence of which the key still lay where it had been placed in the lock.

The window, though not secured on the interior, was closed--a circumstance not a little puzzling, as it afforded the only other mode of escape from the room; it looked out, too, upon a kind of courtyard, round which the old buildings stood, formerly accessible by a narrow doorway and passage lying in the oldest side of the quadrangle, but which had since been built up, so as to preclude all ingress or egress. The room was also upon the second story, and the height of the window considerable. Near the bed were found a pair of razors belonging to the murdered man, one of them upon the ground and both of them open. The weapon which had inflicted the mortal wound was not to be found in the room, nor were any footsteps or other traces of the murderer discoverable.

At the suggestion of Sir Arthur himself, a coroner was instantly summoned to attend, and an inquest was held; nothing, however, in any degree conclusive was elicited. The walls, ceiling, and floor of the room were carefully examined in order to ascertain whether they contained a trap-door or other concealed mode of entrance--but no such thing appeared.

Such was the minuteness of investigation employed that although the grate had contained a large fire during the night, they proceeded to examine even the very chimney, in order to discover whether escape by it were possible; but this attempt, too, was fruitless, for the chimney, built in the old fashion, rose in a perfectly perpendicular line from the hearth to a height of nearly fourteen feet above the roof, affording in its interior scarcely the possibility of ascent, the flue being smoothly plastered, and sloping towards the top like an inverted funnel. Even if the summit of the chimney were attained, it promised, owing to its great height, but a precarious descent upon the sharp and steep-ridged roof. The ashes, too, which lay in the grate, and the soot, as far as it could be seen, were undisturbed, a circumstance almost conclusive.

Sir Arthur was of course examined; his evidence was given with a clearness and unreserve which seemed calculated to silence all suspicion. He stated that up to the day and night immediately preceding the catastrophe, he had lost to a heavy amount, but that, at their last sitting, he had not only won back his original loss, but upwards of four thousand pounds in addition; in evidence of which he produced an acknowledgment of debt to that amount in the handwriting of the deceased, and bearing the date of the fatal night. He had mentioned the circumstance to his lady, and in presence of some of the domestics; which statement was supported by their respective evidence.
One of the jury shrewdly observed that the circumstance of Mr. Tisdall's having sustained so heavy a loss might have suggested to some ill-minded persons, accidentally hearing it, the plan of robbing him, after having murdered him, in such a manner as might make it appear that he had committed suicide; a supposition which was strongly supported by the razors having been found thus displaced, and removed from their case. Two persons had probably been engaged in the attempt, one watching by the sleeping man, and ready to strike him in case of his awakening suddenly, while the other was procuring the razors and employed in inflicting the fatal gash, so as to make it appear to have been the act of the murdered man himself. It was said that while the juror was making this suggestion Sir Arthur changed colour.

Nothing, however, like legal evidence appeared against him, and the consequence was that the verdict was found against a person or persons unknown; and for some time the matter was suffered to rest, until, after about five months, my father received a letter from a person signing himself Andrew Collis, and representing himself to be the cousin of the deceased. This letter stated that Sir Arthur was likely to incur not merely suspicion, but personal risk, unless he could account for certain circumstances connected with the recent murder, and contained a copy of a letter written by the deceased, and bearing date--the day of the week, and of the month--upon the night the deed of blood had been perpetrated. Tisdall's note ran as follows:--

"DEAR COLLIS,--I have had sharp work with Sir Arthur; he tried some of his stale tricks, but soon found that _I_ was Yorkshire too; it would not do--you understand me. We went to the work like good ones, head, heart and soul; and, in fact, since I came here, I have lost no time. I am rather fagged, but I am sure to be well paid for my hardship; I never want sleep so long as I can have the music of a dice-box, and wherewithal to pay the piper. As I told you, he tried some of his queer turns, but I foiled him like a man, and, in return, gave him more than he could relish of the genuine _dead knowledge_.

"In short, I have plucked the old baronet as never baronet was plucked before; I have scarce left him the stump of a quill; I have got promissory notes in his hand to the amount of--if you like round numbers, say, thirty thousand pounds, safely deposited in my portable strong-box, _alias_ double-clasped pocket-book. I leave this ruinous old rat-hole early on to-morrow, for two reasons--first, I do not want to play with Sir Arthur deeper than I think his security, that is, his money, or his money's worth, would warrant; and, secondly, because I am safer a hundred miles from Sir Arthur than in the house with him. Look you, my worthy, I tell you this between ourselves--I may be wrong, but, by G----, I am as sure as that I am now living, that Sir A---- attempted to poison me last night. So much for old friendship on both sides!

"When I won the last stake, a heavy one enough, my friend leant his forehead upon his hands, and you'll laugh when I tell you that his head literally smoked like a hot dumpling. I do not know whether his agitation was produced by the plan which he had against me, or by his having lost so heavily--though it must be allowed that he had reason to be a little funked, whichever way his thoughts went; but he pulled the bell, and ordered two bottles of champagne. While the fellow was bringing them he drew out a promissory note to the full amount, which he signed, and, as the man came in with the bottles and glasses, he desired him to be off; he filled out a glass for me, and, while he thought my eyes were off, for I was putting up his note at the time, he dropped something slyly into it, no doubt to sweeten it; but I saw it all, and when he handed it to me, I said, with an emphasis which he might or might not understand:

"'There is some sediment in this; I'll not drink it.'

"'Is there?' said he, and at the same time snatched it from my hand and threw it into the fire. What do you think of that? have I not a tender chicken to manage? Win or lose, I will not play beyond five thousand to-night, and to-morrow sees me safe out of the reach of Sir Arthur's champagne. So, all things considered, I think you must allow that you are not the last who have found a knowing boy in

"Yours to command,
"HUGH TISDALL."

Of the authenticity of this document I never heard my father express a doubt; and I am satisfied that, owing to his strong conviction in favour of his brother, he would not have admitted it without sufficient inquiry, inasmuch as it tended to confirm the suspicions which already existed to his prejudice.

Now, the only point in this letter which made strongly against my uncle was the mention of the "double-clasped pocket-book" as the receptacle of the papers likely to involve him, for this pocket-book was not forthcoming, nor anywhere to be found, nor had any papers referring to his gaming transactions been found upon the dead man. However, whatever might have been the original intention of this Collis, neither my uncle nor my father ever heard more of him; but he published the letter in Faulkner's Newspaper, which was shortly afterwards made the vehicle of a much more mysterious attack. The passage in that periodical to which I allude appeared about four years afterwards, and while the fatal occurrence was still fresh in public recollection. It commenced by a rambling preface, stating that "a _certain person_ whom _certain_ persons thought to be dead, was not so, but living, and in full possession of his memory, and moreover ready and able to make _great_ delinquents tremble." It then went on to describe the murder, without, however, mentioning names; and in doing so, it entered into minute and circumstantial particulars of which none but an _eye-witness_ could have been possessed, and by implications almost too unequivocal to be regarded in the light of insinuation, to involve the "_titled gambler_" in the guilt of the transaction.

My father at once urged Sir Arthur to proceed against the paper in an action of libel; but he would not hear of it, nor consent to my father's taking any legal steps whatever in the matter. My father, however, wrote in a threatening tone to Faulkner, demanding a surrender of the author of the obnoxious article. The answer to this application is still in my possession, and is penned in an apologetic tone: it states that the manuscript had been handed in, paid for, and inserted as an advertisement, without sufficient inquiry, or any knowledge as to whom it referred.

No step, however, was taken to clear my uncle's character in the judgment of the public; and as he immediately sold a small property, the application of the proceeds of which was known to none, he was said to have disposed of it to enable himself to buy off the threatened information. However the truth might have been, it is certain that no charges respecting the mysterious murder were afterwards publicly made against my uncle, and, as far as external disturbances were concerned, he enjoyed henceforward perfect security and quiet.

A deep and lasting impression, however, had been made upon the public mind, and Sir Arthur T----n was no longer visited or noticed by the gentry and aristocracy of the county, whose attention and courtesies he had hitherto received. He accordingly affected to despise these enjoyments which he could not procure, and shunned even that society which he might have commanded.

This is all that I need recapitulate of my uncle's history, and I now recur to my own. Although my father had never, within my recollection, visited, or been visited by, my uncle, each being of sedentary, procrastinating, and secluded habits, and their respective residences being very far apart--the one lying in the county of Galway, the other in that of Cork--he was strongly attached to his brother, and evinced his affection by an active correspondence, and by deeply and proudly resenting that neglect which had marked Sir Arthur as unfit to mix in society.

When I was about eighteen years of age, my father, whose health had been gradually declining, died, leaving me in heart wretched and desolate, and, owing to his previous seclusion, with few acquaintances, and almost no friends.

The provisions of his will were curious, and when I had sufficiently come to myself to listen to or comprehend them, surprised me not a little: all his vast property was left to me, and to the heirs of my body, for ever; and, in default of such heirs, it was to go after my death to my uncle, Sir Arthur, without any entail.

At the same time, the will appointed him my guardian, desiring that I might be received within his house, and reside with his family, and under his care, during the term of my minority; and in consideration of the increased expense consequent upon such an arrangement, a handsome annuity was allotted to him during the term of my proposed residence.

The object of this last provision I at once understood: my father desired, by making it the direct, apparent interest of Sir Arthur that I should die without issue, while at the same time placing me wholly in his power, to prove to the world how great and unshaken was his confidence in his brother's innocence and honour, and also to afford him an opportunity of showing that this mark of confidence was not unworthily bestowed.

It was a strange, perhaps an idle scheme; but as I had been always brought up in the habit of considering my uncle as a deeply-injured man, and had been taught, almost as a part of my religion, to regard him as the very soul of honour, I felt no further uneasiness respecting the arrangement than that likely to result to a timid girl of secluded habits from the immediate prospect of taking up her abode for the first time in her life among total strangers. Previous to leaving my home, which I felt I should do with a heavy heart, I received a most tender and affectionate letter from my uncle, calculated, if anything could do so, to remove the bitterness of parting from scenes familiar and dear from my earliest childhood, and in some degree to reconcile me to the change.

It was during a fine autumn that I approached the old domain of Carrickleigh. I shall not soon forget the impression of sadness and of gloom which all that I saw produced upon my mind; the sunbeams were falling with a rich and melancholy tint upon the fine old trees, which stood in lordly groups, casting their long, sweeping shadows over rock and sward. There was an air of desolation and decay about the spot, which amounted almost to desolation; the symptoms of this increased in number as we approached the building itself, near which the ground had been originally more artificially and carefully cultivated than elsewhere, and the neglect consequently more immediately and strikingly betrayed itself.

As we proceeded, the road wound near the beds of what had been formerly two fish-ponds--now nothing more than stagnant swamps, overgrown with rank weeds, and here and there encroached upon by the straggling underwood. The avenue itself was much broken, and in many places the stones were almost concealed by grass and nettles; the loose stone walls which had here and there intersected the broad park were, in many places, broken down, so as no longer to answer their original purpose as fences; piers were now and then to be seen, but the gates were gone. And, to add to the general air of dilapidation, some huge trunks were lying scattered through the venerable old trees, either the work of the winter storms, or perhaps the victims of some extensive but desultory scheme of denudation, which the projector had not capital or perseverance to carry into full effect.

After the carriage had travelled a mile of this avenue, we reached the summit of rather an abrupt eminence, one of the many which added to the picturesqueness, if not to the convenience of this rude passage. From the top of this ridge the grey walls of Carrickleigh were visible, rising at a small distance in front, and darkened by the hoary wood which crowded around them. It was a quadrangular building of considerable extent, and the front which lay towards us, and in which the great entrance was placed, bore unequivocal marks of antiquity; the time-worn, solemn aspect of the old building, the ruinous and deserted appearance of the whole place, and the associations which connected it with a dark page in the history of my family, combined to depress spirits already predisposed for the reception of sombre and dejecting impressions.

When the carriage drew up in the grass-grown courtyard before the hall door, two lazy-looking men, whose appearance well accorded with that of the place which they tenanted, alarmed by the obstreperous barking of a great chained dog, ran out from some half-ruinous out-houses, and took charge of the horses; the hall door stood open, and I entered a gloomy and imperfectly lighted apartment, and found no one within. However, I had not long to wait in this awkward predicament, for before my luggage had been deposited in the house--indeed, before I had well removed my cloak and other wraps, so as to enable me to look around--a young girl ran lightly into the hall, and kissing me heartily, and somewhat boisterously, exclaimed:

"My dear cousin, my dear Margaret, I am so delighted, so out of breath. We did not expect you till ten o'clock; my father is somewhere about the place; he must be close at hand. James, Corney--run out and tell your master--my brother is seldom at home, at least at any reasonable hour--you must be so tired, so fatigued, let me show you to your room. See that Lady Margaret's luggage is all brought up, you must lie down and rest yourself. Deborah, bring some coffee-- Up these stairs! We are so delighted to see you, you cannot think how lonely I have been. How steep these stairs are, are they not? I am so glad you are come; I could hardly bring myself to believe that you were really coming; how good of you, dear Lady Margaret."

There was real good nature and delight in my cousin's greeting, and a kind of constitutional confidence of manner which placed me at once at ease, and made me feel immediately upon terms of intimacy with her. The room into which she ushered me, although partaking in the general air of decay which pervaded the mansion and all about it, had nevertheless been fitted up with evident attention to comfort, and even with some dingy attempt at luxury; but what pleased me most was that it opened, by a second door, upon a lobby which communicated with my fair cousin's apartment; a circumstance which divested the room, in my eyes, of the air of solitude and sadness which would otherwise have characterized it, to a degree almost painful to one so dejected in spirits as I was.

After such arrangements as I found necessary were completed, we both went down to the parlour, a large wainscoted room, hung round with grim old portraits, and, as I was not sorry to see, containing in its ample grate a large and cheerful fire. Here my cousin had leisure to talk more at ease; and from her I learned something of the manners and the habits of the two remaining members of her family, whom I had not yet seen.

On my arrival I had known nothing of the family among whom I was come to reside, except that it consisted of three individuals, my uncle, and his son and daughter, Lady T----n having been long dead. In

addition to this very scanty stock of information, I shortly learned from my communicative companion that my uncle was, as I had suspected, completely reserved in his habits, and besides that, having been so far back as she could well recollect, always rather strict (as reformed rakes frequently become), he had latterly been growing more gloomily and sternly religious than heretofore.
Her account of her brother was far less favourable, though she did not say anything directly to his disadvantage. From all that I could gather from her, I was led to suppose that he was a specimen of the idle, coarse-mannered, profligate, low-minded "squire-archy"--a result which might naturally have flowed from the circumstance of his being, as it were, outlawed from society, and driven for companionship to grades below his own; enjoying, too, the dangerous prerogative of spending much money.

However, you may easily suppose that I found nothing in my cousin's communication fully to bear me out in so very decided a conclusion.

I awaited the arrival of my uncle, which was every moment to be expected, with feelings half of alarm, half of curiosity--a sensation which I have often since experienced, though to a less degree, when upon the point of standing for the first time in the presence of one of whom I have long been in the habit of hearing or thinking with interest.

It was, therefore, with some little perturbation that I heard, first a light bustle at the outer door, then a slow step traverse the hall, and finally witnessed the door open, and my uncle enter the room. He was a striking-looking man; from peculiarities both of person and of garb, the whole effect of his appearance amounted to extreme singularity. He was tall, and when young his figure must have been strikingly elegant; as it was, however, its effect was marred by a very decided stoop. His dress was of a sober colour, and in fashion anterior to anything which I could remember. It was, however, handsome, and by no means carelessly put on. But what completed the singularity of his appearance was his uncut white hair, which hung in long, but not at all neglected curls, even so far as his shoulders, and which combined with his regularly classic features and fine dark eyes, to bestow upon him an air of venerable dignity and pride which I have never seen equalled elsewhere. I rose as he entered, and met him about the middle of the room; he kissed my cheek and both my hands, saying:

"You are most welcome, dear child, as welcome as the command of this poor place and all that it contains can make you. I am most rejoiced to see you--truly rejoiced. I trust that you are not much fatigued--pray be seated again." He led me to my chair, and continued: "I am glad to perceive you have made acquaintance with Emily already; I see, in your being thus brought together, the foundation of a lasting friendship. You are both innocent, and both young. God bless you--God bless you, and make you all that I could wish!"

He raised his eyes, and remained for a few moments silent, as if in secret prayer. I felt that it was impossible that this man, with feelings so quick, so warm, so tender, could be the wretch that public opinion had represented him to be. I was more than ever convinced of his innocence.

His manner was, or appeared to me, most fascinating; there was a mingled kindness and courtesy in it which seemed to speak benevolence itself. It was a manner which I felt cold art could never have taught; it owed most of its charm to its appearing to emanate directly from the heart; it must be a genuine index of the owner's mind. So I thought.

My uncle having given me fully to understand that I was most welcome, and might command whatever was his own, pressed me to take some refreshment; and on my refusing, he observed that previously to bidding me good-night, he had one duty further to perform, one in whose observance he was convinced I would cheerfully acquiesce.

He then proceeded to read a chapter from the Bible; after which he took his leave with the same affectionate kindness with which he had greeted me, having repeated his desire that I should consider everything in his house as altogether at my disposal. It is needless to say that I was much pleased with my uncle--it was impossible to avoid being so; and I could not help saying to myself, if such a man as this is not safe from the assaults of slander, who is? I felt much happier than I had done since my father's death, and enjoyed that night the first refreshing sleep which had visited me since that event.

My curiosity respecting my male cousin did not long remain unsatisfied--he appeared the next day at dinner. His manners, though not so coarse as I had expected, were exceedingly disagreeable; there was an assurance and a forwardness for which I was not prepared; there was less of the vulgarity of manner, and almost more of that of the mind, than I had anticipated. I felt quite uncomfortable in his presence; there was just that confidence in his look and tone which would read encouragement even in mere toleration; and I felt more disgusted and annoyed at the coarse and extravagant compliments which he was pleased from time to time to pay me, than perhaps the extent of the atrocity might fully have warranted. It was, however, one consolation that he did not often appear, being much engrossed by pursuits about which I neither knew nor cared anything; but when he did appear, his attentions, either with a view to his amusement or to some more serious advantage, were so obviously and perseveringly directed to me, that young and inexperienced as I was, even _I_ could not be ignorant of his preference. I felt more provoked by this odious persecution than I can express, and discouraged him with so much vigour, that I employed even rudeness to convince him his assiduities were unwelcome; but all in vain.

This had gone on for nearly a twelvemonth, to my infinite annoyance, when one day as I was sitting at some needlework with my companion Emily, as was my habit, in the parlour, the door opened, and my cousin Edward entered the room. There was something, I thought, odd in his manner; a kind of struggle between shame and impudence--a kind of flurry and ambiguity which made him appear, if possible, more than ordinarily disagreeable.

"Your servant, ladies," he said, seating himself at the same time; "sorry to spoil your _tête-à-tête_, but never mind! I'll only take Emily's place for a minute or two; and then we part for a while, fair cousin. Emily, my father wants you in the corner turret. No shilly-shally; he's in a hurry." She hesitated. "Be off--tramp, march!" he exclaimed, in a tone which the poor girl dared not disobey.

She left the room, and Edward followed her to the door. He stood there for a minute or two, as if reflecting what he should say, perhaps satisfying himself that no one was within hearing in the hall.

At length he turned about, having closed the door, as if carelessly, with his foot; and advancing slowly, as if in deep thought, he took his seat at the side of the table opposite to mine.

There was a brief interval of silence, after which he said:

"I imagine that you have a shrewd suspicion of the object of my early visit; but I suppose I must go into particulars. Must I?"

"I have no conception," I replied, "what your object may be."

"Well, well," said he, becoming more at his ease as he proceeded, "it may be told in a few words. You know that it is totally impossible--quite out of the question--that an off-hand young fellow like me, and a good-looking girl like yourself, could meet continually, as you and I have done, without an attachment--a liking growing up on one side or other; in short, I think I have let you know as plain as if I spoke it, that I have been in love with you almost from the first time I saw you."

He paused; but I was too much horrified to speak. He interpreted my silence favourably.

"I can tell you," he continued, "I'm reckoned rather hard to please, and very hard to _hit_. I can't say when I was taken with a girl before; so you see fortune reserved me----"

Here the odious wretch wound his arm round my waist. The action at once restored me to utterance, and with the most indignant vehemence I released myself from his hold, and at the same time said:

"I have not been insensible, sir, of your most disagreeable attentions--they have long been a source of much annoyance to me; and you must be aware that I have marked my disapprobation--my disgust—as unequivocally as I possibly could, without actual indelicacy."

I paused, almost out of breath from the rapidity with which I had spoken; and, without giving him time to renew the conversation, I hastily quitted the room, leaving him in a paroxysm of rage and mortification.

As I ascended the stairs, I heard him open the parlour-door with violence, and take two or three rapid strides in the direction in which I was moving. I was now much frightened, and ran the whole way until I reached my room; and having locked the door, I listened breathlessly, but heard no sound. This relieved me for the present; but so much had I been overcome by the agitation and annoyance attendant upon the scene which I had just gone through, that when Emily knocked at my door, I was weeping in strong hysterics.

You will readily conceive my distress, when you reflect upon my strong dislike to my cousin Edward, combined with my youth and extreme inexperience. Any proposal of such a nature must have agitated me; but that it should have come from the man whom of all others I most loathed and abhorred, and to whom I had, as clearly as manner could do it, expressed the state of my feelings, was almost too overwhelming to be borne. It was a calamity, too, in which I could not claim the sympathy of my cousin Emily, which had always been extended to me in my minor grievances. Still I hoped that it might not be unattended with good; for I thought that one inevitable and most welcome consequence would result from this painful _eclaircissement_, in the discontinuance of my cousin's odious persecution.

When I arose next morning, it was with the fervent hope that I might never again behold the face, or even hear the name, of my cousin Edward; but such a consummation, though devoutly to be wished, was hardly likely to occur. The painful impressions of yesterday were too vivid to be at once erased; and I could not help feeling some dim foreboding of coming annoyance and evil.

To expect on my suitor's part anything like delicacy or consideration for me was out of the question. I saw that he had set his heart upon my property, and that he was not likely easily to forego such an acquisition--possessing what might have been considered opportunities and facilities almost to compel my compliance.

I now keenly felt the unreasonableness of my father's conduct in placing me to reside with a family of all whose members, with one exception, he was wholly ignorant, and I bitterly felt the helplessness of my situation. I determined, however, in case of my cousin's persevering in his addresses, to lay all the particulars before my uncle (although he had never in kindness or intimacy gone a step beyond our first interview), and to throw myself upon his hospitality and his sense of honour for protection against a repetition of such scenes.

My cousin's conduct may appear to have been an inadequate cause for such serious uneasiness; but my alarm was caused neither by his acts nor words, but entirely by his manner, which was strange and even intimidating to excess. At the beginning of yesterday's interview there was a sort of bullying swagger in his air, which towards the close gave place to the brutal vehemence of an undisguised ruffian--a transition which had tempted me into a belief that he might seek even forcibly to extort from me a consent to his wishes, or by means still more horrible, of which I scarcely dared to trust myself to think, to possess himself of my property.

I was early next day summoned to attend my uncle in his private room, which lay in a corner turret of the old building; and thither I accordingly went, wondering all the way what this unusual measure might prelude. When I entered the room, he did not rise in his usual courteous way to greet me, but simply pointed to a chair opposite to his own. This boded nothing agreeable. I sat down, however, silently waiting until he should open the conversation.

"Lady Margaret," at length he said, in a tone of greater sternness than I had thought him capable of using, "I have hitherto spoken to you as a friend, but I have not forgotten that I am also your guardian, and that my authority as such gives me a right to control your conduct. I shall put a question to you, and I expect and will demand a plain, direct answer. Have I rightly been informed that you have contemptuously rejected the suit and hand of my son Edward?"

I stammered forth with a good deal of trepidation:

"I believe--that is, I have, sir, rejected my cousin's proposals; and my coldness and discouragement might have convinced him that I had determined to do so."

"Madam," replied he, with suppressed, but, as it appeared to me, intense anger, "I have lived long enough to know that coldness and discouragement, and such terms, form the common cant of a worthless coquette. You know to the full, as well as I, that _coldness and discouragement_ may be so exhibited as to convince their object that he is neither distasteful nor indifferent to the person who wears this manner. You know, too, none better, that an affected neglect, when skilfully managed, is amongst the most formidable of the engines which artful beauty can employ. I tell you, madam, that having, without one word spoken in discouragement, permitted my son's most marked attentions for a twelvemonth or more, you have no right to dismiss him with no further explanation than demurely telling him that you had always looked coldly upon him; and neither your wealth nor your _ladyship_" (there was an emphasis of scorn on the word, which would have become Sir Giles Overreach himself) "can warrant you in treating with contempt the affectionate regard of an honest heart."

I was too much shocked at this undisguised attempt to bully me into an acquiescence in the interested and unprincipled plan for their own aggrandizement, which I now perceived my uncle and his son to have deliberately entered into, at once to find strength or collectedness to frame an answer to what he had said. At length I replied, with some firmness:

"In all that you have just now said, sir, you have grossly misstated my conduct and motives. Your information must have been most incorrect as far as it regards my conduct towards my cousin; my manner towards him could have conveyed nothing but dislike; and if anything could have added to the strong aversion which I have long felt towards him, it would be his attempting thus to trick and frighten me into a marriage which he knows to be revolting to me, and which is sought by him only as a means for securing to himself whatever property is mine."

As I said this, I fixed my eyes upon those of my uncle, but he was too old in the world's ways to falter beneath the gaze of more searching eyes than mine; he simply said:

"Are you acquainted with the provisions of your father's will?"

I answered in the affirmative; and he continued:

"Then you must be aware that if my son Edward were--which God forbid--the unprincipled, reckless man you pretend to think him"--(here he spoke very slowly, as if he intended that every word which escaped him should be registered in my memory, while at the same time the expression of his countenance underwent a gradual but horrible change, and the eyes which he fixed upon me became so darkly vivid, that I almost lost sight of everything else)--"if he were what you have described him, think you, girl, he could find no briefer means than wedding contracts to gain his ends? 'twas but to gripe your slender neck until the breath had stopped, and lands, and lakes, and all were his."

I stood staring at him for many minutes after he had ceased to speak, fascinated by the terrible serpent-like gaze, until he continued with a welcome change of countenance:

"I will not speak again to you upon this topic until one month has passed. You shall have time to consider the relative advantages of the two courses which are open to you. I should be sorry to hurry you to a decision. I am satisfied with having stated my feelings upon the subject, and pointed out to you the path of duty. Remember this day month--not one word sooner."

He then rose, and I left the room, much agitated and exhausted.

This interview, all the circumstances attending it, but most particularly the formidable expression of my uncle's countenance while he talked, though hypothetically, of murder, combined to arouse all my worst suspicions of him. I dreaded to look upon the face that had so recently worn the appalling livery of guilt and malignity. I regarded it with the mingled fear and loathing with which one looks upon an object which has tortured them in a nightmare.

In a few days after the interview, the particulars of which I have just related, I found a note upon my toilet-table, and on opening it I read as follows:

"MY DEAR LADY MARGARET,

"You will be perhaps surprised to see a strange face in your room to-day. I have dismissed your Irish maid, and secured a French one to wait upon you--a step rendered necessary by my proposing shortly to visit the Continent, with all my family.

"Your faithful guardian,
"ARTHUR T----N."

On inquiry, I found that my faithful attendant was actually gone, and far on her way to the town of Galway; and in her stead there appeared a tall, raw-boned, ill-looking, elderly Frenchwoman, whose sullen and presuming manners seemed to imply that her vocation had never before been that of a lady's maid. I could not help regarding her as a creature of my uncle's, and therefore to be dreaded, even had she been in no other way suspicious.

Days and weeks passed away without any, even a momentary doubt upon my part, as to the course to be pursued by me. The allotted period had at length elapsed; the day arrived on which I was to communicate my decision to my uncle. Although my resolution had never for a moment wavered, I could not shake off the dread of the approaching colloquy;

and my heart sank within me as I heard the expected summons.

I had not seen my cousin Edward since the occurrence of the grand _eclaircissement_; he must have studiously avoided me--I suppose from policy, it could not have been from delicacy. I was prepared for a terrific burst of fury from my uncle, as soon as I should make known my determination; and I not unreasonably feared that some act of violence or of intimidation would next be resorted to.

Filled with these dreary forebodings, I fearfully opened the study door, and the next minute I stood in my uncle's presence. He received me with a politeness which I dreaded, as arguing a favourable anticipation respecting the answer which I was to give; and after some slight delay, he began by saying:

"It will be a relief to both of us, I believe, to bring this conversation as soon as possible to an issue. You will excuse me, then, my dear niece, for speaking with an abruptness which, under other circumstances, would be unpardonable. You have, I am certain, given the subject of our last interview fair and serious consideration; and I trust that you are now prepared with candour to lay your answer before me. A few words will suffice--we perfectly understand one another."

He paused, and I, though feeling that I stood upon a mine which might in an instant explode, nevertheless answered with perfect composure:

"I must now, sir, make the same reply which I did upon the last occasion, and I reiterate the declaration which I then made, that I never can nor will, while life and reason remain, consent to a union with my cousin Edward."

This announcement wrought no apparent change in Sir Arthur, except that he became deadly, almost lividly pale. He seemed lost in dark thought for a minute, and then with a slight effort said:

"You have answered me honestly and directly; and you say your resolution is unchangeable. Well, would it had been otherwise--would it had been otherwise; but be it as it is, I am satisfied."

He gave me his hand--it was cold and damp as death; under an assumed calmness, it was evident that he was fearfully agitated. He continued to hold my hand with an almost painful pressure, while, as if unconsciously, seeming to forget my presence, he muttered:

"Strange, strange, strange, indeed! fatuity, helpless fatuity!" there was here a long pause. "Madness indeed to strain a cable that is rotten to the very heart--it must break--and then--all goes."

There was again a pause of some minutes, after which, suddenly changing his voice and manner to one of wakeful alacrity, he exclaimed:

"Margaret, my son Edward shall plague you no more. He leaves this country on to-morrow for France--he shall speak no more upon this subject--never, never more--whatever events depended upon your answer must now take their own course; but, as for this fruitless proposal, it has been tried enough; it can be repeated no more."

At these words he coldly suffered my hand to drop, as if to express his total abandonment of all his projected schemes of alliance; and certainly the action, with the accompanying words, produced upon my mind a more solemn and depressing effect than I believed possible to have been caused by the course which I had determined to pursue; it struck upon my heart with an awe and heaviness which _will_ accompany the accomplishment of an important and irrevocable act, even though no doubt or scruple remains to make it possible that the agent should wish it undone.

"Well," said my uncle, after a little time, "we now cease to speak upon this topic, never to resume it again. Remember you shall have no further uneasiness from Edward; he leaves Ireland for France on to-morrow; this will be a relief to you. May I depend upon your honour that no word touching the subject of this interview shall ever escape you?"

I gave him the desired assurance; he said:

"It is well--I am satisfied; we have nothing more, I believe, to say upon either side, and my presence must be a restraint upon you, I shall therefore bid you farewell."

I then left the apartment, scarcely knowing what to think of the strange interview which had just taken place.

On the next day my uncle took occasion to tell me that Edward had actually sailed, if his intention had not been interfered with by adverse circumstances; and two days subsequently he actually produced a letter from his son, written, as it said, on board, and despatched while the ship was getting under weigh. This was a great satisfaction to me and as being likely to prove so, it was no doubt communicated to me by Sir Arthur.

During all this trying period, I had found infinite consolation in the society and sympathy of my dear cousin Emily. I never in after-life formed a friendship so close, so fervent, and upon which, in all its progress, I could look back with feelings of such unalloyed pleasure, upon whose termination I must ever dwell with so deep, yet so unembittered regret. In cheerful converse with her I soon recovered my spirits considerably, and passed my time agreeably enough, although still in the strictest seclusion.
Matters went on sufficiently smooth, although I could not help sometimes feeling a momentary, but horrible uncertainty respecting my uncle's character; which was not altogether unwarranted by the circumstances of the two trying interviews whose particulars I have just detailed. The unpleasant impression which these conferences were calculated to leave upon my mind was fast wearing away, when there occurred a circumstance, slight indeed in itself, but calculated irresistibly to awaken all my worst suspicions, and to overwhelm me again with anxiety and terror.

I had one day left the house with my cousin Emily, in order to take a ramble of considerable length, for the purpose of sketching some favourite views, and she had walked about half a mile, when I perceived that we had forgotten our drawing materials, the absence of which would have defeated the object of our walk. Laughing at our own thoughtlessness, we returned to the house, and leaving Emily without, I ran upstairs to procure the drawing-books and pencils, which lay in my bedroom.

As I ran up the stairs I was met by the tall, ill-looking Frenchwoman, evidently a good deal flurried.

"Que veut, madame?" said she, with a more decided effort to be polite than I had ever known her make before.

"No, no--no matter," said I, hastily running by her in the direction of my room.

"Madame," cried she, in a high key, "restez ici, s'il vous plait; votre chambre n'est pas faite--your room is not ready for your reception yet."

I continued to move on without heeding her. She was some way behind me, and feeling that she could not otherwise prevent my entrance, for I was now upon the very lobby, she made a desperate attempt to seize hold of my person: she succeeded in grasping the end of my shawl, which she drew from my shoulders; but slipping at the same time upon the polished oak floor, she fell at full length upon the boards.

A little frightened as well as angry at the rudeness of this strange woman, I hastily pushed open the door of my room, at which I now stood, in order to escape from her; but great was my amazement on entering to find the apartment occupied.

The window was open, and beside it stood two male figures; they appeared to be examining the fastenings of the casement, and their backs were turned towards the door. One of them was my uncle; they both turned on my entrance, as if startled. The stranger was booted and cloaked, and wore a heavy broad-leafed hat over his brows. He turned but for a moment, and averted his face; but I had seen enough to convince me that he was no other than my cousin Edward. My uncle had some iron instrument in his hand, which he hastily concealed behind his back; and, coming towards me, said something as if in an explanatory tone; but I was too much shocked and confounded to understand what it might be. He said something about "repairs--window-frames--cold, and safety."

I did not wait, however, to ask or to receive explanations, but hastily left the room. As I went down the stairs I thought I heard the voice of the French woman in all the shrill volubility of excuse, which was met, however, by suppressed but vehement imprecations, or what seemed to me to be such, in which the voice of my cousin Edward distinctly mingled.

I joined my cousin Emily quite out of breath. I need not say that my head was too full of other things to think much of drawing for that day. I imparted to her frankly the cause of my alarms, but at the same time as gently as I could; and with tears she promised vigilance, and devotion, and love. I never had reason for a moment to repent the unreserved confidence which I then reposed in her. She was no less surprised than I at the unexpected appearance of her brother, whose departure for France neither of us had for a moment doubted, but which was now proved by his actual presence to be nothing more than an imposture, practised, I feared, for no good end.

The situation in which I had found my uncle had removed completely all my doubts as to his designs. I magnified suspicions into certainties, and dreaded night after night that I should be murdered in my bed. The nervousness produced by sleepless nights and days of anxious fears increased the horrors of my situation to such a degree, that I at length wrote a letter to a Mr. Jefferies, an old and faithful friend of my father's, and perfectly acquainted with all his affairs, praying him, for God's sake, to relieve me from my present terrible situation, and communicating without reserve the nature and grounds of my suspicions.

This letter I kept sealed and directed for two or three days always about my person--for discovery would have been ruinous--in expectation of an opportunity which might be safely trusted, whereby to have it placed in the post-office. As neither Emily nor I was permitted to pass beyond the precincts of the demesne itself, which was surrounded by high walls formed of dry stone, the difficulty of procuring such an opportunity was greatly enhanced.

At this time Emily had a short conversation with her father, which she reported to me instantly.

After some indifferent matter, he had asked her whether she and I were upon good terms, and whether I was unreserved in my disposition. She answered in the affirmative; and he then inquired whether I had been much surprised to find him in my chamber on the other day. She answered that I had been both surprised and amused.

"And what did she think of George Wilson's appearance?"

"Who?" inquired she.

"Oh, the architect," he answered, "who is to contract for the repairs of the house; he is accounted a handsome fellow."

"She could not see his face," said Emily, "and she was in such a hurry to escape that she scarcely noticed him."

Sir Arthur appeared satisfied, and the conversation ended.

This slight conversation, repeated accurately to me by Emily, had the effect of confirming, if indeed anything was required to do so, all

that I had before believed as to Edward's actual presence; and I naturally became, if possible, more anxious than ever to despatch the letter to Mr. Jefferies. An opportunity at length occurred.
As Emily and I were walking one day near the gate of the demesne, a man from the village happened to be passing down the avenue from the house; the spot was secluded, and as this person was not connected by service with those whose observation I dreaded, I committed the letter to his keeping, with strict injunctions that he should put it without delay into the receiver of the town post-office; at the same time I added a suitable gratuity, and the man, having made many protestations of punctuality, was soon out of sight.

He was hardly gone when I began to doubt my discretion in having trusted this person; but I had no better or safer means of despatching the letter, and I was not warranted in suspecting him of such wanton dishonesty as an inclination to tamper with it; but I could not be quite satisfied of its safety until I had received an answer, which could not arrive for a few days. Before I did, however, an event occurred which a little surprised me.

I was sitting in my bedroom early in the day, reading by myself, when I heard a knock at the door.

"Come in," said I; and my uncle entered the room.

"Will you excuse me?' said he. "I sought you in the parlour, and thence I have come here. I desire to say a word with you. I trust that you have hitherto found my conduct to you such as that of a guardian towards his ward should be."

I dared not withhold my assent.

"And," he continued, "I trust that you have not found me harsh or unjust, and that you have perceived, my dear niece, that I have sought to make this poor place as agreeable to you as may be."

I assented again; and he put his hand in his pocket, whence he drew a folded paper, and dashing it upon the table with startling emphasis, he said,--

"Did you write that letter?"

The sudden and fearful alteration of his voice, manner, and face, but, more than all, the unexpected production of my letter to Mr. Jefferies, which I at once recognized, so confounded and terrified me that I felt almost choking.

I could not utter a word.

"Did you write that letter?" he repeated, with slow and intense emphasis. "You did, liar and hypocrite! You dared to write this foul and infamous libel; but it shall be your last. Men will universally believe you mad, if I choose to call for an inquiry. I can make you appear so. The suspicions expressed in this letter are the hallucinations and alarms of moping lunacy. I have defeated your first attempt, madam; and by the holy God, if ever you make another, chains, straw, darkness, and the keeper's whip shall be your lasting portion!"

With these astounding words he left the room, leaving me almost fainting.

I was now almost reduced to despair; my last cast had failed; I had no course left but that of eloping secretly from the castle and placing myself under the protection of the nearest magistrate. I felt if this were not done, and speedily, that I should be _murdered_.

No one, from mere description, can have an idea of the unmitigated horror of my situation--a helpless, weak, inexperienced girl, placed under the power and wholly at the mercy of evil men, and feeling that she had it not in her power to escape for a moment from the malignant influences under which she was probably fated to fall; and with a consciousness that if violence, if murder were designed, her dying shriek would be lost in void space; no human being would be near to aid her, no human interposition could deliver her.

I had seen Edward but once during his visit, and, as I did not meet with him again, I began to think that he must have taken his departure--a conviction which was to a certain degree satisfactory, as I regarded his absence as indicating the removal of immediate danger.

Emily also arrived circuitously at the same conclusion, and not without good grounds, for she managed indirectly to learn that Edward's black horse had actually been for a day and part of a night in the castle stables, just at the time of her brother's supposed visit. The horse had gone and, as she argued, the rider must have departed with it.

This point being so far settled, I felt a little less uncomfortable; when, being one day alone in my bedroom, I happened to look out from the window, and, to my unutterable horror, I beheld, peering through an opposite casement, my cousin Edward's face. Had I seen the evil one himself in bodily shape, I could not have experienced a more sickening revulsion.

I was too much appalled to move at once from the window, but I did so soon enough to avoid his eye. He was looking fixedly into the narrow quadrangle upon which the window opened. I shrank back unperceived, to pass the rest of the day in terror and despair. I went to my room early that night, but I was too miserable to sleep.

At about twelve o'clock, feeling very nervous, I determined to call my cousin Emily, who slept, you will remember, in the next room, which communicated with mine by a second door. By this private entrance I found my way into her chamber, and without difficulty persuaded her to return to my room and sleep with me. We accordingly lay down together, she undressed, and I with my clothes on, for I was every moment walking up and down the room, and felt too nervous and miserable to think of rest or comfort.

Emily was soon fast asleep, and I lay awake, fervently longing for the first pale gleam of morning; reckoning every stroke of the old clock with an impatience which made every hour appear like six.

It must have been about one o'clock when I thought I heard a slight noise at the partition-door between Emily's room and mine, as if caused by somebody turning the key in the lock. I held my breath, and the same sound was repeated at the second door of my room--that which opened upon the lobby--the sound was here distinctly caused by the revolution of the bolt in the lock, and it was followed by a slight pressure upon the door itself, as if to ascertain the security of the lock.
The person, whoever it might be, was probably satisfied, for I heard the old boards of the lobby creak and strain, as if under the weight of somebody moving cautiously over them. My sense of hearing became unnaturally, almost painfully acute. I suppose my imagination added distinctness to sounds vague in themselves. I thought that I could actually hear the breathing of the person who was slowly returning down the lobby. At the head of the staircase there appeared to occur a pause;

and I could distinctly hear two or three sentences hastily whispered; the steps then descended the stairs with apparently less caution. I now ventured to walk quickly and lightly to the lobby door, and attempted to open it; it was indeed fast locked upon the outside, as was also the other.

I now felt that the dreadful hour was come; but one desperate expedient remained--it was to awaken Emily, and by our united strength to attempt to force the partition-door, which was slighter than the other, and through this to pass to the lower part of the house, whence it might be possible to escape to the grounds, and forth to the village.

I returned to the bedside and shook Emily, but in vain. Nothing that I could do availed to produce from her more than a few incoherent words--it was a deathlike sleep. She had certainly drunk of some narcotic, as had I probably also, spite of all the caution with which I had examined everything presented to us to eat or drink.

I now attempted, with as little noise as possible, to force first one door, then the other; but all in vain. I believe no strength could have effected my object, for both doors opened inwards. I therefore collected whatever movables I could carry thither, and piled them against the doors, so as to assist me in whatever attempts I should make to resist the entrance of those without. I then returned to the bed and endeavoured again, but fruitlessly, to awaken my cousin. It was not sleep, it was torpor, lethargy, death. I knelt down and prayed with an agony of earnestness; and then seating myself upon the bed, I awaited my fate with a kind of terrible tranquillity.

I heard a faint clanking sound from the narrow court which I have already mentioned, as if caused by the scraping of some iron instrument against stones or rubbish. I at first determined not to disturb the calmness which I now felt by uselessly watching the proceedings of those who sought my life; but as the sounds continued, the horrible curiosity which I felt overcame every other emotion, and I determined, at all hazards, to gratify it. I therefore crawled upon my knees to the window, so as to let the smallest portion of my head appear above the sill.

The moon was shining with an uncertain radiance upon the antique grey buildings, and obliquely upon the narrow court beneath, one side of which was therefore clearly illuminated, while the other was lost in obscurity; the sharp outlines of the old gables, with their nodding clusters of ivy, being at first alone visible.

Whoever or whatever occasioned the noise which had excited my curiosity, was concealed under the shadow of the dark side of the quadrangle. I placed my hand over my eyes to shade them from the moonlight, which was so bright as to be almost dazzling, and, peering into the darkness, I first dimly, but afterwards gradually almost with full distinctness, beheld the form of a man engaged in digging what appeared to be a rude hole close under the wall. Some implements, probably a shovel and pickaxe, lay beside him, and to these he every now and then applied himself as the nature of the ground required. He pursued his task
rapidly, and with as little noise as possible.

"So," thought I, as, shovelful after shovelful, the dislodged rubbish mounted into a heap, "they are digging the grave in which, before two hours pass, I must lie, a cold, mangled corpse. I am _theirs_--I cannot escape."

I felt as if my reason was leaving me. I started to my feet, and in mere despair I applied myself again to each of the two doors alternately. I strained every nerve and sinew, but I might as well have attempted, with my single strength, to force the building itself from its foundation. I threw myself madly upon the ground, and clasped my hands over my eyes as if to shut out the horrible images which crowded upon me.

The paroxysm passed away. I prayed once more, with the bitter, agonized fervour of one who feels that the hour of death is present and inevitable. When I arose, I went once more to the window and looked out, just in time to see a shadowy figure glide stealthily along the wall. The task was finished. The catastrophe of the tragedy must soon be accomplished.

I determined now to defend my life to the last; and that I might be able to do so with some effect, I searched the room for something which might serve as a weapon; but either through accident, or from an anticipation of such a possibility, everything which might have been made available for such a purpose had been carefully removed. I must then die tamely, and without an effort to defend myself.

A thought suddenly struck me--might it not be possible to escape through the door, which the assassin must open in order to enter the room? I resolved to make the attempt. I felt assured that the door through which ingress to the room would be effected was that which opened upon the lobby. It was the more direct way, besides being, for obvious reasons, less liable to interruption than the other. I resolved, then, to place myself behind a projection of the wall, whose shadow would serve fully to conceal me, and when the door should be opened, and before they should have discovered the identity of the occupant of the bed, to creep noiselessly from the room, and then to trust to Providence for escape.

In order to facilitate this scheme, I removed all the lumber which I had heaped against the door; and I had nearly completed my arrangements, when I perceived the room suddenly darkened by the close approach of some shadowy object to the window. On turning my eyes in that direction, I observed at the top of the casement, as if suspended from above, first the feet, then the legs, then the body, and at length the whole figure of a man present himself. It was Edward T----n.

He appeared to be guiding his descent so as to bring his feet upon the centre of the stone block which occupied the lower part of the window; and, having secured his footing upon this, he kneeled down and began to gaze into the room. As the moon was gleaming into the chamber, and the bed-curtains were drawn, he was able to distinguish the bed itself and its contents. He appeared satisfied with his scrutiny, for he looked up and made a sign with his hand, upon which the rope by which his descent had been effected was slackened from above, and he proceeded to disengage it from his waist; this accomplished, he applied his hands to the window-frame, which must have been ingeniously contrived for the purpose, for, with apparently no resistance, the whole frame, containing casement and all, slipped from its position in the wall, and was by him lowered into the room.

The cold night wind waved the bed-curtains, and he paused for a moment; all was still again, and he stepped in upon the floor of the room.
He held in his hand what appeared to be a steel instrument, shaped something like a hammer, but larger and sharper at the extremities. This he held rather behind him, while, with three long, tip-toe strides, he brought himself to the bedside.

I felt that the discovery must now be made, and held my breath in momentary expectation of the execration in which he would vent his surprise and disappointment. I closed my eyes--there was a pause, but it was a short one. I heard two dull blows, given in rapid succession: a quivering sigh, and the long-drawn, heavy breathing of the sleeper was for ever suspended. I unclosed my eyes, and saw the murderer fling the quilt across the head of his victim: he then, with the instrument of death still in his hand, proceeded to the lobby door, upon which he tapped sharply twice or thrice. A quick step was then heard approaching, and a voice whispered something from without. Edward answered, with a kind of chuckle, "Her ladyship is past complaining; unlock the door, in the devil's name, unless you're afraid to come in, and help me to lift the body out of the window."

The key was turned in the lock--the door opened, and my uncle entered the room.

I have told you already that I had placed myself under the shade of a projection of the wall, close to the door. I had instinctively shrunk down, cowering towards the ground, on the entrance of Edward through the window. When my uncle entered the room, he and his son both stood so very close to me that his hand was every moment upon the point of touching my face. I held my breath, and remained motionless as death.

"You had no interruption from the next room?" said my uncle.

"No," was the brief reply.
"Secure the jewels, Ned; the French harpy must not lay her claws upon them. You're a steady hand, by G----! not much blood--eh?"

"Not twenty drops," replied his son, "and those on the quilt."

"I'm glad it's over," whispered my uncle again. "We must lift the--the _thing_ through the window and lay the rubbish over it."

They then turned to the bedside, and, winding the bed-clothes round the body, carried it between them slowly to the window, and, exchanging a few brief words with some one below, they shoved it over the window-sill, and I heard it fall heavily on the ground underneath.

"I'll take the jewels," said my uncle; "there are two caskets in the lower drawer."

He proceeded, with an accuracy which, had I been more at ease, would have furnished me with matter of astonishment, to lay his hand upon the very spot where my jewels lay; and having possessed himself of them, he called to his son:

"Is the rope made fast above?"

"I'm not a fool--to be sure it is," replied he.

They then lowered themselves from the window. I now rose lightly and cautiously, scarcely daring to breathe, from my place of concealment, and was creeping towards the door, when I heard my cousin's voice, in a sharp whisper, exclaim: "Scramble up again! G--d d----n you, you've forgot to lock the room-door!" and I perceived, by the straining of the rope which hung from above, that the mandate was instantly obeyed.

Not a second was to be lost. I passed through the door, which was only closed, and moved as rapidly as I could, consistently with stillness, along the lobby. Before I had gone many yards, I heard the door through which I had just passed double-locked on the inside. I glided down the stairs in terror, lest, at every corner, I should meet the murderer or one of his accomplices.

I reached the hall, and listened for a moment, to ascertain whether all was silent around; no sound was audible. The parlour windows opened on the park, and through one of them I might, I thought, easily effect my escape. Accordingly, I hastily entered; but, to my consternation, a candle was burning in the room, and by its light I saw a figure seated at the dinner-table, upon which lay glasses, bottles, and the other accompaniments of a drinking-party. Two or three chairs were placed about the table irregularly, as if hastily abandoned by their occupants.

A single glance satisfied me that the figure was that of my French attendant. She was fast asleep, having probably drunk deeply. There was something malignant and ghastly in the calmness of this bad woman's features, dimly illuminated as they were by the flickering blaze of the candle. A knife lay upon the table, and the terrible thought, struck me--"Should I kill this sleeping accomplice, and thus secure my retreat?"

Nothing could be easier--it was but to draw the blade across her throat--the work of a second. An instant's pause, however, corrected me. "No," thought I, "the God who has conducted me thus far through the valley of the shadow of death, will not abandon me now. I will fall into their hands, or I will escape hence, but it shall be free from the stain of blood. His will be done!"

I felt a confidence arising from this reflection, an assurance of protection which I cannot describe. There was no other means of escape, so I advanced, with a firm step and collected mind, to the window. I noiselessly withdrew the bars and unclosed the shutters--I pushed open the casement, and, without waiting to look behind me, I ran with my utmost speed, scarcely feeling the ground under me, down the avenue, taking care to keep upon the grass which bordered it.

I did not for a moment slacken my speed, and I had now gained the centre point between the park-gate and the mansion-house. Here the avenue made a wider circuit, and in order to avoid delay, I directed my way across the smooth sward round which the pathway wound, intending, at the opposite side of the flat, at a point which I distinguished by a group of old birch-trees, to enter again upon the beaten track, which was from thence tolerably direct to the gate.

I had, with my utmost speed, got about half way across this broad flat, when the rapid treading of a horse's hoofs struck upon my ear. My heart swelled in my bosom as though I would smother. The clattering of galloping hoofs approached--I was pursued--they were now upon the sward on which I was running--there was not a bush or a bramble to shelter me--and, as if to render escape altogether desperate, the moon, which had hitherto been obscured, at this moment shone forth with a broad clear light, which made every object distinctly visible.

The sounds were now close behind me. I felt my knees bending under me, with the sensation which torments one in dreams. I reeled--I stumbled—I fell--and at the same instant the cause of my alarm wheeled past me at full gallop. It was one of the young fillies which pastured loose about the park, whose frolics had thus all but maddened me with terror. I scrambled to my feet, and rushed on with weak but rapid steps, my sportive companion still galloping round and round me with many a frisk and fling, until, at length, more dead than alive, I reached the avenue-gate, and crossed the stile, I scarce knew how.

I ran through the village, in which all was silent as the grave, until my progress was arrested by the hoarse voice of a sentinel, who cried, "Who goes there?" I felt that I was now safe. I turned in the direction of the voice, and fell fainting at the soldier's feet. When I came to myself, I was sitting in a miserable hovel, surrounded by strange faces, all bespeaking curiosity and compassion.

Many soldiers were in it also: indeed, as I afterwards found, it was employed as a guard-room by a detachment of troops quartered for that night in the town. In a few words I informed their officer of the circumstances which had occurred, describing also the appearance of the persons engaged in the murder; and he, without loss of time, proceeded to the mansion-house of Carrickleigh, taking with him a party of his men. But the villains had discovered their mistake, and had effected their escape before the arrival of the military.

The Frenchwoman was, however, arrested in the neighbourhood upon the next day. She was tried and condemned upon the ensuing assizes; and previous to her execution, confessed that "_she had a hand in making Hugh Tisdall's bed_." She had been a housekeeper in the castle at the time, and a kind of _chère amie_ of my uncle's. She was, in reality, able to speak English like a native, but had exclusively used the French language, I suppose, to facilitate her disguise. She died the same hardened wretch she had lived, confessing her crimes only, as she alleged, that her doing so might involve Sir Arthur T----n, the great author of her guilt and misery, and whom she now regarded with unmitigated detestation.

With the particulars of Sir Arthur's and his son's escape, as far as they are known, you are acquainted. You are also in possession of their after fate--the terrible, the tremendous retribution which, after long delays of many years, finally overtook and crushed them. Wonderful and inscrutable are the dealings of God with His creatures.

Deep and fervent as must always be my gratitude to Heaven for my deliverance, effected by a chain of providential occurrences, the failing of a single link of which must have ensured my destruction, I was long before I could look back upon it with other feelings than those of bitterness, almost of agony. The only being that had ever really loved me, my nearest and dearest friend, ever ready to sympathize, to counsel, and to assist--the gayest, the gentlest, the warmest heart; the only creature on earth that cared for me--_her_ life had been the price of my deliverance; and I then uttered the wish, which no event of my long and sorrowful life has taught me to recall, that she had been spared, and that, in her stead, _I_ were mouldering in the grave, forgotten and at rest.

# STRANGE EVENT IN THE LIFE OF SCHALKEN THE PAINTER (1859)

You will no doubt be surprised, my dear friend, at the subject of the following narrative. What had I to do with Schalken, or Schalken with me? He had returned to his native land, and was probably dead and buried before I was born; I never visited Holland, nor spoke with a native of that country. So much I believe you already know. I must, then, give you my authority, and state to you frankly the ground upon which rests the credibility of the strange story which I am about to lay before you.

I was acquainted, in my early days, with a Captain Vandael, whose father had served King William in the Low Countries, and also in my own unhappy land during the Irish campaigns. I know not how it happened that I liked this man's society, spite of his politics and religion: but so it was; and it was by means of the free intercourse to which our intimacy gave rise that I became possessed of the curious tale which you are about to hear.

I had often been struck, while visiting Vandael, by a remarkable picture, in which, though no _connoisseur_ myself, I could not fail to discern some very strong peculiarities, particularly in the distribution of light and shade, as also a certain oddity in the design itself, which interested my curiosity. It represented the interior of what might be a chamber in some antique religious building--the foreground was occupied by a female figure, arrayed in a species of white robe, part of which was arranged so as to form a veil. The dress, however, was not strictly that of any religious order. In its hand the figure bore a lamp, by whose light alone the form and face were illuminated; the features were marked by an arch smile, such as pretty women wear when engaged in successfully practising some roguish trick; in the background, and (excepting where the dim red light of an expiring fire serves to define the form) totally in the shade, stood the figure of a man equipped in the old fashion, with doublet and so forth, in an attitude of alarm, his hand being placed upon the hilt of his sword, which he appeared to be in the act of drawing.

"There are some pictures," said I to my friend, "which impress one, I know not how, with a conviction that they represent not the mere ideal shapes and combinations which have floated through the imagination of the artist, but scenes, faces, and situations which have actually existed. When I look upon that picture, something assures me that I behold the representation of a reality."

Vandael smiled, and, fixing his eyes upon the painting musingly, he said,--

"Your fancy has not deceived you, my good friend, for that picture is the record, and I believe a faithful one, of a remarkable and mysterious occurrence. It was painted by Schalken, and contains, in the face of the female figure which occupies the most prominent place in the design, an accurate portrait of Rose Velderkaust, the niece of Gerard Douw, the first and, I believe, the only love of Godfrey Schalken. My father knew the painter well, and from Schalken himself he learned the story of the mysterious drama, one scene of which the picture has embodied. This painting, which is accounted a fine specimen of Schalken's style, was bequeathed to my father by the artist's will, and, as you have observed, is a very striking and interesting production."

I had only to request Vandael to tell the story of the painting in order to be gratified; and thus it is that I am enabled to submit to you a faithful recital of what I heard myself, leaving you to reject or to allow the evidence upon which the truth of the tradition depends--with this one assurance, that Schalken was an honest, blunt Dutchman, and, I believe, wholly incapable of committing a flight of imagination; and further, that Vandael, from whom I heard the story, appeared firmly convinced of its truth.

There are few forms upon which the mantle of mystery and romance could seem to hang more ungracefully than upon that of the uncouth and clownish Schalken--the Dutch boor--the rude and dogged, but most cunning worker in oils, whose pieces delight the initiated of the present day almost as much as his manners disgusted the refined of his own; and yet this man, so rude, so dogged, so slovenly, I had almost said so savage in mien and manner, during his after successes, had been selected by the capricious goddess, in his early life, to figure as the hero of a romance by no means devoid of interest or of mystery.

Who can tell how meet he may have been in his young days to play the part of the lover or of the hero? who can say that in early life he had been the same harsh, unlicked, and rugged boor that, in his maturer age, he proved? or how far the neglected rudeness which afterwards marked his air, and garb, and manners, may not have been the growth of that reckless apathy not unfrequently produced by bitter misfortunes and disappointments in early life?

These questions can never now be answered.

We must content ourselves, then, with a plain statement of facts, leaving matters of speculation to those who like them.

When Schalken studied under the immortal Gerard Douw, he was a young man; and in spite of the phlegmatic constitution and excitable manner which he shared, we believe, with his countrymen, he was not incapable of deep and vivid impressions, for it is an established fact that the young painter looked with considerable interest upon the beautiful niece of his wealthy master.

Rose Velderkaust was very young, having, at the period of which we speak, not yet attained her seventeenth year; and, if tradition speaks truth, she possessed all the soft dimpling charms of the fair, light-haired Flemish maidens. Schalken had not studied long in the school of Gerard Douw when he felt this interest deepening into something of a keener and intenser feeling than was quite consistent with the tranquillity of his honest Dutch heart; and at the same time he perceived, or thought he perceived, flattering symptoms of a reciprocal attachment, and this was quite sufficient to determine whatever indecision he might have heretofore experienced, and to lead him to devote exclusively to her every hope and feeling of his heart. In short, he was as much in love as a Dutchman could be. He was not long in making his passion known to the pretty maiden herself, and his declaration was followed by a corresponding confession upon her part.

Schalken, howbeit, was a poor man, and he possessed no counterbalancing advantages of birth or position to induce the old man to consent to a union which must involve his niece and ward in the strugglings and difficulties of a young and nearly friendless artist. He was, therefore, to wait until time had furnished him with opportunity, and accident with success; and then, if his labours were found sufficiently lucrative, it was to be hoped that his proposals might at least be listened to by her jealous guardian. Months passed away, and, cheered by the smiles of the little Rose, Schalken's labours were redoubled, and with such effect and improvement as reasonably to promise the realization of his hopes, and no contemptible eminence in his art, before many years should have elapsed.

The even course of this cheering prosperity was, unfortunately, destined to experience a sudden and formidable interruption, and that, too, in a manner so strange and mysterious as to baffle all investigation, and throw upon the events themselves a shadow of almost supernatural horror.

Schalken had one evening remained in the master's studio considerably longer than his more volatile companions, who had gladly availed themselves of the excuse which the dusk of evening afforded to withdraw from their several tasks, in order to finish a day of labour in the jollity and conviviality of the tavern.

But Schalken worked for improvement, or rather for love. Besides, he was now engaged merely in sketching a design, an operation which, unlike that of colouring, might be continued as long as there was light sufficient to distinguish between canvas and charcoal. He had not then, nor, indeed, until long after, discovered the peculiar powers of his pencil; and he was engaged in composing a group of extremely roguish-looking and grotesque imps and demons, who were inflicting various ingenious torments upon a perspiring and pot-bellied St. Anthony, who reclined in the midst of them, apparently in the last stage of drunkenness.

The young artist, however, though incapable of executing, or even of appreciating, anything of true sublimity, had nevertheless discernment enough to prevent his being by any means satisfied with his work; and many were the patient erasures and corrections which the limbs and features of saint and devil underwent, yet all without producing in their new arrangement anything of improvement or increased effect.

The large, old-fashioned room was silent, and, with the exception of himself, quite deserted by its usual inmates. An hour had passed--nearly two--without any improved result. Daylight had already declined, and twilight was fast giving way to the darkness of night. The patience of the young man was exhausted, and he stood before his unfinished production, absorbed in no very pleasing ruminations, one hand buried in the folds of his long dark hair, and the other holding the piece of charcoal which had so ill executed its office, and which he now rubbed, without much regard to the sable streaks which it produced, with irritable pressure upon his ample Flemish inexpressibles.

"Pshaw!" said the young man aloud, "would that picture, devils, saint, and all, were where they should be--in hell!"

A short, sudden laugh, uttered startlingly close to his ear, instantly responded to the ejaculation.

The artist turned sharply round, and now for the first time became aware that his labours had been overlooked by a stranger.

Within about a yard and a half, and rather behind him, there stood what was, or appeared to be, the figure of an elderly man: he wore a short cloak, and broad-brimmed hat with a conical crown, and in his hand, which was protected with a heavy, gauntlet-shaped glove, he carried a long ebony walking-stick, surmounted with what appeared, as it glittered dimly in the twilight to be a massive head of gold; and upon his breast, through the folds of the cloak, there shone the links of a rich chain of the same metal.

The room was so obscure that nothing further of the appearance of the figure could be ascertained, and the face was altogether overshadowed by the heavy flap of the beaver which overhung it, so that no feature could be clearly discerned. A quantity of dark hair escaped from beneath this sombre hat, a circumstance which, connected with the firm, upright carriage of the intruder, proved that his years could not yet exceed threescore or thereabouts.

There was an air of gravity and importance about the garb of this person, and something indescribably odd--I might say awful--in the perfect, stone-like movelessness of the figure, that effectually checked the testy comment which had at once risen to the lips of the irritated artist. He therefore, as soon as he had sufficiently recovered the surprise, asked the stranger, civilly, to be seated, and desired to know if he had any message to leave for his master.

"Tell Gerard Douw," said the unknown, without altering his attitude in the smallest degree, "that Mynher Vanderhausen, of Rotterdam, desires to speak with him to-morrow evening at this hour, and, if he please, in this room, upon matters of weight; that is all. Good-night."

The stranger, having finished this message, turned abruptly, and, with a quick but silent step quitted the room before Schalken had time to say a word in reply.

The young man felt a curiosity to see in what direction the burgher of Rotterdam would turn on quitting the studio, and for that purpose he went directly to the window which commanded the door.

A lobby of considerable extent intervened between the inner door of the painter's room and the street entrance, so that Schalken occupied the post of observation before the old man could possibly have reached the street.

He watched in vain, however. There was no other mode of exit.

Had the old man vanished, or was he lurking about the recesses of the lobby for some bad purpose? This last suggestion filled the mind of Schalken with a vague horror, which was so unaccountably intense as to make him alike afraid to remain in the room alone and reluctant to pass through the lobby.

However, with an effort which appeared very disproportioned to the occasion, he summoned resolution to leave the room, and, having double-locked the door, and thrust the key in his pocket, without looking to the right or left, he traversed the passage which had so recently, perhaps still, contained the person of his mysterious visitant, scarcely venturing to breathe till he had arrived in the open street.

"Mynher Vanderhausen," said Gerard Douw, within himself, as the appointed hour approached; "Mynher Vanderhausen, of Rotterdam! I never heard of the man till yesterday. What can he want of me? A portrait, perhaps, to be painted; or a younger son or a poor relation to be apprenticed; or a collection to be valued; or--pshaw! there's no one in Rotterdam to leave me a legacy. Well, whatever the business may be, we shall soon know it all."

It was now the close of day, and every easel, except that of Schalken, was deserted. Gerard Douw was pacing the apartment with the restless step of impatient expectation, every now and then humming a passage from a piece of music which he was himself composing; for, though no great proficient, he admired the art; sometimes pausing to glance over the work of one of his absent pupils, but more frequently placing himself at the window, from whence he might observe the passengers who threaded the obscure by-street in which his studio was placed.

"Said you not, Godfrey," exclaimed Douw, after a long and fruitless gaze from his post of observation, and turning to Schalken--"said you not the hour of appointment was at about seven by the clock of the Stadhouse?"

"It had just told seven when I first saw him, sir," answered the student.

"The hour is close at hand, then," said the master, consulting a horologe as large and as round as a full-grown orange. "Mynher Vanderhausen, from Rotterdam--is it not so?"

"Such was the name."

"And an elderly man, richly clad?" continued Douw.

"As well as I might see," replied his pupil. "He could not be young, nor yet very old neither, and his dress was rich and grave, as might become a citizen of wealth and consideration."

At this moment the sonorous boom of the Stadhouse clock told, stroke after stroke, the hour of seven; the eyes of both master and student were directed to the door; and it was not until the last peal of the old bell had ceased to vibrate, that Douw exclaimed,--

"So, so; we shall have his worship presently--that is, if he means to keep his hour; if not, thou mayst wait for him, Godfrey, if you court the acquaintance of a capricious burgomaster. As for me, I think our old Leyden contains a sufficiency of such commodities, without an importation from Rotterdam."

Schalken laughed, as in duty bound; and, after a pause of some minutes, Douw suddenly exclaimed,--

"What if it should all prove a jest, a piece of mummery got up by Vankarp, or some such worthy! I wish you had run all risks, and cudgelled the old burgomaster, stadholder, or whatever else he may be, soundly. I would wager a dozen of Rhenish, his worship would have pleaded old acquaintance before the third application."

"Here he comes, sir," said Schalken, in a low, admonitory tone; and instantly, upon turning towards the door, Gerard Douw observed the same figure which had, on the day before, so unexpectedly greeted the vision of his pupil Schalken.

There was something in the air and mien of the figure which at once satisfied the painter that there was no mummery in the case, and that he really stood in the presence of a man of worship; and so, without hesitation, he doffed his cap, and courteously saluting the stranger, requested him to be seated.

The visitor waved his hand slightly, as if in acknowledgment of the courtesy, but remained standing.

"I have the honour to see Mynher Vanderhausen, of Rotterdam?" said Gerard Douw.

"The same," was the laconic reply.

"I understand your worship desires to speak with me," continued Douw, "and I am here by appointment to wait your commands."

"Is that a man of trust?" said Vanderhausen, turning towards Schalken, who stood at a little distance behind his master.

"Certainly," replied Gerard.

"Then let him take this box and get the nearest jeweller or goldsmith to value its contents, and let him return hither with a certificate of the valuation."

At the same time he placed a small case, about nine inches square, in the hands of Gerard Douw, who was as much amazed at its weight as at the strange abruptness with which it was handed to him.

In accordance with the wishes of the stranger, he delivered it into the hands of Schalken, and repeating _his_ directions, despatched him upon the mission.

Schalken disposed his precious charge securely beneath the folds of his cloak, and rapidly traversing two or three narrow streets, he stopped at a corner house, the lower part of which was then occupied by the shop of a Jewish goldsmith.

Schalken entered the shop, and calling the little Hebrew into the obscurity of its back recesses, he proceeded to lay before him Vanderhausen's packet.

On being examined by the light of a lamp, it appeared entirely cased with lead, the outer surface of which was much scraped and soiled, and nearly white with age. This was with difficulty partially removed, and disclosed beneath a box of some dark and singularly hard wood; this, too, was forced, and after the removal of two or three folds of linen, its contents proved to be a mass of golden ingots, close packed, and, as the Jew declared, of the most perfect quality.

Every ingot underwent the scrutiny of the little Jew, who seemed to feel an epicurean delight in touching and testing these morsels of the glorious metal; and each one of them was replaced in the box with the exclamation,--

"_Mein Gott_, how very perfect! not one grain of alloy--beautiful, beautiful!"

The task was at length finished, and the Jew certified under his hand that the value of the ingots submitted to his examination amounted to many thousand rix-dollars.

With the desired document in his bosom, and the rich box of gold carefully pressed under his arm, and concealed by his cloak, he retraced his way, and, entering the studio, found his master and the stranger in close conference.

Schalken had no sooner left the room, in order to execute the commission he had taken in charge, than Vanderhausen addressed Gerard Douw in the following terms:

"I may not tarry with you to-night more than a few minutes, and so I shall briefly tell you the matter upon which I come. You visited the town of Rotterdam some four months ago, and then I saw in the church of St. Lawrence your niece, Rose Velderkaust. I desire to marry her, and if I satisfy you as to the fact that I am very wealthy--more wealthy than any husband you could dream of for her--I expect that you will forward my views to the utmost of your authority. If you approve my proposal, you must close with it at once, for I cannot command time enough to wait for calculations and delays."

Gerard Douw was, perhaps, as much astonished as anyone could be by the very unexpected nature of Mynher Vanderhausen's communication; but he did not give vent to any unseemly expression of surprise. In addition to the motives supplied by prudence and politeness, the painter experienced a kind of chill and oppressive sensation--a feeling like that which is supposed to affect a man who is placed unconsciously in immediate contact with something to which he has a natural antipathy--an undefined horror and dread--while standing in the presence of the eccentric stranger, which made him very unwilling to say anything that might reasonably prove offensive.

"I have no doubt," said Gerard, after two or three prefatory hems, "that the connection which you propose would prove alike advantageous and honourable to my niece; but you must be aware that she has a will of her own, and may not acquiesce in what _we_ may design for her advantage."

"Do not seek to deceive me, Sir Painter," said Vanderhausen; "you are her guardian--she is your ward. She is mine if _you_ like to make her so."

The man of Rotterdam moved forward a little as he spoke, and Gerard Douw, he scarce knew why, inwardly prayed for the speedy return of Schalken.

"I desire," said the mysterious gentleman, "to place in your hands at once an evidence of my wealth, and a security for my liberal dealing with your niece. The lad will return in a minute or two with a sum in value five times the fortune which she has a right to expect from a husband. This shall lie in your hands, together with her dowry, and you may apply the united sum as suits her interest best; it shall be all exclusively hers while she lives. Is that liberal?"

Douw assented, and inwardly thought that fortune had been extraordinarily kind to his niece. The stranger, he deemed, must be most wealthy and generous, and such an offer was not to be despised, though made by a humorist, and one of no very prepossessing presence.

Rose had no very high pretensions, for she was almost without dowry; indeed, altogether so, excepting so far as the deficiency had been supplied by the generosity of her uncle. Neither had she any right to raise any scruples against the match on the score of birth, for her own origin was by no means elevated; and as to other objections, Gerard resolved, and, indeed, by the usages of the time was warranted in resolving, not to listen to them for a moment.

"Sir," said he, addressing the stranger, "your offer is most liberal, and whatever hesitation I may feel in closing with it immediately, arises solely from my not having the honour of knowing anything of your family or station. Upon these points you can, of course, satisfy me without difficulty?"

"As to my respectability," said the stranger, drily, "you must take that for granted at present; pester me with no inquiries; you can discover nothing more about me than I choose to make known. You shall have sufficient security for my respectability--my word, if you are honourable; if you are sordid, my gold."

"A testy old gentleman," thought Douw; "he must have his own way. But, all things considered, I am justified in giving my niece to him. Were she my own daughter, I would do the like by her. I will not pledge myself unnecessarily, however."

"You will not pledge yourself unnecessarily," said Vanderhausen, strangely uttering the very words which had just floated through the mind of his companion; "but you will do so if it _is_ necessary, I presume; and I will show you that I consider it indispensable. If the gold I mean to leave in your hands satisfies you, and if you desire that my proposal shall not be at once withdrawn, you must, before I leave this room, write your name to this engagement."

Having thus spoken, he placed a paper in the hands of Gerard, the contents of which expressed an engagement entered into by Gerard Douw, to give to Wilken Vanderhausen, of Rotterdam, in marriage, Rose Velderkaust, and so forth, within one week of the date hereof.

While the painter was employed in reading this covenant, Schalken, as we have stated, entered the studio, and having delivered the box and the valuation of the Jew into the hands of the stranger, he was about to retire, when Vanderhausen called to him to wait; and, presenting the case and the certificate to Gerard Douw, he waited in silence until he had satisfied himself by an inspection of both as to the value of the pledge left in his hands. At length he said:

"Are you content?"

The painter said "he would fain have another day to consider."

"Not an hour," said the suitor, coolly.

"Well, then," said Douw, "I am content; it is a bargain."

"Then sign at once," said Vanderhausen; "I am weary."

At the same time he produced a small case of writing materials, and Gerard signed the important document.

"Let this youth witness the covenant," said the old man; and Godfrey Schalken unconsciously signed the instrument which bestowed upon another that hand which he had so long regarded as the object and reward of all his labours.

The compact being thus completed, the strange visitor folded up the paper, and stowed it safely in an inner pocket.

"I will visit you to-morrow night, at nine of the clock, at your house, Gerard Douw, and will see the subject of our contract. Farewell." And so saying, Wilken Vanderhausen moved stiffly, but rapidly out of the room.

Schalken, eager to resolve his doubts, had placed himself by the window in order to watch the street entrance; but the experiment served only to support his suspicions, for the old man did not issue from the door. This was very strange, very odd, very fearful. He and his master returned together, and talked but little on the way, for each had his own subjects of reflection, of anxiety, and of hope.

Schalken, however, did not know the ruin which threatened his cherished schemes.

Gerard Douw knew nothing of the attachment which had sprung up between his pupil and his niece; and even if he had, it is doubtful whether he would have regarded its existence as any serious obstruction to the wishes of Mynher Vanderhausen.

Marriages were then and there matters of traffic and calculation; and it would have appeared as absurd in the eyes of the guardian to make a mutual attachment an essential element in a contract of marriage, as it would have been to draw up his bonds and receipts in the language of chivalrous romance.

The painter, however, did not communicate to his niece the important step which he had taken in her behalf, and his resolution arose not from any anticipation of opposition on her part, but solely from a ludicrous consciousness that if his ward were, as she very naturally might do, to ask him to describe the appearance of the bridegroom whom he destined for her, he would be forced to confess that he had not seen his face, and, if called upon, would find it impossible to identify him.

Upon the next day, Gerard Douw having dined, called his niece to him, and having scanned her person with an air of satisfaction, he took her hand, and looking upon her pretty, innocent face with a smile of kindness, he said:

"Rose, my girl, that face of yours will make your fortune." Rose blushed and smiled. "Such faces and such tempers seldom go together, and, when they do, the compound is a love-potion which few heads or hearts can resist. Trust me, thou wilt soon be a bride, girl. But this is trifling, and I am pressed for time, so make ready the large room by eight o'clock to-night, and give directions for supper at nine. I expect a friend to-night; and observe me, child, do thou trick thyself out handsomely. I would not have him think us poor or sluttish."

With these words he left the chamber, and took his way to the room to which we have already had occasion to introduce our readers--that in which his pupils worked.

When the evening closed in, Gerard called Schalken, who was about to take his departure to his obscure and comfortless lodgings, and asked him to come home and sup with Rose and Vanderhausen.

The invitation was of course accepted, and Gerard Douw and his pupil soon found themselves in the handsome and somewhat antique-looking room which had been prepared for the reception of the stranger.

A cheerful wood-fire blazed in the capacious hearth; a little at one side an old-fashioned table, with richly-carved legs, was placed--destined, no doubt, to receive the supper, for which preparations were going forward; and ranged with exact regularity stood the tall-backed chairs whose ungracefulness was more than counterbalanced by their comfort.

The little party, consisting of Rose, her uncle, and the artist, awaited the arrival of the expected visitor with considerable impatience.

Nine o'clock at length came, and with it a summons at the street-door, which, being speedily answered, was followed by a slow and emphatic tread upon the staircase; the steps moved heavily across the lobby, the door of the room in which the party which we have described were assembled slowly opened, and there entered a figure which startled, almost appalled, the phlegmatic Dutchmen, and nearly made Rose scream with affright; it was the form, and arrayed in the garb, of Mynher Vanderhausen; the air, the gait, the height was the same, but the features had never been seen by any of the party before.

The stranger stopped at the door of the room, and displayed his form and face completely. He wore a dark-coloured cloth cloak, which was short and full, not falling quite to the knees; his legs were cased in dark purple silk stockings, and his shoes were adorned with roses of the same colour. The opening of the cloak in front showed the under-suit to consist of some very dark, perhaps sable material, and his hands were enclosed in a pair of heavy leather gloves which ran up considerably above the wrist, in the manner of a gauntlet. In one hand he carried his walking-stick and his hat, which he had removed, and the other hung heavily by his side. A quantity of grizzled hair descended in long tresses from his head, and its folds rested upon the plaits of a stiff ruff, which effectually concealed his neck.

So far all was well; but the face!--all the flesh of the face was coloured with the bluish leaden hue which is sometimes produced by the operation of metallic medicines administered in excessive quantities; the eyes were enormous, and the white appeared both above and below the iris, which gave to them an expression of insanity, which was heightened by their glassy fixedness; the nose was well enough, but the mouth was writhed considerably to one side, where it opened in order to give egress to two long, discoloured fangs, which projected from the upper jaw, far below the lower lip; the hue of the lips themselves bore the usual relation to that of the face, and was consequently nearly black. The character of the face was malignant, even satanic, to the last degree; and, indeed, such a combination of horror could hardly be accounted for, except by supposing the corpse of some atrocious malefactor, which had long hung blackening upon the gibbet, to have at length become the habitation of a demon--the frightful sport of satanic possession.

It was remarkable that the worshipful stranger suffered as little as possible of his flesh to appear, and that during his visit he did not once remove his gloves.

Having stood for some moments at the door, Gerard Douw at length found breath and collectedness to bid him welcome, and, with a mute inclination of the head, the stranger stepped forward into the room.

There was something indescribably odd, even horrible about all his motions, something undefinable, something unnatural, unhuman--it was as if the limbs were guided and directed by a spirit unused to the management of bodily machinery.

The stranger said hardly anything during his visit, which did not exceed half an hour; and the host himself could scarcely muster courage enough to utter the few necessary salutations and courtesies: and, indeed, such was the nervous terror which the presence of Vanderhausen inspired, that very little would have made all his entertainers fly bellowing from the room.

They had not so far lost all self-possession, however, as to fail to observe two strange peculiarities of their visitor.

During his stay he did not once suffer his eyelids to close, nor even to move in the slightest degree; and further, there was a death-like stillness in his whole person, owing to the total absence of the heaving motion of the chest caused by the process of respiration.

These two peculiarities, though when told they may appear trifling, produced a very striking and unpleasant effect when seen and observed. Vanderhausen at length relieved the painter of Leyden of his inauspicious presence; and with no small gratification the little party heard the street door close after him.

"Dear uncle," said Rose, "what a frightful man! I would not see him again for the wealth of the States!"

"Tush, foolish girl!" said Douw, whose sensations were anything but comfortable. "A man may be as ugly as the devil, and yet if his heart and actions are good, he is worth all the pretty-faced, perfumed puppies that walk the Mall. Rose, my girl, it is very true he has not thy pretty face, but I know him to be wealthy and liberal; and were he ten times more ugly--"

"Which is inconceivable," observed Rose.

"These two virtues would be sufficient," continued her uncle, "to counterbalance all his deformity; and if not of power sufficient actually to alter the shape of the features, at least of efficacy enough to prevent one thinking them amiss."

"Do you know, uncle," said Rose, "when I saw him standing at the door, I could not get it out of my head that I saw the old, painted, wooden figure that used to frighten me so much in the church of St. Laurence at Rotterdam."

Gerard laughed, though he could not help inwardly acknowledging the justness of the comparison. He was resolved, however, as far as he could, to check his niece's inclination to ridicule the ugliness of her intended bridegroom, although he was not a little pleased to observe that she appeared totally exempt from that mysterious dread of the stranger, which, he could not disguise it from himself, considerably affected him, as it also did his pupil Godfrey Schalken.

Early on the next day there arrived from various quarters of the town, rich presents of silks, velvets, jewellery, and so forth, for Rose; and also a packet directed to Gerard Douw, which, on being opened, was found to contain a contract of marriage, formally drawn up, between Wilken Vanderhausen of the Boom-quay, in Rotterdam, and Rose Velderkaust of Leyden, niece to Gerard Douw, master in the art of painting, also of the same city; and containing engagements on the part of Vanderhausen to make settlements upon his bride far more splendid than he had before led her guardian to believe likely, and which were to be secured to her use in the most unexceptionable manner possible--the money being placed in the hands of Gerard Douw himself.

I have no sentimental scenes to describe, no cruelty of guardians or magnanimity of wards, or agonies of lovers. The record I have to make is one of sordidness, levity, and interest. In less than a week after the first interview which we have just described, the contract of marriage was fulfilled, and Schalken saw the prize which he would have risked anything to secure, carried off triumphantly by his formidable rival.

For two or three days he absented himself from the school; he then returned and worked, if with less cheerfulness, with far more dogged resolution than before; the dream of love had given place to that of ambition.

Months passed away, and, contrary to his expectation, and, indeed, to the direct promise of the parties, Gerard Douw heard nothing of his niece or her worshipful spouse. The interest of the money, which was to have been demanded in quarterly sums, lay unclaimed in his hands. He began to grow extremely uneasy.

Mynher Vanderhausen's direction in Rotterdam he was fully possessed of. After some irresolution he finally determined to journey thither--a trifling undertaking, and easily accomplished--and thus to satisfy himself of the safety and comfort of his ward, for whom he entertained an honest and strong affection.

His search was in vain, however. No one in Rotterdam had ever heard of Mynher Vanderhausen.

Gerard Douw left not a house in the Boom-quay untried; but all in vain. No one could give him any information whatever touching the object of his inquiry; and he was obliged to return to Leyden, nothing wiser than when he had left it.

On his arrival he hastened to the establishment from which Vanderhausen had hired the lumbering, though, considering the times, most luxurious vehicle which the bridal party had employed to convey them to Rotterdam. From the driver of this machine he learned, that having proceeded by slow stages, they had late in the evening approached Rotterdam; but that before they entered the city, and while yet nearly a mile from it, a small party of men, soberly clad, and after the old fashion, with peaked beards and moustaches, standing in the centre of the road, obstructed the further progress of the carriage. The driver reined in his horses, much fearing, from the obscurity of the hour, and the loneliness of the road, that some mischief was intended.

His fears were, however, somewhat allayed by his observing that these strange men carried a large litter, of an antique shape, and which they immediately set down upon the pavement, whereupon the bridegroom, having opened the coach-door from within, descended, and having assisted his bride to do likewise, led her, weeping bitterly and wringing her hands, to the litter, which they both entered. It was then raised by the men who surrounded it, and speedily carried towards the city, and before it had proceeded many yards the darkness concealed it from the view of the Dutch chariot.

In the inside of the vehicle he found a purse, whose contents more than thrice paid the hire of the carriage and man. He saw and could tell nothing more of Mynher Vanderhausen and his beautiful lady. This mystery was a source of deep anxiety and almost of grief to Gerard Douw.

There was evidently fraud in the dealing of Vanderhausen with him, though for what purpose committed he could not imagine. He greatly doubted how far it was possible for a man possessing in his countenance so strong an evidence of the presence of the most demoniac feelings to be in reality anything but a villain; and every day that passed without his hearing from or of his niece, instead of inducing him to forget his fears, tended more and more to intensify them.
The loss of his niece's cheerful society tended also to depress his spirits; and in order to dispel this despondency, which often crept upon his mind after his daily employment was over, he was wont frequently to prevail upon Schalken to accompany him home, and by his presence to dispel, in some degree, the gloom of his otherwise solitary supper.

One evening, the painter and his pupil were sitting by the fire, having accomplished a comfortable supper. They had yielded to that silent pensiveness sometimes induced by the process of digestion, when their reflections were disturbed by a loud sound at the street-door, as if occasioned by some person rushing forcibly and repeatedly against it. A domestic had run without delay to ascertain the cause of the disturbance, and they heard him twice or thrice interrogate the applicant for admission, but without producing an answer or any cessation of the sounds.

They heard him then open the hall door, and immediately there followed a light and rapid tread upon the staircase. Schalken laid his hand on his sword, and advanced towards the door. It opened before he reached it, and Rose rushed into the room. She looked wild and haggard, and pale with exhaustion and terror; but her dress surprised them as much even as her unexpected appearance. It consisted of a kind of white woollen wrapper, made close about the neck, and descending to the very ground. It was much deranged and travel-soiled. The poor creature had hardly entered the chamber when she fell senseless on the floor. With some difficulty they succeeded in reviving her, and on recovering her senses she instantly exclaimed, in a tone of eager, terrified impatience,--

"Wine, wine, quickly, or I'm lost!"

Much alarmed at the strange agitation in which the call was made, they at once administered to her wishes, and she drank some wine with a haste and eagerness which surprised him. She had hardly swallowed it, when she exclaimed with the same urgency,--

"Food, food, at once, or I perish!"

A considerable fragment of a roast joint was upon the table, and Schalken immediately proceeded to cut some, but he was anticipated; for no sooner had she become aware of its presence than she darted at it with the rapacity of a vulture, and, seizing it in her hands, she tore off the flesh with her teeth and swallowed it.

When the paroxysm of hunger had been a little appeased, she appeared suddenly to become aware how strange her conduct had been, or it may have been that other more agitating thoughts recurred to her mind, for she began to weep bitterly, and to wring her hands.

"Oh! send for a minister of God," said she; "I am not safe till he comes; send for him speedily."

Gerard Douw despatched a messenger instantly, and prevailed on his niece to allow him to surrender his bedchamber to her use; he also persuaded her to retire to it at once and to rest; her consent was extorted upon the condition that they would not leave her for a moment.

"Oh that the holy man were here!" she said; "he can deliver me. The dead and the living can never be one--God has forbidden it."

With these mysterious words she surrendered herself to their guidance, and they proceeded to the chamber which Gerard Douw had assigned to her use.

"Do not--do not leave me for a moment," said she. "I am lost for ever if you do."

Gerard Douw's chamber was approached through a spacious apartment, which they were now about to enter. Gerard Douw and Schalken each carried a wax candle, so that a sufficient degree of light was cast upon all surrounding objects. They were now entering the large chamber, which, as I have said, communicated with Douw's apartment, when Rose suddenly stopped, and, in a whisper which seemed to thrill with horror, she said,--

"O God! he is here--he is here! See, see--there he goes!"

She pointed towards the door of the inner room, and Schalken thought he saw a shadowy and ill-defined form gliding into that apartment. He drew his sword, and raising the candle so as to throw its light with increased distinctness upon the objects in the room, he entered the chamber into which the figure had glided. No figure was there--nothing but the furniture which belonged to the room, and yet he could not be deceived as to the fact that something had moved before them into the chamber.

A sickening dread came upon him, and the cold perspiration broke out in heavy drops upon his forehead; nor was he more composed when he heard the increased urgency, the agony of entreaty, with which Rose implored them not to leave her for a moment.

"I saw him," said she. "He's here! I cannot be deceived--I know him. He's by me--he's with me--he's in the room. Then, for God's sake, as you would save, do not stir from beside me!"

They at length prevailed upon her to lie down upon the bed, where she continued to urge them to stay by her. She frequently uttered incoherent sentences, repeating again and again, "The dead and the living cannot be one--God has forbidden it!" and then again, "Rest to the wakeful--sleep to the sleep-walkers."

These and such mysterious and broken sentences she continued to utter until the clergyman arrived.

Gerard Douw began to fear, naturally enough, that the poor girl, owing to terror or ill-treatment, had become deranged; and he half suspected, by the suddenness of her appearance, and the unseasonableness of the hour, and, above all, from the wildness and terror of her manner, that she had made her escape from some place of confinement for lunatics, and was in immediate fear of pursuit. He resolved to summon medical advice as soon as the mind of his niece had been in some measure set at rest by the offices of the clergyman whose attendance she had so earnestly desired; and until this object had been attained, he did not venture to put any questions to her, which might possibly, by reviving painful or horrible recollections, increase her agitation.

The clergyman soon arrived—a man of ascetic countenance and venerable age--one whom Gerard Douw respected much, forasmuch as he was a veteran polemic, though one, perhaps, more dreaded as a combatant than beloved as a Christian--of pure morality, subtle brain, and frozen heart. He entered the chamber which communicated with that in which Rose reclined, and immediately on his arrival she requested him to pray for her, as for one who lay in the hands of Satan, and who could hope for deliverance only from Heaven.

That our readers may distinctly understand all the circumstances of the event which we are about imperfectly to describe, it is necessary to state the relative positions of the parties who were engaged in it. The old clergyman and Schalken were in the ante-room of which we have already spoken; Rose lay in the inner chamber, the door of which was open; and by the side of the bed, at her urgent desire, stood her guardian; a candle burned in the bedchamber, and three were lighted in the outer apartment.

The old man now cleared his voice, as if about to commence; but before he had time to begin, a sudden gust of air blew out the candle which served to illuminate the room in which the poor girl lay, and she with hurried alarm, exclaimed:

"Godfrey, bring in another candle; the darkness is unsafe."

Gerard Douw, forgetting for the moment her repeated injunctions in the immediate impulse, stepped from the bedchamber into the other, in order to supply what she desired.

"O God! do not go, dear uncle!' shrieked the unhappy girl; and at the same time she sprang from the bed and darted after him, in order, by her grasp, to detain him.

But the warning came too late, for scarcely had he passed the threshold, and hardly had his niece had time to utter the startling exclamation, when the door which divided the two rooms closed violently after him, as if swung to by a strong blast of wind.

Schalken and he both rushed to the door, but their united and desperate efforts could not avail so much as to shake it.
Shriek after shriek burst from the inner chamber, with all the piercing loudness of despairing terror. Schalken and Douw applied every energy and strained every nerve to force open the door; but all in vain.

There was no sound of struggling from within, but the screams seemed to increase in loudness, and at the same time they heard the bolts of the latticed window withdrawn, and the window itself grated upon the sill as if thrown open.

One last shriek, so long and piercing and agonized as to be scarcely human, swelled from the room, and suddenly there followed a death-like silence.

A light step was heard crossing the floor, as if from the bed to the window; and almost at the same instant the door gave way, and yielding to the pressure of the external applicants, they were nearly precipitated into the room. It was empty. The window was open, and Schalken sprang to a chair and gazed out upon the street and at the canal below. He saw no form, but he beheld, or thought he beheld, the waters of the broad canal beneath settling ring after ring in heavy circular ripples, as if a moment before disturbed by the immersion of some large and heavy mass.

No trace of Rose was ever after discovered, nor was anything certain respecting her mysterious wooer detected or even suspected; no clue whereby to trace the intricacies of the labyrinth, and to arrive at a distinct conclusion was to be found. But an incident occurred, which, though it will not be received by our rational readers as at all approaching to evidence upon the matter, nevertheless produced a strong and a lasting impression upon the mind of Schalken.

Many years after the events which we have detailed, Schalken, then remotely situated, received an intimation of his father's death, and of his intended burial upon a fixed day in the church of Rotterdam. It was necessary that a very considerable journey should be performed by the funeral procession, which, as it will readily be believed, was not very numerously attended. Schalken with difficulty arrived in Rotterdam late in the day upon which the funeral was appointed to take place. The procession had not then arrived. Evening closed in, and still it did not appear.

Schalken strolled down to the church--he found it open; notice of the arrival of the funeral had been given, and the vault in which the body was to be laid had been opened. The official who corresponds to our sexton, on seeing a well-dressed gentleman, whose object was to attend the expected funeral, pacing the aisle of the church, hospitably invited him to share with him the comforts of a blazing wood fire, which as was his custom in winter time upon such occasions, he had kindled on the hearth of a chamber which communicated by a flight of steps with the vault below.

In this chamber Schalken and his entertainer seated themselves; and the sexton, after some fruitless attempts to engage his guest in conversation, was obliged to apply himself to his tobacco-pipe and can to solace his solitude.

In spite of his grief and cares, the fatigues of a rapid journey of nearly forty hours gradually overcame the mind and body of Godfrey Schalken, and he sank into a deep sleep, from which he was awakened by some one shaking him gently by the shoulder. He first thought that the old sexton had called him, but _he_ was no longer in the room.

He roused himself, and as soon as he could clearly see what was around him, he perceived a female form, clothed in a kind of light robe of muslin, part of which was so disposed as to act as a veil, and in her hand she carried a lamp. She was moving rather away from him, and towards the flight of steps which conducted towards the vaults.

Schalken felt a vague alarm at the sight of this figure, and at the same time an irresistible impulse to follow its guidance. He followed it towards the vaults, but when it reached the head of the stairs, he paused; the figure paused also, and turning gently round, displayed, by the light of the lamp it carried, the face and features of his first love, Rose Velderkaust. There was nothing horrible, or even sad, in the countenance. On the contrary, it wore the same arch smile which used to enchant the artist long before in his happy days.

A feeling of awe and of interest, too intense to be resisted, prompted him to follow the spectre, if spectre it were. She descended the stairs--he followed; and, turning to the left, through a narrow passage she led him, to his infinite surprise, into what appeared to be an old-fashioned Dutch apartment, such as the pictures of Gerard Douw have served to immortalize.

Abundance of costly antique furniture was disposed about the room, and in one corner stood a four-post bed, with heavy black cloth curtains around it. The figure frequently turned towards him with the same arch smile; and when she came to the side of the bed, she drew the curtains, and by the light of the lamp which she held towards its contents, she disclosed to the horror-stricken painter, sitting bolt upright in the bed, the livid and demoniac form of Vanderhausen. Schalken had hardly seen him when he fell senseless upon the floor, where he lay until discovered, on the next morning, by persons employed in closing the passages into the vaults. He was lying in a cell of considerable size, which had not been disturbed for a long time, and he had fallen beside a large coffin which was supported upon small stone pillars, a security against the attacks of vermin.

To his dying day Schalken was satisfied of the reality of the vision which he had witnessed, and he has left behind him a curious evidence of the impression which it wrought upon his fancy, in a painting executed shortly after the event we have narrated, and which is valuable as exhibiting not only the peculiarities which have made Schalken's pictures sought after, but even more so as presenting a portrait, as close and faithful as one taken from memory can be, of his early love, Rose Velderkaust, whose mysterious fate must ever remain matter of speculation.

The picture represents a chamber of antique masonry, such as might be found in most old cathedrals, and is lighted faintly by a lamp carried in the hand of a female figure, such as we have above attempted to describe; and in the background, and to the left of him who examines the painting, there stands the form of a man apparently aroused from sleep, and by his attitude, his hand being laid upon his sword, exhibiting considerable alarm; this last figure is illuminated only by the expiring glare of a wood or charcoal fire.

The whole production exhibits a beautiful specimen of that artful and singular distribution of light and shade which has rendered the name of Schalken immortal among the artists of his country. This tale is traditionary, and the reader will easily perceive, by our studiously omitting to heighten many points of the narrative, when a little additional colouring might have added effect to the recital, that we have desired to lay before him, not a figment of the brain, but a curious tradition connected with, and belonging to, the biography of a famous artist.

# THE FORTUNES OF SIR ROBERT ARDAGH (1859)

"The earth hath bubbles as the water hath--
And these are of them."

In the south of Ireland, and on the borders of the county of Limerick, there lies a district of two or three miles in length, which is rendered interesting by the fact that it is one of the very few spots throughout this country in which some vestiges of aboriginal forests still remain. It has little or none of the lordly character of the American forest, for the axe has felled its oldest and its grandest trees; but in the close wood which survives live all the wild and pleasing peculiarities of nature: its complete irregularity, its vistas, in whose perspective the quiet cattle are browsing; its refreshing glades, where the grey rocks arise from amid the nodding fern; the silvery shafts of the old birch-trees; the knotted trunks of the hoary oak, the grotesque but graceful branches which never shed their honours under the tyrant pruning-hook; the soft green sward; the chequered light and shade; the wild luxuriant weeds; the lichen and the moss--all are beautiful alike in the green freshness of spring or in the sadness and sere of autumn. Their beauty is of that kind which makes the heart full with joy--appealing to the affections with a power which belongs to nature only. This wood runs up, from below the base, to the ridge of a long line of irregular hills, having perhaps, in primitive times, formed but the skirting of some mighty forest which occupied the level below.

But now, alas! whither have we drifted? whither has the tide of civilization borne us? It has passed over a land unprepared for it--it has left nakedness behind it; we have lost our forests, but our marauders remain; we have destroyed all that is picturesque, while we have retained everything that is revolting in barbarism. Through the midst of this woodland there runs a deep gully or glen, where the stillness of the scene is broken in upon by the brawling of a mountain-stream, which, however, in the winter season, swells into a rapid and formidable torrent.

There is one point at which the glen becomes extremely deep and narrow; the sides descend to the depth of some hundred feet, and are so steep as to be nearly perpendicular. The wild trees which have taken root in the crannies and chasms of the rock are so intersected and entangled, that one can with difficulty catch a glimpse of the stream which wheels, flashes, and foams below, as if exulting in the surrounding silence and solitude.

This spot was not unwisely chosen, as a point of no ordinary strength, for the erection of a massive square tower or keep, one side of which rises as if in continuation of the precipitous cliff on which it is based. Originally, the only mode of ingress was by a narrow portal in the very wall which overtopped the precipice, opening upon a ledge of rock which afforded a precarious pathway, cautiously intersected, however, by a deep trench cut out with great labour in the living rock; so that, in its pristine state, and before the introduction of artillery into the art of war, this tower might have been pronounced, and that not presumptuously, impregnable.

The progress of improvement and the increasing security of the times had, however, tempted its successive proprietors, if not to adorn, at least to enlarge their premises, and about the middle of the last century, when the castle was last inhabited, the original square tower formed but a small part of the edifice.

The castle, and a wide tract of the surrounding country, had from time immemorial belonged to a family which, for distinctness, we shall call by the name of Ardagh; and owing to the associations which, in Ireland, almost always attach to scenes which have long witnessed alike the exercise of stern feudal authority, and of that savage hospitality which distinguished the good old times, this building has become the subject and the scene of many wild and extraordinary traditions. One of them I have been enabled, by a personal acquaintance with an eye-witness of the events, to trace to its origin; and yet it is hard to say whether the events which I am about to record appear more strange and improbable as seen through the distorting medium of tradition, or in the appalling dimness of uncertainty which surrounds the reality.

Tradition says that, sometime in the last century, Sir Robert Ardagh, a young man, and the last heir of that family, went abroad and served in foreign armies; and that, having acquired considerable honour and emolument, he settled at Castle Ardagh, the building we have just now attempted to describe. He was what the country people call a _dark_ man; that is, he was considered morose, reserved, and ill-tempered; and, as it was supposed from the utter solitude of his life, was upon no terms of cordiality with the other members of his family.

The only occasion upon which he broke through the solitary monotony of his life was during the continuance of the racing season, and immediately subsequent to it; at which time he was to be seen among the busiest upon the course, betting deeply and unhesitatingly, and invariably with success. Sir Robert was, however, too well known as a man of honour, and of too high a family, to be suspected of any unfair dealing. He was, moreover, a soldier, and a man of intrepid as well as of a haughty character; and no one cared to hazard a surmise, the consequences of which would be felt most probably by its originator only.

Gossip, however, was not silent; it was remarked that Sir Robert never appeared at the race-ground, which was the only place of public resort which he frequented, except in company with a certain strange-looking person, who was never seen elsewhere, or under other circumstances. It was remarked, too, that this man, whose relation to Sir Robert was never distinctly ascertained, was the only person to whom he seemed to speak unnecessarily; it was observed that while with the country gentry he exchanged no further communication than what was unavoidable in arranging his sporting transactions, with this person he would converse earnestly and frequently. Tradition asserts that, to enhance the curiosity which this unaccountable and exclusive preference excited, the stranger possessed some striking and unpleasant peculiarities of person and of garb--though it is not stated, however, what these were--but they, in conjunction with Sir Robert's secluded habits and extraordinary run of luck--a success which was supposed to result from the suggestions and immediate advice of the unknown--were sufficient to warrant report in pronouncing that there was something _queer_ in the wind, and in surmising that Sir Robert was playing a fearful and a hazardous game, and that, in short, his strange companion was little better than the Devil himself.

Years rolled quietly away, and nothing very novel occurred in the arrangements of Castle Ardagh, excepting that Sir Robert parted with his odd companion, but as nobody could tell whence he came, so nobody could say whither he had gone. Sir Robert's habits, however, underwent no consequent change; he continued regularly to frequent the race meetings, without mixing at all in the convivialities of the gentry, and immediately afterwards to relapse into the secluded monotony of his ordinary life.

It was said that he had accumulated vast sums of money--and, as his bets were always successful and always large, such must have been the case. He did not suffer the acquisition of wealth, however, to influence his hospitality or his house-keeping--he neither purchased land, nor extended his establishment; and his mode of enjoying his money must have been altogether that of the miser--consisting merely in the pleasure of touching and telling his gold, and in the consciousness of wealth.

Sir Robert's temper, so far from improving, became more than ever gloomy and morose. He sometimes carried the indulgence of his evil dispositions to such a height that it bordered upon insanity. During these paroxysms he would neither eat, drink, nor sleep. On such occasions he insisted on perfect privacy, even from the intrusion of his most trusted servants; his voice was frequently heard, sometimes in earnest supplication, sometimes raised, as if in loud and angry altercation with some unknown visitant. Sometimes he would for hours together walk to and fro throughout the long oak-wainscoted apartment which he generally occupied, with wild gesticulations and agitated pace, in the manner of one who has been roused to a state of unnatural excitement by some sudden and appalling intimation.

These paroxysms of apparent lunacy were so frightful, that during their continuance even his oldest and most faithful domestics dared not approach him; consequently his hours of agony were never intruded upon, and the mysterious causes of his sufferings appeared likely to remain hidden for ever.

On one occasion a fit of this kind continued for an unusual time; the ordinary term of their duration--about two days--had been long past, and the old servant who generally waited upon Sir Robert after these visitations, having in vain listened for the well-known tinkle of his master's hand-bell, began to feel extremely anxious; he feared that his master might have died from sheer exhaustion, or perhaps put an end to his own existence during his miserable depression. These fears at length became so strong, that having in vain urged some of his brother servants to accompany him, he determined to go up alone, and himself see whether any accident had befallen Sir Robert.

He traversed the several passages which conducted from the new to the more ancient parts of the mansion, and having arrived in the old hall of the castle, the utter silence of the hour--for it was very late in the night--the idea of the nature of the enterprise in which he was engaging himself, a sensation of remoteness from anything like human companionship, but, more than all, the vivid but undefined anticipation of something horrible, came upon him with such oppressive weight that he hesitated as to whether he should proceed. Real uneasiness, however, respecting the fate of his master, for whom he felt that kind of attachment which the force of habitual intercourse not unfrequently engenders respecting objects not in themselves amiable, and also a latent unwillingness to expose his weakness to the ridicule of his fellow-servants, combined to overcome his reluctance; and he had just placed his foot upon the first step of the staircase which conducted to his master's chamber, when his attention was arrested by a low but distinct knocking at the hall-door. Not, perhaps, very sorry at finding thus an excuse even for deferring his intended expedition, he placed the candle upon a stone block which lay in the hall and approached the door, uncertain whether his ears had not deceived him. This doubt was justified by the circumstance that the hall entrance had been for nearly fifty years disused as a mode of ingress to the castle. The situation of this gate also, which we have endeavoured to describe, opening upon a narrow ledge of rock which overhangs a perilous cliff, rendered it at all times, but particularly at night, a dangerous entrance. This shelving platform of rock, which formed the only avenue to the door, was divided, as I have already stated, by a broad chasm, the planks across which had long disappeared, by decay or otherwise; so that it seemed at least highly improbable that any man could have found his way across the passage in safety to the door, more particularly on a night like this, of singular darkness. The old man, therefore, listened attentively, to ascertain whether the first application should be followed by another. He had not long to wait. The same low but singularly distinct knocking was repeated; so low that it seemed as if the applicant had employed no harder or heavier instrument than his hand, and yet, despite the immense thickness of the door, with such strength that the sound was distinctly audible.

The knock was repeated a third time, without any increase of loudness; and the old man, obeying an impulse for which to his dying hour he could never account, proceeded to remove, one by one, the three great oaken bars which secured the door. Time and damp had effectually corroded the iron chambers of the lock, so that it afforded little resistance. With some effort, as he believed, assisted from without, the old servant succeeded in opening the door; and a low, square-built figure, apparently that of a man wrapped in a large black cloak, entered the hall. The servant could not see much of this visitor with any distinctness; his dress appeared foreign, the skirt of his ample cloak was thrown over one shoulder; he wore a large felt hat, with a very heavy leaf, from under which escaped what appeared to be a mass of long sooty-black hair; his feet were cased in heavy riding-boots. Such were the few particulars which the servant had time and light to observe. The stranger desired him to let his master know instantly that a friend had come, by appointment, to settle some business with him. The servant hesitated, but a slight motion on the part of his visitor, as if to possess himself of the candle, determined him; so, taking it in his hand, he ascended the castle stairs, leaving the guest in the hall.

On reaching the apartment which opened upon the oak-chamber he was surprised to observe the door of that room partly open, and the room itself lit up. He paused, but there was no sound; he looked in, and saw Sir Robert, his head and the upper part of his body reclining on a table, upon which two candles burned; his arms were stretched forward on either side, and perfectly motionless; it appeared that, having been sitting at the table, he had thus sunk forward, either dead or in a swoon. There was no sound of breathing; all was silent, except the sharp ticking of a watch, which lay beside the lamp. The servant coughed twice or thrice, but with no effect; his fears now almost amounted to certainty, and he was approaching the table on which his master partly lay, to satisfy himself of his death, when Sir Robert slowly raised his head, and, throwing himself back in his chair, fixed his eyes in a ghastly and uncertain gaze upon his attendant. At length he said, slowly and painfully, as if he dreaded the answer,--

"In God's name, what are you?"

"Sir," said the servant, "a strange gentleman wants to see you below."

At this intimation Sir Robert, starting to his feet and tossing his arms wildly upwards, uttered a shriek of such appalling and despairing terror that it was almost too fearful for human endurance; and long after the sound had ceased it seemed to the terrified imagination of the old servant to roll through the deserted passages in bursts of unnatural laughter. After a few moments Sir Robert said,--

"Can't you send him away? Why does he come so soon? O Merciful Powers! let him leave me for an hour; a little time. I can't see him now; try to get him away. You see I can't go down now; I have not strength. O God! O God! let him come back in an hour; it is not long to wait. He cannot lose anything by it; nothing, nothing, nothing. Tell him that! Say anything to him."

The servant went down. In his own words, he did not feel the stairs under him till he got to the hall. The figure stood exactly as he had left it. He delivered his master's message as coherently as he could. The stranger replied in a careless tone:

"If Sir Robert will not come down to me; I must go up to him."

The man returned, and to his surprise he found his master much more composed in manner. He listened to the message, and though the cold perspiration rose in drops upon his forehead faster than he could wipe it away, his manner had lost the dreadful agitation which had marked it before. He rose feebly, and casting a last look of agony behind him, passed from the room to the lobby, where he signed to his attendant not to follow him. The man moved as far as the head of the staircase, from whence he had a tolerably distinct view of the hall, which was imperfectly lighted by the candle he had left there.

He saw his master reel, rather than walk, down the stairs, clinging all the way to the banisters. He walked on, as if about to sink every moment from weakness. The figure advanced as if to meet him, and in passing struck down the light. The servant could see no more; but there was a sound of struggling, renewed at intervals with silent but fearful energy. It was evident, however, that the parties were approaching the door, for he heard the solid oak sound twice or thrice, as the feet of the combatants, in shuffling hither and thither over the floor, struck upon it. After a slight pause, he heard the door thrown open with such violence that the leaf seemed to strike the side-wall of the hall, for it was so dark without that this could only be surmised by the sound. The struggle was renewed with an agony and intenseness of energy that betrayed itself in deep-drawn gasps. One desperate effort, which terminated in the breaking of some part of the door, producing a sound as if the door-post was wrenched from its position, was followed by another wrestle, evidently upon the narrow ledge which ran outside the door, overtopping the precipice. This proved to be the final struggle; it was followed by a crashing sound as if some heavy body had fallen over, and was rushing down the precipice through the light boughs that crossed near the top. All then became still as the grave, except when the moan of the night-wind sighed up the wooded glen.

The old servant had not nerve to return through the hall, and to him the darkness seemed all but endless; but morning at length came, and with it the disclosure of the events of the night. Near the door, upon the ground, lay Sir Robert's sword-belt, which had given way in the scuffle. A huge splinter from the massive door-post had been wrenched off by an almost superhuman effort--one which nothing but the gripe of a despairing man could have severed--and on the rocks outside were left the marks of the slipping and sliding of feet.

At the foot of the precipice, not immediately under the castle, but dragged some way up the glen, were found the remains of Sir Robert, with hardly a vestige of a limb or feature left distinguishable. The right hand, however, was uninjured, and in its fingers were clutched, with the fixedness of death, a long lock of coarse sooty hair--the only direct circumstantial evidence of the presence of a second person.

# THE DREAM (1859)

Dreams! What age, or what country of the world, has not felt and acknowledged the mystery of their origin and end? I have thought not a little upon the subject, seeing it is one which has been often forced upon my attention, and sometimes strangely enough; and yet I have never arrived at anything which at all appeared a satisfactory conclusion. It does appear that a mental phenomenon so extraordinary cannot be wholly without its use. We know, indeed, that in the olden times it has been made the organ of communication between the Deity and His creatures; and when a dream produces upon a mind, to all appearance hopelessly reprobate and depraved, an effect so powerful and so lasting as to break down the inveterate habits, and to reform the life of an abandoned sinner, we see in the result, in the reformation of morals which appeared incorrigible, in the reclamation of a human soul which seemed to be irretrievably lost, something more than could be produced by a mere chimera of the slumbering fancy, something more than could arise from the capricious images of a terrified imagination. And while Reason rejects as absurd the superstition which will read a prophecy in every dream, she may, without violence to herself, recognize, even in the wildest and most incongruous of the wanderings of a slumbering intellect, the evidences and the fragments of a language which may be spoken, which _has_ been spoken, to terrify, to warn and to command. We have reason to believe too, by the promptness of action which in the age of the prophets followed all intimations of this kind, and by the strength of conviction and strange permanence of the effects resulting from certain dreams in latter times--which effects we ourselves may have witnessed--that when this medium of communication has been employed by the Deity, the evidences of His presence have been unequivocal. My thoughts were directed to this subject in a manner to leave a lasting impression upon my mind, by the events which I shall now relate, the statement of which, however extraordinary, is nevertheless accurate.

About the year 17--, having been appointed to the living of C----h, I rented a small house in the town which bears the same name: one morning in the month of November, I was awakened before my usual time by my servant, who bustled into my bedroom for the purpose of announcing a sick call. As the Catholic Church holds her last rites to be totally indispensable to the safety of the departing sinner, no conscientious clergyman can afford a moment's unnecessary delay, and in little more than five minutes I stood ready, cloaked and booted for the road, in the small front parlour in which the messenger, who was to act as my guide, awaited my coming. I found a poor little girl crying piteously near the door, and after some slight difficulty I ascertained that her father was either dead or just dying.

"And what may be your father's name, my poor child?" said I. She held down her head as if ashamed. I repeated the question, and the wretched little creature burst into floods of tears still more bitter than she had shed before. At length, almost angered by conduct which appeared to me so unreasonable, I began to lose patience, and I said rather harshly,--

"If you will not tell me the name of the person to whom you would lead me, your silence can arise from no good motive, and I might be justified in refusing to go with you at all."

"Oh, don't say that--don't say that!" cried she. "Oh, sir, it was that I was afeard of when I would not tell you--I was afeard, when you heard his name, you would not come with me; but it is no use hidin' it now--it's Pat Connell, the carpenter, your honour."

She looked in my face with the most earnest anxiety, as if her very existence depended upon what she should read there. I relieved the child at once. The name, indeed, was most unpleasantly familiar to me; but, however fruitless my visits and advice might have been at another time, the present was too fearful an occasion to suffer my doubts of their utility, or my reluctance to re-attempting what appeared a hopeless task, to weigh even against the lightest chance that a consciousness of his imminent danger might produce in him a more docile and tractable disposition. Accordingly I told the child to lead the way, and followed her in silence. She hurried rapidly through the long narrow street which forms the great thoroughfare of the town. The darkness of the hour, rendered still deeper by the close approach of the old-fashioned houses, which lowered in tall obscurity on either side of the way; the damp, dreary chill which renders the advance of morning peculiarly cheerless, combined with the object of my walk--to visit the death-bed of a presumptuous sinner, to endeavour, almost against my own conviction, to infuse a hope into the heart of a dying reprobate--a drunkard but too probably perishing under the consequences of some mad fit of intoxication; all these circumstances served to enhance the gloom and solemnity of my feelings, as I silently followed my little guide, who with quick steps traversed the uneven pavement of the Main Street. After a walk of about five minutes, she turned off into a narrow lane, of that obscure and comfortless class which is to be found in almost all small old-fashioned towns, chill, without ventilation, reeking with all manner of offensive effluviæ, and lined by dingy, smoky, sickly and pent-up buildings, frequently not only in a wretched but in a dangerous condition.

"Your father has changed his abode since I last visited him, and, I am afraid, much for the worse," said I.

"Indeed he has, sir; but we must not complain," replied she. "We have to thank God that we have lodging and food, though it's poor enough, it is, your honour."

Poor child! thought I. How many an older head might learn wisdom from thee--how many a luxurious philosopher, who is skilled to preach but not to suffer, might not thy patient words put to the blush! The manner and language of my companion were alike above her years and station; and, indeed, in all cases in which the cares and sorrows of life have anticipated their usual date, and have fallen, as they sometimes do, with melancholy prematurity to the lot of childhood, I have observed the result to have proved uniformly the same. A young mind, to which joy and indulgence have been strangers, and to which suffering and self-denial have been familiarized from the first, acquires a solidity and an elevation which no other discipline could have bestowed, and which, in the present case, communicated a striking but mournful peculiarity to the manners, even to the voice, of the child. We paused before a narrow, crazy door, which she opened by means of a latch, and we forthwith began to ascend the steep and broken stairs which led to the sick man's room. As we mounted flight after flight towards the garret-floor, I heard more and more distinctly the hurried talking of many voices. I could also distinguish the low sobbing of a female. On arriving upon the uppermost lobby, these sounds became fully audible.

"This way, your honour," said my little conductress; at the same time, pushing open a door of patched and half-rotten plank, she admitted me into the squalid chamber of death and misery. But one candle, held in the fingers of a scared and haggard-looking child, was burning in the room, and that so dim that all was twilight or darkness except within its immediate influence. The general obscurity, however, served to throw into prominent and startling relief the death-bed and its occupant. The light fell with horrible clearness upon the blue and swollen features of the drunkard. I did not think it possible that a human countenance could look so terrific. The lips were black and drawn apart; the teeth were firmly set; the eyes a little unclosed, and nothing but the whites appearing. Every feature was fixed and livid, and the whole face wore a ghastly and rigid expression of despairing terror such as I never saw equalled. His hands were crossed upon his breast, and firmly clenched; while, as if to add to the corpse-like effect of the whole, some white cloths, dipped in water, were wound about the forehead and temples.

As soon as I could remove my eyes from this horrible spectacle, I observed my friend Dr. D----, one of the most humane of a humane profession, standing by the bedside. He had been attempting, but unsuccessfully, to bleed the patient, and had now applied his finger to the pulse.

"Is there any hope?" I inquired in a whisper.

A shake of the head was the reply. There was a pause, while he continued to hold the wrist; but he waited in vain for the throb of life--it was not there: and when he let go the hand, it fell stiffly back into its former position upon the other.

"The man is dead," said the physician, as he turned from the bed where the terrible figure lay.

Dead! thought I, scarcely venturing to look upon the tremendous and revolting spectacle. Dead! without an hour for repentance, even a moment for reflection. Dead! without the rites which even the best should have. Was there a hope for him? The glaring eyeball, the grinning mouth, the distorted brow--that unutterable look in which a painter would have sought to embody the fixed despair of the nethermost hell--These were my answer.

The poor wife sat at a little distance, crying as if her heart would break--the younger children clustered round the bed, looking with wondering curiosity upon the form of death, never seen before.

When the first tumult of uncontrollable sorrow had passed away, availing myself of the solemnity and impressiveness of the scene, I desired the heart-stricken family to accompany me in prayer, and all knelt down while I solemnly and fervently repeated some of those prayers which appeared most applicable to the occasion. I employed myself thus in a manner which I trusted was not unprofitable, at least to the living, for about ten minutes; and having accomplished my task, I was the first to arise.

I looked upon the poor, sobbing, helpless creatures who knelt so humbly around me, and my heart bled for them. With a natural transition I turned my eyes from them to the bed in which the body lay; and, great God! what was the revulsion, the horror which I experienced on seeing the corpse-like, terrific thing seated half upright before me. The white cloths which had been wound about the head had now partly slipped from their position, and were hanging in grotesque festoons about the face and shoulders, while the distorted eyes leered from amid them--

"A sight to dream of, not to tell."

I stood actually riveted to the spot. The figure nodded its head and lifted its arm, I thought, with a menacing gesture. A thousand confused and horrible thoughts at once rushed upon my mind. I had often read that the body of a presumptuous sinner, who, during life, had been the willing creature of every satanic impulse, had been known, after the human tenant had deserted it, to become the horrible sport of demoniac possession.

I was roused by the piercing scream of the mother, who now, for the first time, perceived the change which had taken place. She rushed towards the bed, but, stunned by the shock and overcome by the conflict of violent emotions, before she reached it she fell prostrate upon the floor.

I am perfectly convinced that had I not been startled from the torpidity of horror in which I was bound by some powerful and arousing stimulant, I should have gazed upon this unearthly apparition until I had fairly lost my senses. As it was, however, the spell was broken--superstition gave way to reason: the man whom all believed to have been actually dead was living!

Dr. D---- was instantly standing by the bedside, and upon examination he found that a sudden and copious flow of blood had taken place from the wound which the lancet had left; and this, no doubt, had effected his sudden and almost preternatural restoration to an existence from which all thought he had been for ever removed. The man was still speechless, but he seemed to understand the physician when he forbade his repeating the painful and fruitless attempts which he made to articulate, and he at once resigned himself quietly into his hands.

I left the patient with leeches upon his temples, and bleeding freely, apparently with little of the drowsiness which accompanies apoplexy. Indeed, Dr. D---- told me that he had never before witnessed a seizure which seemed to combine the symptoms of so many kinds, and yet which belonged to none of the recognized classes; it certainly was not apoplexy, catalepsy, nor _delirium tremens_, and yet it seemed, in some degree, to partake of the properties of all. It was strange, but stranger things are coming.

During two or three days Dr. D---- would not allow his patient to converse in a manner which could excite or exhaust him, with anyone; he suffered him merely as briefly as possible to express his immediate wants. And it was not until the fourth day after my early visit, the particulars of which I have just detailed, that it was thought expedient that I should see him, and then only because it appeared that his extreme importunity and impatience to meet me were likely to retard his recovery more than the mere exhaustion attendant upon a short conversation could possibly do. Perhaps, too, my friend entertained some hope that if by holy confession his patient's bosom were eased of the perilous stuff which no doubt oppressed it, his recovery would be more assured and rapid. It was then, as I have said, upon the fourth day after my first professional call, that I found myself once more in the dreary chamber of want and sickness.

The man was in bed, and appeared low and restless. On my entering the room he raised himself in the bed, and muttered, twice or thrice,--

"Thank God! thank God!"

I signed to those of his family who stood by to leave the room, and took a chair beside the bed. So soon as we were alone, he said, rather doggedly,--

"There's no use in telling me of the sinfulness of bad ways--I know it all. I know where they lead to--I have seen everything about it with my own eyesight, as plain as I see you." He rolled himself in the bed, as if to hide his face in the clothes; and then suddenly raising himself, he exclaimed with startling vehemence, "Look, sir! there is no use in mincing the matter: I'm blasted with the fires of hell; I have been in hell. What do you think of that? In hell--I'm lost for ever--I have not a chance. I am damned already--damned--damned!"

The end of this sentence he actually shouted. His vehemence was perfectly terrific; he threw himself back, and laughed, and sobbed hysterically. I poured some water into a tea-cup, and gave it to him. After he had swallowed it, I told him if he had anything to communicate, to do so as briefly as he could, and in a manner as little agitating to himself as possible; threatening at the same time, though I had no intention of doing so, to leave him at once in case he again gave way to such passionate excitement.

"It's only foolishness," he continued, "for me to try to thank you for coming to such a villain as myself at all. It's no use for me to wish good to you, or to bless you; for such as me has no blessings to give."

I told him that I had but done my duty, and urged him to proceed to the matter which weighed upon his mind. He then spoke nearly as follows:--

"I came in drunk on Friday night last, and got to my bed here; I don't remember how. Sometime in the night it seemed to me I wakened, and feeling unasy in myself, I got up out of the bed. I wanted the fresh air; but I would not make a noise to open the window, for fear I'd waken the crathurs. It was very dark and throublesome to find the door; but at last I did get it, and I groped my way out, and went down as asy as I could. I felt quite sober, and I counted the steps one after another, as I was going down, that I might not stumble at the bottom.

"When I came to the first landing-place--God be about us always!--the floor of it sunk under me, and I went down--down--down, till the senses almost left me. I do not know how long I was falling, but it seemed to me a great while. When I came rightly to myself at last, I was sitting near the top of a great table; and I could not see the end of it, if it had any, it was so far off. And there was men beyond reckoning sitting down all along by it, at each side, as far as I could see at all. I did not know at first was it in the open air; but there was a close smothering feel in it that was not natural. And there was a kind of light that my eyesight never saw before, red and unsteady; and I did not see for a long time where it was coming from, until I looked straight up, and then I seen that it came from great balls of blood-coloured fire that were rolling high overhead with a sort of rushing, trembling sound, and I perceived that they shone on the ribs of a great roof of rock that was arched overhead instead of the sky. When I seen this, scarce knowing what I did, I got up, and I said, 'I have no right to be here; I must go.' And the man that was sitting at my left hand only smiled, and said, 'Sit down again; you can _never_ leave this place.' And his voice was weaker than any child's voice I ever heerd; and when he was done speaking he smiled again.

"Then I spoke out very loud and bold, and I said, 'In the name of God, let me out of this bad place.' And there was a great man that I did not see before, sitting at the end of the table that I was near; and he was taller than twelve men, and his face was very proud and terrible to look at. And he stood up and stretched out his hand before him; and when he stood up, all that was there, great and small, bowed down with a sighing sound; and a dread came on my heart, and he looked at me, and I could not speak. I felt I was his own, to do what he liked with, for I knew at once who he was; and he said, 'If you promise to return, you may depart for a season;' and the voice he spoke with was terrible and mournful, and the echoes of it went rolling and swelling down the endless cave, and mixing with the trembling of the fire overhead; so that when he sat down there was a sound after him, all through the place, like the roaring of a furnace. And I said, with all the strength I had, 'I promise to come back--in God's name let me go!'

"And with that I lost the sight and the hearing of all that was there, and when my senses came to me again, I was sitting in the bed with the blood all over me, and you and the rest praying around the room."

Here he paused, and wiped away the chill drops which hung upon his forehead.

I remained silent for some moments. The vision which he had just described struck my imagination not a little, for this was long before Vathek and the "Hall of Eblis" had delighted the world; and the description which he gave had, as I received it, all the attractions of novelty beside the impressiveness which always belongs to the narration of an _eye-witness_, whether in the body or in the spirit, of the scenes which he describes. There was something, too, in the stern horror with which the man related these things, and in the incongruity of his description with the vulgarly received notions of the great place of punishment, and of its presiding spirit, which struck my mind with awe, almost with fear. At length he said, with an expression of horrible, imploring earnestness, which I shall never forget,--

"Well, sir, is there any hope; is there any chance at all? or is my soul pledged and promised away for ever? is it gone out of my power? must I go back to the place?"

In answering him, I had no easy task to perform; for however clear might be my internal conviction of the groundlessness of his fears, and however strong my scepticism respecting the reality of what he had described, I nevertheless felt that his impression to the contrary, and his humility and terror resulting from it, might be made available as no mean engines in the work of his conversion from profligacy, and of his restoration to decent habits and to religious feeling.

I therefore told him that he was to regard his dream rather in the light of a warning than in that of a prophecy; that our salvation depended not upon the word or deed of a moment, but upon the habits of a life; that, in fine, if he at once discarded his idle companions and evil habits, and firmly adhered to a sober, industrious, and religious course of life, the powers of darkness might claim his soul in vain, for that there were higher and firmer pledges than human tongue could utter, which promised salvation to him who should repent and lead a new life.

I left him much comforted, and with a promise to return upon the next day. I did so, and found him much more cheerful, and without any remains of the dogged sullenness which I suppose had arisen from his despair. His promises of amendment were given in that tone of deliberate earnestness which belongs to deep and solemn determination; and it was with no small delight that I observed, after repeated visits, that his good resolutions, so far from failing, did but gather strength by time; and when I saw that man shake off the idle and debauched companions whose society had for years formed alike his amusement and his ruin, and revive his long-discarded habits of industry and sobriety, I said within myself, There is something more in all this than the operation of an idle dream.

One day, some time after his perfect restoration to health, I was surprised, on ascending the stairs for the purpose of visiting this man, to find him busily employed in nailing down some planks upon the landing-place, through which, at the commencement of his mysterious vision, it seemed to him that he had sunk. I perceived at once that he was strengthening the floor with a view to securing himself against such a catastrophe, and could scarcely forbear a smile as I bid "God bless his work."

He perceived my thoughts, I suppose, for he immediately said:

"I can never pass over that floor without trembling. I'd leave this house if I could, but I can't find another lodging in the town so cheap, and I'll not take a better till I've paid off all my debts, please God; but I could not be asy in my mind till I made it as safe as I could. You'll hardly believe me, your honour, that while I'm working, maybe a mile away, my heart is in a flutter the whole way back, with the bare thoughts of the two little steps I have to walk upon this bit of a floor. So it's no wonder, sir, I'd thry to make it sound and firm with any idle timber I have."

I applauded his resolution to pay off his debts, and the steadiness with which he perused his plans of conscientious economy, and passed on.

Many months elapsed, and still there appeared no alteration in his resolutions of amendment. He was a good workman, and with his better habits he recovered his former extensive and profitable employment. Everything seemed to promise comfort and respectability. I have little more to add, and that shall be told quickly. I had one evening met Pat Connell, as he returned from his work, and as usual, after a mutual, and on his side respectful salutation, I spoke a few words of encouragement and approval. I left him industrious, active, healthy--when next I saw him, not three days after, he was a corpse.

The circumstances which marked the event of his death were somewhat strange--I might say fearful. The unfortunate man had accidentally met an old friend just returned, after a long absence; and in a moment of excitement, forgetting everything in the warmth of his joy, he yielded to his urgent invitation to accompany him into a public house, which lay close by the spot where the encounter had taken place. Connell, however, previously to entering the room, had announced his determination to take nothing more than the strictest temperance would warrant.

But oh! who can describe the inveterate tenacity with which a drunkard's habits cling to him through life? He may repent, he may reform, he may look with actual abhorrence upon his past profligacy; but amid all this reformation and compunction, who can tell the moment in which the base and ruinous propensity may not recur, triumphing over resolution, remorse, shame, everything, and prostrating its victim once more in all that is destructive and revolting in that fatal vice?

The wretched man left the place in a state of utter intoxication. He was brought home nearly insensible, and placed in his bed. The younger part of the family retired to rest much after their usual hour; but the poor wife remained up sitting by the fire, too much grieved and shocked at the occurrence of what she had so little expected, to settle to rest. Fatigue, however, at length overcame her, and she sank gradually into an uneasy slumber. She could not tell how long she had remained in this state; but when she awakened, and immediately on opening her eyes, she perceived by the faint red light of the smouldering turf embers, two persons, one of whom she recognized as her husband, noiselessly gliding out of the room.

"Pat, darling, where are you going?" said she.

There was no answer--the door closed after them; but in a moment she was startled and terrified by a loud and heavy crash, as if some ponderous body had been hurled down the stair.

Much alarmed, she started up, and going to the head of the staircase, she called repeatedly upon her husband, but in vain.

She returned to the room, and with the assistance of her daughter, whom I had occasion to mention before, she succeeded in finding and lighting a candle, with which she hurried again to the head of the staircase.

At the bottom lay what seemed to be a bundle of clothes, heaped together, motionless, lifeless--it was her husband. In going down the stairs, for what purpose can never now be known, he had fallen helplessly and violently to the bottom, and coming head foremost, the spine of the neck had been dislocated by the shock, and instant death must have ensued.

The body lay upon that landing-place to which his dream had referred.

It is scarcely worth endeavouring to clear up a single point in a narrative where all is mystery; yet I could not help suspecting that the second figure which had been seen in the room by Connell's wife on the night of his death might have been no other than his own shadow.

I suggested this solution of the difficulty; but she told me that the unknown person had been considerably in advance of her husband, and on reaching the door, had turned back as if to communicate something to his companion.

It was, then, a mystery.

Was the dream verified?--whither had the disembodied spirit sped? who can say? We know not. But I left the house of death that day in a state of horror which I could not describe. It seemed to me that I was scarce awake. I heard and saw everything as if under the spell of a nightmare. The coincidence was terrible.

# A CHAPTER IN THE HISTORY OF A TYRONE FAMILY (1859)

In the following narrative I have endeavoured to give as nearly as possible the _ipsissima verba_ of the valued friend from whom I received it, conscious that any aberration from _her_ mode of telling the tale of her own life would at once impair its accuracy and its effect.

Would that, with her words, I could also bring before you her animated gesture, the expressive countenance, the solemn and thrilling air and accent with which she related the dark passages in her strange story; and, above all, that I could communicate the impressive consciousness that the narrator had seen with her own eyes, and personally acted in the scenes which she described. These accompaniments, taken with the additional circumstance that she who told the tale was one far too deeply and sadly impressed with religious principle to misrepresent or fabricate what she repeated as fact, gave to the tale a depth of interest which the recording of the events themselves could hardly have produced.

I became acquainted with the lady from whose lips I heard this narrative nearly twenty years since, and the story struck my fancy so much that I committed it to paper while it was still fresh in my mind; and should its perusal afford you entertainment for a listless half hour, my labour shall not have been bestowed in vain.

I find that I have taken the story down as she told it, in the first person, and perhaps this is as it should be.

She began as follows:

My maiden name was Richardson, the designation of a family of some distinction in the county of Tyrone. I was the younger of two daughters, and we were the only children. There was a difference in our ages of nearly six years, so that I did not, in my childhood, enjoy that close companionship which sisterhood, in other circumstances, necessarily involves; and while I was still a child, my sister was married.

The person upon whom she bestowed her hand was a Mr. Carew, a gentleman of property and consideration in the north of England.

I remember well the eventful day of the wedding; the thronging carriages, the noisy menials, the loud laughter, the merry faces, and the gay dresses. Such sights were then new to me, and harmonized ill with the sorrowful feelings with which I regarded the event which was to separate me from a sister whose tenderness alone had hitherto more than supplied all that I wanted in my mother's affection.

The day soon arrived which was to remove the happy couple from Ashtown House. The carriage stood at the hall-door, and my poor sister kissed me again and again, telling me that I should see her soon.

The carriage drove away, and I gazed after it until my eyes filled with tears, and, returning slowly to my chamber, I wept more bitterly and, so to speak, more desolately, than ever I had wept before.

My father had never seemed to love or to take an interest in me. He had desired a son, and I think he never thoroughly forgave me my unfortunate sex.

My having come into the world at all as his child he regarded as a kind of fraudulent intrusion; and as his antipathy to me had its origin in an imperfection of mine too radical for removal, I never even hoped to stand high in his good graces.

My mother was, I dare say, as fond of me as she was of anyone; but she was a woman of a masculine and a worldly cast of mind. She had no tenderness or sympathy for the weaknesses, or even for the affections, of woman's nature, and her demeanour towards me was peremptory, and often even harsh.

It is not to be supposed, then, that I found in the society of my parents much to supply the loss of my sister. About a year after her marriage, we received letters from Mr. Carew, containing accounts of my sister's health, which, though not actually alarming, were calculated to make us seriously uneasy. The symptoms most dwelt upon were loss of appetite, and a cough.

The letters concluded by intimating that he would avail himself of my father and mother's repeated invitation to spend some time at Ashtown, particularly as the physician who had been consulted as to my sister's health had strongly advised a removal to her native air.

There were added repeated assurances that nothing serious was apprehended, as it was supposed that a deranged state of the liver was the only source of the symptoms which at first had seemed to intimate consumption.

In accordance with this announcement, my sister and Mr. Carew arrived in Dublin, where one of my father's carriages awaited them, in readiness to start upon whatever day or hour they might choose for their departure.

It was arranged that Mr. Carew was, as soon as the day upon which they were to leave Dublin was definitely fixed, to write to my father, who intended that the two last stages should be performed by his own horses, upon whose speed and safety far more reliance might be placed than upon those of the ordinary post-horses, which were at that time, almost without exception, of the very worst order. The journey, one of about ninety miles, was to be divided; the larger portion being reserved for the second day.

On Sunday a letter reached us, stating that the party would leave Dublin on Monday, and in due course reach Ashtown upon Tuesday evening.

Tuesday came: the evening closed in, and yet no carriage; darkness came on, and still no sign of our expected visitors.

Hour after hour passed away, and it was now past twelve; the night was remarkably calm, scarce a breath stirring, so that any sound, such as that produced by the rapid movement of a vehicle, would have been audible at a considerable distance. For some such sound I was feverishly listening.
It was, however, my father's rule to close the house at nightfall, and the window-shutters being fastened, I was unable to reconnoitre the avenue as I would have wished. It was nearly one o'clock, and we began almost to despair of seeing them upon that night, when I thought I distinguished the sound of wheels, but so remote and faint as to make me at first very uncertain. The noise approached; it became louder and clearer; it stopped for a moment.

I now heard the shrill screaming of the rusty iron, as the avenue gate revolved on its hinges; again came the sound of wheels in rapid motion.

"It is they," said I, starting up; "the carriage is in the avenue."

We all stood for a few moments breathlessly listening. On thundered the vehicle with the speed of the whirlwind; crack went the whip, and clatter went the wheels, as it rattled over the uneven pavement of the court. A general and furious barking from all the dogs about the house hailed its arrival.

We hurried to the hall in time to hear the steps let down with the sharp clanging noise peculiar to the operation, and the hum of voices exerted in the bustle of arrival. The hall door was now thrown open, and we all stepped forth to greet our visitors.

The court was perfectly empty; the moon was shining broadly and brightly upon all around; nothing was to be seen but the tall trees with their long spectral shadows, now wet with the dews of midnight.

We stood gazing from right to left as if suddenly awakened from a dream; the dogs walked suspiciously, growling and snuffling about the court, and by totally and suddenly ceasing their former loud barking, expressed the predominance of fear.

We stared one upon another in perplexity and dismay, and I think I never beheld more pale faces assembled. By my father's directions, we looked about to find anything which might indicate or account for the noise which we had heard; but no such thing was to be seen--even the mire which lay upon the avenue was undisturbed. We returned to the house, more panic-struck than I can describe.
On the next day, we learned by a messenger, who had ridden hard the greater part of the night, that my sister was dead. On Sunday evening she had retired to bed rather unwell, and on Monday her indisposition declared itself unequivocally to be malignant fever. She became hourly worse, and, on Tuesday night, a little after midnight, she expired.

I mention this circumstance, because it was one upon which a thousand wild and fantastical reports were founded, though one would have thought that the truth scarcely required to be improved upon; and again, because it produced a strong and lasting effect upon my spirits, and indeed, I am inclined to think, upon my character.

I was, for several years after this occurrence, long after the violence of my grief subsided, so wretchedly low-spirited and nervous, that I could scarcely be said to live; and during this time, habits of indecision, arising out of a listless acquiescence in the will of others, a fear of encountering even the slightest opposition, and a disposition to shrink from what are commonly called amusements, grew upon me so strongly, that I have scarcely even yet altogether overcome them.

We saw nothing more of Mr. Carew. He returned to England as soon as the melancholy rites attendant upon the event which I have just mentioned were performed; and not being altogether inconsolable, he married again within two years; after which, owing to the remoteness of our relative situations, and other circumstances, we gradually lost sight of him.

I was now an only child; and, as my elder sister had died without issue, it was evident that, in the ordinary course of things, my father's property, which was altogether in his power, would go to me; and the consequence was, that before I was fourteen, Ashtown House was besieged by a host of suitors. However, whether it was that I was too young, or that none of the aspirants to my hand stood sufficiently high in rank or wealth, I was suffered by both parents to do exactly as I pleased; and well was it for me, as I afterwards found, that fortune, or rather Providence, had so ordained it, that I had not suffered my affections to become in any degree engaged, for my mother would never have suffered any silly fancy of mine, as she was in the habit of styling an attachment, to stand in the way of her ambitious views--views which she was determined to carry into effect in defiance of every obstacle, and in order to accomplish which she would not have hesitated to sacrifice anything so unreasonable and contemptible as a girlish passion.

When I reached the age of sixteen, my mother's plans began to develop themselves; and, at her suggestion, we moved to Dublin to sojourn for the winter, in order that no time might be lost in disposing of me to the best advantage.

I had been too long accustomed to consider myself as of no importance whatever, to believe for a moment that I was in reality the cause of all the bustle and preparation which surrounded me; and being thus relieved from the pain which a consciousness of my real situation would have inflicted, I journeyed towards the capital with a feeling of total indifference.

My father's wealth and connection had established him in the best society, and consequently, upon our arrival in the metropolis, we commanded whatever enjoyment or advantages its gaieties afforded.

The tumult and novelty of the scenes in which I was involved did not fail considerably to amuse me, and my mind gradually recovered its tone, which was naturally cheerful.

It was almost immediately known and reported that I was an heiress, and of course my attractions were pretty generally acknowledged.

Among the many gentlemen whom it was my fortune to please, one, ere long, established himself in my mother's good graces, to the exclusion of all less important aspirants. However, I had not understood or even remarked his attentions, nor in the slightest degree suspected his or my mother's plans respecting me, when I was made aware of them rather abruptly by my mother herself.

We had attended a splendid ball, given by Lord M----, at his residence in Stephen's Green, and I was, with the assistance of my waiting-maid, employed in rapidly divesting myself of the rich ornaments which, in profuseness and value, could scarcely have found their equals in any private family in Ireland.

I had thrown myself into a lounging-chair beside the fire, listless and exhausted after the fatigues of the evening, when I was aroused from the reverie into which I had fallen by the sound of footsteps approaching my chamber, and my mother entered.

"Fanny, my dear," said she, in her softest tone, "I wish to say a word or two with you before I go to rest. You are not fatigued, love, I hope?"

"No, no, madam, I thank you," said I, rising at the same time from my seat, with the formal respect so little practised now.

"Sit down, my dear," said she, placing herself upon a chair beside me; "I must chat with you for a quarter of an hour or so. Saunders" (to the maid), "you may leave the room; do not close the room door, but shut that of the lobby."

This precaution against curious ears having been taken as directed, my mother proceeded:

"You have observed, I should suppose, my dearest Fanny--indeed, you _must_ have observed Lord Glenfallen's marked attentions to you?"

"I assure you, madam--" I began.

"Well, well, that is all right," interrupted my mother. "Of course, you must be modest upon the matter; but listen to me for a few moments, my love, and I will prove to your satisfaction that your modesty is quite unnecessary in this case. You have done better than we could have hoped, at least, so very soon. Lord Glenfallen is in love with you. I give you joy of your conquest;" and, saying this, my mother kissed my forehead.

"In love with me!" I exclaimed in unfeigned astonishment.

"Yes, in love with you," repeated my mother; "devotedly, distractedly in love with you. Why, my dear, what is there wonderful in it? Look in the glass, and look at these," she continued, pointing, with a smile, to the jewels which I had just removed from my person, and which now lay in a glittering heap upon the table.

"May there not--" said I, hesitating between confusion and real alarm, "is it not possible that some mistake may be at the bottom of all this?"

"Mistake, dearest! none," said my mother. "None; none in the world. Judge for yourself; read this, my love." And she placed in my hand a letter, addressed to herself, the seal of which was broken. I read it through with no small surprise. After some very fine complimentary flourishes upon my beauty and perfections, as also upon the antiquity and high reputation of our family, it went on to make a formal proposal of marriage, to be communicated or not to me at present, as my mother should deem expedient; and the letter wound up by a request that the writer might be permitted, upon our return to Ashtown House, which was soon to take place, as the spring was now tolerably advanced, to visit us for a few days, in case his suit was approved.

"Well, well, my dear," said my mother, impatiently; "do you know who Lord Glenfallen is?"

"I do, madam," said I, rather timidly; for I dreaded an altercation with my mother.

"Well, dear, and what frightens you?" continued she. "Are you afraid of a title? What has he done to alarm you? He is neither old nor ugly."

I was silent, though I might have said, "He is neither young nor handsome."

"My dear Fanny," continued my mother, "in sober seriousness, you have been most fortunate in engaging the affections of a nobleman such as Lord Glenfallen, young and wealthy, with first-rate--yes, acknowledged _first-rate_ abilities, and of a family whose influence is not exceeded by that of any in Ireland. Of course, you see the offer in the same light that I do--indeed, I think you _must_."

This was uttered in no very dubious tone. I was so much astonished by the suddenness of the whole communication, that I literally did not know what to say.

"You are not in love?' said my mother, turning sharply, and fixing her dark eyes upon me with severe scrutiny.

"No, madam," said I, promptly; horrified--what young lady would not have been?--at such a query.

"I'm glad to hear it," said my mother, drily. "Once, nearly twenty years ago, a friend of mine consulted me as to how he should deal with a daughter who had made what they call a love-match--beggared herself, and disgraced her family; and I said, without hesitation, take no care for her, but cast her off. Such punishment I awarded for an offence committed against the reputation of a family not my own; and what I advised respecting the child of another, with full as small compunction I would _do_ with mine. I cannot conceive anything more unreasonable or intolerable than that the fortune and the character of a family should be marred by the idle caprices of a girl."

She spoke this with great severity, and paused as if she expected some observation from me.

I, however, said nothing.

"But I need not explain to you, my dear Fanny," she continued, "my views upon this subject; you have always known them well, and I have never yet had reason to believe you are likely to offend me voluntarily, or to abuse or neglect any of those advantages which reason and duty tell you should be improved. Come hither, my dear; kiss me, and do not look so frightened. Well, now, about this letter--you need not answer it yet; of course, you must be allowed time to make up your mind. In the meantime, I will write to his lordship to give him my permission to visit us at Ashtown. Good-night, my love."

And thus ended one of the most disagreeable, not to say astounding, conversations I had ever had. It would not be easy to describe exactly what were my feelings towards Lord Glenfallen;--whatever might have been my mother's suspicions, my heart was perfectly disengaged--and hitherto, although I had not been made in the slightest degree acquainted with his real views, I had liked him very much as an agreeable, well-informed man, whom I was always glad to meet in society. He had served in the navy in early life, and the polish which his manners received in his after intercourse with courts and cities had not served to obliterate that frankness of manner which belongs proverbially to the sailor.

Whether this apparent candour went deeper than the outward bearing, I was yet to learn. However, there was no doubt that, as far as I had seen of Lord Glenfallen, he was, though perhaps not so young as might have been desired in a lover, a singularly pleasing man; and whatever feeling unfavourable to him had found its way into my mind, arose altogether from the dread, not an unreasonable one, that constraint might be practised upon my inclinations. I reflected, however, that Lord Glenfallen was a wealthy man, and one highly thought of; and although I could never expect to love him in the romantic sense of the term, yet I had no doubt but that, all things considered, I might be more happy with him than I could hope to be at home.

When next I met him it was with no small embarrassment; his tact and good breeding, however, soon reassured me, and effectually prevented my awkwardness being remarked upon. And I had the satisfaction of leaving Dublin for the country with the full conviction that nobody, not even those most intimate with me, even suspected the fact of Lord Glenfallen's having made me a formal proposal.

This was to me a very serious subject of self-gratulation, for, besides my instinctive dread of becoming the topic of the speculations of gossip, I felt that if the situation which I occupied in relation to him were made publicly known, I should stand committed in a manner which would scarcely leave me the power of retraction.

The period at which Lord Glenfallen had arranged to visit Ashtown House was now fast approaching, and it became my mother's wish to form me thoroughly to her will, and to obtain my consent to the proposed marriage before his arrival, so that all things might proceed smoothly, without apparent opposition or objection upon my part. Whatever objections, therefore, I had entertained were to be subdued; whatever disposition to resistance I had exhibited or had been supposed to feel, were to be completely eradicated before he made his appearance; and my mother addressed herself to the task with a decision and energy against which even the barriers her imagination had created could hardly have stood.

If she had, however, expected any determined opposition from me, she was agreeably disappointed. My heart was perfectly free, and all my feelings of liking and preference were in favour of Lord Glenfallen; and I well knew that in case I refused to dispose of myself as I was desired, my mother had alike the power and the will to render my existence as utterly miserable as even the most ill-assorted marriage could possibly have made it.

You will remember, my good friend, that I was very young and very completely under the control of my parents, both of whom, my mother particularly, were unscrupulously determined in matters of this kind, and willing, when voluntary obedience on the part of those within their power was withheld, to compel a forced acquiescence by an unsparing use of all the engines of the most stern and rigorous domestic discipline.

All these combined, not unnaturally induced me to resolve upon yielding at once, and without useless opposition, to what appeared almost to be my fate.

The appointed time was come, and my now accepted suitor arrived; he was in high spirits, and, if possible, more entertaining than ever.

I was not, however, quite in the mood to enjoy his sprightliness; but whatever I wanted in gaiety was amply made up in the triumphant and gracious good-humour of my mother, whose smiles of benevolence and exultation were showered around as bountifully as the summer sunshine.

I will not weary you with unnecessary details. Let it suffice to say, that I was married to Lord Glenfallen with all the attendant pomp and circumstance of wealth, rank, and grandeur. According to the usage of the times, now humanely reformed, the ceremony was made, until long past midnight, the season of wild, uproarious, and promiscuous feasting and revelry.

Of all this I have a painfully vivid recollection, and particularly of the little annoyances inflicted upon me by the dull and coarse jokes of the wits and wags who abound in all such places, and upon all such occasions.

I was not sorry when, after a few days, Lord Glenfallen's carriage appeared at the door to convey us both from Ashtown; for any change would have been a relief from the irksomeness of ceremonial and formality which the visits received in honour of my newly-acquired titles hourly entailed upon me.

It was arranged that we were to proceed to Cahergillagh, one of the Glenfallen estates, lying, however, in a southern county; so that, owing to the difficulty of the roads at the time, a tedious journey of three days intervened.

I set forth with my noble companion, followed by the regrets of some, and by the envy of many; though God knows I little deserved the latter. The three days of travel were now almost spent, when passing the brow of a wild heathy hill, the domain of Cahergillagh opened suddenly upon our view.

It formed a striking and a beautiful scene. A lake of considerable extent stretching away towards the west, and reflecting from its broad, smooth waters the rich glow of the setting sun, was overhung by steep hills, covered by a rich mantle of velvet sward, broken here and there by the grey front of some old rock, and exhibiting on their shelving sides and on their slopes and hollows every variety of light and shade. A thick wood of dwarf oak, birch, and hazel skirted these hills, and clothed the shores of the lake, running out in rich luxuriance upon every promontory, and spreading upward considerably upon the side of the hills.

"There lies the enchanted castle," said Lord Glenfallen, pointing towards a considerable level space intervening between two of the picturesque hills which rose dimly around the lake.

This little plain was chiefly occupied by the same low, wild wood which covered the other parts of the domain; but towards the centre, a mass of taller and statelier forest trees stood darkly grouped together, and among them stood an ancient square tower, with many buildings of a humbler character, forming together the manor-house, or, as it was more usually called, the Court of Cahergillagh.

As we approached the level upon which the mansion stood, the winding road gave us many glimpses of the time-worn castle and its surrounding buildings; and seen as it was through the long vistas of the fine old trees, and with the rich glow of evening upon it, I have seldom beheld an object more picturesquely striking.

I was glad to perceive, too, that here and there the blue curling smoke ascended from stacks of chimneys now hidden by the rich, dark ivy which, in a great measure, covered the building. Other indications of comfort made themselves manifest as we approached; and indeed, though the place was evidently one of considerable antiquity, it had nothing whatever of the gloom of decay about it.

"You must not, my love," said Lord Glenfallen, "imagine this place worse than it is. I have no taste for antiquity--at least I should not choose a house to reside in because it is old. Indeed, I do not recollect that I was even so romantic as to overcome my aversion to rats and rheumatism, those faithful attendants upon your noble relics of feudalism; and I much prefer a snug, modern, unmysterious bedroom, with well-aired sheets, to the waving tapestry, mildewed cushions, and all the other interesting appliances of romance. However, though I cannot promise you all the discomfort generally belonging to an old castle, you will find legends and ghostly lore enough to claim your respect; and if old Martha be still to the fore, as I trust she is, you will soon have a supernatural and appropriate anecdote for every closet and corner of the mansion. But here we are--so, without more ado, welcome to Cahergillagh!"

We now entered the hall of the castle, and while the domestics were employed in conveying our trunks and other luggage which we had brought with us for immediate use, to the apartments which Lord Glenfallen had selected for himself and me, I went with him into a spacious sitting-room, wainscoted with finely-polished black oak, and hung round with the portraits of various worthies of the Glenfallen family.

This room looked out upon an extensive level covered with the softest green sward, and irregularly bounded by the wild wood I have before mentioned, through the leafy arcade formed by whose boughs and trunks the level beams of the setting sun were pouring. In the distance a group of dairy-maids were plying their task, which they accompanied throughout with snatches of Irish songs which, mellowed by the distance, floated not unpleasingly to the ear; and beside them sat or lay, with all the grave importance of conscious protection, six or seven large dogs of various kinds. Farther in the distance, and through the cloisters of the arching wood, two or three ragged urchins were employed in driving such stray kine as had wandered farther than the rest to join their fellows.

As I looked upon the scene which I have described, a feeling of tranquillity and happiness came upon me, which I have never experienced in so strong a degree; and so strange to me was the sensation that my eyes filled with tears.

Lord Glenfallen mistook the cause of my emotion, and taking me kindly and tenderly by the hand, he said:

"Do not suppose, my love, that it is my intention to _settle_ here. Whenever you desire to leave this, you have only to let me know your wish, and it shall be complied with; so I must entreat of you not to suffer any circumstances which I can control to give you one moment's uneasiness. But here is old Martha; you must be introduced to her, one of the heirlooms of our family."

A hale, good-humoured, erect old woman was Martha, and an agreeable contrast to the grim, decrepit hag which my fancy had conjured up, as the depositary of all the horrible tales in which I doubted not this old place was most fruitful.

She welcomed me and her master with a profusion of gratulations, alternately kissing our hands and apologizing for the liberty; until at length Lord Glenfallen put an end to this somewhat fatiguing ceremonial by requesting her to conduct me to my chamber, if it were prepared for my reception.

I followed Martha up an old-fashioned oak staircase into a long, dim passage, at the end of which lay the door which communicated with the apartments which had been selected for our use; here the old woman stopped, and respectfully requested me to proceed.

I accordingly opened the door, and was about to enter, when something like a mass of black tapestry, as it appeared, disturbed by my sudden approach, fell from above the door, so as completely to screen the aperture; the startling unexpectedness of the occurrence, and the rustling noise which the drapery made in its descent, caused me involuntarily to step two or three paces backward. I turned, smiling and half-ashamed, to the old servant, and said,--

"You see what a coward I am."

The woman looked puzzled, and, without saying any more, I was about to draw aside the curtain and enter the room, when, upon turning to do so, I was surprised to find that nothing whatever interposed to obstruct the passage.

I went into the room, followed by the servant-woman, and was amazed to find that it, like the one below, was wainscoted, and that nothing like drapery was to be found near the door.

"Where is it?" said I; "what has become of it?"

"What does your ladyship wish to know?" said the old woman.

"Where is the black curtain that fell across the door, when I attempted first to come to my chamber?" answered I.

"The cross of Christ about us!" said the old woman, turning suddenly pale.

"What is the matter, my good friend?" said I; "you seem frightened."

"Oh no, no, your ladyship," said the old woman, endeavouring to conceal her agitation; but in vain, for tottering towards a chair, she sank into it, looking so deadly pale and horror-struck that I thought every moment she would faint.

"Merciful God, keep us from harm and danger!" muttered she at length.

"What can have terrified you so?" said I, beginning to fear that she had seen something more than had met my eye. "You appear ill, my poor woman!"

"Nothing, nothing, my lady," said she, rising. "I beg your ladyship's pardon for making so bold. May the great God defend us from misfortune!"

"Martha," said I, "something _has_ frightened you very much, and I insist on knowing what it is; your keeping me in the dark upon the subject will make me much more uneasy than anything you could tell me. I desire you, therefore, to let me know what agitates you; I command you to tell me."

"Your ladyship said you saw a black curtain falling across the door when you were coming into the room," said the old woman.

"I did," said I; "but though the whole thing appears somewhat strange, I cannot see anything in the matter to agitate you so excessively."

"It's for no good you saw that, my lady," said the crone; "something terrible is coming. It's a sign, my lady--a sign that never fails."

"Explain, explain what you mean, my good woman," said I, in spite of myself, catching more than I could account for, of her superstitious terror.

"Whenever something--something _bad_ is going to happen to the Glenfallen family, some one that belongs to them sees a black handkerchief or curtain just waved or falling before their faces. I saw it myself," continued she, lowering her voice, "when I was only a little girl, and I'll never forget it. I often heard of it before, though I never saw it till then, nor since, praised be God. But I was going into Lady Jane's room to waken her in the morning; and sure enough when I got first to the bed and began to draw the curtain, something dark was waved across the division, but only for a moment; and when I saw rightly into the bed, there she was lying cold and dead, God be merciful to me! So, my lady, there is small blame to me to be daunted when any one of the family sees it; for it's many the story I heard of it, though I saw it but once."

I was not of a superstitious turn of mind, yet I could not resist a feeling of awe very nearly allied to the fear which my companion had so unreservedly expressed; and when you consider my situation, the loneliness, antiquity, and gloom of the place, you will allow that the weakness was not without excuse.

In spite of old Martha's boding predictions, however, time flowed on in an unruffled course. One little incident, however, though trifling in itself, I must relate, as it serves to make what follows more intelligible.

Upon the day after my arrival, Lord Glenfallen of course desired to make me acquainted with the house and domain; and accordingly we set forth upon our ramble. When returning, he became for some time silent and moody, a state so unusual with him as considerably to excite my surprise.

I endeavoured by observations and questions to arouse him--but in vain. At length, as we approached the house, he said, as if speaking to himself,--

"'Twere madness--madness--madness," repeating the words bitterly; "sure and speedy ruin."

There was here a long pause; and at length, turning sharply towards me, in a tone very unlike that in which he had hitherto addressed me, he said,--

"Do you think it possible that a woman can keep a secret?"

"I am sure," said I, "that women are very much belied upon the score of talkativeness, and that I may answer your question with the same directness with which you put it--I reply that I _do_ think a woman can keep a secret."

"But I do not," said he, drily.

We walked on in silence for a time. I was much astonished at his unwonted abruptness--I had almost said rudeness.

After a considerable pause he seemed to recollect himself, and with an effort resuming his sprightly manner, he said,--

"Well, well, the next thing to keeping a secret well is not to desire to possess one; talkativeness and curiosity generally go together. Now I shall make test of you, in the first place, respecting the latter of these qualities. I shall be your _Bluebeard_--tush, why do I trifle thus? Listen to me, my dear Fanny; I speak now in solemn earnest. What I desire is intimately, inseparably connected with your happiness and honour as well as my own; and your compliance with my request will not be difficult. It will impose upon you a very trifling restraint during your sojourn here, which certain events which have occurred since our arrival have determined me shall not be a long one. You must promise me, upon your sacred honour, that you will visit _only_ that part of the castle which can be reached from the front entrance, leaving the back entrance and the part of the building commanded immediately by it to the menials, as also the small garden whose high wall you see yonder; and never at any time seek to pry or peep into them, nor to open the door which communicates from the front part of the house through the corridor with the back. I do not urge this in jest or in caprice, but from a solemn conviction that danger and misery will be the certain consequences of your not observing what I prescribe. I cannot explain myself further at present. Promise me, then, these things, as you hope for peace here and for mercy hereafter."

I did make the promise as desired, and he appeared relieved; his manner recovered all its gaiety and elasticity: but the recollection of the strange scene which I have just described dwelt painfully upon my mind.

More than a month passed away without any occurrence worth recording; but I was not destined to leave Cahergillagh without further adventure. One day, intending to enjoy the pleasant sunshine in a ramble through the woods, I ran up to my room to procure my hat and cloak. Upon entering the chamber I was surprised and somewhat startled to find it occupied. Beside the fireplace, and nearly opposite the door, seated in a large, old-fashioned elbow-chair, was placed the figure of a lady. She appeared to be nearer fifty than forty, and was dressed suitably to her age, in a handsome suit of flowered silk; she had a profusion of trinkets and jewellery about her person, and many rings upon her fingers. But although very rich, her dress was not gaudy or in ill taste. But what was remarkable in the lady was, that although her features were handsome, and upon the whole pleasing, the pupil of each eye was dimmed with the whiteness of cataract, and she was evidently stone-blind. I was for some seconds so surprised at this unaccountable apparition, that I could not find words to address her.

"Madam," said I, "there must be some mistake here--this is my bedchamber."

"Marry come up," said the lady, sharply; "_your_ chamber! Where is Lord Glenfallen?"

"He is below, madam," replied I; "and I am convinced he will be not a little surprised to find you here."

"I do not think he will," said she, "with your good leave; talk of what you know something about. Tell him I want him. Why does the minx dilly-dally so?"

In spite of the awe which this grim lady inspired, there was something in her air of confident superiority which, when I considered our relative situations, was not a little irritating.

"Do you know, madam, to whom you speak?" said I.

"I neither know nor care," said she; "but I presume that you are some one about the house, so again I desire you, if you wish to continue here, to bring your master hither forthwith."

"I must tell you, madam," said I, "that I am Lady Glenfallen."

"What's that?" said the stranger, rapidly.

"I say, madam," I repeated, approaching her that I might be more distinctly heard, "that I am Lady Glenfallen."

"It's a lie, you trull!" cried she, in an accent which made me start, and at the same time, springing forward, she seized me in her grasp, and shook me violently, repeating, "It's a lie--it's a lie!" with a rapidity and vehemence which swelled every vein of her face. The violence of her action, and the fury which convulsed her face, effectually terrified me, and disengaging myself from her grasp, I screamed as loud as I could for help. The blind woman continued to pour out a torrent of abuse upon me, foaming at the mouth with rage, and impotently shaking her clenched fist towards me.

I heard Lord Glenfallen's step upon the stairs, and I instantly ran out; as I passed him I perceived that he was deadly pale, and just caught the words: "I hope that demon has not hurt you?"

I made some answer, I forget what, and he entered the chamber, the door of which he locked upon the inside. What passed within I know not; but I heard the voices of the two speakers raised in loud and angry altercation.

I thought I heard the shrill accents of the woman repeat the words, "Let her look to herself;" but I could not be quite sure. This short sentence, however, was, to my alarmed imagination, pregnant with fearful meaning.

The storm at length subsided, though not until after a conference of more than two long hours. Lord Glenfallen then returned, pale and agitated.

"That unfortunate woman," said he, "is out of her mind. I daresay she treated you to some of her ravings; but you need not dread any further interruption from her: I have brought her so far to reason. She did not hurt you, I trust."

"No, no," said I; "but she terrified me beyond measure."

"Well," said he, "she is likely to behave better for the future; and I dare swear that neither you nor she would desire, after what has passed, to meet again."

This occurrence, so startling and unpleasant, so involved in mystery, and giving rise to so many painful surmises, afforded me no very agreeable food for rumination.

All attempts on my part to arrive at the truth were baffled; Lord Glenfallen evaded all my inquiries, and at length peremptorily forbade any further allusion to the matter. I was thus obliged to rest satisfied with what I had actually seen, and to trust to time to resolve the perplexities in which the whole transaction had involved me.

Lord Glenfallen's temper and spirits gradually underwent a complete and most painful change; he became silent and abstracted, his manner to me was abrupt and often harsh, some grievous anxiety seemed ever present to his mind; and under its influence his spirits sank and his temper became soured.

I soon perceived that his gaiety was rather that which the stir and excitement of society produce, than the result of a healthy habit of mind; every day confirmed me in the opinion, that the considerate good-nature which I had so much admired in him was little more than a mere manner; and to my infinite grief and surprise, the gay, kind, open-hearted nobleman who had for months followed and flattered me, was rapidly assuming the form of a gloomy, morose, and singularly selfish man. This was a bitter discovery, and I strove to conceal it from myself as long as I could; but the truth was not to be denied, and I was forced to believe that my husband no longer loved me, and that he was at little pains to conceal the alteration in his sentiments.
One morning after breakfast, Lord Glenfallen had been for some time walking silently up and down the room, buried in his moody reflections, when pausing suddenly, and turning towards me, he exclaimed:

"I have it--I have it! We must go abroad, and stay there too; and if that does not answer, why--why, we must try some more effectual expedient. Lady Glenfallen, I have become involved in heavy embarrassments. A wife, you know, must share the fortunes of her husband, for better for worse; but I will waive my right if you prefer remaining here--here at Cahergillagh. For I would not have you seen elsewhere without the state to which your rank entitles you; besides, it would break your poor mother's heart," he added, with sneering gravity. "So make up your mind--Cahergillagh or France. I will start if possible in a week, so determine between this and then."

He left the room, and in a few moments I saw him ride past the window, followed by a mounted servant. He had directed a domestic to inform me that he should not be back until the next day.

I was in very great doubt as to what course of conduct I should pursue as to accompanying him in the continental tour so suddenly determined upon. I felt that it would be a hazard too great to encounter; for at Cahergillagh I had always the consciousness to sustain me, that if his temper at any time led him into violent or unwarrantable treatment of me, I had a remedy within reach, in the protection and support of my own family, from all useful and effective communication with whom, if once in France, I should be entirely debarred.

As to remaining at Cahergillagh in solitude, and, for aught I knew, exposed to hidden dangers, it appeared to me scarcely less objectionable than the former proposition; and yet I feared that with one or other I must comply, unless I was prepared to come to an actual breach with Lord Glenfallen. Full of these unpleasing doubts and perplexities, I retired to rest.

I was wakened, after having slept uneasily for some hours, by some person shaking me rudely by the shoulder; a small lamp burned in my room, and by its light, to my horror and amazement, I discovered that my visitant was the self-same blind old lady who had so terrified me a few weeks before.

I started up in the bed, with a view to ring the bell, and alarm the domestics; but she instantly anticipated me by saying:

"Do not be frightened, silly girl! If I had wished to harm you, I could have done it while you were sleeping; I need not have wakened you. Listen to me, now, attentively and fearlessly, for what I have to say interests you to the full as much as it does me. Tell me here, in the presence of God, did Lord Glenfallen marry you--_actually marry you_? Speak the truth, woman."

"As surely as I live and speak," I replied, "did Lord Glenfallen marry me, in presence of more than a hundred witnesses."

"Well," continued she, "he should have told you _then_, before you married him, that he had a wife living,--that I am his wife. I feel you tremble--tush! do not be frightened. I do not mean to harm you. Mark me now--you are _not_ his wife. When I make my story known you will be so neither in the eye of God nor of man. You must leave this house upon to-morrow. Let the world know that your husband has another wife living; go you into retirement, and leave him to justice, which will surely overtake him. If you remain in this house after to-morrow, you will reap the bitter fruits of your sin."

So saying, she quitted the room, leaving me very little disposed to sleep.

Here was food for my very worst and most terrible suspicions; still there was not enough to remove all doubt. I had no proof of the truth of this woman's statement.

Taken by itself, there was nothing to induce me to attach weight to it; but when I viewed it in connection with the extraordinary mystery of some of Lord Glenfallen's proceedings, his strange anxiety to exclude me from certain portions of the mansion, doubtless lest I should encounter this person--the strong influence, nay, command which she possessed over him, a circumstance clearly established by the very fact of her residing in the very place where, of all others, he should least have desired to find her--her thus acting, and continuing to act in direct contradiction to his wishes; when, I say, I viewed her disclosure in connection with all these circumstances, I could not help feeling that there was at least a fearful verisimilitude in the allegations which she had made.

Still I was not satisfied, nor nearly so. Young minds have a reluctance almost insurmountable to believing, upon anything short of unquestionable proof, the existence of premeditated guilt in anyone whom they have ever trusted; and in support of this feeling I was assured that if the assertion of Lord Glenfallen, which nothing in this woman's manner had led me to disbelieve, were true, namely that her mind was unsound, the whole fabric of my doubts and fears must fall to the ground.

I determined to state to Lord Glenfallen freely and accurately the substance of the communication which I had just heard, and in his words and looks to seek for its proof or refutation. Full of these thoughts, I remained wakeful and excited all night, every moment fancying that I heard the step or saw the figure of my recent visitor, towards whom I felt a species of horror and dread which I can hardly describe.

There was something in her face, though her features had evidently been handsome, and were not, at first sight, unpleasing, which, upon a nearer inspection, seemed to indicate the habitual prevalence and indulgence of evil passions, and a power of expressing mere animal anger with an intenseness that I have seldom seen equalled, and to which an almost unearthly effect was given by the convulsive quivering of the sightless eyes.

You may easily suppose that it was no very pleasing reflection to me to consider that, whenever caprice might induce her to return, I was within the reach of this violent and, for aught I knew, insane woman, who had, upon that very night, spoken to me in a tone of menace, of which her mere words, divested of the manner and look with which she uttered them, can convey but a faint idea.

Will you believe me when I tell you that I was actually afraid to leave my bed in order to secure the door, lest I should again encounter the dreadful object lurking in some corner or peeping from behind the window-curtains, so very a child was I in my fears?

The morning came, and with it Lord Glenfallen. I knew not, and indeed I cared not, where he might have been; my thoughts were wholly engrossed by the terrible fears and suspicions which my last night's conference had suggested to me. He was, as usual, gloomy and abstracted, and I feared in no very fitting mood to hear what I had to say with patience, whether the charges were true or false.

I was, however, determined not to suffer the opportunity to pass, or Lord Glenfallen to leave the room, until, at all hazards, I had unburdened my mind.

"My lord," said I, after a long silence, summoning up all my firmness, "my lord, I wish to say a few words to you upon a matter of very great importance, of very deep concernment to you and to me."

I fixed my eyes upon him to discern, if possible, whether the announcement caused him any uneasiness; but no symptom of any such feeling was perceptible.

"Well, my dear," said he, "this is no doubt a very grave preface, and portends, I have no doubt, something extraordinary. Pray let us have it without more ado."

He took a chair, and seated himself nearly opposite to me.

"My lord," said I, "I have seen the person who alarmed me so much a short time since, the blind lady, again, upon last night." His face, upon which my eyes were fixed, turned pale; he hesitated for a moment, and then said:

"And did you, pray, madam, so totally forget or spurn my express command, as to enter that portion of the house from which your promise, I might say your oath, excluded you? Answer me that!" he added fiercely.

"My lord," said I, "I have neither forgotten your _commands_, since such they were, nor disobeyed them. I was, last night, wakened from my sleep, as I lay in my own chamber, and accosted by the person whom I have mentioned. How she found access to the room I cannot pretend to say."

"Ha! this must be looked to,' said he, half reflectively. "And pray," added he quickly, while in turn he fixed his eyes upon me, "what did this person say? since some comment upon her communication forms, no doubt, the sequel to your preface."

"Your lordship is not mistaken," said I; "her statement was so extraordinary that I could not think of withholding it from you. She told me, my lord, that you had a wife living at the time you married me, and that she was that wife."

Lord Glenfallen became ashy pale, almost livid; he made two or three efforts to clear his voice to speak, but in vain, and turning suddenly from me, he walked to the window. The horror and dismay which, in the olden time, overwhelmed the woman of Endor when her spells unexpectedly conjured the dead into her presence, were but types of what I felt when thus presented with what appeared to be almost unequivocal evidence of the guilt whose existence I had before so strongly doubted.

There was a silence of some moments, during which it were hard to conjecture whether I or my companion suffered most.

Lord Glenfallen soon recovered his self-command; he returned to the table, again sat down, and said:

"What you have told me has so astonished me, has unfolded such a tissue of motiveless guilt, and in a quarter from which I had so little reason to look for ingratitude or treachery, that your announcement almost deprived me of speech; the person in question, however, has one excuse, her mind is, as I told you before, unsettled. You should have remembered that, and hesitated to receive as unexceptionable evidence against the honour of your husband, the ravings of a lunatic. I now tell you that this is the last time I shall speak to you upon this subject, and, in the presence of the God who is to judge me, and as I hope for mercy in the day of judgment, I swear that the charge thus brought against me is utterly false, unfounded, and ridiculous. I defy the world in any point to taint my honour; and, as I have never taken the opinion of madmen touching your character or morals, I think it but fair to require that you will evince a like tenderness for me; and now, once for all, never again dare to repeat to me your insulting suspicions, or the clumsy and infamous calumnies of fools. I shall instantly let the worthy lady who contrived this somewhat original device understand fully my opinion upon the matter. Good morning."

And with these words he left me again in doubt, and involved in all the horrors of the most agonizing suspense.

I had reason to think that Lord Glenfallen wreaked his vengeance upon the author of the strange story which I had heard, with a violence which was not satisfied with mere words, for old Martha, with whom I was a great favourite, while attending me in my room, told me that she feared her master had ill-used the poor blind Dutchwoman, for that she had heard her scream as if the very life were leaving her, but added a request that I should not speak of what she had told me to any one, particularly to the master.

"How do you know that she is a Dutchwoman?" inquired I, anxious to learn anything whatever that might throw a light upon the history of this person, who seemed to have resolved to mix herself up in my fortunes.

"Why, my lady," answered Martha, "the master often calls her the Dutch hag, and other names you would not like to hear, and I am sure she is neither English nor Irish; for, whenever they talk together, they speak some queer foreign lingo, and fast enough, I'll be bound. But I ought not to talk about her at all; it might be as much as my place is worth to mention her, only you saw her first yourself, so there can be no great harm in speaking of her now."

"How long has this lady been here?" continued I.

"She came early on the morning after your ladyship's arrival," answered she; "but do not ask me any more, for the master would think nothing of turning me out of doors for daring to speak of her at all, much less to _you_, my lady."
I did not like to press the poor woman further, for her reluctance to speak on this topic was evident and strong.

You will readily believe that upon the very slight grounds which my information afforded, contradicted as it was by the solemn oath of my husband, and derived from what was, at best, a very questionable source, I could not take any very decisive measures whatever; and as to the menace of the strange woman who had thus unaccountably twice intruded herself into my chamber, although, at the moment, it occasioned me some uneasiness, it was not, even in my eyes, sufficiently formidable to induce my departure from Cahergillagh.

A few nights after the scene which I have just mentioned, Lord Glenfallen having, as usual, retired early to his study, I was left alone in the parlour to amuse myself as best I might.

It was not strange that my thoughts should often recur to the agitating scenes in which I had recently taken a part.

The subject of my reflections, the solitude, the silence, and the lateness of the hour, as also the depression of spirits to which I had of late been a constant prey, tended to produce that nervous excitement which places us wholly at the mercy of the imagination.

In order to calm my spirits I was endeavouring to direct my thoughts into some more pleasing channel, when I heard, or thought I heard, uttered within a few yards of me, in an odd, half-sneering tone, the words,--

"There is blood upon your ladyship's throat."

So vivid was the impression that I started to my feet, and involuntarily placed my hand upon my neck.

I looked around the room for the speaker, but in vain.

I went then to the room-door, which I opened, and peered into the passage, nearly faint with horror lest some leering, shapeless thing should greet me upon the threshold.
When I had gazed long enough to assure myself that no strange object was within sight,--

"I have been too much of a rake lately; I am racking out my nerves," said I, speaking aloud, with a view to reassure myself.

I rang the bell, and, attended by old Martha, I retired to settle for the night.

While the servant was--as was her custom--arranging the lamp which I have already stated always burned during the night in my chamber, I was employed in undressing, and, in doing so, I had recourse to a large looking-glass which occupied a considerable portion of the wall in which it was fixed, rising from the ground to a height of about six feet; this mirror filled the space of a large panel in the wainscoting opposite the foot of the bed.

I had hardly been before it for the lapse of a minute when something like a black pall was slowly waved between me and it.

"Oh, God! there it is," I exclaimed, wildly. "I have seen it again, Martha--the black cloth."

"God be merciful to us, then!" answered she, tremulously crossing herself. "Some misfortune is over us."

"No, no, Martha," said I, almost instantly recovering my collectedness; for, although of a nervous temperament, I had never been superstitious. "I do not believe in omens. You know I saw, or fancied I saw, this thing before, and nothing followed."

"The Dutch lady came the next morning," replied she.

"But surely her coming scarcely deserved such a dreadful warning," I replied.

"She is a strange woman, my lady," said Martha; "and she is not _gone_ yet--mark my words."

"Well, well, Martha," said I, "I have not wit enough to change your opinions, nor inclination to alter mine; so I will talk no more of the matter. Good-night," and so I was left to my reflections.

After lying for about an hour awake, I at length fell into a kind of doze; but my imagination was very busy, for I was startled from this unrefreshing sleep by fancying that I heard a voice close to my face exclaim as before,--

"There is blood upon your ladyship's throat."

The words were instantly followed by a loud burst of laughter.

Quaking with horror, I awakened, and heard my husband enter the room. Even this was a relief.

Scared as I was, however, by the tricks which my imagination had played me, I preferred remaining silent, and pretending to sleep, to attempting to engage my husband in conversation, for I well knew that his mood was such, that his words would not, in all probability, convey anything that had not better be unsaid and unheard.

Lord Glenfallen went into his dressing-room, which lay upon the right-hand side of the bed. The door lying open, I could see him by himself, at full length upon a sofa, and, in about half an hour, I became aware, by his deep and regularly drawn respiration, that he was fast asleep.

When slumber refuses to visit one, there is something peculiarly irritating, not to the temper, but to the nerves, in the consciousness that some one is in your immediate presence, actually enjoying the boon which you are seeking in vain; at least, I have always found it so, and never more than upon the present occasion.

A thousand annoying imaginations harassed and excited me; every object which I looked upon, though ever so familiar, seemed to have acquired a strange phantom-like character, the varying shadows thrown by the flickering of the lamplight seemed shaping themselves into grotesque and unearthly forms, and whenever my eyes wandered to the sleeping figure of my husband, his features appeared to undergo the strangest and most demoniacal contortions.

Hour after hour was told by the old clock, and each succeeding one found me, if possible, less inclined to sleep than its predecessor.

It was now considerably past three; my eyes, in their involuntary wanderings, happened to alight upon the large mirror which was, as I have said, fixed in the wall opposite the foot of the bed. A view of it was commanded from where I lay, through the curtains. As I gazed fixedly upon it, I thought I perceived the broad sheet of glass shifting its position in relation to the bed; I riveted my eyes upon it with intense scrutiny; it was no deception, the mirror, as if acting of its own impulse, moved slowly aside, and disclosed a dark aperture in the wall, nearly as large as an ordinary door; a figure evidently stood in this, but the light was too dim to define it accurately.

It stepped cautiously into the chamber, and with so little noise, that had I not actually seen it, I do not think I should have been aware of its presence. It was arrayed in a kind of woollen night-dress, and a white handkerchief or cloth was bound tightly about the head; I had no difficulty, spite of the strangeness of the attire, in recognizing the blind woman whom I so much dreaded.

She stooped down, bringing her head nearly to the ground, and in that attitude she remained motionless for some moments, no doubt in order to ascertain if any suspicious sounds were stirring.

She was apparently satisfied by her observations, for she immediately recommenced her silent progress towards a ponderous mahogany dressing-table of my husband's. When she had reached it, she paused again, and appeared to listen attentively for some minutes; she then noiselessly opened one of the drawers, from which, having groped for some time, she took something, which I soon perceived to be a case of razors. She opened it, and tried the edge of each of the two instruments upon the skin of her hand; she quickly selected one, which she fixed firmly in her grasp. She now stooped down as before, and having listened for a time, she, with the hand that was disengaged, groped her way into the dressing-room where Lord Glenfallen lay fast asleep.

I was fixed as if in the tremendous spell of a nightmare. I could not stir even a finger; I could not lift my voice; I could not even breathe; and though I expected every moment to see the sleeping man murdered, I could not even close my eyes to shut out the horrible spectacle which I had not the power to avert.

I saw the woman approach the sleeping figure, she laid the unoccupied hand lightly along his clothes, and having thus ascertained his identity, she, after a brief interval, turned back and again entered my chamber; here she bent down again to listen.

I had now not a doubt but that the razor was intended for my throat; yet the terrific fascination which had locked all my powers so long, still continued to bind me fast.

I felt that my life depended upon the slightest ordinary exertion, and yet I could not stir one joint from the position in which I lay, nor even make noise enough to waken Lord Glenfallen.

The murderous woman now, with long, silent steps, approached the bed; my very heart seemed turning to ice; her left hand, that which was disengaged, was upon the pillow; she gradually slid it forward towards my head, and in an instant, with the speed of lightning, it was clutched in my hair, while, with the other hand, she dashed the razor at my throat.

A slight inaccuracy saved me from instant death; the blow fell short, the point of the razor grazing my throat. In a moment, I know not how, I found myself at the other side of the bed, uttering shriek after shriek; the wretch was however determined, if possible, to murder me.

Scrambling along by the curtains, she rushed round the bed towards me; I seized the handle of the door to make my escape. It was, however, fastened. At all events, I could not open it. From the mere instinct of recoiling terror, I shrunk back into a corner. She was now within a yard of me. Her hand was upon my face.

I closed my eyes fast, expecting never to open them again, when a blow, inflicted from behind by a strong arm, stretched the monster senseless at my feet. At the same moment the door opened, and several domestics, alarmed by my cries, entered the apartment.

I do not recollect what followed, for I fainted. One swoon succeeded another, so long and death-like, that my life was considered very doubtful.

At about ten o'clock, however, I sank into a deep and refreshing sleep, from which I was awakened at about two, that I might swear my deposition before a magistrate, who attended for that purpose.

I accordingly did so, as did also Lord Glenfallen, and the woman was fully committed to stand her trial at the ensuing assizes.

I shall never forget the scene which the examination of the blind woman and of the other parties afforded.

She was brought into the room in the custody of two servants. She wore a kind of flannel wrapper, which had not been changed since the night before. It was torn and soiled, and here and there smeared with blood, which had flowed in large quantities from a wound in her head. The white handkerchief had fallen off in the scuffle, and her grizzled hair fell in masses about her wild and deadly pale countenance.

She appeared perfectly composed, however, and the only regret she expressed throughout, was at not having succeeded in her attempt, the object of which she did not pretend to conceal.

On being asked her name, she called herself the Countess Glenfallen, and refused to give any other title.

"The woman's name is Flora Van-Kemp," said Lord Glenfallen.

"It _was_, it _was_, you perjured traitor and cheat!" screamed the woman; and then there followed a volley of words in some foreign language. "Is there a magistrate here?" she resumed; "I am Lord Glenfallen's wife--I'll prove it--write down my words. I am willing to be hanged or burned, so _he_ meets his deserts. I did try to kill that doll of his; but it was he who put it into my head to do it--two wives were too many; I was to murder her, or she was to hang me: listen to all I have to say."

Here Lord Glenfallen interrupted.

"I think, sir," said he, addressing the magistrate "that we had better proceed to business; this unhappy woman's furious recriminations but waste our time. If she refuses to answer your questions, you had better, I presume, take my depositions."

"And are you going to swear away my life, you black-perjured murderer?" shrieked the woman. "Sir, sir, sir, you must hear me," she continued, addressing the magistrate; "I can convict him--he bid me murder that girl, and then, when I failed, he came behind me, and struck me down, and now he wants to swear away my life. Take down all I say."

"If it is your intention," said the magistrate, "to confess the crime with which you stand charged, you may, upon producing sufficient evidence, criminate whom you please."

"Evidence!--I have no evidence but myself," said the woman. "I will swear it all--write down my testimony--write it down, I say--we shall hang side by side, my brave lord--all your own handy-work, my gentle husband!"

This was followed by a low, insolent, and sneering laugh, which, from one in her situation, was sufficiently horrible.

"I will not at present hear anything," replied he, "but distinct answers to the questions which I shall put to you upon this matter."

"Then you shall hear nothing,' replied she sullenly, and no inducement or intimidation could bring her to speak again.

Lord Glenfallen's deposition and mine were then given, as also those of the servants who had entered the room at the moment of my rescue. The magistrate then intimated that she was committed, and must proceed directly to gaol, whither she was brought in a carriage of Lord Glenfallen's, for his lordship was naturally by no means indifferent to the effect which her vehement accusations against himself might produce, if uttered before every chance hearer whom she might meet with between Cahergillagh and the place of confinement whither she was despatched.

During the time which intervened between the committal and the trial of the prisoner, Lord Glenfallen seemed to suffer agonies of mind which baffled all description; he hardly ever slept, and when he did, his slumbers seemed but the instruments of new tortures, and his waking hours were, if possible, exceeded in intensity of terror by the dreams which disturbed his sleep.

Lord Glenfallen rested, if to lie in the mere attitude of repose were to do so, in his dressing-room, and thus I had an opportunity of witnessing, far oftener than I wished it, the fearful workings of his mind. His agony often broke out into such fearful paroxysms that delirium and total loss of reason appeared to be impending. He frequently spoke of flying from the country, and bringing with him all the witnesses of the appalling scene upon which the prosecution was founded; then, again, he would fiercely lament that the blow which he had inflicted had not ended all.

The assizes arrived, however, and upon the day appointed Lord Glenfallen and I attended in order to give our evidence.

The cause was called on, and the prisoner appeared at the bar.

Great curiosity and interest were felt respecting the trial, so that the court was crowded to excess.

The prisoner, however, without appearing to take the trouble of listening to the indictment, pleaded guilty, and no representations on the part of the court availed to induce her to retract her plea.

After much time had been wasted in a fruitless attempt to prevail upon her to reconsider her words, the court proceeded, according to the usual form, to pass sentence.

This having been done, the prisoner was about to be removed, when she said, in a low, distinct voice:

"A word--a word, my lord!--Is Lord Glenfallen here in the court?"

On being told that he was, she raised her voice to a tone of loud menace, and continued:

"Hardress, Earl of Glenfallen, I accuse you here in this court of justice of two crimes,--first, that you married a second wife while the first was living; and again, that you prompted me to the murder, for attempting which I am to die. Secure him--chain him--bring him here!"

There was a laugh through the court at these words, which were naturally treated by the judge as a violent extemporary recrimination, and the woman was desired to be silent.

"You won't take him, then?" she said; "you won't try him? You'll let him go free?"

It was intimated by the court that he would certainly be allowed "to go free," and she was ordered again to be removed.

Before, however, the mandate was executed, she threw her arms wildly into the air, and uttered one piercing shriek so full of preternatural rage and despair, that it might fitly have ushered a soul into those realms where hope can come no more.

The sound still rang in my ears, months after the voice that had uttered it was for ever silent.

The wretched woman was executed in accordance with the sentence which had been pronounced.

For some time after this event, Lord Glenfallen appeared, if possible, to suffer more than he had done before, and altogether his language, which often amounted to half confessions of the guilt imputed to him, and all the circumstances connected with the late occurrences, formed a mass of evidence so convincing that I wrote to my father, detailing the grounds of my fears, and imploring him to come to Cahergillagh without delay, in order to remove me from my husband's control, previously to taking legal steps for a final separation.

Circumstanced as I was, my existence was little short of intolerable, for, besides the fearful suspicions which attached to my husband, I plainly perceived that if Lord Glenfallen were not relieved, and that speedily, insanity must supervene. I therefore expected my father's arrival, or at least a letter to announce it, with indescribable impatience.

About a week after the execution had taken place, Lord Glenfallen one morning met me with an unusually sprightly air.

"Fanny," said he, "I have it now for the first time in my power to explain to your satisfaction everything which has hitherto appeared suspicious or mysterious in my conduct. After breakfast come with me to my study, and I shall, I hope, make all things clear."

This invitation afforded me more real pleasure than I had experienced for months. Something had certainly occurred to tranquillize my husband's mind in no ordinary degree, and I thought it by no means impossible that he would, in the proposed interview, prove himself the most injured and innocent of men.

Full of this hope, I repaired to his study at the appointed hour. He was writing busily when I entered the room, and just raising his eyes, he requested me to be seated.

I took a chair as he desired, and remained silently awaiting his leisure, while he finished, folded, directed, and sealed his letter. Laying it then upon the table with the address downward, he said,--

"My dearest Fanny, I know I must have appeared very strange to you and very unkind--often even cruel. Before the end of this week I will show you the necessity of my conduct--how impossible it was that I should have seemed otherwise. I am conscious that many acts of mine must have inevitably given rise to painful suspicions--suspicions which, indeed, upon one occasion, you very properly communicated to me. I have got two letters from a quarter which commands respect, containing information as to the course by which I may be enabled to prove the negative of all the crimes which even the most credulous suspicion could lay to my charge. I expected a third by this morning's post, containing documents which will set the matter for ever at rest, but owing, no doubt, to some neglect, or perhaps to some difficulty in collecting the papers, some inevitable delay, it has not come to hand this morning, according to my expectation. I was finishing one to the very same quarter when you came in, and if a sound rousing be worth anything, I think I shall have a special messenger before two days have passed. I have been anxiously considering with myself, as to whether I had better imperfectly clear up your doubts by submitting to your inspection the two letters which I have already received, or wait till I can triumphantly vindicate myself by the production of the documents which I have already mentioned, and I have, I think, not unnaturally decided upon the latter course. However, there is a person in the next room whose testimony is not without its value--excuse me for one moment."

So saying, he arose and went to the door of a closet which opened from the study; this he unlocked, and half opening the door, he said, "It is only I," and then slipped into the room, and carefully closed and locked the door behind him.

I immediately heard his voice in animated conversation. My curiosity upon the subject of the letter was naturally great, so, smothering any little scruples which I might have felt, I resolved to look at the address of the letter which lay, as my husband had left it, with its face upon the table. I accordingly drew it over to me, and turned up the direction.

For two or three moments I could scarce believe my eyes, but there could be no mistake--in large characters were traced the words, "To the Archangel Gabriel in Heaven."

I had scarcely returned the letter to its original position, and in some degree recovered the shock which this unequivocal proof of insanity produced, when the closet door was unlocked, and Lord Glenfallen re-entered the study, carefully closing and locking the door again upon the outside.

"Whom have you there?" inquired I, making a strong effort to appear calm.

"Perhaps," said he, musingly, "you might have some objection to seeing her, at least for a time."

"Who is it?" repeated I.

"Why," said he, "I see no use in hiding it--the blind Dutchwoman. I have been with her the whole morning. She is very anxious to get out of that closet; but you know she is odd, she is scarcely to be trusted."

A heavy gust of wind shook the door at this moment with a sound as if something more substantial were pushing against it.

"Ha, ha, ha!--do you hear her?" said he, with an obstreperous burst of laughter.

The wind died away in a long howl, and Lord Glenfallen, suddenly checking his merriment, shrugged his shoulders, and muttered:

"Poor devil, she has been hardly used."

"We had better not tease her at present with questions," said I, in as unconcerned a tone as I could assume, although I felt every moment as if I should faint.

"Humph! may be so," said he. "Well, come back in an hour or two, or when you please, and you will find us here."

He again unlocked the door, and entered with the same precautions which he had adopted before, locking the door upon the inside; and as I hurried from the room, I heard his voice again exerted as if in eager parley.

I can hardly describe my emotions; my hopes had been raised to the highest, and now, in an instant, all was gone: the dreadful consummation was accomplished--the fearful retribution had fallen upon the guilty man--the mind was destroyed, the power to repent was gone.

The agony of the hours which followed what I would still call my awful interview with Lord Glenfallen, I cannot describe; my solitude was, however, broken in upon by Martha, who came to inform me of the arrival of a gentleman, who expected me in the parlour.

I accordingly descended, and, to my great joy, found my father seated by the fire.

This expedition upon his part was easily accounted for: my communications had touched the honour of the family. I speedily informed him of the dreadful malady which had fallen upon the wretched man.

My father suggested the necessity of placing some person to watch him, to prevent his injuring himself or others.

I rang the bell, and desired that one Edward Cooke, an attached servant of the family, should be sent to me.

I told him distinctly and briefly the nature of the service required of him, and, attended by him, my father and I proceeded at once to the study. The door of the inner room was still closed, and everything in the outer chamber remained in the same order in which I had left it.

We then advanced to the closet-door, at which we knocked, but without receiving any answer.

We next tried to open the door, but in vain; it was locked upon the inside. We knocked more loudly, but in vain.

Seriously alarmed, I desired the servant to force the door, which was, after several violent efforts, accomplished, and we entered the closet.

Lord Glenfallen was lying on his face upon a sofa.
"Hush!" said I; "he is asleep." We paused for a moment.

"He is too still for that," said my father.

We all of us felt a strong reluctance to approach the figure.

"Edward," said I, "try whether your master sleeps."

The servant approached the sofa where Lord Glenfallen lay. He leant his ear towards the head of the recumbent figure, to ascertain whether the sound of breathing was audible. He turned towards us, and said:

"My lady, you had better not wait here; I am sure he is dead!"

"Let me see the face," said I, terribly agitated; "you _may_ be mistaken."

The man then, in obedience to my command, turned the body round, and, gracious God! what a sight met my view.

The whole breast of the shirt, with its lace frill, was drenched with his blood, as was the couch underneath the spot where he lay.

The head hung back, as it seemed, almost severed from the body by a frightful gash, which yawned across the throat. The razor which had inflicted the wound was found under his body.

All, then, was over; I was never to learn the history in whose termination I had been so deeply and so tragically involved.

The severe discipline which my mind had undergone was not bestowed invain. I directed my thoughts and my hopes to that place where there is no more sin, nor danger, nor sorrow.

Thus ends a brief tale whose prominent incidents many will recognize as having marked the history of a distinguished family; and though it refers to a somewhat distant date, we shall be found not to have taken, upon that account, any liberties with the facts.

# Royal_Hibernian_Military_School

(as referenced in "About the Author")

By National Library of Ireland on The Commons - Unidentified building in unknown location?, Public Domain, https://commons.wikimedia.org/w/index.php?curid=59891887

Printed in Great Britain
by Amazon

63030505R00338